Harry Potter
AND THE ORDER OF THE PHOENIX

J.K. ROWLING

5

英汉对照版

哈利·波特与凤凰社 [上]

Harry Potter

〔英〕J.K. 罗琳／著

马爱农 马爱新／译

WIZARDING WORLD

人民文学出版社
PEOPLE'S LITERATURE PUBLISHING HOUSE

著作权合同登记号　图字　01-2024-1022

Harry Potter and the Order of the Phoenix
First published in Great Britain in 2003 by Bloomsbury Publishing Plc.
Text © 2003 by J.K. Rowling
Interior illustrations by Mary GrandPré © 2003 by Warner Bros.
Wizarding World, Publishing and Theatrical Rights © J.K. Rowling
Wizarding World characters, names and related indicia are TM and © Warner Bros. Entertainment Inc.
Wizarding World TM & © Warner Bros. Entertainment Inc.
Cover illustrations by Mary GrandPré © 2003 by Warner Bros.

图书在版编目（CIP）数据

哈利·波特与凤凰社：英汉对照版：上下／（英）J.K.罗琳著；马爱农，马爱新译. —北京：人民文学出版社，2020（2025.5重印）
ISBN 978-7-02-015071-7

Ⅰ.①哈… Ⅱ.①J…②马…③马… Ⅲ.①儿童小说—长篇小说—英国—现代—英、汉 Ⅳ.①I561.84

中国版本图书馆CIP数据核字（2019）第042705号

责任编辑	翟　灿
美术编辑	刘　静
责任印制	苏文强

出版发行	人民文学出版社
社　　址	北京市朝内大街166号
邮政编码	100705

印　　刷	三河市龙林印务有限公司
经　　销	全国新华书店等

字　　数	2025千字
开　　本	640毫米×960毫米　1/16
印　　张	90.5　插页6
印　　数	120001—126000
版　　次	2020年4月北京第1版
印　　次	2025年5月第10次印刷
书　　号	978-7-02-015071-7
定　　价	168.00元（上、下册）

如有印装质量问题，请与本社图书销售中心调换。电话：010-65233595

To Neil, Jessica and David,
who make my world magical

献　给

使我的世界充满神奇的

尼尔、杰西卡和戴维

HOGSMEADE

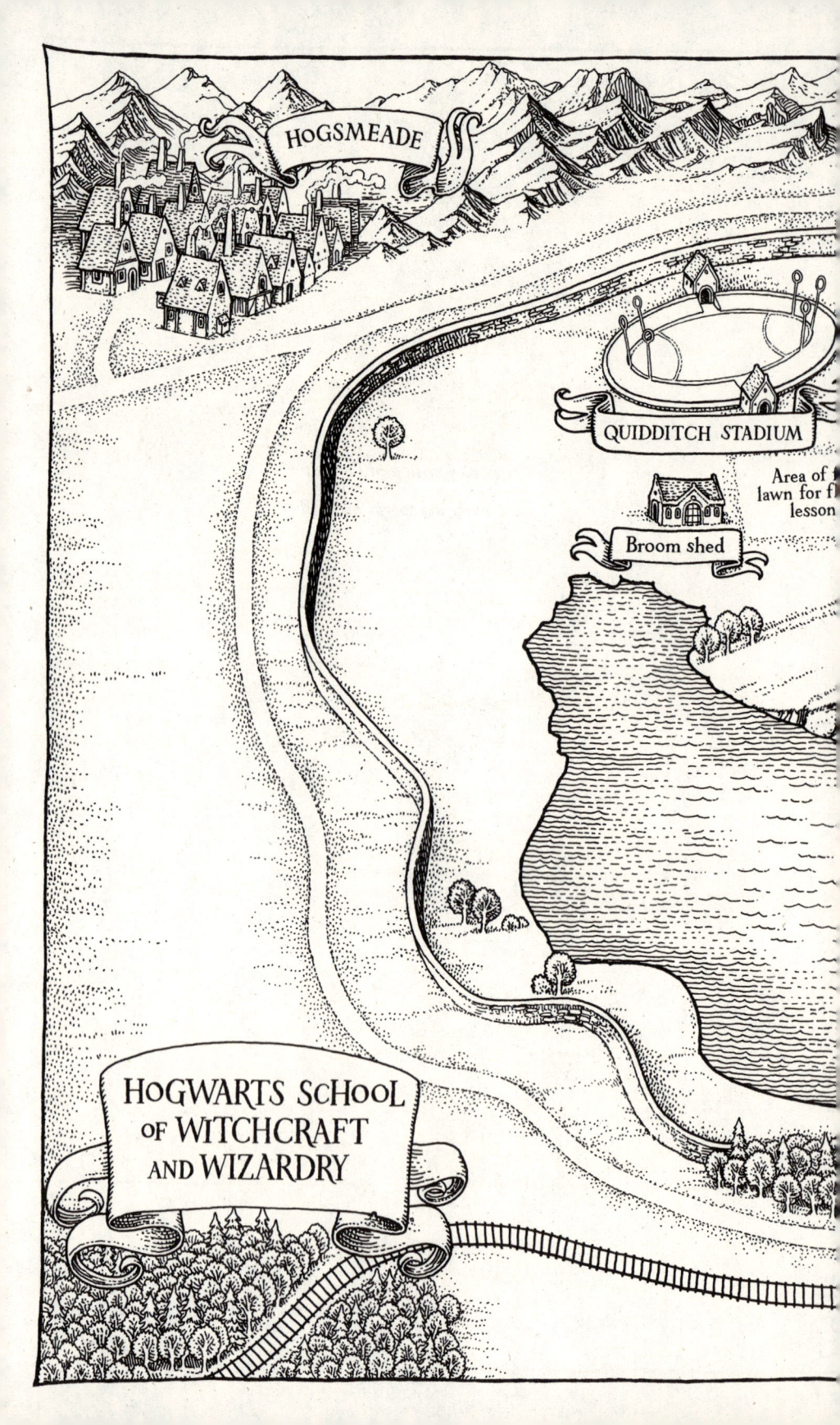

QUIDDITCH STADIUM

Area of
lawn for fl
lesson

Broom shed

HOGWARTS SCHOOL
OF WITCHCRAFT
AND WIZARDRY

HAGRID'S HUT
FORBIDDEN FOREST
WHOMPING WILLOW
GREENHOUSES
HOGWARTS CASTLE
HOGSMEADE STATION

CONTENTS

CHAPTER ONE	Dudley Demented	008
CHAPTER TWO	A Peck of Owls	040
CHAPTER THREE	The Advance Guard	078
CHAPTER FOUR	Number Twelve, Grimmauld Place	108
CHAPTER FIVE	The Order of the Phoenix	142
CHAPTER SIX	The Noble and Most Ancient House of Black	174
CHAPTER SEVEN	The Ministry of Magic	212
CHAPTER EIGHT	The Hearing	238
CHAPTER NINE	The Woes of Mrs Weasley	262
CHAPTER TEN	Luna Lovegood	310
CHAPTER ELEVEN	The Sorting Hat's New Song	344
CHAPTER TWELVE	Professor Umbridge	380
CHAPTER THIRTEEN	Detention with Dolores	430
CHAPTER FOURTEEN	Percy and Padfoot	480
CHAPTER FIFTEEN	The Hogwarts High Inquisitor	526
CHAPTER SIXTEEN	In the Hog's Head	566
CHAPTER SEVENTEEN	Educational Decree Number Twenty-Four	600
CHAPTER EIGHTEEN	Dumbledore's Army	636
CHAPTER NINETEEN	The Lion and the Serpent	674
CHAPTER TWENTY	Hagrid's Tale	714
CHAPTER TWENTY-ONE	The Eye of the Snake	748
CHAPTER TWENTY-TWO	St Mungo's Hospital for Magical Maladies and Injuries	788
CHAPTER TWENTY-THREE	Christmas on the Closed Ward	830

目 录

第 1 章	达力遭遇摄魂怪	009
第 2 章	一群猫头鹰	041
第 3 章	先遣警卫	079
第 4 章	格里莫广场 12 号	109
第 5 章	凤凰社	143
第 6 章	最古老而高贵的布莱克家族	175
第 7 章	魔法部	213
第 8 章	受审	239
第 9 章	韦斯莱夫人的烦恼	263
第 10 章	卢娜·洛夫古德	311
第 11 章	分院帽的新歌	345
第 12 章	乌姆里奇教授	381
第 13 章	被多洛雷斯关禁闭	431
第 14 章	珀西和大脚板	481
第 15 章	霍格沃茨的高级调查官	527
第 16 章	在猪头酒吧	567
第 17 章	第二十四号教育令	601
第 18 章	邓布利多军	637
第 19 章	狮子与蛇	675
第 20 章	海格的故事	715
第 21 章	蛇眼	749
第 22 章	圣芒戈魔法伤病医院	789
第 23 章	封闭病房中的圣诞节	831

CHAPTER TWENTY-FOUR	Occlumency	868
CHAPTER TWENTY-FIVE	The Beetle at Bay	910
CHAPTER TWENTY-SIX	Seen and Unforeseen	952
CHAPTER TWENTY-SEVEN	The Centaur and the Sneak	996
CHAPTER TWENTY-EIGHT	Snape's Worst Memory	1038
CHAPTER TWENTY-NINE	Careers Advice	1084
CHAPTER THIRTY	Grawp	1124
CHAPTER THIRTY-ONE	O.W.L.s	1168
CHAPTER THIRTY-TWO	Out of the Fire	1210
CHAPTER THIRTY-THREE	Fight and Flight	1246
CHAPER THIRTY-FOUR	The Department of Mysteries	1268
CHAPTER THIRTY-FIVE	Beyond the Veil	1296
CHAPTER THIRTY-SIX	The Only One He Ever Feared	1340
CHAPTER THIRTY-SEVEN	The Lost Prophecy	1362
CHAPTER THIRTY-EIGHT	The Second War Begins	1404

第 24 章	大脑封闭术	869
第 25 章	无奈的甲虫	911
第 26 章	梦境内外	953
第 27 章	马人和告密生	997
第 28 章	斯内普最痛苦的记忆	1039
第 29 章	就业指导	1085
第 30 章	格洛普	1125
第 31 章	O.W.L. 考试	1169
第 32 章	从火中归来	1211
第 33 章	战斗与飞行	1247
第 34 章	神秘事务司	1269
第 35 章	帷幔那边	1297
第 36 章	他唯一害怕的人	1341
第 37 章	丢失的预言	1363
第 38 章	第二场战争开始了	1405

CHAPTER ONE

Dudley Demented

The hottest day of the summer so far was drawing to a close and a drowsy silence lay over the large, square houses of Privet Drive. Cars that were usually gleaming stood dusty in their drives and lawns that were once emerald green lay parched and yellowing – for the use of hosepipes had been banned due to drought. Deprived of their usual car-washing and lawn-mowing pursuits, the inhabitants of Privet Drive had retreated into the shade of their cool houses, windows thrown wide in the hope of tempting in a non-existent breeze. The only person left outdoors was a teenage boy who was lying flat on his back in a flower-bed outside number four.

He was a skinny, black-haired, bespectacled boy who had the pinched, slightly unhealthy look of someone who has grown a lot in a short space of time. His jeans were torn and dirty, his T-shirt baggy and faded, and the soles of his trainers were peeling away from the uppers. Harry Potter's appearance did not endear him to the neighbours, who were the sort of people who thought scruffiness ought to be punishable by law, but as he had hidden himself behind a large hydrangea bush this evening he was quite invisible to passers-by. In fact, the only way he would be spotted was if his Uncle Vernon or Aunt Petunia stuck their heads out of the living-room window and looked straight down into the flowerbed below.

On the whole, Harry thought he was to be congratulated on his idea of hiding here. He was not, perhaps, very comfortable lying on the hot, hard earth but, on the other hand, nobody was glaring at him, grinding their teeth so loudly that he could not hear the news, or shooting nasty questions at him, as had happened every time he had tried sitting down in the living room to watch television with his aunt and uncle.

Almost as though this thought had fluttered through the open window,

第 1 章

达力遭遇摄魂怪

夏季以来最炎热的一天终于快要结束了,女贞路上那些方方正正的大房子笼罩在一片令人昏昏欲睡的寂静中。平日里光亮照人的汽车,这会儿全都灰扑扑地停在车道上,曾经葱翠欲滴的草地,已变得枯黄——由于旱情严重,浇水软管已被禁止使用。女贞路上的居民,平常的消遣就是擦车和割草,现在这两件事都做不成了,只好躲进阴凉的房子里,把窗户开得大大的,指望着能吹进一丝并不存在的凉风。只有一个人还待在户外,是一个十多岁的男孩,此时他正平躺在女贞路4号外面的花坛里。

他是一个瘦瘦的男孩,黑头发,戴着眼镜,看上去有些羸弱,略带病态,似乎是因为在短时间里个头蹿得太快。他身上的牛仔裤又破又脏,T恤衫松松垮垮的,已经褪了颜色,运动鞋的鞋底与鞋帮分了家。哈利·波特的这副模样,是无法讨得邻居们喜欢的。他们认为破烂邋遢应该受到法律制裁。不过哈利这天傍晚藏在一大丛绣球花后面,过路人都不会看见他。实际上,只有他的姨父弗农或姨妈佩妮从起居室的窗户探出脑袋,径直朝下面的花坛里望去,哈利才有可能被他们发现。

总的来说,哈利觉得他能想到藏在这里真是万幸。躺在热乎乎、硬邦邦的泥土上也许并不舒服,但这里不会有人狠狠地瞪着他,把牙齿咬得咯咯响,害得他听不清新闻里讲的是什么,也不会有人连珠炮似的问他一些烦人的问题。每次他想坐在客厅里跟姨妈姨父一起看看电视的时候,他们总是搅得他不得安宁。

就好像他的这些想法插上翅膀,飞进了敞开的窗户,哈利的姨父

CHAPTER ONE — Dudley Demented

Vernon Dursley, Harry's uncle, suddenly spoke.

'Glad to see the boy's stopped trying to butt in. Where is he, anyway?'

'I don't know,' said Aunt Petunia, unconcerned. 'Not in the house.'

Uncle Vernon grunted.

'*Watching the news* ...' he said scathingly. 'I'd like to know what he's really up to. As if a normal boy cares what's on the news – Dudley hasn't got a clue what's going on; doubt he knows who the Prime Minister is! Anyway, it's not as if there'd be anything about *his lot* on *our* news –'

'Vernon, *shh*!' said Aunt Petunia. 'The window's open!'

'Oh – yes – sorry, dear.'

The Dursleys fell silent. Harry listened to a jingle about Fruit 'n' Bran breakfast cereal while he watched Mrs Figg, a batty cat-loving old lady from nearby Wisteria Walk, amble slowly past. She was frowning and muttering to herself. Harry was very pleased he was concealed behind the bush, as Mrs Figg had recently taken to asking him round for tea whenever she met him in the street. She had rounded the corner and vanished from view before Uncle Vernon's voice floated out of the window again.

'Dudders out for tea?'

'At the Polkisses',' said Aunt Petunia fondly. 'He's got so many little friends, he's so popular ...'

Harry suppressed a snort with difficulty. The Dursleys really were astonishingly stupid about their son, Dudley. They had swallowed all his dim-witted lies about having tea with a different member of his gang every night of the summer holidays. Harry knew perfectly well that Dudley had not been to tea anywhere; he and his gang spent every evening vandalising the play park, smoking on street corners and throwing stones at passing cars and children. Harry had seen them at it during his evening walks around Little Whinging; he had spent most of the holidays wandering the streets, scavenging newspapers from bins along the way.

The opening notes of the music that heralded the seven o'clock news reached Harry's ears and his stomach turned over. Perhaps tonight – after a month of waiting – would be the night.

'*Record numbers of stranded holidaymakers fill airports as the Spanish baggage-handlers' strike reaches its second week –*'

第1章 达力遭遇摄魂怪

弗农·德思礼突然说起话来。

"谢天谢地,那小子总算不来探头探脑了。呃,他到底上哪儿去了?"

"不知道,"佩妮姨妈漠不关心地说,"反正不在家。"

弗农姨父不满地嘟哝着。

"看新闻……"他刻薄地说,"我倒想知道他究竟想干什么。一个正常的男孩,谁会去关心新闻哪——达力对时事一无所知,我怀疑他连首相是谁都不知道!见鬼,我们的新闻里怎么会有跟他们那类人有关的——"

"弗农,嘘!"佩妮姨妈说,"窗户开着呢!"

"哦——是的——对不起,亲爱的。"

德思礼夫妇不说话了。哈利听着一段关于水果麦麸营养早餐的广告短歌,一边望着费格太太慢吞吞地走过去——那是一个住在离这儿不远的紫藤路上的、脾气古怪的、爱猫如命的老太太。她皱着眉头,嘴里念念有词。哈利想幸亏自己藏在灌木丛后面,因为最近费格太太在街上一碰到哈利,就要邀请他过去喝茶。她拐过街角不见了,这时弗农姨父的声音又从窗口飘了出来。

"达达出去喝茶了?"

"到波奇斯家去了。"佩妮姨妈慈爱地说,"他交了这么多小朋友,大家都这么喜欢他……"

哈利拼命克制自己,才没有从鼻子里哼出声来。德思礼两口子在对待他们的宝贝儿子达力的问题上,真是愚蠢得出奇。达力在暑假的每个晚上都编造愚蠢的谎话,说是到他那帮狐朋狗友中的某个人家去喝茶,而他的父母居然就信了。哈利知道得很清楚,达力压根儿就没去什么地方喝茶,他和他那些哥们儿每天晚上都在游乐场毁坏公物,在街角抽烟,朝过路的汽车和孩子扔石子儿。哈利晚上在小惠金区散步时,曾看见过他们的这些行径。这个暑假的大部分时间哈利都在街头游荡,从路边的垃圾箱里捡报纸看。

七点钟新闻片头曲的前奏传到了哈利耳朵里,他紧张得连五脏六腑都翻腾起来。也许今晚——在等待了一个月之后——就在今晚。

西班牙行李搬运工的罢工进入第二周,大批度假者滞留机场——

CHAPTER ONE   Dudley Demented

'Give 'em a lifelong siesta, I would,' snarled Uncle Vernon over the end of the newsreader's sentence, but no matter: outside in the flowerbed, Harry's stomach seemed to unclench. If anything had happened, it would surely have been the first item on the news; death and destruction were more important than stranded holidaymakers.

He let out a long, slow breath and stared up at the brilliant blue sky. Every day this summer had been the same: the tension, the expectation, the temporary relief, and then mounting tension again ... and always, growing more insistent all the time, the question of *why* nothing had happened yet.

He kept listening, just in case there was some small clue, not recognised for what it really was by the Muggles – an unexplained disappearance, perhaps, or some strange accident ... but the baggage-handlers' strike was followed by news about the drought in the Southeast ('I hope he's listening next door!' bellowed Uncle Vernon. 'Him with his sprinklers on at three in the morning!'), then a helicopter that had almost crashed in a field in Surrey, then a famous actress's divorce from her famous husband ('As if we're interested in their sordid affairs,' sniffed Aunt Petunia, who had followed the case obsessively in every magazine she could lay her bony hands on).

Harry closed his eyes against the now blazing evening sky as the newsreader said, '*– and finally, Bungy the budgie has found a novel way of keeping cool this summer. Bungy, who lives at the Five Feathers in Barnsley, has learned to water ski! Mary Dorkins went to find out more.*'

Harry opened his eyes. If they had reached water-skiing budgerigars, there would be nothing else worth hearing. He rolled cautiously on to his front and raised himself on to his knees and elbows, preparing to crawl out from under the window.

He had moved about two inches when several things happened in very quick succession.

A loud, echoing *crack* broke the sleepy silence like a gunshot; a cat streaked out from under a parked car and flew out of sight; a shriek, a bellowed oath and the sound of breaking china came from the Dursleys' living room, and as though this was the signal Harry had been waiting for he jumped to his feet, at the same time pulling from the waistband of his jeans a thin wooden wand as if he were unsheathing a sword – but before

第1章 达力遭遇摄魂怪

"要是我,就让他们终身享受午睡。"新闻广播员的话音刚落,弗农姨父就恶狠狠地吼道。但是没关系,外面花坛里的哈利心头已经一块石头落地。如果真的发生了什么事,肯定是头条新闻,死亡和灾难远比滞留机场的度假者重要。

他慢慢地长舒一口气,仰望着清澈湛蓝的天空。这个夏天的每个日子都是这样:紧张,期待,暂时松一口气,然后弦又一点点地绷紧……但一个问题越来越迫切:为什么还没有事情发生?

他继续听下去,生怕有一些不起眼的线索,麻瓜们还没有弄清究竟是怎么回事——比如有人不明原因地失踪,或出了奇怪的意外事故……可是行李搬运工罢工的新闻之后,是东南部地区的旱情("我希望隔壁那个人好好听听!"弗农姨父气冲冲地嚷道,"他凌晨三点就把洒水器开着了!"),然后是一架直升机差点在萨里郡的田野坠毁,接着是某位大名鼎鼎的女演员跟她那位大名鼎鼎的丈夫离婚("就好像我们谁关心他们那些破事儿似的。"佩妮姨妈轻蔑地说,实际上她近乎痴迷地关注着这件事,翻遍了她那双骨瘦如柴的手能拿到的每一本杂志)。

哈利闭上眼睛,天空的晚霞变得刺眼了,这时新闻广播员说道:

——最后,虎皮鹦鹉邦吉今年夏天找到了一个保持凉爽的新办法。生活在巴恩斯利五根羽毛街的邦吉,学会了用水橇滑水!玛丽·多尔金详细报道。

哈利睁开眼睛。既然已经说到虎皮鹦鹉滑水橇,看来不会再有什么值得一听的新闻了。他小心翼翼地翻过身,用膝盖和胳膊肘撑着爬起来,准备手脚并用爬离窗户。

刚爬了两英寸,就接二连三地发生了好几件事,真是说时迟那时快。一记响亮的、带有回音的爆裂声,像一声枪响,划破了令人昏昏欲睡的寂静;一只猫从一辆停着的汽车底下蹿出来,不见了踪影;德思礼家的客厅里传来一声尖叫、一句叫骂,还有瓷器摔碎的声音。哈利似乎一直在等这个信号,他猛地站起身,同时像拔剑一样从牛仔裤裤腰里掏出一根细细的木质魔杖——可是还没等他完全站直身体,他

CHAPTER ONE — Dudley Demented

he could draw himself up to full height, the top of his head collided with the Dursleys' open window. The resultant *crash* made Aunt Petunia scream even louder.

Harry felt as though his head had been split in two. Eyes streaming, he swayed, trying to focus on the street to spot the source of the noise, but he had barely staggered upright when two large purple hands reached through the open window and closed tightly around his throat.

'*Put – it – away!*' Uncle Vernon snarled into Harry's ear. '*Now! Before – anyone – sees!*'

'*Get – off – me!*' Harry gasped. For a few seconds they struggled, Harry pulling at his uncle's sausage-like fingers with his left hand, his right maintaining a firm grip on his raised wand; then, as the pain in the top of Harry's head gave a particularly nasty throb, Uncle Vernon yelped and released Harry as though he had received an electric shock. Some invisible force seemed to have surged through his nephew, making him impossible to hold.

Panting, Harry fell forwards over the hydrangea bush, straightened up and stared around. There was no sign of what had caused the loud cracking noise, but there were several faces peering through various nearby windows. Harry stuffed his wand hastily back into his jeans and tried to look innocent.

'Lovely evening!' shouted Uncle Vernon, waving at Mrs Number Seven opposite, who was glaring from behind her net curtains. 'Did you hear that car backfire just now? Gave Petunia and me quite a turn!'

He continued to grin in a horrible, manic way until all the curious neighbours had disappeared from their various windows, then the grin became a grimace of rage as he beckoned Harry back towards him.

Harry moved a few steps closer, taking care to stop just short of the point at which Uncle Vernon's outstretched hands could resume their strangling.

'What the *devil* do you mean by it, boy?' asked Uncle Vernon in a croaky voice that trembled with fury.

'What do I mean by what?' said Harry coldly. He kept looking left and right up the street, still hoping to see the person who had made the cracking noise.

'Making a racket like a starting pistol right outside our –'

'I didn't make that noise,' said Harry firmly.

的脑袋就撞在了德思礼家敞开的窗户上。砰的一声,吓得佩妮姨妈叫得更响了。

哈利觉得脑袋似乎被劈成了两半,眼睛里充满泪水。他摇晃着身体,看着街上,努力想让模糊的视线变得清晰,好弄明白刚才的声音是从哪儿发出来的。可是他刚勉强站直身子,就有两只紫红色的大手从敞开的窗口伸出来,紧紧掐住了他的喉咙。

"把它——收起来!"弗农姨父冲着哈利的耳朵吼道,"快点!别让——人家——看见!"

"放——开——我!"哈利喘着气说。他们扭打了几秒钟,哈利用左手去掰姨父香肠般粗大的手指,右手还牢牢地握着举起的魔杖。接着,哈利本来就疼痛难忍的头顶突然一阵钻心的剧痛,弗农姨父大叫一声,就像遭到电击一般,松开了哈利。似乎他外甥体内涌起一股看不见的力量,使他没法抓住他。

哈利气喘吁吁地扑倒在绣球花中,然后直起身体,朝四周张望。他看不出刚才那声爆响是从哪儿发出的,但周围各式各样的窗户里探出了几张人脸。哈利赶紧把魔杖塞进牛仔裤里,装出一副什么事也没有的样子。

"多么迷人的夜晚!"弗农姨父朝住在对面7号的、正从网眼窗帘后面朝外瞪视的那位太太挥挥手,大声说道,"听见刚才汽车回火的声音了吗?把我和佩妮吓了一大跳!"

他脸上一直堆着那种难看的、疯子般的怪笑,直到那些好奇的邻居从各式各样的窗口消失。这时他的笑容突然变成狰狞的怒容,他示意哈利回到他的面前。

哈利朝前挪动几步,很小心地及时停住了,以免弗农姨父伸出的双手再掐住他的喉咙。

"你这到底搞的什么鬼,小子?"弗农姨父用气得微微发抖的低沉声音问。

"我搞什么啦?"哈利冷冷地问。他不停地朝街上张望,仍然希望看见是谁弄出了刚才那声爆响。

"弄出那噪音,像发令枪开火,就在我们家窗户外——"

"那声音不是我弄出来的。"哈利坚决地说。

CHAPTER ONE — Dudley Demented

Aunt Petunia's thin, horsy face now appeared beside Uncle Vernon's wide, purple one. She looked livid.

'Why were you lurking under our window?'

'Yes – yes, good point, Petunia! *What were you doing under our window, boy?*'

'Listening to the news,' said Harry in a resigned voice.

His aunt and uncle exchanged looks of outrage.

'Listening to the news! *Again?*'

'Well, it changes every day, you see,' said Harry.

'Don't you be clever with me, boy! I want to know what you're really up to – and don't give me any more of this *listening to the news* tosh! You know perfectly well that *your lot* –'

'Careful, Vernon!' breathed Aunt Petunia, and Uncle Vernon lowered his voice so that Harry could barely hear him, '– that *your lot* don't get on *our* news!'

'That's all you know,' said Harry.

The Dursleys goggled at him for a few seconds, then Aunt Petunia said, 'You're a nasty little liar. What are all those –' she, too, lowered her voice so that Harry had to lip-read the next word, '– *owls* doing if they're not bringing you news?'

'Aha!' said Uncle Vernon in a triumphant whisper. 'Get out of that one, boy! As if we didn't know you get all your news from those pestilential birds!'

Harry hesitated for a moment. It cost him something to tell the truth this time, even though his aunt and uncle could not possibly know how bad he felt at admitting it.

'The owls ... aren't bringing me news,' he said tonelessly.

'I don't believe it,' said Aunt Petunia at once.

'No more do I,' said Uncle Vernon forcefully.

'We know you're up to something funny,' said Aunt Petunia.

'We're not stupid, you know,' said Uncle Vernon.

'Well, *that's* news to me,' said Harry, his temper rising, and before the Dursleys could call him back, he had wheeled about, crossed the front lawn, stepped over the low garden wall and was striding off up the street.

He was in trouble now and he knew it. He would have to face his aunt and

第1章 达力遭遇摄魂怪

这时，弗农姨父紫红色的宽脸膛旁边，出现了佩妮姨妈那张瘦长的马脸，脸色铁青。

"你为什么鬼鬼祟祟地躲在我们家窗户底下？"

"好——好，问得好，佩妮！你在我们家窗户底下搞什么鬼，小子？"

"听新闻。"哈利用无奈的声音说。

姨妈和姨父气呼呼地交换了一下目光。

"听新闻！还听？"

"是啊，新闻每天都在变的，你知道。"哈利说。

"别跟我耍小聪明，小子！我想知道你到底打的什么主意——别再跟我说什么听新闻之类的鬼话！你明明知道，你们那类人——"

"留神，弗农！"佩妮姨妈紧张地说，于是弗农姨父一下子把声音压得很低，哈利简直听不清他在说什么，"——你们那类人不会出现在我们的新闻里！"

"那是你的想法。"哈利说。

德思礼夫妇狠狠地瞪了他几秒钟，然后佩妮姨妈说："你真是个坏透了的小骗子。那些——"她也突然放低了声音，哈利只能凭着她嘴唇的动作才听懂了她下面的话，"——猫头鹰不是给你传递消息又是在做什么呢？"

"啊哈！"弗农姨父得意地小声说，"快说实话吧，小子！好像我们不知道你能从那些讨厌的大鸟那儿得到所有的消息似的！"

哈利迟疑了片刻。这次他真不愿意说实话，尽管姨妈和姨父不可能知道他承认这件事心里有多难过。

"猫头鹰——不是在给我传递消息。"他干巴巴地说。

"我不相信。"佩妮姨妈立刻说。

"我也不相信。"弗农姨父强硬地跟了一句。

"我们知道你想做出点出格的事了。"佩妮姨妈说。

"我们不是傻瓜，你知道。"弗农姨父说。

"哦，那对我来说倒是新闻。"哈利说，他的火气上来了，不等德思礼夫妇把他叫回去，就一转身跑过门前的草地，跨过花园的矮墙，大步流星地走到了街上。

他惹麻烦了，他知道。待会儿他将不得不面对姨妈姨父，为他刚

uncle later and pay the price for his rudeness, but he did not care very much just at the moment; he had much more pressing matters on his mind.

Harry was sure the cracking noise had been made by someone Apparating or Disapparating. It was exactly the sound Dobby the house-elf made when he vanished into thin air. Was it possible that Dobby was here in Privet Drive? Could Dobby be following him right at this very moment? As this thought occurred he wheeled around and stared back down Privet Drive, but it appeared to be completely deserted and Harry was sure that Dobby did not know how to become invisible.

He walked on, hardly aware of the route he was taking, for he had pounded these streets so often lately that his feet carried him to his favourite haunts automatically. Every few steps he glanced back over his shoulder. Someone magical had been near him as he lay among Aunt Petunia's dying begonias, he was sure of it. Why hadn't they spoken to him, why hadn't they made contact, why were they hiding now?

And then, as his feeling of frustration peaked, his certainty leaked away.

Perhaps it hadn't been a magical sound after all. Perhaps he was so desperate for the tiniest sign of contact from the world to which he belonged that he was simply overreacting to perfectly ordinary noises. Could he be *sure* it hadn't been the sound of something breaking inside a neighbour's house?

Harry felt a dull, sinking sensation in his stomach and before he knew it the feeling of hopelessness that had plagued him all summer rolled over him once again.

Tomorrow morning he would be woken by the alarm at five o'clock so he could pay the owl that delivered the *Daily Prophet* – but was there any point continuing to take it? Harry merely glanced at the front page before throwing it aside these days; when the idiots who ran the paper finally realised that Voldemort was back it would be headline news, and that was the only kind Harry cared about.

If he was lucky, there would also be owls carrying letters from his best friends Ron and Hermione, though any expectation he'd had that their letters would bring him news had long since been dashed.

We can't say much about you-know-what, obviously ... We've been told not to say anything important in case our letters go astray ... We're quite busy but I can't give you details here ... There's a fair amount going on, we'll tell you everything when we see you ...

才的无礼言行付出代价，但现在管不了那么多了，他脑子里有更迫切的事情需要考虑。

哈利可以肯定，刚才那声爆响是有人幻影显形或幻影移形发出的。家养小精灵多比每次消失在空气中时，发出的都是这种声音。难道多比跑到这女贞路来了？难道多比此刻正在跟踪他？想到这里，哈利猛地转过身，望着身后的女贞路，但是路上看不见一个人，而哈利相信多比是不知道怎样隐形的。

他继续朝前走，几乎没去注意脚下的路。最近他经常拖着沉重的脚步在这些街道上走来走去，两只脚自动就把他带往他最爱去的地方。他每走几步，就扭头张望。刚才他躺在佩妮姨妈那丛奄奄一息的秋海棠中时，某个会魔法的人就在近旁，这是肯定的。他们为什么不跟他说话？他们为什么不与他取得联系？他们为什么现在躲起来了？

随着他心头的失望渐渐达到高峰，他的自信开始动摇。

也许那根本就不是什么魔法声音。也许他太渴望得到来自他那个世界的哪怕是最微弱的联络信号了，结果被一些再普通不过的声音搞得大惊小怪。他能肯定那不是邻居家里什么东西被打碎了吗？

哈利内心产生了一种沮丧、失落的感觉，接着，整个夏天都在折磨着他的绝望感又一次不期而然地把他淹没了。

明天早晨五点钟，他会被闹钟吵醒，付钱买下猫头鹰送来的《预言家日报》——可是继续订阅这份报纸有什么用呢？这些日子，哈利每天只扫一眼第一版，就把报纸扔到一边。这些办报纸的白痴，一旦知道伏地魔回来了，肯定会把这个消息作为头版头条，这才是哈利唯一关心的事情。

如果他运气好，猫头鹰会送来他最好的朋友罗恩和赫敏的来信，他原来指望他们的来信会给他带来消息，但这份期待早就破灭了。

关于那件事，我们不能说得太多……有人叫我们不要谈及任何重要事情，以免信件被送错地方……我们现在很忙，但我在这里不能跟你细说……发生了许多事情，我们跟你见面时都会告诉你的……

CHAPTER ONE   Dudley Demented

But when were they going to see him? Nobody seemed too bothered with a precise date. Hermione had scribbled *I expect we'll be seeing you quite soon* inside his birthday card, but how soon was soon? As far as Harry could tell from the vague hints in their letters, Hermione and Ron were in the same place, presumably at Ron's parents' house. He could hardly bear to think of the pair of them having fun at The Burrow when he was stuck in Privet Drive. In fact, he was so angry with them he had thrown away, unopened, the two boxes of Honeydukes chocolates they'd sent him for his birthday. He'd regretted it later, after the wilted salad Aunt Petunia had provided for dinner that night.

And what were Ron and Hermione busy with? Why wasn't he, Harry, busy? Hadn't he proved himself capable of handling much more than them? Had they all forgotten what he had done? Hadn't it been *he* who had entered that graveyard and watched Cedric being murdered, and been tied to that tombstone and nearly killed?

Don't think about that, Harry told himself sternly for the hundredth time that summer. It was bad enough that he kept revisiting the graveyard in his nightmares, without dwelling on it in his waking moments too.

He turned a corner into Magnolia Crescent; halfway along he passed the narrow alleyway down the side of a garage where he had first clapped eyes on his godfather. Sirius, at least, seemed to understand how Harry was feeling. Admittedly, his letters were just as empty of proper news as Ron and Hermione's, but at least they contained words of caution and consolation instead of tantalising hints:

I know this must be frustrating for you ... Keep your nose clean and everything will be OK ... Be careful and don't do anything rash ...

Well, thought Harry, as he crossed Magnolia Crescent, turned into Magnolia Road and headed towards the darkening play park, he had (by and large) done as Sirius advised. He had at least resisted the temptation to tie his trunk to his broomstick and set off for The Burrow by himself. In fact, Harry thought his behaviour had been very good considering how frustrated and angry he felt at being stuck in Privet Drive so long, reduced to hiding in flowerbeds in the hope of hearing something that might point to what Lord Voldemort was doing. Nevertheless, it was quite galling to be told not to be

第1章 达力遭遇摄魂怪

可是他们什么时候才能见到他呢？谁也不肯说出一个具体日期。赫敏在给他的生日贺卡上草草写道：我想我们很快就能见到你。可是到底多快呢？哈利从他们信里透露的蛛丝马迹可以看出，赫敏和罗恩是在同一个地方，很可能是在罗恩父母的家里。一想到他们俩在陋居玩得开心，而他却困在女贞路动弹不得，他就觉得简直受不了。他太生他们的气了，过生日时他们寄来的两盒蜂蜜公爵糖果店的巧克力，他没有打开就扔掉了。那天晚上，吃完佩妮姨妈端出来当晚饭的热酱汁拌沙拉后，他又觉得很后悔。

罗恩和赫敏到底在忙些什么呢？为什么他，哈利，整天无所事事？难道他没有证明自己处理事情的能力比他们强得多吗？难道他们都忘记了他做过的事情吗？难道不是他进入那片墓地，亲眼目睹塞德里克被杀，并且被绑在那块墓碑上，差点丧命吗？

别想那些事啦，哈利严厉地对自己说，暑假以来他已是第一百次这样警告自己。夜里不断做噩梦回到那片墓地，已经够糟糕的了，如果醒着时也想这件事，就更让人难以忍受了。

他转了个弯，来到木兰花新月街。在这条街上走到一半，经过了车库旁那条狭窄的小巷，他就是在那里第一次看见他教父的。至少，小天狼星似乎能明白哈利的感受。必须承认，他的信与罗恩和赫敏的一样，也没有向哈利透露他想知道的消息，但小天狼星的信里写了一些告诫和宽慰的话，而不是半掩半露，逗得人心痒难忍。

> 我知道这对你来说一定很沮丧……只要安分守己，一切都会很好的……千万小心，不要做任何鲁莽的事情……

是啊，他（基本上）还是照小天狼星的叮嘱去做的。哈利这么想着，一边穿过木兰花新月街，拐进了木兰花路，朝逐渐变得昏暗的游乐场走去。是啊，他至少抵挡住了诱惑，没有索性把箱子绑在飞天扫帚上，直接飞到陋居去。实际上，哈利认为自己的表现一直非常好，他被困在女贞路这么长时间，为了能听见一点透露伏地魔所作所为的只言片语，不得不藏在花坛里，这让他感到多么沮丧和生气啊。然而，居然

CHAPTER ONE   Dudley Demented

rash by a man who had served twelve years in the wizard prison, Azkaban, escaped, attempted to commit the murder he had been convicted for in the first place, then gone on the run with a stolen Hippogriff.

Harry vaulted over the locked park gate and set off across the parched grass. The park was as empty as the surrounding streets. When he reached the swings he sank on to the only one that Dudley and his friends had not yet managed to break, coiled one arm around the chain and stared moodily at the ground. He would not be able to hide in the Dursleys' flowerbed again. Tomorrow, he would have to think of some fresh way of listening to the news. In the meantime, he had nothing to look forward to but another restless, disturbed night, because even when he escaped the nightmares about Cedric he had unsettling dreams about long dark corridors, all finishing in dead ends and locked doors, which he supposed had something to do with the trapped feeling he had when he was awake. Often the old scar on his forehead prickled uncomfortably, but he did not fool himself that Ron or Hermione or Sirius would find that very interesting any more. In the past, his scar hurting had warned that Voldemort was getting stronger again, but now that Voldemort was back they would probably remind him that its regular irritation was only to be expected ... nothing to worry about ... old news ...

The injustice of it all welled up inside him so that he wanted to yell with fury. If it hadn't been for him, nobody would even have known Voldemort was back! And his reward was to be stuck in Little Whinging for four solid weeks, completely cut off from the magical world, reduced to squatting among dying begonias so that he could hear about water-skiing budgerigars! How could Dumbledore have forgotten him so easily? Why had Ron and Hermione got together without inviting him along, too? How much longer was he supposed to endure Sirius telling him to sit tight and be a good boy; or resist the temptation to write to the stupid *Daily Prophet* and point out that Voldemort had returned? These furious thoughts whirled around in Harry's head, and his insides writhed with anger as a sultry, velvety night fell around him, the air full of the smell of warm, dry grass, and the only sound that of the low grumble of traffic on the road beyond the park railings.

He did not know how long he had sat on the swing before the sound of voices interrupted his musings and he looked up. The street lamps from the

第1章 达力遭遇摄魂怪

是小天狼星叮嘱他不要鲁莽,这真叫人恼怒。要知道小天狼星就是被关在阿兹卡班巫师监狱十二年,然后逃出来,试图完成他原先被指控的那起谋杀罪,最后骑着一头偷来的鹰头马身有翼兽逃之夭夭的。

游乐场的门锁着,哈利一跃而过,踏着干枯的草地往前走。游乐场里和周围的街道一样空无一人。他来到秋千那儿,找到仅剩的一架达力和他那些朋友还没来得及毁坏的秋千坐了上去,一只胳膊挽着铁链,目光忧郁地望着地面。他再也不能藏在德思礼家的花坛里了。明天,必须想出另外的办法偷听新闻。眼下,他没有什么可指望的,摆在面前的又是一个混乱不安的夜晚。就算侥幸逃过关于塞德里克的噩梦,他也会梦见一条条漫长而昏暗的走廊,每条走廊的尽头都是死胡同或紧锁的房门。这些梦境弄得他心神不宁,他猜想这大概和他醒着时产生的困兽般的情绪有关。额头上的伤疤经常刺痛,很不舒服,但他知道,罗恩、赫敏和小天狼星不会对这件事很感兴趣了。过去,伤疤疼痛发作预示着伏地魔的力量正在再次变得强大起来,但既然伏地魔已经回来了,他们大概会说早就料到会有这种定期发作的疼痛……没什么可担心的……已经不是什么新闻了……

这太不公平了,他内心的怨愤不断堆积,他真想大声怒吼出来。如果不是他,甚至谁都不会知道伏地魔回来了!而他得到的回报呢,却是被困在小惠金区整整四个星期,完全与魔法世界失去了联系,不得不去蹲在那些快要枯死的秋海棠丛中,就是为了能够听到虎皮鹦鹉滑水橇的消息!邓布利多怎么能这么轻易地就把他忘记呢?为什么罗恩和赫敏聚到一起,却没有叫上他呢?他还需要在这里忍耐多久?听着小天狼星告诉自己要循规蹈矩,不要轻举妄动;抵挡住内心的冲动,不给愚蠢的《预言家日报》写信,告诉他们伏地魔已经回来了?这些愤怒的想法在哈利脑海里翻腾,搅得他内心乱糟糟的。夜幕已经降临,一个闷热而柔和的夜晚到来了,空气里弥漫着热乎乎的干草味,四下里只能听见游乐场栏杆外的道路上传来低沉的车辆声。

他不知道在秋千上坐了多久,后来别人的说话声打断了他的沉思。他抬起头,周围街道上的路灯投下一片朦胧的光影。只见一伙人影正在穿过游乐场,其中一个大声哼着一首粗俗的歌,其他人哈哈大笑。

CHAPTER ONE   Dudley Demented

surrounding roads were casting a misty glow strong enough to silhouette a group of people making their way across the park. One of them was singing a loud, crude song. The others were laughing. A soft ticking noise came from several expensive racing bikes that they were wheeling along.

Harry knew who those people were. The figure in front was unmistakeably his cousin, Dudley Dursley, wending his way home, accompanied by his faithful gang.

Dudley was as vast as ever, but a year's hard dieting and the discovery of a new talent had wrought quite a change in his physique. As Uncle Vernon delightedly told anyone who would listen, Dudley had recently become the Junior Heavyweight Inter-School Boxing Champion of the Southeast. 'The noble sport', as Uncle Vernon called it, had made Dudley even more formidable than he had seemed to Harry in their primary school days when he had served as Dudley's first punchball. Harry was not remotely afraid of his cousin any more but he still didn't think that Dudley learning to punch harder and more accurately was cause for celebration. Neighbourhood children all around were terrified of him – even more terrified than they were of 'that Potter boy' who, they had been warned, was a hardened hooligan and attended St Brutus's Secure Centre for Incurably Criminal Boys.

Harry watched the dark figures crossing the grass and wondered who they had been beating up tonight. *Look round,* Harry found himself thinking as he watched them. *Come on ... look round ... I'm sitting here all alone ... come and have a go ...*

If Dudley's friends saw him sitting here, they would be sure to make a beeline for him, and what would Dudley do then? He wouldn't want to lose face in front of the gang, but he'd be terrified of provoking Harry ... it would be really fun to watch Dudley's dilemma, to taunt him, watch him, with him powerless to respond ... and if any of the others tried hitting Harry, he was ready – he had his wand. Let them try ... he'd love to vent some of his frustration on the boys who had once made his life hell.

But they didn't turn around, they didn't see him, they were almost at the railings. Harry mastered the impulse to call after them ... seeking a fight was not a smart move ... he must not use magic ... he would be risking expulsion again.

The voices of Dudley's gang died away; they were out of sight, heading along Magnolia Road.

There you go, Sirius, Harry thought dully. *Nothing rash. Kept my nose clean. Exactly the opposite of what you'd have done.*

还有轻微的丁丁声传来,那是他们推着的几辆价格不菲的竞速自行车发出的声音。

哈利知道那些人是谁。打头的那个毫无疑问就是他的表哥达力·德思礼,他正由那帮狐朋狗友陪着朝家里走去。

达力还像以前一样人高马大,但一年来严格控制伙食,再加上新开发了一项才能,他的体格大有改观。弗农姨父逢人就高兴地说,达力最近成了东南部少年重量级校际拳击比赛冠军。弗农姨父所说的这项"高贵的运动",使达力变得更加令人生畏。哈利上小学时充当的是达力练习拳击的第一个吊球,那时他就觉得达力够厉害的。现在哈利对表哥已经没有丝毫畏惧感,但他认为,达力出拳越来越狠、越来越准,总不是什么值得庆贺的事情。左邻右舍的孩子都很害怕达力——甚至超过害怕那个"波特小子",大人们曾经警告过他们,那个波特是个屡教不改的小流氓,正在圣布鲁斯安全中心少年犯学校接受管教。

哈利望着那几个黑乎乎的身影走过草地,不知他们今晚又把谁痛打了一顿。回过头来,哈利发现自己一边望着他们一边这么想:快呀……回过头来……我一个人坐在这里呢……过来比试比试吧……

达力的朋友们如果看见他坐在这里,肯定会径直朝他冲过来的,那么达力会怎么做呢?他肯定不愿在朋友面前丢脸,但又不敢招惹哈利……看着达力左右为难,嘲弄他,欣赏他无力反抗的难受样儿,真是太好玩了……如果有谁敢来打哈利,他也有准备——他手里有魔杖呢。来试试吧……他正巴不得把失望的情绪发泄在这些曾使他的生活变得像地狱一样的男孩们身上呢。

但是他们没有回过头来,没有看见哈利,他们已经快走到栏杆那儿了。哈利克制住把他们叫回来的冲动……找人打架可不是明智之举……他绝不可以使用魔法……不然又有被学校开除的危险。

达力那伙人的声音渐渐地听不见了,他们顺着木兰花路越走越远,从哈利的视线中消失了。

你可以放心了,小天狼星,哈利闷闷不乐地想,不做鲁莽的事情……安分守己。跟你会做的事情正好相反。

CHAPTER ONE   Dudley Demented

He got to his feet and stretched. Aunt Petunia and Uncle Vernon seemed to feel that whenever Dudley turned up was the right time to be home, and any time after that was much too late. Uncle Vernon had threatened to lock Harry in the shed if he came home after Dudley ever again, so, stifling a yawn, and still scowling, Harry set off towards the park gate.

Magnolia Road, like Privet Drive, was full of large, square houses with perfectly manicured lawns, all owned by large, square owners who drove very clean cars similar to Uncle Vernon's. Harry preferred Little Whinging by night, when the curtained windows made patches of jewel-bright colour in the darkness and he ran no danger of hearing disapproving mutters about his 'delinquent' appearance when he passed the householders. He walked quickly, so that halfway along Magnolia Road Dudley's gang came into view again; they were saying their farewells at the entrance to Magnolia Crescent. Harry stepped into the shadow of a large lilac tree and waited.

'... squealed like a pig, didn't he?' Malcolm was saying, to guffaws from the others.

'Nice right hook, Big D,' said Piers.

'Same time tomorrow?' said Dudley.

'Round at my place, my parents will be out,' said Gordon.

'See you then,' said Dudley.

'Bye, Dud!'

'See ya, Big D!'

Harry waited for the rest of the gang to move on before setting off again. When their voices had faded once more he headed around the corner into Magnolia Crescent and by walking very quickly he soon came within hailing distance of Dudley, who was strolling along at his ease, humming tunelessly.

'Hey, Big D!'

Dudley turned.

'Oh,' he grunted. 'It's you.'

'How long have you been "Big D" then?' said Harry.

'Shut it,' snarled Dudley, turning away.

'Cool name,' said Harry, grinning and falling into step beside his cousin. 'But you'll always be "Ickle Diddykins" to me.'

他从秋千上下来,伸了个懒腰。佩妮姨妈和弗农姨父似乎觉得达力什么时间露面,这个时间就是应该回家的时候;只要是在这个时间之后,就是太晚了。弗农姨父曾经威胁说,如果哈利再在达力之后回家,就把他关进棚子里。于是,哈利忍住哈欠,愁眉苦脸地朝游乐场的大门走去。

木兰花路和女贞路一样,布满了一座座方方正正的大房子,草地修剪得完美无瑕。房子主人都是一些方方正正的大块头,像弗农姨父那样开着一尘不染的汽车。哈利更喜欢晚上的小惠金区,那些拉着窗帘的窗户,在黑暗中呈现出一个个珠宝般明亮的色块。白天,每当他经过那些户主面前,总会听见对他这个"少年犯"不满的嘀咕声,但现在就不会有这种危险。他走得很快,在木兰花路一半的地方,又看见了达力那帮家伙。他们正在木兰花新月街的入口处互相告别。哈利走进一棵大丁香树的阴影里等着。

"……他像猪一样嗷嗷叫唤,是吧?"莫肯说,其他人发出粗野的笑声。

"漂亮的右勾拳,D哥。"皮尔说。

"明天还是那个时候?"达力问。

"在我家外面,我爸妈明天出去。"戈登说。

"到时候见。"达力说。

"回见,达!"

"再见,D哥!"

哈利等其他人都走开了才从树下走出来。那些人的声音又一次远去了,他拐过街角,走上了木兰花新月街。他走得很快,一会儿就跟上了达力,能跟他打招呼了。达力悠闲自在地迈着步子,嘴里哼着不成调的小曲儿。

"喂,D哥!"

达力转过身来。

"噢,"他嘟哝道,"是你啊。"

"你什么时候成'D哥'了?"哈利问道。

"闭嘴!"达力恶狠狠地吼道,转过身去。

"这名字蛮酷的,"哈利说,他咧嘴笑着,跟表哥齐步往前走,"但在我看来,你永远都是'达达小宝贝'。"

CHAPTER ONE   Dudley Demented

'I said, SHUT IT!' said Dudley, whose ham-like hands had curled into fists.

'Don't the boys know that's what your mum calls you?'

'Shut your face.'

'You don't tell *her* to shut her face. What about "Popkin" and "Dinky Diddydums", can I use them then?'

Dudley said nothing. The effort of keeping himself from hitting Harry seemed to demand all his self-control.

'So who've you been beating up tonight?' Harry asked, his grin fading. 'Another ten-year-old? I know you did Mark Evans two nights ago –'

'He was asking for it,' snarled Dudley.

'Oh yeah?'

'He cheeked me.'

'Yeah? Did he say you look like a pig that's been taught to walk on its hind legs? 'Cause that's not cheek, Dud, that's true.'

A muscle was twitching in Dudley's jaw. It gave Harry enormous satisfaction to know how furious he was making Dudley; he felt as though he was siphoning off his own frustration into his cousin, the only outlet he had.

They turned right down the narrow alleyway where Harry had first seen Sirius and which formed a short cut between Magnolia Crescent and Wisteria Walk. It was empty and much darker than the streets it linked because there were no street lamps. Their footsteps were muffled between garage walls on one side and a high fence on the other.

'Think you're a big man carrying that thing, don't you?' Dudley said after a few seconds.

'What thing?'

'That – that thing you are hiding.'

Harry grinned again.

'Not as stupid as you look, are you, Dud? But I s'pose, if you were, you wouldn't be able to walk and talk at the same time.'

Harry pulled out his wand. He saw Dudley look sideways at it.

'You're not allowed,' Dudley said at once. 'I know you're not. You'd get expelled from that freak school you go to.'

"我叫你闭嘴!"达力说,两只火腿般粗胖的手捏成了拳头。

"那些男孩不知道你妈妈叫你什么吗?"

"住口!"

"你可没有叫你妈妈住口啊。'宝贝蛋儿'和'达达小心肝',我能用这些名字叫你吗?"

达力没有说话。他在拼命克制自己,没有动手揍哈利,这似乎用去了他所有的自制力。

"你们今天晚上把谁打了一顿?"哈利问,脸上的笑容隐去了,"又是个十岁大的男孩?我知道你们两天前的晚上打了马克·伊万斯——"

"他自找的。"达力没好气地说。

"哦,是吗?"

"他侮辱我。"

"是吗?他是不是说你像一头被训练着用两条腿走路的猪?嘿,那可不是侮辱,达达,那是事实呀。"

达力牙关上的肌肉在抽动。哈利看到自己惹得达力这么生气,心里别提多满足了。他觉得似乎把自己的沮丧情绪转移到了表哥身上,这是他唯一的发泄方式。

他们拐进了哈利第一次看见小天狼星的那条窄巷,那是木兰花新月街和紫藤路之间的一条近道。空荡荡的小巷,因为没有路灯,比它连接的那两条街道黑暗得多。小巷一边是车库的围墙,另一边是高高的栅栏,因此他们的脚步声听上去很沉闷。

"你拿着那玩意儿,就觉得自己是个男子汉了,是吗?"达力愣了几秒钟后说。

"什么玩意儿?"

"那个——你藏起来的东西。"

哈利脸上又露出坏笑。

"你看起来很笨,实际上并不笨哪,达达?我想,如果你真的很笨,就不会一边走路一边说话了。"

哈利抽出魔杖。他看见达力斜眼瞄着魔杖。

"你不能用它,"达力反应很快地说,"我知道你不能。你会被你上的那个怪胎学校开除的。"

CHAPTER ONE   Dudley Demented

'How d'you know they haven't changed the rules, Big D?'

'They haven't,' said Dudley, though he didn't sound completely convinced.

Harry laughed softly.

'You haven't got the guts to take me on without that thing, have you?' Dudley snarled.

'Whereas you just need four mates behind you before you can beat up a ten-year-old. You know that boxing title you keep banging on about? How old was your opponent? Seven? Eight?'

'He was sixteen, for your information,' snarled Dudley, 'and he was out cold for twenty minutes after I'd finished with him and he was twice as heavy as you. You just wait till I tell Dad you had that thing out –'

'Running to Daddy now, are you? Is his ickle boxing champ frightened of nasty Harry's wand?'

'Not this brave at night, are you?' sneered Dudley.

'This *is* night, Diddykins. That's what we call it when it goes all dark like this.'

'I mean when you're in bed!' Dudley snarled.

He had stopped walking. Harry stopped too, staring at his cousin. From the little he could see of Dudley's large face, he was wearing a strangely triumphant look.

'What d'you mean, I'm not brave when I'm in bed?' said Harry, completely nonplussed. 'What am I supposed to be frightened of, pillows or something?'

'I heard you last night,' said Dudley breathlessly. 'Talking in your sleep. *Moaning.*'

'What d'you mean?' Harry said again, but there was a cold, plunging sensation in his stomach. He had revisited the graveyard last night in his dreams.

Dudley gave a harsh bark of laughter, then adopted a high-pitched whimpering voice.

'"Don't kill Cedric! Don't kill Cedric!" Who's Cedric – your boyfriend?'

'I – you're lying,' said Harry automatically. But his mouth had gone dry. He knew Dudley wasn't lying – how else would he know about Cedric?

'"Dad! Help me, Dad! He's going to kill me, Dad! Boo hoo!"'

'Shut up,' said Harry quietly. 'Shut up, Dudley, I'm warning you!'

030

"你怎么知道他们没有改变章程呢，D哥？"

"那不可能。"达力说，不过声音显得不那么肯定。

哈利轻轻笑出声来。

"你如果不拿着那玩意儿，根本没有胆子跟我较量，是不是？"达力怒气冲冲地问。

"那你呢，你需要四个伙计给你撑腰，才能打败一个十岁的毛孩子？你知道你到处吹嘘的那个拳击称号吗？你的对手有几岁？七岁？八岁？"

"告诉你吧，他十六岁了。"达力恶狠狠地说，"我把他撂倒后，他整整昏迷了二十分钟，而且他的身体比你的重两倍。你等着吧，我要告诉爸爸你掏出了那玩意儿——"

"跑回家去找爸爸，是吗？他的拳击小冠军还会害怕哈利这根讨厌的魔杖？"

"晚上你就没这么勇敢了，是不是？"达力讥笑道。

"现在就是晚上，达达小宝贝。天黑成这样，不是晚上是什么？"

"我是说等你上床以后！"达力气势汹汹地说。

他停下脚步，哈利也站住了，盯着表哥。他只能看见达力那张大脸的一部分，可以看出那上面透着一种古怪的得意。

"你说什么，我躺在床上就不勇敢啦？"哈利问，完全被弄糊涂了，"我有什么可害怕的，是枕头还是什么？"

"我昨天夜里听见了，"达力喘着粗气说，"你说梦话。哼哼来着。"

"你说什么？"哈利又问了一遍，但他的心突然一阵发冷，忽地往下一沉。昨夜他在梦中又回到了那片墓地。

达力声音粗哑地笑了起来，然后发出一阵呜呜咽咽的尖厉声音。

"'别杀塞德里克！别杀塞德里克！'谁是塞德里克——你的男朋友吗？"

"我——你在胡说。"哈利本能地说。但他突然嘴里发干。他知道达力没有胡说——不然达力怎么会知道塞德里克呢？

"爸！救救我，爸！他要来杀我了，爸！呜呜！'"

"闭嘴！"哈利小声说，"闭嘴，达力，我警告你！"

CHAPTER ONE
Dudley Demented

'"Come and help me, Dad! Mum, come and help me! He's killed Cedric! Dad, help me! He's going to –" *Don't you point that thing at me!*'

Dudley backed into the alley wall. Harry was pointing the wand directly at Dudley's heart. Harry could feel fourteen years' hatred of Dudley pounding in his veins – what wouldn't he give to strike now, to jinx Dudley so thoroughly he'd have to crawl home like an insect, struck dumb, sprouting feelers ...

'Don't ever talk about that again,' Harry snarled. 'D'you understand me?'

'Point that thing somewhere else!'

'I said, *do you understand me?*'

'*Point it somewhere else!*'

'DO YOU UNDERSTAND ME?'

'GET THAT THING AWAY FROM –'

Dudley gave an odd, shuddering gasp, as though he had been doused in icy water.

Something had happened to the night. The star-strewn indigo sky was suddenly pitch black and lightless – the stars, the moon, the misty street lamps at either end of the alley had vanished. The distant rumble of cars and the whisper of trees had gone. The balmy evening was suddenly piercingly, bitingly cold. They were surrounded by total, impenetrable, silent darkness, as though some giant hand had dropped a thick, icy mantle over the entire alleyway, blinding them.

For a split second Harry thought he had done magic without meaning to, despite the fact that he'd been resisting as hard as he could – then his reason caught up with his senses – he didn't have the power to turn off the stars. He turned his head this way and that, trying to see something, but the darkness pressed on his eyes like a weightless veil.

Dudley's terrified voice broke in Harry's ear.

'W-what are you d-doing? St-stop it!'

'I'm not doing anything! Shut up and don't move!'

'I c-can't see! I've g-gone blind! I –'

'I said shut up!'

Harry stood stock-still, turning his sightless eyes left and right. The cold was so intense he was shivering all over; goose bumps had erupted up his

第1章 达力遭遇摄魂怪

"'快来救救我,爸!妈,快来救救我!他杀死了塞德里克!爸,救救我!他要——'不许你用那玩意儿指着我!"

达力退缩到墙根下。哈利将魔杖直接对准了达力的心脏。哈利感觉到他对达力十四年的仇恨此刻正在血管里汹涌冲撞——他真愿意放弃一切,只要能痛痛快快地出手,给达力念一个厉害的恶咒,让他只能像虫子一样爬回家,嘴里说不出话来,头顶上忽忽冒出两根触角……

"不许再提这件事,"哈利厉声说,"明白了吗?"

"把那玩意儿指着别处!"

"我问你呢,明白了吗?"

"把它指着别处!"

"你明白了吗?"

"把那玩意儿拿开——"

达力突然奇怪地打了个寒战,抽了口冷气,好像被冰冰的水浇了个透湿。

黑夜里,怪事发生了。洒满星星的深蓝色夜空一下子变得漆黑,没有一丝光亮——星星、月亮、小巷两端昏黄的路灯,突然全都消失了。远处汽车开过的隆隆声、近处树叶的沙沙声,也都听不见了。刚才温和宜人的夜晚瞬间变得寒冷刺骨。他们被包围在无法穿透的深邃而无声的黑暗中,仿佛一只巨手用一层冷冰冰的厚厚帘幕覆盖住了整条小巷,使他们看不见任何东西。

刹那间,哈利以为他在不知不觉中施了魔法,尽管他一直在拼命克制自己——然后他反应过来了——他没有能力让星星熄灭。他把脑袋转来转去,想看到点什么,但黑暗像一层轻薄的面纱贴在他眼睛上。

达力恐惧的声音刺进了哈利的耳膜。

"你—你在做—做什么?快停—停下!"

"我什么也没做!你快闭嘴,不许动!"

"我—我看不见!我—我眼睛瞎了!我——"

"我叫你闭嘴!"

哈利一动不动地站着,失去视力的眼睛转向左边又转向右边。四下里冷得要命,他禁不住浑身发抖,手臂上起了一层鸡皮疙瘩,脖子

CHAPTER ONE   Dudley Demented

arms and the hairs on the back of his neck were standing up – he opened his eyes to their fullest extent, staring blankly around, unseeing.

It was impossible ... they couldn't be here ... not in Little Whinging ... he strained his ears ... he would hear them before he saw them ...

'I'll t-tell Dad!' Dudley whimpered. 'W-where are you? What are you d-do–?'

'Will you shut up?' Harry hissed, 'I'm trying to lis–'

But he fell silent. He had heard just the thing he had been dreading.

There was something in the alleyway apart from themselves, something that was drawing long, hoarse, rattling breaths. Harry felt a horrible jolt of dread as he stood trembling in the freezing air.

'C-cut it out! Stop doing it! I'll h-hit you, I swear I will!'

'Dudley, shut–'

WHAM.

A fist made contact with the side of Harry's head, lifting him off his feet. Small white lights popped in front of his eyes. For the second time in an hour Harry felt as though his head had been cleaved in two; next moment, he had landed hard on the ground and his wand had flown out of his hand.

'You moron, Dudley!' Harry yelled, his eyes watering with pain as he scrambled to his hands and knees, feeling around frantically in the blackness. He heard Dudley blundering away, hitting the alley fence, stumbling.

'DUDLEY, COME BACK! YOU'RE RUNNING RIGHT AT IT!'

There was a horrible squealing yell and Dudley's footsteps stopped. At the same moment, Harry felt a creeping chill behind him that could mean only one thing. There was more than one.

'DUDLEY, KEEP YOUR MOUTH SHUT! WHATEVER YOU DO, KEEP YOUR MOUTH SHUT! Wand!' Harry muttered frantically, his hands flying over the ground like spiders. 'Where's – wand – come on – *lumos!*'

He said the spell automatically, desperate for light to help him in his search – and to his disbelieving relief, light flared inches from his right hand – the wand-tip had ignited. Harry snatched it up, scrambled to his feet and turned around.

后面的汗毛根根竖立起来——他极力睁大眼睛,茫然地瞪着四周,但是什么也看不见。

这不可能……它们不会来这里……不会来小惠金区……他竖起耳朵……要在看到它们之前先听到它们的声音……

"我要告—告诉爸爸!"达力抽抽搭搭地说,"你—你在哪里?你在—在做什——?"

"你能不能闭嘴?"哈利从牙缝里挤出声音说道,"我正在听——"

但他停住了。他听见了一直害怕的东西。

小巷里除了他们俩还有另外的东西,正在发出呼噜呼噜的长长的沙哑喘息声。哈利瑟瑟发抖地站在寒冷刺骨的黑夜里,感到一阵强烈的恐惧。

"停—停下!住手!我—我要揍你,我说到做到!"

"达力,闭——"

砰!

一拳击中了哈利的脑袋,打得他双脚失去平衡,眼前直冒金星。哈利在一小时内第二次觉得脑袋被劈成了两半。接着,他重重地跌倒在地,魔杖脱手飞了出去。

"你这个笨蛋,达力!"哈利喊道,疼得眼睛里涌出了泪水。他挣扎着手脚并用,在黑暗中胡乱摸索。他听见达力跟跟跄跄冲过去,撞在小巷边的栅栏上,脚底下摇摇晃晃。

"达力,快回来!你正好冲着它去了!"

一声可怕的、尖厉刺耳的喊叫,达力的脚步声停止了。与此同时,哈利感到身后一阵寒意袭来,这只能说明一点——它们不止一个。

"**达力,把嘴巴闭上!不管你做什么,千万要把嘴巴闭上!魔杖!**"哈利狂乱地说,两只手像蜘蛛一样在地面快速摸索,"我的——魔杖呢——快点——荧光闪烁!"

他本能地念出这个咒语,急于想得到一点亮光帮他找到魔杖——突然,在离他右手几英寸的地方冒出一道亮光,他简直不敢相信,心中松了口气——魔杖头被点亮了。哈利一把抓起魔杖,挣扎着站起来,急忙转身。

CHAPTER ONE   Dudley Demented

His stomach turned over.

A towering, hooded figure was gliding smoothly towards him, hovering over the ground, no feet or face visible beneath its robes, sucking on the night as it came.

Stumbling backwards, Harry raised his wand.

'*Expecto patronum!*'

A silvery wisp of vapour shot from the tip of the wand and the Dementor slowed, but the spell hadn't worked properly; tripping over his own feet, Harry retreated further as the Dementor bore down upon him, panic fogging his brain – *concentrate* –

A pair of grey, slimy, scabbed hands slid from inside the Dementor's robes, reaching for him. A rushing noise filled Harry's ears.

'*Expecto patronum!*'

His voice sounded dim and distant. Another wisp of silver smoke, feebler than the last, drifted from the wand – he couldn't do it any more, he couldn't work the spell.

There was laughter inside his own head, shrill, high-pitched laughter ... he could smell the Dementor's putrid, death-cold breath filling his own lungs, drowning him – *think ... something happy ...*

But there was no happiness in him ... the Dementor's icy fingers were closing on his throat – the high-pitched laughter was growing louder and louder, and a voice spoke inside his head: '*Bow to death, Harry ... it might even be painless ... I would not know ... I have never died ...*'

He was never going to see Ron and Hermione again –

And their faces burst clearly into his mind as he fought for breath.

'*EXPECTO PATRONUM!*'

An enormous silver stag erupted from the tip of Harry's wand; its antlers caught the Dementor in the place where the heart should have been; it was thrown backwards, weightless as darkness, and as the stag charged, the Dementor swooped away, bat-like and defeated.

'THIS WAY!' Harry shouted at the stag. Wheeling around, he sprinted down the alleyway, holding the lit wand aloft. 'DUDLEY? DUDLEY!'

He had run barely a dozen steps when he reached them: Dudley was curled up on the ground, his arms clamped over his face. A second Dementor

他的五脏六腑都翻腾起来了。

一个戴着兜帽的庞大身影无声地朝他滑来。那身影高高地悬浮在地面上，长袍下看不见脚也看不见脸，移动时仿佛在一点点地吞噬着黑暗。

哈利跌跌撞撞地退后几步，举起魔杖。

"呼神护卫！"

一股银色的烟雾从魔杖头上冒出来，摄魂怪的动作放慢了，但咒语并没有完全生效。看到摄魂怪朝自己袭来，哈利脚底绊了一下，又往后退了两步，恐慌使他的大脑变得模糊一片——集中意念——

一双结痂的黏糊糊的灰手从摄魂怪的长袍里伸出来抓他。窸窸窣窣的声音灌满了哈利的耳朵。

"呼神护卫！"

他的声音显得模糊而遥远。又是一股银色的烟雾，比刚才更加淡薄无力，从魔杖头上喷了出来——他无能为力了，他念不成这个咒语了。

脑海里响起了笑声，尖厉而刺耳的笑声……他已经感到摄魂怪那股腐臭的死亡般阴冷的气息灌满了他的肺部，憋得他喘不过气来——想一想……快乐的事情……

可是他内心已经没有丝毫喜悦……摄魂怪冰冷的手指就要掐住他的喉咙了——那尖厉刺耳的笑声越来越响，他脑海里有一个声音在说："朝死亡屈服吧，哈利……甚至没有任何痛苦……我不知道……我从来没有尝过死亡的滋味……"

他再也见不到罗恩和赫敏了——

他拼命地喘息，他们的脸一下子清晰地浮现在他脑海里。

"呼神护卫！"

一头巨大的银色牡鹿从哈利的魔杖头上喷了出来，两根鹿角直刺向摄魂怪应该是心脏的位置。摄魂怪被撞得连连后退，它们像周围的黑暗一样没有重量。牡鹿冲上前去，摄魂怪像蝙蝠一般扑闪到一边，匆匆逃走了。

"这边！"哈利朝牡鹿喊道。他转身在小巷里奔跑，手里高高举着点亮的魔杖。"达力？达力？"

他跑了十几步就赶到了他们跟前。达力蜷缩在地上，两只胳膊死

CHAPTER ONE   Dudley Demented

was crouching low over him, gripping his wrists in its slimy hands, prising them slowly, almost lovingly apart, lowering its hooded head towards Dudley's face as though about to kiss him.

'GET IT!' Harry bellowed, and with a rushing, roaring sound, the silver stag he had conjured came galloping past him. The Dementor's eyeless face was barely an inch from Dudley's when the silver antlers caught it; the thing was thrown up into the air and, like its fellow, it soared away and was absorbed into the darkness; the stag cantered to the end of the alleyway and dissolved into silver mist.

Moon, stars and street lamps burst back into life. A warm breeze swept the alleyway. Trees rustled in neighbouring gardens and the mundane rumble of cars in Magnolia Crescent filled the air again. Harry stood quite still, all his senses vibrating, taking in the abrupt return to normality. After a moment, he became aware that his T-shirt was sticking to him; he was drenched in sweat.

He could not believe what had just happened. Dementors *here*, in Little Whinging.

Dudley lay curled up on the ground, whimpering and shaking. Harry bent down to see whether he was in a fit state to stand up, but then he heard loud, running footsteps behind him. Instinctively raising his wand again, he spun on his heel to face the newcomer.

Mrs Figg, their batty old neighbour, came panting into sight. Her grizzled grey hair was escaping from its hairnet, a clanking string shopping bag was swinging from her wrist and her feet were halfway out of her tartan carpet slippers. Harry made to stow his wand hurriedly out of sight, but –

'Don't put it away, idiot boy!' she shrieked. 'What if there are more of them around? Oh, I'm going to *kill* Mundungus Fletcher!'

死地护着脸。第二个摄魂怪正矮身蹲在他身边,用两只黏糊糊的手抓住达力的手腕,几乎很温柔地把两只胳膊慢慢掰开,那颗戴着兜帽的脑袋朝达力的脸垂了下去,似乎要去亲吻他。

"**抓住它!**"哈利喊道,随着一阵快速的呼啸声,他变出来的那头银色牡鹿从身边跑过。摄魂怪那没有眼睛的脸离达力的脸不到一英寸了,说时迟那时快,银色的鹿角刺中了它,把它挑起来抛到半空。它像刚才那个同伴一样,腾空逃走,被黑暗吞没。牡鹿慢跑到小巷尽头,化为一股银色的烟雾消失了。

月亮、星星和路灯一下子又发出了亮光。小巷里吹过一阵温暖的微风。附近花园里的沙沙树叶声、木兰花新月街那尘世里的汽车声,又充斥着夜空。哈利一动不动地站着,所有的感官都跳动不止,以适应这突如其来的变化。过了一会儿,他才意识到 T 恤衫粘在身上,他全身已经被汗水湿透了。

他无法相信刚才的事情。摄魂怪出现在这里,在小惠金区。

达力蜷着身子躺在地上,抽抽搭搭,浑身发抖。哈利弯腰看看达力有没有可能站起来。就在这时,他听见身后传来奔跑的重重脚步声。他又本能地举起魔杖,急转过身面对着这个新来的人。

费格太太,那位脾气古怪的老邻居,气喘吁吁地出现在他们面前。她花白相间的头发从发网里散落出来,手腕上挂着一个叮当作响的网袋,两只脚都快从格子呢厚拖鞋里滑出来了。哈利刚想赶紧把魔杖藏起来,只听——

"别藏啦,傻孩子!"她尖叫着说,"如果周围还有那些东西怎么办?哦,我非宰了蒙顿格斯·弗莱奇不可!"

CHAPTER TWO

A Peck of Owls

'What?' said Harry blankly.

'He left!' said Mrs Figg, wringing her hands. 'Left to see someone about a batch of cauldrons that fell off the back of a broom! I told him I'd flay him alive if he went, and now look! Dementors! It's just lucky I put Mr Tibbles on the case! But we haven't got time to stand around! Hurry, now, we've got to get you back! Oh, the trouble this is going to cause! I will *kill* him!'

'But –' The revelation that his batty old cat-obsessed neighbour knew what Dementors were was almost as big a shock to Harry as meeting two of them down the alleyway. 'You're – you're a *witch*?'

'I'm a Squib, as Mundungus knows full well, so how on earth was I supposed to help you fight off Dementors? He left you completely without cover when I'd *warned* him –'

'This Mundungus has been following me? Hang on – it was *him*! He Disapparated from the front of my house!'

'Yes, yes, *yes*, but luckily I'd stationed Mr Tibbles under a car just in case, and Mr Tibbles came and warned me, but by the time I got to your house you'd gone – and now – oh, *what's* Dumbledore going to say? You!' she shrieked at Dudley, still supine on the alley floor. 'Get your fat bottom off the ground, quick!'

'You know Dumbledore?' said Harry, staring at her.

'Of course I know Dumbledore, who doesn't know Dumbledore? But come *on* – I'll be no help if they come back, I've never so much as Transfigured a teabag.'

She stooped down, seized one of Dudley's massive arms in her wizened hands and tugged.

第 2 章

一群猫头鹰

"什么？"哈利迷惑地问。

"他离开了！"费格太太绞着两只手说，"去见一个人，为了一批从飞天扫帚上掉下来的坩埚！我对他说，如果他敢去，我就活剥他的皮，结果你看看现在！摄魂怪！幸亏我叫踢踢给我通风报信！哎呀，我们没时间在这里闲站着了！快，我们得赶紧把你送回去！哦，这会惹来多大的麻烦哪！我非宰了他不可！"

"可是——"哈利突然得知这位脾气古怪、爱猫如命的老邻居居然知道摄魂怪，这份惊讶不亚于他刚才在小巷里碰见两个摄魂怪，"你——你是个巫师？"

"我是个哑炮，蒙顿格斯什么都知道，所以我怎么可能帮助你赶跑摄魂怪呢？他自个儿跑了，留下你毫无掩护，我还提醒过他——"

"这个蒙顿格斯一直在跟踪我？慢着——原来是他！他在我家门口幻影移形了！"

"是啊，是啊，是啊，幸亏我安排踢踢躲在一辆汽车下面以防万一。踢踢跑过来告诉了我，可是等我赶到你家时你已经走了——结果现在——哦，邓布利多会怎么说呢？你！"她尖着嗓子朝仍然躺在小巷里的达力嚷道，"把你的肥屁股从地上抬起来，快点！"

"你认识邓布利多？"哈利吃惊地瞪着她问道。

"我当然认识邓布利多，谁不认识邓布利多呢？可是快点吧——如果它们再回来，我可帮不上什么忙。我没有多少本事，连给一只茶叶包变形都不会。"

她弯下腰，用皱巴巴的手抓住达力一只肥粗的胳膊使劲拉着。

CHAPTER TWO   A Peck of Owls

'Get *up*, you useless lump, get *up*!'

But Dudley either could not or would not move. He remained on the ground, trembling and ashen-faced, his mouth shut very tight.

'I'll do it.' Harry took hold of Dudley's arm and heaved. With an enormous effort he managed to hoist him to his feet. Dudley seemed to be on the point of fainting. His small eyes were rolling in their sockets and sweat was beading his face; the moment Harry let go of him he swayed dangerously.

'Hurry up!' said Mrs Figg hysterically.

Harry pulled one of Dudley's massive arms around his own shoulders and dragged him towards the road, sagging slightly under the weight. Mrs Figg tottered along in front of them, peering anxiously around the corner.

'Keep your wand out,' she told Harry, as they entered Wisteria Walk. 'Never mind the Statute of Secrecy now, there's going to be hell to pay anyway, we might as well be hanged for a dragon as an egg. Talk about the Reasonable Restriction of Underage Sorcery … this was *exactly* what Dumbledore was afraid of – What's that at the end of the street? Oh, it's just Mr Prentice … don't put your wand away, boy, don't I keep telling you I'm no use?'

It was not easy to hold a wand steady and haul Dudley along at the same time. Harry gave his cousin an impatient dig in the ribs, but Dudley seemed to have lost all desire for independent movement. He was slumped on Harry's shoulder, his large feet dragging along the ground.

'Why didn't you tell me you're a Squib, Mrs Figg?' asked Harry, panting with the effort to keep walking. 'All those times I came round your house – why didn't you say anything?'

'Dumbledore's orders. I was to keep an eye on you but not say anything, you were too young. I'm sorry I gave you such a miserable time, Harry, but the Dursleys would never have let you come if they'd thought you enjoyed it. It wasn't easy, you know … but oh my word,' she said tragically, wringing her hands once more, 'when Dumbledore hears about this – how could Mundungus have left, he was supposed to be on duty until midnight – *where is he*? How am I going to tell Dumbledore what's happened? I can't Apparate.'

'I've got an owl, you can borrow her.' Harry groaned, wondering whether his spine was going to snap under Dudley's weight.

第2章 一群猫头鹰

"站起来,你这个没用的傻大个儿。快站起来!"

达力不知是动不了还是压根儿就不愿意动弹,还是躺在地上,浑身发抖,脸如死灰,嘴巴闭得紧紧的。

"我来吧。"哈利抓住达力的胳膊用力拽,他费了九牛二虎之力,总算把达力拖得站了起来。达力似乎随时都会昏过去,他的小眼睛在眼窝里转来转去,脸上沁出粒粒汗珠。哈利刚松开手,他就摇晃起来,好像要摔倒的样子。

"快走!"费格太太心急火燎地说。

哈利抓起达力一只粗大无比的胳膊,搭在自己的肩膀上,拖着他往路上走。达力的重量把他压得腰都直不起来了。费格太太跌跌撞撞地走在前面,不安地注视着拐角里的动静。

"把你的魔杖拿出来,"他们走进紫藤路时,她对哈利说,"现在别管什么《保密法》啦,反正免不了受罚,为一条火龙是一死,为一个火龙蛋也是一死。说到《对未成年巫师加以合理约束法》——这正是邓布利多一直担心的——路口那儿是什么?噢,是普伦提斯先生……别把魔杖收起来,孩子,我不是一直跟你说吗,我是不管用的!"

既要稳稳地举着魔杖,又要拖着达力往前走,这真不是件容易的事。哈利不耐烦地捅了捅表哥的肋骨,可是达力似乎完全丧失了自己行动的愿望,他瘫倒在哈利的肩膀上,两只大脚拖在地面上。

"你以前为什么没有告诉我你是个哑炮,费格太太?"哈利问,他不敢停脚,累得气喘吁吁,"我那么多次到你家去——你为什么一字不提呢?"

"邓布利多盼咐的,要我留心照看你,但什么也不能说,你当时还太小呢。对不起,我那时弄得你很不开心,哈利,但如果德思礼家的人觉得你喜欢上我家来,就再也不会让你来了。这挺不容易的,你知道……可是,哎呀,"她悲痛地说,又一次把双手紧紧地绞在一起,"如果邓布利多听说了这件事——蒙顿格斯怎么能离开呢,他应该值班到午夜的——他去了哪儿呢?我怎么去向邓布利多汇报这件事呢?我不会幻影显形啊。"

"我有一只猫头鹰,可以借给你。"哈利嘴里直哼哼,怀疑他的脊椎骨都要被达力压断了。

'Harry, you don't understand! Dumbledore will need to act as quickly as possible, the Ministry have their own ways of detecting underage magic, they'll know already, you mark my words.'

'But I was getting rid of Dementors, I had to use magic – they're going to be more worried about what Dementors were doing floating around Wisteria Walk, surely?'

'Oh, my dear, I wish it were so, but I'm afraid – MUNDUNGUS FLETCHER, I AM GOING TO KILL YOU!'

There was a loud *crack* and a strong smell of drink mingled with stale tobacco filled the air as a squat, unshaven man in a tattered overcoat materialised right in front of them. He had short, bandy legs, long straggly ginger hair and bloodshot, baggy eyes that gave him the doleful look of a basset hound. He was also clutching a silvery bundle that Harry recognised at once as an Invisibility Cloak.

''S'up, Figgy?' he said, staring from Mrs Figg to Harry and Dudley. 'What 'appened to staying undercover?'

'I'll give you *undercover*!' cried Mrs Figg. '*Dementors*, you useless, skiving sneak thief!'

'Dementors?' repeated Mundungus, aghast. 'Dementors, 'ere?'

'Yes, here, you worthless pile of bat droppings, here!' shrieked Mrs Figg. 'Dementors attacking the boy on your watch!'

'Blimey,' said Mundungus weakly, looking from Mrs Figg to Harry, and back again. 'Blimey, I –'

'And you off buying stolen cauldrons! Didn't I tell you not to go? *Didn't I?*'

'I – well, I –' Mundungus looked deeply uncomfortable. 'It – it was a very good business opportunity, see –'

Mrs Figg raised the arm from which her string bag dangled and whacked Mundungus around the face and neck with it; judging by the clanking noise it made it was full of cat food.

'Ouch – gerroff – gerroff, you mad old bat! Someone's gotta tell Dumbledore!'

'Yes – they – have!' yelled Mrs Figg, swinging the bag of cat food at every bit of Mundungus she could reach. 'And – it – had – better – be – you – and – you – can – tell – him – why – you – weren't – there – to – help!'

"哈利，你不明白！邓布利多需要尽快采取行动，因为魔法部有一套办法侦查未成年人使用魔法的情况，他们恐怕已经知道了，信不信由你。"

"但我要摆脱摄魂怪呀，不得不使用魔法——他们肯定更关心为什么摄魂怪在紫藤路飘来飘去，是不是？"

"哦，我亲爱的，我也巴不得是这样呢，但我担心——蒙顿格斯·弗莱奇，我要宰了你！"

啪，随着一声刺耳的爆响，空气里升起一股烟酒混合的恶臭，一个身穿一件破烂外套、胡子拉碴的矮胖子突然出现在他们面前。两条短短的罗圈腿，一头又长又乱的姜黄色头发，一双肿胀充血的眼睛，使他看上去像一只短腿猎狗那样愁苦。他手里还抓着一包银色的东西，哈利一眼认出那是一件隐形衣。

"出什么事了，费格？"他问，眼睛望望费格太太，望望哈利，又望望达力，"不是说不暴露身份的吗？"

"去你的不暴露身份！"费格太太嚷道，"摄魂怪来了，你这个逃避责任的没用的贼！"

"摄魂怪？"蒙顿格斯重复了一句，吓坏了，"摄魂怪，在这儿？"

"没错，就在这儿，你这坨一无是处的臭大粪，就在这儿！"费格太太尖声嚷道，"摄魂怪袭击了你负责监护的孩子！"

"天哪，"蒙顿格斯轻声叫道，看看费格太太，看看哈利，又看看费格太太，"天哪，我——"

"你去买那些偷来的坩埚了！我不是叫你别去的吗？是不是？"

"我——唉，我——"蒙顿格斯显得心烦意乱，"这——这笔生意可是机会难得啊，你看——"

费格太太举起拎网袋的胳膊，用网袋使劲抽打蒙顿格斯的脸和脖子。从叮叮当当的声音推测，网袋里肯定装满了猫食。

"哎哟——够了——够了，你这只发疯的老蝙蝠！得派人去告诉邓布利多呀！"

"是的——摄魂怪——来了！"费格太太一边嚷，一边把那袋猫食没头没脑地砸向蒙顿格斯，"最好——你——自己去说——你可以——告诉他——你为什么——没在这里——帮忙！"

CHAPTER TWO A Peck of Owls

'Keep your 'airnet on!' said Mundungus, his arms over his head, cowering. 'I'm going, I'm going!'

And with another loud *crack*, he vanished.

'I hope Dumbledore *murders* him!' said Mrs Figg furiously. 'Now come *on*, Harry, what are you waiting for?'

Harry decided not to waste his remaining breath on pointing out that he could barely walk under Dudley's bulk. He gave the semi-conscious Dudley a heave and staggered onwards.

'I'll take you to the door,' said Mrs Figg, as they turned into Privet Drive. 'Just in case there are more of them around ... oh my word, what a catastrophe ... and you had to fight them off yourself ... and Dumbledore said we were to keep you from doing magic at all costs ... well, it's no good crying over spilt potion, I suppose ... but the cat's among the pixies now.'

'So,' Harry panted, 'Dumbledore's ... been having ... me followed?'

'Of course he has,' said Mrs Figg impatiently. 'Did you expect him to let you wander around on your own after what happened in June? Good Lord, boy, they told me you were intelligent ... right ... get inside and stay there,' she said, as they reached number four. 'I expect someone will be in touch with you soon enough.'

'What are you going to do?' asked Harry quickly.

'I'm going straight home,' said Mrs Figg, staring around the dark street and shuddering. 'I'll need to wait for more instructions. Just stay in the house. Goodnight.'

'Hang on, don't go yet! I want to know –'

But Mrs Figg had already set off at a trot, carpet slippers flopping, string bag clanking.

'Wait!' Harry shouted after her. He had a million questions to ask anyone who was in contact with Dumbledore; but within seconds Mrs Figg was swallowed by the darkness. Scowling, Harry readjusted Dudley on his shoulder and made his slow, painful way up number four's garden path.

The hall light was on. Harry stuck his wand back inside the waistband of his jeans, rang the bell and watched Aunt Petunia's outline grow larger and larger, oddly distorted by the rippling glass in the front door.

'Diddy! About time too, I was getting quite – quite – *Diddy, what's the matter?*'

"别发火了！"蒙顿格斯用胳膊护住脑袋，往后退缩着说，"我这就去，我这就去！"

啪，又是一声刺耳的爆响，他消失了。

"真希望邓布利多取了他的小命！"费格太太气呼呼地说，"好了，快走吧，哈利，你还等什么呀？"

哈利已经累得气都喘不匀了，心想还是不要浪费口舌向费格太太解释说达力压得他几乎走不动路吧。他使劲拉了一下半昏半醒的达力，继续跟跟跄跄地往前走。

"我送你们到门口，"他们拐进女贞路时，费格太太说，"以防附近还有摄魂怪……哎呀呀，真是一场大祸啊……你不得不独自把它们赶跑……而邓布利多说我们要不惜一切代价阻止你使用魔法……唉，得啦，药水已经洒了，哭也没有用……这就像狸猫闯进了小精灵堆。"

"这么说，"哈利喘着气说，"邓布利多……一直在……派人跟踪我？"

"当然是这样，"费格太太不耐烦地说，"六月份发生了那件事之后，你难道还指望他让你一个人四处乱逛？孩子，他们告诉我说你很聪明……好了……进去吧，待着别出来。"他们已经到了4号门前，"我想很快就会有人跟你联系的。"

"你准备做什么？"哈利赶紧问道。

"我直接回家，"费格太太说，朝漆黑的街道张望了一下，打了个冷战，"我需要等候新的命令。待在家里别出来。晚安。"

"等等，先别走！我还想知道——"

但是费格太太已经一溜烟跑远了，厚拖鞋啪嗒啪嗒，网袋叮叮当当。

"等一下！"哈利对着她的背影喊道。他心里有数不清的问题要问任何一个与邓布利多有联系的人，但是一眨眼的工夫，费格太太的身影就被黑暗吞没了。哈利紧锁眉头，重新调整了一下瘫在他肩膀上的达力，拖着沉重的脚步，慢慢走上女贞路4号的花园小径。

门厅里亮着灯。哈利把魔杖重新插进牛仔裤的腰带，摁响了门铃。佩妮姨妈的身影越来越大，被前门的波浪纹玻璃折射得奇形怪状。

"达达！回来得正是时候，我正感到非常——非常——达达，怎么回事？"

CHAPTER TWO A Peck of Owls

Harry looked sideways at Dudley and ducked out from under his arm just in time. Dudley swayed on the spot for a moment, his face pale green ... then he opened his mouth and vomited all over the doormat.

'DIDDY! Diddy, what's the matter with you? Vernon? VERNON!'

Harry's uncle came galumphing out of the living room, walrus moustache blowing hither and thither as it always did when he was agitated. He hurried forwards to help Aunt Petunia negotiate a weak-kneed Dudley over the threshold while avoiding stepping in the pool of sick.

'He's ill, Vernon!'

'What is it, son? What's happened? Did Mrs Polkiss give you something foreign for tea?'

'Why are you all covered in dirt, darling? Have you been lying on the ground?'

'Hang on – you haven't been mugged, have you, son?'

Aunt Petunia screamed.

'Phone the police, Vernon! Phone the police! Diddy, darling, speak to Mummy! What did they do to you?'

In all the kerfuffle nobody seemed to have noticed Harry, which suited him perfectly. He managed to slip inside just before Uncle Vernon slammed the door and, while the Dursleys made their noisy progress down the hall towards the kitchen, Harry moved carefully and quietly towards the stairs.

'Who did it, son? Give us names. We'll get them, don't worry.'

'Shh! He's trying to say something, Vernon! What is it, Diddy? Tell Mummy!'

Harry's foot was on the bottom-most stair when Dudley found his voice.

'*Him.*'

Harry froze, foot on the stair, face screwed up, braced for the explosion.

'BOY! COME HERE!'

With a feeling of mingled dread and anger, Harry removed his foot slowly from the stair and turned to follow the Dursleys.

The scrupulously clean kitchen had an oddly unreal glitter after the darkness outside. Aunt Petunia was ushering Dudley into a chair; he was still

第 2 章 一群猫头鹰

哈利侧脸望着达力，及时从他胳膊下脱出身来。达力原地摇晃了几下，脸色发青……然后他张开大嘴，哇的一口，全吐在门垫子上了。

"达达，达达，你怎么啦？弗农？**弗农！**"

哈利的姨父拖着笨重的身体从起居室赶来，那些海象胡子乱七八糟地飘了起来，每当他激动不安时总是这样。他三步并作两步赶上来，和佩妮姨妈一起搀扶着膝盖发软的达力跨过门槛，同时小心别踩到达力吐出来的那堆脏东西。

"他病了，弗农！"

"怎么回事，儿子？出了什么事？波奇斯太太在茶点上给你吃什么不合适的东西了？"

"你怎么身上都是土，亲爱的？你一直躺在地上吗？"

"慢着——你没有挨打吧，儿子，嗯？"

佩妮姨妈尖叫起来。

"给警察打电话，弗农！给警察打电话！达达，亲爱的，跟妈妈说说！他们把你怎么啦？"

在一片混乱中，似乎谁也没有注意哈利，这正合他的心意。他赶在弗农姨父重重关上房门前溜了进来。当德思礼一家闹哄哄地穿过门厅走向厨房时，哈利小心地蹑手蹑脚地朝楼梯走去。

"这是谁干的，儿子？快把他们的名字告诉我们。我们会抓住他们的，不用担心。"

"嘘！他正要说话呢，弗农！怎么回事，达达？快告诉妈妈！"

哈利的脚刚踏上第一级楼梯，达力终于发出了声音。

"他。"

哈利怔住了，一只脚踏在楼梯上，脸扭成一团，鼓起勇气准备迎接一场大爆炸。

"小子！你给我过来！"

哈利怀着恐惧和愤怒的心情，慢慢地把脚从楼梯上撤下来，转身跟上了德思礼一家。

刚从外面的夜色中进来，哈利觉得擦洗得一尘不染的厨房明晃晃

CHAPTER TWO   A Peck of Owls

very green and clammy-looking. Uncle Vernon was standing in front of the draining board, glaring at Harry through tiny, narrowed eyes.

'What have you done to my son?' he said in a menacing growl.

'Nothing,' said Harry, knowing perfectly well that Uncle Vernon wouldn't believe him.

'What did he do to you, Diddy?' Aunt Petunia said in a quavering voice, now sponging sick from the front of Dudley's leather jacket. 'Was it – was it you-know-what, darling? Did he use – his *thing*?'

Slowly, tremulously, Dudley nodded.

'I didn't!' Harry said sharply, as Aunt Petunia let out a wail and Uncle Vernon raised his fists. 'I didn't do anything to him, it wasn't me, it was –'

But at that precise moment a screech owl swooped in through the kitchen window. Narrowly missing the top of Uncle Vernon's head, it soared across the kitchen, dropped the large parchment envelope it was carrying in its beak at Harry's feet, turned gracefully, the tips of its wings just brushing the top of the fridge, then zoomed outside again and off across the garden.

'OWLS!' bellowed Uncle Vernon, the well-worn vein in his temple pulsing angrily as he slammed the kitchen window shut. 'OWLS AGAIN! I WILL NOT HAVE ANY MORE OWLS IN MY HOUSE!'

But Harry was already ripping open the envelope and pulling out the letter inside, his heart pounding somewhere in the region of his Adam's apple.

> Dear Mr Potter,
>
> We have received intelligence that you performed the Patronus Charm at twenty-three minutes past nine this evening in a Muggle-inhabited area and in the presence of a Muggle.
>
> The severity of this breach of the Decree for the Reasonable Restriction of Underage Sorcery has resulted in your expulsion from Hogwarts School of Witchcraft and Wizardry. Ministry representatives will be calling at your place of residence shortly to destroy your wand.
>
> As you have already received an official warning for a previous offence under Section 13 of the International Confederation of Warlocks' Statute of Secrecy, we regret to inform you that your

第2章 一群猫头鹰

的，显得怪异而不真实。佩妮姨妈领着达力坐到一把椅子上。达力仍然脸色发青，一副病恹恹的样子。弗农姨父站在滴水板前，眯起一对小眼睛，狠狠地瞪着哈利。

"你对我儿子做了什么？"他气势汹汹地吼道。

"什么也没做。"哈利说，他很清楚弗农姨父根本不会相信他的话。

"他对你做了什么，达达？"佩妮姨妈一边用湿海绵擦去达力皮夹克上的脏东西，一边用发抖的声音问道，"是——是那玩意儿吗，亲爱的？他用了——他的家伙？"

达力颤抖着慢慢点点头。

"我没有！"哈利急切地说，佩妮姨妈发出一声号啕，弗农姨父举起两个拳头，"我没有把他怎么样，那不是我，那是——"

就在这时，一只长耳猫头鹰忽地从窗户飞进了厨房，擦着弗农姨父的头顶，轻盈地从厨房那头飞过来，把嘴里叼着的一个羊皮纸大信封丢在哈利脚边，然后优雅地一转身，翅膀尖正好扫过冰箱顶，嗖的一声飞了出去，掠过花园上空消失了。

"猫头鹰！"弗农姨父气得大吼，狠狠地把厨房窗户砰的一声关上了，太阳穴上的那根经常暴起的血管又在突突跳动。"又是猫头鹰！再也不许猫头鹰进我的家里！"

哈利已经扯开信封，抽出了里面的信，他的心怦怦狂跳，已经快要跳到嗓子眼了。

亲爱的波特先生：

　　我们接到情报，你于今晚九点二十三分在一个麻瓜居住区，当着一个麻瓜的面施用了守护神咒。

　　这一行为严重违反了《对未成年巫师加以合理约束法》，因此你已被霍格沃茨魔法学校开除。魔法部将很快派代表前往你的住所，销毁你的魔杖。

　　鉴于你此前已因违反《国际巫师联合会保密法》的第十三条而受到正式警告，我们很遗憾地通知你，你必须在八月十二日上

presence is required at a disciplinary hearing at the Ministry of Magic at 9 a.m. on the twelfth of August.

Hoping you are well,

Yours sincerely,

Mafalda Hopkirk

Improper Use of Magic Office

Ministry of Magic

Harry read the letter through twice. He was only vaguely aware of Uncle Vernon and Aunt Petunia talking. Inside his head, all was icy and numb. One fact had penetrated his consciousness like a paralysing dart. He was expelled from Hogwarts. It was all over. He was never going back.

He looked up at the Dursleys. Uncle Vernon was purple-faced, shouting, his fists still raised; Aunt Petunia had her arms around Dudley, who was retching again.

Harry's temporarily stupefied brain seemed to reawaken. *Ministry representatives will be calling at your place of residence shortly to destroy your wand.* There was only one thing for it. He would have to run – now. Where he was going to go, Harry didn't know, but he was certain of one thing: at Hogwarts or outside it, he needed his wand. In an almost dreamlike state, he pulled his wand out and turned to leave the kitchen.

'Where d'you think you're going?' yelled Uncle Vernon. When Harry didn't reply, he pounded across the kitchen to block the doorway into the hall. 'I haven't finished with you, boy!'

'Get out of the way,' said Harry quietly.

'You're going to stay here and explain how my son –'

'If you don't get out of the way I'm going to jinx you,' said Harry, raising the wand.

'You can't pull that one on me!' snarled Uncle Vernon. 'I know you're not allowed to use it outside that madhouse you call a school!'

'The madhouse has chucked me out,' said Harry. 'So I can do whatever I like. You've got three seconds. One – two –'

A resounding CRACK filled the kitchen. Aunt Petunia screamed, Uncle Vernon yelled and ducked, but for the third time that night Harry was

第2章 一群猫头鹰

午九时前往魔法部受审。

希望你多多保重。

你忠实的

马法尔达·霍普柯克

魔法部禁止滥用魔法办公室

哈利把信连读了两遍。他只模模糊糊地意识到弗农姨父和佩妮姨妈在那儿说着什么。他脑海里一片冰冷，一片空白。一个事实像一把致人瘫痪的飞镖扎进了他的意识。他被霍格沃茨开除了。一切都完了。他再也回不去了。

他抬头望着德思礼一家。弗农姨父的脸涨成了猪肝色，他大声吼叫着，两只拳头仍然高高地举着。佩妮姨妈用两只胳膊搂着又在干呕不止的达力。

哈利暂时麻木的思维似乎慢慢苏醒了过来。魔法部将很快派代表前往你的住所，销毁你的魔杖。只有一个办法。他必须逃走——事不宜迟。究竟去哪儿呢，哈利不知道，但有一点是肯定的：不管在霍格沃茨校内还是校外，他都离不开他的魔杖。在一种几乎是半梦半醒的状态中，他抽出魔杖，转身想离开厨房。

"你打算上哪儿去？"弗农姨父嚷道。看到哈利没有回答，他嘟嘟囔囔地从厨房那头走过来，挡在通往门厅的门口，"你的事儿还没完呢，小子！"

"闪开！"哈利轻声说。

"你必须待在这里，老实交代我的儿子怎么会——"

"如果你不闪开，我就给你念一个恶咒。"哈利说着举起了魔杖。

"你别想用它来对付我！"弗农姨父恶狠狠地说，"我知道，你出了那所你称为学校的疯人院，是不允许摆弄它的！"

"疯人院已经把我赶出来了，"哈利说，"所以我愿意干什么就干什么。现在给你三秒钟。——一——二——"

厨房里发出一声**爆响**，回音不绝。佩妮姨妈失声尖叫，弗农姨父吼叫着弯腰躲避，而哈利呢，他在寻找一场不是由他造成的混乱的源头，

CHAPTER TWO   A Peck of Owls

searching for the source of a disturbance he had not made. He spotted it at once: a dazed and ruffled-looking barn owl was sitting outside on the kitchen sill, having just collided with the closed window.

Ignoring Uncle Vernon's anguished yell of 'OWLS!' Harry crossed the room at a run and wrenched the window open. The owl stuck out its leg, to which a small roll of parchment was tied, shook its feathers, and took off the moment Harry had taken the letter. Hands shaking, Harry unfurled the second message, which was written very hastily and blotchily in black ink.

> Harry -
>
> Dumbledore's just arrived at the Ministry and he's trying to sort it all out. DO NOT LEAVE YOUR AUNT AND UNCLE'S HOUSE. DO NOT DO ANY MORE MAGIC. DO NOT SURRENDER YOUR WAND.
>
> Arthur Weasley

Dumbledore was trying to sort it all out ... what did that mean? How much power did Dumbledore have to override the Ministry of Magic? Was there a chance that he might be allowed back to Hogwarts, then? A small shoot of hope burgeoned in Harry's chest, almost immediately strangled by panic – how was he supposed to refuse to surrender his wand without doing magic? He'd have to duel with the Ministry representatives, and if he did that, he'd be lucky to escape Azkaban, let alone expulsion.

His mind was racing ... he could run for it and risk being captured by the Ministry, or stay put and wait for them to find him here. He was much more tempted by the former course, but he knew Mr Weasley had his best interests at heart ... and after all, Dumbledore had sorted out much worse than this before.

'Right,' Harry said, 'I've changed my mind, I'm staying.'

He flung himself down at the kitchen table and faced Dudley and Aunt Petunia. The Dursleys appeared taken aback at his abrupt change of mind. Aunt Petunia glanced despairingly at Uncle Vernon. The vein in his purple temple was throbbing worse than ever.

'Who are all these ruddy owls from?' he growled.

'The first one was from the Ministry of Magic, expelling me,' said Harry calmly. He was straining his ears to catch any noises outside, in case the

这已经是这个晚上的第三次了。他立刻发现了：一只昏头昏脑、羽毛蓬乱的谷仓猫头鹰，正蹲在厨房外的窗台上，刚才它撞在关着的窗户玻璃上了。

弗农姨父痛苦地嚷道："猫头鹰！"哈利没有理睬他，径直跑到厨房那头，猛地打开窗户。猫头鹰伸出一条腿，上面拴着一小卷羊皮纸。它抖了抖羽毛，哈利刚把信取下来它就飞走了。哈利颤抖着双手，展开这第二封信，上面用黑墨水草草地写着几行字，纸上污渍斑斑。

哈利：

邓布利多刚赶到魔法部，正在尽力解决这件事。**不要离开你姨妈和姨父的家。不要再施魔法。不要交出你的魔杖。**

亚瑟·韦斯莱

邓布利多正在尽力解决这件事……这是什么意思呢？邓布利多有多大的权力来推翻魔法部的决定呢？这么说，哈利还有可能重新回到霍格沃茨？一线小小的希望在哈利心中迅速升起，但几乎立刻就被惊慌的情绪扼杀了——他不施魔法，怎么可能拒绝交出魔杖呢？他必须与魔法部的代表展开较量。如果他那么做了，能够逃脱阿兹卡班监狱已算侥幸，更别说被学校开除了。

他脑子飞快地转着……他可以赶快逃走，冒着被魔法部抓到的危险，也可以待在原地，等着他们来这里找他。他觉得第一条路更有吸引力，但知道韦斯莱先生肯定考虑过怎样对他最有利……而且，邓布利多以前处理过比这糟糕得多的事情呢。

"好吧，"哈利说，"我改变主意了，我不走了。"

他飞快地扑到厨房桌子旁，面对达力和佩妮姨妈。德思礼一家似乎对他这样突然改变主意吃惊不小。佩妮姨妈绝望地望着弗农姨父。弗农姨父紫红色太阳穴上的血管跳得比以前更厉害了。

"这些讨厌透顶的猫头鹰是谁派来的？"他凶狠地吼道。

"第一只是魔法部派来的，把我开除了。"哈利平静地说。他竖起两只耳朵，专心听着外面的动静，生怕魔法部的代表已经来了。现在

CHAPTER TWO A Peck of Owls

Ministry representatives were approaching, and it was easier and quieter to answer Uncle Vernon's questions than to have him start raging and bellowing. 'The second one was from my friend Ron's dad, who works at the Ministry.'

'*Ministry of Magic?*' bellowed Uncle Vernon. 'People like you in *government*? Oh, this explains everything, everything, no wonder the country's going to the dogs.'

When Harry did not respond, Uncle Vernon glared at him, then spat out, 'And why have you been expelled?'

'Because I did magic.'

'AHA!' roared Uncle Vernon, slamming his fist down on top of the fridge, which sprang open; several of Dudley's low-fat snacks toppled out and burst on the floor. 'So you admit it! *What did you do to Dudley?*'

'Nothing,' said Harry, slightly less calmly. 'That wasn't me –'

'*Was*,' muttered Dudley unexpectedly, and Uncle Vernon and Aunt Petunia instantly made flapping gestures at Harry to quieten him while they both bent low over Dudley.

'Go on, son,' said Uncle Vernon, 'what did he do?'

'Tell us, darling,' whispered Aunt Petunia.

'Pointed his wand at me,' Dudley mumbled.

'Yeah, I did, but I didn't use –' Harry began angrily, but –

'SHUT UP!' roared Uncle Vernon and Aunt Petunia in unison.

'Go on, son,' repeated Uncle Vernon, moustache blowing about furiously.

'All went dark,' Dudley said hoarsely, shuddering. 'Everything dark. And then I h-heard ... *things*. Inside m-my head.'

Uncle Vernon and Aunt Petunia exchanged looks of utter horror. If their least favourite thing in the world was magic – closely followed by neighbours who cheated more than they did on the hosepipe ban – people who heard voices were definitely in the bottom ten. They obviously thought Dudley was losing his mind.

'What sort of things did you hear, Popkin?' breathed Aunt Petunia, very white-faced and with tears in her eyes.

But Dudley seemed incapable of saying. He shuddered again and shook his large blond head, and despite the sense of numb dread that had settled on

第2章 一群猫头鹰

与其让弗农姨父大发雷霆、怒吼咆哮，还不如回答他的问题更容易，也更安静。"第二只是我朋友罗恩的爸爸派来的，他在魔法部工作。"

"魔法部？"弗农姨父恶声恶气地说，"你们这样的人也能在政府工作？哦，我总算都明白了，都明白了，怪不得这个国家如今一天不如一天呢。"

哈利没有回答。弗农姨父气呼呼地瞪着他，然后厉声问："你为什么会被开除？"

"因为我使用了魔法。"

"**啊哈！**"弗农姨父吼道，拳头重重地砸在冰箱顶上，冰箱的门忽地弹开，达力的几包低脂肪小食品掉了出来，散落在地上，"这么说你承认了！你对达力做了什么？"

"什么也没有，"哈利说，不像刚才那么平静了，"那不是我——"

"是你！"达力出人意料地冒出一句，弗农姨父和佩妮姨妈立刻朝哈利挥舞着胳膊让他闭嘴，然后两人都俯身看着达力。

"说下去，儿子，"弗农姨父说，"他做了什么？"

"告诉我们，亲爱的。"佩妮姨妈小声说。

"他用魔杖指着我。"达力含混不清地说。

"是啊，我指着他，但并没有用——"哈利气愤地说，然而——

"**闭嘴！**"弗农姨父和佩妮姨妈异口同声地吼道。

"说下去，儿子。"弗农姨父又说了一遍，小胡子上下乱舞。

"全黑了，"达力打着寒战，声音嘶哑地说，"四下里一片漆黑。然后我听——听见……有东西。在我——我的脑袋里。"

弗农姨父和佩妮姨妈交换了一个惊恐万状的眼神。如果说在这个世界上他们最不喜欢的东西是魔法——其次就是邻居在禁用浇水软管的事情上弄虚作假，做得比他们更过分——那么听到自己脑子里有人说话，肯定也是最糟糕的事情之一。他们显然认为达力已经精神错乱了。

"你听见什么样的话了，宝贝？"佩妮姨妈压低声音问，脸色白得吓人，眼里含着泪水。

可是达力似乎不会说话了。他又打了个寒战，摇了摇那颗金色头发的大脑袋。尽管第一只猫头鹰到来后，哈利的内心已因恐惧而近乎

CHAPTER TWO   A Peck of Owls

Harry since the arrival of the first owl, he felt a certain curiosity. Dementors caused a person to relive the worst moments of their life. What would spoiled, pampered, bullying Dudley have been forced to hear?

'How come you fell over, son?' said Uncle Vernon, in an unnaturally quiet voice, the kind of voice he might adopt at the bedside of a very ill person.

'T-tripped,' said Dudley shakily. 'And then –'

He gestured at his massive chest. Harry understood. Dudley was remembering the clammy cold that filled the lungs as hope and happiness were sucked out of you.

'Horrible,' croaked Dudley. 'Cold. Really cold.'

'OK,' said Uncle Vernon, in a voice of forced calm, while Aunt Petunia laid an anxious hand on Dudley's forehead to feel his temperature. 'What happened then, Dudders?'

'Felt ... felt ... felt ... as if ... as if ...'

'As if you'd never be happy again,' Harry supplied tonelessly.

'Yes,' Dudley whispered, still trembling.

'So!' said Uncle Vernon, voice restored to full and considerable volume as he straightened up. 'You put some crackpot spell on my son so he'd hear voices and believe he was – was doomed to misery, or something, did you?'

'How many times do I have to tell you?' said Harry, temper and voice both rising. '*It wasn't me!* It was a couple of Dementors!'

'A couple of – what's this codswallop?'

'De – men – tors,' said Harry slowly and clearly. 'Two of them.'

'And what the ruddy hell are Dementors?'

'They guard the wizard prison, Azkaban,' said Aunt Petunia.

Two seconds of ringing silence followed these words before Aunt Petunia clapped her hand over her mouth as though she had let slip a disgusting swear word. Uncle Vernon was goggling at her. Harry's brain reeled. Mrs Figg was one thing – but *Aunt Petunia?*

'How d'you know that?' he asked her, astonished.

Aunt Petunia looked quite appalled with herself. She glanced at Uncle Vernon in fearful apology, then lowered her hand slightly to reveal her horsy teeth.

'I heard – that awful boy – telling *her* about them – years ago,' she said

第2章 一群猫头鹰

麻木，但此刻他也感到有些好奇。摄魂怪能使人重新经历一生中最痛苦的时刻。那么，这个被溺爱的养尊处优、横行霸道的达力，会被迫听到什么呢？

"你是怎么摔倒的，儿子？"弗农姨父问，用的是一种很不自然的轻声细语，就像在一个病入膏肓的病人床边说话。

"绊——绊了一跤，"达力发着抖说，"后来——"

他指了指自己肥阔的胸脯。哈利明白了。达力想起了希望和快乐被吸走时灌满他肺部的那股阴森森的寒气。

"可怕，"达力声音嘶哑地说，"冷。冷极了。"

"好吧，"弗农姨父说，尽量使声音显得平静，"接下来发生了什么事，达力？"佩妮姨妈焦急地把手放在达力的额头上，试试他发不发烧。

"觉得……觉得……觉得……好像……好像……"

"好像你再也不会感到快乐了。"哈利干巴巴地替他说道。

"就是这样。"达力小声说，仍然抖个不停。

"知道了！"弗农姨父直起身，重新扯开了嗓子，声音震耳欲聋，"你给我儿子念了一个古怪的咒语，害得他听见自己脑子里有人说话，还以为自己——自己一辈子也快活不起来了，是不是？"

"我还要告诉你们多少遍？"哈利说，声音和火气同时上升，"不是我。是两个摄魂怪！"

"两个——什么乱七八糟的东西？"

"摄——魂——怪，"哈利慢慢地一字一顿地说，"两个。"

"这摄魂怪又是什么古怪玩意儿？"

"他们看守阿兹卡班巫师监狱。"佩妮姨妈说。

话一出口，是两秒钟的死寂，然后佩妮姨妈猛地用手捂住嘴巴，似乎刚才不小心说了一句令人恶心的脏话。弗农姨父瞪大眼睛看着她。哈利脑子里一片混乱。费格太太倒也罢了——可是佩妮姨妈？

"你怎么知道？"他惊讶极了，问道。

佩妮姨妈似乎被自己吓坏了。她战战兢兢带着歉意地看了一眼弗农姨父，手微微下垂，露出嘴里的长牙。

"好多年前——我听见——那个可怕的男孩——对她说起过它们。"

CHAPTER TWO   A Peck of Owls

jerkily.

'If you mean my mum and dad, why don't you use their names?' said Harry loudly, but Aunt Petunia ignored him. She seemed horribly flustered.

Harry was stunned. Except for one outburst years ago, in the course of which Aunt Petunia had screamed that Harry's mother had been a freak, he had never heard her mention her sister. He was astounded that she had remembered this scrap of information about the magical world for so long, when she usually put all her energies into pretending it didn't exist.

Uncle Vernon opened his mouth, closed it again, opened it once more, shut it, then, apparently struggling to remember how to talk, opened it for a third time and croaked, 'So – so – they – er – they – er – they actually exist, do they – er – Dementy-whatsits?'

Aunt Petunia nodded.

Uncle Vernon looked from Aunt Petunia to Dudley to Harry as if hoping somebody was going to shout 'April Fool!' When nobody did, he opened his mouth yet again, but was spared the struggle to find more words by the arrival of the third owl of the evening. It zoomed through the still-open window like a feathery cannonball and landed with a clatter on the kitchen table, causing all three of the Dursleys to jump with fright. Harry tore a second official-looking envelope from the owl's beak and ripped it open as the owl swooped back out into the night.

'Enough – effing – *owls*,' muttered Uncle Vernon distractedly, stomping over to the window and slamming it shut again.

> **Dear Mr Potter,**
> Further to our letter of approximately twenty-two minutes ago, the Ministry of Magic has revised its decision to destroy your wand forthwith. You may retain your wand until your disciplinary hearing on the twelfth of August, at which time an official decision will be taken.
> Following discussions with the Headmaster of Hogwarts School of Witchcraft and Wizardry, the Ministry has agreed that the question of your expulsion will also be decided at that time. You should therefore consider yourself suspended from

第2章 一群猫头鹰

她断断续续地说。

"如果你是指我的爸爸妈妈,你为什么不说他们的名字呢?"哈利大声问,但佩妮姨妈没有理睬他。她似乎惊慌失措到了极点。

哈利感到非常震惊。几年前有一次佩妮姨妈情绪爆发,尖叫着说哈利的妈妈是个怪物,除此之外,哈利从没听她提起过自己的妹妹。而她居然记得魔法世界的这点细节,这么长时间都没有忘记。哈利真是惊讶极了,平常佩妮姨妈总是竭力假装魔法世界并不存在的呀。

弗农姨父张了张嘴又闭上,接着又张了张又闭上,然后,显然是在挣扎着回忆怎样说话。他第三次把嘴张开,声音嘶哑地说:"这么说——这么说——他们——呃——他们——呃——真的存在,他们——呃——这些死魂怪什么的?"

佩妮姨妈点了点头。

弗农姨父的目光从佩妮姨妈身上转向达力,又转向哈利,似乎希望有人大喊一声:"愚人节!"看到没有人这么做,他又把嘴巴张开了,而就在这时,今晚的第三只猫头鹰飞来了,他也就不用费力地再说什么。猫头鹰像一枚长着羽毛的炮弹,嗖的一声飞进仍然开着的窗户,啪嗒嗒地落在厨房的桌子上,吓得德思礼一家三口都跳了起来。哈利从猫头鹰嘴里扯下第二封公函样的信封,撕开封口,猫头鹰腾身飞回了外面的夜色中。

"够了——粗鲁的——猫头鹰。"弗农姨父心烦意乱地说,噔噔噔地走到窗口,又把窗户重重地关上。

亲爱的波特先生:

  我们约二十二分钟前曾致函于你,之后魔法部改变了立即销毁你的魔杖的决定。我们允许你保留魔杖,直到八月十二日受审时再做正式决定。

  经与霍格沃茨魔法学校校长商量,魔法部同意将开除你学籍的问题也留到那时再做决定。因此,你可以认为自己是暂时停学,

CHAPTER TWO   A Peck of Owls

school pending further enquiries.
With best wishes,
Yours sincerely,
Mafalda Hopkirk
Improper Use of Magic Office
Ministry of Magic

Harry read this letter through three times in quick succession. The miserable knot in his chest loosened slightly with the relief of knowing he was not yet definitely expelled, though his fears were by no means banished. Everything seemed to hang on this hearing on the twelfth of August.

'Well?' said Uncle Vernon, recalling Harry to his surroundings. 'What now? Have they sentenced you to anything? Do your lot have the death penalty?' he added as a hopeful afterthought.

'I've got to go to a hearing,' said Harry.

'And they'll sentence you there?'

'I suppose so.'

'I won't give up hope, then,' said Uncle Vernon nastily.

'Well, if that's all,' said Harry, getting to his feet. He was desperate to be alone, to think, perhaps to send a letter to Ron, Hermione or Sirius.

'NO, IT RUDDY WELL IS NOT ALL!' bellowed Uncle Vernon. 'SIT BACK DOWN!'

'What *now*?' said Harry impatiently.

'DUDLEY!' roared Uncle Vernon. 'I want to know exactly what happened to my son!'

'FINE!' yelled Harry, and in his temper, red and gold sparks shot out of the end of his wand, still clutched in his hand. All three Dursleys flinched, looking terrified.

'Dudley and I were in the alleyway between Magnolia Crescent and Wisteria Walk,' said Harry, speaking fast, fighting to control his temper. 'Dudley thought he'd be smart with me, I pulled out my wand but didn't use it. Then two Dementors turned up –'

'But what ARE Dementoids?' asked Uncle Vernon furiously. 'What do they DO?'

第2章 一群猫头鹰

等候进一步的调查。

顺致问候。

你忠实的

马法尔达·霍普柯克

魔法部禁止滥用魔法办公室

哈利飞快地将信连看了三遍。知道自己还没有肯定被开除，心头那个令人难受的疙瘩总算解开了一点，但他的担心丝毫没有消除。似乎所有的事情都取决于八月十二日的受审。

"怎么了？"弗农姨父说，把哈利一下子拉回到现实中，"现在又怎么啦？他们给你判决了没有？"他突然产生了一个念头，满怀希望地跟着问了这一句，"你们那类人有没有死刑啊？"

"我要去受审。"哈利说。

"他们在那儿给你判决？"

"我想是吧。"

"我不会放弃希望的。"弗农姨父满脸凶相地说。

"好吧，如果完事了的话——"哈利说着站了起来。他迫不及待地想清静一会儿，好好想一想，也许还要给罗恩、赫敏或小天狼星写一封信。

"**没有，事情还没有完！**"弗农姨父吼道，"**坐下去！**"

"还有什么？"哈利不耐烦地问。

"**达力！**"弗农姨父咆哮着说，"我想知道我的儿子到底出了什么事！"

"**很好！**"哈利大喊一声。他气坏了，手里仍然攥着的魔杖杖头上冒出了红色和金色的火星。德思礼一家三口纷纷后退，一副大惊失色的样子。

"达力和我走在木兰花新月街和紫藤路之间的小巷里，"哈利语速极快地说，他拼命克制着自己的火气，"达力跟我斗嘴，我抽出了魔杖，但并没有用它。这时两个摄魂怪出现了——"

"这个摄魂鬼**是**什么东西？"弗农姨父狂怒地问，"它们是**做**什么的？"

CHAPTER TWO   A Peck of Owls

'I told you – they suck all the happiness out of you,' said Harry, 'and if they get the chance, they kiss you –'

'Kiss you?' said Uncle Vernon, his eyes popping slightly. '*Kiss* you?'

'It's what they call it when they suck the soul out of your mouth.'

Aunt Petunia uttered a soft scream.

'His *soul*? They didn't take – he's still got his –'

She seized Dudley by the shoulders and shook him, as though testing to see whether she could hear his soul rattling around inside him.

'Of course they didn't get his soul, you'd know if they had,' said Harry, exasperated.

'Fought 'em off, did you, son?' said Uncle Vernon loudly, with the appearance of a man struggling to bring the conversation back on to a plane he understood. 'Gave 'em the old one-two, did you?'

'You can't give a Dementor *the old one-two*,' said Harry through clenched teeth.

'Why's he all right, then?' blustered Uncle Vernon. 'Why isn't he all empty, then?'

'Because I used the Patronus –'

WHOOSH. With a clattering, a whirring of wings and a soft fall of dust, a fourth owl came shooting out of the kitchen fireplace.

'FOR GOD'S SAKE!' roared Uncle Vernon, pulling great clumps of hair out of his moustache, something he hadn't been driven to do in a long time. 'I WILL NOT HAVE OWLS HERE, I WILL NOT TOLERATE THIS, I TELL YOU!'

But Harry was already pulling a roll of parchment from the owl's leg. He was so convinced that this letter had to be from Dumbledore, explaining everything – the Dementors, Mrs Figg, what the Ministry was up to, how he, Dumbledore, intended to sort everything out – that for the first time in his life he was disappointed to see Sirius's handwriting. Ignoring Uncle Vernon's ongoing rant about owls, and narrowing his eyes against a second cloud of dust as the most recent owl took off back up the chimney, Harry read Sirius's message.

第2章 一群猫头鹰

"我告诉过你了——它们吸光你内心所有的快乐,"哈利说,"如果逮着机会,它们还会亲吻你——"

"亲吻?"弗农姨父说,眼珠子微微凸了出来,"亲吻?"

"把灵魂从你的嘴里吸出来,它们管这叫'亲吻'。"

佩妮姨妈发出一声低低的惊叫。

"他的灵魂?它们没有吸走——他的灵魂没有被吸——"

佩妮姨妈抓住达力的两个肩膀拼命摇晃,好像要试试能不能听见他的灵魂在身体里哗啦啦作响似的。

"它们当然没有吸走他的灵魂,如果真是那样,你们会知道的。"哈利气恼地说。

"你把它们打跑了,是吗,儿子?"弗农姨父大声说,看他那模样,似乎正挣扎着把谈话拖回到他能理解的水平上,"你给了它们一个'左直拳接右直拳',是不是?"

"他不可能给摄魂怪一个左直拳接右直拳。"哈利从牙缝里挤出声音说道。

"那他怎么会没事?"弗农姨父气势汹汹地问,"他怎么没有被吸空,嗯?"

"因为我念了守护神——"

呼呼。随着一阵撞击声,翅膀扇动,灰尘轻轻落处,第四只猫头鹰从厨房的壁炉里冲了出来。

"**看在老天的分儿上!**"弗农姨父大叫,把一撮撮胡子连根拔了下来,他已经很长时间没有被逼到这个地步了,"**不许猫头鹰到这里来,我受不了啦,你给我听着!**"

可是哈利已经从猫头鹰脚上扯下了一卷羊皮纸。他相信这封信肯定是邓布利多寄来的,而且解释清楚了所有的事情——摄魂怪、费格太太、魔法部的勾当,还有他邓布利多打算怎样把事情摆平——因此,平生第一次,他看到小天狼星的笔迹后感到非常失望。他没有理睬弗农姨父继续对猫头鹰的事大叫大嚷,刚来的猫头鹰扑扇着翅膀从烟囱里飞出去时又搅起一片灰尘,他只好眯起眼睛,读着小天狼星的来信。

CHAPTER TWO A Peck of Owls

Arthur has just told us what's happened.
Don't leave the house again, whatever you do.

Harry found this such an inadequate response to everything that had happened tonight that he turned the piece of parchment over, looking for the rest of the letter, but there was nothing else.

And now his temper was rising again. Wasn't *anybody* going to say 'well done' for fighting off two Dementors single-handed? Both Mr Weasley and Sirius were acting as though he'd misbehaved, and were saving their tellings-off until they could ascertain how much damage had been done.

'... a peck, I mean, pack of owls shooting in and out of my house. I won't have it, boy, I won't –'

'I can't stop the owls coming,' Harry snapped, crushing Sirius's letter in his fist.

'I want the truth about what happened tonight!' barked Uncle Vernon. 'If it was Demenders who hurt Dudley, how come you've been expelled? You did you-know-what, you've admitted it!'

Harry took a deep, steadying breath. His head was beginning to ache again. He wanted more than anything to get out of the kitchen, and away from the Dursleys.

'I did the Patronus Charm to get rid of the Dementors,' he said, forcing himself to remain calm. 'It's the only thing that works against them.'

'But what were Dementoids *doing* in Little Whinging?' said Uncle Vernon in an outraged tone.

'Couldn't tell you,' said Harry wearily. 'No idea.'

His head was pounding in the glare of the strip-lighting now. His anger was ebbing away. He felt drained, exhausted. The Dursleys were all staring at him.

'It's you,' said Uncle Vernon forcefully. 'It's got something to do with you, boy, I know it. Why else would they turn up here? Why else would they be down that alleyway? You've got to be the only – the only –' Evidently, he couldn't bring himself to say the word 'wizard'. 'The only *you-know-what* for miles.'

'I don't know why they were here.'

第2章 一群猫头鹰

亚瑟刚把事情告诉了我们。无论如何,你千万别再离开那所房子。

哈利觉得,对今晚发生的事做出这样的反应实在太不够意思了。他把羊皮纸翻过来,以为反面还有话,但什么也没有。

他的火气又上来了。他只身一人打跑了两个摄魂怪,难道就没有一个人对他说一声"干得漂亮"?看韦斯莱先生和小天狼星的反应,就好像他做了什么错事,他们要等弄清他造成了多大的破坏,再好好地训斥他一顿。

"……一堆,我的意思是,一群猫头鹰在我家里飞进飞出。我不允许,小子,我不——"

"猫头鹰要来,我也没有办法。"哈利没好气地说,使劲把小天狼星的来信捏在手心里。

"我想知道今晚事情的真相!"弗农姨父厉声吼道,"如果是摄魂怪伤害了达力,为什么你会被开除?你干了那事,你已经承认了!"

哈利深深吸了口气,镇定一下情绪。他的头又开始疼了。他最渴望的就是离开这间厨房,离开德思礼一家三口。

"为了摆脱摄魂怪,我念了守护神咒,"他说,竭力使自己保持平静,"对付它们只有这个办法管用。"

"可是摄魂怪跑到小惠金区来做什么?"弗农姨父怒不可遏地问。

"没法告诉你。"哈利疲倦地说,"不知道。"

现在他的脑袋在灯管投射出的强光下突突作响。他的愤怒逐渐消退,人觉得特别疲倦,浑身一点力气也没有了。德思礼一家三口都在瞪着他。

"是你,"弗农姨父恶狠狠地说,"肯定跟你有点关系,小子,我知道。不然它们为什么会出现在这儿?不然它们为什么会跑到那条小巷子里?方圆多少英里,你是唯一的一个——唯一的——"显然,他没有勇气说出"巫师"这个词,"一个你知道是什么的货色。"

"我也不知道它们为什么会上这儿来。"

但是听了弗农姨父的话,哈利已经极度疲劳的大脑又开始吱吱嘎

CHAPTER TWO A Peck of Owls

But at Uncle Vernon's words, Harry's exhausted brain had ground back into action. Why *had* the Dementors come to Little Whinging? How *could* it be coincidence that they had arrived in the alleyway where Harry was? Had they been sent? Had the Ministry of Magic lost control of the Dementors? Had they deserted Azkaban and joined Voldemort, as Dumbledore had predicted they would?

'These Demembers guard some weirdo prison?' asked Uncle Vernon, lumbering along in the wake of Harry's train of thought.

'Yes,' said Harry.

If only his head would stop hurting, if only he could just leave the kitchen and get to his dark bedroom and *think* ...

'Oho! They were coming to arrest you!' said Uncle Vernon, with the triumphant air of a man reaching an unassailable conclusion. 'That's it, isn't it, boy? You're on the run from the law!'

'Of course I'm not,' said Harry, shaking his head as though to scare off a fly, his mind racing now.

'Then why –?'

'He must have sent them,' said Harry quietly, more to himself than to Uncle Vernon.

'What's that? Who must have sent them?'

'Lord Voldemort,' said Harry.

He registered dimly how strange it was that the Dursleys, who flinched, winced and squawked if they heard words like 'wizard', 'magic' or 'wand', could hear the name of the most evil wizard of all time without the slightest tremor.

'Lord – hang on,' said Uncle Vernon, his face screwed up, a look of dawning comprehension coming into his piggy eyes. 'I've heard that name ... that was the one who –'

'Murdered my parents, yes,' Harry said.

'But he's gone,' said Uncle Vernon impatiently, without the slightest sign that the murder of Harry's parents might be a painful topic. 'That giant bloke said so. He's gone.'

'He's back,' said Harry heavily.

It felt very strange to be standing here in Aunt Petunia's surgically clean

第2章 一群猫头鹰

嘎地运转起来。摄魂怪为什么到小惠金区来？它们正好落在哈利所在的小巷里，这怎么可能是巧合呢？它们是被派来的吗？难道魔法部失去了对摄魂怪的控制？难道摄魂怪擅自逃离了阿兹卡班，加入了伏地魔一伙，就像邓布利多曾经预言的那样？

"这些死魂怪是看守一家古怪监狱的？"弗农姨父问，吃力地紧跟着哈利的思路。

"是的。"哈利说。

只希望脑袋能够不疼，只希望能够离开厨房，回到黑暗的卧室，好好想想……

"啊哈！它们是来抓你的！"弗农姨父一脸得意地说，像是得出了一个不容辩驳的结论，"就是这么回事，对不对，小子？你想逃脱法律的制裁！"

"当然不是这样。"哈利说，使劲晃晃脑袋，像要赶走一只苍蝇，他的脑子在快速地运转。

"那为什么——？"

"一定是他派它们来的。"哈利轻声说，与其说是他在对弗农姨父说话，不如说是他自言自语。

"什么意思？一定是谁派它们来的？"

"伏地魔。"哈利说。

他模模糊糊地意识到眼前的情景多么奇怪：德思礼一家听到"巫师""魔法"和"魔杖"这样的词都会吓得连连退缩，失声尖叫，而听到有史以来最邪恶的魔头的名字，居然没有一丝一毫的惊慌。

"伏——慢着，"弗农姨父说，他的脸皱成一团，猪眼似的小眼睛里慢慢露出恍然大悟的神情，"我听说过这个名字……他就是那个——"

"杀死我爸爸妈妈的人，没错。"哈利说。

"可是他走了，"弗农姨父不耐烦地说，丝毫没有显出哈利父母被害是一个痛苦的话题，"那个大块头说的。他走了。"

"他又回来了。"哈利语气沉重地说。

他站在佩妮姨妈那像手术室一样整洁干净的厨房里，挨着最高档的冰箱和超宽屏幕电视机，心平气和地跟弗农姨父谈论伏地魔，这感

CHAPTER TWO   A Peck of Owls

kitchen, beside the top-of-the-range fridge and the wide-screen television, talking calmly of Lord Voldemort to Uncle Vernon. The arrival of the Dementors in Little Whinging seemed to have breached the great, invisible wall that divided the relentlessly non-magical world of Privet Drive and the world beyond. Harry's two lives had somehow become fused and everything had been turned upside-down; the Dursleys were asking for details about the magical world, and Mrs Figg knew Albus Dumbledore; Dementors were soaring around Little Whinging, and he might never return to Hogwarts. Harry's head throbbed more painfully.

'Back?' whispered Aunt Petunia.

She was looking at Harry as she had never looked at him before. And all of a sudden, for the very first time in his life, Harry fully appreciated that Aunt Petunia was his mother's sister. He could not have said why this hit him so very powerfully at this moment. All he knew was that he was not the only person in the room who had an inkling of what Lord Voldemort being back might mean. Aunt Petunia had never in her life looked at him like that before. Her large, pale eyes (so unlike her sister's) were not narrowed in dislike or anger, they were wide and fearful. The furious pretence that Aunt Petunia had maintained all Harry's life – that there was no magic and no world other than the world she inhabited with Uncle Vernon – seemed to have fallen away.

'Yes,' Harry said, talking directly to Aunt Petunia now. 'He came back a month ago. I saw him.'

Her hands found Dudley's massive leather-clad shoulders and clutched them.

'Hang on,' said Uncle Vernon, looking from his wife to Harry and back again, apparently dazed and confused by the unprecedented understanding that seemed to have sprung up between them. 'Hang on. This Lord Voldything's back, you say.'

'Yes.'

'The one who murdered your parents.'

'Yes.'

'And now he's sending Dismembers after you?'

'Looks like it,' said Harry.

'I see,' said Uncle Vernon, looking from his white-faced wife to Harry

觉真是非常怪异。今晚摄魂怪光临小惠金区，似乎打破了一堵挡在女贞路这个冷漠的非魔法世界和另一个世界之间的无形高墙。哈利的两种不同生活好像融在了一起，一切都乱了套。德思礼夫妇在询问魔法世界的详细情况，费格太太居然认识阿不思·邓布利多，摄魂怪在小惠金区上空飘来荡去，而他可能再也不能回到霍格沃茨去了。哈利的脑袋一跳一跳地疼得更厉害了。

"回来了？"佩妮姨妈压低声音问。

她望着哈利，那目光是以前从没有过的。突然之间，哈利有生以来第一次充分意识到佩妮姨妈是他妈妈的姐姐。他不明白为什么此刻这样强烈地感受到这一点。他只知道，这个屋子里不只他一个人模糊地意识到伏地魔的复出意味着什么。佩妮姨妈这辈子从没用这种目光看过他。她那双浅色的大眼睛（与她妹妹的眼睛如此不同）不再因厌恶和愤怒而眯起，而是睁得大大的，充满恐惧。哈利一直看着佩妮姨妈在激烈地维护一种假象——魔法根本不存在，除了她和弗农姨父共同生活的这个世界，根本不存在另一个世界——而现在这种假象似乎消失了。

"是的，"哈利说，现在他直接对佩妮姨妈说话了，"他一个月前回来的。我看见过他。"

佩妮姨妈的手摸索着抓住达力穿着皮夹克的肥阔肩膀，紧紧地抓着。

"慢着，"弗农姨父望望妻子，望望哈利，然后又望望妻子，似乎被他们之间突然出现的前所未有的相互理解弄糊涂了，"慢着。你是说，那个叫伏地魔的家伙回来了？"

"是的。"

"就是杀死你父母的那个人？"

"是的。"

"现在他派摄魂灵来追杀你？"

"看来是这样。"哈利说。

"我明白了。"弗农姨父说，目光从妻子苍白的脸上转向哈利，然后把裤子往上提了提。他整个人似乎正在膨胀，那张紫红色的大脸膛

CHAPTER TWO   A Peck of Owls

and hitching up his trousers. He seemed to be swelling, his great purple face stretching before Harry's eyes. 'Well, that settles it,' he said, his shirt front straining as he inflated himself, *'you can get out of this house, boy!'*

'What?' said Harry.

'You heard me – OUT!' Uncle Vernon bellowed, and even Aunt Petunia and Dudley jumped. 'OUT! OUT! I should've done this years ago! Owls treating the place like a rest home, puddings exploding, half the lounge destroyed, Dudley's tail, Marge bobbing around on the ceiling and that flying Ford Anglia – OUT! OUT! You've had it! You're history! You're not staying here if some loony's after you, you're not endangering my wife and son, you're not bringing trouble down on us. If you're going the same way as your useless parents, I've had it! OUT!'

Harry stood rooted to the spot. The letters from the Ministry, Mr Weasley and Sirius were all crushed in his left hand. *Don't leave the house again, whatever you do. DO NOT LEAVE YOUR AUNT AND UNCLE'S HOUSE.*

'You heard me!' said Uncle Vernon, bending forwards now, his massive purple face coming so close to Harry's, he actually felt flecks of spit hit his face. 'Get going! You were all keen to leave half an hour ago! I'm right behind you! Get out and never darken our doorstep again! Why we ever kept you in the first place, I don't know. Marge was right, it should have been the orphanage. We were too damn soft for our own good, thought we could squash it out of you, thought we could turn you normal, but you've been rotten from the beginning and I've had enough – *owls!*'

The fifth owl zoomed down the chimney so fast it actually hit the floor before zooming into the air again with a loud screech. Harry raised his hand to seize the letter, which was in a scarlet envelope, but it soared straight over his head, flying directly at Aunt Petunia, who let out a scream and ducked, her arms over her face. The owl dropped the red envelope on her head, turned, and flew straight back up the chimney.

Harry darted forwards to pick up the letter, but Aunt Petunia beat him to it.

'You can open it if you like,' said Harry, 'but I'll hear what it says anyway. That's a Howler.'

'Let go of it, Petunia!' roared Uncle Vernon. 'Don't touch it, it could be dangerous!'

第2章 一群猫头鹰

在哈利眼前拉长了。"好了，这下子全解决了，"他吸足了气，衬衫的前胸绷得紧紧的，"你可以从这个家里滚出去了，小子！"

"什么？"哈利问。

"我说过了——**出去**！"弗农姨父吼道，就连佩妮姨妈和达力也吓得跳了起来，"**出去！出去**！我好多年前就应该这么做了！猫头鹰把这里当成了疗养所，布丁炸开了花，半个起居室被糟蹋得不成样子，达力长出了尾巴，玛姬在天花板上飘来飘去，还有那辆会飞的福特安格里亚车——**出去！出去**！你玩够了！你该退出了！如果有疯子在追杀你，你就不能留在这里，不能威胁到我的妻子和儿子，不能给我们带来麻烦。如果你要跟你那没用的父母走同一条路，我受够了！**出去**！"

哈利站在原地，脚底像生了根。魔法部、韦斯莱先生和小天狼星的来信都捏在他的左手里。无论如何，你千万别再离开那所房子。**不要离开你姨妈和姨父的家。**

"你听见我的话了！"弗农姨父向前探过身子，那张紫红色的大阔脸凑近哈利的脸，哈利都能感觉到他的唾沫星子喷到自己脸上，"快走！你半小时前不是急着要离开吗？我支持你！滚出去，永远不要再玷污我们家的门槛！我真不明白当初我们怎么会把你留下？玛姬说得对，应该把你送到孤儿院去。我们心肠太软了，到头来自己倒霉，还以为能铲除你身上的孽根，以为能把你变成一个正常人，没想到你从一开始就不可救药，我受够了——猫头鹰！"

第五只猫头鹰嗖的一声从烟囱里蹿了下来，因为速度太快，在它能够再次起飞之前一头撞在地上。它尖厉地叫了一声，又忽地腾空飞起。哈利举起一只手去抓那个深红色的信封，可猫头鹰掠过他的头顶，径直朝佩妮姨妈飞去。佩妮姨妈尖叫一声，抬起两只胳膊护住脸，闪身躲避。猫头鹰把红信封扔在她头上，转身又从烟囱里飞了出去。

哈利冲过去捡那封信，但佩妮姨妈抢先把信拿在了手里。

"如果你愿意，你可以打开，"哈利说，"反正我能听见里面说些什么。这是一封吼叫信。"

"扔掉它，佩妮！"弗农姨父大声吼道，"别碰它，可能会有危险！"

"信是写给我的，"佩妮姨妈声音颤抖地说，"写着我的名字，弗农，

CHAPTER TWO   A Peck of Owls

'It's addressed to me,' said Aunt Petunia in a shaking voice. 'It's addressed to *me*, Vernon, look! *Mrs Petunia Dursley, The Kitchen, Number Four, Privet Drive* –'

She caught her breath, horrified. The red envelope had begun to smoke.

'Open it!' Harry urged her. 'Get it over with! It'll happen anyway.'

'No.'

Aunt Petunia's hand was trembling. She looked wildly around the kitchen as though looking for an escape route, but too late – the envelope burst into flames. Aunt Petunia screamed and dropped it.

An awful voice filled the kitchen, echoing in the confined space, issuing from the burning letter on the table.

'*Remember my last, Petunia.*'

Aunt Petunia looked as though she might faint. She sank into the chair beside Dudley, her face in her hands. The remains of the envelope smouldered into ash in the silence.

'What is this?' Uncle Vernon said hoarsely. 'What – I don't – Petunia?'

Aunt Petunia said nothing. Dudley was staring stupidly at his mother, his mouth hanging open. The silence spiralled horribly. Harry was watching his aunt, utterly bewildered, his head throbbing fit to burst.

'Petunia, dear?' said Uncle Vernon timidly. 'P-Petunia?'

She raised her head. She was still trembling. She swallowed.

'The boy – the boy will have to stay, Vernon,' she said weakly.

'W-what?'

'He stays,' she said. She was not looking at Harry. She got to her feet again.

'He ... but Petunia ...'

'If we throw him out, the neighbours will talk,' she said. She was rapidly regaining her usual brisk, snappish manner, though she was still very pale. 'They'll ask awkward questions, they'll want to know where he's gone. We'll have to keep him.'

Uncle Vernon was deflating like an old tyre.

'But Petunia, dear –'

Aunt Petunia ignored him. She turned to Harry.

'You're to stay in your room,' she said. 'You're not to leave the house. Now

你看！女贞路4号，厨房，佩妮·德思礼夫人——"

她喘不过气来，完全吓坏了。这时红信封开始冒烟。

"快打开！"哈利催促道，"让它快点结束！你逃不过去的。"

"不。"

佩妮姨妈的手在颤抖。她惊慌失措地环顾厨房，似乎在寻找一条逃生之路，可是来不及了——信封蹿出了火苗。佩妮姨妈失声尖叫，扔掉了信封。

一个可怕的声音，从落在桌上的那封燃烧的信里传出来，充满了整个厨房，在有限的空间里回荡着。

记住我最后的，佩妮。

佩妮姨妈看上去似乎要晕倒了。她跌坐在达力旁边的椅子上，两只手捂着脸。信封剩下的残片在寂静中化成了灰烬。

"这是什么？"弗农姨父声音嘶哑地问，"什么——我不明——佩妮？"

佩妮姨妈什么也没说。达力呆呆地瞪着母亲，嘴巴张得大大的。寂静在可怕地升级。哈利无比惊愕地望着姨妈，脑袋疼得像要裂开一般。

"佩妮，亲爱的？"弗农姨父怯生生地问，"佩—佩妮？"

佩妮姨妈抬起头。她仍然抖个不停，费力地咽了口唾沫。

"那孩子——那孩子必须留在这里，弗农。"她有气无力地说。

"什—什么？"

"他留在这里。"她说，但眼睛没有望着哈利。她重新站了起来。

"他……可是佩妮……"

"如果我们把他赶出去，邻居们会说闲话的。"她说。她很快恢复了平日里那种精干、严厉的做派，尽管脸色仍然十分苍白，"他们会问一些令人尴尬的问题，他们会打听他上哪儿去了。我们必须把他留下。"

弗农姨父像只旧轮胎一样泄了气。

"可是佩妮，亲爱的——"

佩妮姨妈没有理睬他，而是转向了哈利。

"你必须待在自己的房间里，"她说，"不许离开这所房子。现在上床去吧。"

CHAPTER TWO   A Peck of Owls

get to bed.'

Harry didn't move.

'Who was that Howler from?'

'Don't ask questions,' Aunt Petunia snapped.

'Are you in touch with wizards?'

'I told you to get to bed!'

'What did it mean? Remember the last what?'

'Go to bed!'

'How come –?'

'YOU HEARD YOUR AUNT, NOW GO UP TO BED!'

哈利没有动弹。

"那封吼叫信是谁寄来的？"

"别问东问西了。"佩妮姨妈厉声呵斥道。

"你跟巫师有联系？"

"我叫你上床去！"

"那句话是什么意思？记住最后的什么？"

"上床去！"

"怎么会——？"

"听见你姨妈的话了吗，快上床去！"

CHAPTER THREE

The Advance Guard

I've just been attacked by Dementors and I might be expelled from Hogwarts. I want to know what's going on and when I'm going to get out of here.

Harry copied these words on to three separate pieces of parchment the moment he reached the desk in his dark bedroom. He addressed the first to Sirius, the second to Ron and the third to Hermione. His owl, Hedwig, was off hunting; her cage stood empty on the desk. Harry paced the bedroom waiting for her to come back, his head pounding, his brain too busy for sleep even though his eyes stung and itched with tiredness. His back ached from hauling Dudley home, and the two lumps on his head where the window and Dudley had hit him were throbbing painfully.

Up and down he paced, consumed with anger and frustration, grinding his teeth and clenching his fists, casting angry looks out at the empty, star-strewn sky every time he passed the window. Dementors sent to get him, Mrs Figg and Mundungus Fletcher tailing him in secret, then suspension from Hogwarts and a hearing at the Ministry of Magic – and still no one was telling him what was going on.

And what, *what*, had that Howler been about? Whose voice had echoed so horribly, so menacingly, through the kitchen?

Why was he still trapped here without information? Why was everyone treating him like some naughty kid? *Don't do any more magic, stay in the house ...*

He kicked his school trunk as he passed it, but far from relieving his anger he felt worse, as he now had a sharp pain in his toe to deal with in addition to the pain in the rest of his body.

第3章

先遣警卫

我刚才遭到摄魂怪的袭击,而且可能会被霍格沃茨开除。我想知道发生了什么事,我什么时候才能离开这里。

哈利走进黑暗的卧室,来到书桌前,立刻把这几句话抄在三张羊皮纸上。第一封信写给小天狼星,第二封信写给罗恩,第三封信写给赫敏。他的猫头鹰海德薇出去捕食了,空空的笼子放在桌上。哈利在卧室里踱来踱去,等着它回来。他的脑袋嗡嗡作响,眼睛累得又疼又涩,但思绪一片混乱,根本不可能睡觉。刚才把达力一路拖回家,现在后背疼得厉害;之前脑袋被窗户撞了一下,又挨了达力一拳,这时两个肿包一跳一跳地疼。

他踱过来踱过去,内心充满了火气和沮丧。他把牙齿咬得咯咯响,拳头捏得紧紧的,每次经过窗口,都把愤怒的目光投向外面群星闪烁的空荡荡的夜空。摄魂怪被派来抓他,费格太太和蒙顿格斯·弗莱奇在偷偷跟踪他,然后他又被霍格沃茨暂时停学,还要到魔法部去受审——而且仍然没有一个人告诉他到底出了什么事。

还有,那封吼叫信说的到底是什么意思?是谁的声音那么可怕、那么气势汹汹地在厨房里回荡?

他为什么仍然被困在这里,得不到半点音讯?为什么每个人都像对待一个调皮捣蛋的孩子那样对待他?不要再施魔法,待在那所房子里……

他走过上学用的箱子时,狠狠地踢了它一脚,可是这非但没有缓解愤怒的心情,反而更糟糕了,现在他不仅要忍受身上其他地方的疼痛,脚趾也钻心地疼。

CHAPTER THREE   The Advance Guard

Just as he limped past the window, Hedwig soared through it with a soft rustle of wings like a small ghost.

'About time!' Harry snarled, as she landed lightly on top of her cage. 'You can put that down, I've got work for you!'

Hedwig's large, round, amber eyes gazed at him reproachfully over the dead frog clamped in her beak.

'Come here,' said Harry, picking up the three small rolls of parchment and a leather thong and tying the scrolls to her scaly leg. 'Take these straight to Sirius, Ron and Hermione and don't come back here without good long replies. Keep pecking them till they've written decent-length answers if you've got to. Understand?'

Hedwig gave a muffled hooting noise, her beak still full of frog.

'Get going, then,' said Harry.

She took off immediately. The moment she'd gone, Harry threw himself down on his bed without undressing and stared at the dark ceiling. In addition to every other miserable feeling, he now felt guilty that he'd been irritable with Hedwig; she was the only friend he had at number four, Privet Drive. But he'd make it up to her when she came back with the answers from Sirius, Ron and Hermione.

They were bound to write back quickly; they couldn't possibly ignore a Dementor attack. He'd probably wake up tomorrow to three fat letters full of sympathy and plans for his immediate removal to The Burrow. And with that comforting idea, sleep rolled over him, stifling all further thought.

But Hedwig didn't return next morning. Harry spent the day in his bedroom, leaving it only to go to the bathroom. Three times that day Aunt Petunia shoved food into his room through the catflap Uncle Vernon had installed three summers ago. Every time Harry heard her approaching he tried to question her about the Howler, but he might as well have interrogated the doorknob for all the answers he got. Otherwise, the Dursleys kept well clear of his bedroom. Harry couldn't see the point of forcing his company on them; another row would achieve nothing except perhaps make him so angry he'd perform more illegal magic.

第3章 先遣警卫

当他一瘸一拐地经过窗口时,海德薇像一个小幽灵似的轻轻扑棱着翅膀飞进了窗户。

"回来得是时候啊!"哈利看到它轻盈地落在笼子顶上,没好气地说,"赶紧把那玩意儿放下,我有活儿等着你干呢!"

海德薇嘴里叼着一只死青蛙,一双圆溜溜的琥珀色大眼睛责备地望着哈利。

"过来。"哈利说着拿起那三小卷羊皮纸和一根皮带子,把羊皮纸拴在海德薇长满鳞片的腿上,"把这些直接送给小天狼星、罗恩和赫敏,必须等拿到长长的回信再回来。如果需要,就不停地用嘴啄他们,逼他们写出长度合适的回信。明白了吗?"

海德薇发出一声含混的叫声,嘴里仍然被青蛙塞得满满的。

"好啦,快走吧。"哈利说。

海德薇立刻出发了。它刚一离开,哈利连衣服都没脱就一头倒在床上,眼睛呆呆地凝视着天花板。现在除了其他痛苦的感觉外,他还为自己刚才对海德薇恶劣的态度而感到内疚。海德薇是他在女贞路4号唯一的朋友。不过,等它拿到小天狼星、罗恩和赫敏的回信回来时,他会好好补偿它的。

他们肯定会很快给他回音的。他们不可能对摄魂怪的攻击无动于衷。没准儿他明天一早醒来,就会看到三封厚厚的信,里面写满了对他的同情,以及安排他立刻转移到陋居的计划。这个想法令他放宽了心,睡意随之袭来,淹没了所有的思绪。

然而,第二天早晨海德薇没有回来。哈利一整天都待在自己的卧室里,只有上厕所时才出去一下。佩妮姨妈一天三次把饭菜通过那扇小活板门塞进他的房间,那还是弗农姨父在三年前的夏天装上的。哈利每次听见佩妮姨妈的脚步声走近,都想问问她那封吼叫信是怎么回事,但这些问题与其问她,还不如去问那只门把手呢。除了送饭,德思礼一家人从不走近他的卧室。哈利也觉得硬跟他们待在一起没有什么意思。再大吵大闹一番不会有任何收获,大概只会惹得自己勃然大怒,忍不住违反法律动用魔法,一错再错。

CHAPTER THREE   The Advance Guard

So it went on for three whole days. Harry was alternately filled with restless energy that made him unable to settle to anything, during which time he paced his bedroom, furious at the whole lot of them for leaving him to stew in this mess; and with a lethargy so complete that he could lie on his bed for an hour at a time, staring dazedly into space, aching with dread at the thought of the Ministry hearing.

What if they ruled against him? What if he *was* expelled and his wand was snapped in half? What would he do, where would he go? He could not return to living full-time with the Dursleys, not now he knew the other world, the one to which he really belonged. Might he be able to move into Sirius's house, as Sirius had suggested a year ago, before he had been forced to flee from the Ministry? Would Harry be allowed to live there alone, given that he was still underage? Or would the matter of where he went next be decided for him? Had his breach of the International Statute of Secrecy been severe enough to land him in a cell in Azkaban? Whenever this thought occurred, Harry invariably slid off his bed and began pacing again.

On the fourth night after Hedwig's departure Harry was lying in one of his apathetic phases, staring at the ceiling, his exhausted mind quite blank, when his uncle entered his bedroom. Harry looked slowly around at him. Uncle Vernon was wearing his best suit and an expression of enormous smugness.

'We're going out,' he said.

'Sorry?'

'We – that is to say, your aunt, Dudley and I – are going out.'

'Fine,' said Harry dully, looking back at the ceiling.

'You are not to leave your bedroom while we are away.'

'OK.'

'You are not to touch the television, the stereo, or any of our possessions.'

'Right.'

'You are not to steal food from the fridge.'

'OK.'

'I am going to lock your door.'

'You do that.'

Uncle Vernon glared at Harry, clearly suspicious of this lack of argument,

第3章 先遣警卫

这种情况整整持续了三天。有时候哈利焦躁不安,根本不能静下心来做任何事情,只是在卧室里踱来踱去,为他们所有的人让他在这里忍受煎熬而气愤。有时候他又完全无精打采,整小时整小时地躺在床上,眼睛失神地望着空中,为想到要去魔法部受审而惶恐不安。

如果他们的判决对他不利怎么办呢?如果他真的被开除,魔杖被折断成两截怎么办呢?他将怎么做?他将去哪里?他不可能再像以前那样整天跟德思礼一家生活在一起,因为他现在已经知道了另一个世界,一个真正属于他的世界。那么,他能不能搬到小天狼星那里去呢?一年前,小天狼星被迫逃避魔法部的追捕之前,曾经提出过这样的建议。现在哈利还没有成年,他们会允许他独自住在那里吗?或者,以后住在哪里的问题也将由别人替他做决定?难道他违反《国际保密法》的行为这么严重,使他不得不到阿兹卡班去坐牢?每次一想到这儿,哈利总忍不住从床上爬起来,又在房间里踱来踱去。

海德薇离开后的第四个夜晚,哈利正处于无精打采的状态,躺在床上,眼睛瞪着天花板,疲倦的大脑里几乎一片空白,这时弗农姨父走进了他的卧室。哈利慢慢地转过脸来望着他。弗农姨父穿着他那套最好的西装,一副得意扬扬的神情。

"我们要出去。"他说。

"对不起,你说什么?"

"我们——也就是说,你姨妈、达力和我——要出去。"

"好吧。"哈利干巴巴地说,眼睛重又望着天花板。

"我们不在的时候,你不许走出你的房间。"

"好的。"

"不许碰电视,碰音响,碰我们的任何东西。"

"行。"

"不准偷吃冰箱里的东西。"

"好的。"

"我要把你的门锁起来。"

"你锁吧。"

弗农姨父朝哈利瞪着眼睛,显然怀疑哈利这样听话有些不对头。

CHAPTER THREE   The Advance Guard

then stomped out of the room and closed the door behind him. Harry heard the key turn in the lock and Uncle Vernon's footsteps walking heavily down the stairs. A few minutes later he heard the slamming of car doors, the rumble of an engine, and the unmistakeable sound of the car sweeping out of the drive.

Harry had no particular feeling about the Dursleys leaving. It made no difference to him whether they were in the house or not. He could not even summon the energy to get up and turn on his bedroom light. The room grew steadily darker around him as he lay listening to the night sounds through the window he kept open all the time, waiting for the blessed moment when Hedwig returned.

The empty house creaked around him. The pipes gurgled. Harry lay there in a kind of stupor, thinking of nothing, suspended in misery.

Then, quite distinctly, he heard a crash in the kitchen below.

He sat bolt upright, listening intently. The Dursleys couldn't be back, it was much too soon, and in any case he hadn't heard their car.

There was silence for a few seconds, then voices.

Burglars, he thought, sliding off the bed on to his feet – but a split second later it occurred to him that burglars would keep their voices down, and whoever was moving around in the kitchen was certainly not troubling to do so.

He snatched up his wand from the bedside table and stood facing his bedroom door, listening with all his might. Next moment, he jumped as the lock gave a loud click and his door swung open.

Harry stood motionless, staring through the open doorway at the dark upstairs landing, straining his ears for further sounds, but none came. He hesitated for a moment, then moved swiftly and silently out of his room to the head of the stairs.

His heart shot upwards into his throat. There were people standing in the shadowy hall below, silhouetted against the streetlight glowing through the glass door; eight or nine of them, all, as far as he could see, looking up at him.

'Lower your wand, boy, before you take someone's eye out,' said a low, growling voice.

Harry's heart was thumping uncontrollably. He knew that voice, but he did not lower his wand.

第3章　先遣警卫

然后他踏着沉重的脚步走出房间，回手把门关上了。哈利听见钥匙在锁眼里转动，又听见弗农姨父的脚步嗵嗵嗵地下楼去了。几分钟后，他听见车门重重关上，发动机隆隆作响，还听见了汽车驶出车道的确切无疑的声音。

哈利对德思礼一家的离去没有什么特别的感觉。对他来说，他们在不在家并无多少差别。他甚至都打不起精神下床把卧室的灯打开。房间里越来越黑了，他躺在那里，倾听着一直敞开的窗口传进来夜的声音，等待着海德薇归来的喜悦时刻。

空荡荡的房子在他周围发出吱吱嘎嘎的响声。管子里的水汩汩流淌。哈利躺在床上，仿佛处于一种麻木状态，脑子里什么也不想，心里焦躁不安。

突然，他清楚地听见下面厨房里传来哗啦一声响。

他腾地坐起，侧耳细听。德思礼一家不可能这么快就回来了，而且他并没有听见他们汽车驶回的声音。

几秒钟的寂静，然后传来了说话声。

盗贼，他想，一边悄悄地从床上下来——但紧接着他又想到，盗贼肯定不敢大声说话，而在厨房里走动的人显然并没有压低自己的声音。

他一把抓起床头柜上的魔杖，脸冲卧室的门站着，全神贯注地倾听。接着，锁咔嚓一响，卧室的门猛地开了，他吓得跳了起来。

哈利一动不动地站着，通过洞开的房门望着漆黑的楼梯平台，竖起耳朵捕捉动静，但再也没有听见任何声音。他迟疑片刻，然后飞快地、悄没声儿地走出自己的房间，来到楼梯口。

他的心一下子蹿到了嗓子眼儿。下面昏暗的门厅里站着好几个人，从玻璃门透进来的路灯的光照出了他们的轮廓。一共有八九个人，而且在哈利看来，他们都在抬头望着他。

"放下你的魔杖，孩子，免得把什么人的眼睛挖出来。"一个粗声粗气的低沉声音说。

哈利的心无法控制地狂跳着。他听出了那个声音，但并没有放下魔杖。

CHAPTER THREE   The Advance Guard

'Professor Moody?' he said uncertainly.

'I don't know so much about "Professor",' growled the voice, 'never got round to much teaching, did I? Get down here, we want to see you properly.'

Harry lowered his wand slightly but did not relax his grip on it, nor did he move. He had very good reason to be suspicious. He had recently spent nine months in what he had thought was Mad-Eye Moody's company only to find out that it wasn't Moody at all, but an impostor; an impostor, moreover, who had tried to kill Harry before being unmasked. But before he could make a decision about what to do next, a second, slightly hoarse voice floated upstairs.

'It's all right, Harry. We've come to take you away.'

Harry's heart leapt. He knew that voice, too, though he hadn't heard it for over a year.

'P-Professor Lupin?' he said disbelievingly. 'Is that you?'

'Why are we all standing in the dark?' said a third voice, this one completely unfamiliar, a woman's. '*Lumos.*'

A wand-tip flared, illuminating the hall with magical light. Harry blinked. The people below were crowded around the foot of the stairs, gazing up at him intently, some craning their heads for a better look.

Remus Lupin stood nearest to him. Though still quite young, Lupin looked tired and rather ill; he had more grey hairs than when Harry had last said goodbye to him and his robes were more patched and shabbier than ever. Nevertheless, he was smiling broadly at Harry, who tried to smile back despite his state of shock.

'Oooh, he looks just like I thought he would,' said the witch who was holding her lit wand aloft. She looked the youngest there; she had a pale heart-shaped face, dark twinkling eyes, and short spiky hair that was a violent shade of violet. 'Wotcher, Harry!'

'Yeah, I see what you mean, Remus,' said a bald black wizard standing furthest back – he had a deep, slow voice and wore a single gold hoop in his ear – 'he looks exactly like James.'

'Except the eyes,' said a wheezy-voiced, silver-haired wizard at the back. 'Lily's eyes.'

第3章 先遣警卫

"穆迪教授？"他不敢肯定地问。

"教授不教授的，我可不太知道。"那个粗粗的声音吼道，"我一直没有捞到多少教书的机会，是不是？下来吧，我们想好好看看你呢。"

哈利把魔杖稍微放低了一点儿，但仍然用手攥得紧紧的，脚下也没有动弹。他完全有理由心存怀疑。就在最近，他曾跟那个他以为是疯眼汉穆迪的人一起待了九个月，结果发现那根本不是穆迪，而是一个冒名顶替的家伙，而且，那家伙在暴露身份前还想杀死他。哈利还没想好下一步该怎么做，这时第二个微微沙哑的声音从楼下飘了上来。

"没问题的，哈利。我们是来带你走的。"

哈利的心欢跳起来。这个声音也是他熟悉的，尽管已经有一年多没有听到了。

"卢——卢平教授？"他不敢相信地问，"是你吗？"

"我们干吗都摸黑站着？"第三个声音说话了，这次是一个完全陌生的声音，一个女人的声音，"荧光闪烁。"

一根魔杖头上突然发出亮光，照亮了门厅。哈利眨了眨眼睛。下面的人都挤在楼梯口，抬头目不转睛地望着他，有几个人还使劲伸长了脖子，好把他看得更清楚一些。

莱姆斯·卢平站得离他最近。卢平尽管还不算老，但显得十分疲惫，神色憔悴。他的白头发比哈利上次跟他分手时更多，身上的长袍也比以前多了几块补丁，更加破旧了。不过，他望着哈利时脸上绽开了灿烂的笑容。哈利呢，尽管心里吃惊得不行，也勉强对他笑着。

"噢，他的模样正跟我原先想的一样。"那个高高举着发光魔杖的女巫说。她似乎是那几个人里最年轻的，有着一张苍白的、心形的脸，一对闪闪发光的黑眼睛，那一头尖钉般的短发是一种鲜艳夺目的紫罗兰色。"你好哇，哈利！"

"啊，我明白你的意思了，莱姆斯，"站在最后面的一个黑皮肤、秃脑袋的巫师说——他声音低沉、缓慢，一边耳朵上戴着一只金环——"他看上去简直和詹姆一模一样。"

"除了那双眼睛，"后面一个满头银发、说话呼哧呼哧的巫师说，"是莉莉的眼睛。"

CHAPTER THREE   The Advance Guard

Mad-Eye Moody, who had long grizzled grey hair and a large chunk missing from his nose, was squinting suspiciously at Harry through his mismatched eyes. One eye was small, dark and beady, the other large, round and electric blue – the magical eye that could see through walls, doors and the back of Moody's own head.

'Are you quite sure it's him, Lupin?' he growled. 'It'd be a nice lookout if we bring back some Death Eater impersonating him. We ought to ask him something only the real Potter would know. Unless anyone brought any Veritaserum?'

'Harry, what form does your Patronus take?' Lupin asked.

'A stag,' said Harry nervously.

'That's him, Mad-Eye,' said Lupin.

Very conscious of everybody still staring at him, Harry descended the stairs, stowing his wand in the back pocket of his jeans as he came.

'Don't put your wand there, boy!' roared Moody. 'What if it ignited? Better wizards than you have lost buttocks, you know!'

'Who d'you know who's lost a buttock?' the violet-haired woman asked Mad-Eye interestedly.

'Never you mind, you just keep your wand out of your back pocket!' growled Mad-Eye. 'Elementary wand-safety, nobody bothers about it any more.' He stumped off towards the kitchen. 'And I saw that,' he added irritably, as the woman rolled her eyes towards the ceiling.

Lupin held out his hand and shook Harry's.

'How are you?' he asked, looking closely at Harry.

'F-fine ...'

Harry could hardly believe this was real. Four weeks with nothing, not the tiniest hint of a plan to remove him from Privet Drive, and suddenly a whole bunch of wizards was standing matter-of-factly in the house as though this was a long-standing arrangement. He glanced at the people surrounding Lupin; they were still gazing avidly at him. He felt very conscious of the fact that he had not combed his hair for four days.

'I'm – you're really lucky the Dursleys are out ...' he mumbled.

'Lucky, ha!' said the violet-haired woman. 'It was me who lured them out of the way. Sent a letter by Muggle post telling them they'd been short-

第3章　先遣警卫

疯眼汉穆迪留着一头长长的灰白头发，鼻子上缺了一大块肉，此刻正眯起两只不对称的眼睛怀疑地盯着哈利。他的一只眼睛又小又黑，晶亮如珠，另一只眼睛则又大又圆，是亮蓝色的——这只魔眼能够看穿墙壁、房门和穆迪自己的后脑勺。

"你能保证这就是他吗，卢平？"他粗声大气地吼道，"如果我们带回去一个冒充他的食死徒，可就闹出大麻烦了。我们最好问他一点只有波特本人才会知道的事情。除非有人带着吐真剂？"

"哈利，你的守护神是什么样子的？"卢平问道。

"一头牡鹿。"哈利紧张地说。

"没错，就是他，疯眼汉。"卢平说。

哈利意识到这么多人直瞪瞪地盯着自己，他一边往楼下走，一边把魔杖插进牛仔裤后面的口袋里。

"别把魔杖插在那儿，孩子！"疯眼汉叫道，"如果它着起火来怎么办？知道吗，比你厉害的巫师都把自己的屁股给烧掉过！"

"你知道谁把屁股给烧掉啦？"紫罗兰色头发的女人很感兴趣地问疯眼汉。

"不用你管，只是别把魔杖放在裤兜里就对了！"疯眼汉气冲冲地说，"这是基本的魔杖安全守则，现在谁也不理会了。"他脚步重重地朝厨房走去。"我看见你了。"那女人冲天花板翻眼珠时，他恼怒地加了一句。

卢平伸出手来，跟哈利握手。

"你怎么样？"他问，一边仔细地打量着哈利。

"还—还好……"

哈利简直不敢相信这一切都是真的。四个星期毫无音讯，没有一点蛛丝马迹显示要将他从女贞路转移出去，可是突然之间，一大群巫师一本正经地站在这个家里，好像这是早就安排好的事情。他望望围在卢平身边的那些人，他们仍然眼巴巴地盯着他。他想起自己已经四天没有梳头，不由得感到很不好意思。

"我——你们来得真巧，德思礼一家出去了……"他吞吞吐吐地说。

"真巧，哈！"紫罗兰色头发的女人说，"是我把他们引出去的，免得碍事。通过麻瓜邮局给他们寄了一封信，说他们在全英格兰最佳近郊草坪

CHAPTER THREE   The Advance Guard

listed for the All-England Best Kept Suburban Lawn Competition. They're heading off to the prize-giving right now ... or they think they are.'

Harry had a fleeting vision of Uncle Vernon's face when he realised there was no All-England Best Kept Suburban Lawn Competition.

'We are leaving, aren't we?' he asked. 'Soon?'

'Almost at once,' said Lupin, 'we're just waiting for the all-clear.'

'Where are we going? The Burrow?' Harry asked hopefully.

'Not The Burrow, no,' said Lupin, motioning Harry towards the kitchen; the little knot of wizards followed, all still eyeing Harry curiously. 'Too risky. We've set up Headquarters somewhere undetectable. It's taken a while ...'

Mad-Eye Moody was now sitting at the kitchen table swigging from a hip flask, his magical eye spinning in all directions, taking in the Dursleys' many labour-saving appliances.

'This is Alastor Moody, Harry,' Lupin continued, pointing towards Moody.

'Yeah, I know,' said Harry uncomfortably. It felt odd to be introduced to somebody he'd thought he'd known for a year.

'And this is Nymphadora –'

'*Don't* call me Nymphadora, Remus,' said the young witch with a shudder, 'it's Tonks.'

'Nymphadora Tonks, who prefers to be known by her surname only,' finished Lupin.

'So would you if your fool of a mother had called you *Nymphadora*,' muttered Tonks.

'And this is Kingsley Shacklebolt.' He indicated the tall black wizard, who bowed. 'Elphias Doge.' The wheezy-voiced wizard nodded. 'Dedalus Diggle –'

'We've met before,' squeaked the excitable Diggle, dropping his violet-coloured top hat.

'Emmeline Vance.' A stately-looking witch in an emerald green shawl inclined her head. 'Sturgis Podmore.' A square-jawed wizard with thick straw-coloured hair winked. 'And Hestia Jones.' A pink-cheeked, black-haired witch waved from next to the toaster.

Harry inclined his head awkwardly at each of them as they were introduced. He wished they would look at something other than him; it was as though he had suddenly been ushered on-stage. He also wondered why so

大奖赛中入围了。他们现在正急着去领奖……或者自以为是去领奖呢。"

哈利眼前闪过当弗农姨父得知根本就没有什么全英格兰最佳近郊草坪大奖赛时,脸上的那副表情。

"我们要离开这里,是不是?"他问,"很快就走?"

"差不多立即动身,"卢平说,"我们在等平安无事的信号。"

"我们去哪儿呢?陋居吗?"哈利满怀希望地问。

"不去陋居,那里不行,"卢平说着示意哈利朝厨房走;那一群巫师都跟在后面,仍然好奇地打量着哈利,"太冒险了。我们在一个别人发现不了的地方建了指挥部。花了一些时间……"

疯眼汉穆迪已经坐在厨房的桌子边,大口大口地喝着弧形酒瓶里的酒,那只魔眼滴溜溜乱转,把德思礼家那许多节省劳力的用具尽收眼底。

"哈利,这是阿拉斯托·穆迪。"卢平指着穆迪继续说道。

"是啊,我知道。"哈利尴尬地说。一个自己以为认识了一年的人,又被别人介绍来重新认识,这感觉真是很奇怪。

"这位是尼法朵拉——"

"莱姆斯,别叫我尼法朵拉。"那个年轻女巫打了个冷战说道,"我是唐克斯。"

"尼法朵拉·唐克斯更喜欢别人只称呼她的姓。"卢平把话说完。

"如果你的傻瓜妈妈管你叫尼法朵拉,你也会这样的。"唐克斯嘟哝道。

"这位是金斯莱·沙克尔,"他指的是那位高个子的黑皮肤巫师,那人欠了欠身。"埃非亚斯·多吉。"那个说话呼哧呼哧的巫师点了点头。"德达洛·迪歌——"

"我们以前见过。"爱激动的迪歌尖声尖气地说,他那顶紫色高顶大礼帽掉了下来。

"爱米琳·万斯。"一位披着深绿色披肩、端庄典雅的女巫微微点了点头;"斯多吉·波德摩。"一个长着一头厚厚的稻草色头发的方下巴巫师眨了眨眼睛;"还有海丝佳·琼斯。"一位头发乌黑、面颊粉嘟嘟的女巫从烤面包炉旁朝他们挥了挥手。

介绍到每个人时,哈利都笨拙地朝对方点头打招呼。他真希望他们能把目光投向别处,别老盯着他看。他感到自己好像突然被请到了

CHAPTER THREE The Advance Guard

many of them were there.

'A surprising number of people volunteered to come and get you,' said Lupin, as though he had read Harry's mind; the corners of his mouth twitched slightly.

'Yeah, well, the more the better,' said Moody darkly. 'We're your guard, Potter.'

'We're just waiting for the signal to tell us it's safe to set off,' said Lupin, glancing out of the kitchen window. 'We've got about fifteen minutes.'

'Very *clean*, aren't they, these Muggles?' said the witch called Tonks, who was looking around the kitchen with great interest. 'My dad's Muggle-born and he's a right old slob. I suppose it varies, just as it does with wizards?'

'Er – yeah,' said Harry. 'Look –' he turned back to Lupin, 'what's going on, I haven't heard anything from anyone, what's Vol–?'

Several of the witches and wizards made odd hissing noises; Dedalus Diggle dropped his hat again and Moody growled, '*Shut up!*'

'What?' said Harry.

'We're not discussing anything here, it's too risky,' said Moody, turning his normal eye on Harry. His magical eye remained focused on the ceiling. '*Damn it*,' he added angrily, putting a hand up to the magical eye, 'it keeps getting stuck – ever since that scum wore it.'

And with a nasty squelching sound much like a plunger being pulled from a sink, he popped out his eye.

'Mad-Eye, you do know that's disgusting, don't you?' said Tonks conversationally.

'Get me a glass of water, would you, Harry,' requested Moody.

Harry crossed to the dishwasher, took out a clean glass and filled it with water at the sink, still watched eagerly by the band of wizards. Their relentless staring was starting to annoy him.

'Cheers,' said Moody, when Harry handed him the glass. He dropped the magical eyeball into the water and prodded it up and down; the eye whizzed around, staring at them all in turn. 'I want three hundred and sixty degrees visibility on the return journey.'

'How're we getting – wherever we're going?' Harry asked.

'Brooms,' said Lupin. 'Only way. You're too young to Apparate, they'll be

舞台上。而且，他不明白为什么一下子来了这么多人。

"没想到那么多人主动提出要来接你。"卢平说，似乎读出了哈利的心思，两个嘴角微微动了动。

"是啊，是啊，越多越好。"穆迪闷闷不乐地说，"我们是你的警卫，波特。"

"现在就等一切平安的信号来了，我们就可以出发。"卢平说着朝厨房窗外望了望，"大概还有十五分钟。"

"弄得真干净啊，这些麻瓜，是不是？"那个姓唐克斯的女巫怀着极大的兴趣打量着厨房，说道，"我爸爸也是麻瓜出身，他是个典型的邋遢鬼。我想麻瓜也是多种多样的，就像巫师一样。"

"呃——是啊。"哈利说，"对了——"他重新转向卢平，"发生了什么事，谁也不给我一点儿消息，伏地——？"

几个巫师嘴里发出古怪的嘘嘘声，德达洛·迪歌的帽子又掉了下来，穆迪低吼道："闭嘴！"

"怎么啦？"哈利问。

"在这里什么也不能说，太危险了。"穆迪说，那只正常的眼睛转向哈利，而那只魔眼还是一动不动地盯着天花板。"该死，"他恼火地说，举起一只手去掏魔眼，"老是卡住——自从那个卑鄙小人戴过以后就出毛病了。"

随着一声令人不适的吧唧声，就像从洗涤池里拔撅子一样，穆迪把魔眼掏了出来。

"疯眼汉，你这样做怪叫人恶心的，你知道吧？"唐克斯随意地说。

"劳驾，给我一杯水，哈利。"穆迪要求道。

哈利走到洗碗机前，拿出一只干净杯子，在水池边接满了清水，而那帮巫师仍然眼巴巴地注视着他。他们这样毫不留情地盯着他看，他开始有点恼怒了。

"谢谢。"哈利把杯子递过去时穆迪说。他把魔眼丢进水里，用手捅得它一沉一浮。那只眼睛嗖嗖地转动,挨个儿瞪着屋里的每个人。"在回去的路上，我希望我能有三百六十度的视野。"

"我们怎么去——我们要去的地方？"哈利问。

"骑扫帚，"卢平说，"只有这个办法。你年纪太小,还不能幻影移形，

CHAPTER THREE   The Advance Guard

watching the Floo Network and it's more than our life's worth to set up an unauthorised Portkey.'

'Remus says you're a good flier,' said Kingsley Shacklebolt in his deep voice.

'He's excellent,' said Lupin, who was checking his watch. 'Anyway, you'd better go and get packed, Harry, we want to be ready to go when the signal comes.'

'I'll come and help you,' said Tonks brightly.

She followed Harry back into the hall and up the stairs, looking around with much curiosity and interest.

'Funny place,' she said. 'It's a bit *too* clean, d'you know what I mean? Bit unnatural. Oh, this is better,' she added, as they entered Harry's bedroom and he turned on the light.

His room was certainly much messier than the rest of the house. Confined to it for four days in a very bad mood, Harry had not bothered tidying up after himself. Most of the books he owned were strewn over the floor where he'd tried to distract himself with each in turn and thrown it aside; Hedwig's cage needed cleaning out and was starting to smell; and his trunk lay open, revealing a jumbled mixture of Muggle clothes and wizards' robes that had spilled on to the floor around it.

Harry started picking up books and throwing them hastily into his trunk. Tonks paused at his open wardrobe to look critically at her reflection in the mirror on the inside of the door.

'You know, I don't think violet's really my colour,' she said pensively, tugging at a lock of spiky hair. 'D'you think it makes me look a bit peaky?'

'Er –' said Harry, looking up at her over the top of *Quidditch Teams of Britain and Ireland*.

'Yeah, it does,' said Tonks decisively. She screwed up her eyes in a strained expression as though she was struggling to remember something. A second later, her hair had turned bubble-gum pink.

'How did you do that?' said Harry, gaping at her as she opened her eyes again.

'I'm a Metamorphmagus,' she said, looking back at her reflection and turning her head so that she could see her hair from all directions. 'It means

飞路网会遭到他们的监视,而如果起用一个未经批准的门钥匙,那要搭上我们的性命还不够呢。"

"莱姆斯说你飞得很出色。"金斯莱·沙克尔用低沉的声音说。

"他飞得棒极了,"卢平说,他看了看手表,"不管怎样,哈利,你最好去收拾一下东西,等信号一来,我们就要上路。"

"我去帮帮你吧。"唐克斯欢快地说。

她跟着哈利回到门厅,往楼上走去,一路兴趣盎然、充满好奇地东张西望。

"这地方真好玩,"她说,"弄得也太干净了。你明白我的意思吧?有点不自然了。哦,这还差不多。"他们走进哈利的卧室,哈利把灯打开时,她说道。

哈利的房间确实比家里其他地方乱得多。整整四天闭门不出,情绪恶劣,哈利根本没有心思收拾东西。他的大部分书都散落在地板上,因为他为了分散注意力,把每本书都翻开看看,又随手扔到一边。海德薇的笼子需要清理了,已经开始发出臭味。他的箱子敞开着,可以看见麻瓜衣服、巫师长袍在里面堆得乱七八糟,有的还散在周围的地板上。

哈利开始把书一本本地捡起来,匆匆扔进箱子。唐克斯停在他打开的衣柜前,挑剔地照着柜门内侧的镜子。

"知道吗,我觉得实际上紫罗兰色并不适合我,"她扯着一绺尖钉般的头发忧虑地说,"你说,它是不是使我的脸显得太苍白了点儿?"

"呃——"哈利的视线越过一本《不列颠和爱尔兰的魁地奇球队》望着她。

"没错,是这样。"唐克斯果断地说。她紧紧地闭上眼睛,脸上是一种紧张的表情,似乎在拼命回忆什么。一秒钟后,她的头发变成了泡泡糖般的粉红色。

"你怎么办到的?"哈利问,吃惊地望着她,这时她把眼睛睁开了。

"我是个易容马格斯,"她说,重新打量着镜子里的自己,脑袋转来转去,从各个角度审视自己的头发,"也就是说,我能够随心所欲地改变我的外貌。"她在镜子里看到身后的哈利脸上露出迷惑不解的表情,便又补充道:"我天生就是。在傲罗培训时,我根本不用学习就得到了

CHAPTER THREE   The Advance Guard

I can change my appearance at will,' she added, spotting Harry's puzzled expression in the mirror behind her. 'I was born one. I got top marks in Concealment and Disguise during Auror training without any study at all, it was great.'

'You're an Auror?' said Harry, impressed. Being a Dark-wizard-catcher was the only career he'd ever considered after Hogwarts.

'Yeah,' said Tonks, looking proud. 'Kingsley is as well, he's a bit higher up than me, though. I only qualified a year ago. Nearly failed on Stealth and Tracking. I'm dead clumsy, did you hear me break that plate when we arrived downstairs?'

'Can you learn how to be a Metamorphmagus?' Harry asked her, straightening up, completely forgetting about packing.

Tonks chuckled.

'Bet you wouldn't mind hiding that scar sometimes, eh?'

Her eyes found the lightning-shaped scar on Harry's forehead.

'No, I wouldn't mind,' Harry mumbled, turning away. He did not like people staring at his scar.

'Well, you'll have to learn the hard way, I'm afraid,' said Tonks. 'Metamorphmagi are really rare, they're born, not made. Most wizards need to use a wand, or potions, to change their appearance. But we've got to get going, Harry, we're supposed to be packing,' she added guiltily, looking around at all the mess on the floor.

'Oh – yeah,' said Harry, grabbing a few more books.

'Don't be stupid, it'll be much quicker if I – *pack*!' cried Tonks, waving her wand in a long, sweeping movement over the floor.

Books, clothes, telescope and scales all soared into the air and flew pell-mell into the trunk.

'It's not very neat,' said Tonks, walking over to the trunk and looking down at the jumble inside. 'My mum's got this knack of getting stuff to fit itself in neatly – she even gets the socks to fold themselves – but I've never mastered how she does it – it's a kind of flick –' She flicked her wand hopefully.

One of Harry's socks gave a feeble sort of wiggle and flopped back on top of the mess in the trunk.

'Ah, well,' said Tonks, slamming the trunk's lid shut, 'at least it's all in.

第3章　先遣警卫

隐藏和伪装的最高分，这可真棒。"

"你是个傲罗？"哈利有些佩服地问道。对于从霍格沃茨毕业以后的职业，他唯一考虑过的就是做一个专门逮捕黑巫师的傲罗。

"是啊，"唐克斯显出很骄傲的样子说，"金斯莱也是，不过他的级别比我还要高一点。我是去年才取得资格的。潜行和跟踪这门课差点儿不及格。我总是笨手笨脚，你听见我们刚到楼下时我打碎那只盘子的声音了吗？"

"能通过学习成为一个易容马格斯吗？"哈利问道。他直起身来，把收拾行李的事抛到了脑后。

唐克斯轻轻地笑了。

"我敢说，你不反对有时候把你的伤疤藏起来吧，嗯？"

她的目光捕捉到哈利额头上的闪电形伤疤。

"不反对，我巴不得呢。"哈利嘟哝着把脸转开了。他不喜欢别人盯着他伤疤。

"噢，那你恐怕得靠自己的努力去学习了。"唐克斯说，"但易容马格斯非常稀罕，都是天生的，不是后天培养的。大多数巫师都需要用魔杖或药剂才能改变自己的外貌。不过我们得抓紧时间了，哈利，我们是来收拾行李的。"她望了望地上那堆乱七八糟的东西愧疚地说。

"噢——是啊。"哈利说着又抓起几本书。

"别犯傻了，可以快得多呢，让我来——收拾！"唐克斯大喊一声，同时用魔杖幅度很大地扫过地面。

书、衣服、望远镜和天平纷纷飘到空中，杂乱无章地飞进了箱子。

"不太整齐。"唐克斯说着，走到箱子旁边低头看了看里面乱糟糟的一堆，"我妈妈有一个诀窍，让东西自动归拢整齐——她还能让袜子自己叠起来呢——但我一直没弄清她是怎么做的——好像是迅速地一抖——"她满怀希望地抖了一下魔杖。

哈利的一只袜子软绵绵地扭动了一下，又落回到箱子里那堆乱七八糟的东西上。

"唉，算啦，"唐克斯说，把箱子盖砰的一声合上了，"至少东西都进去了。那玩意儿也需要打扫了。"她用魔杖指着海德薇的笼子。"清

CHAPTER THREE The Advance Guard

That could do with a bit of cleaning, too.' She pointed her wand at Hedwig's cage. '*Scourgify*.' A few feathers and droppings vanished. 'Well, that's a *bit* better – I've never quite got the hang of these householdy sort of spells. Right – got everything? Cauldron? Broom? Wow! – A *Firebolt*?'

Her eyes widened as they fell on the broomstick in Harry's right hand. It was his pride and joy, a gift from Sirius, an international-standard broomstick.

'And I'm still riding a Comet Two Sixty,' said Tonks enviously. 'Ah well ... wand still in your jeans? Both buttocks still on? OK, let's go. *Locomotor trunk*.'

Harry's trunk rose a few inches into the air. Holding her wand like a conductor's baton, Tonks made the trunk hover across the room and out of the door ahead of them, Hedwig's cage in her left hand. Harry followed her down the stairs carrying his broomstick.

Back in the kitchen Moody had replaced his eye, which was spinning so fast after its cleaning it made Harry feel sick to look at it. Kingsley Shacklebolt and Sturgis Podmore were examining the microwave and Hestia Jones was laughing at a potato peeler she had come across while rummaging in the drawers. Lupin was sealing a letter addressed to the Dursleys.

'Excellent,' said Lupin, looking up as Tonks and Harry entered. 'We've got about a minute, I think. We should probably get out into the garden so we're ready. Harry, I've left a letter telling your aunt and uncle not to worry –'

'They won't,' said Harry.

'– that you're safe –'

'That'll just depress them.'

'– and you'll see them next summer.'

'Do I have to?'

Lupin smiled but made no answer.

'Come here, boy,' said Moody gruffly, beckoning Harry towards him with his wand. 'I need to Disillusion you.'

'You need to what?' said Harry nervously.

'Disillusionment Charm,' said Moody, raising his wand. 'Lupin says you've got an Invisibility Cloak, but it won't stay on while we're flying; this'll disguise you better. Here you go –'

理一新。"几片羽毛和一些粪便顿时消失了。"哈，这下子好点儿了——对这些家务活儿方面的咒语，我一向不太在行。好了——东西都带齐了吗？坩埚？扫帚？哇！——火弩箭？"

她的目光落在哈利右手拿着的飞天扫帚上，眼睛顿时瞪大了。这是哈利的骄傲和欢乐，是小天狼星送给他的礼物，一把国际标准的飞天扫帚。

"我骑的还是一把彗星260呢。"唐克斯羡慕地说，"啊，好了……魔杖还插在你的牛仔裤里？两边的屁股还都在？好吧，我们走！箱子移动。"

哈利的箱子飘浮到离地面几英寸的高度。唐克斯像指挥家拿着指挥棒一样举着她的魔杖，让箱子在他们前面摇摇晃晃地飘过房间，飘出房门，她用左手拎着海德薇的笼子。哈利拿着他的飞天扫帚跟着她下了楼梯。

他们回到厨房时，穆迪已经把魔眼装上了，清洗过的眼睛转得飞快，哈利看了只觉得恶心想吐。金斯莱·沙克尔和斯多吉·波德摩在仔细研究微波炉，海丝佳·琼斯刚才在抽屉里东翻西翻，发现了一个削土豆器，现在正对着它哈哈大笑。卢平给德思礼一家写了封信，正在封口。

"太好了，"卢平抬头看到唐克斯和哈利走进来，说道，"大概还有一分钟。我们应该到外面的花园里去做好准备。哈利，我留下了一封信，告诉你的姨妈和姨父不要担心——"

"他们不会担心的。"哈利说。

"——说你很安全——"

"这只会让他们感到失望。"

"——还说你明年夏天再来看他们。"

"非得这样吗？"

卢平微微一笑，没有回答。

"过来，孩子，"穆迪声音粗哑地说，用魔杖示意哈利到他跟前去，"我需要给你幻身。"

"你需要什么？"哈利不安地问。

"幻身咒。"穆迪说着举起魔杖，"卢平说你有一件隐形衣，但待会儿我们飞起来，它不会很贴身的。用幻身咒会把你伪装得更好。这就开始啦——"

CHAPTER THREE The Advance Guard

He rapped him hard on the top of the head and Harry felt a curious sensation as though Moody had just smashed an egg there; cold trickles seemed to be running down his body from the point the wand had struck.

'Nice one, Mad-Eye,' said Tonks appreciatively, staring at Harry's midriff.

Harry looked down at his body, or rather, what had been his body, for it didn't look anything like his any more. It was not invisible; it had simply taken on the exact colour and texture of the kitchen unit behind him. He seemed to have become a human chameleon.

'Come on,' said Moody, unlocking the back door with his wand.

They all stepped outside on to Uncle Vernon's beautifully kept lawn.

'Clear night,' grunted Moody, his magical eye scanning the heavens. 'Could've done with a bit more cloud cover. Right, you,' he barked at Harry, 'we're going to be flying in close formation. Tonks'll be right in front of you, keep close on her tail. Lupin'll be covering you from below. I'm going to be behind you. The rest'll be circling us. We don't break ranks for anything, got me? If one of us is killed –'

'Is that likely?' Harry asked apprehensively, but Moody ignored him.

'– the others keep flying, don't stop, don't break ranks. If they take out all of us and you survive, Harry, the rear guard are standing by to take over; keep flying east and they'll join you.'

'Stop being so cheerful, Mad-Eye, he'll think we're not taking this seriously,' said Tonks, as she strapped Harry's trunk and Hedwig's cage into a harness hanging from her broom.

'I'm just telling the boy the plan,' growled Moody. 'Our job's to deliver him safely to Headquarters and if we die in the attempt –'

'No one's going to die,' said Kingsley Shacklebolt in his deep, calming voice.

'Mount your brooms, that's the first signal!' said Lupin sharply, pointing into the sky.

Far, far above them, a shower of bright red sparks had flared among the stars. Harry recognised them at once as wand sparks. He swung his right leg over his Firebolt, gripped its handle tightly and felt it vibrating very slightly, as though it was as keen as he was to be up in the air once more.

'Second signal, let's go!' said Lupin loudly as more sparks, green this time,

第3章 先遣警卫

他重重地敲了敲哈利的头顶,哈利有一种很奇怪的感觉,似乎穆迪在他脑袋上敲碎了一个鸡蛋,仿佛有一股冷冰冰的东西从魔杖敲打的地方流进了他的身体。

"干得漂亮,疯眼汉。"唐克斯瞪大眼睛望着哈利的上腹,欣赏地说。

哈利低头看了看自己的身体,确切地说,本该是自己身体的地方。现在它看上去好像根本不属于他了,倒没有隐形不见,但是颜色和质地变得与他身后的厨房设备一模一样。他似乎成了一只人形的变色龙。

"走吧。"穆迪用魔杖打开了后门的锁。

他们一个接一个地出了门,来到弗农姨父修剪得漂漂亮亮的草坪上。

"晴朗的夜空,"穆迪嘟哝着,那只魔眼扫视着天空,"如果能多点儿云彩做掩护就好了。好吧,你听着,"他粗声粗气地对哈利说,"我们排成紧密的队形往前飞。唐克斯在你的正前方,你紧紧跟在她后面。卢平在下面掩护你。我在你后面。其他人把我们围在中间。不管怎样都不能乱了队形,明白吗?如果我们中间有谁遇害——"

"那可能吗?"哈利担忧地问,但穆迪没有理他。

"——其他人继续往前飞,不能停下,不能乱了队形。如果他们把我们都干掉了,只有你还活着,哈利,还有后续的警卫随时准备接替上来。不停地往东飞,他们就会与你会合。"

"不要这样兴高采烈,疯眼汉,不然他会以为我们不是当真的。"唐克斯一边说,一边把哈利的箱子和海德薇的笼子绑在她扫帚上挂着的一根吊带上。

"我只是在把计划告诉孩子。"穆迪没好气地说,"我们的工作是把他安全护送到指挥部,如果我们半路就死了——"

"没有人会死的。"金斯莱·沙克尔用令人感到安心的低沉声音说。

"骑上扫帚,那是第一个信号!"卢平指着天空果断地说。

在他们头顶上空很高很高的地方,群星中突然绽开一片鲜红色的火花。哈利立刻看出那是魔杖变出的火花。他把右腿跨在火弩箭上,紧紧地抓住扫帚把,感觉到扫帚在微微颤动,似乎也和他一样迫不及待地渴望再次飞上天空。

"第二个信号,我们走吧!"卢平大声说,高空中又绽开一片火花,

CHAPTER THREE   The Advance Guard

exploded high above them.

Harry kicked off hard from the ground. The cool night air rushed through his hair as the neat square gardens of Privet Drive fell away, shrinking rapidly into a patchwork of dark greens and blacks, and every thought of the Ministry hearing was swept from his mind as though the rush of air had blown it out of his head. He felt as though his heart was going to explode with pleasure; he was flying again, flying away from Privet Drive as he'd been fantasising about all summer, he was going home … for a few glorious moments, all his problems seemed to recede to nothing, insignificant in the vast, starry sky.

'Hard left, hard left, there's a Muggle looking up!' shouted Moody from behind him. Tonks swerved and Harry followed her, watching his trunk swinging wildly beneath her broom. 'We need more height … give it another quarter of a mile!'

Harry's eyes watered in the chill as they soared upwards; he could see nothing below now but tiny pinpricks of light that were car headlights and street lamps. Two of those tiny lights might belong to Uncle Vernon's car … the Dursleys would be heading back to their empty house right now, full of rage about the non-existent Lawn Competition … and Harry laughed aloud at the thought, though his voice was drowned by the flapping robes of the others, the creaking of the harness holding his trunk and the cage, and the whoosh of the wind in their ears as they sped through the air. He had not felt this alive in a month, or this happy.

'Bearing south!' shouted Mad-Eye. 'Town ahead!'

They soared right to avoid passing directly over the glittering spider's web of lights below.

'Bear southeast and keep climbing, there's some low cloud ahead we can lose ourselves in!' called Moody.

'We're not going through clouds!' shouted Tonks angrily, 'we'll get soaked, Mad-Eye!'

Harry was relieved to hear her say this; his hands were growing numb on the Firebolt's handle. He wished he had thought to put on a coat; he was starting to shiver.

They altered their course every now and then according to Mad-Eye's instructions. Harry's eyes were screwed up against the rush of icy wind that

第3章 先遣警卫

这次是绿色的。

哈利使劲蹬离地面。黑夜里凉爽的微风吹拂着他的头发,女贞路上那些方方正正的花园越来越远,迅速缩小成一幅由墨绿和黑色拼缀而成的图案,到魔法部受审的事被抛到了九霄云外,似乎嗖嗖掠过的空气把这个念头从脑海里吹跑了。哈利觉得他的心快乐得都要爆炸了。终于又飞上了天空,终于离开了女贞路,这可是他整个暑假都梦寐以求的事啊,他要回家了……一时间他心花怒放,似乎所有的烦恼都不存在了,都在星光灿烂的辽阔夜空中变得微不足道。

"快向左,向左,有个麻瓜在抬头往上看呢!"穆迪在他后面喊道。唐克斯猛地一拐,哈利紧紧跟上,望着自己的箱子在唐克斯的扫帚底下剧烈地晃来晃去。"我们需要飞得再高一些……再飞高四分之一英里!"

他们忽忽地上升,哈利的眼睛被寒冷的空气刺得涌出了泪水。下面什么也看不见了,只有一个个针孔般的亮点,是路灯和汽车前灯发出的光,其中两个亮点可能属于弗农姨父的汽车……此刻德思礼一家大概正在赶回他们的空屋子呢,一路上为那个并不存在的草坪大奖赛气得肚子鼓鼓的……想到这里,哈利开心地大笑起来,但是其他巫师长袍飘动的呼呼声、那根拴住他箱子和鸟笼的吊带的嘎吱声,以及他们飞速掠过夜空时灌进耳朵里的呼啸风声,把他的笑声淹没了。一个月来,他从没有感觉这样快活、这样扬眉吐气。

"向南!"疯眼汉大叫,"前面是小镇!"

他们向右一拐,以免直接从蛛网般的万家灯火上空飞过。

"向东南飞,继续上升,前面有一片低云,我们可以飞进去,隐藏在里面!"穆迪喊道。

"可别在云里头飞!"唐克斯气呼呼地大声说,"我们会变成落汤鸡的,疯眼汉!"

哈利听她这么说,松了一口气。他的双手一直抓着火弩箭的扫帚把,已经有点发麻。真后悔刚才没想到再穿一件外套,他禁不住打起哆嗦来。

他们根据疯眼汉的指令,不时地改变路线。凛冽的寒风迎面吹来,哈利不得不紧紧眯起眼睛,耳朵也冻得生疼。在他的记忆中,只有一

CHAPTER THREE   The Advance Guard

was starting to make his ears ache; he could remember being this cold on a broom only once before, during the Quidditch match against Hufflepuff in his third year, which had taken place in a storm. The guard around him was circling continuously like giant birds of prey. Harry lost track of time. He wondered how long they had been flying, it felt like an hour at least.

'Turning southwest!' yelled Moody. 'We want to avoid the motorway!'

Harry was now so chilled he thought longingly of the snug, dry interiors of the cars streaming along below, then, even more longingly, of travelling by Floo powder; it might be uncomfortable to spin around in fireplaces but it was at least warm in the flames ... Kingsley Shacklebolt swooped around him, bald pate and earring gleaming slightly in the moonlight ... now Emmeline Vance was on his right, her wand out, her head turning left and right ... then she, too, swooped over him, to be replaced by Sturgis Podmore ...

'We ought to double back for a bit, just to make sure we're not being followed!' Moody shouted.

'ARE YOU MAD, MAD-EYE?' Tonks screamed from the front. 'We're all frozen to our brooms! If we keep going off-course we're not going to get there until next week! Besides, we're nearly there now!'

'Time to start the descent!' came Lupin's voice. 'Follow Tonks, Harry!'

Harry followed Tonks into a dive. They were heading for the largest collection of lights he had yet seen, a huge, sprawling crisscrossing mass, glittering in lines and grids, interspersed with patches of deepest black. Lower and lower they flew, until Harry could see individual headlights and street lamps, chimneys and television aerials. He wanted to reach the ground very much, though he felt sure someone would have to unfreeze him from his broom.

'Here we go!' called Tonks, and a few seconds later she had landed.

Harry touched down right behind her and dismounted on a patch of unkempt grass in the middle of a small square. Tonks was already unbuckling Harry's trunk. Shivering, Harry looked around. The grimy fronts of the surrounding houses were not welcoming; some of them had broken windows, glimmering dully in the light from the street lamps, paint was peeling from many of the doors and heaps of rubbish lay outside several sets of front steps.

'Where are we?' Harry asked, but Lupin said quietly, 'In a minute.'

第3章 先遣警卫

次也是这么冷骑在扫帚上，那是三年级时跟赫奇帕奇的那场魁地奇比赛，是在暴风雨中进行的。警卫们不停地在他周围绕着圈子，像一只只巨大的猛禽。哈利已经失去了时间概念。他不知道他们已经飞了多长时间，感觉至少有一个小时了。

"转向西南！"穆迪嚷道，"我们要避开高速公路！"

哈利已经感到冷得不行了，他渴望地想到下面公路上疾驶的汽车里的舒服干爽，甚至更渴望地想到撒飞路粉旅行时的感觉。在壁炉里转来转去也许不太舒服，但至少是热乎乎地被火焰烤着的呀……金斯莱·沙克尔呼呼地绕着他飞，秃脑袋和耳环在月光下微微闪烁……这时候爱米琳·万斯飞到他的右边，举着魔杖，警惕地转动着脑袋……然后她也嗖的一声超过了他，斯多吉·波德摩立刻补了上来……

"我们最好原路折回去一段，以确保没有被人跟踪！"穆迪大声说。

"你疯了吗，疯眼汉？"唐克斯在前面尖叫道，"我们都快在扫帚上冻僵了！如果这样不停地偏离路线，大概下个星期都到不了那儿！而且，我们差不多已经到了！"

"是应该开始降落了！"卢平的声音传了过来，"哈利，跟牢唐克斯！"

哈利跟着唐克斯往下俯冲。他们朝着一大片光亮飞去，哈利从没见过这么多灯光汇集在一起，纵横交错，星罗棋布，向四面八方延伸，其间点缀着一个个深黑色的方块。他们飞得越来越低，最后哈利能够看清一盏盏车灯和路灯、一个个烟囱和一根根电视天线了。他多么渴望赶紧落到地面啊，不过肯定需要有人先给他解冻，他才能从扫帚上下来。

"我们到了！"唐克斯大喊一声。几秒钟后，她落在了地面上。

哈利紧跟在她后面降落下来，在一个小广场中央一片凌乱荒芜的草地上跨下扫帚。唐克斯已经在把哈利的箱子从吊带上解下来。哈利浑身发抖，四下张望。周围的房屋门脸阴森森的，一副拒人千里之外的样子。有些房屋的窗户都破了，在路灯的映照下闪着惨淡的光，许多门上油漆剥落，还有几户的前门台阶外堆满了垃圾。

"这是什么地方？"哈利问。可是卢平小声说："等一等。"

CHAPTER THREE   The Advance Guard

Moody was rummaging in his cloak, his gnarled hands clumsy with cold.

'Got it,' he muttered, raising what looked like a silver cigarette lighter into the air and clicking it.

The nearest streetlamp went out with a pop. He clicked the unlighter again; the next lamp went out; he kept clicking until every lamp in the square was extinguished and the only remaining light came from curtained windows and the sickle moon overhead.

'Borrowed it from Dumbledore,' growled Moody, pocketing the Put-Outer. 'That'll take care of any Muggles looking out of the window, see? Now come on, quick.'

He took Harry by the arm and led him from the patch of grass, across the road and on to the pavement; Lupin and Tonks followed, carrying Harry's trunk between them, the rest of the guard, all with their wands out, flanking them.

The muffled pounding of a stereo was coming from an upper window in the nearest house. A pungent smell of rotting rubbish came from the pile of bulging bin-bags just inside the broken gate.

'Here,' Moody muttered, thrusting a piece of parchment towards Harry's Disillusioned hand and holding his lit wand close to it, so as to illuminate the writing. 'Read quickly and memorise.'

Harry looked down at the piece of paper. The narrow handwriting was vaguely familiar. It said:

> *The Headquarters of the Order of the Phoenix may be found at number twelve, Grimmauld Place, London.*

第3章 先遣警卫

穆迪在他的斗篷里翻找,骨节粗大的双手已经冻得不听使唤。

"找到了。"他嘟哝着举起一个像是银色打火机一样的东西,咔嗒摁了一下。

最近的一盏路灯噗的一声熄灭了。他又咔嗒摁了一下那灭灯的玩意儿,第二盏灯也灭了。他不停地咔嗒咔嗒,最后广场上的所有路灯都熄灭了,只有那些拉着窗帘的窗户里透出亮光,还有夜空中弯弯的月亮洒下些许清辉。

"向邓布利多借的,"穆迪粗声粗气地说,把熄灯器装进口袋,"防止麻瓜从窗户里往外看,明白吗?现在走吧,快点儿。"

他拉着哈利的胳膊,领着他走出那片草地,穿过马路,来到人行道上。卢平和唐克斯搬着哈利的箱子跟在后面,其他人都拿出魔杖,在两侧掩护他们。

从最近一座房屋的楼上窗户里隐隐传来立体声音响的隆隆声。一股腐烂垃圾的刺鼻臭味儿,从破败的大门里那堆鼓鼓囊囊的垃圾口袋里散发出来。

"这儿,"穆迪粗声说着,把一张羊皮纸塞进哈利被幻身的手里,并举起他发光的魔杖凑过来照亮了纸上的字,"快读一读,牢牢记住。"

哈利低头看着那张羊皮纸,上面细细长长的笔迹似乎在哪儿见过,写的是:

凤凰社指挥部位于伦敦格里莫广场12号。

CHAPTER FOUR

Number Twelve, Grimmauld Place

'What's the Order of the –?' Harry began.

'Not here, boy!' snarled Moody. 'Wait till we're inside!'

He pulled the piece of parchment out of Harry's hand and set fire to it with his wand-tip. As the message curled into flames and floated to the ground, Harry looked around at the houses again. They were standing outside number eleven; he looked to the left and saw number ten; to the right, however, was number thirteen.

'But where's –?'

'Think about what you've just memorised,' said Lupin quietly.

Harry thought, and no sooner had he reached the part about number twelve, Grimmauld Place, than a battered door emerged out of nowhere between numbers eleven and thirteen, followed swiftly by dirty walls and grimy windows. It was as though an extra house had inflated, pushing those on either side out of its way. Harry gaped at it. The stereo in number eleven thudded on. Apparently the Muggles inside hadn't felt anything.

'Come on, hurry,' growled Moody, prodding Harry in the back.

Harry walked up the worn stone steps, staring at the newly materialised door. Its black paint was shabby and scratched. The silver doorknocker was in the form of a twisted serpent. There was no keyhole or letterbox.

Lupin pulled out his wand and tapped the door once. Harry heard many loud, metallic clicks and what sounded like the clatter of a chain. The door creaked open.

'Get in quick, Harry,' Lupin whispered, 'but don't go far inside and don't touch anything.'

Harry stepped over the threshold into the almost total darkness of the hall.

第 4 章

格里莫广场 12 号

"什么是凤——?"哈利刚要发问。

"别在这儿说,孩子!"穆迪厉声吼道,"等我们进去再说!"

他抽走了哈利手里的羊皮纸,用魔杖头把它点燃了。纸片卷曲着燃烧起来,飘落到地上。哈利抬头打量着周围的房屋,他们此时正站在 11 号的前面。他望望左边,看见的是 10 号,望望右边,却是 13 号。

"可是怎么不见——?"

"想想你刚才记住的话。"卢平轻声说。

哈利专心地想着,刚想到格里莫广场 12 号,就有一扇破破烂烂的门在 11 号和 13 号之间凭空冒了出来,接着肮脏的墙壁和阴森森的窗户也出现了,看上去就像一座额外的房子突然膨胀出来,把两边的东西都挤开了。哈利看得目瞪口呆。11 号的立体声音响还在沉闷地响着,显然住在里面的麻瓜们什么也没有感觉到。

"走吧,快点儿。"穆迪粗声吼道,捅了一下哈利的后背。

哈利一边走上破烂的石头台阶,一边睁大眼睛望着刚变出来的房门。门上的黑漆都剥落了,布满左一道右一道的划痕。银质门环是一条盘曲的大蛇形状。门上没有钥匙孔,也没有信箱。

卢平抽出魔杖,在门上敲了一下。哈利听见许多金属撞击的响亮声音,以及像链条发出的哗啦哗啦声。门吱吱呀呀地打开了。

"快点进去,哈利,"卢平小声说,"但是别往里走得太远,别碰任何东西。"

哈利跨过门槛,走进几乎一片漆黑的门厅。他闻到了湿乎乎、灰

CHAPTER FOUR   Number Twelve, Grimmauld Place

He could smell damp, dust and a sweetish, rotting smell; the place had the feeling of a derelict building. He looked over his shoulder and saw the others filing in behind him, Lupin and Tonks carrying his trunk and Hedwig's cage. Moody was standing on the top step releasing the balls of light the Put-Outer had stolen from the street lamps; they flew back to their bulbs and the square glowed momentarily with orange light before Moody limped inside and closed the front door, so that the darkness in the hall became complete.

'Here –'

He rapped Harry hard over the head with his wand; Harry felt as though something hot was trickling down his back this time and knew that the Disillusionment Charm must have lifted.

'Now stay still, everyone, while I give us a bit of light in here,' Moody whispered.

The others' hushed voices were giving Harry an odd feeling of foreboding; it was as though they had just entered the house of a dying person. He heard a soft hissing noise and then old-fashioned gas lamps sputtered into life all along the walls, casting a flickering insubstantial light over the peeling wallpaper and threadbare carpet of a long, gloomy hallway, where a cobwebby chandelier glimmered overhead and age-blackened portraits hung crooked on the walls. Harry heard something scuttling behind the skirting board. Both the chandelier and the candelabra on a rickety table nearby were shaped like serpents.

There were hurried footsteps and Ron's mother, Mrs Weasley, emerged from a door at the far end of the hall. She was beaming in welcome as she hurried towards them, though Harry noticed that she was rather thinner and paler than she had been last time he had seen her.

'Oh, Harry, it's lovely to see you!' she whispered, pulling him into a rib-cracking hug before holding him at arm's length and examining him critically. 'You're looking peaky; you need feeding up, but you'll have to wait a bit for dinner, I'm afraid.'

She turned to the gang of wizards behind him and whispered urgently, 'He's just arrived, the meeting's started.'

The wizards behind Harry all made noises of interest and excitement and began filing past him towards the door through which Mrs Weasley had just

扑扑的气味，还有一股甜滋滋的腐烂味儿。这地方给人的感觉像是一座废弃的空房子。他扭头望望后面，看见其他人正跟着鱼贯而入。卢平和唐克斯抬着他的箱子，拎着海德薇的笼子。穆迪站在外面最上面一级台阶上，把刚才熄灯器从路灯上偷来的一个个光球释放出去。光球一个接一个地跳进了各自的灯泡，转眼间广场又被橘黄色灯光照得通亮。穆迪一瘸一拐地走了进来，关上前门，这下子门厅更是黑得伸手不见五指了。

"这儿——"

他用魔杖重重地敲了一下哈利的脑袋。这次哈利觉得仿佛有一股热乎乎的东西顺着后背流淌下去，他知道幻身咒被解除了。

"好了，大家都待着别动，我给这里弄出点儿亮光。"穆迪轻声说。

听到别人这样压低声音说话，哈利产生了一种奇怪的不祥之感，就好像他们走进了一座将死之人的房子。他听见了一阵窸窸窣窣的声音，然后墙上一排老式气灯都亮了，投下一片晃晃悠悠的不真实的亮光，照着长长的阴森森的门厅里剥落的墙纸，和磨光绽线的地毯。头顶上一盏蛛网状的枝形吊灯闪烁着微光，墙上歪歪斜斜地挂着一些因年深日久而发黑的肖像。哈利听见壁脚板后面有什么东西急匆匆跑过。枝形吊灯和旁边一张摇晃不稳的桌子上的枝形烛台都做成了大蛇的形状。

随着一阵匆匆的脚步声，罗恩的母亲韦斯莱夫人从门厅另一端的一扇门里走了出来。她三步并作两步地朝他们走来，脸上洋溢着热情的笑容，不过哈利注意到，她比他上回见到时消瘦和苍白了许多。

"哦，哈利，见到你真是太高兴了！"她低声说，一把将哈利搂到怀里，差点儿把他的肋骨都搂断了，然后又把他推开一点，仔仔细细地端详着，"你看上去怎么这么憔悴，需要多吃点东西，不过恐怕你得等一会儿才能吃晚饭。"

她又转向哈利身后的那伙巫师，口气急促地小声说："他刚来，会议已经开始了。"

哈利身后的巫师们都发出了关注和兴奋的声音，开始从他身边朝韦斯莱夫人刚才出来的那扇门走去。哈利正要跟着卢平过去，韦斯莱

CHAPTER FOUR   Number Twelve, Grimmauld Place

come. Harry made to follow Lupin, but Mrs Weasley held him back.

'No, Harry, the meeting's only for members of the Order. Ron and Hermione are upstairs, you can wait with them until the meeting's over, then we'll have dinner. And keep your voice down in the hall,' she added in an urgent whisper.

'Why?'

'I don't want anything to wake up.'

'What d'you –?'

'I'll explain later, I've got to hurry, I'm supposed to be at the meeting – I'll just show you where you're sleeping.'

Pressing her finger to her lips, she led him on tiptoe past a pair of long, moth-eaten curtains, behind which Harry supposed there must be another door, and after skirting a large umbrella stand that looked as though it had been made from a severed troll's leg they started up the dark staircase, passing a row of shrunken heads mounted on plaques on the wall. A closer look showed Harry that the heads belonged to house-elves. All of them had the same rather snout-like nose.

Harry's bewilderment deepened with every step he took. What on earth were they doing in a house that looked as though it belonged to the Darkest of wizards?

'Mrs Weasley, why –?'

'Ron and Hermione will explain everything, dear, I've really got to dash,' Mrs Weasley whispered distractedly. 'There –' they had reached the second landing, '– you're the door on the right. I'll call you when it's over.'

And she hurried off downstairs again.

Harry crossed the dingy landing, turned the bedroom doorknob, which was shaped like a serpent's head, and opened the door.

He caught a brief glimpse of a gloomy high-ceilinged, twin-bedded room; then there was a loud twittering noise, followed by an even louder shriek, and his vision was completely obscured by a large quantity of very bushy hair. Hermione had thrown herself on to him in a hug that nearly knocked him flat, while Ron's tiny owl, Pigwidgeon, zoomed excitedly round and round their heads.

'HARRY! Ron, he's here, Harry's here! We didn't hear you arrive! Oh,

夫人把他拉住了。

"不行,哈利,只有凤凰社的成员才能参加会议。罗恩和赫敏都在楼上呢,你可以跟他们一起等到会议结束,然后我们就吃晚饭。在门厅里说话要压低声音。"她又用急促的语气小声说。

"为什么?"

"我不想吵醒任何东西。"

"你说什——?"

"我待会儿再给你解释,现在我得赶紧过去了,我应该在会上的——我来告诉你睡在什么地方。"

她用一根手指压在嘴唇上,领着哈利蹑手蹑脚地走过两道长长的、布满虫眼的窗帘——哈利猜想那后面一定是另外一扇门,接着他们绕过一个看上去是用巨怪的一条断腿做成的大伞架,然后顺着黑暗的楼梯往上走,旁边墙上的饰板上聚着一排皱巴巴的脑袋。哈利仔细一看,发现那都是些家养小精灵的脑袋。他们都长着同样难看的大鼻子。

哈利每走一步,内心的困惑就更多一层。他们在这座看上去属于最邪恶的黑巫师的房子里做什么呢?

"韦斯莱夫人,为什么——?"

"罗恩和赫敏会把一切都给你解释清楚的,亲爱的,我真的得赶紧过去了。"韦斯莱夫人心不在焉地小声说,"到了——"他们来到了楼梯的第二个平台上,"——你在右边的那个门。会开完了我来叫你们。"

说完,她就急匆匆地又下楼去了。

哈利走过昏暗的楼梯平台,转动了一下蛇头形状的卧室门把手,把门打开了。

他只匆匆扫了一眼这个光线昏暗的房间、高高的天花板、并排放着的两张单人床,就听见一阵刺耳的吱吱叫声,继而是一声更尖厉的惊叫,接着他的视线就被一大堆毛茸茸、乱糟糟的头发完全挡住了。赫敏猛地扑到他身上,差点儿把他撞得仰面摔倒,罗恩的那只小猫头鹰小猪,兴奋地在他们头顶上一圈一圈飞个不停。

"**哈利**!罗恩,他来了,哈利来了!我们没有听见你进来!哦,你怎么样?一切都好吧?是不是生我们的气了?肯定生气了。我知道我

CHAPTER FOUR   Number Twelve, Grimmauld Place

how *are* you? Are you all right? Have you been furious with us? I bet you have, I know our letters were useless – but we couldn't tell you anything, Dumbledore made us swear we wouldn't, oh, we've got so much to tell you, and you've got things to tell us – the Dementors! When we heard – and that Ministry hearing – it's just outrageous, I've looked it all up, they can't expel you, they just can't, there's provision in the Decree for the Reasonable Restriction of Underage Sorcery for the use of magic in life-threatening situations –'

'Let him breathe, Hermione,' said Ron, grinning as he closed the door behind Harry. He seemed to have grown several more inches during their month apart, making him taller and more gangly looking than ever, though the long nose, bright red hair and freckles were the same.

Still beaming, Hermione let go of Harry, but before she could say another word there was a soft whooshing sound and something white soared from the top of a dark wardrobe and landed gently on Harry's shoulder.

'Hedwig!'

The snowy owl clicked her beak and nibbled his ear affectionately as Harry stroked her feathers.

'She's been in a right state,' said Ron. 'Pecked us half to death when she brought your last letters, look at this –'

He showed Harry the index finger of his right hand, which sported a half-healed but clearly deep cut.

'Oh, yeah,' Harry said. 'Sorry about that, but I wanted answers, you know –'

'We wanted to give them to you, mate,' said Ron. 'Hermione was going spare, she kept saying you'd do something stupid if you were stuck all on your own without news, but Dumbledore made us –'

'– swear not to tell me,' said Harry. 'Yeah, Hermione's already said.'

The warm glow that had flared inside him at the sight of his two best friends was extinguished as something icy flooded the pit of his stomach. All of a sudden – after yearning to see them for a solid month – he felt he would rather Ron and Hermione left him alone.

There was a strained silence in which Harry stroked Hedwig automatically, not looking at either of the others.

们的信都是没用的废话——但是我们什么也不能告诉你，邓布利多要我们发誓什么都不说的。哦，我们有太多的事情要告诉你啊，你也有好多事情要告诉我们——摄魂怪！当我们听说——还有那个到魔法部受审的事——真是太不像话了。我仔细查过了，他们不能开除你，绝对不能，《对未成年巫师加以合理约束法》里规定，在生命受到威胁的情况下可以使用魔法——"

"让他喘口气吧，赫敏。"罗恩一边说一边微笑着在哈利身后把门关上。在他们分开的这个月里，罗恩似乎又长高了几英寸，这使他比以前显得更瘦长、更笨拙了，不过那个长鼻子、那头红色的头发，还有那一脸的雀斑仍然和以前一模一样。

赫敏放开了哈利，仍然满脸喜色，但没等她再说什么，就听见传来一阵轻微的呼呼声，一个白色的东西从黑黑的衣柜顶上飞过来，轻捷地落在哈利肩头。

"海德薇！"

哈利抚摸着这只雪白的猫头鹰的羽毛，它嘴巴发出咔嗒咔嗒的声音，爱怜地轻轻啄着哈利的耳朵。

"它一直烦躁不安，"罗恩说，"它捎来你最后那两封信时，差点把我们啄个半死，你看看这个——"

他举起右手的食指给哈利看，上面有一个已经快要愈合但显然很深的伤口。

"哎呀，"哈利说，"真是对不起，但我想得到回信，你知道——"

"我们也想给你回信啊，哥们儿，"罗恩说，"赫敏担忧得要命，她不停地说，如果你一直困在那里，得不到一点儿消息，肯定会做出什么傻事来的。但邓布利多让我们——"

"——发誓不告诉我，"哈利说，"是啊，赫敏已经说过了。"

此刻，见到两个最要好朋友时的那种热乎乎的喜悦慢慢熄灭了，一股冷冰冰的东西涌进了他的内心深处。突然之间——虽然整整一个月眼巴巴地渴望见到他们——他觉得情愿罗恩和赫敏走开，让他独自待着。

一阵令人紧张的沉默，哈利机械地抚摸着海德薇，眼睛连看都不看他们俩。

CHAPTER FOUR   Number Twelve, Grimmauld Place

'He seemed to think it was best,' said Hermione rather breathlessly. 'Dumbledore, I mean.'

'Right,' said Harry. He noticed that her hands, too, bore the marks of Hedwig's beak and found that he was not at all sorry.

'I think he thought you were safest with the Muggles –' Ron began.

'Yeah?' said Harry, raising his eyebrows. 'Have either of *you* been attacked by Dementors this summer?'

'Well, no – but that's why he's had people from the Order of the Phoenix tailing you all the time –'

Harry felt a great jolt in his guts as though he had just missed a step going downstairs. So everyone had known he was being followed, except him.

'Didn't work that well, though, did it?' said Harry, doing his utmost to keep his voice even. 'Had to look after myself after all, didn't I?'

'He was so angry,' said Hermione, in an almost awestruck voice. 'Dumbledore. We saw him. When he found out Mundungus had left before his shift had ended. He was scary.'

'Well, I'm glad he left,' Harry said coldly. 'If he hadn't, I wouldn't have done magic and Dumbledore would probably have left me at Privet Drive all summer.'

'Aren't you … aren't you worried about the Ministry of Magic hearing?' said Hermione quietly.

'No,' Harry lied defiantly. He walked away from them, looking around, with Hedwig nestled contentedly on his shoulder, but this room was not likely to raise his spirits. It was dank and dark. A blank stretch of canvas in an ornate picture frame was all that relieved the bareness of the peeling walls, and as Harry passed it he thought he heard someone, who was lurking out of sight, snigger.

'So why's Dumbledore been so keen to keep me in the dark?' Harry asked, still trying hard to keep his voice casual. 'Did you – er – bother to ask him at all?'

He glanced up just in time to see them exchanging a look that told him he was behaving just as they had feared he would. It did nothing to improve his temper.

'We told Dumbledore we wanted to tell you what was going on,' said Ron.

第4章 格里莫广场12号

"他似乎觉得这样做最合适,"赫敏呼吸有点急促地说,"我指的是邓布利多。"

"是啊。"哈利说。他注意到赫敏的手上也留着被海德薇啄伤的疤痕,而他却没有丝毫歉意。

"我想,他大概认为你跟麻瓜待在一起是最安全的——"罗恩说道。

"是吗?"哈利扬起眉毛反问道,"你们这个暑假里谁遭到摄魂怪的袭击啦?"

"噢,没有——正因为那样,他才派了凤凰社的人随时跟踪你呀——"

哈利感到心里猛地忽悠一下,好像下楼梯时一脚踏空了。这么说大家都知道他被人跟踪,只有他一个人蒙在鼓里。

"看来并不怎么管用,是不是?"哈利说,拼命使声音保持平静,"我还是得自己保护自己,是不是?"

"他气极了,"赫敏用一种几乎战战兢兢的口吻说,"邓布利多。我们看见他了。当他弄清蒙顿格斯不到换岗时间就擅自离开时,他那副样子简直吓人。"

"噢,我倒巴不得蒙顿格斯离开呢。"哈利冷冰冰地说,"如果他不离开,我就不会使用魔法,邓布利多大概会让我整个暑假都待在女贞路吧。"

"你对……对到魔法部受审不感到担心吗?"赫敏轻声问。

"不。"哈利倔强地没说实话。他从他们身边走开,四下打量着,海德薇心满意足地歇在他的肩头,但这个房间似乎并不能使他的情绪有所好转。这里阴暗、潮湿。墙皮剥落的墙面上空荡荡的,只有一张空白的油画布镶在一个华丽的相框里。哈利从它旁边经过时,仿佛听见有谁躲在暗处轻声发笑。

"那么,邓布利多为什么这样热心地把我蒙在鼓里呢?"哈利问,仍然竭力保持着淡漠的声音,"你们——呃——有没有费心问问他呢?"

他一抬头,正好瞥见他们俩交换了一个眼神,似乎在说他的表现正像他们所担心的一样。这并没有使他的情绪好转一点。

"我们对邓布利多说,我们很想告诉你到底发生了什么事情,"罗

CHAPTER FOUR   Number Twelve, Grimmauld Place

'We did, mate. But he's really busy now, we've only seen him twice since we came here and he didn't have much time, he just made us swear not to tell you important stuff when we wrote, he said the owls might be intercepted.'

'He could still've kept me informed if he'd wanted to,' Harry said shortly. 'You're not telling me he doesn't know ways to send messages without owls.'

Hermione glanced at Ron and then said, 'I thought that, too. But he didn't want you to know *anything*.'

'Maybe he thinks I can't be trusted,' said Harry, watching their expressions.

'Don't be thick,' said Ron, looking highly disconcerted.

'Or that I can't take care of myself.'

'Of course he doesn't think that!' said Hermione anxiously.

'So how come I have to stay at the Dursleys' while you two get to join in everything that's going on here?' said Harry, the words tumbling over one another in a rush, his voice growing louder with every word. 'How come you two are allowed to know everything that's going on?'

'We're not!' Ron interrupted. 'Mum won't let us near the meetings, she says we're too young –'

But before he knew it, Harry was shouting.

'SO YOU HAVEN'T BEEN IN THE MEETINGS, BIG DEAL! YOU'VE STILL BEEN HERE, HAVEN'T YOU? YOU'VE STILL BEEN TOGETHER! ME, I'VE BEEN STUCK AT THE DURSLEYS' FOR A MONTH! AND I'VE HANDLED MORE THAN YOU TWO'VE EVER MANAGED AND DUMBLEDORE KNOWS IT – WHO SAVED THE PHILOSOPHER'S STONE? WHO GOT RID OF RIDDLE? WHO SAVED BOTH YOUR SKINS FROM THE DEMENTORS?'

Every bitter and resentful thought Harry had had in the past month was pouring out of him: his frustration at the lack of news, the hurt that they had all been together without him, his fury at being followed and not told about it – all the feelings he was half ashamed of finally burst their boundaries. Hedwig took fright at the noise and soared off to the top of the wardrobe again; Pigwidgeon twittered in alarm and zoomed even faster around their heads.

'WHO HAD TO GET PAST DRAGONS AND SPHINXES AND EVERY OTHER FOUL THING LAST YEAR? WHO SAW *HIM* COME

恩说,"我们真的说了,哥们儿。但他现在忙得要命,我们到这里之后只见过他两次。他没有多少时间,他只是叫我们保证写信时不把重要的事情告诉你,他说猫头鹰可能会被人半路截走。"

"如果他真的愿意,还是可以把消息告诉我的。"哈利粗暴地说,"难道除了猫头鹰,他就不知道还有其他送信的办法吗?"

赫敏扫了罗恩一眼,说道:"这点我也想过。但他就是不想让你知道任何事情。"

"也许他认为我不可信任。"哈利一边说一边观察着他们的表情。

"别说傻话啦。"罗恩说,显得有点儿惊慌失措。

"或者认为我不能照顾好自己。"

"他当然不是这么想的!"赫敏焦急地说。

"那么我为什么不得不留在德思礼家,而你们俩却参与了这里发生的每件事情?"他的话一句接一句地喷出来,声音越来越高,"为什么你们俩就有资格知道所有发生的事情?"

"不是这样的!"罗恩打断了他,"妈妈不让我们走进他们开会的地方,她说我们年纪太小——"

哈利不知不觉地喊了起来:

"这么说你们没能参加会议,真是太遗憾了!但你们一直待在这里,是不是?你们一直待在一起!而我呢,我被困在德思礼家整整一个月!可我解决过的事情比你们俩都多,邓布利多明明知道这一点——是谁保住了魔法石?是谁除掉了里德尔?是谁从摄魂怪手里救了你们两个人的命?"

过去一个月里哈利有过的每一个痛苦、怨恨的想法,现在都一股脑儿地涌了出来:得不到消息时的焦虑不安,得知他们一直待在一起、唯独把他撇在一边时的委屈,被人跟踪、自己却蒙在鼓里的愤怒——所有这些令他有一种屈辱的感觉,现在这种感觉终于像决堤的洪水一样冲了出来。海德薇被他的声音吓坏了,抖抖翅膀飞回到衣柜顶上去了。小猪惊慌地吱吱叫着,在他们头顶上嗖嗖地越飞越快。

"是谁去年不得不穿越火龙和斯芬克斯,以及其他每一种令人恶心的东西?是谁亲眼看见了那家伙的复活?是谁不得不逃脱他的魔爪?"

CHAPTER FOUR — Number Twelve, Grimmauld Place

BACK? WHO HAD TO ESCAPE FROM HIM? ME!'

Ron was standing there with his mouth half open, clearly stunned and at a loss for anything to say, whilst Hermione looked on the verge of tears.

'BUT WHY SHOULD I KNOW WHAT'S GOING ON? WHY SHOULD ANYONE BOTHER TO TELL ME WHAT'S BEEN HAPPENING?'

'Harry, we wanted to tell you, we really did –' Hermione began.

'CAN'T'VE WANTED TO THAT MUCH, CAN YOU, OR YOU'D HAVE SENT ME AN OWL, BUT *DUMBLEDORE MADE YOU SWEAR* –'

'Well, he did –'

'FOUR WEEKS I'VE BEEN STUCK IN PRIVET DRIVE, NICKING PAPERS OUT OF BINS TO TRY AND FIND OUT WHAT'S BEEN GOING ON –'

'We wanted to –'

'I SUPPOSE YOU'VE BEEN HAVING A REAL LAUGH, HAVEN'T YOU, ALL HOLED UP HERE TOGETHER –'

'No, honest –'

'Harry, we're really sorry!' said Hermione desperately, her eyes now sparkling with tears. 'You're absolutely right, Harry – I'd be furious if it was me!'

Harry glared at her, still breathing deeply, then turned away from them again, pacing up and down. Hedwig hooted glumly from the top of the wardrobe. There was a long pause, broken only by the mournful creak of the floorboards below Harry's feet.

'What *is* this place, anyway?' he shot at Ron and Hermione.

'Headquarters of the Order of the Phoenix,' said Ron at once.

'Is anyone going to bother telling me what the Order of the Phoenix –?'

'It's a secret society,' said Hermione quickly. 'Dumbledore's in charge, he founded it. It's the people who fought against You-Know-Who last time.'

'Who's in it?' said Harry, coming to a halt with his hands in his pockets.

'Quite a few people –'

'We've met about twenty of them,' said Ron, 'but we think there are more.'

Harry glared at them.

'*Well?*' he demanded, looking from one to the other.

第4章 格里莫广场12号

是我！"

罗恩站在那里，半张着嘴巴，目瞪口呆，完全不知道该说什么，赫敏看上去快要哭了。

"可是，我凭什么知道现在的情况呢？别人凭什么要费心告诉我正在发生什么事情呢？"

"哈利，我们是想告诉你来着，我们真的——"赫敏急切地说。

"大概也不是特别想吧，不然你们就会派一只猫头鹰给我送信了，可是邓布利多叫你们发誓——"

"是啊，他确实——"

"我被困在女贞路整整四个星期，从垃圾箱里捡报纸看，就为了弄清情况到底怎么——"

"我们想——"

"我想你们一定开心得要命，是不是？舒舒服服地一块儿藏在这里——"

"不，说老实话——"

"哈利，我们真的很抱歉！"赫敏不顾一切地说，眼睛里已经闪着泪花，"你说得非常对，哈利——换了我也会生气的！"

哈利气冲冲地瞪着她，仍然急促地喘着粗气，然后一转身离开了他们俩，在房间里踱来踱去。海德薇在衣柜顶上闷闷不乐地尖叫。一阵长长的沉默，只有哈利脚下的地板发出哀怨的嘎吱声。

"这里到底是什么地方？"他向罗恩和赫敏抛出了这个问题。

"凤凰社的总部。"罗恩毫不迟疑地回答。

"有没有谁能行行好，告诉我什么是凤凰社——"

"这是一个秘密社团，"赫敏赶紧说道，"由邓布利多负责，是他创建的。社团里都是上次跟神秘人做斗争的一些人。"

"里面都有谁？"哈利停住脚步，双手插在口袋里。

"有好些人呢——"

"我们见过其中的二十来个，"罗恩说，"但肯定不止这些。"

哈利向他投去愤怒的目光。

"然后呢？"他问道，目光从一个转向另一个。

CHAPTER FOUR   Number Twelve, Grimmauld Place

'Er,' said Ron. 'Well what?'

'*Voldemort!*' said Harry furiously, and both Ron and Hermione winced. 'What's happening? What's he up to? Where is he? What are we doing to stop him?'

'We've *told* you, the Order don't let us in on their meetings,' said Hermione nervously. 'So we don't know the details – but we've got a general idea,' she added hastily, seeing the look on Harry's face.

'Fred and George have invented Extendable Ears, see,' said Ron. 'They're really useful.'

'Extendable –?'

'Ears, yeah. Only we've had to stop using them lately because Mum found out and went berserk. Fred and George had to hide them all to stop Mum binning them. But we got a good bit of use out of them before Mum realised what was going on. We know some of the Order are following known Death Eaters, keeping tabs on them, you know –'

'Some of them are working on recruiting more people to the Order –' said Hermione.

'And some of them are standing guard over something,' said Ron. 'They're always talking about guard duty.'

'Couldn't have been me, could it?' said Harry sarcastically.

'Oh, yeah,' said Ron, with a look of dawning comprehension.

Harry snorted. He walked around the room again, looking anywhere but at Ron and Hermione. 'So, what have you two been doing, if you're not allowed in meetings?' he demanded. 'You said you'd been busy.'

'We have,' said Hermione quickly. 'We've been decontaminating this house, it's been empty for ages and stuff's been breeding in here. We've managed to clean out the kitchen, most of the bedrooms and I think we're doing the drawing room tomo– AARGH!'

With two loud cracks, Fred and George, Ron's elder twin brothers, had materialised out of thin air in the middle of the room. Pigwidgeon twittered more wildly than ever and zoomed off to join Hedwig on top of the wardrobe.

'Stop *doing* that!' Hermione said weakly to the twins, who were as vividly red-haired as Ron, though stockier and slightly shorter.

'Hello, Harry,' said George, beaming at him. 'We thought we heard your

第4章 格里莫广场12号

"呃,"罗恩说,"然后什么?"

"伏地魔!"哈利气愤地喊道,罗恩和赫敏都吓得缩起了脖子,"发生了什么事?他想干什么?他在哪儿?我们采取什么办法阻止他?"

"我们已经对你说过了,凤凰社不让我们参加他们的会议,"赫敏不安地说,"所以一些具体细节我们也不清楚——不过我们好歹知道一点儿大概。"看到哈利脸上的表情,她赶紧补充道。

"弗雷德和乔治发明了伸缩耳,明白吗,"罗恩说,"真的很管用。"

"伸缩——?"

"伸缩耳,对呀。可是我们最近只好不用它们了,因为妈妈发现了,气得要命。弗雷德和乔治不得不把它们藏了起来,免得妈妈把它们扔到垃圾箱里去。不过在妈妈发现是怎么回事之前,我们可用它们派了大用场呢。我们知道凤凰社的一些成员正在跟踪那些已暴露身份的食死徒,密切注意他们的行踪,你知道——"

"他们当中有些人正在吸收更多的人加入凤凰社——"赫敏说。

"还有些人正在为什么事情站岗放哨,"罗恩说,"他们一直在谈论什么警卫任务。"

"不会是保护我吧,啊?"哈利讥讽地说。

"哦,没错。"罗恩说,脸上露出了恍然大悟的神情。

哈利轻蔑地哼了一声。他又在房间里一圈圈地踱起步来,看看这里看看那里,就是不看罗恩和赫敏。"那么你们俩最近在做什么呢,既然不让你们参加会议?"他问道,"你们说你们一直很忙。"

"是很忙啊,"赫敏急忙说,"我们给这座房子来了个彻底大扫除,这房子已经空了许多年头,里面滋生繁殖了许多东西。我们总算把厨房和大部分卧室打扫干净了,我想明天该去对付客厅——**哎呀!**"

啪、啪,随着两声刺耳的爆响,罗恩的两个双胞胎哥哥——弗雷德和乔治突然出现在房间中央。小猪吱吱地叫得更慌乱了,嗖地飞过去和海德薇一起栖在衣柜顶上。

"不许这么做!"赫敏惊魂未定地对双胞胎说。他们和罗恩一样长着一头红得耀眼的头发,不过身材比罗恩壮实,个头比罗恩略矮一些。

"你好,哈利,"乔治一边说一边朝哈利开心地笑着,"我们刚才好

CHAPTER FOUR Number Twelve, Grimmauld Place

dulcet tones.'

'You don't want to bottle up your anger like that, Harry, let it all out,' said Fred, also beaming. 'There might be a couple of people fifty miles away who didn't hear you.'

'You two passed your Apparition tests, then?' asked Harry grumpily.

'With distinction,' said Fred, who was holding what looked like a piece of very long, flesh-coloured string.

'It would have taken you about thirty seconds longer to walk down the stairs,' said Ron.

'Time is Galleons, little brother,' said Fred. 'Anyway, Harry, you're interfering with reception. Extendable Ears,' he added in response to Harry's raised eyebrows, and held up the string which Harry now saw was trailing out on to the landing. 'We're trying to hear what's going on downstairs.'

'You want to be careful,' said Ron, staring at the Ear, 'if Mum sees one of them again ...'

'It's worth the risk, that's a major meeting they're having,' said Fred.

The door opened and a long mane of red hair appeared.

'Oh, hello, Harry!' said Ron's younger sister, Ginny, brightly. 'I thought I heard your voice.'

Turning to Fred and George, she said, 'It's no-go with the Extendable Ears, she's gone and put an Imperturbable Charm on the kitchen door.'

'How d'you know?' said George, looking crestfallen.

'Tonks told me how to find out,' said Ginny. 'You just chuck stuff at the door and if it can't make contact the door's been Imperturbed. I've been flicking Dungbombs at it from the top of the stairs and they just soar away from it, so there's no way the Extendable Ears will be able to get under the gap.'

Fred heaved a deep sigh.

'Shame. I really fancied finding out what old Snape's been up to.'

'Snape!' said Harry quickly. 'Is he here?'

'Yeah,' said George, carefully closing the door and sitting down on one of the beds; Fred and Ginny followed. 'Giving a report. Top secret.'

'Git,' said Fred idly.

'He's on our side now,' said Hermione reprovingly.

像听见你悦耳动听的声音了。"

"你用不着那样压抑自己的怒火,哈利,把它都发泄出来吧,"弗雷德也是满脸带笑,"五十英里之外大概还有两个人听不见你的声音呢。"

"这么说,你们俩通过幻影显形的考试啦?"哈利没好气地问。

"成绩优异。"弗雷德说,他手里拿着一个东西,像是一根长长的肉色细绳。

"从楼梯上下来也就不过多花三十秒钟。"罗恩说。

"时间就是金加隆,弟弟。"弗雷德说,"不管怎么说,哈利,你干扰接收了。伸缩耳,"他看到哈利扬起眉毛,又接着解释道,并举起了那根细绳,哈利这才看到它一直通到外面的楼梯平台上,"我们想听听楼下的动静。"

"你们可得小心点儿,"罗恩盯着伸缩耳说,"如果又给妈妈看见了……"

"值得冒险,他们在开一个重要会议。"弗雷德说。

门开了,露出一头红色的长发。

"噢,你好,哈利!"罗恩的妹妹金妮高兴地说,"我好像听见你的声音了。"

她又转向弗雷德和乔治,对他们说:"伸缩耳不管用了,妈妈竟然给厨房门念了个抗扰咒。"

"你怎么知道的?"乔治问,一副垂头丧气的样子。

"是唐克斯告诉我怎么验证的。"金妮说,"你只要往门上扔东西,如果东西碰不到门,就说明念了抗扰咒。我一直在楼梯顶上往门上扔粪弹,可它们全都避开门飞到了别处,所以伸缩耳根本不可能从门缝底下钻进去了。"

弗雷德长长地叹了一口气。

"可惜。我真想知道斯内普那老家伙想干什么。"

"斯内普!"哈利立刻问道,"他也在这儿?"

"是啊。"乔治说着小心地关上房门,坐在一张床上。弗雷德和金妮也跟了过来。"他正在念一份报告。绝密的。"

"烦人精。"弗雷德懒洋洋地说。

"他现在是我们这边的人了。"赫敏责备地说。

CHAPTER FOUR Number Twelve, Grimmauld Place

Ron snorted. 'Doesn't stop him being a git. The way he looks at us when he sees us.'

'Bill doesn't like him, either,' said Ginny, as though that settled the matter.

Harry was not sure his anger had abated yet; but his thirst for information was now overcoming his urge to keep shouting. He sank on to the bed opposite the others.

'Is Bill here?' he asked. 'I thought he was working in Egypt?'

'He applied for a desk job so he could come home and work for the Order,' said Fred. 'He says he misses the tombs, but,' he smirked, 'there are compensations.'

'What d'you mean?'

'Remember old Fleur Delacour?' said George. 'She's got a job at Gringotts to *eemprove 'er Eeenglish* –'

'And Bill's been giving her a lot of private lessons,' sniggered Fred.

'Charlie's in the Order, too,' said George, 'but he's still in Romania. Dumbledore wants as many foreign wizards brought in as possible, so Charlie's trying to make contacts on his days off.'

'Couldn't Percy do that?' Harry asked. The last he had heard, the third Weasley brother was working in the Department of International Magical Co-operation at the Ministry of Magic.

At Harry's words, all the Weasleys and Hermione exchanged darkly significant looks.

'Whatever you do, don't mention Percy in front of Mum and Dad,' Ron told Harry in a tense voice.

'Why not?'

'Because every time Percy's name's mentioned, Dad breaks whatever he's holding and Mum starts crying,' Fred said.

'It's been awful,' said Ginny sadly.

'I think we're well shot of him,' said George, with an uncharacteristically ugly look on his face.

'What's happened?' Harry said.

'Percy and Dad had a row,' said Fred. 'I've never seen Dad row with anyone like that. It's normally Mum who shouts.'

第 4 章 格里莫广场 12 号

罗恩哼了一声："那也不能说他就不是烦人精了。瞧他看着我们时的那种眼神。"

"比尔也不喜欢他。"金妮说，似乎这就一锤定音了。

哈利不知道自己的火气是不是熄灭了，他此刻迫不及待地想知道更多的情况，这份渴望压过了他大叫大嚷的冲动。他一屁股坐在其他人对面的那张床上。

"比尔也在这儿？"他问，"他不是在埃及工作吗？"

"他申请了一个坐办公室的工作，这样就能回家，为凤凰社做事了。"弗雷德说，"他说他很想念那些古墓。不过，"他调皮地笑了，"也有所补偿啊。"

"什么意思？"

"还记得那个芙蓉·德拉库尔吗？"乔治说，"她在古灵阁找了一份工作，为了提高英语——"

"比尔一直在给她许多个别辅导。"弗雷德咯咯地笑着说。

"查理也加入了凤凰社，"乔治说，"但他人还在罗马尼亚。邓布利多希望尽量多吸收一些国外的巫师，所以查理在不上班时就与人广泛接触。"

"珀西不能那么做吗？"哈利问。据他上次所知道的情况，韦斯莱家的第三个儿子在魔法部的国际魔法合作司工作。

听了哈利的话，韦斯莱家的几个兄妹和赫敏交换了一个忧郁而意味深长的眼神。

"你可千万别在妈妈和爸爸面前提到珀西。"罗恩用紧张的口气对哈利说。

"为什么呢？"

"因为每次提到珀西的名字，爸爸就把手里拿的东西砸得粉碎，妈妈就放声大哭。"弗雷德说。

"真是太可怕了。"金妮悲哀地说。

"我想我们总算摆脱他了。"乔治说，脸上一反常态露出阴沉的表情。

"出什么事了？"哈利问。

"珀西和爸爸大吵了一架。"弗雷德说，"我从没见过爸爸跟谁吵成那样。平常总是妈妈大吵大嚷。"

CHAPTER FOUR — Number Twelve, Grimmauld Place

'It was the first week back after term ended,' said Ron. 'We were about to come and join the Order. Percy came home and told us he'd been promoted.'

'You're kidding?' said Harry.

Though he knew perfectly well that Percy was highly ambitious, Harry's impression was that Percy had not made a great success of his first job at the Ministry of Magic. Percy had committed the fairly large oversight of failing to notice that his boss was being controlled by Lord Voldemort (not that the Ministry had believed it — they all thought Mr Crouch had gone mad).

'Yeah, we were all surprised,' said George, 'because Percy got into a load of trouble about Crouch, there was an inquiry and everything. They said Percy ought to have realised Crouch was off his rocker and informed a superior. But you know Percy, Crouch left him in charge, he wasn't going to complain.'

'So how come they promoted him?'

'That's exactly what we wondered,' said Ron, who seemed very keen to keep normal conversation going now that Harry had stopped yelling. 'He came home really pleased with himself — even more pleased than usual, if you can imagine that — and told Dad he'd been offered a position in Fudge's own office. A really good one for someone only a year out of Hogwarts: Junior Assistant to the Minister. He expected Dad to be all impressed, I think.'

'Only Dad wasn't,' said Fred grimly.

'Why not?' said Harry.

'Well, apparently Fudge has been storming round the Ministry checking that nobody's having any contact with Dumbledore,' said George.

'Dumbledore's name is mud with the Ministry these days, see,' said Fred. 'They all think he's just making trouble saying You-Know-Who's back.'

'Dad says Fudge has made it clear that anyone who's in league with Dumbledore can clear out their desks,' said George.

'Trouble is, Fudge suspects Dad, he knows he's friendly with Dumbledore, and he's always thought Dad's a bit of a weirdo because of his Muggle obsession.'

'But what's that got to do with Percy?' asked Harry, confused.

'I'm coming to that. Dad reckons Fudge only wants Percy in his office

第 4 章　格里莫广场 12 号

"那是学期结束后的第一个星期,"罗恩说,"我们正准备来凤凰社。珀西回家了,告诉我们他被提拔了。"

"你在开玩笑吧?"哈利说。

哈利虽然很清楚珀西一直野心勃勃,但他有个印象,似乎珀西在魔法部的第一份工作干得并不是很成功。珀西犯了比较严重的失察错误,没有发现他的上司是受伏地魔控制的(就连魔法部也不相信——他们都以为克劳奇先生疯了)。

"是啊,我们也都感到很意外,"乔治说,"因为珀西在克劳奇的事情上惹了一大堆麻烦,后来又是调查又是什么的。他们说珀西应该意识到克劳奇精神失常,并及时向上级报告。但你是了解珀西的,克劳奇让他独当一面,他正巴不得呢。"

"那他们怎么还会提拔他呢?"

"我们也为这个感到纳闷呢。"罗恩说,看到哈利不再大嚷大叫,他似乎特别愿意让谈话正常地进行下去,"他回家时一副得意扬扬的样子——比平常还要得意,你就想象一下吧——他告诉爸爸,他们给了他一个福吉部长办公室里的职位。对于一个从霍格沃茨刚毕业一年的人来说,这真是一份求之不得的好差使:部长初级助理啊。我想,他大概指望爸爸会很高兴呢。"

"可是爸爸没有。"弗雷德忧郁地说。

"为什么呢?"哈利问。

"嗯,显然是因为福吉在部里大发雷霆,禁止任何人跟邓布利多有任何接触。"乔治说。

"这些日子邓布利多在部里名声扫地,知道吗?"弗雷德说,"他们都认为他散布神秘人回来了的消息是故意制造事端。"

"爸爸说福吉明确指出,凡是与邓布利多有任何瓜葛的人都不能再待在部里。"乔治说。

"问题是,福吉怀疑到爸爸头上了。他知道爸爸跟邓布利多关系不错,而且福吉一直觉得爸爸有点儿古怪,居然对麻瓜那么着迷。"

"这跟珀西有什么关系呢?"哈利迷惑不解地问。

"我正要说到这一点上呢。爸爸琢磨,福吉把珀西安排在自己的办

CHAPTER FOUR   Number Twelve, Grimmauld Place

because he wants to use him to spy on the family – and Dumbledore.'

Harry let out a low whistle.

'Bet Percy loved that.'

Ron laughed in a hollow sort of way.

'He went completely berserk. He said – well, he said loads of terrible stuff. He said he's been having to struggle against Dad's lousy reputation ever since he joined the Ministry and that Dad's got no ambition and that's why we've always been – you know – not had a lot of money, I mean –'

'*What?*' said Harry in disbelief, as Ginny made a noise like an angry cat.

'I know,' said Ron in a low voice. 'And it got worse. He said Dad was an idiot to run around with Dumbledore, that Dumbledore was heading for big trouble and Dad was going to go down with him, and that he – Percy – knew where his loyalty lay and it was with the Ministry. And if Mum and Dad were going to become traitors to the Ministry he was going to make sure everyone knew he didn't belong to our family any more. And he packed his bags the same night and left. He's living here in London now.'

Harry swore under his breath. He had always liked Percy least of Ron's brothers, but he had never imagined he would say such things to Mr Weasley.

'Mum's been in a right state,' said Ron. 'You know – crying and stuff. She came up to London to try and talk to Percy but he slammed the door in her face. I dunno what he does if he meets Dad at work – ignores him, I s'pose.'

'But Percy *must* know Voldemort's back,' said Harry slowly. 'He's not stupid, he must know your mum and dad wouldn't risk everything without proof.'

'Yeah, well, your name got dragged into the row,' said Ron, shooting Harry a furtive look. 'Percy said the only evidence was your word and ... I dunno ... he didn't think it was good enough.'

'Percy takes the *Daily Prophet* seriously,' said Hermione tartly, and the others all nodded.

'What are you talking about?' Harry asked, looking around at them all. They were all regarding him warily.

'Haven't – haven't you been getting the *Daily Prophet*?' Hermione asked nervously.

'Yeah, I have!' said Harry.

公室,是想利用他监视我们家——监视邓布利多。"

哈利轻轻吹出一声口哨。

"我猜珀西肯定很爱听这话。"

罗恩发出空洞的笑声。

"他简直气疯了。他说——唉,他说了一大堆可怕的话。说他自从进了部里,就一直不得不拼命挣扎,摆脱爸爸的坏名声;他还说爸爸没有一点抱负,害得我们一直过得——你知道的——我指的是一直没有多少钱——"

"什么?"哈利不敢相信地说,金妮发出一种怒猫般的叫声。

"我知道,"罗恩放低声音说,"后来更过分了。他说爸爸与邓布利多为伍真是蠢到了家,还说邓布利多眼看着就要有大麻烦了,爸爸会跟着他一块儿倒霉的,还说他——珀西——知道自己应该为谁效忠,他要忠于魔法部。他还说,如果妈妈和爸爸硬要背叛魔法部,他就要让每一个人知道他已经不再属于我们这个家了。当天晚上他就收拾行李走了。他眼下就住在伦敦这儿呢。"

哈利不出声地骂了几句。在罗恩的几个哥哥中间,他一直最不喜欢珀西,但压根儿也没想到珀西居然对韦斯莱先生说出那样的话。

"妈妈一直烦躁不安,"罗恩说,"你知道,哭哭啼啼的。她赶到伦敦,想和珀西谈谈,但珀西当着她的面把门重重地关上了。我不知道珀西上班时碰见爸爸是怎么做的——大概假装没看见吧。"

"但是珀西肯定知道伏地魔回来了,"哈利说,"他不是傻瓜,他肯定知道如果没有证据,你们的爸爸妈妈是不会轻易冒险的。"

"是啊,后来,你的名字就被扯到争吵里来了,"罗恩说着偷偷瞥了哈利一眼,"珀西说,唯一的证据就是你说的话,而……我也说不好……他认为光凭这个是不够的。"

"珀西把《预言家日报》当真了。"赫敏尖刻地说,其他人都点了点头。

"你们在说什么呀?"哈利问,挨个儿看看他们每个人。他们都小心翼翼地注视着他。

"你不是——你不是一直收到《预言家日报》吗?"赫敏不安地问。

"是啊,一直收到!"哈利说。

'Have you – er – been reading it thoroughly?' Hermione asked, still more anxiously.

'Not cover to cover,' said Harry defensively. 'If they were going to report anything about Voldemort it would be headline news, wouldn't it?'

The others flinched at the sound of the name. Hermione hurried on, 'Well, you'd need to read it cover to cover to pick it up, but they – um – they mention you a couple of times a week.'

'But I'd have seen –'

'Not if you've only been reading the front page, you wouldn't,' said Hermione, shaking her head. 'I'm not talking about big articles. They just slip you in, like you're a standing joke.'

'What d'you –?'

'It's quite nasty, actually,' said Hermione in a voice of forced calm. 'They're just building on Rita's stuff.'

'But she's not writing for them any more, is she?'

'Oh, no, she's kept her promise – not that she's got any choice,' Hermione added with satisfaction. 'But she laid the foundation for what they're trying to do now.'

'Which is *what*?' said Harry impatiently.

'OK, you know she wrote that you were collapsing all over the place and saying your scar was hurting and all that?'

'Yeah,' said Harry, who was not likely to forget Rita Skeeter's stories about him in a hurry.

'Well, they're writing about you as though you're this deluded, attention-seeking person who thinks he's a great tragic hero or something,' said Hermione, very fast, as though it would be less unpleasant for Harry to hear these facts quickly. 'They keep slipping in snide comments about you. If some far-fetched story appears, they say something like, "A tale worthy of Harry Potter", and if anyone has a funny accident or anything it's, "Let's hope he hasn't got a scar on his forehead or we'll be asked to worship him next" –'

'I don't want anyone to worship –' Harry began hotly.

'I know you don't,' said Hermione quickly, looking frightened. 'I *know*, Harry. But you see what they're doing? They want to turn you into someone nobody will believe. Fudge is behind it, I'll bet anything. They want wizards

第4章 格里莫广场12号

"你有没有——呃——你没有仔细看它吗?"赫敏问,口气更加不安了。

"没有从头到尾地看。"哈利以一种防卫的语气说,"如果他们要报道伏地魔的事情,肯定是头版头条的新闻,是不是?"

听到那个名字,其他人都吓得一缩脖子。赫敏急匆匆地说了下去:"噢,你需要从头到尾看一遍才会发现,他们——呃——他们每星期都要提到你一两次呢。"

"那我应该看见——"

"你如果光看第一版,是不会看到的。"赫敏说着摇了摇脑袋,"我说的不是大块文章。他们只是顺带着提你一笔,把你当成一个笑料。"

"你说什——?"

"确实,这非常可恶,"赫敏强使自己的声音保持平静,"他们的根据就是丽塔的那些胡言乱语。"

"但她不是不再给他们写稿了吗,是不是?"

"噢,不写了,她遵守了自己的诺言——她也没有别的选择呀,"赫敏得意地解释道,"但是,她为他们现在要做的事情打下了基础。"

"什么基础?"哈利不耐烦地问。

"是这样,你知道的,她在文章里说你到处昏倒,嚷嚷你的伤疤疼什么的。"

"是啊。"哈利说,他不太可能一下子就忘记丽塔·斯基特编派他的那些鬼话。

"现在他们在文章里提到你的时候,似乎你就是这样一个执迷不悟的、千方百计引起别人注意的人,以为自己是个悲壮的大英雄什么的。"赫敏说,语速很快,似乎让哈利很快听到这些事实就会减少一些不快似的,"他们不断假装不经意地说几句关于你的刻毒评论。碰到一篇毫无根据的报道,他们就会说'这只有哈利·波特才编得出来'之类的话;如果有人出了点可笑的事故,他们就会说'但愿他的额头上别弄出一道伤疤,不然他接下来会要求我们崇拜他了——'"

"我并不想得到任何人的崇拜——"哈利气愤地说。

"我知道你不想,"赫敏似乎吓坏了,赶紧说道,"我知道,哈利。但你明白他们在做什么吗?他们是想把你变成一个没有人会相信的人。

CHAPTER FOUR Number Twelve, Grimmauld Place

on the street to think you're just some stupid boy who's a bit of a joke, who tells ridiculous tall stories because he loves being famous and wants to keep it going.'

'I didn't ask – I didn't want – *Voldemort killed my parents*!' Harry spluttered. 'I got famous because he murdered my family but couldn't kill me! Who wants to be famous for that? Don't they think I'd rather it'd never –'

'We *know*, Harry,' said Ginny earnestly.

'And of course, they didn't report a word about the Dementors attacking you,' said Hermione. 'Someone's told them to keep that quiet. That should've been a really big story, out-of-control Dementors. They haven't even reported that you broke the International Statute of Secrecy. We thought they would, it would tie in so well with this image of you as some stupid show-off. We think they're biding their time until you're expelled, then they're really going to go to town – I mean, *if* you're expelled, obviously,' she went on hastily. 'You really shouldn't be, not if they abide by their own laws, there's no case against you.'

They were back on the hearing and Harry did not want to think about that. He cast around for another change of subject, but was saved the necessity of finding one by the sound of footsteps coming up the stairs.

'Uh oh.'

Fred gave the Extendable Ear a hearty tug; there was another loud crack and he and George vanished. Seconds later, Mrs Weasley appeared in the bedroom doorway.

'The meeting's over, you can come down and have dinner now. Everyone's dying to see you, Harry. And who's left all those Dungbombs outside the kitchen door?'

'Crookshanks,' said Ginny unblushingly. 'He loves playing with them.'

'Oh,' said Mrs Weasley, 'I thought it might have been Kreacher, he keeps doing odd things like that. Now don't forget to keep your voices down in the hall. Ginny, your hands are filthy, what have you been doing? Go and wash them before dinner, please.'

Ginny grimaced at the others and followed her mother out of the room, leaving Harry alone with Ron and Hermione. Both of them were watching him apprehensively, as though they feared he would start shouting again now

第4章 格里莫广场12号

福吉是幕后操纵者，我敢打赌。他们想使外面的巫师都认为你只是一个蠢笨的男孩，是个笑料，尽说一些荒唐的无稽之谈，就为了使自己出人头地，使这种状况保持下去。"

"我并没有要求——我不想——伏地魔杀死了我的父母！"哈利气急败坏地说，"我出名是因为他杀死了我的亲人却没能杀死我！谁想为了这个出名？他们难道不知道，我宁愿从来没有——"

"我们知道的，哈利。"金妮真诚地说。

"当然啦，他们一个字也没有提到摄魂怪攻击你的事。"赫敏说，"准是有人叫他们对这件事隐瞒不报。不然那应该是一个轰动性的好题材啊。失控的摄魂怪！他们甚至没有报道你违反《国际保密法》的事。我们猜想他们肯定是愿意报道的，那太符合你作为一个爱出风头的傻瓜的形象了。我们认为他们是在等到你被开除的那一天，然后他们就真的可以肆无忌惮了——我的意思是，万一你被开除了，但显然，"她急急忙忙地往下说，"实际上你不会，只要他们遵守他们自己的法律，情况就不会对你不利。"

又回到受审的话题上来了，而哈利不愿意去想这件事。他想重新换个话题，就在这时楼梯上传来了脚步声，他也就没必要费心去找话题了。

"哎哟。"

弗雷德使劲扯了一下伸缩耳。随着又一声爆响，他和乔治都不见了。几秒钟后，韦斯莱夫人出现在卧室门口。

"会开完了，现在你们可以下楼来吃晚饭了。哈利，大伙儿都盼着见到你呢。对了，谁在厨房门外丢了那么多粪弹？"

"克鲁克山。"金妮毫不脸红地说，"它最喜欢玩粪弹了。"

"噢，"韦斯莱夫人说，"我还以为是克利切呢，他总是做出这种古怪的事情。好了，在门厅里别忘了压低声音说话。金妮，你怎么两只手这么脏，干什么去了？快去洗干净再吃晚饭。"

金妮朝其他人做了个鬼脸，跟着妈妈走了出去，房间里只留下哈利和罗恩、赫敏。那两人都忧心忡忡地望着哈利，似乎担心其他人一走，他又会大吵大嚷起来。看到他们俩神情这么紧张，哈利觉得有点儿不

CHAPTER FOUR   Number Twelve, Grimmauld Place

that everyone else had gone. The sight of them looking so nervous made him feel slightly ashamed.

'Look ...' he muttered, but Ron shook his head, and Hermione said quietly, 'We knew you'd be angry, Harry, we really don't blame you, but you've got to understand, we *did* try to persuade Dumbledore –'

'Yeah, I know,' said Harry shortly.

He cast around for a topic that didn't involve his headmaster, because the very thought of Dumbledore made Harry's insides burn with anger again.

'Who's Kreacher?' he asked.

'The house-elf who lives here,' said Ron. 'Nutter. Never met one like him.'

Hermione frowned at Ron.

'He's not a *nutter*, Ron.'

'His life's ambition is to have his head cut off and stuck up on a plaque just like his mother,' said Ron irritably. 'Is that normal, Hermione?'

'Well – well, if he is a bit strange, it's not his fault.'

Ron rolled his eyes at Harry.

'Hermione still hasn't given up on S.P.E.W.'

'It's not S.P.E.W.!' said Hermione heatedly. 'It's the Society for the Promotion of Elfish Welfare. And it's not just me, Dumbledore says we should be kind to Kreacher too.'

'Yeah, yeah,' said Ron. 'C'mon, I'm starving.'

He led the way out of the door and on to the landing, but before they could descend the stairs –

'Hold it!' Ron breathed, flinging out an arm to stop Harry and Hermione walking any further. 'They're still in the hall, we might be able to hear something.'

The three of them looked cautiously over the banisters. The gloomy hallway below was packed with witches and wizards, including all of Harry's guard. They were whispering excitedly together. In the very centre of the group Harry saw the dark, greasy-haired head and prominent nose of his least favourite teacher at Hogwarts, Professor Snape. Harry leant further over the banisters. He was very interested in what Snape was doing for the Order of the Phoenix ...

A thin piece of flesh-coloured string descended in front of Harry's eyes.

好意思。

"这个……"他吞吞吐吐地说,但罗恩摇了摇头,赫敏轻声说道:"我们知道你会生气的,哈利,我们真的不怪你,但你一定要理解,我们确实试着说服邓布利多——"

"好啦,我知道了。"哈利简短地说。

他想赶紧换一个与校长无关的话题,每次一想到邓布利多,哈利的内心就又呼呼地怒火直冒。

"克利切是谁?"他问。

"一个住在这里的家养小精灵,"罗恩说,"一个疯子。从没见过像他这样的。"

赫敏冲罗恩皱起眉头。

"他不是疯子,罗恩。"

"他人生的最大理想就是像他妈妈那样,脑袋被割下来,粘在一块饰板上。"罗恩不耐烦地说,"那正常吗,赫敏?"

"这个——可是,就算他有点儿古怪,那也不是他的过错。"

罗恩朝哈利翻翻眼睛。

"赫敏仍然没有放弃她的'呕吐'。"

"不是'呕吐'!"赫敏恼火地说,"是家养小精灵权益促进会。而且不光是我,邓布利多也说我们应该仁慈地对待克利切。"

"是啊,是啊。"罗恩说,"快走吧,我都饿坏了。"

他领头出了房门来到楼梯平台上,但没等他们开始下楼——

"慢着!"罗恩轻声说,伸出一只胳膊不让哈利和赫敏再往前走,"他们还在门厅里,说不定我们能听见什么呢。"

他们三个小心翼翼地从栏杆上往下看。下面昏暗的门厅里挤满了巫师,包括先前给哈利当警卫的那几个人。他们都在激动地小声议论着什么。在人群的最中间,哈利看见了那个头发乌黑油亮的脑袋和那个突出的大鼻子,那是他在霍格沃茨最不喜欢的老师——斯内普教授。哈利从栏杆上探出脑袋,他很想知道斯内普究竟在为凤凰社做些什么……

一根细细的肉色绳子在哈利眼前垂了下去。他一抬头,看见弗雷德

CHAPTER FOUR Number Twelve, Grimmauld Place

Looking up, he saw Fred and George on the landing above, cautiously lowering the Extendable Ear towards the dark knot of people below. A moment later, however, they all began to move towards the front door and out of sight.

'Dammit,' Harry heard Fred whisper, as he hoisted the Extendable Ear back up again.

They heard the front door open, then close.

'Snape never eats here,' Ron told Harry quietly. 'Thank God. C'mon.'

'And don't forget to keep your voice down in the hall, Harry,' Hermione whispered.

As they passed the row of house-elf heads on the wall, they saw Lupin, Mrs Weasley and Tonks at the front door, magically sealing its many locks and bolts behind those who had just left.

'We're eating down in the kitchen,' Mrs Weasley whispered, meeting them at the bottom of the stairs. 'Harry, dear, if you'll just tiptoe across the hall it's through this door here –'

CRASH.

'*Tonks*!' cried Mrs Weasley in exasperation, turning to look behind her.

'I'm sorry!' wailed Tonks, who was lying flat on the floor. 'It's that stupid umbrella stand, that's the second time I've tripped over –'

But the rest of her words were drowned by a horrible, ear-splitting, blood-curdling screech.

The moth-eaten velvet curtains Harry had passed earlier had flown apart, but there was no door behind them. For a split second, Harry thought he was looking through a window, a window behind which an old woman in a black cap was screaming and screaming as though she were being tortured – then he realised it was simply a life-size portrait, but the most realistic, and the most unpleasant, he had ever seen in his life.

The old woman was drooling, her eyes were rolling, the yellowing skin of her face stretched taut as she screamed; and all along the hall behind them, the other portraits awoke and began to yell, too, so that Harry actually screwed up his eyes at the noise and clapped his hands over his ears.

Lupin and Mrs Weasley darted forward and tried to tug the curtains shut over the old woman, but they would not close and she screeched louder than

和乔治正在上一层楼梯平台上小心地把伸缩耳降落到下面黑压压的人群中间。然而，没过一会儿，那伙人就开始朝前门走去，很快就不见了。

"见鬼！"哈利听见弗雷德小声骂了一句，把伸缩耳又拽了上去。

他们听见前门打开了，然后又关上了。

"斯内普从不在这里吃饭，"罗恩小声地告诉哈利，"谢天谢地。我们走吧。"

"在门厅里别忘了压低声音说话，哈利。"赫敏悄声说。

他们经过墙上那一排家养小精灵的脑袋时，看见那些人离开后，卢平、韦斯莱夫人和唐克斯站在门前，用魔法把门上的许多道门锁和门闩封住。

"我们在下面的厨房里吃饭。"韦斯莱夫人在楼梯底下等他们时压低声音说，"哈利，亲爱的，你只要轻手轻脚地穿过门厅，再穿过这里的这道门——"

砰。

"唐克斯！"韦斯莱夫人恼火地喊道，转身去看身后。

"对不起！"唐克斯惨叫道——她仰面朝天躺在地上，"都怪那个倒霉的伞架，我已经是第二次被它绊倒——"

她的话没说完，就被一阵可怕的、震耳欲聋的、令人毛骨悚然的尖叫声淹没了。

哈利先前经过的那两道布满虫眼的天鹅绒帷幔，现在突然被掀开了，但后面并没有门。哈利一刹那间以为那是一扇窗户，窗户后面一个戴黑帽子的老太太正在拼命地尖叫，一声紧似一声，好像正在经受严刑毒打——接着哈利才意识到，这只是一幅真人大小的肖像，但是他有生以来从没见过这么逼真、这么令人不快的肖像。

那老太太流着口水，眼珠滴溜溜地转着，脸上的黄皮肤因为尖叫而绷得紧紧的。在他们身后的门厅里，其他肖像都被吵醒了，也开始尖叫起来，那声音简直把人的耳朵都吵聋了。哈利只好紧紧闭上眼睛，用手捂住耳朵。

卢平和韦斯莱夫人三步并作两步冲了过去，想拉上帷幔，把老太太遮在里面，但怎么也拉不上。老太太的叫声越发刺耳了，她还挥动

CHAPTER FOUR Number Twelve, Grimmauld Place

ever, brandishing clawed hands as though trying to tear at their faces.

'*Filth! Scum! By-products of dirt and vileness! Half-breeds, mutants, freaks, begone from this place! How dare you befoul the house of my fathers –*'

Tonks apologised over and over again, dragging the huge, heavy troll's leg back off the floor; Mrs Weasley abandoned the attempt to close the curtains and hurried up and down the hall, Stunning all the other portraits with her wand; and a man with long black hair came charging out of a door facing Harry.

'Shut up, you horrible old hag, shut UP!' he roared, seizing the curtain Mrs Weasley had abandoned.

The old woman's face blanched.

'*Yoooou!*' she howled, her eyes popping at the sight of the man. '*Blood traitor, abomination, shame of my flesh!*'

'I said – shut – UP!' roared the man, and with a stupendous effort he and Lupin managed to force the curtains closed again.

The old woman's screeches died and an echoing silence fell.

Panting slightly and sweeping his long dark hair out of his eyes, Harry's godfather Sirius turned to face him.

'Hello, Harry,' he said grimly, 'I see you've met my mother.'

着利爪般的双手,好像要来抓他们的脸。

"畜生!贱货!肮脏和罪恶的孽子!杂种,怪胎,丑八怪,快从这里滚出去!你们怎么敢玷污我祖上的家宅——"

唐克斯一个劲儿地道歉,一边把那条庞大而笨重的巨怪腿重新拖到原来的位置。韦斯莱夫人不再试着拉上帷幔了,而是转身匆匆朝门厅那头走去,一边用魔杖给其他肖像都念了昏迷咒。接着,一个留着一头黑色长发的男人从哈利对面的一扇门里冲了出来。

"闭嘴,你这个可怕的老女妖,**闭嘴**!"他吼道,一把抓住韦斯莱夫人刚才丢下的帷幔。

老太太顿时脸色煞白。

"你——你!"她一看见那个男人就瞪大了双眼,厉声叫道,"败家子,家族的耻辱,我生下的孽种!"

"我说过了——闭——嘴!"那男人吼道,他和卢平一起费了九牛二虎之力,总算把帷幔又拉上了。

老太太的尖叫声消失了,接着是一片余音回荡的寂静。

微微喘着粗气,撩开挡着眼睛的长长黑发,哈利的教父小天狼星转过身来看着哈利。

"你好,哈利,"他板着脸说,"看来你已经见过我的母亲了。"

CHAPTER FIVE

The Order of the Phoenix

'Your –?'

'My dear old mum, yeah,' said Sirius. 'We've been trying to get her down for a month but we think she put a Permanent Sticking Charm on the back of the canvas. Let's get downstairs, quick, before they all wake up again.'

'But what's a portrait of your mother doing here?' Harry asked, bewildered, as they went through the door from the hall and led the way down a flight of narrow stone steps, the others just behind them.

'Hasn't anyone told you? This was my parents' house,' said Sirius. 'But I'm the last Black left, so it's mine now. I offered it to Dumbledore for Headquarters – about the only useful thing I've been able to do.'

Harry, who had expected a better welcome, noted how hard and bitter Sirius's voice sounded. He followed his godfather to the bottom of the steps and through a door leading into the basement kitchen.

It was scarcely less gloomy than the hall above, a cavernous room with rough stone walls. Most of the light was coming from a large fire at the far end of the room. A haze of pipe smoke hung in the air like battle fumes, through which loomed the menacing shapes of heavy iron pots and pans hanging from the dark ceiling. Many chairs had been crammed into the room for the meeting and a long wooden table stood in the middle of them, littered with rolls of parchment, goblets, empty wine bottles, and a heap of what appeared to be rags. Mr Weasley and his eldest son Bill were talking quietly with their heads together at the end of the table.

Mrs Weasley cleared her throat. Her husband, a thin, balding, red-haired man who wore horn-rimmed glasses, looked around and jumped to his feet.

第 5 章

凤 凰 社

"**你**的——？"

"是啊，我亲爱的好妈妈。"小天狼星说，"一个月来，我们一直想把她弄下来，但她似乎在画布后面念了一个永久粘贴咒。我们下楼去吧，快点儿，别等他们又醒过来。"

"可是你母亲的肖像放在这里做什么？"哈利疑惑地问，这时他们已经穿过那扇门出了门厅，正顺着一道狭窄的石头台阶往下走，其他人都跟在后面。

"没有人告诉过你吗？这是我父母的房子。"小天狼星说，"但布莱克家族就剩下我一个人了，所以这房子现在归我所有。我把它交给邓布利多当指挥部——我大概也只能做这点有用的事情了。"

哈利原来以为自己会得到更热情的欢迎，却发现小天狼星说话的口气那么生硬、冷漠。他跟着教父走到楼梯底下，穿过一道门，进入了地下室的厨房。

这里几乎和上面的门厅里一样昏暗，一个洞穴般幽深的房间，四周是粗糙的石头墙壁。大部分光线都来自房间那头的一个大壁炉。管子里冒出的烟雾弥漫在空气中，如同战场上的硝烟，黑乎乎的天花板上挂下来的沉甸甸的铁锅铁盆，在烟雾中显得面目狰狞、阴森可怖。因为开会，房间里摆满了许多椅子，中间是一张长长的木头桌子，桌上散乱地放着羊皮纸卷、高脚酒杯、空酒瓶和一堆看上去像是破布的东西。韦斯莱先生和他的长子比尔坐在桌子那一头，脑袋凑在一起小声说着什么。

韦斯莱夫人清了清嗓子。她的丈夫，一个秃顶、红发、戴着角质架眼镜的瘦男人抬头望了望，赶紧站了起来。

CHAPTER FIVE   The Order of the Phoenix

'Harry!' Mr Weasley said, hurrying forward to greet him, and shaking his hand vigorously. 'Good to see you!'

Over his shoulder Harry saw Bill, who still wore his long hair in a ponytail, hastily rolling up the lengths of parchment left on the table.

'Journey all right, Harry?' Bill called, trying to gather up twelve scrolls at once. 'Mad-Eye didn't make you come via Greenland, then?'

'He tried,' said Tonks, striding over to help Bill and immediately toppling a candle on to the last piece of parchment. 'Oh no – *sorry* –'

'Here, dear,' said Mrs Weasley, sounding exasperated, and she repaired the parchment with a wave of her wand. In the flash of light caused by Mrs Weasley's charm Harry caught a glimpse of what looked like the plan of a building.

Mrs Weasley had seen him looking. She snatched the plan off the table and stuffed it into Bill's already overladen arms.

'This sort of thing ought to be cleared away promptly at the end of meetings,' she snapped, before sweeping off towards an ancient dresser from which she started unloading dinner plates.

Bill took out his wand, muttered, '*Evanesco!*' and the scrolls vanished.

'Sit down, Harry,' said Sirius. 'You've met Mundungus, haven't you?'

The thing Harry had taken to be a pile of rags gave a prolonged, grunting snore, then jerked awake.

'Some'n say m'name?' Mundungus mumbled sleepily. 'I 'gree with Sirius ...' He raised a very grubby hand in the air as though voting, his droopy, bloodshot eyes unfocused.

Ginny giggled.

'The meeting's over, Dung,' said Sirius, as they all sat down around him at the table. 'Harry's arrived.'

'Eh?' said Mundungus, peering balefully at Harry through his matted ginger hair. 'Blimey, so 'e 'as. Yeah ... you all right, 'Arry?'

'Yeah,' said Harry.

Mundungus fumbled nervously in his pockets, still staring at Harry, and pulled out a grimy black pipe. He stuck it in his mouth, ignited the end of it with his wand and took a deep pull on it. Great billowing clouds of greenish

第5章 凤凰社

"哈利！"韦斯莱先生说着，三步并作两步走过来迎接他，热情地同他握手，"见到你真是太高兴了！"

哈利的目光越过他的肩头，看见比尔匆匆卷起留在桌上的羊皮纸，他脑袋后面仍然扎着长长的马尾辫。

"路上还顺利吧，哈利？"比尔大声问道，同时试着一下子抱起十二卷羊皮纸，"这么说，疯眼汉没有让你取道格陵兰岛过来？"

"他想这么做来着。"唐克斯快步走过去想帮比尔一把，但转眼间就把一根蜡烛碰倒在最后一卷羊皮纸上，"哦，糟糕——对不起——"

"没关系，亲爱的。"韦斯莱夫人说，声音显得有点恼火。她一挥魔杖，把羊皮纸修复好了。韦斯莱夫人念咒时闪过一道亮光，哈利瞥见那纸上好像是一座建筑物的平面图。

韦斯莱夫人发现哈利在看，赶紧把平面图从桌上抓起来，塞进比尔已经不堪重负的怀里。

"这些东西应该会议一结束就赶紧收起来。"她厉声说，然后快步走向一个很古老的碗柜，从里面拿出晚餐的盘子。

比尔抽出魔杖，低声说了一句："消失不见！"那些羊皮纸卷一下子就不见了。

"坐下吧，哈利。"小天狼星说，"你已经见过蒙顿格斯了，是不是？"

哈利刚才以为是一堆破布的东西，这时发出一声长长的呼噜呼噜的鼾声，猛地惊醒过来。

"谁在说我的名字？"蒙顿格斯迷迷糊糊地嘟哝道，"我同意小天狼星的……"他高高举起一只脏兮兮的手，像是要投票表决，那双眼皮耷拉的、充血的眼睛茫然地瞪着。

金妮咯咯地笑了。

"会议结束了，顿格。"小天狼星说，他们都围着蒙顿格斯在桌旁坐下，"哈利来了。"

"嗯？"蒙顿格斯说着，目光透过乱糟糟的姜黄色头发狠狠地望着哈利，"天哪，他来了。没错……你好吗，哈利？"

"挺好的。"哈利说。

蒙顿格斯局促不安地在几个口袋里摸索，但眼睛仍然盯着哈利，最后他掏出一个满是污垢的黑烟斗。他把烟斗塞进嘴里，用魔杖把它点燃，

CHAPTER FIVE The Order of the Phoenix

smoke obscured him within seconds.

'Owe you a 'pology,' grunted a voice from the middle of the smelly cloud.

'For the last time, Mundungus,' called Mrs Weasley, 'will you please *not* smoke that thing in the kitchen, especially not when we're about to eat!'

'Ah,' said Mundungus. 'Right. Sorry, Molly.'

The cloud of smoke vanished as Mundungus stowed his pipe back in his pocket, but an acrid smell of burning socks lingered.

'And if you want dinner before midnight I'll need a hand,' Mrs Weasley said to the room at large. 'No, you can stay where you are, Harry dear, you've had a long journey.'

'What can I do, Molly?' said Tonks enthusiastically, bounding forwards.

Mrs Weasley hesitated, looking apprehensive.

'Er – no, it's all right, Tonks, you have a rest too, you've done enough today.'

'No, no, I want to help!' said Tonks brightly, knocking over a chair as she hurried towards the dresser, from which Ginny was collecting cutlery.

Soon, a series of heavy knives were chopping meat and vegetables of their own accord, supervised by Mr Weasley, while Mrs Weasley stirred a cauldron dangling over the fire and the others took out plates, more goblets and food from the pantry. Harry was left at the table with Sirius and Mundungus, who was still blinking at him mournfully.

'Seen old Figgy since?' he asked.

'No,' said Harry, 'I haven't seen anyone.'

'See, I wouldn't 'ave left,' said Mundungus, leaning forward, a pleading note in his voice, 'but I 'ad a business opportunity –'

Harry felt something brush against his knees and started, but it was only Crookshanks, Hermione's bandy-legged ginger cat, who wound himself once around Harry's legs, purring, then jumped on to Sirius's lap and curled up. Sirius scratched him absent-mindedly behind the ears as he turned, still grim-faced, to Harry.

'Had a good summer so far?'

'No, it's been lousy,' said Harry.

For the first time, something like a grin flitted across Sirius's face.

深深地吸了一口。几秒钟后,大股大股泛着绿色的烟雾就把他包围了。

"我得向你道歉。"一个声音从那团臭烘烘的烟雾中间嘟哝着说。

"我最后再提醒你一次,蒙顿格斯,"韦斯莱夫人大声说道,"拜托,你能不能不要在厨房里抽那玩意儿,特别是我们马上就要吃饭了!"

"啊,"蒙顿格斯说,"好的。对不起,莫丽。"

蒙顿格斯把烟斗重新塞进口袋,烟雾散去了,但那股袜子烧焦的刺鼻气味迟迟没有散尽。

"如果你们想在午夜之前吃到晚饭,就需要有人来帮我一把。"韦斯莱夫人对房间里所有的人说,"不,你坐在那里别动,哈利,亲爱的,你刚经过长途旅行。"

"我能做点什么,莫丽?"唐克斯热情洋溢地说,跳起来冲了过去。

韦斯莱夫人迟疑着,显得心有余悸。

"呃——不用,没事儿,唐克斯,你也休息一会儿吧,今天你已经做了不少了。"

"不,不,我想帮帮你!"唐克斯欢快地说,匆匆奔向金妮正在拿餐具的碗柜,不留神撞翻了一把椅子。

很快,一套沉甸甸的刀子就在韦斯莱先生的监督下,开始自动切肉剁菜。韦斯莱夫人搅拌着一只悬挂在火上的大锅,其他人从食品储藏间拿出盘子、高脚酒杯和食物。哈利陪小天狼星和蒙顿格斯留在桌边,蒙顿格斯仍然悲哀地冲他眨巴着眼睛。

"后来又看见费格老太了吗?"他问。

"没有,"哈利说,"我谁也没看见。"

"你看,我不应该离开的,"蒙顿格斯探着身子,声音里带着请求,"但我有机会做成一笔大买卖——"

哈利感到什么东西正蹭着他的膝盖,不禁吓了一跳,原来是克鲁克山——赫敏那只姜黄色的罗圈腿猫,它把身体绕在哈利的腿上,呼噜呼噜叫着,然后一下子跳到小天狼星的膝头,蜷作一团。小天狼星心不在焉地挠着它的耳根,同时转过脸来望着哈利,脸上表情仍然很沉重。

"这个夏天过得还好吧?"

"不好,糟糕透了。"哈利说。

小天狼星的脸上第一次掠过一丝若有若无的笑容。

CHAPTER FIVE   The Order of the Phoenix

'Don't know what you're complaining about, myself.'

'*What?*' said Harry incredulously.

'Personally, I'd have welcomed a Dementor attack. A deadly struggle for my soul would have broken the monotony nicely. You think you've had it bad, at least you've been able to get out and about, stretch your legs, get into a few fights ... I've been stuck inside for a month.'

'How come?' asked Harry, frowning.

'Because the Ministry of Magic's still after me, and Voldemort will know all about me being an Animagus by now, Wormtail will have told him, so my big disguise is useless. There's not much I can do for the Order of the Phoenix ... or so Dumbledore feels.'

There was something about the slightly flattened tone of voice in which Sirius uttered Dumbledore's name that told Harry that Sirius, too, was not very happy with the Headmaster. Harry felt a sudden upsurge of affection for his godfather.

'At least you've known what's been going on,' he said bracingly.

'Oh yeah,' said Sirius sarcastically. 'Listening to Snape's reports, having to take all his snide hints that he's out there risking his life while I'm sat on my backside here having a nice comfortable time ... asking me how the cleaning's going –'

'What cleaning?' asked Harry.

'Trying to make this place fit for human habitation,' said Sirius, waving a hand around the dismal kitchen. 'No one's lived here for ten years, not since my dear mother died, unless you count her old house-elf, and he's gone round the twist – hasn't cleaned anything in ages.'

'Sirius,' said Mundungus, who did not appear to have paid any attention to the conversation, but had been minutely examining an empty goblet. 'This solid silver, mate?'

'Yes,' said Sirius, surveying it with distaste. 'Finest fifteenth-century goblin-wrought silver, embossed with the Black family crest.'

'That'd come orf, though,' muttered Mundungus, polishing it with his cuff.

'Fred – George – NO, JUST CARRY THEM!' Mrs Weasley shrieked.

Harry, Sirius and Mundungus looked round and, within a split second, they had dived away from the table. Fred and George had bewitched a

"我真不知道你还有什么可抱怨的。"

"什么？"哈利不敢相信地说。

"就我个人来说，我还巴不得摄魂怪来袭击我呢。为保卫我的灵魂而殊死搏斗，这多好啊，可以打破令人厌烦的单调生活。你以为你的日子很难熬，但你至少可以出门到处走动走动，伸展伸展腿脚，跟人打打架什么的……我已经在屋里困了一个月了。"

"怎么会呢？"哈利皱起眉头问道。

"因为魔法部仍然在追捕我，伏地魔这会儿已经知道我是一个阿尼马格斯，虫尾巴肯定告诉他了，所以我再怎么伪装也没有用了。我已经不能为凤凰社做多少事情——至少邓布利多是这样感觉的。"

小天狼星说出邓布利多的名字时声音显得有点儿消沉，这使哈利明白，小天狼星对校长也有些不满。哈利顿时对教父产生了一种亲切的情感。

"至少你知道正在发生什么事情吧。"他安慰道。

"哦，是啊，"小天狼星讥讽地说，"听斯内普的长篇报告，忍受他的冷嘲热讽，似乎他冒着生命危险，出生入死，而我却安坐在这里，舒舒服服地混日子……他还问我大扫除搞得怎么样了——"

"什么大扫除？"哈利问。

"把这个地方搞得可以住人，"小天狼星说，又挥手指了指阴暗破败的厨房，"这里已经十年没有人居住，自从我亲爱的母亲去世之后就没住过人，除非算上她留下的家养小精灵，但那个小精灵已经变得疯疯癫癫——好长时间没做任何打扫了。"

"小天狼星，"蒙顿格斯说话了，他似乎根本没注意他们在说什么，而是在细细地端详一个空高脚酒杯，"这是纯银的吧，伙计？"

"是的，"小天狼星厌恶地看了看杯子，说道，"十五世纪小妖精制造的最精美的银器，上面还刻着布莱克家族的饰章。"

"这倒真是好东西。"蒙顿格斯含混地说，用袖口把杯子擦亮。

"弗雷德——乔治——**别这样，把它们端起来！**"韦斯莱夫人尖叫道。

哈利、小天狼星和蒙顿格斯扭头一看，说时迟那时快，三人赶紧一猫腰，从桌子旁躲开了。弗雷德和乔治动用魔法把一大锅炖菜、一

large cauldron of stew, an iron flagon of Butterbeer and a heavy wooden breadboard, complete with knife, to hurtle through the air towards them. The stew skidded the length of the table and came to a halt just before the end, leaving a long black burn on the wooden surface; the flagon of Butterbeer fell with a crash, spilling its contents everywhere; the bread knife slipped off the board and landed, point down and quivering ominously, exactly where Sirius's right hand had been seconds before.

'FOR HEAVEN'S SAKE!' screamed Mrs Weasley. 'THERE WAS NO NEED – I'VE HAD ENOUGH OF THIS – JUST BECAUSE YOU'RE ALLOWED TO USE MAGIC NOW, YOU DON'T HAVE TO WHIP YOUR WANDS OUT FOR EVERY TINY LITTLE THING!'

'We were just trying to save a bit of time!' said Fred, hurrying forward to wrench the bread knife out of the table. 'Sorry, Sirius, mate – didn't mean to –'

Harry and Sirius were both laughing; Mundungus, who had toppled backwards off his chair, was swearing as he got to his feet; Crookshanks had given an angry hiss and shot off under the dresser, from where his large yellow eyes glowed in the darkness.

'Boys,' Mr Weasley said, lifting the stew back into the middle of the table, 'your mother's right, you're supposed to show a sense of responsibility now you've come of age –'

'None of your brothers caused this sort of trouble!' Mrs Weasley raged at the twins as she slammed a fresh flagon of Butterbeer on to the table, and spilling almost as much again. 'Bill didn't feel the need to Apparate every few feet! Charlie didn't charm everything he met! Percy –'

She stopped dead, catching her breath with a frightened look at her husband, whose expression was suddenly wooden.

'Let's eat,' said Bill quickly.

'It looks wonderful, Molly,' said Lupin, ladling stew on to a plate for her and handing it across the table.

For a few minutes there was silence but for the chink of plates and cutlery and the scraping of chairs as everyone settled down to their food. Then Mrs Weasley turned to Sirius.

'I've been meaning to tell you, Sirius, there's something trapped in that writing desk in the drawing room, it keeps rattling and shaking. Of course, it

大铁壶黄油啤酒、一块沉重的切面包板，外加一把刀子，一股脑儿地朝他们猛抛过来。那锅炖菜咪溜溜滑过整个桌面，正好在桌子边缘停住，木头桌面上留下了一长条烧焦发黑的痕迹。那壶黄油啤酒哗啦一声翻倒了，啤酒洒得到处都是。切面包的刀子从板上掉下来，刀尖朝下扎进了桌子，凶险地微微颤动，那正好是几秒钟前小天狼星的右手放着的地方。

"看在老天的分儿上！"韦斯莱夫人大声嚷道，"没必要这么做——这一套我受够了——就算现在允许你们使用魔法了，你们也用不着做每件鸡毛蒜皮的小事都挥动魔杖吧！"

"我们只是为了节约一点时间！"弗雷德说着匆忙赶过来，把切面包的刀子拔出桌面，"对不起，小天狼星，伙计——不是故意的——"

哈利和小天狼星都放声大笑。蒙顿格斯刚才向后栽下了椅子，这会儿正骂骂咧咧地爬起身来。克鲁克山愤怒地嘶嘶叫了一声，箭一般地钻到碗柜底下去了，那双黄澄澄的大眼睛在黑暗中闪闪发亮。

"儿子们，"韦斯莱先生把那锅炖菜重新端到桌子中央，说道，"你们的妈妈说得对，你们现在已经长大成人，应该表现出一点责任感了——"

"你们的几个哥哥就从没闹出过这种乱子！"韦斯莱夫人一边朝双胞胎儿子吼道，一边把另一壶黄油啤酒重重地放在桌上，洒出的啤酒几乎跟上一壶一样多，"比尔觉得没必要几步路就幻影移形！查理不会碰到什么东西都施魔法！珀西——"

她猛地停住话头，屏住呼吸，惊慌地望了丈夫一眼，韦斯莱先生的表情突然僵住了。

"我们吃饭吧。"比尔赶紧说道。

"看上去很不错啊，莫丽。"卢平说着，替她盛了一些炖菜在盘子里，隔着桌子递了过去。

几分钟没有人说话，只有大家坐下来就餐时盘子和餐具发出的碰撞声，还有椅子的摩擦声。然后，韦斯莱夫人转脸望着小天狼星。

"小天狼星，我一直想告诉你，客厅的那张写字台里面关着个什么东西，它不停地摇晃，发出咯啦啦的声音。也许只是一个博格特，但

could just be a Boggart, but I thought we ought to ask Alastor to have a look at it before we let it out.'

'Whatever you like,' said Sirius indifferently.

'The curtains in there are full of Doxys, too,' Mrs Weasley went on. 'I thought we might try and tackle them tomorrow.'

'I look forward to it,' said Sirius. Harry heard the sarcasm in his voice, but he was not sure that anyone else did.

Opposite Harry, Tonks was entertaining Hermione and Ginny by transforming her nose between mouthfuls. Screwing up her eyes each time with the same pained expression she had worn back in Harry's bedroom, her nose swelled to a beak-like protuberance that resembled Snape's, shrank to the size of a button mushroom and then sprouted a great deal of hair from each nostril. Apparently this was a regular mealtime entertainment, because Hermione and Ginny were soon requesting their favourite noses.

'Do that one like a pig snout, Tonks.'

Tonks obliged, and Harry, looking up, had the fleeting impression that a female Dudley was grinning at him from across the table.

Mr Weasley, Bill and Lupin were having an intense discussion about goblins.

'They're not giving anything away yet,' said Bill. 'I still can't work out whether or not they believe he's back. Course, they might prefer not to take sides at all. Keep out of it.'

'I'm sure they'd never go over to You-Know-Who,' said Mr Weasley, shaking his head. 'They've suffered losses too; remember that goblin family he murdered last time, somewhere near Nottingham?'

'I think it depends what they're offered,' said Lupin. 'And I'm not talking about gold. If they're offered the freedoms we've been denying them for centuries they're going to be tempted. Have you still not had any luck with Ragnok, Bill?'

'He's feeling pretty anti-wizard at the moment,' said Bill, 'he hasn't stopped raging about the Bagman business, he reckons the Ministry did a cover-up, those goblins never got their gold from him, you know –'

A gale of laughter from the middle of the table drowned the rest of Bill's words. Fred, George, Ron and Mundungus were rolling around in their seats.

我想我们还是先请阿拉斯托来看看再把它放出来。"

"随便吧。"小天狼星兴味索然地说。

"还有,那儿的窗帘里都是狐媚子,"韦斯莱夫人接着说道,"我想明天我们得想办法把它们处理一下。"

"我正巴不得呢。"小天狼星说。哈利听出了他声音里的讽刺意味,但不知道其他人有没有听出来。

在哈利对面,唐克斯一边吃饭一边给她的鼻子变形,逗赫敏和金妮开心。每次她都紧紧地闭上眼睛,露出她在哈利卧室里时露出的那种痛苦表情,她的鼻子忽而肿胀得像鸟嘴一样,看上去活脱脱是斯内普的鼻子,忽而又缩回去,变成圆球蘑菇一般大小,然后每个鼻孔里都冒出一大堆鼻毛。这显然是吃饭时的固定娱乐节目,因为很快赫敏和金妮就要求她变出她们最喜欢的鼻子。

"变出一只猪鼻子来,唐克斯。"

唐克斯照办了,哈利抬起头,刹那间,他还以为一个女版达力正隔着桌子朝他咧嘴微笑呢。

韦斯莱先生、比尔和卢平正在进行一场关于妖精的激烈讨论。

"他们还是滴水不漏,什么也不肯说,"比尔说,"我仍然弄不清楚他们是不是相信他回来了。当然,他们大概不想支持任何一方,不想卷到这里头来。"

"我相信他们决不会倒向神秘人那边,"韦斯莱先生摇着头说道,"他们的损失也很惨重。还记得他上次杀害的那一家妖精吗,就在诺丁汉附近?"

"我想,那得看人家给他们开出了什么价码,"卢平说,"我说的不是金子。如果有人向他们提供我们几个世纪以来不肯给他们的自由,他们就会抵挡不住诱惑。比尔,拉格诺那边还是没有丝毫转机吗?"

"他目前在感情上对巫师还是很排斥的,"比尔说,"他还为巴格曼的那档子事气得要命呢,觉得魔法部掩盖了真相。你们知道,那些妖精始终没能从他手里拿到他们的金子——"

桌子中央传来一阵大笑,淹没了比尔没说完的话。弗雷德、乔治、罗恩和蒙顿格斯在椅子上笑得前仰后合。

CHAPTER FIVE   The Order of the Phoenix

'... and then,' choked Mundungus, tears running down his face, 'and then, if you'll believe it, 'e says to me, 'e says, "'Ere, Dung, where didja get all them toads from? 'Cos some son of a Bludger's gone and nicked all mine!" And I says, "Nicked all your toads, Will, what next? So you'll be wanting some more, then?" And if you'll believe me, lads, the gormless gargoyle buys all 'is own toads back orf me for a lot more'n what 'e paid in the first place –'

'I don't think we need to hear any more of your business dealings, thank you very much, Mundungus,' said Mrs Weasley sharply, as Ron slumped forwards on to the table, howling with laughter.

'Beg pardon, Molly,' said Mundungus at once, wiping his eyes and winking at Harry. 'But, you know, Will nicked 'em orf Warty Harris in the first place so I wasn't really doing nothing wrong.'

'I don't know where you learned about right and wrong, Mundungus, but you seem to have missed a few crucial lessons,' said Mrs Weasley coldly.

Fred and George buried their faces in their goblets of Butterbeer; George was hiccoughing. For some reason, Mrs Weasley threw a very nasty look at Sirius before getting to her feet and going to fetch a large rhubarb crumble for pudding. Harry looked round at his godfather.

'Molly doesn't approve of Mundungus,' said Sirius in an undertone.

'How come he's in the Order?' Harry said, very quietly.

'He's useful,' Sirius muttered. 'Knows all the crooks – well, he would, seeing as he's one himself. But he's also very loyal to Dumbledore, who helped him out of a tight spot once. It pays to have someone like Dung around, he hears things we don't. But Molly thinks inviting him to stay for dinner is going too far. She hasn't forgiven him for slipping off duty when he was supposed to be tailing you.'

Three helpings of rhubarb crumble and custard later and the waistband on Harry's jeans was feeling uncomfortably tight (which was saying something as the jeans had once been Dudley's). As he laid down his spoon there was a lull in the general conversation: Mr Weasley was leaning back in his chair, looking replete and relaxed; Tonks was yawning widely, her nose now back to normal; and Ginny, who had lured Crookshanks out from under the dresser, was sitting cross-legged on the floor, rolling Butterbeer corks for him to chase.

第5章 凤凰社

"……后来,"蒙顿格斯笑得喘不过气来,眼泪直顺着他的面颊往下流,他说,"后来,信不信由你们吧,他对我说,他说:'咦,顿格,这些癞蛤蟆你是从哪儿弄来的?不知道哪个杂种把我的癞蛤蟆全偷走了!'我就说了:'有人把你的癞蛤蟆全偷走了,威尔,那怎么办呢?所以你才需要再买一些呀,对不对?'你们信不信,孩子们,那个没头脑的滴水嘴石兽居然从我手里把他自己的癞蛤蟆全都买了回去,价钱比他原先买的时候还要高得多——"

"我们不需要听你唠叨这些生意经,蒙顿格斯,非常感谢。"韦斯莱夫人严厉地说。罗恩扑在桌子上,放声大笑。

"对不起,莫丽,"蒙顿格斯立刻说道,他擦擦眼泪,朝哈利眨了眨眼睛,"可是,你知道,癞蛤蟆是威尔从瓦提·海里斯那里偷出来的,所以我其实并没有做什么坏事。"

"我不知道你的是非观是在哪儿学的,蒙顿格斯,但你似乎漏掉了最关键的几课。"韦斯莱夫人冷冷地说。

弗雷德和乔治把脸埋在盛着黄油啤酒的高脚酒杯上,乔治笑得直打嗝。不知为什么,韦斯莱夫人狠狠地白了小天狼星一眼,然后起身拿来一个大黄馅的酥皮派做甜点。哈利扭头望着他的教父。

"莫丽不大认可蒙顿格斯。"小天狼星压低声音说。

"那他怎么会加入凤凰社的?"哈利悄声地问。

"他有用啊,"小天狼星小声嘀咕道,"认识所有的骗子毛贼——哼,这也难怪,他自己就是那一类货色。不过他对邓布利多倒是忠心耿耿,邓布利多有一次还帮助他摆脱了困境。弄一个顿格这样的人在身边也有好处,他能听到我们听不到的东西。但莫丽认为请他留下来吃晚饭太过分了。莫丽还没有原谅他在应该跟踪你的时候擅离职守。"

吃了三块大黄馅的酥皮派和蛋奶糕,哈利牛仔裤的裤腰紧得难受了(这就很能说明问题了,因为那条牛仔裤本来是达力的)。哈利放下勺子时,饭桌上的谈话逐渐平静了下来。韦斯莱先生靠在椅子背上,一副吃饱喝足、身心放松的样子。唐克斯张着大嘴打哈欠,她的鼻子已经恢复了正常。金妮把克鲁克山从碗柜下面引了出来,这会儿正盘腿坐在地上,把一些黄油啤酒的软木塞滚来滚去,让克鲁克山追着玩儿。

CHAPTER FIVE   The Order of the Phoenix

'Nearly time for bed, I think,' said Mrs Weasley with a yawn.

'Not just yet, Molly,' said Sirius, pushing away his empty plate and turning to look at Harry. 'You know, I'm surprised at you. I thought the first thing you'd do when you got here would be to start asking questions about Voldemort.'

The atmosphere in the room changed with the rapidity Harry associated with the arrival of Dementors. Where seconds before it had been sleepily relaxed, it was now alert, even tense. A frisson had gone around the table at the mention of Voldemort's name. Lupin, who had been about to take a sip of wine, lowered his goblet slowly, looking wary.

'I did!'said Harry indignantly.'I asked Ron and Hermione but they said we're not allowed in the Order, so –'

'And they're quite right,'said Mrs Weasley. 'You're too young.'

She was sitting bolt upright in her chair, her fists clenched on its arms, every trace of drowsiness gone.

'Since when did someone have to be in the Order of the Phoenix to ask questions?' asked Sirius. 'Harry's been trapped in that Muggle house for a month. He's got the right to know what's been happen—'

'Hang on!'interrupted George loudly.

'How come Harry gets his questions answered?'said Fred angrily.

'*We've* been trying to get stuff out of you for a month and you haven't told us a single stinking thing!' said George.

'"*You're too young, you're not in the Order,*"' said Fred, in a high-pitched voice that sounded uncannily like his mother's. 'Harry's not even of age!'

'It's not my fault you haven't been told what the Order's doing,'said Sirius calmly,'that's your parents'decision. Harry, on the other hand –'

'It's not down to you to decide what's good for Harry!' said Mrs Weasley sharply. The expression on her normally kind face looked dangerous. 'You haven't forgotten what Dumbledore said, I suppose?'

'Which bit?' Sirius asked politely, but with the air of a man readying himself for a fight.

'The bit about not telling Harry more than he *needs to know*,' said Mrs Weasley, placing a heavy emphasis on the last three words.

第5章 凤凰社

"差不多该上床睡觉了,我想。"韦斯莱夫人打着哈欠说。

"还没有呢,莫丽。"小天狼星把面前的空盘子推到一边,转脸望着哈利,"知道吗,我真为你感到吃惊。我以为你到这里的第一件事就是询问伏地魔的情况。"

屋里的气氛突然变了,速度如此之快,哈利还以为是摄魂怪来了。几秒钟前还是那样轻松悠闲,令人昏昏欲睡,现在却变得警觉,甚至是紧张了。听到伏地魔的名字,饭桌周围掠过一阵战栗。卢平刚才端起杯子正要喝酒,这时慢慢放下酒杯,露出警惕的神情。

"我问了!"哈利气愤地说,"我问了罗恩和赫敏,但他们说我们没被批准加入凤凰社,所以——"

"他们说得对呀,"韦斯莱夫人说,"你们年纪还太小。"

她笔直地坐在椅子上,两个拳头捏得紧紧的抱在怀里,睡意消失得无影无踪。

"从什么时候开始,我们必须先加入凤凰社才能提问题?"小天狼星问,"哈利在那个麻瓜家里困了整整一个月。他有权利知道发生了什么——"

"等一等!"乔治大声打断了他。

"为什么哈利的问题就能得到答复?"弗雷德气呼呼地问。

"一个月来我们一直想从你们嘴里问出点什么来,但你们什么也不肯告诉我们!"乔治说。

"你们年纪太小了,你们没有加入凤凰社。"弗雷德说,那又尖又细的声音活脱脱就是他母亲的,听着简直不可思议,"而哈利甚至还没有成年呢!"

"没有人告诉你们凤凰社在做什么,这可不能怪我呀,"小天狼星平静地说,"这是你们父母的决定。而哈利则不同——"

"用不着你来决定怎么对哈利有好处!"韦斯莱夫人厉声说,平日和蔼亲切的脸上此刻露出的表情很吓人,"我想,你没有忘记邓布利多说的话吧?"

"哪一部分?"小天狼星不失礼貌地问,但神情却像一个准备迎战的人。

"就是不告诉哈利他不需要知道的。"韦斯莱夫人说,着重强调了最后几个字。

CHAPTER FIVE The Order of the Phoenix

Ron, Hermione, Fred and George's heads swivelled from Sirius to Mrs Weasley as though they were following a tennis rally. Ginny was kneeling amid a pile of abandoned Butterbeer corks, watching the conversation with her mouth slightly open. Lupin's eyes were fixed on Sirius.

'I don't intend to tell him more than he *needs to know*, Molly,' said Sirius. 'But as he was the one who saw Voldemort come back' (again, there was a collective shudder around the table at the name) 'he has more right than most to –'

'He's not a member of the Order of the Phoenix!' said Mrs Weasley. 'He's only fifteen and –'

'And he's dealt with as much as most in the Order,' said Sirius, 'and more than some.'

'No one's denying what he's done!' said Mrs Weasley, her voice rising, her fists trembling on the arms of her chair. 'But he's still –'

'He's not a child!' said Sirius impatiently.

'He's not an adult either!' said Mrs Weasley, the colour rising in her cheeks. 'He's not *James*, Sirius!'

'I'm perfectly clear who he is, thanks, Molly,' said Sirius coldly.

'I'm not sure you are!' said Mrs Weasley. 'Sometimes, the way you talk about him, it's as though you think you've got your best friend back!'

'What's wrong with that?' said Harry.

'What's wrong, Harry, is that you are *not* your father, however much you might look like him!' said Mrs Weasley, her eyes still boring into Sirius. 'You are still at school and adults responsible for you should not forget it!'

'Meaning I'm an irresponsible godfather?' demanded Sirius, his voice rising.

'Meaning you have been known to act rashly, Sirius, which is why Dumbledore keeps reminding you to stay at home and –'

'We'll leave my instructions from Dumbledore out of this, if you please!' said Sirius loudly.

'Arthur!' said Mrs Weasley, rounding on her husband. 'Arthur, back me up!'

Mr Weasley did not speak at once. He took off his glasses and cleaned them slowly on his robes, not looking at his wife. Only when he had replaced

第5章 凤凰社

罗恩、赫敏、弗雷德和乔治的脑袋在小天狼星和韦斯莱夫人之间转来转去，仿佛在观看网球场上的来回对打。金妮跪在一堆丢弃的黄油啤酒软木塞中间，呆呆地望着他们谈话，嘴巴微微张着。卢平眼睛一眨不眨地盯着小天狼星。

"我只打算告诉哈利他需要知道的，莫丽。"小天狼星说，"当时是他看见伏地魔（听到这个名字，饭桌周围的人又是一阵战栗）恢复肉身的，他比大多数人都更有权利——"

"他还不是凤凰社的成员呢！"韦斯莱夫人说，"他才十五岁，而且——"

"但他经历的事情不比凤凰社的大多数人少，"小天狼星说，"甚至比有些人还多。"

"没有人否认他做过的事情！"韦斯莱夫人说，声音越来越高，放在椅子扶手上的拳头在微微颤抖，"但他仍然——"

"他不是个孩子了！"小天狼星不耐烦地说。

"但他也不是个成年人！"韦斯莱夫人说，血液冲上了她的面颊，"他不是詹姆，小天狼星！"

"谢谢，我很清楚他是谁，莫丽。"小天狼星冷冷地说。

"我看不一定！"韦斯莱夫人说，"有时你谈起他时的语气，就好像你以为你最好的朋友又回来了似的！"

"那又有什么错呢？"哈利说。

"错就错在你不是你的父亲，哈利，不管你长得多么像他！"韦斯莱夫人说，眼睛仍然死死地盯着小天狼星，"你还在上学，对你负责任的成年人不应该忘记这一点！"

"你是说我是个不负责任的教父？"小天狼星问道，声音提高了。

"我是说大家都知道你做事莽撞，小天狼星，所以邓布利多才不断提醒你待在家里——"

"对不起，希望我们的谈话不要扯进邓布利多对我的指教。"小天狼星大声说。

"亚瑟！"韦斯莱夫人说，突然转向了她的丈夫，"亚瑟，你支持我一下！"

韦斯莱先生没有马上说话，而是摘下眼镜，在长袍上慢慢地擦拭镜片，眼睛也不看自己的妻子。他小心翼翼地把眼镜重新戴好，才开

them carefully on his nose did he reply.

'Dumbledore knows the position has changed, Molly. He accepts that Harry will have to be filled in, to a certain extent, now that he is staying at Headquarters.'

'Yes, but there's a difference between that and inviting him to ask whatever he likes!'

'Personally,' said Lupin quietly, looking away from Sirius at last, as Mrs Weasley turned quickly to him, hopeful that finally she was about to get an ally, 'I think it better that Harry gets the facts – not all the facts, Molly, but the general picture – from us, rather than a garbled version from ... others.'

His expression was mild, but Harry felt sure Lupin, at least, knew that some Extendable Ears had survived Mrs Weasley's purge.

'Well,' said Mrs Weasley, breathing deeply and looking around the table for support that did not come, 'well ... I can see I'm going to be overruled. I'll just say this: Dumbledore must have had his reasons for not wanting Harry to know too much, and speaking as someone who has Harry's best interests at heart –'

'He's not your son,' said Sirius quietly.

'He's as good as,' said Mrs Weasley fiercely. 'Who else has he got?'

'He's got me!'

'Yes,' said Mrs Weasley, her lip curling, 'the thing is, it's been rather difficult for you to look after him while you've been locked up in Azkaban, hasn't it?'

Sirius started to rise from his chair.

'Molly, you're not the only person at this table who cares about Harry,' said Lupin sharply. 'Sirius, sit *down*.'

Mrs Weasley's lower lip was trembling. Sirius sank slowly back into his chair, his face white.

'I think Harry ought to be allowed a say in this,' Lupin continued, 'he's old enough to decide for himself.'

'I want to know what's been going on,' Harry said at once.

He did not look at Mrs Weasley. He had been touched by what she had said about his being as good as a son, but he was also impatient with her mollycoddling. Sirius was right, he was *not* a child.

了口。

"邓布利多知道情况有了变化,莫丽。他同意在一定程度上必须把最新的消息告诉给哈利,既然哈利现在已经住在指挥部了。"

"没错,但那跟鼓励他随便发问还是有区别的!"

"就我个人来说,"卢平终于把目光从小天狼星身上移开,轻声细语地说话了,韦斯莱夫人立刻转向他,满心指望自己总算有了一个支持者,"我认为最好让哈利从我们这里了解到事实真相——不是所有的事实,莫丽,而是一个大致的情况,免得他从……别人那里得到一些混乱不清的说法。"

他的表情很温和,但哈利可以肯定,至少卢平知道有几只伸缩耳逃脱了韦斯莱夫人的清理扫荡。

"好吧,"韦斯莱夫人说,深深吸了口气,扫视了一圈饭桌,希望能得到支持,但没有人响应,"好吧……看来我的意见是要被否决了。我只想说一句,邓布利多不想让哈利知道得太多肯定有他的道理,我作为一个关心哈利切身利益的人——"

"他不是你的儿子。"小天狼星轻声说。

"但和我的儿子差不多。"韦斯莱夫人恼怒地说,"他还有谁?"

"他有我!"

"是啊,"韦斯莱夫人撇着嘴说,"问题是,你自己被关在阿兹卡班,根本就难以照顾他,是不是?"

小天狼星忍不住要从椅子上跳起来。

"莫丽,这张桌子旁关心哈利的人不止你一个。"卢平严厉地说,"小天狼星,坐下。"

韦斯莱夫人的下嘴唇颤抖着,小天狼星缓缓地跌回椅子上,脸色煞白。

"我认为这件事最好允许哈利发表意见,"卢平接着说,"他年纪不小了,可以自己决定了。"

"我想知道到底发生了什么事情。"哈利立刻说道。

他没有看韦斯莱夫人。刚才韦斯莱夫人说他就像她的亲生儿子一样,他很感动,但同时也被韦斯莱夫人对自己的过分溺爱弄得很不耐烦。小天狼星说得对,他已经不是一个孩子了。

CHAPTER FIVE   The Order of the Phoenix

'Very well,' said Mrs Weasley, her voice cracking. 'Ginny – Ron – Hermione – Fred – George – I want you out of this kitchen, now.'

There was instant uproar.

'We're of age!' Fred and George bellowed together.

'If Harry's allowed, why can't I?' shouted Ron.

'Mum, I *want* to hear!' wailed Ginny.

'NO!' shouted Mrs Weasley, standing up, her eyes overbright. 'I absolutely forbid –'

'Molly, you can't stop Fred and George,' said Mr Weasley wearily. 'They *are* of age.'

'They're still at school.'

'But they're legally adults now,' said Mr Weasley, in the same tired voice.

Mrs Weasley was now scarlet in the face.

'I – oh, all right then, Fred and George can stay, but Ron –'

'Harry'll tell me and Hermione everything you say anyway!' said Ron hotly. 'Won't – won't you?' he added uncertainly, meeting Harry's eyes.

For a split second, Harry considered telling Ron that he wouldn't tell him a single word, that he could try a taste of being kept in the dark and see how he liked it. But the nasty impulse vanished as they looked at each other.

'Course I will,' Harry said.

Ron and Hermione beamed.

'Fine!' shouted Mrs Weasley. 'Fine! Ginny – BED!'

Ginny did not go quietly. They could hear her raging and storming at her mother all the way up the stairs, and when she reached the hall Mrs Black's ear-splitting shrieks were added to the din. Lupin hurried off to the portrait to restore calm. It was only after he had returned, closing the kitchen door behind him and taking his seat at the table again, that Sirius spoke.

'OK, Harry ... what do you want to know?'

Harry took a deep breath and asked the question that had obsessed him for the last month.

'Where's Voldemort?' he said, ignoring the renewed shudders and winces at the name. 'What's he doing? I've been trying to watch the Muggle news, and there hasn't been anything that looks like him yet, no funny deaths or anything.'

第5章 凤凰社

"很好。"韦斯莱夫人说,声音都嘶哑了,"金妮——罗恩——赫敏——弗雷德——乔治——我要你们离开这间厨房,马上。"

立刻,屋子里像炸了窝一样。

"我们已经成年了!"弗雷德和乔治同时嚷道。

"哈利能知道,为什么我就不能?"罗恩大叫。

"妈妈,我也想听听!"金妮尖声喊。

"**不行!**"韦斯莱夫人大吼一声,腾地站起来,眼睛里放出奇亮的光芒,"我绝对不允许——"

"莫丽,你不能阻拦弗雷德和乔治,"韦斯莱先生疲倦地说,"他们已经成年了。"

"他们还在上学。"

"但他们是合法的成年人了。"韦斯莱先生还是用那疲倦的声音说。

韦斯莱夫人的脸此时涨得通红。

"我——哦,好吧,弗雷德和乔治可以留下,但是罗恩——"

"反正哈利会把你们说的一切都告诉我和赫敏的!"罗恩愤愤不平地说,"你——会吗?"他迎住哈利的目光,没有把握地追问了一句。

刹那间,哈利想对罗恩说他一个字也不会告诉他,也让他尝尝被蒙在鼓里的滋味,看看好受不好受。但是当两人目光相对时,他那种小心眼的冲动一下子就消失了。

"我当然会。"哈利说。

罗恩和赫敏顿时喜上眉梢。

"很好!"韦斯莱夫人大声喝道,"很好!金妮——**上床睡觉!**"

金妮并不是乖乖离开的。他们听见她上楼时一路冲她妈妈连喊带叫,大发脾气。到了门厅里,布莱克夫人又发出震耳欲聋的尖叫,使喧闹声变得更加无法忍受。卢平赶紧冲到那幅肖像前使它恢复了平静。等他回来返身关上厨房的门,重新在桌子旁坐下,小天狼星才开口说话。

"好吧,哈利……你想知道什么?"

哈利深深吸了口气,问出了最近一个月来一直困扰着他的那个问题。

"伏地魔在哪儿?"他问,别人听到这个名字又是一阵战栗和畏缩,但他只当没看见,"他在做什么?我一直在想办法看麻瓜的新闻,但没有发现他的一点蛛丝马迹,没有人蹊跷地死去,什么也没有发生。"

CHAPTER FIVE The Order of the Phoenix

'That's because there haven't been any funny deaths yet,' said Sirius, 'not as far as we know, anyway ... and we know quite a lot.'

'More than he thinks we do, anyway,' said Lupin.

'How come he's stopped killing people?' Harry asked. He knew Voldemort had murdered more than once in the last year alone.

'Because he doesn't want to draw attention to himself,' said Sirius. 'It would be dangerous for him. His comeback didn't come off quite the way he wanted it to, you see. He messed it up.'

'Or rather, you messed it up for him,' said Lupin, with a satisfied smile.

'How?' Harry asked, perplexed.

'You weren't supposed to survive!' said Sirius. 'Nobody apart from his Death Eaters was supposed to know he'd come back. But you survived to bear witness.'

'And the very last person he wanted alerted to his return the moment he got back was Dumbledore,' said Lupin. 'And you made sure Dumbledore knew at once.'

'How has that helped?' Harry asked.

'Are you kidding?' said Bill incredulously. 'Dumbledore was the only one You-Know-Who was ever scared of!'

'Thanks to you, Dumbledore was able to recall the Order of the Phoenix about an hour after Voldemort returned,' said Sirius.

'So, what's the Order been doing?' said Harry, looking around at them all.

'Working as hard as we can to make sure Voldemort can't carry out his plans,' said Sirius.

'How d'you know what his plans are?' Harry asked quickly.

'Dumbledore's got a shrewd idea,' said Lupin, 'and Dumbledore's shrewd ideas normally turn out to be accurate.'

'So what does Dumbledore reckon he's planning?'

'Well, firstly, he wants to build up his army again,' said Sirius. 'In the old days he had huge numbers at his command: witches and wizards he'd bullied or bewitched into following him, his faithful Death Eaters, a great variety of Dark creatures. You heard him planning to recruit the giants; well, they'll be just one of the groups he's after. He's certainly not going to try and take on the Ministry of Magic with only a dozen Death Eaters.'

第5章 凤凰社

"那是因为到现在为止还没有人蹊跷地死去,"小天狼星说,"反正据我们所知是这样……而我们知道不少情况。"

"至少他想不到我们会知道得这么多。"卢平说。

"他怎么会停止杀人呢?"哈利问。他知道伏地魔光是去年就不止一次地杀过人。

"因为他不想引起别人对他的注意,"小天狼星说,"那对他来说是很危险的。你知道,他这次回来并不像他所希望的那样顺利。他的安排被打乱了。"

"或者说,是你打乱了他的安排。"卢平说着,脸上露出满意的微笑。

"怎么会呢?"哈利困惑不解地问。

"你本来不应该活下来的!"小天狼星说,"除了他的食死徒,谁都不应该知道他已经回来。而你活下来成了证人。"

"他最不希望他一回来就惊动的人是邓布利多,"卢平说,"而你确保了邓布利多立刻就知道了这件事。"

"那又有什么用呢?"哈利问。

"你在开玩笑吗?"比尔不敢相信地说,"邓布利多是神秘人有生以来唯一害怕的人!"

"多亏了你,邓布利多才能够在伏地魔回来后不到一小时就重新召集了凤凰社。"小天狼星说。

"那么,凤凰社一直在做些什么呢?"哈利问,挨个儿望着大家。

"尽我们最大的努力,确保伏地魔无法实施他的计划。"小天狼星说。

"你们怎么知道他的计划是什么呢?"哈利立刻问道。

"邓布利多有敏锐的感觉,"卢平说,"而邓布利多的敏锐感觉一般都被证明是准确的。"

"那么邓布利多认为伏地魔的计划是什么呢?"

"是这样,首先,伏地魔想重新纠集他的人马。"小天狼星说,"过去,他有一大批人听他指挥,那些迫于他的淫威或受他蒙蔽而跟随他的巫师,那些忠心耿耿的食死徒,还有各种黑魔法生物。听说他还打算把巨人也拉拢过去。其实,他们只是他想纠集的大批人马中的一部分。他显然不会只带着十几个食死徒就来跟魔法部较量。"

CHAPTER FIVE The Order of the Phoenix

'So you're trying to stop him getting more followers?'

'We're doing our best,' said Lupin.

'How?'

'Well, the main thing is to try and convince as many people as possible that You-Know-Who really has returned, to put them on their guard,' said Bill. 'It's proving tricky, though.'

'Why?'

'Because of the Ministry's attitude,' said Tonks. 'You saw Cornelius Fudge after You-Know-Who came back, Harry. Well, he hasn't shifted his position at all. He's absolutely refusing to believe it's happened.'

'But why?' said Harry desperately. 'Why's he being so stupid? If Dumbledore –'

'Ah, well, you've put your finger on the problem,' said Mr Weasley with a wry smile. '*Dumbledore*.'

'Fudge is frightened of him, you see,' said Tonks sadly.

'Frightened of Dumbledore?' said Harry incredulously.

'Frightened of what he's up to,' said Mr Weasley. 'Fudge thinks Dumbledore's plotting to overthrow him. He thinks Dumbledore wants to be Minister for Magic.'

'But Dumbledore doesn't want –'

'Of course he doesn't,' said Mr Weasley. 'He's never wanted the Minister's job, even though a lot of people wanted him to take it when Millicent Bagnold retired. Fudge came to power instead, but he's never quite forgotten how much popular support Dumbledore had, even though Dumbledore never applied for the job.'

'Deep down, Fudge knows Dumbledore's much cleverer than he is, a much more powerful wizard, and in the early days of his Ministry he was forever asking Dumbledore for help and advice,' said Lupin. 'But it seems he's become fond of power, and much more confident. He loves being Minister for Magic and he's managed to convince himself that he's the clever one and Dumbledore's simply stirring up trouble for the sake of it.'

'How can he think that?' said Harry angrily. 'How can he think Dumbledore would just make it all up – that *I'd* make it all up?'

'Because accepting that Voldemort's back would mean trouble like the

"所以你们想阻止他得到更多的追随者？"

"我们在尽力而为。"卢平说。

"怎么做呢？"

"是这样，主要是尽量让更多的人相信神秘人真的回来了，让他们保持警惕，"比尔说，"不过这件事做起来很棘手。"

"为什么呢？"

"因为魔法部的态度。"唐克斯说，"哈利，神秘人回来后，你是见过康奈利·福吉的。哼，他丝毫也没有改变立场。他死活不肯相信这件事真的发生了。"

"可是为什么呢？"哈利烦躁地问，"他为什么这样愚蠢？既然邓布利多——"

"啊，好了，你指出了问题的关键，"韦斯莱先生苦笑着说，"邓布利多。"

"福吉害怕他，明白吗？"唐克斯悲哀地说。

"害怕邓布利多？"哈利不敢相信地问。

"害怕他想做的事情。"韦斯莱先生说，"福吉认为邓布利多在密谋推翻他。他认为邓布利多自己想当魔法部部长。"

"可是邓布利多并不想——"

"他当然不想，"韦斯莱先生说，"他从来没想过要当部长，尽管米里森·巴格诺退休时，许多人想让邓布利多接替部长职位。后来福吉掌了大权，但他一直没有忘记曾经有多少人支持邓布利多，尽管其实邓布利多从来没有申请过这个职位。"

"在内心深处，福吉知道邓布利多比他有智慧得多，法力也比他强大得多。他刚开始当部长的时候，还三天两头地向邓布利多讨教、求助。"卢平说，"但是后来他似乎喜欢上了权力，信心也增强了。他迷恋当魔法部部长的感觉，而且他使自己相信，他才是有智慧的人，邓布利多只是故意制造事端。"

"他怎么能那么想呢？"哈利生气地说，"他怎么能认为邓布利多会凭空编造——我会凭空编造呢？"

"因为如果承认伏地魔回来了，就意味着有大麻烦，这种麻烦魔法

Ministry hasn't had to cope with for nearly fourteen years,' said Sirius bitterly. 'Fudge just can't bring himself to face it. It's so much more comfortable to convince himself Dumbledore's lying to destabilise him.'

'You see the problem,' said Lupin. 'While the Ministry insists there is nothing to fear from Voldemort it's hard to convince people he's back, especially as they really don't want to believe it in the first place. What's more, the Ministry's leaning heavily on the *Daily Prophet* not to report any of what they're calling Dumbledore's rumour-mongering, so most of the wizarding community are completely unaware anything's happened, and that makes them easy targets for the Death Eaters if they're using the Imperius Curse.'

'But you're telling people, aren't you?' said Harry, looking around at Mr Weasley, Sirius, Bill, Mundungus, Lupin and Tonks. 'You're letting people know he's back?'

They all smiled humourlessly.

'Well, as everyone thinks I'm a mad mass-murderer and the Ministry's put a ten thousand Galleon price on my head, I can hardly stroll up the street and start handing out leaflets, can I?' said Sirius restlessly.

'And I'm not a very popular dinner guest with most of the community,' said Lupin. 'It's an occupational hazard of being a werewolf.'

'Tonks and Arthur would lose their jobs at the Ministry if they started shooting their mouths off,' said Sirius, 'and it's very important for us to have spies inside the Ministry, because you can bet Voldemort will have them.'

'We've managed to convince a couple of people, though,' said Mr Weasley. 'Tonks here, for one – she's too young to have been in the Order of the Phoenix last time, and having Aurors on our side is a huge advantage – Kingsley Shacklebolt's been a real asset, too; he's in charge of the hunt for Sirius, so he's been feeding the Ministry information that Sirius is in Tibet.'

'But if none of you are putting the news out that Voldemort's back –' Harry began.

'Who said none of us are putting the news out?' said Sirius. 'Why d'you think Dumbledore's in such trouble?'

'What d'you mean?' Harry asked.

'They're trying to discredit him,' said Lupin. 'Didn't you see the

第5章 凤凰社

部已经有将近十四年没有碰到了。"小天狼星尖刻地说,"福吉只是没有勇气面对这件事。他让自己相信邓布利多是在散布谣言,破坏他的稳定地位,这样一想就轻松多了。"

"你说到点子上了。"卢平说,"既然魔法部坚持说不用担心伏地魔,我们就很难让人们相信他回来了,特别是在人们其实也不愿意相信这个事实的情况下。还有,魔法部一直在对《预言家日报》施加压力,不让他们报道有关的任何消息,他们现在称这些消息为邓布利多的谣言,因此,巫师界的大部分人都完全不知道有事情发生了,这样一来,他们就很容易成为食死徒的攻击目标,如果食死徒使用夺魂咒的话。"

"可是你们在告诉人们真相,是不是?"哈利说,轮番看着韦斯莱先生、小天狼星、比尔、蒙顿格斯、卢平和唐克斯,"你们在让人们知道他已经回来了?"

他们全都苦笑着。

"唉,所有的人都认为我是一个杀人不眨眼的疯子,魔法部悬赏一万加隆捉我归案,所以我不可能溜溜达达地在大街上散发传单,是不是?"小天狼星焦躁不安地说。

"在大多数人眼里,我不是一个很受欢迎的晚宴贵宾。"卢平说,"身为狼人,真是一种职业性的危害。"

"唐克斯和亚瑟如果信口开河,就会丢掉他们在魔法部的工作。"小天狼星说,"而我们在部里安插内线是很重要的,伏地魔肯定也有他们自己的奸细。"

"不过我们还是说服了几个人,"韦斯莱先生说,"比如这位唐克斯——她年纪太轻,上次没能加入凤凰社,能把傲罗争取到我们这边是一个很大的优势——金斯莱·沙克尔也是一个无价之宝。他负责追捕小天狼星,所以他一直向部里提供消息说小天狼星在西藏。"

"但是如果你们谁也不公布伏地魔回来的消息——"哈利话没说完。

"谁说我们没有公布这个消息?"小天狼星说,"你认为邓布利多为什么会陷入这样的麻烦境地?"

"你这话是什么意思?"哈利问。

"他们拼命想败坏他的名声,"卢平说,"你没看上个星期的《预言

CHAPTER FIVE   The Order of the Phoenix

Daily Prophet last week? They reported that he'd been voted out of the Chairmanship of the International Confederation of Wizards because he's getting old and losing his grip, but it's not true; he was voted out by Ministry wizards after he made a speech announcing Voldemort's return. They've demoted him from Chief Warlock on the Wizengamot – that's the Wizard High Court – and they're talking about taking away his Order of Merlin, First Class, too.'

'But Dumbledore says he doesn't care what they do as long as they don't take him off the Chocolate Frog Cards,' said Bill, grinning.

'It's no laughing matter,' said Mr Weasley sharply. 'If he carries on defying the Ministry like this he could end up in Azkaban, and the last thing we want is to have Dumbledore locked up. While You-Know-Who knows Dumbledore's out there and wise to what he's up to he's going to go cautiously. If Dumbledore's out of the way – well, You-Know-Who will have a clear field.'

'But if Voldemort's trying to recruit more Death Eaters it's bound to get out that he's come back, isn't it?' asked Harry desperately.

'Voldemort doesn't march up to people's houses and bang on their front doors, Harry,' said Sirius. 'He tricks, jinxes and blackmails them. He's well-practised at operating in secret. In any case, gathering followers is only one thing he's interested in. He's got other plans too, plans he can put into operation very quietly indeed, and he's concentrating on those for the moment.'

'What's he after apart from followers?' Harry asked swiftly. He thought he saw Sirius and Lupin exchange the most fleeting of looks before Sirius answered.

'Stuff he can only get by stealth.'

When Harry continued to look puzzled, Sirius said, 'Like a weapon. Something he didn't have last time.'

'When he was powerful before?'

'Yes.'

'Like what kind of weapon?' said Harry. 'Something worse than the Avada Kedavra –?'

'That's enough!'

Mrs Weasley spoke from the shadows beside the door. Harry hadn't

家日报》吗？他们报道说他经过投票被解除了国际巫师联合会会长的职位，因为他已经年迈，力不从心，但那根本不是事实。他发表了一篇讲话，宣布伏地魔回来了，之后魔法部的巫师们就投票使他被解职了。他们给他降了级，他不再是威森加摩——就是最高巫师法庭——的首席魔法师，他们还在讨论收回他的梅林爵士团一级勋章。"

"可是邓布利多说，只要不把他从巧克力蛙的画片中撤下来，他们做什么他都不在乎。"比尔咧嘴笑着说。

"这不是什么好笑的事情。"韦斯莱先生严厉地说，"如果他一直这样公然与魔法部对着干，最后他可能会被关进阿兹卡班的，而我们最不希望看到的就是邓布利多被关起来。既然神秘人知道邓布利多在外面并且清楚他打算做什么，他就必须谨慎行事。如果邓布利多这个障碍被清除了——唉，神秘人就可以肆意妄为了。"

"但是，如果伏地魔想吸收更多的人成为食死徒，他回来的消息肯定会传出去的，是不是？"哈利急躁地问。

"伏地魔并不是大摇大摆地走到别人家门口，砰砰地敲他们的门，哈利，"小天狼星说，"他对他们施魔法，念恶咒，威逼利诱。他搞秘密活动是很有一套的。不管怎么说，网罗追随者只是他感兴趣的事情之一。他还有其他计划，可以神不知鬼不觉地实施的计划，眼下他的全部注意力都在那上面。"

"除了追随者以外，他还想得到什么呢？"哈利反应敏捷地问。他仿佛看到小天狼星和卢平飞快地交换了一下眼神，然后小天狼星才做出了回答。

"某种只有偷偷摸摸才能得到的东西。"

看到哈利还是一脸迷惑，小天狼星说："比如一件武器。他以前所没有的东西。"

"他以前得势的时候？"

"是的。"

"比如什么样的武器呢？"哈利说，"比阿瓦达索命咒还要厉害——"

"够了！"韦斯莱夫人站在门旁的阴影里说。

哈利没有注意到她送金妮上楼已经回来了。她抱着双臂，满脸怒气。

noticed her return from taking Ginny upstairs. Her arms were crossed and she looked furious.

'I want you in bed, now. All of you,' she added, looking around at Fred, George, Ron and Hermione.

'You can't boss us –' Fred began.

'Watch me,' snarled Mrs Weasley. She was trembling slightly as she looked at Sirius. 'You've given Harry plenty of information. Any more and you might just as well induct him into the Order straightaway.'

'Why not?' said Harry quickly. 'I'll join, I want to join, I want to fight.'

'No.'

It was not Mrs Weasley who spoke this time, but Lupin.

'The Order is comprised only of overage wizards,' he said. 'Wizards who have left school,' he added, as Fred and George opened their mouths. 'There are dangers involved of which you can have no idea, any of you ... I think Molly's right, Sirius. We've said enough.'

Sirius half-shrugged but did not argue. Mrs Weasley beckoned imperiously to her sons and Hermione. One by one they stood up and Harry, recognising defeat, followed suit.

第5章 凤凰社

"我希望你们赶紧上床睡觉。大家都去!"她补充了一句,挨个儿扫视着弗雷德、乔治、罗恩和赫敏。

"你不能对我们发号施令——"弗雷德想反抗。

"你看我能不能!"韦斯莱夫人吼道,她身体微微颤抖,望着小天狼星,"你告诉哈利的情况够多的了。再说下去,你就可以马上吸收他加入凤凰社了。"

"为什么不呢?"哈利立刻问道,"我想参加,我愿意参加。我希望参加战斗。"

"不行。"

这次说话的不是韦斯莱夫人,而是卢平。

"凤凰社的成员只能是达到一定年龄的巫师,"他说,"已经从学校毕业的巫师。"他看到弗雷德和乔治张嘴想要说什么,便又补充说,"这里头有很多危险,你们根本就不可能知道,你们谁也不知道……我认为莫丽说得对,小天狼星。我们说得够多的了。"

小天狼星微微耸了耸肩膀,但没有再说什么。韦斯莱夫人盛气凌人地招呼她的几个儿子和赫敏。他们一个接一个地站起身,哈利看到没什么希望了,也只好跟着站了起来。

CHAPTER SIX

The Noble and Most Ancient House of Black

Ms Weasley followed them upstairs looking grim. 'I want you all to go straight to bed, no talking,' she said as they reached the first landing, 'we've got a busy day tomorrow. I expect Ginny's asleep,' she added to Hermione, 'so try not to wake her up.'

'Asleep, yeah, right,' said Fred in an undertone, after Hermione bade them goodnight and they were climbing to the next floor. 'If Ginny's not lying awake waiting for Hermione to tell her everything they said downstairs then I'm a Flobberworm ...'

'All right, Ron, Harry,' said Mrs Weasley on the second landing, pointing them into their bedroom. 'Off to bed with you.'

''Night,' Harry and Ron said to the twins.

'Sleep tight,' said Fred, winking.

Mrs Weasley closed the door behind Harry with a sharp snap. The bedroom looked, if anything, even danker and gloomier than it had on first sight. The blank picture on the wall was now breathing very slowly and deeply, as though its invisible occupant was asleep. Harry put on his pyjamas, took off his glasses and climbed into his chilly bed while Ron threw Owl Treats up on top of the wardrobe to pacify Hedwig and Pigwidgeon, who were clattering around and rustling their wings restlessly.

'We can't let them out to hunt every night,' Ron explained as he pulled on his maroon pyjamas. 'Dumbledore doesn't want too many owls swooping around the square, thinks it'll look suspicious. Oh yeah ... I forgot ...'

He crossed to the door and bolted it.

'What're you doing that for?'

第6章

最古老而高贵的布莱克家族

韦斯莱夫人跟着他们上楼,脸板得叫人害怕。

"我希望你们每个人立刻上床睡觉,不许说话。"他们走到楼梯的第一个平台时,她说道,"明天我们有许多事情要做。我想金妮已经睡着了。"她又对赫敏说:"尽量不要把她吵醒。"

"睡着了,是啊,没错。"弗雷德压低声音说,这时赫敏已经向他们道了晚安,他们正继续往楼上走去,"金妮肯定醒着,等着赫敏把他们在楼下说的话原原本本地告诉她,如果不是这样,我就是一只弗洛伯毛虫……"

"好了,罗恩,哈利,"韦斯莱夫人在楼梯的第二个平台上说,指着卧室,叫他们快点走进去,"快上床睡觉吧。"

"晚安。"哈利和罗恩对双胞胎说。

"睡个好觉。"弗雷德眨了眨眼睛说。

韦斯莱夫人在哈利身后重重地把门关上了。卧室看上去要说有什么不一样的话,倒是比第一次见到时更昏暗、更阴森了。墙上那幅空白油画此刻缓缓地、一起一伏地呼吸着,似乎住在里头的那个看不见的人已经进入了梦乡。哈利换上睡衣,摘下眼镜,爬到冰冷的床上;罗恩往衣柜顶上扔了一些猫头鹰食,安抚了一下海德薇和小猪,它们不停地呱着嘴,焦躁地扑扇着翅膀。

"我们不能每天晚上放它们出去捕食。"罗恩一边穿上他的褐紫红色睡衣,一边解释说,"邓布利多不想让太多的猫头鹰在广场上飞来飞去,他认为那样会显得很可疑。哦,对了……我忘记了……"

他走过去把门闩上了。

"为什么要这么做?"

CHAPTER SIX   The Noble and Most Ancient House of Black

'Kreacher,' said Ron as he turned off the light. 'First night I was here he came wandering in at three in the morning. Trust me, you don't want to wake up and find him prowling around your room. Anyway ...' he got into his bed, settled down under the covers then turned to look at Harry in the darkness; Harry could see his outline by the moonlight filtering in through the grimy window, *'what d'you reckon?'*

Harry didn't need to ask what Ron meant.

'Well, they didn't tell us much we couldn't have guessed, did they?' he said, thinking of all that had been said downstairs. 'I mean, all they've really said is that the Order's trying to stop people joining Vol–'

There was a sharp intake of breath from Ron.

'*–demort*,' said Harry firmly. 'When are you going to start using his name? Sirius and Lupin do.'

Ron ignored this last comment.

'Yeah, you're right,' he said, 'we already knew nearly everything they told us, from using the Extendable Ears. The only new bit was –'

Crack.

'OUCH!'

'Keep your voice down, Ron, or Mum'll be back up here.'

'You two just Apparated on my knees!'

'Yeah, well, it's harder in the dark.'

Harry saw the blurred outlines of Fred and George leaping down from Ron's bed. There was a groan of bedsprings and Harry's mattress descended a few inches as George sat down near his feet.

'So, got there yet?' said George eagerly.

'The weapon Sirius mentioned?' said Harry.

'Let slip, more like,' said Fred with relish, now sitting next to Ron. 'We didn't hear about *that* on the old Extendables, did we?'

'What d'you reckon it is?' said Harry.

'Could be anything,' said Fred.

'But there can't be anything worse than the Avada Kedavra Curse, can there?' said Ron. 'What's worse than death?'

"克利切，"罗恩一边关灯一边说道，"我来这里的第一天夜里，他凌晨三点钟摸进了我的房间。相信我，你总不愿意醒过来看见他在你房间里鬼鬼祟祟地转悠吧。算了……"他爬到床上，钻进被窝，转过脸在黑暗中望着哈利。哈利就着从肮脏的窗户中透进来的月光，勉强能够分辨出罗恩的轮廓。"你是怎么想的？"

哈利不需要询问罗恩的问话是什么意思。

"哦，他们告诉我们的情况，我们基本上都能猜得出来，是不是？"他说，想着刚才他们在楼下说过的所有那些话，"我的意思是，实际上他们只说了一点，就是凤凰社正在竭力阻止人们加入伏——"

罗恩呼地倒抽了一口冷气。

"——地魔，"哈利坚决地说，"你什么时候才能对他直呼其名呢？小天狼星和卢平就能做到。"

罗恩假装没听见最后这句话。

"是啊，你说得对，"他说，"他们告诉我们的事情，我们使用伸缩耳差不多都已经知道了。唯一的新消息就是——"

砰！

"哎哟！"

"你声音小点儿，罗恩，不然妈妈又该跑回来了。"

"你们俩幻影移形，正好落在我的膝盖上了！"

"是啊，没办法，摸着黑总是不太容易。"

哈利看见弗雷德和乔治的模糊身影从罗恩的床上跳了下来。乔治一屁股坐在哈利脚边，哈利床垫的弹簧发出一阵呻吟，床垫往下陷了几英寸。

"怎么样，明白了吧？"乔治急切地问。

"小天狼星提到的那件武器？"哈利说。

"估计是不小心说漏了嘴，"弗雷德兴致勃勃地说，他已坐在了罗恩身边，"我们以前用伸缩耳可没听到这一点，是不是？"

"你们想那会是什么呢？"哈利问。

"什么都有可能。"弗雷德说。

"但是不可能有比阿瓦达索命咒还厉害的东西了，是不是？"罗恩说，"还有什么比死亡更可怕呢？"

CHAPTER SIX — The Noble and Most Ancient House of Black

'Maybe it's something that can kill loads of people at once,' suggested George.

'Maybe it's some particularly painful way of killing people,' said Ron fearfully.

'He's got the Cruciatus Curse for causing pain,' said Harry, 'he doesn't need anything more efficient than that.'

There was a pause and Harry knew that the others, like him, were wondering what horrors this weapon could perpetrate.

'So who d'you think's got it now?' asked George.

'I hope it's our side,' said Ron, sounding slightly nervous.

'If it is, Dumbledore's probably keeping it,' said Fred.

'Where?' said Ron quickly. 'Hogwarts?'

'Bet it is!' said George. 'That's where he hid the Philosopher's Stone.'

'A weapon's going to be a lot bigger than the Stone, though!' said Ron.

'Not necessarily,' said Fred.

'Yeah, size is no guarantee of power,' said George. 'Look at Ginny.'

'What d'you mean?' said Harry.

'You've never been on the receiving end of one of her Bat-Bogey Hexes, have you?'

'Shhh!' said Fred, half rising from the bed. 'Listen!'

They fell silent. Footsteps were coming up the stairs.

'Mum,' said George and without further ado there was a loud *crack* and Harry felt the weight vanish from the end of his bed. A few seconds later, they heard the floorboard creak outside their door; Mrs Weasley was plainly listening to check whether or not they were talking.

Hedwig and Pigwidgeon hooted dolefully. The floorboard creaked again and they heard her heading upstairs to check on Fred and George.

'She doesn't trust us at all, you know,' said Ron regretfully.

Harry was sure he would not be able to fall asleep; the evening had been so packed with things to think about that he fully expected to lie awake for hours mulling it all over. He wanted to continue talking to Ron, but Mrs Weasley was now creaking back downstairs again, and once she had gone he distinctly heard others making their way upstairs ... in fact, many-legged creatures were cantering softly up and down outside the bedroom door, and Hagrid the Care of Magical Creatures teacher was saying, *'Beauties, aren' they, eh, Harry? We'll be studyin' weapons this term ...'* and Harry saw that the creatures

"也许是一种可以一下子杀死好多人的武器。"乔治猜测道。

"也许是一种特别痛苦的杀人办法。"罗恩恐惧地说。

"他已经有了可以让人痛苦的钻心咒,"哈利说,"不会再需要比那个更有效的东西了。"

一阵沉默,哈利知道其他人像他一样,都在猜想这件秘密武器能做出什么恐怖的坏事。

"那么你们说,这武器如今在谁的手里呢?"乔治问。

"我希望在我们这边。"罗恩说,声音里微微透着紧张。

"如果是这样,准是由邓布利多保管着。"弗雷德说。

"在哪儿?"罗恩立刻问道,"在霍格沃茨?"

"肯定没错!"乔治说,"当年他就把魔法石藏在了那儿。"

"可是,一件武器肯定要比魔法石大得多呀!"罗恩说。

"不一定。"弗雷德说。

"是啊,威力大小不在于个头。"乔治说,"看看金妮吧。"

"你这是什么意思?"哈利说。

"你从来没有领教过她的蝙蝠精咒吧?"

"嘘!"弗雷德说着从床上欠起身子,"听!"

他们屏住呼吸。有脚步声从楼梯上传来。

"妈妈。"乔治说,说时迟那时快,随着啪的一声爆响,哈利觉得压在他床上的重量突然消失了。几秒钟后,他们听见门外的地板吱吱嘎嘎地响了起来,韦斯莱夫人显然在听他们是不是还在说话。

海德薇和小猪闷闷不乐地叫着。地板又吱吱嘎嘎地响了,他们听见她在继续往楼上走,去检查弗雷德和乔治了。

"你看,她根本就不相信我们。"罗恩懊丧地说。

哈利知道自己肯定是睡不着了。这一晚上发生的事情太多了,他需要好好想想,他估计自己会躺在床上,翻来覆去地寻思几个小时。他很想继续跟罗恩说说话,但韦斯莱夫人又吱吱嘎嘎地走下楼来了。她刚一走远,哈利又清清楚楚地听见其他人在往楼上走……实际上,那是一些多腿的动物在卧室门外悄没声地跑来跑去,保护神奇动物课的老师海格在说:"它们多漂亮啊,是不是,哈利?我们这学期要学习武

CHAPTER SIX   The Noble and Most Ancient House of Black

had cannons for heads and were wheeling to face him ... he ducked ...

The next thing he knew, he was curled into a warm ball under his bedclothes and George's loud voice was filling the room.

'Mum says get up, your breakfast is in the kitchen and then she needs you in the drawing room, there are loads more Doxys than she thought and she's found a nest of dead Puffskeins under the sofa.'

Half an hour later Harry and Ron, who had dressed and breakfasted quickly, entered the drawing room, a long, high-ceilinged room on the first floor with olive green walls covered in dirty tapestries. The carpet exhaled little clouds of dust every time someone put their foot on it and the long, moss green velvet curtains were buzzing as though swarming with invisible bees. It was around these that Mrs Weasley, Hermione, Ginny, Fred and George were grouped, all looking rather peculiar as they had each tied a cloth over their nose and mouth. Each of them was also holding a large bottle of black liquid with a nozzle at the end.

'Cover your faces and take a spray,' Mrs Weasley said to Harry and Ron the moment she saw them, pointing to two more bottles of black liquid standing on a spindle-legged table. 'It's Doxycide. I've never seen an infestation this bad – *what* that house-elf's been doing for the last ten years –'

Hermione's face was half concealed by a tea towel but Harry distinctly saw her throw a reproachful look at Mrs Weasley.

'Kreacher's really old, he probably couldn't manage –'

'You'd be surprised what Kreacher can manage when he wants to, Hermione,' said Sirius, who had just entered the room carrying a bloodstained bag of what appeared to be dead rats. 'I've just been feeding Buckbeak,' he added, in reply to Harry's enquiring look. 'I keep him upstairs in my mother's bedroom. Anyway ... this writing desk ...'

He dropped the bag of rats into an armchair, then bent over to examine the locked cabinet which, Harry now noticed for the first time, was shaking slightly.

'Well, Molly, I'm pretty sure this is a Boggart,' said Sirius, peering through the keyhole, 'but perhaps we ought to let Mad-Eye have a shufti at it before we let it out – knowing my mother, it could be something much worse.'

'Right you are, Sirius,' said Mrs Weasley.

器……"哈利突然看见那些动物的脑袋变成了一门门大炮,正转过来对准了他……他闪身躲藏……

接下来,他发现自己在被窝里蜷缩成一个温暖的球,乔治响亮的声音在房间里回荡。

"妈妈说该起床了,你们的早饭在厨房里,然后她要你们都到客厅去,那里的狐媚子比她原来想的还要多得多,她还在沙发底下发现了一窝死蒲绒绒。"

半小时后,哈利和罗恩三下五除二地穿好衣服,吃过早饭,来到了客厅。这是二楼的一个长长的、天花板很高的房间,橄榄绿色的墙壁上挂着肮脏的挂毯。每次有人把脚踩在地毯上,就会扬起一小股灰尘,长长的、黄绿色的天鹅绒窗帘嗡嗡作响,好像里面飞着许多看不见的蜜蜂。韦斯莱夫人、赫敏、金妮、弗雷德和乔治正围在窗帘前面,脸上都蒙着一块布,掩住了鼻子和嘴巴,样子显得特别滑稽。他们每个人手里都拿着一大瓶黑色的液体,瓶口有一个喷嘴。

"把脸蒙住,拿一瓶喷雾剂,"韦斯莱夫人一看见哈利和罗恩就说,一边指着一张细长腿桌子上的两瓶黑色液体,"这是狐媚子灭剂。我从没见过害虫这样泛滥成灾的——那个家养小精灵这十年来都做什么了——"

赫敏的脸被一块茶巾遮去了一半,但哈利清清楚楚地看见她朝韦斯莱夫人投去了不满的一瞥。

"克利切已经很老了,他大概不能做——"

"克利切只要想做,他能做的事情准会使你大吃一惊,赫敏。"小天狼星说,他刚刚走进房间,手里拎着一只血迹斑斑的口袋,里面装的像是死老鼠。"我刚才在喂巴克比克,"看到哈利脸上询问的神色,他解释道,"我把它关在了楼上我母亲的卧室里。不管怎么说……这张写字台……"

他把那袋死老鼠扔在一把扶手椅上,俯身查看那个锁着的柜子,哈利这才第一次注意到柜子在微微颤动。

"没错,莫丽,我可以肯定这是一个博格特,"小天狼星从钥匙孔里往里瞅着说道,"但或许我们最好先让疯眼汉看看再把它放出来——据我对我妈的了解,搞不好是比博格特更可怕的东西。"

"你说得对,小天狼星。"韦斯莱夫人说。

CHAPTER SIX

The Noble and Most Ancient House of Black

They were both speaking in carefully light, polite voices that told Harry quite plainly that neither had forgotten their disagreement of the night before.

A loud, clanging bell sounded from downstairs, followed at once by the cacophony of screams and wails that had been triggered the previous night by Tonks knocking over the umbrella stand.

'I keep telling them not to ring the doorbell!' said Sirius exasperatedly, hurrying out of the room. They heard him thundering down the stairs as Mrs Black's screeches echoed up through the house once more:

'*Stains of dishonour, filthy half-breeds, blood traitors, children of filth ...*'

'Close the door, please, Harry,' said Mrs Weasley.

Harry took as much time as he dared to close the drawing-room door; he wanted to listen to what was going on downstairs. Sirius had obviously managed to shut the curtains over his mother's portrait because she had stopped screaming. He heard Sirius walking down the hall, then the clattering of the chain on the front door, and then a deep voice he recognised as Kingsley Shacklebolt's saying, 'Hestia's just relieved me, so she's got Moody's Cloak now, thought I'd leave a report for Dumbledore ...'

Feeling Mrs Weasley's eyes on the back of his head, Harry regretfully closed the drawing-room door and rejoined the Doxy party.

Mrs Weasley was bending over to check the page on Doxys in *Gilderoy Lockhart's Guide to Household Pests*, which was lying open on the sofa.

'Right, you lot, you need to be careful, because Doxys bite and their teeth are poisonous. I've got a bottle of antidote here, but I'd rather nobody needed it.'

She straightened up, positioned herself squarely in front of the curtains and beckoned them all forward.

'When I say the word, start spraying immediately,' she said. 'They'll come flying out at us, I expect, but it says on the sprays one good squirt will paralyse them. When they're immobilised, just throw them in this bucket.'

She stepped carefully out of their line of fire, and raised her own spray.

'All right – *squirt*!'

Harry had been spraying only a few seconds when a fully-grown Doxy came soaring out of a fold in the material, shiny beetle-like wings whirring, tiny needle-sharp teeth bared, its fairy-like body covered with thick black hair

第6章 最古老而高贵的布莱克家族

两人说话都小心翼翼，客客气气，哈利明白他们俩都还没有忘记前一天晚上的争吵。

楼下传来叮叮当当刺耳的门铃声，紧接着是昨天晚上唐克斯撞翻伞架时触发的那种凄厉的尖叫哀号。

"我告诉他们多少次了，不要摁门铃！"小天狼星恼火地说，匆匆离开了房间。他们听见他脚步声很重地跑下楼去，而布莱克夫人的尖叫声又一次在整个房子里回荡起来：

"伤风败俗的家伙，肮脏的杂种，家族的败类，龌龊的孽子……"

"劳驾你把门关上，哈利。"韦斯莱夫人说。

哈利大着胆子，尽量拖延关上客厅房门的时间。他想听听楼下的动静。小天狼星显然已经把帷幔拉上盖住了他母亲的肖像，因为老太太不再尖叫了。哈利听见小天狼星走过门厅，然后前门上的链条一阵哗啦啦作响，一个低沉的声音说话了，哈利听出那是金斯莱·沙克尔："海丝佳刚把我替下，现在她穿上了穆迪的隐形斗篷，不过我要给邓布利多留一份报告……"

哈利感觉到韦斯莱夫人的眼睛在盯着他的后脑勺，便只好遗憾地关上客厅的门，重新加入了消灭狐媚子的行列。

韦斯莱夫人俯下身，查看着摊放在沙发上的《吉德罗·洛哈特教你清除家庭害虫》里关于灭狐媚子的那一页。

"听着，你们大家，你们必须格外留神，狐媚子的牙齿是有毒的，被它们咬了之后会中毒。我这里有一瓶解毒剂，但愿没有人需要它。"

她直起身，在窗帘前面摆开架势，示意他们都过去。

"我一发口令，就立刻开始喷。"她说，"我想它们会飞出来攻击我们，但喷雾剂上说，只要足足地喷一下，就能使它们瘫痪。等它们不能动弹了，就把它们扔进这只桶里。"

她小心地走出大家的喷射范围，举起她自己的喷雾剂。

"预备——喷！"

哈利刚喷了几秒钟，就有一只成年的狐媚子从窗帘的褶皱里飞了出来，甲虫般亮晶晶的翅膀嗡嗡扇动着，尖针般的小牙齿露在外面，小巧玲珑的身体上布满浓密的黑毛，四只小拳头愤怒地攥得紧紧的。哈利用

and its four tiny fists clenched with fury. Harry caught it full in the face with a blast of Doxycide. It froze in midair and fell, with a surprisingly loud *thunk*, on to the worn carpet below. Harry picked it up and threw it in the bucket.

'Fred, what are you doing?' said Mrs Weasley sharply. 'Spray that at once and throw it away!'

Harry looked round. Fred was holding a struggling Doxy between his forefinger and thumb.

'Right-o,' Fred said brightly, spraying the Doxy quickly in the face so that it fainted, but the moment Mrs Weasley's back was turned he pocketed it with a wink.

'We want to experiment with Doxy venom for our Skiving Snackboxes,' George told Harry under his breath.

Deftly spraying two Doxys at once as they soared straight for his nose, Harry moved closer to George and muttered out of the corner of his mouth, 'What are Skiving Snackboxes?'

'Range of sweets to make you ill,' George whispered, keeping a wary eye on Mrs Weasley's back. 'Not seriously ill, mind, just ill enough to get you out of a class when you feel like it. Fred and I have been developing them this summer. They're double-ended, colour-coded chews. If you eat the orange half of the Puking Pastilles, you throw up. Moment you've been rushed out of the lesson for the hospital wing, you swallow the purple half –'

'"– which restores you to full fitness, enabling you to pursue the leisure activity of your own choice during an hour that would otherwise have been devoted to unprofitable boredom." That's what we're putting in the adverts, anyway,' whispered Fred, who had edged over out of Mrs Weasley's line of vision and was now sweeping a few stray Doxys from the floor and adding them to his pocket. 'But they still need a bit of work. At the moment our testers are having a bit of trouble stopping themselves puking long enough to swallow the purple end.'

'Testers?'

'Us,' said Fred. 'We take it in turns. George did the Fainting Fancies – we both tried the Nosebleed Nougat –'

'Mum thought we'd been duelling,' said George.

'Joke shop still on, then?' Harry muttered, pretending to be adjusting the nozzle on his spray.

'Well, we haven't had a chance to get premises yet,' said Fred, dropping

狐媚子灭剂将它喷了个正着。它僵在半空中不动了，然后掉在下面满是虫眼的地毯上，当的一声，响得出奇。哈利把它捡起来丢进了桶里。

"弗雷德，你在做什么呢？"韦斯莱夫人严厉地问，"快喷它一下，然后扔掉！"

哈利转过头，看见弗雷德正用大拇指和食指捏住一只不断挣扎的狐媚子。

"好——嘞。"弗雷德欢快地说，迅速地朝那只狐媚子喷了一下，狐媚子昏了过去，但韦斯莱夫人刚一转身，弗雷德就挤挤眼睛，把狐媚子装进了口袋。

"我们想用狐媚子的毒液做实验，研制我们的速效逃课糖。"乔治压低声音对哈利说。

哈利敏捷地同时喷中了两只迎面飞来的狐媚子，凑到乔治身边，几乎不动嘴唇地低声问："什么是速效逃课糖？"

"各种各样让你犯病的糖果，"乔治小声说，一边警惕地留意着韦斯莱夫人的背影，"记住，不是犯重病，而是刚好能在你不想上课的时候让你离开课堂。我和弗雷德这个夏天一直在研制它们。是一种双色口香糖，一头是橘黄色的，另一头是紫色的。如果你吃下这种吐吐糖的橘黄色一半，就会呕吐。等你冲出教室到医院去时，再吞下紫色的一半——"

"——它又让你变得活蹦乱跳，使你能够在一个小时里进行你喜欢的休闲活动，不然那一小时肯定是枯燥乏味、毫无收获的。反正我们的广告词就是这么说的，"他侧着身子移到韦斯莱夫人看不见的地方，把掉在地上的几只狐媚子划拉到一起，装进了口袋，"但是还需要再做一些工作。目前，我们的试验者吐起来没完没了，无法歇口气吞下紫色的一半。"

"试验者？"

"我们，"弗雷德说，"我们轮流试验。乔治试验昏迷花糖——我们俩还共同试验鼻血牛轧糖——"

"妈妈还以为我们在决斗呢。"乔治说。

"那么，笑话店还开着吧？"哈利小声问，一边假装调整喷雾器的喷嘴。

"唉，我们还没有机会去找房子呢，"弗雷德说，把声音压得更低了，

CHAPTER SIX   The Noble and Most Ancient House of Black

his voice even lower as Mrs Weasley mopped her brow with her scarf before returning to the attack, 'so we're running it as a mail-order service at the moment. We put advertisements in the *Daily Prophet* last week.'

'All thanks to you, mate,' said George. 'But don't worry ... Mum hasn't got a clue. She won't read the *Daily Prophet* any more, 'cause of it telling lies about you and Dumbledore.'

Harry grinned. He had forced the Weasley twins to take the thousand Galleons prize money he had won in the Triwizard Tournament to help them realise their ambition to open a joke shop, but he was still glad to know that his part in furthering their plans was unknown to Mrs Weasley. She did not think running a joke shop was a suitable career for two of her sons.

The de-Doxying of the curtains took most of the morning. It was past midday when Mrs Weasley finally removed her protective scarf, sank into a sagging armchair and sprang up again with a cry of disgust, having sat on the bag of dead rats. The curtains were no longer buzzing; they hung limp and damp from the intensive spraying. At the foot of them unconscious Doxys lay crammed in the bucket beside a bowl of their black eggs, at which Crookshanks was now sniffing and Fred and George were shooting covetous looks.

'I think we'll tackle *those* after lunch.' Mrs Weasley pointed at the dusty glass-fronted cabinets standing on either side of the mantelpiece. They were crammed with an odd assortment of objects: a selection of rusty daggers, claws, a coiled snakeskin, a number of tarnished silver boxes inscribed with languages Harry could not understand and, least pleasant of all, an ornate crystal bottle with a large opal set into the stopper, full of what Harry was quite sure was blood.

The clanging doorbell rang again. Everyone looked at Mrs Weasley.

'Stay here,' she said firmly, snatching up the bag of rats as Mrs Black's screeches started up again from down below. 'I'll bring up some sandwiches.'

She left the room, closing the door carefully behind her. At once, everyone dashed over to the window to look down on the doorstep. They could see the top of an unkempt gingery head and a stack of precariously balanced cauldrons.

'Mundungus!' said Hermione. 'What's he brought all those cauldrons for?'

'Probably looking for a safe place to keep them,' said Harry. 'Isn't that what he was doing the night he was supposed to be tailing me? Picking up

这时韦斯莱夫人用围巾擦了擦额头上的汗，又返身投入战斗，"所以目前还只是办理邮购业务。上个星期我们在《预言家日报》上登了广告。"

"还得感谢你呢，伙计。"乔治说，"不用担心……妈妈什么也不知道。她再也不肯看《预言家日报》了，因为报上尽给你和邓布利多造谣。"

哈利咧嘴笑了。他曾经硬要韦斯莱家的这对双胞胎收下他在三强争霸赛中得到的一千加隆，以帮助他们实现开一个笑话店的雄心壮志，不过得知韦斯莱夫人不知道他资助了双胞胎，他还是感到松了口气。韦斯莱夫人认为，对她这两个儿子来说，开一家笑话店不是一个合适的职业。

消灭窗帘里的狐媚子花了几乎一上午的时间。一直到过了中午，韦斯莱夫人才摘掉防护的围巾，一屁股坐在一把中间凹陷的扶手椅上，紧接着又厌恶地大叫一声，跳了起来——她坐在那一袋死老鼠上了。窗帘不再发出嗡嗡的响声，它们软绵绵地垂着，因为喷了太多的药水而湿漉漉的。在它们的下面，失去知觉的狐媚子密密麻麻地躺在桶里，旁边一个碗里是它们黑色的卵，克鲁克山用鼻子嗅来嗅去，弗雷德和乔治眼馋地朝它们望着。

"我想，我们吃过午饭后再来对付那些吧。"韦斯莱夫人指着壁炉架两边布满灰尘的玻璃门柜子，那里面塞满了各种各样的古怪玩意儿：一批锈迹斑斑的短剑、动物的脚爪、一条盘起来的蛇皮，还有一大堆颜色暗淡发乌的银盒子，上面刻着哈利看不懂的文字，最让人不喜欢的是一个装饰用的水晶瓶，塞子上嵌着一块很大的蛋白石，瓶子里盛满了哈利相信是血的东西。

门铃又叮叮当当地响了起来。大伙儿都望着韦斯莱夫人。

"待在这儿，"她不容置疑地说，一把抓起那袋死老鼠，下面又传来了布莱克夫人凄厉刺耳的尖叫声，"我会带一些三明治上来。"

她走出房间，回手把门小心地关上了。立刻，大家都冲到窗口，朝下面的前门台阶望去。他们看见的是一个乱蓬蓬的姜黄色头顶，还有一大摞东倒西歪、眼看就要倒下来的坩埚。

"蒙顿格斯！"赫敏说，"他带那么多坩埚来干什么？"

"大概想找个安全的地方藏起来吧。"哈利说，"他本该跟踪我的那

CHAPTER SIX The Noble and Most Ancient House of Black

dodgy cauldrons?'

'Yeah, you're right!' said Fred, as the front door opened; Mundungus heaved his cauldrons through it and disappeared from view. 'Blimey, Mum won't like that ...'

He and George crossed to the door and stood beside it, listening intently. Mrs Black's screaming had stopped.

'Mundungus is talking to Sirius and Kingsley,' Fred muttered, frowning with concentration. 'Can't hear properly ... d'you reckon we can risk the Extendable Ears?'

'Might be worth it,' said George. 'I could sneak upstairs and get a pair –'

But at that precise moment there was an explosion of sound from downstairs that rendered Extendable Ears quite unnecessary. All of them could hear exactly what Mrs Weasley was shouting at the top of her voice.

'WE ARE NOT RUNNING A HIDEOUT FOR STOLEN GOODS!'

'I love hearing Mum shouting at someone else,' said Fred, with a satisfied smile on his face as he opened the door an inch or so to allow Mrs Weasley's voice to permeate the room better, 'it makes such a nice change.'

'– COMPLETELY IRRESPONSIBLE, AS IF WE HAVEN'T GOT ENOUGH TO WORRY ABOUT WITHOUT YOU DRAGGING STOLEN CAULDRONS INTO THE HOUSE –'

'The idiots are letting her get into her stride,' said George, shaking his head. 'You've got to head her off early otherwise she builds up a head of steam and goes on for hours. And she's been dying to have a go at Mundungus ever since he sneaked off when he was supposed to be following you, Harry – and there goes Sirius's mum again.'

Mrs Weasley's voice was lost amid fresh shrieks and screams from the portraits in the hall.

George made to shut the door to drown the noise, but before he could do so, a house-elf edged into the room.

Except for the filthy rag tied like a loincloth around its middle, it was completely naked. It looked very old. Its skin seemed to be several times too big for it and, though it was bald like all house-elves, there was a quantity of white hair growing out of its large, batlike ears. Its eyes were a bloodshot and watery grey and its fleshy nose was large and rather snoutlike.

天晚上，去办的不就是这件事吗？抢购来路不明的坩埚？"

"没错，你说得对！"弗雷德说，这时前门打开了，蒙顿格斯费力地搬着那些坩埚进了门，从他们的视野中消失了，"天哪，妈妈肯定不高兴……"

他和乔治走过去站在房门旁，仔细地听着。布莱克夫人的叫声已经停止了。

"蒙顿格斯在跟小天狼星和金斯莱说话，"弗雷德小声说，同时皱紧眉头专心地听着，"听不太清楚……你说我们可不可以冒险用一次伸缩耳？"

"值得一试，"乔治说，"我可以悄悄上楼拿一副——"

可是就在这个时候，楼下传来爆炸般的声响，伸缩耳变得完全没有必要了。每个人都能清清楚楚地听见韦斯莱夫人扯足嗓子的叫嚷。

"我们这里不是窝藏赃物的地方！"

"我真喜欢听妈妈冲别人嚷嚷，"弗雷德脸上带着满足的微笑说道，他把门打开了一两英寸，好让韦斯莱夫人的声音更清楚地传进屋里，"换换口味真不赖。"

"——完全不负责任，好像我们的烦心事还不够多似的，你还要把这一大堆偷来的坩埚拖进屋子——"

"那些傻瓜怎么会让她由着性子发火呢。"乔治摇摇头说，"必须趁早转移她的注意力，不然她的火气会越来越大，接连几小时嚷嚷个没完没了。哈利，自从蒙顿格斯在应该跟踪你的时候偷偷溜走之后，妈妈就一直盼着狠狠地教训他一顿——哦，小天狼星的妈妈又叫起来了。"

韦斯莱夫人的声音几乎被门厅里那些肖像发出的一片尖厉刺耳的叫声淹没。

乔治想关上房门，把声音挡在外面，但没等他来得及这么做，一个家养小精灵侧身闪了进来。

除了腰上围了一条脏兮兮的破布，就像热带国家男子用来遮体的腰布，他全身几乎一丝不挂。他的模样很老了，皮肤似乎比他的身体实际需要的多出了好几倍，脑袋像所有家养小精灵一样光秃秃的，但那两只蝙蝠般的大耳朵里长出了一大堆白毛。他两眼充血，水汪汪灰蒙蒙的，肉乎乎的鼻子很大，简直像猪的鼻子一样。

CHAPTER SIX   The Noble and Most Ancient House of Black

The elf took absolutely no notice of Harry and the rest. Acting as though it could not see them, it shuffled hunchbacked, slowly and doggedly, towards the far end of the room, all the while muttering under its breath in a hoarse, deep voice like a bullfrog's.

'... smells like a drain and a criminal to boot, but she's no better, nasty old blood traitor with her brats messing up my mistress's house, oh, my poor mistress, if she knew, if she knew the scum they've let into her house, what would she say to old Kreacher, oh, the shame of it, Mudbloods and werewolves and traitors and thieves, poor old Kreacher, what can he do ...'

'Hello, Kreacher,' said Fred very loudly, closing the door with a snap.

The house-elf froze in his tracks, stopped muttering, and gave a very pronounced and very unconvincing start of surprise.

'Kreacher did not see young master,' he said, turning around and bowing to Fred. Still facing the carpet, he added, perfectly audibly, 'Nasty little brat of a blood traitor it is.'

'Sorry?' said George. 'Didn't catch that last bit.'

'Kreacher said nothing,' said the elf, with a second bow to George, adding in a clear undertone, 'and there's its twin, unnatural little beasts they are.'

Harry didn't know whether to laugh or not. The elf straightened up, eyeing them all malevolently, and apparently convinced that they could not hear him as he continued to mutter.

'... and there's the Mudblood, standing there bold as brass, oh, if my mistress knew, oh, how she'd cry, and there's a new boy, Kreacher doesn't know his name. What is he doing here? Kreacher doesn't know ...'

'This is Harry, Kreacher,' said Hermione tentatively. 'Harry Potter.'

Kreacher's pale eyes widened and he muttered faster and more furiously than ever.

'The Mudblood is talking to Kreacher as though she is my friend, if Kreacher's mistress saw him in such company, oh, what would she say —'

'Don't call her a Mudblood!' said Ron and Ginny together, very angrily.

'It doesn't matter,' Hermione whispered, 'he's not in his right mind, he doesn't know what he's —'

'Don't kid yourself, Hermione, he knows *exactly* what he's saying,' said

小精灵根本没有注意哈利和其他人。他就像看不见他们似的，弓着背，拖着脚，慢慢地、固执地朝房间那头走去，一边用牛蛙般沙哑、低沉的声音不停地轻声念叨：

"……闻着就像阴沟和罪犯的气味。她也好不到哪儿去，讨厌的老败类，领着她的小崽子糟蹋我女主人的房子。哦，我可怜的女主人哪，如果她地下有知，如果她知道他们把什么样的渣滓弄进了她的家门，她会对老克利切说些什么呢。哦，真丢人哪，泥巴种、狼人、叛徒和小偷，可怜的老克利切，他能怎么办呢……"

"你好，克利切。"弗雷德声音很大地说，一边重重地把门关上了。

家养小精灵顿时僵住了，嘴里不再念念有词，而是做出非常明显但很不可信的吃惊样子。

"克利切刚才没有看见小少爷。"他说，转身朝弗雷德鞠了一躬。他的脸仍然对着地毯，又用别人完全能够听见的声音说道："是老败类的讨厌的小崽子。"

"对不起？"乔治说，"最后那句话我没听清。"

"克利切什么也没说，"小精灵又朝乔治鞠了一躬，然后用虽然很轻但清清楚楚的声音说，"这是他的双胞胎兄弟，一对古怪的小野崽子。"

哈利不知道要不要放声大笑。小精灵直起身，用恶毒的目光望了望他们大家，显然相信他们都听不见他的话，因为他又继续念叨开了：

"……还有那个泥巴种，大大咧咧、肆无忌惮地站在那里，如果我的女主人知道，哦，她该哭得多么伤心哪，这里又新来了一个男孩，克利切不知道他叫什么名字。他在这里做什么呢？克利切不知道……"

"克利切，这是哈利，"赫敏犹豫地说，"哈利·波特。"

克利切那两只浅色的眼睛突然睁大了，嘴里念叨得比以前更快更充满火气：

"那泥巴种居然跟克利切说话，就好像她是我的朋友似的，如果克利切的女主人看见他跟这样的人在一起，哦，她会说什么呢——"

"不许叫她泥巴种！"罗恩和金妮非常生气地同时说道。

"没关系，"赫敏小声说，"他脑子不正常，不知道自己在说——"

"你别自欺欺人了，赫敏，他很清楚自己在说什么。"弗雷德一边

CHAPTER SIX   The Noble and Most Ancient House of Black

Fred, eyeing Kreacher with great dislike.

Kreacher was still muttering, his eyes on Harry.

'Is it true? Is it Harry Potter? Kreacher can see the scar, it must be true, that's the boy who stopped the Dark Lord, Kreacher wonders how he did it –'

'Don't we all, Kreacher,' said Fred.

'What do you want, anyway?' George asked.

Kreacher's huge eyes darted towards George.

'Kreacher is cleaning,' he said evasively.

'A likely story,' said a voice behind Harry.

Sirius had come back; he was glowering at the elf from the doorway. The noise in the hall had abated; perhaps Mrs Weasley and Mundungus had moved their argument down into the kitchen. At the sight of Sirius, Kreacher flung himself into a ridiculously low bow that flattened his snoutlike nose on the floor.

'Stand up straight,' said Sirius impatiently. 'Now, what are you up to?'

'Kreacher is cleaning,' the elf repeated. 'Kreacher lives to serve the Noble House of Black –'

'And it's getting blacker every day, it's filthy,' said Sirius.

'Master always liked his little joke,' said Kreacher, bowing again, and continuing in an undertone, 'Master was a nasty ungrateful swine who broke his mother's heart –'

'My mother didn't have a heart, Kreacher,' snapped Sirius. 'She kept herself alive out of pure spite.'

Kreacher bowed again as he spoke.

'Whatever Master says,' he muttered furiously. 'Master is not fit to wipe slime from his mother's boots, oh, my poor mistress, what would she say if she saw Kreacher serving him, how she hated him, what a disappointment he was –'

'I asked you what you were up to,' said Sirius coldly. 'Every time you show up pretending to be cleaning, you sneak something off to your room so we can't throw it out.'

'Kreacher would never move anything from its proper place in Master's house,' said the elf, then muttered very fast, 'Mistress would never forgive Kreacher if the tapestry was thrown out, seven centuries it's been in the family, Kreacher must save it, Kreacher will not let Master and the blood

说一边非常厌恶地瞪着克利切。

克利切嘴里仍然念念有词，眼睛望着哈利。

"这是真的吗？真的是哈利·波特？克利切看见伤疤了，肯定是真的，就是那个阻止了黑魔王的男孩，克利切不知道他是怎么做到的——"

"我们都不知道，克利切。"弗雷德说。

"你到底想要什么呀？"乔治问。

克利切的一对大眼睛猛地朝乔治望去。

"克利切在打扫卫生。"他躲躲闪闪地说。

"说得倒很像是真的。"哈利身后的一个声音说。

小天狼星回来了，他在门口怒气冲冲地瞪着小精灵。门厅里的声音平息了，也许韦斯莱夫人和蒙顿格斯把他们的争吵转移到厨房里去了。克利切一看见小天狼星立刻深鞠一躬，身子低得简直滑稽可笑，猪鼻子一般的大鼻子压扁在地上。

"快站起来。"小天狼星不耐烦地说，"好了，你想干什么？"

"克利切在打扫卫生，"小精灵又说了一遍，"克利切终生为高贵的布莱克家族效力——"

"可是房子一天比一天黑暗，它太脏了。"小天狼星说。

"少爷总是喜欢开点儿小玩笑，"克利切说着又鞠了一躬，随即压低声音念叨开了，"少爷是个讨厌的、忘恩负义的下流坏子，伤透了他母亲的心——"

"我母亲没有心，克利切，"小天狼星没好气地说，"她完全是靠怨恨维持生命的。"

克利切说话时又鞠了一躬。

"不管少爷怎么说，"他愤愤不平地嘟哝道，"少爷连给他母亲擦鞋底都不配，哦，我可怜的女主人哪，如果她看见克利切在服侍少爷会怎么说呢，女主人是多么恨他啊，他多么令人失望——"

"我问你到底打算干什么。"小天狼星冷冷地说，"每次你出来假装打扫卫生，可是却把什么东西都偷偷拿到你的房间，不让我们扔掉。"

"克利切永远不会把少爷家里的任何东西从合适的地方拿走。"小精灵说，然后又很快地念叨起来，"如果挂毯被扔掉了，女主人永远都不会原谅克利切的，挂毯在这个家里已经有七个世纪了，克利切一定要保

CHAPTER SIX   The Noble and Most Ancient House of Black

traitors and the brats destroy it –'

'I thought it might be that,' said Sirius, casting a disdainful look at the opposite wall. 'She'll have put another Permanent Sticking Charm on the back of it, I don't doubt, but if I can get rid of it I certainly will. Now go away, Kreacher.'

It seemed that Kreacher did not dare disobey a direct order; nevertheless, the look he gave Sirius as he shuffled out past him was full of deepest loathing and he muttered all the way out of the room.

'– comes back from Azkaban ordering Kreacher around, oh, my poor mistress, what would she say if she saw the house now, scum living in it, her treasures thrown out, she swore he was no son of hers and he's back, they say he's a murderer too –'

'Keep muttering and I will be a murderer!' said Sirius irritably as he slammed the door shut on the elf.

'Sirius, he's not right in the head,' Hermione pleaded, 'I don't think he realises we can hear him.'

'He's been alone too long,' said Sirius, 'taking mad orders from my mother's portrait and talking to himself, but he was always a foul little –'

'If you could just set him free,' said Hermione hopefully, 'maybe –'

'We can't set him free, he knows too much about the Order,' said Sirius curtly. 'And anyway, the shock would kill him. You suggest to him that he leaves this house, see how he takes it.'

Sirius walked across the room to where the tapestry Kreacher had been trying to protect hung the length of the wall. Harry and the others followed.

The tapestry looked immensely old; it was faded and looked as though Doxys had gnawed it in places. Nevertheless, the golden thread with which it was embroidered still glinted brightly enough to show them a sprawling family tree dating back (as far as Harry could tell) to the Middle Ages. Large words at the very top of the tapestry read:

**THE NOBLE AND
MOST ANCIENT
HOUSE OF BLACK
'TOUJOURS PUR'**

住它,克利切绝不让少爷,还有那些血统叛徒和小崽子把挂毯毁掉——"

"我就知道是这么回事。"小天狼星说,朝对面墙上投去轻蔑的一瞥,"她会在挂毯后面再念一个永久粘贴咒,对此我毫不怀疑,但是如果我能摆脱它,我绝不会犹豫。好了,你走吧,克利切。"

克利切似乎不敢违抗直接的命令,不过,当他拖着两只脚走出去时,他投给小天狼星的目光充满了刻骨铭心的憎恨,而且他走出房间时嘴里一直念念有词:

"——从阿兹卡班回来,倒对克利切指手画脚了,哦,我可怜的女主人,如果她看到房子变成这样,会说什么呢,卑鄙小人住了进来,她的宝贝被扔了出去,她发誓不认这个儿子的,如今他又回来了,据说还是个杀人犯——"

"你再念叨,我就真的要杀人啦!"小天狼星烦躁地说,对着小精灵把门重重地关上了。

"小天狼星,他的脑子不正常,"赫敏恳求道,"我想他并不知道我们能听见他的话。"

"他独自待的时间太长了,"小天狼星说,"从我母亲的肖像里接受了一些疯疯癫癫的命令,自己对自己说话,不过他以前就是一个可恶的小——"

"如果你放他自由呢,"赫敏抱有希望地说,"说不定——"

"我们不能放他自由,他对凤凰社的事情知道得太多了。"小天狼星粗暴地说,"而且,不管怎么说,那份惊吓也会要了他的命。你突然对他提出要他离开这个家,看看他会有什么反应。"

小天狼星走到房间那头,克利切千方百计要保护的那个挂毯覆盖着整面墙壁。哈利和其他人跟了过去。

挂毯看上去很旧很旧了,颜色已经暗淡,似乎狐媚子把好几处都咬坏了。不过,上面绣的金线仍然闪闪发亮,他们清楚地看到了一幅枝枝蔓蔓的家谱图,一直可以追溯到(就哈利所知)中世纪。挂毯顶上绣着几个大字:

最古老

而高贵的

布莱克家族

永远纯洁

CHAPTER SIX The Noble and Most Ancient House of Black

'You're not on here!' said Harry, after scanning the bottom of the tree.

'I used to be there,' said Sirius, pointing at a small, round, charred hole in the tapestry, rather like a cigarette burn. 'My sweet old mother blasted me off after I ran away from home – Kreacher's quite fond of muttering the story under his breath.'

'You ran away from home?'

'When I was about sixteen,' said Sirius. 'I'd had enough.'

'Where did you go?' asked Harry, staring at him.

'Your dad's place,' said Sirius. 'Your grandparents were really good about it; they sort of adopted me as a second son. Yeah, I camped out at your dad's in the school holidays, and when I was seventeen I got a place of my own. My Uncle Alphard had left me a decent bit of gold – he's been wiped off here, too, that's probably why – anyway, after that I looked after myself. I was always welcome at Mr and Mrs Potter's for Sunday lunch, though.'

'But ... why did you ...?'

'Leave?' Sirius smiled bitterly and ran his fingers through his long, unkempt hair. 'Because I hated the whole lot of them: my parents, with their pure-blood mania, convinced that to be a Black made you practically royal ... my idiot brother, soft enough to believe them ... that's him.'

Sirius jabbed a finger at the very bottom of the tree, at the name 'Regulus Black'. A date of death (some fifteen years previously) followed the date of birth.

'He was younger than me,' said Sirius, 'and a much better son, as I was constantly reminded.'

'But he died,' said Harry.

'Yeah,' said Sirius. 'Stupid idiot ... he joined the Death Eaters.'

'You're kidding!'

'Come on, Harry, haven't you seen enough of this house to tell what kind of wizards my family were?' said Sirius testily.

'Were – were your parents Death Eaters as well?'

'No, no, but believe me, they thought Voldemort had the right idea, they were all for the purification of the wizarding race, getting rid of Muggle-borns and having pure-bloods in charge. They weren't alone, either, there

"你不在上面！"哈利看了看家谱最底下的一行说道。

"曾经在上面的。"小天狼星指了指挂毯上一个焦黑的小圆洞，那像是被香烟烧焦留下的痕迹，"我从家里逃走之后，我亲爱的老母亲就把我销毁了——克利切很喜欢低声念叨这个故事。"

"你从家里逃走？"

"那年我大约十六岁，"小天狼星说，"我受够了。"

"你去了哪儿？"哈利盯着他问道。

"你爸爸家里，"小天狼星说，"你的爷爷奶奶非常善解人意，他们差不多把我当成了第二个儿子。是啊，学校放假时，我就暂时住在你爸爸家里，到了十七岁，我就自己找了个地方。我叔叔阿尔法德给我留下了数量可观的金子——他也是从这里被清除出去的，大概惺惺相惜吧——反正，从那以后，我就自己照顾自己了，不过，波特先生和夫人总是欢迎我每个星期天到他们家吃午饭。"

"可是……你为什么……？"

"离家出走？"小天狼星苦笑了一下，用手梳理着他乱蓬蓬的长发，"因为我讨厌他们所有的人。我的父母，疯狂地痴迷纯血统，他们相信，身为布莱克家族的人，天生就是高贵的……我那个傻瓜弟弟，性情太软弱，居然相信了他们的话……这就是他。"

小天狼星伸出一个手指，指了指家谱图最下面的一个名字：雷古勒斯·布莱克。出生日期后面有一个死亡日期（大约在十五年前）。

"他比我小，"小天狼星说，"不断地有人提醒我，他这个儿子比我强得多。"

"可是他死了。"哈利说。

"是啊，"小天狼星说，"愚蠢的白痴……他加入了食死徒的行列。"

"你在开玩笑吧！"

"我说，哈利，你看了这所房子的情形，难道还不明白我的家人都是什么样的巫师吗？"小天狼星不耐烦地说。

"你的——你父母也是食死徒吗？"

"不，不是，可是相信我，他们认为伏地魔的主张是正确的，他们都赞成维护巫师血统的纯正，摆脱麻瓜出身的人，让纯血统的人掌握大权。他们并不是唯一这么想的人，在伏地魔露出他的真实面孔之前，

CHAPTER SIX   The Noble and Most Ancient House of Black

were quite a few people, before Voldemort showed his true colours, who thought he had the right idea about things ... they got cold feet when they saw what he was prepared to do to get power, though. But I bet my parents thought Regulus was a right little hero for joining up at first.'

'Was he killed by an Auror?' Harry asked tentatively.

'Oh, no,' said Sirius. 'No, he was murdered by Voldemort. Or on Voldemort's orders, more likely; I doubt Regulus was ever important enough to be killed by Voldemort in person. From what I found out after he died, he got in so far, then panicked about what he was being asked to do and tried to back out. Well, you don't just hand in your resignation to Voldemort. It's a lifetime of service or death.'

'Lunch,' said Mrs Weasley's voice.

She was holding her wand high in front of her, balancing a huge tray loaded with sandwiches and cake on its tip. She was very red in the face and still looked angry. The others moved over to her, eager for some food, but Harry remained with Sirius, who had bent closer to the tapestry.

'I haven't looked at this for years. There's Phineas Nigellus ... my great-great-grandfather, see? ... least popular Headmaster Hogwarts ever had ... and Araminta Meliflua ... cousin of my mother's ... tried to force through a Ministry Bill to make Muggle-hunting legal ... and dear Aunt Elladora ... she started the family tradition of beheading house-elves when they got too old to carry tea trays ... of course, any time the family produced someone halfway decent they were disowned. I see Tonks isn't on here. Maybe that's why Kreacher won't take orders from her – he's supposed to do whatever anyone in the family asks him –'

'You and Tonks are related?' Harry asked, surprised.

'Oh, yeah, her mother Andromeda was my favourite cousin,' said Sirius, examining the tapestry carefully. 'No, Andromeda's not on here either, look –'

He pointed to another small round burn mark between two names, Bellatrix and Narcissa.

'Andromeda's sisters are still here because they made lovely, respectable pure-blood marriages, but Andromeda married a Muggle-born, Ted Tonks, so –'

许多人都认为他对一些事情的主张是正确的……不过，当他们发现他为了获得权势而不择手段时，他们都胆怯、退缩了。但是我想，我的父母一开始一定认为雷古勒斯加入其中，算得上一个勇敢的小英雄。"

"他是被傲罗杀死的吗？"哈利不很确定地问。

"哦，不是，"小天狼星说，"不是，他是被伏地魔杀害的。或者，更有可能是在伏地魔的指使下被害的。我怀疑雷古勒斯还没有那么重要，需要伏地魔亲自动手把他干掉。从他死后我了解的情况看，他已经陷得很深，后来他对别人要他做的事情感到恐惧，就想退出。唉，你不可能向伏地魔递一份辞职报告就算完事。要么卖命终身，要么死路一条。"

"吃饭了。"韦斯莱夫人叫道。

她把魔杖高高地举在面前，魔杖尖上顶着一个托盘，里面堆着许多三明治和蛋糕。韦斯莱夫人的脸涨得通红，仍然一副怒气冲冲的样子。其他人都向她围拢过去，争先恐后地拿东西吃，哈利留在小天狼星身边没有动。小天狼星弯腰更仔细地看着挂毯。

"我已经好几年没有看这个东西了。这是菲尼亚斯·奈杰勒斯……我的高祖父，看见了吗？……是霍格沃茨历史上最不受欢迎的校长……还有阿拉明塔·梅利弗伦……我母亲的堂妹……试图强行通过一条魔法部法令，使捕杀麻瓜的行为合法化……还有我亲爱的埃拉朵拉婶婶……家养小精灵老得端不动盘子时就砍下他们的脑袋，这个家族传统就是她开创的……当然啦，每当家族中产生一个还算正派的人物时，他们就声明与他断绝关系。我看到唐克斯也不在上面。也许就是因为这个，克利切才不听从她的命令——克利切应该对家族里所有的人都俯首听命的——"

"你和唐克斯是亲戚？"哈利吃惊地问。

"哦，是啊，她的母亲安多米达是我最喜欢的堂姐，"小天狼星一边说一边认真地研究家谱图，"没有，安多米达也不在上面，你看——"

他指着贝拉特里克斯和纳西莎两个名字之间的另一个被烧煳的小圆斑。

"安多米达的姐妹们都在上面，因为她们嫁给了可爱的、值得尊敬的纯血统巫师，只有安多米达嫁给了一个麻瓜出身的人——泰德·唐克斯，所以——"

CHAPTER SIX   The Noble and Most Ancient House of Black

Sirius mimed blasting the tapestry with a wand and laughed sourly. Harry, however, did not laugh; he was too busy staring at the names to the right of Andromeda's burn mark. A double line of gold embroidery linked Narcissa Black with Lucius Malfoy and a single vertical gold line from their names led to the name Draco.

'You're related to the Malfoys!'

'The pure-blood families are all interrelated,' said Sirius. 'If you're only going to let your sons and daughters marry pure-bloods your choice is very limited; there are hardly any of us left. Molly and I are cousins by marriage and Arthur's something like my second cousin once removed. But there's no point looking for them on here – if ever a family was a bunch of blood traitors it's the Weasleys.'

But Harry was now looking at the name to the left of Andromeda's burn: Bellatrix Black, which was connected by a double line to Rodolphus Lestrange.

'Lestrange ...' Harry said aloud. The name had stirred something in his memory; he knew it from somewhere, but for a moment he couldn't think where, though it gave him an odd, creeping sensation in the pit of his stomach.

'They're in Azkaban,' said Sirius shortly.

Harry looked at him curiously.

'Bellatrix and her husband Rodolphus came in with Barty Crouch junior,' said Sirius, in the same brusque voice. 'Rodolphus's brother rabastan was with them, too.'

Then Harry remembered. He had seen Bellatrix Lestrange inside Dumbledore's Pensieve, the strange device in which thoughts and memories could be stored: a tall dark woman with heavy-lidded eyes, who had stood at her trial and proclaimed her continuing allegiance to Lord Voldemort, her pride that she had tried to find him after his downfall and her conviction that she would one day be rewarded for her loyalty.

'You never said she was your –'

'Does it matter if she's my cousin?' snapped Sirius. 'As far as I'm concerned, they're not my family. *She's* certainly not my family. I haven't seen her since I was your age, unless you count a glimpse of her coming into Azkaban. D'you think I'm proud of having a relative like her?'

第6章 最古老而高贵的布莱克家族

小天狼星用魔杖做了一个向挂毯射击的动作，苦涩地笑了几声。但哈利没有笑，他正目不转睛地盯着安多米达的焦痕右边的几个名字。一根双股的金线把纳西莎·布莱克与卢修斯·马尔福连接在了一起，然后一根单股的垂直金线从他们的名字连向了德拉科的名字。

"你跟马尔福一家是亲戚！"

"纯血统的家庭之间都有亲戚关系。"小天狼星说，"如果你只想让你的儿女同纯血统的人结婚，那你的选择余地就非常有限了。我们这种人已经所剩无几了。莫丽和我是姻亲关系的表姐弟，亚瑟大概算是我远方表亲吧。但在这上面不可能找到他们——如果有哪个家里都是一伙玷污血统的败类，那准是韦斯莱一家了。"

哈利这时又望着安多米达的焦痕左边的那个名字：贝拉特里克斯·布莱克，一根双股金线将它与罗道夫斯·莱斯特兰奇的名字连接在一起。

"莱斯特兰奇……"哈利大声说。这名字触动了他记忆中的某个东西，他在什么地方见过它，现在一时想不起是在哪儿，但是他内心深处产生了一种奇怪的、阴森森的感觉。

"他们被关在了阿兹卡班。"小天狼星简短地说。

哈利好奇地望着他。

"贝拉特里克斯和她丈夫罗道夫斯是和小巴蒂·克劳奇一起进去的。"小天狼星还是用那种简慢生硬的声音说，"罗道夫斯的弟弟拉巴斯坦也和他们在一起。"

哈利想起来了。他在邓布利多的冥想盆里见过贝拉特里克斯·莱斯特兰奇。冥想盆是一种储存思想和记忆的奇特装置。贝拉特里克斯是一个高个子的黑皮肤女人，厚厚的眼帘耷拉着，她当时在接受审判，声明她继续为伏地魔效忠，并说她为自己在伏地魔失势后想方设法寻找他而感到骄傲，还说她坚信总有一天会因自己的忠诚而得到回报。

"你从没说过她是你的——"

"就算她是我的堂姐又有什么关系呢？"小天狼星没好气地说，"就我而言，他们根本就不是我的亲人。她当然更不能算我的亲人，我从你这么大以后就再没有见过她，除非算上我看见她被关进阿兹卡班时的匆匆一瞥。你认为我会因为有她这样一个亲戚而感到自豪吗？"

CHAPTER SIX The Noble and Most Ancient House of Black

'Sorry,' said Harry quickly, 'I didn't mean – I was just surprised, that's all –'

'It doesn't matter, don't apologise,' Sirius mumbled. He turned away from the tapestry, his hands deep in his pockets. 'I don't like being back here,' he said, staring across the drawing room. 'I never thought I'd be stuck in this house again.'

Harry understood completely. He knew how he would feel, when he was grown up and thought he was free of the place for ever, to return and live at number four, Privet Drive.

'It's ideal for Headquarters, of course,' Sirius said. 'My father put every security measure known to wizardkind on it when he lived here. It's unplottable, so Muggles could never come and call – as if they'd ever have wanted to – and now Dumbledore's added his protection, you'd be hard put to find a safer house anywhere. Dumbledore is Secret Keeper for the Order, you know – nobody can find Headquarters unless he tells them personally where it is – that note Moody showed you last night, that was from Dumbledore ...' Sirius gave a short, bark-like laugh. 'If my parents could see the use their house was being put to now ... well, my mother's portrait should give you some idea ...'

He scowled for a moment, then sighed.

'I wouldn't mind if I could just get out occasionally and do something useful. I've asked Dumbledore whether I can escort you to your hearing – as Snuffles, obviously – so I can give you a bit of moral support, what d'you think?'

Harry felt as though his stomach had sunk through the dusty carpet. He had not thought about the hearing once since dinner the previous evening; in the excitement of being back with the people he liked best, and hearing everything that was going on, it had completely flown his mind. At Sirius's words, however, the crushing sense of dread returned to him. He stared at Hermione and the Weasleys, all tucking into their sandwiches, and thought how he would feel if they went back to Hogwarts without him.

'Don't worry,' Sirius said. Harry looked up and realised that Sirius had been watching him. 'I'm sure they'll clear you, there's definitely something in the International Statute of Secrecy about being allowed to use magic to save your own life.'

"对不起,"哈利赶紧说道,"我不是这个意思——我只是感到很意外,没别的——"

"没关系,用不着道歉。"小天狼星轻声嘀咕道。他转身离开了挂毯,两只手深深插在口袋里。"我真不愿意回到这里,"他一边说一边将目光投向了客厅的另一头,"我从来没想过我会又被困在这所房子里。"

哈利完全能够理解。他知道,如果他长大成人,以为永远摆脱女贞路4号了,结果又回到那个地方生活,会是一种什么感觉。

"当然,用它做指挥部再合适不过了。"小天狼星说,"我父亲住在这里时,对它采取了巫师界所知道的所有保密措施。这房子无法在地图上标绘出来,因此麻瓜们不可能登门拜访——就好像有谁愿意来似的——现在邓布利多又增加了一些他的保护措施,你简直不可能在别处找到一所比这更安全的房子了。知道吗,邓布利多是凤凰社的保密人——谁也不可能找到指挥部,除非邓布利多亲自告诉他们地址——昨天晚上穆迪给你看的那张纸条,就是从邓布利多那里拿来的……"小天狼星发出一声短促、刺耳的笑声,"如果我父母看见他们的房子现在派上了这样的用场……唉,我母亲的肖像画应该给了你一些想象空间……"

他板着脸沉默了一会儿,叹了口气。

"如果我能偶尔出去一下,做一些有用的事情就好了。我问过邓布利多,我能不能陪你去参加受审——当然是以伤风的身份——这样我能给你一些精神支持,你说呢?"

哈利觉得他的心似乎一下子沉到肮脏的地毯下面去了。自从前一天晚上吃完饭之后,他就再没有想过受审的事。他终于回到了他最喜欢的人身边,听他们讲述正在发生的事情,这使他非常兴奋,早就把这件事忘到了九霄云外。现在听了小天狼星的话,那种万念俱灰的恐惧感又回来了。他呆呆地望着正在狼吞虎咽吃三明治的赫敏和韦斯莱兄弟,想着如果自己不能跟他们一起回霍格沃茨,该是一种什么滋味。

"别担心。"小天狼星说。哈利抬起头,这才发现小天狼星一直在注视着自己。"我相信他们一定会宣告你无罪,《国际保密法》里肯定有允许人们为了保全性命而使用魔法的条款。"

CHAPTER SIX   The Noble and Most Ancient House of Black

'But if they do expel me,' said Harry quietly, 'can I come back here and live with you?'

Sirius smiled sadly.

'We'll see.'

'I'd feel a lot better about the hearing if I knew I didn't have to go back to the Dursleys',' Harry pressed him.

'They must be bad if you prefer this place,' said Sirius gloomily.

'Hurry up, you two, or there won't be any food left,' Mrs Weasley called.

Sirius heaved another great sigh, cast a dark look at the tapestry, then he and Harry went to join the others.

Harry tried his best not to think about the hearing while they emptied the glass-fronted cabinets that afternoon. Fortunately for him, it was a job that required a lot of concentration, as many of the objects in there seemed very reluctant to leave their dusty shelves. Sirius sustained a bad bite from a silver snuffbox; within seconds his bitten hand had developed an unpleasant crusty covering like a tough brown glove.

'It's OK,' he said, examining the hand with interest before tapping it lightly with his wand and restoring its skin to normal, 'must be Wartcap powder in there.'

He threw the box aside into the sack where they were depositing the debris from the cabinets; Harry saw George wrap his own hand carefully in a cloth moments later and sneak the box into his already Doxy-filled pocket.

They found an unpleasant-looking silver instrument, something like a many-legged pair of tweezers, which scuttled up Harry's arm like a spider when he picked it up, and attempted to puncture his skin. Sirius seized it and smashed it with a heavy book entitled *Nature's Nobility: A Wizarding Genealogy*. There was a musical box that emitted a faintly sinister, tinkling tune when wound, and they all found themselves becoming curiously weak and sleepy, until Ginny had the sense to slam the lid shut; a heavy locket that none of them could open; a number of ancient seals; and, in a dusty box, an Order of Merlin, First Class, that had been awarded to Sirius's grandfather for 'services to the Ministry'.

'It means he gave them a load of gold,' said Sirius contemptuously, throwing the medal into the rubbish sack.

第6章 最古老而高贵的布莱克家族

"但如果他们真的开除了我,"哈利小声问,"我能回到这里跟你住在一起吗?"

小天狼星露出忧伤的笑容。

"到时候看吧。"

"如果我知道不用回到德思礼家去,我就不那么害怕受审了。"哈利央求道。

"你竟然宁愿住在这里,想必他们对你非常恶劣。"小天狼星忧郁地说。

"快点儿,你们两个,不然就什么吃的也没有了。"韦斯莱夫人喊道。

小天狼星又沉重地长叹了一声,朝挂毯投去悲哀的一瞥,便和哈利一起来到其他人身边。

那天下午,他们清除玻璃门柜子时,哈利尽量克制住自己不去想受审的事。幸好,这项工作需要注意力非常集中,因为柜子里的许多东西似乎很不情愿离开落满灰尘的搁板。小天狼星被一只银鼻烟盒狠狠地咬了一口,几秒钟内,被咬的手就结了一层难看的硬壳,好像戴了一只粗糙的褐色手套。

"没事。"他一边说一边很有兴趣地查看着那只手,然后用魔杖轻轻一点,手上的皮肤又恢复了正常,"里面一定是肉瘤粉。"

他把鼻烟盒扔进了专门放柜里垃圾的袋子里。片刻之后,哈利看见乔治小心地用一块布包着手,偷偷把盒子塞进了他那已经装满狐媚子的口袋里。

他们发现了一个样子特别难看的银器具,像是一把多脚的镊子。哈利刚把它拿起来,它就像蜘蛛一样飞快地顺着哈利的胳膊往上爬,而且还想刺破他的皮肤。小天狼星一把抓了过去,用一本名为《生而高贵:巫师家谱》的书把它拍碎了。还有一个音乐盒,一拧发条,就隐隐约约地发出叮叮咚咚的不祥乐曲,接着他们都发现自己莫名其妙地变得虚弱无力,昏昏欲睡,幸亏金妮脑子还算清楚,赶紧将盖子关上了。还有一个谁也打不开的沉甸甸的挂坠盒。一大堆古色古香的印章。此外,在一个灰扑扑的盒子里,放着一枚梅林一级勋章,是授予小天狼星的祖父的,奖励他"为魔法部做出的贡献"。

"意思是给了他们一大堆金子。"小天狼星轻蔑地说,把勋章扔进了装垃圾的袋子。

CHAPTER SIX The Noble and Most Ancient House of Black

Several times Kreacher sidled into the room and attempted to smuggle things away under his loincloth, muttering horrible curses every time they caught him at it. When Sirius wrested a large golden ring bearing the Black crest from his grip, Kreacher actually burst into furious tears and left the room sobbing under his breath and calling Sirius names Harry had never heard before.

'It was my father's,' said Sirius, throwing the ring into the sack. 'Kreacher wasn't *quite* as devoted to him as to my mother, but I still caught him snogging a pair of my father's old trousers last week.'

Mrs Weasley kept them all working very hard over the next few days. The drawing room took three days to decontaminate. Finally, the only undesirable things left in it were the tapestry of the Black family tree, which resisted all their attempts to remove it from the wall, and the rattling writing desk. Moody had not dropped by Headquarters yet, so they could not be sure what was inside it.

They moved from the drawing room to a dining room on the ground floor where they found spiders as large as saucers lurking in the dresser (Ron left the room hurriedly to make a cup of tea and did not return for an hour and a half). The china, which bore the Black crest and motto, was all thrown unceremoniously into a sack by Sirius, and the same fate met a set of old photographs in tarnished silver frames, all of whose occupants squealed shrilly as the glass covering them smashed.

Snape might refer to their work as 'cleaning', but in Harry's opinion they were really waging war on the house, which was putting up a very good fight, aided and abetted by Kreacher. The house-elf kept appearing wherever they were congregated, his muttering becoming more and more offensive as he attempted to remove anything he could from the rubbish sacks. Sirius went as far as to threaten him with clothes, but Kreacher fixed him with a watery stare and said, 'Master must do as Master wishes,' before turning away and muttering very loudly, 'but Master will not turn Kreacher away, no, because Kreacher knows what they are up to, oh yes, he is plotting against the Dark Lord, yes, with these Mudbloods and traitors and scum ...'

At which Sirius, ignoring Hermione's protests, seized Kreacher by the

第6章 最古老而高贵的布莱克家族

克利切好几次偷偷溜进房间，想把一些东西藏在他的腰布下面带走；每次被人抓住时，他都会说出许多非常难听的脏话。当小天狼星把一个刻着布莱克家族饰章的大金戒指从他手里硬夺过来时，克利切居然气得流出了眼泪，小声啜泣着走出房间，一边用哈利从来没听过的字眼诅咒小天狼星。

"这是我父亲的东西，"小天狼星说着把戒指扔进了袋子，"克利切对他不像对我母亲那样忠心耿耿，但我上个星期还是看见他在亲吻我父亲的一条旧裤子。"

接下来的几天，韦斯莱夫人让他们干得非常辛苦。给客厅消毒花了三天时间。最后，房间里还剩下两件令人不快的东西，一个就是那块布莱克家谱图的挂毯，他们想尽各种办法都不能把它从墙上弄下来，还有就是那个咔啦啦作响的写字台。穆迪还没有来指挥部，所以他们不敢肯定那里面到底是什么东西。

他们从客厅转移到一层的一个餐厅，发现那儿的碗柜里藏着大得像茶托一般的蜘蛛（罗恩急急忙忙跑出房间去给自己倒杯茶喝，一个半小时都没有回来）。那些印着布莱克家族饰章和铭词的瓷器都被小天狼星马马虎虎地扔进了一个袋子。装在褪色银相框里的一些老照片也遭到了同样的命运，当玻璃稀里哗啦地碎裂时，相框里的人都发出凄厉的尖叫。

斯内普大概喜欢把他们的工作称为"大扫除"，但在哈利看来，他们实际上是在对老房子发动一场战争。老房子在克利切的帮助下，进行着十分顽强的抵抗。这个家养小精灵总是出现在他们集中干活的地方，千方百计想从装垃圾的袋子里拿走一些东西，同时嘴里念叨着越来越难听的话。小天狼星最后甚至威胁说要给他衣服穿，克利切用水汪汪的眼睛盯着他说："少爷愿意做什么就做什么。"但不等转身，他又大声念叨说："可是少爷不会把克利切打发走的，不会的，因为克利切知道他们想干什么，噢，是的，他在密谋反抗黑魔王，是的，带着这些泥巴种、叛徒和渣滓……"

听了这话，小天狼星不理睬赫敏的抗议，一把从后面揪住克利切

CHAPTER SIX   The Noble and Most Ancient House of Black

back of his loincloth and threw him bodily from the room.

The doorbell rang several times a day, which was the cue for Sirius's mother to start shrieking again, and for Harry and the others to attempt to eavesdrop on the visitor, though they gleaned very little from the brief glimpses and snatches of conversation they were able to sneak before Mrs Weasley recalled them to their tasks. Snape flitted in and out of the house several times more, though to Harry's relief they never came face to face; Harry also caught sight of his Transfiguration teacher Professor McGonagall, looking very odd in a Muggle dress and coat, and she also seemed too busy to linger. Sometimes, however, the visitors stayed to help. Tonks joined them for a memorable afternoon in which they found a murderous old ghoul lurking in an upstairs toilet, and Lupin, who was staying in the house with Sirius but who left it for long periods to do mysterious work for the Order, helped them repair a grandfather clock that had developed the unpleasant habit of shooting heavy bolts at passers-by. Mundungus redeemed himself slightly in Mrs Weasley's eyes by rescuing Ron from an ancient set of purple robes that had tried to strangle him when he removed them from their wardrobe.

Despite the fact that he was still sleeping badly, still having dreams about corridors and locked doors that made his scar prickle, Harry was managing to have fun for the first time all summer. As long as he was busy he was happy; when the action abated, however, whenever he dropped his guard, or lay exhausted in bed watching blurred shadows move across the ceiling, the thought of the looming Ministry hearing returned to him. Fear jabbed at his insides like needles as he wondered what was going to happen to him if he was expelled. The idea was so terrible that he did not dare voice it aloud, not even to Ron and Hermione, who, though he often saw them whispering together and casting anxious looks in his direction, followed his lead in not mentioning it. Sometimes, he could not prevent his imagination showing him a faceless Ministry official who was snapping his wand in two and ordering him back to the Dursleys' ... but he would not go. He was determined on that. He would come back here to Grimmauld Place and live with Sirius.

He felt as though a brick had dropped into his stomach when Mrs Weasley turned to him during dinner on Wednesday evening and said quietly, 'I've ironed your best clothes for tomorrow morning, Harry, and I want you to

的腰布，把他扔到了房间外面。

每天门铃都要响几次，一听到铃声，小天狼星的母亲就开始刺耳地尖叫，哈利和其他人则努力想偷听来访者的谈话，但每次只能匆匆瞥上几眼，听几句零星的对话，就被韦斯莱夫人叫回去干活了，根本没有捞到多少有用的情报。斯内普又来了几次，每次都没有逗留太长时间，不过让哈利感到欣慰的是，他们一直没有正面碰见过。哈利还看见了他的变形术老师麦格教授，她穿着麻瓜的衣服和外套，显得十分古怪。她似乎也非常忙碌，来去匆匆。不过，有的时候来访者也会留下来帮忙。唐克斯和他们一起度过了一个难忘的下午，他们在楼上的一间厕所里发现了一只凶恶残忍的老食尸鬼。卢平本来是和小天狼星一起住在房子里的，但总时不时地离开很长一段时间，为凤凰社做秘密工作。但他帮助他们修好了一台老爷钟，那钟不知怎的染上了一个令人讨厌的坏毛病：朝过路人发射硬邦邦的螺丝钉。蒙顿格斯稍微挽回了一些自己在韦斯莱夫人心目中的形象，他把罗恩从一套古旧的紫色长袍里救了出来。当罗恩把那套袍子从衣柜里拿出来时，袍子缠住了他，要把他勒死。

哈利夜里还是睡得不踏实，梦境里仍然会出现那些长长的走廊和紧锁的房门，引起伤疤的阵阵刺痛，但在整个暑假里他总算第一次感到开心了。只要手里有活儿干，他就高兴。而当活儿告一段落，他松懈下来，或精疲力竭地躺在床上望着模糊的阴影在天花板上移动时，就又会想起即将到魔法部受审的可怕事情。一想到如果被开除他会怎么办，恐惧就像无数根尖针一样刺着他的心。这个想法太可怕了，他不敢大声把它说出来，就连对罗恩和赫敏也不敢说，而他们俩呢，尽管哈利经常看见他们凑在一起嘀嘀咕咕，并不时朝他这边投来担忧的目光，却也跟他一样，对这件事只字不提。有时，他忍不住会展开想象：面前出现了一个面目不清的魔法部官员，咔嚓一声把他的魔杖撅成了两截，命令他回到德思礼家去……他是绝对不会去的。在这一点上他已拿定主意。他要到格里莫广场这儿来跟小天狼星住在一起。

星期三晚上吃饭的时候，韦斯莱夫人转过脸来轻声对他说："我已经把你最好的衣服熨平，你明天早晨穿上，哈利，我希望你今晚再把头发洗洗。好的第一印象是会创造奇迹的。"哈利听了这话，觉得就像

CHAPTER SIX The Noble and Most Ancient House of Black

wash your hair tonight, too. A good first impression can work wonders.'

Ron, Hermione, Fred, George and Ginny all stopped talking and looked over at him. Harry nodded and tried to keep eating his chop, but his mouth had become so dry he could not chew.

'How am I getting there?' he asked Mrs Weasley, trying to sound unconcerned.

'Arthur's taking you to work with him,' said Mrs Weasley gently.

Mr Weasley smiled encouragingly at Harry across the table.

'You can wait in my office until it's time for the hearing,' he said.

Harry looked over at Sirius, but before he could ask the question, Mrs Weasley had answered it.

'Professor Dumbledore doesn't think it's a good idea for Sirius to go with you, and I must say I –'

'– think he's *quite right*,' said Sirius through clenched teeth.

Mrs Weasley pursed her lips.

'When did Dumbledore tell you that?' Harry said, staring at Sirius.

'He came last night, when you were in bed,' said Mr Weasley.

Sirius stabbed moodily at a potato with his fork. Harry lowered his own eyes to his plate. The thought that Dumbledore had been in the house on the eve of his hearing and not asked to see him made him feel, if it were possible, even worse.

一块砖头砸进了他心里。

　　罗恩、赫敏、弗雷德、乔治和金妮都停止了谈话，朝他这边望着。哈利点点头，还想继续吃他的排骨，但嘴里突然变得很干，简直没法咀嚼了。

　　"我怎么去呢？"他问韦斯莱夫人，努力使声音听上去显得不太在乎。

　　"亚瑟上班时带你一起去。"韦斯莱夫人温和地说。

　　韦斯莱先生隔着桌子朝哈利鼓励地微笑着。

　　"你可以先待在我的办公室，等受审的时间到了再去。"他说。

　　哈利朝小天狼星望去，但没等他发问，韦斯莱夫人就回答了：

　　"邓布利多教授认为小天狼星陪你一起去不太合适，我必须说我——"

　　"——认为他非常正确。"小天狼星从紧咬的牙缝中挤出声音说。

　　韦斯莱夫人噘起了嘴巴。

　　"邓布利多是什么时候对你说这个话的？"哈利问，眼睛望着小天狼星。

　　"他昨夜来了一趟，那时你已经睡着了。"韦斯莱先生说。

　　小天狼星闷闷不乐地把叉子扎进一个土豆。哈利垂眼望着自己的盘子。邓布利多在他受审的前夜来过这所房子，却没有提出要见他，想到这一点，他原本就糟糕透顶的心情更加恶劣了。

CHAPTER SEVEN

The Ministry of Magic

Harry awoke at half past five the next morning as abruptly and completely as if somebody had yelled in his ear. For a few moments he lay immobile as the prospect of the disciplinary hearing filled every tiny particle of his brain, then, unable to bear it, he leapt out of bed and put on his glasses. Mrs Weasley had laid out his freshly laundered jeans and T-shirt at the foot of his bed. Harry scrambled into them. The blank picture on the wall sniggered.

Ron was lying sprawled on his back with his mouth wide open, fast asleep. He did not stir as Harry crossed the room, stepped out on to the landing and closed the door softly behind him. Trying not to think of the next time he would see Ron, when they might no longer be fellow students at Hogwarts, Harry walked quietly down the stairs, past the heads of Kreacher's ancestors, and down into the kitchen.

He had expected it to be empty, but when he reached the door he heard the soft rumble of voices on the other side. He pushed it open and saw Mr and Mrs Weasley, Sirius, Lupin and Tonks sitting there almost as though they were waiting for him. All were fully dressed except Mrs Weasley, who was wearing a quilted purple dressing gown. She leapt to her feet the moment Harry entered.

'Breakfast,' she said as she pulled out her wand and hurried over to the fire.

'M – m – morning, Harry,' yawned Tonks. Her hair was blonde and curly this morning. 'Sleep all right?'

'Yeah,' said Harry.

'I've b – b – been up all night,' she said, with another shuddering yawn. 'Come and sit down ...'

第 7 章

魔 法 部

第二天早晨五点半,哈利猛地一下完全清醒过来,就好像有人冲他耳朵里大喊了一声。他一动不动地躺在那里,慢慢地,要去魔法部受审的事充满了他大脑的每个细胞。他再也无法忍受了,就从床上跳下来,戴上了眼镜。韦斯莱夫人已经把洗熨一新的牛仔裤和 T 恤衫放在了他的床脚边。哈利摸索着穿上它们。墙上那幅空白的画布在咻咻发笑。

罗恩四肢舒展地仰面躺在床上,嘴巴张得大大的,睡得正香。哈利穿过房间,来到门外的楼梯平台上,反手把门轻轻关上,罗恩一直没有动弹。哈利竭力不去想当他下次再见到罗恩时,他们可能已经不再是霍格沃茨的同学了。他轻手轻脚地走下楼梯,经过克利切祖先的那些脑袋,来到下面的厨房里。

他本来以为厨房里没有人,可他刚走到门口,就听见门后传来低低的说话声。他推开门,看见韦斯莱先生、韦斯莱夫人、小天狼星、卢平和唐克斯都坐在那里,好像正在等他似的。他们都穿得整整齐齐,只有韦斯莱夫人穿的是一件紫色的夹晨衣。哈利一进去,她就立刻站了起来。

"吃早饭。"她一边说一边抽出魔杖,匆匆地朝火炉走去。

"早——早——早上好,哈利。"唐克斯打着哈欠说。今天早晨她的头发是金黄色的,打着卷儿。"睡得好吗?"

"挺好。"哈利说。

"我一夜没—没—没睡。"她说,又浑身颤抖着打了一个大哈欠,"过来坐下吧……"

CHAPTER SEVEN   The Ministry of Magic

She drew out a chair, knocking over the one beside it in the process.

'What do you want, Harry?' Mrs Weasley called. 'Porridge? Muffins? Kippers? Bacon and eggs? Toast?'

'Just – just toast, thanks,' said Harry.

Lupin glanced at Harry, then said to Tonks, 'What were you saying about Scrimgeour?'

'Oh ... yeah ... well, we need to be a bit more careful, he's been asking Kingsley and me funny questions ...'

Harry felt vaguely grateful that he was not required to join in the conversation. His insides were squirming. Mrs Weasley placed a couple of pieces of toast and marmalade in front of him; he tried to eat, but it was like chewing carpet. Mrs Weasley sat down on his other side and started fussing with his T-shirt, tucking in the label and smoothing out the creases across his shoulders. He wished she wouldn't.

'... and I'll have to tell Dumbledore I can't do night duty tomorrow, I'm just t – t – too tired,' Tonks finished, yawning hugely again.

'I'll cover for you,' said Mr Weasley. 'I'm OK, I've got a report to finish anyway ...'

Mr Weasley was not wearing wizards' robes but a pair of pinstriped trousers and an old bomber jacket. He turned from Tonks to Harry.

'How are you feeling?'

Harry shrugged.

'It'll all be over soon,' Mr Weasley said bracingly. 'In a few hours' time you'll be cleared.'

Harry said nothing.

'The hearing's on my floor, in Amelia Bones's office. She's Head of the Department of Magical Law Enforcement, and the one who'll be questioning you.'

'Amelia Bones is OK, Harry,' said Tonks earnestly. 'She's fair, she'll hear you out.'

Harry nodded, still unable to think of anything to say.

'Don't lose your temper,' said Sirius abruptly. 'Be polite and stick to the facts.'

Harry nodded again.

第7章 魔法部

她拖出一把椅子,结果把旁边一把椅子撞翻了。

"你想吃什么,哈利?"韦斯莱夫人大声问,"粥?松饼?熏鱼?熏咸肉和鸡蛋?面包?"

"就——就来面包好了,谢谢。"哈利说。

卢平看了一眼哈利,然后对唐克斯说:"你刚才说斯克林杰怎么啦?"

"哦……对了……是这样,我们需要更小心点儿了,他开始问我和金斯莱一些古怪的问题……"

他们没有要求哈利加入谈话,他感到松了口气。他心里一直局促不安。韦斯莱夫人把两片面包和橘子酱放在他面前,他费力地吃着,食不甘味。韦斯莱夫人在他的另一边坐了下来,开始格外细致地关心他的T恤衫,一会儿把标签塞进去,一会儿又把肩膀上的接缝抹平。哈利真希望她不要这么做。

"……我得跟邓布利多说说,我明天可不能再值夜班了,我太——太——太累啦。"唐克斯说着,又打了一个大大的哈欠。

"我来替你吧,"韦斯莱先生说,"我没事儿,反正要赶一份报告……"

韦斯莱先生没有穿巫师长袍,而是穿着一条细条纹裤子和一件旧的短夹克衫。他把目光从唐克斯身上转向哈利。

"你感觉怎么样?"

哈利耸了耸肩。

"很快就会结束的。"韦斯莱先生给他打气说,"再过几个小时,你就什么事儿都没有了。"

哈利什么也没说。

"受审地点就在我那层楼,在阿米莉亚·博恩斯的办公室。她是法律执行司的司长,到时候就由她来向你提问。"

"阿米莉亚·博恩斯挺好的,哈利,"唐克斯真心诚意地说,"她很公正,会听你把话说完的。"

哈利点点头,仍然想不出一句话来说。

"不要发脾气,"小天狼星突然说,"态度要彬彬有礼,实事求是。"

哈利又点点头。

CHAPTER SEVEN The Ministry of Magic

'The law's on your side,' said Lupin quietly. 'Even underage wizards are allowed to use magic in life-threatening situations.'

Something very cold trickled down the back of Harry's neck; for a moment he thought someone was putting a Disillusionment Charm on him, then he realised that Mrs Weasley was attacking his hair with a wet comb. She pressed hard on the top of his head.

'Doesn't it ever lie flat?' she said desperately.

Harry shook his head.

Mr Weasley checked his watch and looked up at Harry.

'I think we'll go now,' he said. 'We're a bit early, but I think you'll be better off at the Ministry than hanging around here.'

'OK,' said Harry automatically, dropping his toast and getting to his feet.

'You'll be all right, Harry,' said Tonks, patting him on the arm.

'Good luck,' said Lupin. 'I'm sure it will be fine.'

'And if it's not,' said Sirius grimly, 'I'll see to Amelia Bones for you ...'

Harry smiled weakly. Mrs Weasley hugged him.

'We've all got our fingers crossed,' she said.

'Right,' said Harry. 'Well ... see you later then.'

He followed Mr Weasley upstairs and along the hall. He could hear Sirius's mother grunting in her sleep behind her curtains. Mr Weasley unbolted the door and they stepped out into the cold, grey dawn.

'You don't normally walk to work, do you?' Harry asked him, as they set off briskly around the square.

'No, I usually Apparate,' said Mr Weasley, 'but obviously you can't, and I think it's best we arrive in a thoroughly non-magical fashion ... makes a better impression, given what you're being disciplined for ...'

Mr Weasley kept his hand inside his jacket as they walked. Harry knew it was clenched around his wand. The run-down streets were almost deserted, but when they arrived at the miserable little underground station they found it already full of early-morning commuters. As ever when he found himself in close proximity to Muggles going about their daily business, Mr Weasley was hard put to contain his enthusiasm.

'Simply fabulous,' he whispered, indicating the automatic ticket machines. 'Wonderfully ingenious.'

第7章 魔法部

"法律会支持你的。"卢平轻声说,"即使是未成年巫师,也应该允许在生命受到威胁的情况下使用魔法。"

一股凉飕飕的东西正顺着哈利的脖子后面往下淌,他一时还以为有人在给他施幻身咒,接着才发现是韦斯莱夫人在用一把湿梳子对付他的头发。她用力按压着他的头顶。

"它服帖下来过吗?"她绝望地说。

哈利摇了摇头。

韦斯莱先生看了看表,抬头望着哈利。

"我想我们现在就走吧,"他说,"稍微早了点儿,但我想你与其在这儿闲待着,还不如在魔法部等着呢。"

"好吧。"哈利机械地说,放下面包,站了起来。

"你不会有事的,哈利。"唐克斯说着拍了拍他的胳膊。

"祝你好运。"卢平说,"我相信一切都会很顺利的。"

"如果不是,"小天狼星沉着脸说,"我就替你去找阿米莉亚·博恩斯算账……"

哈利勉强笑了笑。韦斯莱夫人使劲拥抱了他一下。

"我们都交叉手指为你祈祷。"她说。

"好的,"哈利说,"那么……待会儿再见吧。"

他跟着韦斯莱先生上了楼,走过门厅。他可以听见帷幔后面小天狼星的母亲在睡梦中喃喃低语。韦斯莱先生拔掉门闩,两人出门来到外面。天刚刚破晓,天色灰蒙蒙的,带着寒意。

"你一般不是步行去上班的,对吗?"他们快步绕过广场时,哈利问他。

"对,我通常是幻影移形,"韦斯莱先生说,"但显然你不会,而且我们最好通过非魔法的方式去那里……给别人一个比较好的印象,要知道你受审是因为……"

韦斯莱先生走路时一只手插在夹克衫里,哈利知道那手里一定攥着魔杖。破败的街道上几乎一个人也没有,可是当他们走进寒酸的、不起眼的地铁车站时,发现里面已经挤满了早晨上班的乘客。韦斯莱先生难以抑制内心的浓厚兴趣,他每次发现自己与正在处理日常事务的麻瓜们近在咫尺时,都是这样。

"真是不可思议,"他小声说,指的是自动售票机,"太奇妙了。"

CHAPTER SEVEN   The Ministry of Magic

'They're out of order,' said Harry, pointing at the sign.

'Yes, but even so ...' said Mr Weasley, beaming at them fondly.

They bought their tickets instead from a sleepy-looking guard (Harry handled the transaction, as Mr Weasley was not very good with Muggle money) and five minutes later they were boarding an underground train that rattled them off towards the centre of London. Mr Weasley kept anxiously checking and rechecking the Underground Map above the windows.

'Four more stops, Harry ... Three stops left now ... Two stops to go, Harry ...'

They got off at a station in the very heart of London, and were swept from the train in a tide of besuited men and women carrying briefcases. Up the escalator they went, through the ticket barrier (Mr Weasley delighted with the way the stile swallowed his ticket), and emerged on to a broad street lined with imposing-looking buildings and already full of traffic.

'Where are we?' said Mr Weasley blankly, and for one heart-stopping moment Harry thought they had got off at the wrong station despite Mr Weasley's continual references to the map; but a second later he said, 'Ah yes ... this way, Harry,' and led him down a side road.

'Sorry,' he said, 'but I never come by train and it all looks rather different from a Muggle perspective. As a matter of fact, I've never even used the visitors' entrance before.'

The further they walked, the smaller and less imposing the buildings became, until finally they reached a street that contained several rather shabby-looking offices, a pub and an overflowing skip. Harry had expected a rather more impressive location for the Ministry of Magic.

'Here we are,' said Mr Weasley brightly, pointing at an old red telephone box, which was missing several panes of glass and stood before a heavily graffitied wall. 'After you, Harry.'

He opened the telephone-box door.

Harry stepped inside, wondering what on earth this was about. Mr Weasley folded himself in beside Harry and closed the door. It was a tight fit; Harry was jammed against the telephone apparatus, which was hanging crookedly from the wall as though a vandal had tried to rip it off. Mr Weasley reached past Harry for the receiver.

第 7 章 魔法部

"已经坏了。"哈利指着告示牌。

"是吗，但即使这样……"韦斯莱先生说，满心喜爱、笑眯眯地望着那些售票机。

他们还是从一个睡眼惺忪的管理员手里买了地铁票（这笔交易是哈利完成的，因为韦斯莱先生不太搞得清麻瓜的货币），五分钟后，他们登上了地铁。地铁载着他们哐当哐当地朝伦敦市中心驶去。韦斯莱先生紧张地一遍遍核对窗户上方的地铁路线图。

"还有四站，哈利……现在还有三站……还有两站，哈利……"

他们在伦敦市中心的一站下了车，人流如潮，他们被无数衣冠楚楚、提着公文包的男男女女推挤着出了地铁。他们上了自动扶梯，通过检票处（韦斯莱先生看到旋转栅门那样灵巧地吞下他的车票，显得非常高兴），来到一条宽阔的街道上，两边都是威严壮观的建筑物，街上已经是车水马龙。

"这是什么地方？"韦斯莱先生茫然地问。哈利以为，虽然韦斯莱先生那样频繁地核对地铁路线图，他们还是下错了车站，顿时吓得心脏都停止了跳动。可是紧接着韦斯莱先生又说："啊，对了……这边走，哈利。"转身领着哈利拐进了一条岔道。

"对不起，"他说，"我从没有乘地铁来过，而且用麻瓜的眼光看起来，一切完全不同。说实在的，我以前一次也没有使用过来宾入口。"

他们往前走着，街道两边的建筑物渐渐不像刚才那样威严壮观了。最后来到一条凄凉的小街上，只有几间看上去破破烂烂的办公室、一家小酒馆和一个满得快要溢出来的垃圾转运箱。哈利原以为魔法部是在一个气派得多的地方呢。

"到了。"韦斯莱先生高兴地说，指着一间破旧的红色电话亭——上面好几块玻璃都不见了，后面紧贴着一堵被涂抹得一塌糊涂的墙，"你先进去，哈利。"

他打开电话亭的门。

哈利走了进去，心里纳闷这到底是怎么回事。韦斯莱先生挤进来站在哈利身边，反手把门关上了。里面真挤，哈利被挤得贴在了电话设备上。那电话歪歪斜斜地从墙上挂下来，似乎曾经有个破坏公物的家伙想用力把它扯掉。韦斯莱先生隔着哈利，伸手拿起了话筒。

CHAPTER SEVEN The Ministry of Magic

'Mr Weasley, I think this might be out of order, too,' Harry said.

'No, no, I'm sure it's fine,' said Mr Weasley, holding the receiver above his head and peering at the dial. 'Let's see ... six ...' he dialled the number, 'two ... four ... and another four ... and another two ...'

As the dial whirred smoothly back into place, a cool female voice sounded inside the telephone box, not from the receiver in Mr Weasley's hand, but as loudly and plainly as though an invisible woman were standing right beside them.

'Welcome to the Ministry of Magic. Please state your name and business.'

'Er ...' said Mr Weasley, clearly uncertain whether or not he should talk into the receiver. He compromised by holding the mouthpiece to his ear, 'Arthur Weasley, Misuse of Muggle Artefacts Office, here to escort Harry Potter, who has been asked to attend a disciplinary hearing ...'

'Thank you,' said the cool female voice. 'Visitor, please take the badge and attach it to the front of your robes.'

There was a click and a rattle, and Harry saw something slide out of the metal chute where returned coins usually appeared. He picked it up: it was a square silver badge with *Harry Potter, Disciplinary Hearing* on it. He pinned it to the front of his T-shirt as the female voice spoke again.

'Visitor to the Ministry, you are required to submit to a search and present your wand for registration at the security desk, which is located at the far end of the Atrium.'

The floor of the telephone box shuddered. They were sinking slowly into the ground. Harry watched apprehensively as the pavement seemed to rise up past the glass windows of the telephone box until darkness closed over their heads. Then he could see nothing at all; he could hear only a dull grinding noise as the telephone box made its way down through the earth. After about a minute, though it felt much longer to Harry, a chink of golden light illuminated his feet and, widening, rose up his body, until it hit him in the face and he had to blink to stop his eyes watering.

'The Ministry of Magic wishes you a pleasant day,' said the woman's voice.

The door of the telephone box sprang open and Mr Weasley stepped out of it, followed by Harry, whose mouth had fallen open.

They were standing at one end of a very long and splendid hall with a highly polished, dark wood floor. The peacock blue ceiling was inlaid with gleaming

第7章 魔法部

"韦斯莱先生,我想这电话可能也坏了。"哈利说。

"不,没有,我相信它没有坏。"韦斯莱先生说着把话筒举过头顶,眼睛望着拨号盘,"让我想想……6……"他拨了这个号码,"2……4……又是一个4……又是一个2……"

随着拨号盘呼呼地转回到原来的位置,电话亭里响起了一个女人冷漠的声音,但那声音并不是从韦斯莱先生拿着的话筒里传出来的,它响亮而清晰,仿佛一个看不见的女人就站在他们身边。

"欢迎来到魔法部,请说出您的姓名和来办事宜。"

"呃……"韦斯莱先生说,显然拿不准是不是应该对着话筒说话。最后他做了让步,把送话口贴在了耳朵上,"亚瑟·韦斯莱,禁止滥用麻瓜物品办公室,是陪哈利·波特来的,部里要求他来受审……"

"谢谢,"那个女人冷漠的声音说,"来宾,请拿起徽章,别在您的衣服前。"

丁零零,哗啦啦,哈利看见什么东西从平常用来退硬币的金属斜槽里滑了出来。他把它拿了起来:是一枚方方正正的银色徽章,上面写着:哈利·波特,受审。他把徽章别在T恤衫前,那个女人的声音又响了起来。

"魔法部的来宾,您需要在安检台接受检查,并登记您的魔杖。安检台位于正厅的尽头。"

电话亭的地面突然颤抖起来。他们慢慢沉入了地下。哈利惊恐地看着电话亭玻璃窗外的人行道越升越高,最后他们头顶上一片黑暗。他什么也看不见了,只能听见电话亭陷入地下时发出的单调、刺耳的摩擦声。过了大约一分钟,但哈利感觉要长得多,一道细细的金光照到他的脚面,随后金光逐渐变宽,扩大到他的身体上,最后直射他的面孔,他不得不使劲眨眼睛,以免眼泪流出来。

"魔法部希望您今天过得愉快。"那个女人的声音说。

电话亭的门猛地打开了,韦斯莱先生走了出去,哈利跟在后面,惊讶得嘴巴都合不拢了。

他们站在一个很长的金碧辉煌的大厅一头,地上是擦得光亮鉴人的深色木地板。孔雀蓝的天花板上镶嵌着闪闪发光的金色符号,不停

CHAPTER SEVEN   The Ministry of Magic

golden symbols that kept moving and changing like some enormous heavenly noticeboard. The walls on each side were panelled in shiny dark wood and had many gilded fireplaces set into them. Every few seconds a witch or wizard would emerge from one of the left-hand fireplaces with a soft *whoosh*. On the right-hand side, short queues were forming before each fireplace, waiting to depart.

Halfway down the hall was a fountain. A group of golden statues, larger than life-size, stood in the middle of a circular pool. Tallest of them all was a noble-looking wizard with his wand pointing straight up in the air. Grouped around him were a beautiful witch, a centaur, a goblin and a house-elf. The last three were all looking adoringly up at the witch and wizard. Glittering jets of water were flying from the ends of their wands, the point of the centaur's arrow, the tip of the goblin's hat and each of the house-elf's ears, so that the tinkling hiss of falling water was added to the *pops* and *cracks* of the Apparators and the clatter of footsteps as hundreds of witches and wizards, most of whom were wearing glum, early-morning looks, strode towards a set of golden gates at the far end of the hall.

'This way,' said Mr Weasley.

They joined the throng, wending their way between the Ministry workers, some of whom were carrying tottering piles of parchment, others battered briefcases; still others were reading the *Daily Prophet* while they walked. As they passed the fountain Harry saw silver Sickles and bronze Knuts glinting up at him from the bottom of the pool. A small smudged sign beside it read:

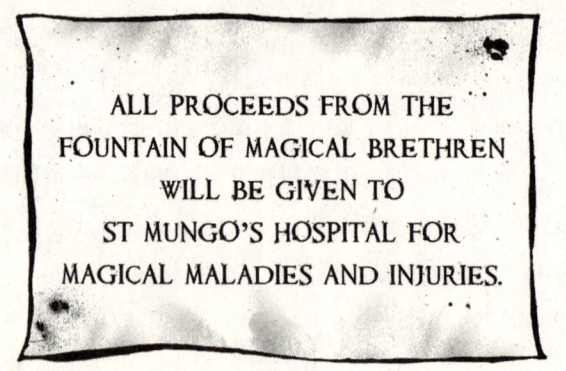

> ALL PROCEEDS FROM THE
> FOUNTAIN OF MAGICAL BRETHREN
> WILL BE GIVEN TO
> ST MUNGO'S HOSPITAL FOR
> MAGICAL MALADIES AND INJURIES.

If I'm not expelled from Hogwarts, I'll put in ten Galleons, Harry found himself thinking desperately.

'Over here, Harry,' said Mr Weasley, and they stepped out of the stream

第7章 魔法部

地活动着、变化着,像是一个巨大的高空布告栏。两旁的墙壁都镶着乌黑油亮的深色木板,木板里嵌着许多镀金的壁炉。每过几秒钟,随着噗的一声轻响,就有一个巫师从左边某个壁炉里突然冒出来。而在右边,每个壁炉前都有几个人在排队等着离开。

门厅中间是一个喷泉。一个圆形的水潭中间竖立着一组纯金雕像,比真人还大。其中最高的是一个气质高贵的男巫,高举着魔杖,直指天空。他周围是一个美丽的女巫、一个马人、一个妖精和一个家养小精灵。马人、妖精和家养小精灵都无限崇拜地抬头望着两个巫师。一道道闪亮的水柱从巫师的魔杖顶端,从马人的箭头上,从妖精的帽子尖,从家养小精灵的两只耳朵里喷射出来。四下里有叮咚叮咚、哗啦哗啦的水声,有幻影显形的人发出的噗、啪的声音,还有几百个男女巫师杂乱的脚步声。他们大多脸上挂着早晨特有的死气沉沉的表情,大步流星地朝门厅那头的一排金色大门走去。

"这边走。"韦斯莱先生说。

他们加入了人群,挤在魔法部工作人员中间往前走。他们有些人怀里抱着一堆堆摇摇欲坠的羊皮纸,有些人提着破破烂烂的公文包,还有些人边走边读《预言家日报》。经过喷泉时,哈利看见水潭底部有许多闪闪发光的银西可和铜纳特,旁边一个污迹斑斑的小牌子上写着:

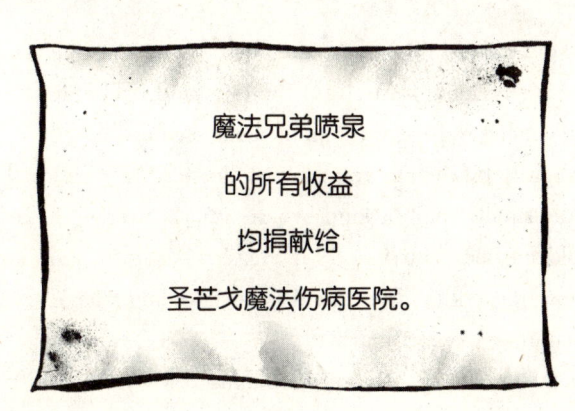

> 魔法兄弟喷泉
>
> 的所有收益
>
> 均捐献给
>
> 圣芒戈魔法伤病医院。

如果不把我从霍格沃茨开除,我就放十个加隆进去,哈利发现自己这样绝望地想道。

"这边走,哈利。"韦斯莱先生说,他们离开了那些朝金色大门走

CHAPTER SEVEN   The Ministry of Magic

of Ministry employees heading for the golden gates. Seated at a desk to the left, beneath a sign saying *Security*, a badly-shaven wizard in peacock blue robes looked up as they approached and put down his *Daily Prophet*.

'I'm escorting a visitor,' said Mr Weasley, gesturing towards Harry.

'Step over here,' said the wizard in a bored voice.

Harry walked closer to him and the wizard held up a long golden rod, thin and flexible as a car aerial, and passed it up and down Harry's front and back.

'Wand,' grunted the security wizard at Harry, putting down the golden instrument and holding out his hand.

Harry produced his wand. The wizard dropped it on to a strange brass instrument, which looked something like a set of scales with only one dish. It began to vibrate. A narrow strip of parchment came speeding out of a slit in the base. The wizard tore this off and read the writing on it.

'Eleven inches, phoenix-feather core, been in use four years. That correct?'

'Yes,' said Harry nervously.

'I keep this,' said the wizard, impaling the slip of parchment on a small brass spike. 'You get this back,' he added, thrusting the wand at Harry.

'Thank you.'

'Hang on ...' said the wizard slowly.

His eyes had darted from the silver visitor's badge on Harry's chest to his forehead.

'Thank you, Eric,' said Mr Weasley firmly, and grasping Harry by the shoulder he steered him away from the desk and back into the stream of wizards and witches walking through the golden gates.

Jostled slightly by the crowd, Harry followed Mr Weasley through the gates into the smaller hall beyond, where at least twenty lifts stood behind wrought golden grilles. Harry and Mr Weasley joined the crowd around one of them. Nearby, stood a big bearded wizard holding a large cardboard box which was emitting rasping noises.

'All right, Arthur?' said the wizard, nodding at Mr Weasley.

'What've you got there, Bob?' asked Mr Weasley, looking at the box.

'We're not sure,' said the wizard seriously. 'We thought it was a bog-standard chicken until it started breathing fire. Looks like a serious breach of the Ban on Experimental Breeding to me.'

第7章 魔法部

去的魔法部职员的人流。在左边的一张桌子旁,在一个写着安全检查的牌子下,坐着一个穿孔雀蓝长袍、胡子刮得很不干净的巫师。他们走近时,他抬起头,放下了手里的《预言家日报》。

"我带了一位来宾。"韦斯莱先生说着指了指哈利。

"到这边来。"那巫师用没精打采的口吻说。

哈利走近他面前,巫师举起一根长长的金棒,像汽车的天线一样细细的,很有韧性,他用它在哈利的前胸后背从上到下扫了一遍。

"魔杖。"安检巫师朝哈利嘟哝了一声,放下那个金色的玩意儿,伸出手来。

哈利把魔杖交了出去。巫师把它扔在一个怪模怪样的、像是一个单盘天平的黄铜机器上。机器开始微微振动。一条窄窄的羊皮纸从底部的一道口子里飞快地吐了出来。巫师把纸扯了下来,读着上面的字。

"十一英寸,杖芯是凤凰羽毛,用了四年。对吗?"

"没错。"哈利紧张不安地说。

"这个我留着,"巫师说着把那张羊皮纸条戳在一根小小的黄铜钉子上,"你把这个拿回去。"他把魔杖塞进了哈利手里。

"谢谢。"

"等一等……"巫师慢吞吞地说。

他的目光从哈利胸前的银色来宾徽章移向了哈利的额头。

"谢谢你,埃里克。"韦斯莱先生果断地说,一把抓住哈利的肩膀,带着他离开了桌子,回到走向金色大门的巫师人潮中。

哈利被人群推挤着,跟韦斯莱先生穿过大门,来到那边一个较小的大厅里。那儿至少有二十部升降梯,被精制的金色栅栏门挡着。哈利和韦斯莱先生走到围在一部升降梯前的人群中。旁边站着一个胡子拉碴的大个子巫师,怀里抱着一个大纸板箱,里面发出刺耳的摩擦声。

"还好吧,亚瑟?"巫师说着冲韦斯莱先生点了点头。

"你那里头是什么东西,鲍勃?"韦斯莱先生望着那纸板箱问道。

"还不能肯定。"巫师一本正经地说,"我们原以为是一只普普通通的鸡,没想到它喷出火来了。在我看来,这似乎严重违反了《禁止为实验目的而饲养》。"

CHAPTER SEVEN   The Ministry of Magic

With a great jangling and clattering a lift descended in front of them; the golden grille slid back and Harry and Mr Weasley stepped into the lift with the rest of the crowd and Harry found himself jammed against the back wall. Several witches and wizards were looking at him curiously; he stared at his feet to avoid catching anyone's eye, flattening his fringe as he did so. The grilles slid shut with a crash and the lift ascended slowly, chains rattling, while the same cool female voice Harry had heard in the telephone box rang out again.

'Level Seven, Department of Magical Games and Sports, incorporating the British and Irish Quidditch League Headquarters, Official Gobstones Club and Ludicrous Patents Office.'

The lift doors opened. Harry glimpsed an untidy-looking corridor, with various posters of Quidditch teams tacked lopsidedly on the walls. One of the wizards in the lift, who was carrying an armful of broomsticks, extricated himself with difficulty and disappeared down the corridor. The doors closed, the lift juddered upwards again and the woman's voice announced:

'Level Six, Department of Magical Transportation, incorporating the Floo Network Authority, Broom Regulatory Control, Portkey Office and Apparition Test Centre.'

Once again the lift doors opened and four or five witches and wizards got out; at the same time, several paper aeroplanes swooped into the lift. Harry stared up at them as they flapped idly around above his head; they were a pale violet colour and he could see *Ministry of Magic* stamped along the edge of their wings.

'Just inter-departmental memos,' Mr Weasley muttered to him. 'We used to use owls, but the mess was unbelievable ... droppings all over the desks ...'

As they clattered upwards again the memos flapped around the lamp swaying from the lift's ceiling.

'Level Five, Department of International Magical Co-operation, incorporating the International Magical Trading Standards Body, the International Magical Office of Law and the International Confederation of Wizards, British Seats.'

When the doors opened, two of the memos zoomed out with a few more of the witches and wizards, but several more memos zoomed in, so that the light from the lamp flickered and flashed overhead as they darted around it.

'Level Four, Department for the Regulation and Control of Magical

第7章 魔法部

随着叮叮当当、咔啦咔啦的一阵响动，一部升降梯降落到他们面前。金色的栅栏门轻轻滑开，哈利和韦斯莱先生与那伙人一起走进升降梯，哈利发现自己被挤得贴在了后面的墙上。几个巫师好奇地打量着他。他低头望着脚尖，避免与别人目光相对，一边用手抹平额前的头发。栅栏门哗啦一声关上了，升降梯慢慢上升，链条咔啦啦作响，哈利在电话亭里听见过的那个冷漠的女声又响了起来。

"第七层，魔法体育运动司，包括不列颠和爱尔兰魁地奇联盟指挥部、官方高布石俱乐部和滑稽产品专利办公室。"

升降梯的门开了，哈利瞥见了一条杂乱无章的走廊，墙上东倒西歪地贴着各种各样的魁地奇球队的海报。升降梯里一位抱着满怀飞天扫帚的巫师费力地挤了出去，在走廊上消失了。门关上了，升降梯微微晃动着继续上升，那女人的声音宣布道：

"第六层，魔法交通司，包括飞路网管理局、飞天扫帚管理控制局、门钥匙办公室和幻影显形测试中心。"

升降梯的门又一次被打开，四五个巫师走了出去。与此同时，几架纸飞机嗖嗖地飞进了升降梯。哈利抬头注视着它们绕着他的头顶慢悠悠地飞，它们的颜色是一种浅紫色，哈利还看见机翼边上盖着魔法部的戳记。

"那是部门之间传递消息的字条。"韦斯莱先生低声告诉他，"以前用的是猫头鹰，可是那种脏乱简直不可思议……办公桌上到处都是粪便……"

升降梯又咔啦咔啦地往上升了，那些字条围着从升降梯天花板上悬挂下来的那盏灯飞舞。

"第五层，国际魔法合作司，包括国际魔法贸易标准协会、国际魔法法律办公室和国际巫师联合会英国分会。"

门开了，两张字条随着几个巫师嗖嗖地飞了出去，但又有几张字条嗖嗖地飞了进来，绕着他们头顶的那盏灯飞来飞去，弄得灯光闪烁不定。

"第四层，神奇动物管理控制司，包括野兽、异类和幽灵办公室、

CHAPTER SEVEN   The Ministry of Magic

Creatures, incorporating Beast, Being and Spirit Divisions, Goblin Liaison Office and Pest Advisory Bureau.'

''S'cuse,' said the wizard carrying the fire-breathing chicken and he left the lift pursued by a little flock of memos. The doors clanged shut yet again.

'Level Three, Department of Magical Accidents and Catastrophes, including the Accidental Magic Reversal Squad, Obliviator Headquarters and Muggle-Worthy Excuse Committee.'

Everybody left the lift on this floor except Mr Weasley, Harry and a witch who was reading an extremely long piece of parchment that was trailing on the floor. The remaining memos continued to soar around the lamp as the lift juddered upwards again, then the doors opened and the voice made its announcement.

'Level Two, Department of Magical Law Enforcement, including the Improper Use of Magic Office, Auror Headquarters and Wizengamot Administration Services.'

'This is us, Harry,' said Mr Weasley, and they followed the witch out of the lift into a corridor lined with doors. 'My office is on the other side of the floor.'

'Mr Weasley,' said Harry, as they passed a window through which sunlight was streaming, 'aren't we still underground?'

'Yes, we are,' said Mr Weasley. 'Those are enchanted windows. Magical Maintenance decide what weather we'll get every day. We had two months of hurricanes last time they were angling for a pay rise ... Just round here, Harry.'

They turned a corner, walked through a pair of heavy oak doors and emerged in a cluttered open area divided into cubicles, which was buzzing with talk and laughter. Memos were zooming in and out of cubicles like miniature rockets. A lopsided sign on the nearest cubicle read: *Auror Headquarters*.

Harry looked surreptitiously through the doorways as they passed. The Aurors had covered their cubicle walls with everything from pictures of wanted wizards and photographs of their families, to posters of their favourite Quidditch teams and articles from the *Daily Prophet*. A scarlet-robed man with a ponytail longer than Bill's was sitting with his boots up on his desk, dictating a report to his quill. A little further along, a witch with a patch over one eye was talking over the top of her cubicle wall to Kingsley Shacklebolt.

'Morning, Weasley,' said Kingsley carelessly, as they drew nearer. 'I've

第 7 章 魔法部

妖精联络处和害虫咨询处。"

"对不起，请让一下。"捧着喷火鸡的巫师说。他走出了升降梯，一小群字条跟着飞了出去。升降梯的门又哐啷啷关上了。

"第三层，魔法事故和灾害司，包括逆转偶发魔法事件小组、记忆注销指挥部和麻瓜问题调解委员会。"

到了这一层，几乎所有的人都出去了，升降梯里只剩韦斯莱先生、哈利和一个女巫。那个女巫正在读一张长得要命、一直拖到地上的羊皮纸。升降梯再次微微摇晃着往上走，剩下的几张字条继续围着灯打转，然后门开了，那个声音宣布道：

"第二层，魔法法律执行司，包括禁止滥用魔法办公室、傲罗指挥部和威森加摩管理机构。"

"我们到了，哈利，"韦斯莱先生说，他们跟着那女巫走出了升降梯，来到一条两边都是房门的走廊上，"我的办公室在这层楼的另一边。"

"韦斯莱先生，"他们走过一个窗户，明亮的阳光洒了进来，哈利问道，"我们不是还在地底下吗？"

"是啊，没错。"韦斯莱先生说，"这些是施了魔法的窗户。魔法维修保养处决定我们每天是什么天气。上次我们这里刮了两个月的飓风，因为他们想涨工资……转过弯就是，哈利。"

他们转过一个拐角，穿过两扇沉重的橡木大门，进入了一片凌乱嘈杂、被分成许多小隔间的开放区域，里面谈笑风生，热闹异常。传递消息的字条从小隔间里飞进飞出，像一枚枚微型火箭。最近的一个小隔间上歪歪斜斜地挂着一个牌子：傲罗指挥部。

他们走过时，哈利偷偷朝门里望了望。傲罗们在他们小隔间的墙上贴满了东西，从被通缉的巫师的头像，到他们家人的照片，再到他们喜欢的魁地奇球队的海报，还有《预言家日报》上剪下来的文章，真是五花八门，包罗万象。一个穿深红色长袍的男人，脑袋后面的马尾辫比比尔的还长，他把靴子高高地跷在桌子上，正在给他的羽毛笔口授一篇报告。再往前走一点，一位一只眼睛蒙着眼罩的女巫正隔着小隔间的挡板跟金斯莱·沙克尔说话。

"早上好，韦斯莱，"看到他们走进来，金斯莱大大咧咧地说，"我

CHAPTER SEVEN   The Ministry of Magic

been wanting a word with you, have you got a second?'

'Yes, if it really is a second,' said Mr Weasley, 'I'm in rather a hurry.'

They were talking as though they hardly knew each other and when Harry opened his mouth to say hello to Kingsley, Mr Weasley stood on his foot. They followed Kingsley along the row and into the very last cubicle.

Harry received a slight shock; blinking down at him from every direction was Sirius's face. Newspaper cuttings and old photographs – even the one of Sirius being best man at the Potters' wedding – papered the walls. The only Sirius-free space was a map of the world in which little red pins were glowing like jewels.

'Here,' said Kingsley brusquely to Mr Weasley, shoving a sheaf of parchment into his hand. 'I need as much information as possible on flying Muggle vehicles sighted in the last twelve months. We've received information that Black might still be using his old motorcycle.'

Kingsley tipped Harry an enormous wink and added, in a whisper, 'Give him the magazine, he might find it interesting.' Then he said in normal tones, 'And don't take too long, Weasley, the delay on that firelegs report held our investigation up for a month.'

'If you had read my report you would know that the term is *firearms*,' said Mr Weasley coolly. 'And I'm afraid you'll have to wait for information on motorcycles; we're extremely busy at the moment.' He dropped his voice and said, 'If you can get away before seven, Molly's making meatballs.'

He beckoned to Harry and led him out of Kingsley's cubicle, through a second set of oak doors, into another passage, turned left, marched along another corridor, turned right into a dimly lit and distinctly shabby corridor, and finally reached a dead end, where a door on the left stood ajar, revealing a broom cupboard, and a door on the right bore a tarnished brass plaque reading: *Misuse of Muggle Artefacts*.

Mr Weasley's dingy office seemed to be slightly smaller than the broom cupboard. Two desks had been crammed inside it and there was barely space to move around them because of all the overflowing filing cabinets lining the walls, on top of which were tottering piles of files. The little wall space available bore witness to Mr Weasley's obsessions: several posters of cars, including one of a dismantled engine; two illustrations of postboxes he

第 7 章 魔法部

一直想跟你说一句话,你能给我一秒钟时间吗?"

"行啊,如果真是一秒钟的话,"韦斯莱先生说,"我现在很忙。"

他们像是互相不怎么熟悉似的谈起话来,哈利张嘴刚想向金斯莱问好,韦斯莱先生踩了一下他的脚。他们跟着金斯莱走过一排小隔间,走进了最尽头的一个小隔间。

哈利微微吃了一惊。从四面八方朝他眨巴眼睛的正是小天狼星的脸。挡板上密密麻麻地贴着剪报和旧照片——包括小天狼星在波特婚礼上当伴郎的那张。只有一块地方没被小天狼星遮住,那里贴着一张世界地图,上面的一个个小红图钉像宝石一样闪闪发亮。

"给。"金斯莱生硬地对韦斯莱先生说,把一卷羊皮纸塞进了他手里,"关于最近十二个月有人看见麻瓜交通工具在天上飞的事,我需要尽可能多地了解情况。我们接到情报,布莱克可能仍在使用他那辆旧摩托车。"

金斯莱朝哈利使劲眨了一下眼睛,压低声音说:"把这份杂志给他,他大概会觉得很有趣的。"然后他又用正常的声音说,"拖的时间不要太长,韦斯莱,那份闪光腿的报告交迟了,害得我们的调查耽搁了一个月。"

"你如果读过我的报告,就会知道那个词是闪光臂。"韦斯莱先生冷冷地说,"恐怕你关于摩托车的情报要等一等了,我们目前忙得要命。"他又压低声音说道:"你争取在七点钟前离开,莫丽在做肉丸子呢。"

他朝哈利示意,领着他走出金斯莱的小隔间,穿过第二道橡木大门,走进另一条过道,然后向左一拐,来到另一条走廊上,再往右一拐,走进一条光线昏暗、破旧不堪的走廊,最后来到走廊尽头,再也不能往前走了。左边有一扇门微微开了道缝,可以看出里面是一个扫帚间,右边的门上有个褪色的黄铜标牌:禁止滥用麻瓜物品办公室。

韦斯莱先生的办公室昏暗寒酸,似乎比扫帚间还要略小一些。两张桌子挤在里面,周围沿墙排着满得都快溢出来的文件柜,柜顶上还堆着一包包摇摇欲坠的文件,简直逼仄得连绕过桌子的空间都没有。从墙上仅有的一点点能够利用的空间,可以看出韦斯莱先生情有独钟的东西:几张汽车广告,其中一张画着拆开的发动机;两张信箱的插

seemed to have cut out of Muggle children's books; and a diagram showing how to wire a plug.

Sitting on top of Mr Weasley's overflowing in-tray was an old toaster that was hiccoughing in a disconsolate way and a pair of empty leather gloves that were twiddling their thumbs. A photograph of the Weasley family stood beside the in-tray. Harry noticed that Percy appeared to have walked out of it.

'We haven't got a window,' said Mr Weasley apologetically, taking off his bomber jacket and placing it on the back of his chair. 'We've asked, but they don't seem to think we need one. Have a seat, Harry, doesn't look as if Perkins is in yet.'

Harry squeezed himself into the chair behind Perkins's desk while Mr Weasley riffled through the sheaf of parchment Kingsley Shacklebolt had given him.

'Ah,' he said, grinning, as he extracted a copy of a magazine entitled *The Quibbler* from its midst, 'yes ...' He flicked through it. 'Yes, he's right, I'm sure Sirius will find that very amusing – oh dear, what's this now?'

A memo had just zoomed in through the open door and fluttered to rest on top of the hiccoughing toaster. Mr Weasley unfolded it and read it aloud.

'"Third regurgitating public toilet reported in Bethnal Green, kindly investigate immediately." This is getting ridiculous ...'

'A regurgitating toilet?'

'Anti-Muggle pranksters,' said Mr Weasley, frowning. 'We had two last week, one in Wimbledon, one in Elephant and Castle. Muggles are pulling the flush and instead of everything disappearing – well, you can imagine. The poor things keep calling in those – *pumbles*, I think they're called – you know, the ones who mend pipes and things.'

'Plumbers?'

'Exactly, yes, but of course they're flummoxed. I only hope we can catch whoever's doing it.'

'Will it be Aurors who catch them?'

'Oh no, this is too trivial for Aurors, it'll be the ordinary Magical Law Enforcement Patrol – ah, Harry, this is Perkins.'

图画,看样子是他从麻瓜儿童图书上剪下来的;还有一张如何安装插座的示意图。

韦斯莱先生的收文篮里满满当当,位于最上面的是个旧的烤面包机,正在闷闷不乐地打嗝,此外还有两只空空的皮手套,正在摆弄着两个大拇指。收文篮旁边是一张韦斯莱全家福照片,哈利注意到珀西似乎已从照片上走了出去。

"这里没有窗户。"韦斯莱先生抱歉地说,一边脱下短夹克衫搭在椅子背上,"我们提出过要求,但他们似乎认为我们并不需要。坐下吧,哈利,看样子珀金斯还没有来。"

哈利勉强挤进珀金斯办公桌后的那把椅子,这时韦斯莱先生飞快地翻查着金斯莱·沙克尔刚才给他的那卷羊皮纸。

"啊,"他咧嘴笑着说,从羊皮纸中间抽出一本名为唱唱反调的杂志,"是的……"他草草地翻看着,"是的,他说得没错,我敢肯定小天狼星会觉得非常有意思——哦,天哪,这又是怎么啦?"

一张字条嗖地飞进了敞开的门,慢悠悠地落在那个不断打嗝的烤面包机上。韦斯莱先生打开字条,大声念道:

"据报告,在贝斯纳绿地发生了第三例公共厕所污水回涌事件,请火速前去调查。这可真是见鬼了……"

"厕所污水回涌?"

"反麻瓜的恶作剧分子干的,"韦斯莱先生皱着眉头说,"上个星期就有过两次,一次是在温布尔顿,另一次是在象堡。麻瓜一冲厕所,脏东西不仅没消失——哎,你自己想象一下吧。可怜的人们不停地叫那些——管子人,我想他们是这么说的吧——你知道的,就是那些修理管子之类东西的人。"

"管道工?"

"对啦,就是这个,但是当然啦,他们也毫无办法。我只希望我们能抓住干这种勾当的人。"

"傲罗不会去抓他们吗?"

"噢,不,这种区区小事不需要傲罗出动,普通的魔法法律执行巡逻队就能对付——啊,哈利,这位是珀金斯。"

CHAPTER SEVEN The Ministry of Magic

A stooped, timid-looking old wizard with fluffy white hair had just entered the room, panting.

'Oh, Arthur!' he said desperately, without looking at Harry. 'Thank goodness, I didn't know what to do for the best, whether to wait here for you or not. I've just sent an owl to your home but you've obviously missed it – an urgent message came ten minutes ago –'

'I know about the regurgitating toilet,' said Mr Weasley.

'No, no, it's not the toilet, it's the Potter boy's hearing – they've changed the time and venue – it starts at eight o'clock now and it's down in old Courtroom Ten –'

'Down in old – but they told me – Merlin's beard!'

Mr Weasley looked at his watch, let out a yelp and leapt from his chair.

'Quick, Harry, we should have been there five minutes ago!'

Perkins flattened himself against the filing cabinets as Mr Weasley left the office at a run, Harry close on his heels.

'Why have they changed the time?' Harry said breathlessly, as they hurtled past the Auror cubicles; people poked out their heads and stared as they streaked past. Harry felt as though he'd left all his insides back at Perkins's desk.

'I've no idea, but thank goodness we got here so early, if you'd missed it, it would have been catastrophic!'

Mr Weasley skidded to a halt beside the lifts and jabbed impatiently at the 'down' button.

'Come ON!'

The lift clattered into view and they hurried inside. Every time it stopped Mr Weasley cursed furiously and pummelled the number nine button.

'Those courtrooms haven't been used in years,' said Mr Weasley angrily. 'I can't think why they're doing it down there – unless – but no –'

A plump witch carrying a smoking goblet entered the lift at that moment, and Mr Weasley did not elaborate.

'The Atrium,' said the cool female voice and the golden grilles slid open, showing Harry a distant glimpse of the golden statues in the fountain. The plump witch got out and a sallow-skinned wizard with a very mournful face got in.

'Morning, Arthur,' he said in a sepulchral voice as the lift began to

第7章 魔法部

一个弯腰驼背、神情有些腼腆、一头松软的花白头发的老巫师微微喘着粗气走进了房间。

"啊,亚瑟!"他没有看哈利,只是着急地说道,"谢天谢地,我本来正发愁该怎么办才好呢,不知道要不要在这里等你们。我刚才打发一只猫头鹰给你家里送信,但你显然没有收到——十分钟前来了一条紧急消息——"

"厕所污水回涌的事我已经知道了。"韦斯莱先生说。

"不,不,不是厕所,是波特那孩子受审的事——他们把时间、地点给改了——改成了八点钟在下面那间旧的第十审判室——"

"在下面那间——可是他们告诉我说——梅林的胡子啊!"

韦斯莱先生看了看表,惊呼一声,从椅子上一跃而起。

"快点儿,哈利,我们应该五分钟前就到那里的!"

珀金斯把身体贴在文件柜上让出道来,韦斯莱先生飞跑出办公室,哈利紧跟在后面。

"他们为什么要改时间呢?"哈利气喘吁吁地问。他们一溜烟地跑过傲罗的那些小隔间,人们纷纷探出头来,惊讶地望着他们飞奔而过。哈利觉得他似乎把五脏六腑都留在珀金斯的办公桌后面了。

"真不明白,幸亏我们这么早就来了。如果你错过了,可就大祸临头了!"

韦斯莱先生在升降梯旁刹住脚步,不耐烦地敲打着"向下"的按钮。

"**快点儿!**"

升降梯咔啦咔啦地出现了,他们闪身进了升降梯。每次升降梯一停,韦斯莱先生都要气愤地咒骂几句,并用拳头使劲击打着九层的按钮。

"那些审判室已经好多年没有使用了,"韦斯莱先生气呼呼地说,"我真不明白他们为什么要选择在那里——除非——不,不会——"

这个时候,一个胖胖的女巫端着一只冒烟的高脚酒杯走进了升降梯,韦斯莱先生便住了嘴。

"正厅。"那个冷冷的女声说道,金色的栅栏门滑开了,哈利远远地看见喷泉中的那几尊黄金雕像。胖胖的女巫走了出去,一个满面菜色的巫师愁眉苦脸地走了进来。

"早上好,亚瑟,"升降梯开始下降时,他用忧郁低沉的声音说,"最

CHAPTER SEVEN   The Ministry of Magic

descend. 'Don't often see you down here.'

'Urgent business, Bode,' said Mr Weasley, who was bouncing on the balls of his feet and throwing anxious looks over at Harry.

'Ah, yes,' said Bode, surveying Harry unblinkingly. 'Of course.'

Harry barely had emotion to spare for Bode, but his unfaltering gaze did not make him feel any more comfortable.

'Department of Mysteries,' said the cool female voice, and left it at that.

'Quick, Harry,' said Mr Weasley as the lift doors rattled open, and they sped up a corridor that was quite different from those above. The walls were bare; there were no windows and no doors apart from a plain black one set at the very end of the corridor. Harry expected them to go through it, but instead Mr Weasley seized him by the arm and dragged him to the left, where there was an opening leading to a flight of steps.

'Down here, down here,' panted Mr Weasley, taking two steps at a time. 'The lift doesn't even come down this far ... *why* they're doing it down there I ...'

They reached the bottom of the steps and ran along yet another corridor, which bore a great resemblance to the one that led to Snape's dungeon at Hogwarts, with rough stone walls and torches in brackets. The doors they passed here were heavy wooden ones with iron bolts and keyholes.

'Courtroom ... Ten ... I think ... we're nearly ... yes.'

Mr Weasley stumbled to a halt outside a grimy dark door with an immense iron lock and slumped against the wall, clutching at a stitch in his chest.

'Go on,' he panted, pointing his thumb at the door. 'Get in there.'

'Aren't – aren't you coming with –?'

'No, no, I'm not allowed. Good luck!'

Harry's heart was beating a violent tattoo against his Adam's apple. He swallowed hard, turned the heavy iron door handle and stepped inside the courtroom.

第7章 魔法部

近不怎么看见你下来。"

"我有急事,博德。"韦斯莱先生说,一边心急火燎地踮着脚尖,并不时用焦急的目光望望哈利。

"啊,是的,"博德眼睛一眨不眨地打量着哈利,说道,"当然是这样。"

哈利几乎没有心情理睬博德,但对方目不转睛的凝视仍使他感到很不舒服。

"神秘事务司。"那个冷冷的女声说完就陷入了沉默。

"快点儿,哈利。"升降梯的门哗啦啦地打开了,韦斯莱先生催促道。他们飞快地跑过一道走廊。这道走廊与上面的那些走廊完全不同,墙上空荡荡的,没有门也没有窗户,只是走廊的尽头有一扇简简单单的黑门。哈利以为他们会走这扇门,不料韦斯莱先生抓住他的胳膊把他拉到左边,这里有个豁口通向一道阶梯。

"下来,下来,"韦斯莱先生气喘吁吁地说,一步跨下两个台阶,"连升降梯都下不到这么深的地方……他们为什么要弄到这里来,我真……"

他们下到阶梯底下,又顺着一道走廊往前跑,这里跟霍格沃茨的那些通向斯内普地下教室的走廊简直一模一样:粗糙的石头墙壁,托架上插着一支支火把。他们在这里经过的门都是沉重的木门,上面嵌着铁门闩和钥匙孔。

"第十……审判室……我想……我们差不多到了……没错。"

在一扇阴森森的挂着一把大铁锁的黑门前,韦斯莱先生跌跌撞撞地停下脚步,精疲力竭地靠在墙上,揪着胸前的衣服直喘粗气。

"走吧,"他喘着气说,用大拇指点着那扇门,"进去吧。"

"你不——你不和我一起——"

"哦,不行。我不能进去。祝你好运!"

哈利狂跳的心脏扑通扑通地撞击着他的喉结。他费力地咽了口唾沫,拧了一下门上沉重的铁把手,走进了审判室。

237

CHAPTER EIGHT

The Hearing

Harry gasped; he could not help himself. The large dungeon he had entered was horribly familiar. He had not only seen it before, he had *been* here before. This was the place he had visited inside Dumbledore's Pensieve, the place where he had watched the Lestranges sentenced to life imprisonment in Azkaban.

The walls were made of dark stone, dimly lit by torches. Empty benches rose on either side of him, but ahead, in the highest benches of all, were many shadowy figures. They had been talking in low voices, but as the heavy door swung closed behind Harry an ominous silence fell.

A cold male voice rang across the courtroom.

'You're late.'

'Sorry,' said Harry nervously. 'I – I didn't know the time had been changed.'

'That is not the Wizengamot's fault,' said the voice. 'An owl was sent to you this morning. Take your seat.'

Harry dropped his gaze to the chair in the centre of the room, the arms of which were covered in chains. He had seen those chains spring to life and bind whoever sat between them. His footsteps echoed loudly as he walked across the stone floor. When he sat gingerly on the edge of the chair the chains clinked threateningly, but did not bind him. Feeling rather sick, he looked up at the people seated at the bench above.

There were about fifty of them, all, as far as he could see, wearing plum-coloured robes with an elaborately worked silver 'W' on the left-hand side of the chest and all staring down their noses at him, some with very austere expressions, others looks of frank curiosity.

第8章

受 审

　　哈利倒抽了一口冷气,他无法控制自己。他走进的这间幽深的地下室对他来说太熟悉了,令他胆战心惊。他不仅以前见过它,而且还曾经来过这里。这就是他在邓布利多的冥想盆里来过的地方,他就是在这里目睹了莱斯特兰奇夫妇被判在阿兹卡班终身监禁。

　　四周的墙壁是用黑黑的石头砌成的,火把的光线昏暗阴森。他的两边是一排排逐渐升高的空板凳,而他的前方,在最高的几条板凳上,赫然浮现着许多黑乎乎的人影。他们刚才一直在窃窃私语,而当沉重的大门在哈利身后关上时,一种不祥的沉寂笼罩下来。

　　一个冷冷的男声在审判室里回荡。

　　"你迟到了。"

　　"对不起,"哈利紧张地说,"我——我不知道时间改了。"

　　"那不是威森加摩的过错。"那个声音说,"今天早晨派一只猫头鹰去通知你了。坐下吧。"

　　哈利垂下目光,望着房间中央的那把椅子,椅子的扶手上是左一道右一道的铁链。他曾经见过这些铁链突然蹿起来,把坐在上面的人捆得结结实实。他的双脚走过石头地面,发出响亮的回音。他小心翼翼地坐在椅子边上,链条凶险地叮叮当当响了起来,但并没有把他捆住。哈利觉得一阵眩晕恶心,抬头望了望坐在上面板凳上的那些人。

　　他所能看见的,大约有五十个人,穿着紫红色的长袍,左前胸上绣着一个精致的银色"W"。他们都垂眼望着他,有的带着严厉的表情,其他人则毫不掩饰内心的好奇。

CHAPTER EIGHT The Hearing

In the very middle of the front row sat Cornelius Fudge, the Minister for Magic. Fudge was a portly man who often sported a lime-green bowler hat, though today he had dispensed with it; he had dispensed, too, with the indulgent smile he had once worn when he spoke to Harry. A broad, square-jawed witch with very short grey hair sat on Fudge's left; she wore a monocle and looked forbidding. On Fudge's right was another witch, but she was sitting so far back on the bench that her face was in shadow.

'Very well,' said Fudge. 'The accused being present – finally – let us begin. Are you ready?' he called down the row.

'Yes, sir,' said an eager voice Harry knew. Ron's brother Percy was sitting at the very end of the front bench. Harry looked at Percy, expecting some sign of recognition from him, but none came. Percy's eyes, behind his horn-rimmed glasses, were fixed on his parchment, a quill poised in his hand.

'Disciplinary hearing of the twelfth of August,' said Fudge in a ringing voice, and Percy began taking notes at once, 'into offences committed under the Decree for the Reasonable Restriction of Underage Sorcery and the International Statute of Secrecy by Harry James Potter, resident at number four, Privet Drive, Little Whinging, Surrey.

'Interrogators: Cornelius Oswald Fudge, Minister for Magic; Amelia Susan Bones, Head of the Department of Magical Law Enforcement; Dolores Jane Umbridge, Senior Undersecretary to the Minister. Court Scribe, Percy Ignatius Weasley –'

'Witness for the defence, Albus Percival Wulfric Brian Dumbledore,' said a quiet voice from behind Harry, who turned his head so fast he cricked his neck.

Dumbledore was striding serenely across the room wearing long midnight-blue robes and a perfectly calm expression. His long silver beard and hair gleamed in the torchlight as he drew level with Harry and looked up at Fudge through the half-moon spectacles that rested halfway down his very crooked nose.

The members of the Wizengamot were muttering. All eyes were now on Dumbledore. Some looked annoyed, others slightly frightened; two elderly witches in the back row, however, raised their hands and waved in welcome.

A powerful emotion had risen in Harry's chest at the sight of Dumbledore, a fortified, hopeful feeling rather like that which phoenix song gave him. He wanted to catch Dumbledore's eye, but Dumbledore was not looking his way;

第8章 受审

在前面一排板凳的正中间，坐着魔法部部长康奈利·福吉。福吉是一个大胖子，经常戴一顶暗黄绿色的圆顶高帽，不过今天他没有戴。另外，以前他对哈利说话时脸上总带着的那种慈祥的微笑，今天也消失不见了。福吉的左边坐着一个宽身材、方下巴的女巫，灰色的头发剪得短短的，戴着一副单片眼镜，脸上的表情令人生畏。福吉的右边坐着另一个女巫，但她在板凳上坐得太靠后了，脸被笼罩在阴影中。

"很好，"福吉说，"被告终于到场了，我们开始吧。你准备好了吗？"他朝板凳那头大声问道。

"是的，先生。"一个哈利熟悉的声音急切地说道。罗恩的哥哥珀西坐在前排板凳的最边上。哈利望着珀西，以为他会显露出认识自己的表情，但是他脸上什么表情也没有。珀西那双藏在角质架眼镜后面的眼睛正专注地盯着面前的羊皮纸，一支羽毛笔拿在手里准备记录。

"八月十二日的审判，"福吉声如洪钟地说，珀西忙不迭地开始做记录，"审理家住萨里郡小惠金区女贞路4号的哈利·詹姆·波特违反《对未成年巫师加以合理约束法》和《国际保密法》一案。

"审问者：魔法部部长康奈利·奥斯瓦尔德·福吉；魔法法律执行司司长阿米莉亚·苏珊·博恩斯；高级副部长多洛雷斯·简·乌姆里奇。审判记录员：珀西·伊格内修斯·韦斯莱——"

"被告方证人：阿不思·珀西瓦尔·伍尔弗里克·布赖恩·邓布利多。"哈利身后一个平静的声音说道。哈利猛一转头，把脖子扭了一下。

邓布利多镇定自若地大步走了过来，他身穿一袭黑蓝色的长袍，脸上是一副极为镇静的表情。他走到与哈利平行的地方，抬起头来，透过架在歪扭鼻梁上的半月形眼镜望着福吉，他长长的银白色胡须和头发在火把的映照下闪闪发光。

威森加摩的成员都在小声地交头接耳。所有的目光都投在邓布利多身上。有人显得很恼火，有人似乎有点儿害怕，而坐在后排的两个上了年纪的女巫竟然挥手表示欢迎。

哈利一看见邓布利多，内心升起一股强烈的情感，让他感到踏实，充满了希望，就像凤凰福克斯歌声曾经带给他的感觉一样。他想与邓布利多对一下目光，但邓布利多没有朝他这边看，而是继续抬眼望着

CHAPTER EIGHT   The Hearing

he was continuing to look up at the obviously flustered Fudge.

'Ah,' said Fudge, who looked thoroughly disconcerted. 'Dumbledore. Yes. You – er – got our – er – message that the time and – er – place of the hearing had been changed, then?'

'I must have missed it,' said Dumbledore cheerfully. 'However, due to a lucky mistake I arrived at the Ministry three hours early, so no harm done.'

'Yes – well – I suppose we'll need another chair – I – Weasley, could you –?'

'Not to worry, not to worry,' said Dumbledore pleasantly; he took out his wand, gave it a little flick, and a squashy chintz armchair appeared out of nowhere next to Harry. Dumbledore sat down, put the tips of his long fingers together and looked at Fudge over them with an expression of polite interest. The Wizengamot was still muttering and fidgeting restlessly; only when Fudge spoke again did they settle down.

'Yes,' said Fudge again, shuffling his notes. 'Well, then. So. The charges. Yes.'

He extricated a piece of parchment from the pile before him, took a deep breath, and read out, 'The charges against the accused are as follows:

'That he did knowingly, deliberately and in full awareness of the illegality of his actions, having received a previous written warning from the Ministry of Magic on a similar charge, produce a Patronus Charm in a Muggle-inhabited area, in the presence of a Muggle, on the second of August at twenty-three minutes past nine, which constitutes an offence under Paragraph C of the Decree for the Reasonable Restriction of Underage Sorcery, 1875, and also under Section 13 of the International Confederation of Warlocks' Statute of Secrecy.

'You are Harry James Potter, of number four, Privet Drive, Little Whinging, Surrey?' Fudge said, glaring at Harry over the top of his parchment.

'Yes,' Harry said.

'You received an official warning from the Ministry for using illegal magic three years ago, did you not?'

'Yes, but –'

'And yet you conjured a Patronus on the night of the second of August?' said Fudge.

'Yes,' said Harry, 'but –'

第8章 受审

显然惊慌失措的福吉。

"啊，"福吉说，看上去完全没了主张，"邓布利多。是的。这么说，你——呃——呃——你收到我们的信——知道审讯的时间、地点都改变了？"

"看来我是没收到，"邓布利多语气欢快地说，"不过，我犯了一个幸运的错误，提前三个小时就来到了魔法部，所以一切都没问题。"

"是的——好吧——我想我们需要再拿一把椅子来——我——韦斯莱，你能不能——？"

"不劳费心，不劳费心。"邓布利多温文尔雅地说。他抽出魔杖，轻轻抖动了一下，一把柔软的磨光印花棉布扶手椅凭空出现在哈利旁边。邓布利多坐了下来，长长的手指尖对接在一起，目光从那上面望着福吉，脸上带着彬彬有礼、饶有兴趣的表情。威森加摩的成员仍然在交头接耳，一个个坐立不安。后来福吉又开口说话时，他们才安静下来。

"是的，"福吉说，把面前的文件移来移去，"那么好吧。现在是……指控。是的。"

他从一堆文件中抽出一张羊皮纸，深深吸了口气，大声念道："指控被告方有如下罪行：

"被告以前曾因类似指控受到魔法部书面警告，这次又在完全知道自己的行为是违法的情况下，蓄意地、明知故犯地于八月二日晚九点二十三分，在一个麻瓜居住区，当着一个麻瓜的面，施用了一个守护神咒，此行为违反了一八七五年颁布的《对未成年巫师加以合理约束法》第三款以及《国际巫师联合会保密法》第十三条。

"你就是居住在萨里郡小惠金区女贞路4号的哈利·詹姆·波特？"福吉一边问一边从羊皮纸上方瞪视着哈利。

"是的。"哈利回答。

"你三年前曾因非法使用魔法而受到魔法部的正式警告，是吗？"

"是的，可是——"

"但你又在八月二日晚用魔法变出了一个守护神？"福吉说。

"是的，"哈利说，"可是——"

'Knowing that you are not permitted to use magic outside school while you are under the age of seventeen?'

'Yes, but –'

'Knowing that you were in an area full of Muggles?'

'Yes, but –'

'Fully aware that you were in close proximity to a Muggle at the time?'

'*Yes*,' said Harry angrily, 'but I only used it because we were –'

The witch with the monocle cut across him in a booming voice.

'You produced a fully-fledged Patronus?'

'Yes,' said Harry, 'because –'

'A corporeal Patronus?'

'A – what?' said Harry.

'Your Patronus had a clearly defined form? I mean to say, it was more than vapour or smoke?'

'Yes,' said Harry, feeling both impatient and slightly desperate, 'it's a stag, it's always a stag.'

'Always?' boomed Madam Bones. 'You have produced a Patronus before now?'

'*Yes*,' said Harry, 'I've been doing it for over a year.'

'And you are fifteen years old?'

'Yes, and –'

'You learned this at school?'

'Yes, Professor Lupin taught me in my third year, because of the –'

'Impressive,' said Madam Bones, staring down at him, 'a true Patronus at his age ... very impressive indeed.'

Some of the wizards and witches around her were muttering again; a few nodded, but others were frowning and shaking their heads.

'It's not a question of how impressive the magic was,' said Fudge in a testy voice, 'in fact, the more impressive the worse it is, I would have thought, given that the boy did it in plain view of a Muggle!'

Those who had been frowning now murmured in agreement, but it was the sight of Percy's sanctimonious little nod that goaded Harry into speech.

第8章 受 审

"你明知道你还不到十七岁,不允许在校外使用魔法?"

"是的,可是——"

"明知道你当时身处一个麻瓜密集的地方?"

"是的,可是——"

"你完全清楚当时近旁就有一个麻瓜?"

"是的,"哈利恼火地说,"但我使用魔法,只是因为我们——"

戴单片眼镜的女巫用洪亮而深沉的声音打断了他。

"你变出了一个完全成熟的守护神?"

"是的,"哈利说,"因为——"

"一个实体守护神?"

"一个——什么?"哈利问。

"你的守护神具有清楚明确的形态?我的意思是,它不仅仅是蒸气或烟雾?"

"是的,"哈利觉得又烦躁又有点绝望,"是一头牡鹿,每次都是一头牡鹿。"

"每次?"博恩斯女士用洪亮的声音问,"你以前也变出过守护神?"

"是的,"哈利说,"我这么做已经有一年多了。"

"你现在是十五岁?"

"是的,而且——"

"你是在学校里学会的?"

"是的,我三年级时,卢平教授教我的,因为——"

"真是了不起,"博恩斯女士从上面望着他说道,"他这个年纪能变出真正的守护神……确实很了不起。"

她周围的一些巫师又开始交头接耳了。有的点点头,有的则露出不悦的神情,连连摇头。

"这不是一个魔法多么了不起的问题,"福吉用恼怒的声音说,"实际上我认为,越是了不起就越糟糕,因为那孩子是当着一个麻瓜的面这么做的!"

那些露出不悦神情的巫师们喃喃地表示同意,哈利看见珀西居然也假装正经地点了点头。他被激怒了,忍不住开了口:

CHAPTER EIGHT   The Hearing

'I did it because of the Dementors!' he said loudly, before anyone could interrupt him again.

He had expected more muttering, but the silence that fell seemed to be somehow denser than before.

'Dementors?' said Madam Bones after a moment, her thick eyebrows rising until her monocle looked in danger of falling out. 'What do you mean, boy?'

'I mean there were two Dementors down that alleyway and they went for me and my cousin!'

'Ah,' said Fudge again, smirking unpleasantly as he looked around at the Wizengamot, as though inviting them to share the joke. 'Yes. Yes, I thought we'd be hearing something like this.'

'Dementors in Little Whinging?' Madam Bones said, in a tone of great surprise. 'I don't understand –'

'Don't you, Amelia?' said Fudge, still smirking. 'Let me explain. He's been thinking it through and decided Dementors would make a very nice little cover story, very nice indeed. Muggles can't see Dementors, can they, boy? Highly convenient, highly convenient ... so it's just your word and no witnesses ...'

'I'm not lying!' said Harry loudly, over another outbreak of muttering from the court. 'There were two of them, coming from opposite ends of the alley, everything went dark and cold and my cousin felt them and ran for it –'

'Enough, enough!' said Fudge, with a very supercilious look on his face. 'I'm sorry to interrupt what I'm sure would have been a very well-rehearsed story –'

Dumbledore cleared his throat. The Wizengamot fell silent again.

'We do, in fact, have a witness to the presence of Dementors in that alleyway,' he said, 'other than Dudley Dursley, I mean.'

Fudge's plump face seemed to slacken, as though somebody had let air out of it. He stared down at Dumbledore for a moment or two, then, with the appearance of a man pulling himself back together, said, 'We haven't got time to listen to more tarradiddles, I'm afraid, Dumbledore. I want this dealt with quickly –'

'I may be wrong,' said Dumbledore pleasantly, 'but I am sure that under the Wizengamot Charter of Rights, the accused has the right to present witnesses for his or her case? Isn't that the policy of the Department of Magical Law Enforcement, Madam Bones?' he continued, addressing the witch in the monocle.

第8章 受审

"我那么做是因为摄魂怪!"他大声说道,没人来得及再次打断他。

他以为人们又会交头接耳,没想到四下里鸦雀无声,似乎比刚才还要肃静。

"摄魂怪?"过了一会儿博恩斯女士说,她两条浓眉扬得高高的,单片眼镜似乎快要滑下来了,"你这是什么意思,孩子?"

"我是说,当时小巷里冒出了两个摄魂怪,直朝我和我表哥逼来!"

"啊,"福吉又说话了,嘴里发出令人讨厌的嘲笑声,一边望着前后左右的威森加摩成员,似乎希望他们对这个笑话也能心领神会,"是啊,是啊,我就知道我们会听到诸如此类的鬼话。"

"摄魂怪在小惠金区?"博恩斯女士说,语气里透着十二万分的惊讶,"我不明白——"

"你不明白吗,阿米莉亚?"福吉仍然嘲笑地说,"让我来解释一下吧。他可真是煞费苦心哪,发现摄魂怪可以成为一个绝妙的托词,确实绝妙。麻瓜是看不见摄魂怪的,是不是,孩子?非常巧妙,非常巧妙……所以没有证人,只有你的一面之词……"

"我没有说谎!"哈利大声说,声音盖过了审判席上再次响起的交头接耳声,"有两个,分别从小巷两头堵了过来,所有的东西都变得那么黑那么冷,我表哥感觉到了它们,拼命想逃跑——"

"够了,够了!"福吉说,脸上带着一副非常傲慢的神情,"很抱歉我打断了他,我敢肯定这是一篇经过精心排练的谎言——"

邓布利多清了清嗓子。威森加摩又安静了下来。

"实际上,我们有一个证人可以证明摄魂怪确实在那条小巷出现了,"他说,"我是说除了达力·德思礼之外。"

福吉肥胖的面孔似乎突然松懈了下来,好像有人放跑了里面的空气。他呆呆地瞪着下面的邓布利多,好一会儿之后,他像是重新振作了起来,说道:"我们恐怕没有时间再听这些胡言乱语了,邓布利多,我希望快点处理这桩——"

"我也许记得不准确,"邓布利多和颜悦色地说,"但我相信根据《威森加摩权利宪章》,被告有权请证人出庭为其作证,对吗?这难道不是魔法法律执行司的政策吗,博恩斯女士?"他问那个戴单片眼镜的女巫。

CHAPTER EIGHT The Hearing

'True,' said Madam Bones. 'Perfectly true.'

'Oh, very well, very well,' snapped Fudge. 'Where is this person?'

'I brought her with me,' said Dumbledore. 'She's just outside the door. Should I –?'

'No – Weasley, you go,' Fudge barked at Percy, who got up at once, ran down the stone steps from the judge's balcony and hurried past Dumbledore and Harry without glancing at them.

A moment later, Percy returned, followed by Mrs Figg. She looked scared and more batty than ever. Harry wished she had thought to change out of her carpet slippers.

Dumbledore stood up and gave Mrs Figg his chair, conjuring a second one for himself.

'Full name?' said Fudge loudly, when Mrs Figg had perched herself nervously on the very edge of her seat.

'Arabella Doreen Figg,' said Mrs Figg in her quavery voice.

'And who exactly are you?' said Fudge, in a bored and lofty voice.

'I'm a resident of Little Whinging, close to where Harry Potter lives,' said Mrs Figg.

'We have no record of any witch or wizard living in Little Whinging, other than Harry Potter,' said Madam Bones at once. 'That situation has always been closely monitored, given ... given past events.'

'I'm a Squib,' said Mrs Figg. 'So you wouldn't have me registered, would you?'

'A Squib, eh?' said Fudge, eyeing her suspiciously. 'We'll be checking that. You'll leave details of your parentage with my assistant Weasley. Incidentally, can Squibs see Dementors?' he added, looking left and right along the bench.

'Yes, we can!' said Mrs Figg indignantly.

Fudge looked back down at her, his eyebrows raised. 'Very well,' he said aloofly. 'What is your story?'

'I had gone out to buy cat food from the corner shop at the end of Wisteria Walk, around about nine o'clock, on the evening of the second of August,' gabbled Mrs Figg at once, as though she had learned what she was saying by heart, 'when I heard a disturbance down the alleyway between Magnolia Crescent and Wisteria Walk. On approaching the mouth of the alleyway I saw Dementors running –'

第8章 受审

"不错,"博恩斯女士说,"确实如此。"

"哦,很好,很好,"福吉没好气地说,"这个人在哪儿?"

"我把她带来了,"邓布利多说,"她就在门外。我是不是——"

"不——韦斯莱,你去。"福吉粗暴地对珀西说。珀西立刻站起来,顺着石头台阶从法官席上跑了下来,匆匆跑过邓布利多和哈利身边,看也不看他们一眼。

片刻之后,珀西回来了,后面跟着费格太太。她显得很害怕,模样比平常更加古怪。哈利真希望她能想到把她那双厚拖鞋换掉。

邓布利多站起身,把椅子让给了费格太太,又给自己变出了一把。

"全名?"福吉大声问,这时费格太太刚刚战战兢兢地在椅子边缘坐下。

"阿拉贝拉·多里恩·费格。"费格太太用微微颤抖的声音说。

"你到底是谁?"福吉用不耐烦而高傲的声音问。

"我是小惠金区的居民,就住在哈利·波特家旁边。"费格太太说。

"在我们的记录上,除了哈利·波特外,没有任何巫师住在小惠金区。"博恩斯女士立刻说道,"那片地区一直受到严密监视,因为……因为以前发生过一些事情。"

"我是个哑炮,"费格太太说,"所以你们不会登记我的名字,是不是?"

"哑炮,嗯?"福吉怀疑地打量着她,说道,"我们会核实的。你待会儿把你父母的情况告诉我的助手韦斯莱。顺便提一句,哑炮能看见摄魂怪吗?"他加了一句,并向左右望了望长凳上的人。

"能,我们能看见!"费格太太气愤地说。

福吉又高高在上地看着她,扬了扬眉毛。"很好,"他冷冷地说,"你的说法是什么?"

"八月二日那天晚上,大约九点钟左右,我出门到紫藤路路口的拐角商店买猫食,"费格太太立刻急促地说开了,就好像她已经把要说的话都背了下来,"后来我听见木兰花新月街和紫藤路之间的小巷里传来骚乱声。我走到小巷口,看见摄魂怪在跑——"

CHAPTER EIGHT   The Hearing

'Running?' said Madam Bones sharply. 'Dementors don't run, they glide.'

'That's what I meant to say,' said Mrs Figg quickly, patches of pink appearing in her withered cheeks. 'Gliding along the alley towards what looked like two boys.'

'What did they look like?' said Madam Bones, narrowing her eyes so that the edge of the monocle disappeared into her flesh.

'Well, one was very large and the other one rather skinny –'

'No, no,' said Madam Bones impatiently. 'The Dementors ... describe them.'

'Oh,' said Mrs Figg, the pink flush creeping up her neck now. 'They were big. Big and wearing cloaks.'

Harry felt a horrible sinking in the pit of his stomach. Whatever Mrs Figg might say, it sounded to him as though the most she had ever seen was a picture of a Dementor, and a picture could never convey the truth of what these beings were like: the eerie way they moved, hovering inches over the ground; or the rotting smell of them; or that terrible rattling noise they made as they sucked on the surrounding air ...

In the second row, a dumpy wizard with a large black moustache leaned close to whisper in the ear of his neighbour, a frizzy-haired witch. She smirked and nodded.

'Big and wearing cloaks,' repeated Madam Bones coolly, while Fudge snorted derisively.

'I see. Anything else?'

'Yes,' said Mrs Figg. 'I felt them. Everything went cold, and this was a very warm summer's night, mark you. And I felt ... as though all happiness had gone from the world ... and I remembered ... dreadful things ...'

Her voice shook and died.

Madam Bones's eyes widened slightly. Harry could see red marks under her eyebrow where the monocle had dug into it.

'What did the Dementors do?' she asked, and Harry felt a rush of hope.

'They went for the boys,' said Mrs Figg, her voice stronger and more confident now, the pink flush ebbing away from her face. 'One of them had fallen. The other was backing away, trying to repel the Dementor. That

第8章 受审

"跑?"博恩斯女士严厉地说,"摄魂怪不会跑,它们只会滑行。"

"我就是这个意思,"费格太太赶紧说道,干瘪的脸上泛起了红晕,"在小巷里滑行,扑向像是两个男孩的人。"

"它们是什么模样?"博恩斯女士说着,紧紧眯起了眼睛,单片眼镜的边缘都陷进肉里去了。

"噢,一个块头很大,另一个瘦瘦的——"

"不,不,"博恩斯女士不耐烦地说,"摄魂怪……形容一下摄魂怪的模样。"

"噢,"费格太太说,现在红晕蔓延到她的脖子上了,"它们很大。很大,穿着斗篷。"

哈利感到他的心可怕地往下一沉。不管费格太太说什么,在他听来她似乎最多只看过摄魂怪的照片,而照片是根本无法传达那些家伙的真正本质的:它们在离地面几英寸的地方悬浮移动时的怪异可怖的样子;它们散发出的那股腐烂的恶臭;还有它们吞噬周围空气时发出的可怕的窸窸窣窣的声音……

在第二排长凳上,一个矮矮胖胖、留着一大蓬黑胡子的男巫师凑到旁边一位头发拳曲的女巫师耳边窃窃私语起来。女巫师露出得意的讥笑,点了点头。

"很大,穿着斗篷。"博恩斯女士冷冷地重复了一遍——福吉讥讽地哼了一声。

"我明白了。还有别的吗?"

"有,"费格太太说,"我感觉到了它们。所有的一切都变得很冷,别忘了当时是很炎热的夏天的夜晚哪。然后我觉得……似乎所有的快乐都从世界上消失了……我想起了……可怕的事情……"

她的声音颤抖着,渐渐听不见了。

博恩斯女士的眼睛微微睁大了。哈利可以看见她眉毛下刚才镜片陷进去的地方留下的红印。

"摄魂怪做了什么?"她问。哈利内心升起一丝希望。

"它们朝两个男孩扑去,"费格太太说,现在她的声音更有力、更自信了,脸上的红晕也退去了,"一个男孩倒下了,另一个一边后退一边试着击退

CHAPTER EIGHT   The Hearing

was Harry. He tried twice and produced only silver vapour. On the third attempt, he produced a Patronus, which charged down the first Dementor and then, with his encouragement, chased the second one away from his cousin. And that ... that is what happened,' Mrs Figg finished, somewhat lamely.

Madam Bones looked down at Mrs Figg in silence. Fudge was not looking at her at all, but fidgeting with his papers. Finally, he raised his eyes and said, rather aggressively, 'That's what you saw, is it?'

'That is what happened,' Mrs Figg repeated.

'Very well,' said Fudge. 'You may go.'

Mrs Figg cast a frightened look from Fudge to Dumbledore, then got up and shuffled off towards the door. Harry heard it thud shut behind her.

'Not a very convincing witness,' said Fudge loftily.

'Oh, I don't know,' said Madam Bones, in her booming voice. 'She certainly described the effects of a Dementor attack very accurately. And I can't imagine why she would say they were there if they weren't.'

'But Dementors wandering into a Muggle suburb and just *happening* to come across a wizard?' snorted Fudge. 'The odds on that must be very, very long. Even Bagman wouldn't have bet –'

'Oh, I don't think any of us believe the Dementors were there by coincidence,' said Dumbledore lightly.

The witch sitting to the right of Fudge, with her face in shadow, moved slightly but everyone else was quite still and silent.

'And what is that supposed to mean?' Fudge asked icily.

'It means that I think they were ordered there,' said Dumbledore.

'I think we might have a record of it if someone had ordered a pair of Dementors to go strolling through Little Whinging!' barked Fudge.

'Not if the Dementors are taking orders from someone other than the Ministry of Magic these days,' said Dumbledore calmly. 'I have already given you my views on this matter, Cornelius.'

'Yes, you have,' said Fudge forcefully, 'and I have no reason to believe that your views are anything other than bilge, Dumbledore. The Dementors

摄魂怪。这是哈利。他试了两次，变出来的只是银色烟雾。第三次再试，他变出了一个守护神。那守护神冲过去撞倒了第一个摄魂怪，然后在哈利的激励之下，又把第二个摄魂怪从他表哥身边赶跑了。这就是……这就是当时发生的事情。"费格太太说完了，她的声音有点儿软弱无力。

博恩斯女士默默地望着费格太太。福吉则看也不看她，只顾摆弄他的文件。最后，他抬起眼睛，有点咄咄逼人地说："那就是你看到的情形，是吗？"

"是当时发生的事情。"费格太太又说了一遍。

"很好，"福吉说，"你可以走了。"

费格太太胆怯地望望福吉，又望望邓布利多，然后站起来，拖着脚朝门口走去。哈利听见门在她身后重重地关上了。

"这个证人不很令人信服。"福吉傲慢地说。

"哦，我看不一定，"博恩斯女士用她洪亮的声音说，"她对摄魂怪发起进攻时的威力描绘得非常准确。而且我不明白，如果摄魂怪不在那里，她为什么要这么说。"

"可是摄魂怪跑到一个城郊的麻瓜住宅区，又正好遇到一个巫师？"福吉轻蔑地说，"这种可能性肯定很小很小，就连巴格曼也不会下赌注——"

"噢，我认为我们谁也不会相信摄魂怪出现在那里是一种巧合。"邓布利多轻言慢语地说。

坐在福吉的右边、脸被笼罩在阴影里的女巫微微动了动，但其他人都一动不动，一言不发。

"这到底是什么意思呢？"福吉冷冰冰地问。

"意思是我认为它们是有人派去的。"邓布利多说。

"我想，如果有人命令两个摄魂怪在小惠金区大摇大摆地溜达，我们应该会有记录的！"福吉粗声吼道。

"如果这两个摄魂怪最近接受了魔法部之外的某个人的指令，那就不一定了吧。"邓布利多平静地说，"我已经把我对这个问题的看法告诉过你，康奈利。"

"是的，你说过，"福吉强硬地说，"而我没有理由相信你的看法不是一派胡言，邓布利多。摄魂怪仍然规规矩矩地待在阿兹卡班，严格

CHAPTER EIGHT   The Hearing

remain in place in Azkaban and are doing everything we ask them to.'

'Then,' said Dumbledore, quietly but clearly, 'we must ask ourselves why somebody within the Ministry ordered a pair of Dementors into that alleyway on the second of August.'

In the complete silence that greeted these words, the witch to the right of Fudge leaned forwards so that Harry saw her for the first time.

He thought she looked just like a large, pale toad. She was rather squat with a broad, flabby face, as little neck as Uncle Vernon and a very wide, slack mouth. Her eyes were large, round and slightly bulging. Even the little black velvet bow perched on top of her short curly hair put him in mind of a large fly she was about to catch on a long sticky tongue.

'The Chair recognises Dolores Jane Umbridge, Senior Undersecretary to the Minister,' said Fudge.

The witch spoke in a fluttery, girlish, high-pitched voice that took Harry aback; he had been expecting a croak.

'I'm sure I must have misunderstood you, Professor Dumbledore,' she said, with a simper that left her big, round eyes as cold as ever. 'So silly of me. But it sounded for a teensy moment as though you were suggesting that the Ministry of Magic had ordered an attack on this boy!'

She gave a silvery laugh that made the hairs on the back of Harry's neck stand up. A few other members of the Wizengamot laughed with her. It could not have been plainer that not one of them was really amused.

'If it is true that the Dementors are taking orders only from the Ministry of Magic, and it is also true that two Dementors attacked Harry and his cousin a week ago, then it follows logically that somebody at the Ministry might have ordered the attacks,' said Dumbledore politely. 'Of course, these particular Dementors may have been outside Ministry control –'

'There are no Dementors outside Ministry control!' snapped Fudge, who had turned brick red.

Dumbledore inclined his head in a little bow.

'Then undoubtedly the Ministry will be making a full inquiry into why two Dementors were so very far from Azkaban and why they attacked without authorisation.'

'It is not for you to decide what the Ministry of Magic does or does not

第8章 受审

服从我们的命令。"

"那么,"邓布利多语调平稳而清晰地说,"我们必须问问我们自己,为什么魔法部的某人会在八月二日命令两个摄魂怪到那条小巷里去。"

这些话一说完,场上一片静默,坐在福吉右边的那个女巫探身向前,哈利这才第一次看清了她的脸。

哈利觉得她活像一只苍白的大癞蛤蟆。她又矮又胖,长着一张宽大的、皮肉松弛的脸,像弗农一样看不见脖子,一张大嘴向下耷拉着。她的眼睛很大,圆圆的,微微向外凸起。就连戴在她短鬈发上的那个黑色天鹅绒小蝴蝶结,也使哈利想到她正准备伸出黏糊糊的长舌头去捕捉一只大苍蝇。

"本主持准许高级副部长多洛雷斯·简·乌姆里奇发言。"福吉说。

于是那女巫用一种小姑娘一样大惊小怪、又尖又细的声音说起话来,哈利大吃了一惊,他还以为会听到一个沙哑的嗓音呢。

"我相信我一定是误会你的意思了,邓布利多教授。"她说,脸上堆着假笑,那两只圆圆的大眼睛仍和刚才一样冷漠,"我可能太愚笨了,但是我觉得刚才有那么一刹那,你似乎在暗示是魔法部下令攻击这个男孩的!"

她发出银铃般的笑声,哈利听得脖子后面的汗毛直竖。几个威森加摩的成员跟她一起笑了起来。但是并没有一个人真的觉得好笑,这是再明显不过了。

"如果摄魂怪确实只接受魔法部的命令,如果那两个摄魂怪一星期前确实袭击过哈利和他表哥,那么按逻辑推断,可能是魔法部的某个人命令摄魂怪去袭击的。"邓布利多温文尔雅地说,"当然啦,上面说的这两个摄魂怪也可能不受魔法部的控制——"

"没有哪个摄魂怪不受魔法部的控制!"福吉厉声说道,脸涨成了褐红色。

邓布利多微微欠身点了点头。

"那么,魔法部无疑会彻底调查为什么那两个摄魂怪会跑到离阿兹卡班这么远的地方,为什么它们没有得到批准就向人发起进攻。"

"邓布利多,魔法部做什么或不做什么,还轮不到你来决定!"福

CHAPTER EIGHT   The Hearing

do, Dumbledore!' snapped Fudge, now a shade of magenta of which Uncle Vernon would have been proud.

'Of course it isn't,' said Dumbledore mildly. 'I was merely expressing my confidence that this matter will not go uninvestigated.'

He glanced at Madam Bones, who readjusted her monocle and stared back at him, frowning slightly.

'I would remind everybody that the behaviour of these Dementors, if indeed they are not figments of this boy's imagination, is not the subject of this hearing!' said Fudge. 'We are here to examine Harry Potter's offences under the Decree for the Reasonable Restriction of Underage Sorcery!'

'Of course we are,' said Dumbledore, 'but the presence of Dementors in that alleyway is highly relevant. Clause Seven of the Decree states that magic may be used before Muggles in exceptional circumstances, and as those exceptional circumstances include situations which threaten the life of the wizard or witch him- or herself, or any witches, wizards or Muggles present at the time of the –'

'We are familiar with Clause Seven, thank you very much!' snarled Fudge.

'Of course you are,' said Dumbledore courteously. 'Then we are in agreement that Harry's use of the Patronus Charm in these circumstances falls precisely into the category of exceptional circumstances the clause describes?'

'If there were Dementors, which I doubt.'

'You have heard it from an eyewitness,' Dumbledore interrupted. 'If you still doubt her truthfulness, call her back, question her again. I am sure she would not object.'

'I – that – not –' blustered Fudge, fiddling with the papers before him. 'It's – I want this over with today, Dumbledore!'

'But naturally, you would not care how many times you heard from a witness, if the alternative was a serious miscarriage of justice,' said Dumbledore.

'Serious miscarriage, my hat!' said Fudge at the top of his voice. 'Have you ever bothered to tot up the number of cock-and-bull stories this boy has come out with, Dumbledore, while trying to cover up his flagrant misuse of magic out of school? I suppose you've forgotten the Hover Charm he used three years ago –'

'That wasn't me, it was a house-elf!' said Harry.

'YOU SEE?' roared Fudge, gesturing flamboyantly in Harry's direction. 'A

第8章 受审

吉粗暴地说，此刻他脸上是一种会令弗农姨父感到骄傲的洋红色。

"当然是这样，"邓布利多不紧不慢地说，"我只是表示我相信这件事一定会被查个水落石出的。"

他扫了一眼博恩斯女士。博恩斯女士重新调整了一下单片眼镜，再次瞪着邓布利多，微微皱起眉头。

"我想提醒诸位，那两个摄魂怪的行为，就算它们不是这个孩子胡思乱想的产物，也不是这次审问的话题！"福吉说，"我们在这里是要审问哈利·波特违反《对未成年巫师加以合理约束法》一案！"

"当然是这样，"邓布利多说，"但摄魂怪在小巷里的出现与本案有着密切关系。该法的第七条写着，在特殊情况下可以在麻瓜面前使用魔法，那些特殊情况就包括当巫师本人或同时在场的其他巫师或麻瓜的生命受到威胁——"

"我们很熟悉第七条的内容，真是多谢你了！"福吉怒吼道。

"当然是这样，"邓布利多不卑不亢地说，"那么我们一致同意，哈利使用守护神咒时的情形正好符合第七条里所描述的特殊情况的范畴喽？"

"那是说如果真有摄魂怪的话，对此我深表怀疑。"

"你已经听一位目击证人叙述过了。"邓布利多打断了他，"如果你仍然怀疑她没说实话，不妨把她再叫进来，重新提问。我想她肯定不会反对的。"

"我——那个——不是——"福吉气急败坏地吼道，摆弄着面前的纸张，"这是——我想今天就把此事了结，邓布利多！"

"可是，你们肯定会不厌其烦地听一个证人的证词，因为草率行事会造成严重的误判。"邓布利多说。

"严重的误判。我的天哪！"福吉扯足了嗓门说，"邓布利多，你有没有费心算一算，这个孩子到底编造了多少荒唐可笑的谎言，就为了掩盖他在校外公然滥用魔法的行径！我想你大概已经忘记他三年前使用的那个悬停咒了吧——"

"那不是我，是一个家养小精灵！"哈利说。

"**看见了吧**？"福吉吼道，一边夸张地朝哈利那边做了个手势，"一

CHAPTER EIGHT The Hearing

house-elf! In a Muggle house! I ask you.'

'The house-elf in question is currently in the employ of Hogwarts School,' said Dumbledore. 'I can summon him here in an instant to give evidence if you wish.'

'I – not – I haven't got time to listen to house-elves! Anyway, that's not the only – he blew up his aunt, for God's sake!' Fudge shouted, banging his fist on the judge's bench and upsetting a bottle of ink.

'And you very kindly did not press charges on that occasion, accepting, I presume, that even the best wizards cannot always control their emotions,' said Dumbledore calmly, as Fudge attempted to scrub the ink off his notes.

'And I haven't even started on what he gets up to at school.'

'But, as the Ministry has no authority to punish Hogwarts students for misdemeanours at school, Harry's behaviour there is not relevant to this hearing,' said Dumbledore, as politely as ever, but now with a suggestion of coolness behind his words.

'Oho!' said Fudge. 'Not our business what he does at school, eh? You think so?'

'The Ministry does not have the power to expel Hogwarts students, Cornelius, as I reminded you on the night of the second of August,' said Dumbledore. 'Nor does it have the right to confiscate wands until charges have been successfully proven; again, as I reminded you on the night of the second of August. In your admirable haste to ensure that the law is upheld, you appear, inadvertently I am sure, to have overlooked a few laws yourself.'

'Laws can be changed,' said Fudge savagely.

'Of course they can,' said Dumbledore, inclining his head. 'And you certainly seem to be making many changes, Cornelius. Why, in the few short weeks since I was asked to leave the Wizengamot, it has already become the practice to hold a full criminal trial to deal with a simple matter of underage magic!'

A few of the wizards above them shifted uncomfortably in their seats. Fudge turned a slightly deeper shade of puce. The toadlike witch on his right, however, merely gazed at Dumbledore, her face quite expressionless.

'As far as I am aware,' Dumbledore continued, 'there is no law yet in place that says this court's job is to punish Harry for every bit of magic he has ever performed. He has been charged with a specific offence and he has presented his defence. All he and I can do now is to await your verdict.'

第8章 受审

个家养小精灵!在一个麻瓜住宅里!请问这可能吗?"

"该家养小精灵目前正受雇于霍格沃茨魔法学校,"邓布利多说,"如果您愿意,我马上就可以把他召到这儿来作证。"

"我——不是——我没有时间听家养小精灵胡扯!而且,不光这一件事——他还把他姑妈吹得膨胀起来,天哪!"福吉大声嚷道,一拳砸在法官席上,把一瓶墨水打翻了。

"你当时非常仁慈地没有提出指控,我想你也同意即使是最优秀的巫师也并不是总能控制自己的情绪。"邓布利多平静地说,而福吉正手忙脚乱地试图擦掉笔记上的墨水。

"他在学校里干的那些坏事我还没有开始说呢。"

"可是,魔法部无权因霍格沃茨学生在校的不端行为而惩罚他们,因此,哈利在那里的所作所为与本案毫无关系。"邓布利多说,还是那样谦和有礼,但此时他的话里透着一种冷峻。

"哦嗬!"福吉说,"他在学校的行为不用我们管,嗯?你是这样认为的?"

"魔法部无权开除霍格沃茨的学生,康奈利,这一点我已在八月二日晚就提醒过你。"邓布利多说,"魔法部也无权没收魔杖,除非那些指控被证明确实成立,这一点,我也在八月二日晚提醒过你。你急于确保法律得到维护的态度是值得称道的,但你自己似乎,我相信是出于一时疏忽,忽略了几条法律。"

"法律是可以修改的。"福吉恶狠狠地说。

"当然是这样,"邓布利多欠了欠身说,"看样子你无疑正在做许多修改,康奈利。是啊,我被请出威森加摩只有短短几个星期,现在一件未成年人使用魔法的区区小事居然要动用正式的刑事法庭来审理!"

上面有几位巫师不安地在座位里动来动去。福吉的脸涨成了紫红的猪肝色。他右边的癞蛤蟆似的女巫则死死地瞪着邓布利多,脸上不带任何表情。

"据我所知,"邓布利多继续说道,"迄今还没有哪条法律规定,这次开庭要让哈利为其有生以来施过的每一个魔法而受罚。他是因一个特定的行为而受到指控的,并已为自己进行了辩护。我和他目前所能做的就是等候你们的裁决!"

CHAPTER EIGHT   The Hearing

Dumbledore put his fingertips together again and said no more. Fudge glared at him, evidently incensed. Harry glanced sideways at Dumbledore, seeking reassurance; he was not at all sure that Dumbledore was right in telling the Wizengamot, in effect, that it was about time they made a decision. Again, however, Dumbledore seemed oblivious to Harry's attempt to catch his eye. He continued to look up at the benches where the entire Wizengamot had fallen into urgent, whispered conversations.

Harry looked at his feet. His heart, which seemed to have swollen to an unnatural size, was thumping loudly under his ribs. He had expected the hearing to last longer than this. He was not at all sure that he had made a good impression. He had not really said very much. He ought to have explained more fully about the Dementors, about how he had fallen over, about how both he and Dudley had nearly been kissed ...

Twice he looked up at Fudge and opened his mouth to speak, but his swollen heart was now constricting his air passages and both times he merely took a deep breath and looked back down at his shoes.

Then the whispering stopped. Harry wanted to look up at the judges, but found that it was really much, much easier to keep examining his laces.

'Those in favour of clearing the accused of all charges?' said Madam Bones's booming voice.

Harry's head jerked upwards. There were hands in the air, many of them ... more than half! Breathing very fast, he tried to count, but before he could finish, Madam Bones had said, 'And those in favour of conviction?'

Fudge raised his hand; so did half a dozen others, including the witch on his right and the heavily-moustached wizard and the frizzy-haired witch in the second row.

Fudge glanced around at them all, looking as though there was something large stuck in his throat, then lowered his own hand. He took two deep breaths and said, in a voice distorted by suppressed rage, 'Very well, very well ... cleared of all charges.'

'Excellent,' said Dumbledore briskly, springing to his feet, pulling out his wand and causing the two chintz armchairs to vanish. 'Well, I must be getting along. Good-day to you all.'

And without looking once at Harry, he swept from the dungeon.

第8章 受审

邓布利多又把十个指尖对接在一起，不再说话了。福吉狠狠地瞪着他，一副恼羞成怒的样子。哈利侧眼望望邓布利多，想从他那里得到一些安慰。邓布利多告诉威森加摩现在就做出裁决，这样做合适不合适呢，他一点把握也没有。可是，邓布利多又一次没有理睬哈利希望与他进行目光交流的愿望。他继续注视着上面那些正在紧张地窃窃私语的威森加摩的全体成员。

哈利望着自己的脚尖。他的心似乎膨胀得很大很大，在肋骨下咚咚地狂跳着。他原来以为审讯的时间会更长一些。他不知道自己是否给人留下了较好的印象。实际上他并没有说几句话。他应该更详细地说一说摄魂怪，说一说他怎么摔倒在地，说一说他和达力怎么差点被摄魂怪吻了……

他两次抬头看了看福吉，张开嘴巴想说话，可是膨胀的心脏憋得他透不过气来，他两次都只是深深地吸了口气，又低下头望着自己脚上的鞋。

窃窃私语的声音停息了。哈利想抬头看看那些审判员，但又觉得继续研究自己的鞋带要轻松得多、容易得多。

"赞成指控不成立的请举手。"博恩斯女士用洪亮的声音说。

哈利猛地把头抬起。一只只手举了起来，数量不少……超过了半数！他呼吸急促起来，想好好数一数，可是没等他数完，博恩斯女士就说："赞成罪行成立的请举手。"

福吉把手举了起来，同时举手的还有其他六七个人，包括福吉右边的那个女巫，那个胡子拉碴的男巫和第二排那个鬈发的女巫。

福吉左右看看大家，喉咙里似乎被一大块东西卡住了，随即他把手放下来，深吸了两口气，因为拼命压抑着火气，声音都变得异样了："很好，很好……指控不成立。"

"太好了。"邓布利多欢快地说，迅速站了起来，抽出魔杖一挥，那两把印花棉布的扶手椅就消失了，"好了，我得走了。祝大家今天过得愉快。"

说完，他看也不看哈利一眼，就快步走出了暗室。

CHAPTER NINE

The Woes of Mrs Weasley

Dumbledore's abrupt departure took Harry completely by surprise. He remained sitting where he was in the chained chair, struggling with his feelings of shock and relief. The Wizengamot were all getting to their feet, talking, gathering up their papers and packing them away. Harry stood up. Nobody seemed to be paying him the slightest bit of attention, except the toadlike witch on Fudge's right, who was now gazing down at him instead of at Dumbledore. Ignoring her, he tried to catch Fudge's eye, or Madam Bones's, wanting to ask whether he was free to go, but Fudge seemed quite determined not to notice Harry, and Madam Bones was busy with her briefcase, so he took a few tentative steps towards the exit and, when nobody called him back, broke into a very fast walk.

He took the last few steps at a run, wrenched open the door and almost collided with Mr Weasley, who was standing right outside, looking pale and apprehensive.

'Dumbledore didn't say –'

'Cleared,' Harry said, pulling the door closed behind him, 'of all charges!'

Beaming, Mr Weasley seized Harry by the shoulders.

'Harry, that's wonderful! Well, of course, they couldn't have found you guilty, not on the evidence, but even so, I can't pretend I wasn't –'

But Mr Weasley broke off, because the courtroom door had just opened again. The Wizengamot were filing out.

'Merlin's beard!' exclaimed Mr Weasley wonderingly, pulling Harry aside to let them all pass. 'You were tried by the full court?'

'I think so,' said Harry quietly.

One or two of the wizards nodded to Harry as they passed and a few,

第9章

韦斯莱夫人的烦恼

邓布利多的突然离去使哈利感到十分意外。他一动不动地坐在缠着链条的椅子上,努力使自己从惊愕和如释重负的感觉中缓过来。威森加摩的成员们纷纷站起身来,一边说着话一边整理收拾文件。哈利也站了起来。似乎没有一个人在注意他,只有福吉右边那个癞蛤蟆般的女巫例外,她刚才一直盯着邓布利多,现在又盯着哈利了。哈利假装没有看见,他试着去捕捉福吉或博恩斯女士的目光,想问问他是不是可以走了,但福吉似乎打定主意不理睬哈利,博恩斯女士则忙着整理自己的公文包。于是哈利犹豫不决地朝门口走了几步,见没有人叫他回去,便赶紧加快了脚步。

他几乎是小跑着走完了最后几步,拧开房门,差点跟站在外面的韦斯莱先生撞了个满怀。韦斯莱先生脸色苍白,显得惶恐不安。

"邓布利多没有说——"

"澄清了,"哈利反手把门关上,说道,"所有的指控都不成立。"

韦斯莱先生顿时眉开眼笑,一把抓住哈利的两个肩膀。

"哈利,真是太棒了!其实,当然啦,他们不可能判你有罪的,你有证据嘛,但我还是不能假装自己不——"

韦斯莱先生猛地顿住了,因为这时审判室的门又开了,威森加摩的成员鱼贯而出。

"梅林的胡子啊!"韦斯莱先生惊讶地喊了起来,把哈利拉到一边,让他们过去,"他们用全席法庭来审判你?"

"我想是的。"哈利轻声说。

一两个巫师走过时冲哈利点了点头,还有几个,包括博恩斯女士,

CHAPTER NINE   The Woes of Mrs Weasley

including Madam Bones, said, 'Morning, Arthur,' to Mr Weasley, but most averted their eyes. Cornelius Fudge and the toadlike witch were almost the last to leave the dungeon. Fudge acted as though Mr Weasley and Harry were part of the wall, but again, the witch looked almost appraisingly at Harry as she passed. Last of all to pass was Percy. Like Fudge, he completely ignored his father and Harry; he marched past clutching a large roll of parchment and a handful of spare quills, his back rigid and his nose in the air. The lines around Mr Weasley's mouth tightened slightly, but other than this he gave no sign that he had seen his third son.

'I'm going to take you straight back so you can tell the others the good news,' he said, beckoning Harry forwards as Percy's heels disappeared up the steps to Level Nine. 'I'll drop you off on the way to that toilet in Bethnal Green. Come on ...'

'So, what will you have to do about the toilet?' Harry asked, grinning. Everything suddenly seemed five times funnier than usual. It was starting to sink in: he was cleared, *he was going back to Hogwarts.*

'Oh, it's a simple enough anti-jinx,' said Mr Weasley as they mounted the stairs, 'but it's not so much having to repair the damage, it's more the attitude behind the vandalism, Harry. Muggle-baiting might strike some wizards as funny, but it's an expression of something much deeper and nastier, and I for one –'

Mr Weasley broke off in mid-sentence. They had just reached the ninth-level corridor and Cornelius Fudge was standing a few feet away from them, talking quietly to a tall man with sleek blond hair and a pointed, pale face.

The second man turned at the sound of their footsteps. He, too, broke off in mid-conversation, his cold grey eyes narrowed and fixed upon Harry's face.

'Well, well, well ... Patronus Potter,' said Lucius Malfoy coolly.

Harry felt winded, as though he had just walked into something solid. He had last seen those cold grey eyes through slits in a Death Eater's hood, and last heard that man's voice jeering in a dark graveyard while Lord Voldemort tortured him. Harry could not believe that Lucius Malfoy dared look him in the face; he could not believe that he was here, in the Ministry of Magic, or that Cornelius Fudge was talking to him, when Harry had told Fudge mere

第9章 韦斯莱夫人的烦恼

对韦斯莱先生说:"早上好,亚瑟。"但大多数人都把眼睛望着别处。康奈利和那个癞蛤蟆般的女巫几乎是最后离开地下室的。福吉只当韦斯莱先生和哈利是墙壁的一部分,而那个女巫走过时,又一次用几乎是审视的目光打量着哈利。最后走过的是珀西,他和福吉一样,完全无视他父亲和哈利的存在。他抓着一大卷羊皮纸和一大把备用的羽毛笔,背挺得直直的,鼻孔朝天,大步流星地走了过去。韦斯莱先生嘴巴周围的线条紧了一紧,但除此之外,他没有表露出见到他三儿子的任何迹象。

"我想直接把你送回去,你可以把这个好消息告诉大家。"他说,当珀西的脚跟消失在通往第九层的阶梯上时,他示意哈利往前走,"我要去贝斯纳绿地的那间厕所,顺便把你捎回去。走吧……"

"那么,你准备怎么对付那间厕所呢?"哈利咧嘴笑着问。突然之间,所有的事情似乎都比平常好玩了五倍。他终于开始明白:他被宣告无罪了,他就要回霍格沃茨了。

"哦,只需一个反恶咒的魔法,再简单不过了。"他们上楼时韦斯莱先生说,"修好被弄坏的东西倒没有什么,要纠正这种破坏行为背后的态度可就不容易了,哈利。有些巫师可能会觉得捉弄麻瓜挺好玩的,但这可能表达了一种更深刻、更丑恶的东西,我作为一个——"

韦斯莱先生话说到一半突然打住了。他们刚走到第九层的走廊上,康奈利·福吉站在离他们几英尺远的地方,正和一个高个子男人小声交谈,那人一头油光水滑的金黄色头发,一张尖脸白煞煞的。

听到他们的脚步声,那个高个子男人转过脸来。他也是话没说完就突然停住了,眯起冷冰冰的灰眼睛,死死地盯着哈利的脸。

"好啊,好啊,好啊……守护神波特!"卢修斯·马尔福冷冷地说。

哈利突然觉得透不过气来,似乎他一脚跨进了某个凝固的东西里。他上次看见这两只冷冰冰的灰眼睛时,它们隐藏在食死徒兜帽的两道狭缝后面;他上次听见这个男人的声音,是在阴暗的墓地里发出的阵阵嘲笑,而当时伏地魔正在折磨他。哈利不敢相信卢修斯·马尔福竟然还敢当面看着他,他不敢相信马尔福竟然出现在这里,在堂堂的魔法部,而康奈利·福吉竟然在跟他说话,要知道哈利几个星期前曾亲

CHAPTER NINE The Woes of Mrs Weasley

weeks ago that Malfoy was a Death Eater.

'The Minister was just telling me about your lucky escape, Potter,' drawled Mr Malfoy. 'Quite astonishing, the way you continue to wriggle out of very tight holes ... *snakelike*, in fact.'

Mr Weasley gripped Harry's shoulder in warning.

'Yeah,' said Harry, 'yeah, I'm good at escaping.'

Lucius Malfoy raised his eyes to Mr Weasley's face.

'And Arthur Weasley too! What are you doing here, Arthur?'

'I work here,' said Mr Weasley curtly.

'Not *here*, surely?' said Mr Malfoy, raising his eyebrows and glancing towards the door over Mr Weasley's shoulder. 'I thought you were up on the second floor ... don't you do something that involves sneaking Muggle artefacts home and bewitching them?'

'No,' Mr Weasley snapped, his fingers now biting into Harry's shoulder.

'What are *you* doing here, anyway?' Harry asked Lucius Malfoy.

'I don't think private matters between myself and the Minister are any concern of yours, Potter,' said Malfoy, smoothing the front of his robes. Harry distinctly heard the gentle clinking of what sounded like a full pocket of gold. 'Really, just because you are Dumbledore's favourite boy, you must not expect the same indulgence from the rest of us ... shall we go up to your office, then, Minister?'

'Certainly,' said Fudge, turning his back on Harry and Mr Weasley. 'This way, Lucius.'

They strode off together, talking in low voices. Mr Weasley did not let go of Harry's shoulder until they had disappeared into the lift.

'Why wasn't he waiting outside Fudge's office if they've got business to do together?' Harry burst out furiously. 'What was he doing down here?'

'Trying to sneak down to the courtroom, if you ask me,' said Mr Weasley, looking extremely agitated and glancing over his shoulder as though making sure they could not be overheard. 'Trying to find out whether you'd been expelled or not. I'll leave a note for Dumbledore when I drop you off, he ought to know Malfoy's been talking to Fudge again.'

'What private business have they got together, anyway?'

'Gold, I expect,' said Mr Weasley angrily. 'Malfoy's been giving generously

第9章 韦斯莱夫人的烦恼

口对福吉说过马尔福是个食死徒。

"部长刚跟我说了你侥幸逃脱的经过,波特,"马尔福先生拿腔作调地说,"真是令人惊诧,你能不断地从很狭窄的洞里钻出来……说实在的,真像蛇一样。"

韦斯莱先生紧紧抓住哈利的肩膀,警告他不要轻举妄动。

"是啊,"哈利说,"是啊,我很善于逃脱。"

卢修斯·马尔福抬起目光望着韦斯莱先生的脸。

"还有亚瑟·韦斯莱!你在这里干什么呢,亚瑟?"

"我在这里工作。"韦斯莱先生没好气地说。

"肯定不是这里吧?"马尔福说着扬起眉毛,扫了一眼韦斯莱先生身后的那扇门,"我记得你好像是在第二层……你的那份工作所涉及的不就是把麻瓜物品偷回家,给它们施魔法吗?"

"不是。"韦斯莱先生粗暴地说,他的手指已深深陷进了哈利的肩膀。

"那么你在这里干什么呢?"哈利问卢修斯·马尔福。

"我认为,我自己和部长之间的一些私事不需要你来过问,波特。"马尔福说着抹了抹他长袍的前襟。哈利清楚地听见了一阵轻微的丁零丁零的声音,似乎马尔福的口袋里装满了金子。"说实在的,你可不能因为自己是邓布利多的宠儿,就指望我们其他人也对你这样放纵……好了,部长,我们这就去你的办公室吧?"

"当然。"福吉说着把背转向了哈利和韦斯莱先生,"这边走,卢修斯。"

他们迈开大步走了,一边低声交谈着。韦斯莱先生一直等到他们消失在升降梯里,才松开了哈利的肩膀。

"如果他们要一起谈事情,他为什么不在福吉的办公室外面等着呢?"哈利气呼呼地问道,"他到这下面来干什么?"

"照我看,他是想偷偷溜进审判室,"韦斯莱先生说,他显得十分心烦意乱,不住地扭头看看有没有人在偷听,"想弄清你到底是不是被开除了。我把你送回去时要给邓布利多留一个短信,他应该知道马尔福又在跟福吉嘀嘀咕咕了。"

"他们之间到底有什么私事呢?"

"我想是金子吧。"韦斯莱先生气愤地说,"许多年来,马尔福一直

CHAPTER NINE The Woes of Mrs Weasley

to all sorts of things for years ... gets him in with the right people ... then he can ask favours ... delay laws he doesn't want passed ... oh, he's very well-connected, Lucius Malfoy.'

The lift arrived; it was empty except for a flock of memos that flapped around Mr Weasley's head as he pressed the button for the Atrium and the doors clanged shut. He waved them away irritably.

'Mr Weasley,' said Harry slowly, 'if Fudge is meeting Death Eaters like Malfoy, if he's seeing them alone, how do we know they haven't put the Imperius Curse on him?'

'Don't think it hasn't occurred to us, Harry,' said Mr Weasley quietly. 'But Dumbledore thinks Fudge is acting of his own accord at the moment – which, as Dumbledore says, is not a lot of comfort. Best not talk about it any more just now, Harry.'

The doors slid open and they stepped out into the now almost-deserted Atrium. Eric the watchwizard was hidden behind his *Daily Prophet* again. They had walked straight past the golden fountain before Harry remembered.

'Wait ...' he told Mr Weasley, and, pulling his money bag from his pocket, he turned back to the fountain.

He looked up into the handsome wizard's face, but close-to Harry thought he looked rather weak and foolish. The witch was wearing a vapid smile like a beauty contestant, and from what Harry knew of goblins and centaurs, they were most unlikely to be caught staring so soppily at humans of any description. Only the house-elf's attitude of creeping servility looked convincing. With a grin at the thought of what Hermione would say if she could see the statue of the elf, Harry turned his money bag upside-down and emptied not just ten Galleons, but the whole contents into the pool.

'I knew it!' yelled Ron, punching the air. 'You always get away with stuff!'

'They were bound to clear you,' said Hermione, who had looked positively faint with anxiety when Harry had entered the kitchen and was now holding a shaking hand over her eyes, 'there was no case against you, none at all.'

'Everyone seems quite relieved, though, considering you all knew I'd get off,' said Harry, smiling.

第9章 韦斯莱夫人的烦恼

对各种各样的事出手很大方……好使自己跟有权势的人攀上交情……然后可以要求特殊照顾……让那些他不想通过的法律一拖再拖……哦,卢修斯·马尔福,他真是能耐不小,神通广大啊。"

升降梯来了,里面没有人,只有一堆字条在韦斯莱先生的头顶上飞来飞去。他按了一下到正厅的按钮,升降梯的门哐啷哐啷关上了。他不耐烦地挥手驱赶着字条。

"韦斯莱先生,"哈利慢吞吞地说,"如果福吉跟马尔福这样的食死徒来往,如果他跟他们单独会面,我们怎么知道他们没有给福吉施夺魂咒呢?"

"别以为我们没有想到这一点,哈利,"韦斯莱先生小声说,"但邓布利多认为福吉目前是按照自己的意愿在行事——不过,用邓布利多的话说,这并不能给人带来多少安慰。现在最好还是别谈这件事,哈利。"

升降梯的门滑开了,他们走了出来,正厅里现在几乎空无一人。值班的巫师埃里克又藏在《预言家日报》后面了。他们径直从金色喷泉旁边走过时,哈利突然想起一件事。

"等一等……"他对韦斯莱先生说,然后从口袋里掏出钱袋,返身朝喷泉走去。

他抬头仔细端详着那位英俊巫师的面孔,现在离得近了,哈利觉得他显得很柔弱,很愚蠢。那女巫脸上堆着一个空洞的笑容,像是在参加选美比赛,而且就哈利对妖精和马人的了解,他们绝不可能这样含情脉脉地仰望任何人。只有家养小精灵那副怯生生的奴隶般的神态还令人信服。不知赫敏看到这个小精灵的雕像会说什么。哈利想到这儿,脸上露出调皮的笑容,他把钱袋倒了过来,不是数出十个加隆,而是把里面的钱全都倒进了水潭。

"我早就知道!"罗恩挥拳击打着空气,喊道,"你总是能够逃脱的!"

"他们肯定会宣告你无罪的,"赫敏说,刚才哈利走进厨房时,她看上去紧张得都快晕倒了,现在正用一只颤抖的手捂住眼睛,"没有理由给你判罪,根本就没有。"

"虽说你们都早就知道我不会有事,但每个人似乎都松了一口气呢。"哈利笑眯眯地说。

CHAPTER NINE The Woes of Mrs Weasley

Mrs Weasley was wiping her face on her apron, and Fred, George and Ginny were doing a kind of war dance to a chant that went: '*He got off, he got off, he got off ...*'

'That's enough! Settle down!' shouted Mr Weasley, though he too was smiling. 'Listen, Sirius, Lucius Malfoy was at the Ministry –'

'What?' said Sirius sharply.

'*He got off, he got off, he got off ...*'

'Be quiet, you three! Yes, we saw him talking to Fudge on Level Nine, then they went up to Fudge's office together. Dumbledore ought to know.'

'Absolutely,' said Sirius. 'We'll tell him, don't worry.'

'Well, I'd better get going, there's a vomiting toilet waiting for me in Bethnal Green. Molly, I'll be late, I'm covering for Tonks, but Kingsley might be dropping in for dinner –'

'*He got off, he got off, he got off ...*'

'That's enough – Fred – George – Ginny!' said Mrs Weasley, as Mr Weasley left the kitchen. 'Harry, dear, come and sit down, have some lunch, you hardly ate breakfast.'

Ron and Hermione sat themselves down opposite him, looking happier than they had done since he had first arrived at Grimmauld Place, and Harry's feeling of giddy relief, which had been somewhat dented by his encounter with Lucius Malfoy, swelled again. The gloomy house seemed warmer and more welcoming all of a sudden; even Kreacher looked less ugly as he poked his snoutlike nose into the kitchen to investigate the source of all the noise.

'Course, once Dumbledore turned up on your side, there was no way they were going to convict you,' said Ron happily, now dishing great mounds of mashed potato on to everyone's plates.

'Yeah, he swung it for me,' said Harry. He felt it would sound highly ungrateful, not to mention childish, to say, 'I wish he'd talked to me, though. Or even *looked* at me.'

And as he thought this, the scar on his forehead burned so badly that he clapped his hand to it.

'What's up?' said Hermione, looking alarmed.

'Scar,' Harry mumbled. 'But it's nothing ... it happens all the time now ...'

第9章 韦斯莱夫人的烦恼

韦斯莱夫人正用她的围裙擦眼泪,弗雷德、乔治和金妮跳起了一种战舞,嘴里一遍又一遍地唱道:"他没事啦,没事啦,没事啦……"

"够了!安静一点儿!"韦斯莱先生喊道,但他脸上也笑眯眯的,"听着,小天狼星,卢修斯·马尔福也在部里——"

"什么?"小天狼星警觉地问。

"他没事啦,没事啦,没事啦……"

"安静,安静,你们三个!是的,我们看见他在第九层跟福吉说话,然后他们一起进了福吉的办公室。这事儿应该让邓布利多知道。"

"一点儿不错,"小天狼星说,"我们会告诉他的,不要担心。"

"好了,我得走了,贝斯纳绿地还有一间正在呕吐的厕所等着我呢。莫丽,我大概会晚点儿回来,我要替换唐克斯,不过金斯莱可能过来吃晚饭——"

"他没事啦,没事啦,没事啦……"

"够了——弗雷德——乔治——金妮!"韦斯莱先生走出厨房后,韦斯莱夫人说道,"哈利,亲爱的,过来坐下吃点午饭吧,你早饭几乎没怎么吃。"

罗恩和赫敏坐在哈利对面,自打他到格里莫广场以来,他们还没显得这么高兴呢。哈利心头那份令他感到晕眩的如释重负的感觉,曾经因为与卢修斯·马尔福狭路相逢而受到一点影响,现在又重新在心里激荡起来。突然之间,这座昏暗阴森的房子显得那么温暖、那么热情好客。就连克利切把脑袋探进厨房,看看这里闹哄哄的在做什么时,他那猪鼻子般的大鼻子看上去也没那么难看了。

"只要邓布利多出面支持你,他们就不可能给你定罪,这是不用说的。"罗恩兴高采烈地说,一边把大团大团的土豆泥分进每人的盘子里。

"是啊,他帮我摆平了这件事。"哈利说。他觉得如果现在说"我希望他跟我说两句话,哪怕看我一眼也好",会显得很不知好歹,更不用说多么幼稚了。

想到这里,他额头上的伤疤突然一阵剧痛,他赶紧伸手捂住了它。

"怎么啦?"赫敏问,显得很惊慌。

"伤疤,"哈利含混地说,"没关系……现在经常有这种情况……"

CHAPTER NINE   The Woes of Mrs Weasley

None of the others had noticed a thing; all of them were now helping themselves to food while gloating over Harry's narrow escape; Fred, George and Ginny were still singing. Hermione looked rather anxious, but before she could say anything, Ron had said happily, 'I bet Dumbledore turns up this evening, to celebrate with us, you know.'

'I don't think he'll be able to, Ron,' said Mrs Weasley, setting a huge plate of roast chicken down in front of Harry. 'He's really very busy at the moment.'

'*HE GOT OFF, HE GOT OFF, HE GOT OFF...*'

'SHUT UP!' roared Mrs Weasley.

Over the next few days Harry could not help noticing that there was one person within number twelve, Grimmauld Place, who did not seem wholly overjoyed that he would be returning to Hogwarts. Sirius had put up a very good show of happiness on first hearing the news, wringing Harry's hand and beaming just like the rest of them. Soon, however, he was moodier and surlier than before, talking less to everybody, even Harry, and spending increasing amounts of time shut up in his mother's room with Buckbeak.

'Don't you go feeling guilty!' said Hermione sternly, after Harry had confided some of his feelings to her and Ron while they scrubbed out a mouldy cupboard on the third floor a few days later. 'You belong at Hogwarts and Sirius knows it. Personally, I think he's being selfish.'

'That's a bit harsh, Hermione,' said Ron, frowning as he attempted to prise off a bit of mould that had attached itself firmly to his finger, '*you* wouldn't want to be stuck inside this house without any company.'

'He'll have company!' said Hermione. 'It's Headquarters to the Order of the Phoenix, isn't it? He just got his hopes up that Harry would be coming to live here with him.'

'I don't think that's true,' said Harry, wringing out his cloth. 'He wouldn't give me a straight answer when I asked him if I could.'

'He just didn't want to get his own hopes up even more,' said Hermione wisely. 'And he probably felt a bit guilty himself, because I think a part of him was really hoping you'd be expelled. Then you'd both be outcasts together.'

'Come off it!' said Harry and Ron together, but Hermione merely shrugged.

第9章 韦斯莱夫人的烦恼

其他人都没有注意到。这会儿他们都在一边动手盛饭菜，一边为哈利的侥幸脱身而欢欣鼓舞。弗雷德、乔治和金妮还在唱歌。赫敏看上去忧心忡忡，但没等她再说什么，罗恩就开心地说："我猜邓布利多今晚肯定会来，你知道的，来跟我们一块儿庆祝呀。"

"我想他可能来不了，罗恩，"韦斯莱夫人说着把一大盘烤鸡放在哈利面前，"他眼下确实忙得够呛。"

"他没事啦，没事啦，没事啦……"

"闭嘴！"韦斯莱夫人大吼一声。

在接下来的几天里，哈利忍不住注意到格里莫广场12号里有一个人似乎对他能够重返霍格沃茨并不十分高兴。最初听到这个消息时，小天狼星表现出非常喜悦的样子，紧紧攥住了哈利的手，像其他人一样满脸喜色。可是，没过多久，他就变得比以前还要沉闷、忧郁，话越来越少，甚至跟哈利也没有几句话可说，他把自己关在他母亲房间里的时间越来越多，只与巴克比克为伴。

"你不要觉得内疚！"赫敏斩钉截铁地说。这已是几天以后，他们三个在四楼擦洗一个发霉的小橱时，哈利把自己内心的想法透露给了她和罗恩，"你属于霍格沃茨，小天狼星知道这一点。我个人认为，他这样很自私。"

"这么说太尖刻了。"罗恩一边说一边皱着眉头，使劲刮掉一块牢牢粘在他手指上的霉斑，"换了你，你也不愿意被困在这个房子里，没有人做伴。"

"会有人跟他做伴的！"赫敏说，"这里是凤凰社的指挥部，是不是？他只是心里起了希望，觉得哈利可能会过来和他住在一起。"

"我认为不是这样。"哈利拧干抹布说道，"当我问他我能不能住在这里时，他都不肯直截了当地回答我。"

"他只是不想让自己的希望变得更强烈。"赫敏显得很有见解地说，"他大概自己也感到有点内疚，因为我想他心里确实隐约希望你被开除。然后你们俩就都是被驱逐的人了。"

"别胡说了！"哈利和罗恩异口同声地说，赫敏只是耸了耸肩膀。

CHAPTER NINE The Woes of Mrs Weasley

'Suit yourselves. But I sometimes think Ron's mum's right and Sirius gets confused about whether you're you or your father, Harry.'

'So you think he's touched in the head?' said Harry heatedly.

'No, I just think he's been very lonely for a long time,' said Hermione simply.

At this point, Mrs Weasley entered the bedroom behind them.

'Still not finished?' she said, poking her head into the cupboard.

'I thought you might be here to tell us to have a break!' said Ron bitterly. 'D'you know how much mould we've got rid of since we arrived here?'

'You were so keen to help the Order,' said Mrs Weasley, 'you can do your bit by making Headquarters fit to live in.'

'I feel like a house-elf,' grumbled Ron.

'Well, now you understand what dreadful lives they lead, perhaps you'll be a bit more active in S.P.E.W.!' said Hermione hopefully, as Mrs Weasley left them to it. 'You know, maybe it wouldn't be a bad idea to show people exactly how horrible it is to clean all the time – we could do a sponsored scrub of Gryffindor common room, all proceeds to S.P.E.W., it would raise awareness as well as funds.'

'I'll sponsor you to shut up about *S.P.E.W.*,' Ron muttered irritably, but only so Harry could hear him.

Harry found himself daydreaming about Hogwarts more and more as the end of the holidays approached; he could not wait to see Hagrid again, to play Quidditch, even to stroll across the vegetable patches to the Herbology greenhouses; it would be a treat just to leave this dusty, musty house, where half of the cupboards were still bolted shut and Kreacher wheezed insults out of the shadows as you passed, though Harry was careful not to say any of this within earshot of Sirius.

The fact was that living at the Headquarters of the anti-Voldemort movement was not nearly as interesting or exciting as Harry would have expected before he'd experienced it. Though members of the Order of the Phoenix came and went regularly, sometimes staying for meals, sometimes only for a few minutes of whispered conversation, Mrs Weasley made sure that Harry and the others were kept well out of earshot (whether Extendable or normal) and nobody, not even Sirius, seemed to feel that Harry needed to

第9章 韦斯莱夫人的烦恼

"随你们怎么想吧。但我有时认为罗恩的妈妈说得对,哈利,小天狼星确实搞不清你到底是你还是你父亲。"

"所以你认为他头脑有点儿不正常?"哈利恼火地问。

"不是,我只是认为他很长时间以来一直很孤独。"赫敏简单地说。

就在这时,韦斯莱夫人走进了他们身后的卧室。

"还没有弄完吗?"她说着把脑袋探进了小橱。

"我还以为你会过来叫我们休息一会儿呢!"罗恩气呼呼地说,"你知道我们来这里已经清除了多少霉菌吗?"

"你们这么热心想帮助凤凰社,"韦斯莱夫人说,"把指挥部打扫得能住人也算是你们的一份贡献嘛。"

"我觉得自己像个家养小精灵。"罗恩嘟哝道。

"是啊,现在你该明白他们过着多么悲惨的生活了吧,也许你会更积极地对待S.P.E.W.了!"赫敏满怀希望地说,韦斯莱夫人径自走开了,"对了,让人们体会到从早到晚都在打扫卫生是多么可怕,这个主意倒不坏——我们可以发起一个打扫格兰芬多公共休息室的筹款活动,所有收益都归S.P.E.W.,这样不仅可以筹集资金,还能提高人们的觉悟。"

"我赞助你,求你别再谈什么'呕吐'了。"罗恩不耐烦地咕哝道,但声音很低,只有哈利能听见。

随着假期即将结束,哈利发现自己一天比一天更想念霍格沃茨了。他迫不及待地想看到海格,想打魁地奇球,甚至想穿过菜地走向草药课的温室。离开这座肮脏、腐臭的老房子真是太让人愉快了,这里还有一半的橱柜都锁得紧紧的,克利切总在你经过时躲在阴影里恶声恶气地谩骂,不过哈利得留心不在小天狼星能听见的地方说这些抱怨的话。

事实上,住在反伏地魔行动的指挥部里,一点儿也不像哈利原先想的那样有趣,那样激动人心。尽管凤凰社的成员定期进进出出,有时留下来吃饭,有时则只停留几分钟,说几句悄悄话,但韦斯莱夫人确保不让哈利和其他人(无论是用人耳还是伸缩耳)听到任何消息。他们都认为哈利除了刚来的那天晚上听到的那些,不再需要知道更多

CHAPTER NINE   The Woes of Mrs Weasley

know anything more than he had heard on the night of his arrival.

On the very last day of the holidays Harry was sweeping up Hedwig's owl droppings from the top of the wardrobe when Ron entered their bedroom carrying a couple of envelopes.

'Booklists have arrived,' he said, throwing one of the envelopes up to Harry, who was standing on a chair. 'About time, I thought they'd forgotten, they usually come much earlier than this ...'

Harry swept the last of the droppings into a rubbish bag and threw the bag over Ron's head into the wastepaper basket in the corner, which swallowed it and belched loudly. He then opened his letter. It contained two pieces of parchment: one the usual reminder that term started on the first of September; the other telling him which books he would need for the coming year.

'Only two new ones,' he said, reading the list, '*The Standard Book of Spells, Grade 5*, by Miranda Goshawk, and *Defensive Magical Theory*, by Wilbert Slinkhard.'

Crack.

Fred and George Apparated right beside Harry. He was so used to them doing this by now that he didn't even fall off his chair.

'We were just wondering who set the Slinkhard book,' said Fred conversationally.

'Because it means Dumbledore's found a new Defence Against the Dark Arts teacher,' said George.

'And about time too,' said Fred.

'What d'you mean?' Harry asked, jumping down beside them.

'Well, we overheard Mum and Dad talking on the Extendable Ears a few weeks back,' Fred told Harry, 'and from what they were saying, Dumbledore was having real trouble finding anyone to do the job this year.'

'Not surprising, is it, when you look at what's happened to the last four?' said George.

'One sacked, one dead, one's memory removed and one locked in a trunk for nine months,' said Harry, counting them off on his fingers. 'Yeah, I see what you mean.'

'What's up with you, Ron?' asked Fred.

Ron did not answer. Harry looked round. Ron was standing very still with his mouth slightly open, gaping at his letter from Hogwarts.

第9章 韦斯莱夫人的烦恼

的事情,就连小天狼星也是这样想的。

假期的最后一天,哈利正在清扫衣柜顶上海德薇的粪便,罗恩拿着两个信封走进了卧室。

"书单来了。"他说,把一个信封扔给了站在椅子上的哈利,"也该来了,我还以为他们忘记了呢,往年早就来了……"

哈利把最后一点粪便扫进垃圾袋,然后从罗恩的头顶上把袋子扔进了墙角的废纸篓。废纸篓吞下垃圾袋,大声打起嗝来。哈利这才拆开他的信,里面有两张羊皮纸:一张照例是提醒他九月一日开学,另一张告诉他下一学年需要哪些书。

"只有两本新书,"他读着那张单子说道,"《标准咒语,五级》,米兰达·戈沙克著,和《魔法防御理论》,威尔伯特·斯林卡著。"

啪!

弗雷德和乔治幻影显形,突然出现在哈利身边。哈利现在对他们这一套已经习以为常,不会再被吓得从椅子上摔下来了。

"我们正在纳闷是谁订下斯林卡的那本书的。"弗雷德随意地说。

"因为这意味着邓布利多找到黑魔法防御术课的新老师了。"乔治说。

"也该找到了。"弗雷德说。

"这是什么意思?"哈利一边问一边跳下来落在他们旁边。

"噢,几个星期前,我们用伸缩耳偷听了妈妈和爸爸的谈话。"弗雷德告诉哈利,"从他们的谈话中可以听出,邓布利多为了找到这学年能胜任这份工作的人,可是费尽了周折。"

"你看看以前那四个老师的遭遇,就觉得这并不奇怪了,是吧?"乔治说。

"一个被开除,一个死了,一个被消除了记忆,还有一个被锁在箱子里整整九个月。"哈利掰着指头一个个地数,"是啊,我明白你们的意思了。"

"罗恩,你怎么啦?"弗雷德问。

罗恩没有回答。哈利转过头一看,罗恩一动不动地站在那里,嘴巴微张,呆呆地望着霍格沃茨给他的那封信。

CHAPTER NINE The Woes of Mrs Weasley

'What's the matter?' said Fred impatiently, moving around Ron to look over his shoulder at the parchment.

Fred's mouth fell open, too.

'Prefect?' he said, staring incredulously at the letter. '*Prefect?*'

George leapt forwards, seized the envelope in Ron's other hand and turned it upside-down. Harry saw something scarlet and gold fall into George's palm.

'No way,' said George in a hushed voice.

'There's been a mistake,' said Fred, snatching the letter out of Ron's grasp and holding it up to the light as though checking for a watermark. 'No one in their right mind would make Ron a prefect.'

The twins' heads turned in unison and both of them stared at Harry.

'We thought you were a cert!' said Fred, in a tone that suggested Harry had tricked them in some way.

'We thought Dumbledore was *bound* to pick you!' said George indignantly.

'Winning the Triwizard and everything!' said Fred.

'I suppose all the mad stuff must've counted against him,' said George to Fred.

'Yeah,' said Fred slowly. 'Yeah, you've caused too much trouble, mate. Well, at least one of you's got their priorities right.'

He strode over to Harry and clapped him on the back while giving Ron a scathing look.

'*Prefect* ... ickle Ronnie the Prefect.'

'Ohh, Mum's going to be revolting,' groaned George, thrusting the prefect badge back at Ron as though it might contaminate him.

Ron, who still had not said a word, took the badge, stared at it for a moment, then held it out to Harry as though asking mutely for confirmation that it was genuine. Harry took it. A large 'P' was superimposed on the Gryffindor lion. He had seen a badge just like this on Percy's chest on his very first day at Hogwarts.

The door banged open. Hermione came tearing into the room, her cheeks flushed and her hair flying. There was an envelope in her hand.

'Did you – did you get –?'

She spotted the badge in Harry's hand and let out a shriek.

第9章 韦斯莱夫人的烦恼

"怎么回事呀？"弗雷德不耐烦地问，一边绕到罗恩身后，从他肩膀上探头望着那张羊皮纸。

弗雷德也吃惊地张大了嘴巴。

"级长？"他不敢相信地瞪着那封信，说道，"级长？"

乔治冲上前，一把抢过罗恩另一只手里的信封，把它倒了过来。哈利看见一个红色和金色的东西掉进了乔治的手心。

"不可能。"乔治压低声音说。

"肯定是弄错了，"弗雷德把信从罗恩手里一把抢了过去，高高举在光线底下，似乎要检查上面的水印，"头脑正常的人，谁会选罗恩当级长呢？"

双胞胎的脑袋齐刷刷地转了过来，四只眼睛同时盯着哈利。

"我们还以为肯定是你呢！"弗雷德说，听他的口气，好像哈利在某种程度上欺骗了他们似的。

"我们以为邓布利多肯定会选你！"乔治愤愤不平地说。

"赢得了三强争霸赛，做了那么多事！"弗雷德说。

"我猜肯定是那些离奇的鬼话拖了他的后腿。"乔治对弗雷德说。

"是啊，"弗雷德慢吞吞地说，"是啊，你制造的麻烦太多了，伙计。嘿，至少你们俩中间有一个是在做正事的。"

他大步走到哈利身边，拍了拍他的后背，同时朝罗恩刻薄地瞪了一眼。

"级长……小罗尼当上了级长。"

"哦哦，妈妈肯定要令人作呕了。"乔治唉声叹气地说，把级长的徽章塞进罗恩手里，好像生怕它会玷污了自己似的。

罗恩仍然一句话也没有说，只是接过徽章呆呆地望了一会儿，然后把它递给了哈利，似乎在无声地请求哈利证实徽章是货真价实的。哈利接了过来。格兰芬多的狮子身上镶着一个大大的字母"P"字。他在进入霍格沃茨的第一天，曾在珀西的胸前看见过一个这样的徽章。

门砰的一声被推开了，赫敏一头冲进房间，脸上红扑扑的，头发都飘了起来。她手里拿着一个信封。

"你——你拿到了——？"

她一眼看到哈利手里的徽章，发出一声尖叫。

CHAPTER NINE   The Woes of Mrs Weasley

'I knew it!' she said excitedly, brandishing her letter. 'Me too, Harry, me too!'

'No,' said Harry quickly, pushing the badge back into Ron's hand. 'It's Ron, not me.'

'It – what?'

'Ron's prefect, not me,' Harry said.

'*Ron?*' said Hermione, her jaw dropping. 'But ... are you sure? I mean –'

She turned red as Ron looked round at her with a defiant expression on his face.

'It's my name on the letter,' he said.

'I ...' said Hermione, looking thoroughly bewildered. 'I ... well ... wow! Well done, Ron! That's really –'

'Unexpected,' said George, nodding.

'No,' said Hermione, blushing harder than ever, 'no it's not ... Ron's done loads of ... he's really ...'

The door behind her opened a little wider and Mrs Weasley backed into the room carrying a pile of freshly laundered robes.

'Ginny said the booklists had come at last,' she said, glancing around at all the envelopes as she made her way over to the bed and started sorting the robes into two piles. 'If you give them to me I'll take them over to Diagon Alley this afternoon and get your books while you're packing. Ron, I'll have to get you more pyjamas, these are at least six inches too short, I can't believe how fast you're growing ... what colour would you like?'

'Get him red and gold to match his badge,' said George, smirking.

'Match his what?' said Mrs Weasley absently, rolling up a pair of maroon socks and placing them on Ron's pile.

'His *badge*,' said Fred, with the air of getting the worst over quickly. 'His lovely shiny new *prefect's badge*.'

Fred's words took a moment to penetrate Mrs Weasley's preoccupation with pyjamas.

'His ... but ... Ron, you're not ...?'

Ron held up his badge.

280

第9章　韦斯莱夫人的烦恼

"我早就知道!"她兴奋地说,挥舞着手里的信封,"我也是,哈利,我也是!"

"不,"哈利赶紧说道,把徽章塞还到罗恩手里,"是罗恩,不是我。"

"是——什么?"

"级长是罗恩,不是我。"哈利说。

"罗恩?"赫敏说,吃惊得嘴巴都合不拢了,"可是……你能肯定吗?我是说——"

这时罗恩转过脸望着她,脸上带着一副挑衅的表情,赫敏的脸腾地红了。

"信上是我的名字。"他说。

"我……"赫敏说,似乎完全被弄糊涂了,"我……好吧……哇!罗恩,太棒了!这真是——"

"没有想到。"乔治说着点了点头。

"不是,"赫敏说,脸红得比刚才更厉害了,"不,不是的……罗恩也做了许多……他真的很……"

她身后的房门又被推开了一点儿,韦斯莱夫人抱着一堆刚洗干净的袍子后退着走了进来。

"金妮说书单终于来了。"她说着扫了一眼大家手里的信封,一边朝床边走去,然后开始把衣服分成两堆,"如果你们把书单给我,我今天下午就到对角巷去给你们把书买来,你们在家收拾行李。罗恩,我要给你再买一套睡衣,这一套短了至少六英寸,真不敢相信你怎么长得这么快……你想要什么颜色的?"

"给他买红色和金色相间的,配他的徽章。"乔治坏笑着说。

"配他的什么?"韦斯莱夫人心不在焉地说,卷起一双褐紫色的袜子放在罗恩的那堆衣服上。

"他的徽章啊,"弗雷德说,似乎长痛不如短痛,索性一口气都说了出来,"他那可爱的、崭新的、闪闪发亮的级长徽章。"

韦斯莱夫人脑子里还在想着睡衣,过了好一会儿她才明白了弗雷德的话。

"他的……可是……罗恩,你该不是……?"

罗恩举起了他的徽章。

CHAPTER NINE The Woes of Mrs Weasley

Mrs Weasley let out a shriek just like Hermione's.

'I don't believe it! I don't believe it! Oh, Ron, how wonderful! A prefect! That's everyone in the family!'

'What are Fred and I, next-door neighbours?' said George indignantly, as his mother pushed him aside and flung her arms around her youngest son.

'Wait until your father hears! Ron, I'm so proud of you, what wonderful news, you could end up Head Boy just like Bill and Percy, it's the first step! Oh, what a thing to happen in the middle of all this worry, I'm just thrilled, oh, *Ronnie* –'

Fred and George were both making loud retching noises behind her back but Mrs Weasley did not notice; arms tight around Ron's neck, she was kissing him all over his face, which had turned a brighter scarlet than his badge.

'Mum ... don't ... Mum, get a grip ...' he muttered, trying to push her away.

She let go of him and said breathlessly, 'Well, what will it be? We gave Percy an owl, but you've already got one, of course.'

'W-what do you mean?' said Ron, looking as though he did not dare believe his ears.

'You've got to have a reward for this!' said Mrs Weasley fondly. 'How about a nice new set of dress robes?'

'We've already bought him some,' said Fred sourly, who looked as though he sincerely regretted this generosity.

'Or a new cauldron, Charlie's old one's rusting through, or a new rat, you always liked Scabbers –'

'Mum,' said Ron hopefully, 'can I have a new broom?'

Mrs Weasley's face fell slightly; broomsticks were expensive.

'Not a really good one!' Ron hastened to add. 'Just – just a new one for a change ...'

Mrs Weasley hesitated, then smiled.

'Of *course* you can ... well, I'd better get going if I've got a broom to buy too. I'll see you all later ... little Ronnie, a prefect! And don't forget to pack your trunks ... a prefect ... oh, I'm all of a dither!'

第9章 韦斯莱夫人的烦恼

韦斯莱夫人发出一声尖叫,跟赫敏刚才一模一样。

"我真不敢相信!我真不敢相信!哦,罗恩,真是太棒了!级长!家里的每个人都是级长!"

"弗雷德和我算什么?隔壁邻居吗?"乔治愤愤不平地说,他妈妈把他推到一边,张开双臂搂住了她最小的儿子。

"你爸爸听说了该多高兴啊!罗恩,我太为你骄傲了,多么令人高兴的消息,你以后可能会像比尔和珀西一样当上男生学生会主席呢,这是第一步啊!哦,最近烦心事这么多,没想到有了这么一个大喜讯,我真是太激动了,哦,罗尼——"

弗雷德和乔治都在韦斯莱夫人后面发出很响的干呕声,但韦斯莱夫人没有注意到。她用胳膊紧紧搂住罗恩的脖子,在他脸上左一下右一下地亲着,罗恩的脸涨得比他的徽章还要鲜红耀眼。

"妈妈……不要……妈妈,控制一下……"他喃喃地说,拼命想把她推开。

韦斯莱夫人放开了罗恩,气喘吁吁地说:"那么,想要什么呢?我们给了珀西一只猫头鹰,可是当然啦,你已经有一只了。"

"你——你说什么?"罗恩说,似乎不敢相信自己的耳朵。

"你必须因此得到奖励!"韦斯莱夫人慈爱地说,"一套漂亮的新礼服长袍怎么样?"

"我们已经给他买了一套。"弗雷德没好气地说,似乎从心底里懊悔他的这份慷慨。

"或者一只新坩埚,查理的那只旧坩埚已经生满了锈,或者一只新老鼠,你以前一直那么喜欢斑斑——"

"妈妈,"罗恩满怀希望地说,"我能得到一把新扫帚吗?"

韦斯莱夫人的脸微微沉了沉,飞天扫帚是很贵的。

"不要特别好的!"罗恩赶紧说道,"只要——只要一把新的,换换感觉……"

韦斯莱夫人犹豫了一下,然后笑了。

"当然可以……好了,我怎么也得走了,还要买一把扫帚呢。我们待会儿再见……小罗尼,级长!你们别忘了收拾箱子……级长……哦,我真是太高兴了!"

She gave Ron yet another kiss on the cheek, sniffed loudly, and bustled from the room.

Fred and George exchanged looks.

'You don't mind if we don't kiss you, do you, Ron?' said Fred in a falsely anxious voice.

'We could curtsey, if you like,' said George.

'Oh, shut up,' said Ron, scowling at them.

'Or what?' said Fred, an evil grin spreading across his face. 'Going to put us in detention?'

'I'd love to see him try,' sniggered George.

'He could if you don't watch out!' said Hermione angrily.

Fred and George burst out laughing, and Ron muttered, 'Drop it, Hermione.'

'We're going to have to watch our step, George,' said Fred, pretending to tremble, 'with these two on our case ...'

'Yeah, it looks like our law-breaking days are finally over,' said George, shaking his head.

And with another loud *crack*, the twins Disapparated.

'Those two!' said Hermione furiously, staring up at the ceiling, through which they could now hear Fred and George roaring with laughter in the room upstairs. 'Don't pay any attention to them, Ron, they're only jealous!'

'I don't think they are,' said Ron doubtfully, also looking up at the ceiling. 'They've always said only prats become prefects ... still,' he added on a happier note, 'they've never had new brooms! I wish I could go with Mum and choose ... she'll never be able to afford a Nimbus, but there's the new Cleansweep out, that'd be great ... yeah, I think I'll go and tell her I like the Cleansweep, just so she knows ...'

He dashed from the room, leaving Harry and Hermione alone.

For some reason, Harry found he did not want to look at Hermione. He turned to his bed, picked up the pile of clean robes Mrs Weasley had laid on it and crossed the room to his trunk.

'Harry?' said Hermione tentatively.

'Well done, Hermione,' said Harry, so heartily it did not sound like his voice at all, and, still not looking at her, 'brilliant. Prefect. Great.'

第9章 韦斯莱夫人的烦恼

她又在罗恩的面颊上亲了一口,很响地抽了抽鼻子,匆匆忙忙地走出了房间。

弗雷德和乔治交换了一下目光。

"我们不亲你,你不介意吧,罗恩?"弗雷德装出一种诚惶诚恐的声音问。

"如果你愿意,我们可以行屈膝礼。"乔治说。

"哦,闭嘴!"罗恩说,气呼呼地瞪着他们。

"不然就怎么样?"弗雷德说,脸上露出一副坏笑,"要给我们关禁闭吗?"

"我倒想看看他敢不敢呢。"乔治哧哧地笑着说。

"如果你们不小心点儿,他就能!"赫敏气愤地说。

弗雷德和乔治哈哈大笑,罗恩低声说:"别这么说,赫敏。"

"乔治,我们以后可得多加小心了,"弗雷德假装浑身发抖地说道,"有这两个人盯着我们……"

"是啊,我们违法乱纪的日子眼看就要结束了。"乔治说着摇了摇头。

随着又一声震耳欲聋的啪,一对双胞胎幻影移形了。

"这两个人!"赫敏气恼地说,抬眼望着天花板,他们可以听见弗雷德和乔治在楼上的房间里放声大笑,"别理睬他们,罗恩,他们只是在嫉妒!"

"我认为不是,"罗恩怀疑地说,也抬头望着天花板,"他们总是说,只有傻瓜才会当级长……不过,"他的语气又高兴起来,"他们从来没得到过新扫帚!真希望我能跟妈妈一起去,亲自挑选……她肯定买不起'光轮',但现在有新款的'横扫'上市了,那肯定很棒……对啊,我想我得去告诉她,我要'横扫',这样她就知道了……"

他一头冲出房间,把哈利和赫敏撇在身后。

不知怎的,哈利发现自己不愿意看着赫敏。他转身走到他的床边,抱起韦斯莱夫人刚才放在床上的那堆干净衣服,朝房间那头他的箱子走去。

"哈利?"赫敏迟疑不决地说。

"太棒了,赫敏,"哈利说,热情得有些夸张,听上去根本不像是他的声音,而且他的眼睛仍然没看赫敏,"太出色了。级长。真了不起。"

CHAPTER NINE   The Woes of Mrs Weasley

'Thanks,' said Hermione. 'Erm – Harry – could I borrow Hedwig so I can tell Mum and Dad? They'll be really pleased – I mean *prefect* is something they can understand.'

'Yeah, no problem,' said Harry, still in the horrible hearty voice that did not belong to him. 'Take her!'

He leaned over his trunk, laid the robes on the bottom of it and pretended to be rummaging for something while Hermione crossed to the wardrobe and called Hedwig down. A few moments passed; Harry heard the door close but remained bent double, listening; the only sounds he could hear were the blank picture on the wall sniggering again and the wastepaper basket in the corner coughing up the owl droppings.

He straightened up and looked behind him. Hermione had left and Hedwig had gone. Harry returned slowly to his bed and sank on to it, gazing unseeingly at the foot of the wardrobe.

He had forgotten completely about prefects being chosen in the fifth year. He had been too anxious about the possibility of being expelled to spare a thought for the fact that badges must be winging their way towards certain people. But if he *had* remembered ... if he *had* thought about it ... what would he have expected?

Not this, said a small and truthful voice inside his head.

Harry screwed up his face and buried it in his hands. He could not lie to himself; if he had known the prefect badge was on its way, he would have expected it to come to him, not Ron. Did this make him as arrogant as Draco Malfoy? Did he think himself superior to everyone else? Did he really believe he was *better* than Ron?

No, said the small voice defiantly.

Was that true? Harry wondered, anxiously probing his own feelings.

I'm better at Quidditch, said the voice. *But I'm not better at anything else.*

That was definitely true, Harry thought; he was no better than Ron in lessons. But what about outside lessons? What about those adventures he, Ron and Hermione had had together since starting at Hogwarts, often risking much worse than expulsion?

Well, Ron and Hermione were with me most of the time, said the voice in Harry's head.

第9章 韦斯莱夫人的烦恼

"谢谢,"赫敏说,"唔——哈利——我能借海德薇用一下吗?我想告诉我的爸爸妈妈。他们肯定会非常高兴的——我是说当级长这件事他们是能明白的。"

"行,没问题,"哈利说,仍然是那种热情过分、不像是他自己的语气,"拿去吧!"

他弯腰俯在箱子上,把那堆衣服放在箱子底下,假装在里面翻找着什么,这时赫敏走到衣柜前唤海德薇下来。过了一会儿,哈利听见门关上了,但他仍然弯着腰,侧耳倾听,四下里没有别的声音,只有墙上那张空白油画布又在咻咻发笑,还有墙角的废纸篓在咳嗽,想把猫头鹰的粪便吐出来。

他直起身,看看身后,赫敏已经走了,海德薇也不见了。哈利慢慢走回到床边,一头倒在床上,两眼失神地望着衣柜的脚。

他已经把五年级要挑选级长的事忘得一干二净。他一直忧心忡忡地担心会被开除,根本没有心思去想徽章正扇动着翅膀朝某些人飞来。但如果他没有忘记……如果他曾经想过……他会希望有什么结果呢?

不是现在这样。他脑袋里一个诚实的小声音说道。

哈利的脸皱成一团,埋在双手里。他不能对自己撒谎。如果他知道要选级长,他肯定希望选中的是自己,而不是罗恩。他这是不是像德拉科·马尔福一样狂妄自大呢?他难道认为自己比别人都了不起?他真的相信自己比罗恩出色?

不。那个小声音斩钉截铁地说。

真的吗?哈利疑惑地想,急于把自己的感觉探究个水落石出。

我打魁地奇球确实打得比他棒,那个声音说,但在其他方面并不比他出色。

那是千真万确的,哈利想道,他的功课并不比罗恩优秀。可是功课以外的事情呢?自从进入霍格沃茨后,他、罗恩和赫敏共同经历的那些奇遇呢?而且还经常冒着比被开除更可怕的危险!

是啊,大多数时候罗恩和赫敏都和我在一起。哈利脑袋里的那个声音说。

CHAPTER NINE The Woes of Mrs Weasley

Not all the time, though, Harry argued with himself. They didn't fight Quirrell with me. They didn't take on Riddle and the Basilisk. They didn't get rid of all those Dementors the night Sirius escaped. They weren't in that graveyard with me, the night Voldemort returned ...

And the same feeling of ill-usage that had overwhelmed him on the night he had arrived rose again. *I've definitely done more*, Harry thought indignantly. *I've done more than either of them!*

But maybe, said the small voice fairly, *maybe Dumbledore doesn't choose prefects because they've got themselves into a load of dangerous situations ... maybe he chooses them for other reasons ... Ron must have something you don't ...*

Harry opened his eyes and stared through his fingers at the wardrobe's clawed feet, remembering what Fred had said: 'No one in their right mind would make Ron a prefect ...'

Harry gave a small snort of laughter. A second later he felt sickened with himself.

Ron had not asked Dumbledore to give him the prefect badge. This was not Ron's fault. Was he, Harry, Ron's best friend in the world, going to sulk because he didn't have a badge, laugh with the twins behind Ron's back, ruin this for Ron when, for the first time, he had beaten Harry at something?

At this point Harry heard Ron's footsteps on the stairs again. He stood up, straightened his glasses, and hitched a grin on to his face as Ron bounded back through the door.

'Just caught her!' he said happily. 'She says she'll get the Cleansweep if she can.'

'Cool,' Harry said, and he was relieved to hear that his voice had stopped sounding hearty. 'Listen – Ron – well done, mate.'

The smile faded off Ron's face.

'I never thought it would be me!' he said, shaking his head. 'I thought it would be you!'

'Nah, I've caused too much trouble,' Harry said, echoing Fred.

'Yeah,' said Ron, 'yeah, I suppose ... well, we'd better get our trunks packed, hadn't we?'

It was odd how widely their possessions seemed to have scattered themselves since they had arrived. It took them most of the afternoon to

第9章 韦斯莱夫人的烦恼

不是总在一起,哈利同自己辩论道。他们没有和我一起同奇洛搏斗。他们没有跟里德尔和蛇怪较量。他们没有在小天狼星逃跑的那天晚上摆脱那些摄魂怪。在伏地魔回来的那天夜里,他们没有在墓地里和我在一起……

想到这里,他刚来的那天晚上感到自己受到不公平待遇的那种强烈感觉又一次在心头翻滚起来。我绝对做得更多,哈利气愤不平地说。我做得比他们俩都多!

可是,那个小声音公正地说,也许邓布利多选级长并不看中他们经历过多少危险处境……也许他选级长看的是其他因素……罗恩肯定具有一些你所没有的东西……

哈利睁开眼睛,透过手指缝望着衣柜爪子形的脚,想起了弗雷德说过的话:"头脑正常的人,谁会选罗恩当级长呢……"

哈利发出一声嘲讽的轻笑,但随即又为自己感到恶心。

罗恩并没有要求邓布利多给他级长的徽章。这不是罗恩的错。而他,哈利,罗恩在世界上最好的朋友,难道就因为自己没有得到徽章,就要闷闷不乐,就要和双胞胎一起在罗恩背后嘲笑他,毁了罗恩的这份快乐吗?就因为罗恩第一次在某件事上胜过了他哈利?

就在这时,哈利听见楼梯上又传来罗恩的脚步声。他站起来,正了正眼镜,急忙在脸上摆出一个微笑,罗恩连蹦带跳地冲了进来。

"正好追上了她!"他高兴地说,"她说如果可能,就给我买'横扫'。"

"真酷!"哈利说,他听见自己热情的声音已不再那么虚假,总算松了口气,"你听我说——罗恩——太棒了,伙计。"

罗恩脸上的笑容消失了。

"我压根儿没想到会是我!"他说着摇了摇头,"我还以为会是你呢!"

"不,我惹的麻烦太多了。"哈利重复着弗雷德的话。

"是啊,"罗恩说,"是啊,我猜也是……好了,我们最好还是收拾箱子吧,好吗?"

真是奇怪,来到这里以后,他们的东西居然散落得到处都是。下午的大部分时间,他们都在从房子的各个角落里找回自己的书本和其

CHAPTER NINE The Woes of Mrs Weasley

retrieve their books and belongings from all over the house and stow them back inside their school trunks. Harry noticed that Ron kept moving his prefect's badge around, first placing it on his bedside table, then putting it into his jeans pocket, then taking it out and laying it on his folded robes, as though to see the effect of the red on the black. Only when Fred and George dropped in and offered to attach it to his forehead with a Permanent Sticking Charm did he wrap it tenderly in his maroon socks and lock it in his trunk.

Mrs Weasley returned from Diagon Alley around six o'clock, laden with books and carrying a long package wrapped in thick brown paper that Ron took from her with a moan of longing.

'Never mind unwrapping it now, people are arriving for dinner, I want you all downstairs,' she said, but the moment she was out of sight Ron ripped off the paper in a frenzy and examined every inch of his new broom, an ecstatic expression on his face.

Down in the basement Mrs Weasley had hung a scarlet banner over the heavily laden dinner table, which read:

> CONGRATULATIONS
> RON AND HERMIONE
> NEW PREFECTS

She looked in a better mood than Harry had seen her all holiday.

'I thought we'd have a little party, not a sit-down dinner,' she told Harry, Ron, Hermione, Fred, George and Ginny as they entered the room. 'Your father and Bill are on their way, Ron. I've sent them both owls and they're *thrilled*,' she added, beaming.

Fred rolled his eyes.

Sirius, Lupin, Tonks and Kingsley Shacklebolt were already there and Mad-Eye Moody stumped in shortly after Harry had got himself a Butterbeer.

'Oh, Alastor, I am glad you're here,' said Mrs Weasley brightly, as Mad-Eye shrugged off his travelling cloak. 'We've been wanting to ask you for ages –

第9章 韦斯莱夫人的烦恼

他东西,重新塞进上学用的箱子。哈利注意到,罗恩不停地把他的级长徽章摆来摆去,先是搁在床头柜上,然后塞进牛仔裤口袋里,接着又拿出来放在叠好的长袍上,似乎要看看红色衬在黑色上的效果如何。后来乔治和弗雷德进来了一下,提出要用永久粘贴咒把徽章粘在他的额头上,罗恩才用褐紫色的袜子把它仔仔细细地包好,锁在了箱子里。

大约六点钟的时候,韦斯莱夫人从对角巷回来了,抱着一大堆书,还拎着一个长长的、棕色厚纸包着的东西,罗恩充满渴望地呻吟了一声,从她手里拿了过来。

"先别忙着打开,大家要来吃晚饭了,我希望你们都下楼去。"韦斯莱夫人说,可是她刚走开,罗恩就急不可耐地扯开包装纸,上上下下、仔仔细细地端详着他的新扫帚,脸上是一种欣喜若狂的表情。

在下面的地下室里,韦斯莱夫人在无比丰盛的饭桌上方挂出一条深红色的横幅,上面写着:

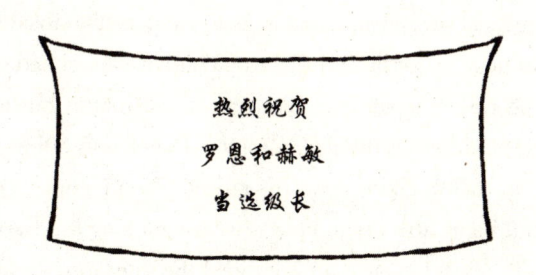

> 热烈祝贺
> 罗恩和赫敏
> 当选级长

她情绪非常好,整个假期哈利都没见她这么高兴过。

"我想我们应该搞一个小小的晚会,而不是一本正经地坐着吃饭,"看到哈利、罗恩、赫敏、弗雷德、乔治和金妮走进厨房,她对他们说道,"你爸爸和比尔正在路上呢,罗恩。我派猫头鹰给他们俩都送了信,他们都激动坏了。"她满脸喜色地补充道。

弗雷德翻了翻眼睛。

小天狼星、卢平、唐克斯和金斯莱·沙克尔已经到了,哈利给自己倒了一杯黄油啤酒后不久,疯眼汉穆迪脚步沉重地走了进来。

"哦,阿拉斯托,你来了我真高兴。"疯眼汉脱掉身上的旅行斗篷时,韦斯莱夫人高兴地说,"我们好长时间一直想问问你——你能不能

CHAPTER NINE   The Woes of Mrs Weasley

could you have a look in the writing desk in the drawing room and tell us what's inside it? We haven't wanted to open it just in case it's something really nasty.'

'No problem, Molly ...'

Moody's electric-blue eye swivelled upwards and stared fixedly through the ceiling of the kitchen.

'Drawing room ...' he growled, as the pupil contracted. 'Desk in the corner? Yeah, I see it ... yeah, it's a Boggart ... want me to go up and get rid of it, Molly?'

'No, no, I'll do it myself later,' beamed Mrs Weasley, 'you have your drink. We're having a little bit of a celebration, actually ...' She gestured at the scarlet banner. 'Fourth prefect in the family!' she said fondly, ruffling Ron's hair.

'Prefect, eh?' growled Moody, his normal eye on Ron and his magical eye swivelling around to gaze into the side of his head. Harry had the very uncomfortable feeling it was looking at him and moved away towards Sirius and Lupin.

'Well, congratulations,' said Moody, still glaring at Ron with his normal eye, 'authority figures always attract trouble, but I suppose Dumbledore thinks you can withstand most major jinxes or he wouldn't have appointed you ...'

Ron looked rather startled at this view of the matter but was saved the trouble of responding by the arrival of his father and eldest brother. Mrs Weasley was in such a good mood she did not even complain that they had brought Mundungus with them; he was wearing a long overcoat that seemed oddly lumpy in unlikely places and declined the offer to remove it and put it with Moody's travelling cloak.

'Well, I think a toast is in order,' said Mr Weasley, when everyone had a drink. He raised his goblet. 'To Ron and Hermione, the new Gryffindor prefects!'

Ron and Hermione beamed as everyone drank to them, and then applauded.

'I was never a prefect myself,' said Tonks brightly from behind Harry as everybody moved towards the table to help themselves to food. Her hair was tomato red and waist-length today; she looked like Ginny's older sister. 'My Head of House said I lacked certain necessary qualities.'

'Like what?' said Ginny, who was choosing a baked potato.

'Like the ability to behave myself,' said Tonks.

第9章 韦斯莱夫人的烦恼

看看客厅的那张写字台,告诉我们里面是什么东西?我们一直不敢打开,生怕那是个特别难对付的家伙。"

"没问题,莫丽……"

穆迪那亮蓝色的眼睛滴溜溜往上一转,死死盯着厨房的天花板。

"客厅……"他粗声粗气地说,魔眼的瞳孔缩小了,"墙角的写字台?啊,我看见了……是的,是一个博格特……需要我上去把它弄出来吗,莫丽?"

"不,不用了,我待会儿自己来吧。"韦斯莱夫人眉开眼笑地说,"你喝点酒吧。实际上,我们在搞一个小小的庆祝活动……"她指了指深红色的横幅,"家里第四位级长!"她揉揉罗恩的头发,慈爱地说。

"级长,哦?"穆迪低吼道,那只正常的眼睛望着罗恩,那只魔眼滴溜溜一转,朝着脑袋里面的一侧凝视着。哈利有一种很不舒服的感觉,似乎那眼睛正在望着自己,他转身朝小天狼星和卢平走去。

"好啊,祝贺祝贺,"穆迪说,仍然用他那只正常的眼睛盯着罗恩,"权威人士总会招来麻烦,但我想邓布利多一定认为你能够抵抗大多数厉害的恶咒,不然他不会选中你的……"

罗恩听到这样的说法,似乎很吃了一惊,但正好这时候他爸爸和大哥回来了,他也就用不着费心做出回答了。韦斯莱夫人喜气洋洋,甚至没有埋怨他们把蒙顿格斯也带了来。蒙顿格斯穿着一件长长的大衣,上面不该鼓起来的地方却鼓鼓囊囊的,显得很奇怪,而且他还不肯把大衣脱下来跟穆迪的旅行斗篷放在一起。

"好了,我想我们可以举杯了,"每个人都拿到饮料后,韦斯莱先生说,举起了他的高脚酒杯,"祝贺罗恩和赫敏当选格兰芬多的级长!"

大家都举杯祝贺,然后热烈鼓掌,罗恩和赫敏高兴得满脸放光。

"我自己从没当过级长。"大家都凑在桌子跟前取食物时,唐克斯在哈利身后兴高采烈地说。今天她的头发红得像西红柿,一直拖到腰际,看上去活像金妮的姐姐。"我们学院的院长说我缺乏某些必要的素质。"

"比如说什么呢?"正在挑一个烤土豆的金妮问道。

"比如不能够循规蹈矩。"唐克斯说。

CHAPTER NINE The Woes of Mrs Weasley

Ginny laughed; Hermione looked as though she did not know whether to smile or not and compromised by taking an extra large gulp of Butterbeer and choking on it.

'What about you, Sirius?' Ginny asked, thumping Hermione on the back.

Sirius, who was right beside Harry, let out his usual bark-like laugh.

'No one would have made me a prefect, I spent too much time in detention with James. Lupin was the good boy, he got the badge.'

'I think Dumbledore might have hoped I would be able to exercise some control over my best friends,' said Lupin. 'I need scarcely say that I failed dismally.'

Harry's mood suddenly lifted. His father had not been a prefect either. All at once the party seemed much more enjoyable; he loaded up his plate, feeling doubly fond of everyone in the room.

Ron was rhapsodising about his new broom to anybody who would listen.

'... nought to seventy in ten seconds, not bad, is it? When you think the Comet Two Ninety's only nought to sixty and that's with a decent tailwind according to *Which Broomstick?*'

Hermione was talking very earnestly to Lupin about her view of elf rights.

'I mean, it's the same kind of nonsense as werewolf segregation, isn't it? It all stems from this horrible thing wizards have of thinking they're superior to other creatures ...'

Mrs Weasley and Bill were having their usual argument about Bill's hair.

'... getting really out of hand, and you're so good-looking, it would look much better shorter, wouldn't it, Harry?'

'Oh – I dunno –' said Harry, slightly alarmed at being asked his opinion; he slid away from them in the direction of Fred and George, who were huddled in a corner with Mundungus.

Mundungus stopped talking when he saw Harry, but Fred winked and beckoned Harry closer.

'It's OK,' he told Mundungus, 'we can trust Harry, he's our financial backer.'

'Look what Dung's got us,' said George, holding out his hand to Harry. It was full of what looked like shrivelled black pods. A faint rattling noise was coming from them, even though they were completely stationary.

第9章 韦斯莱夫人的烦恼

金妮哈哈大笑。赫敏似乎不知道是不是也该笑一笑,便采取个折中的办法,端起杯子喝了一大口黄油啤酒,结果被呛着了。

"你呢,小天狼星?"金妮拍着赫敏的后背问道。

坐在哈利旁边的小天狼星发出他惯常的那种短促刺耳的笑声。

"没有人会选我当级长的,我花了那么多时间跟詹姆一起关禁闭。卢平是个好孩子,他得到了徽章。"

"我想,邓布利多大概希望我能对我最好的朋友进行一些管束。"卢平说,"不用说,我很悲惨地失败了。"

哈利的情绪突然好了起来。他爸爸当年也不是级长。顿时,晚会似乎变得好玩多了。他把盘子装得满满的,觉得自己加倍地喜爱房间里的每一个人。

罗恩逢人就热情洋溢地介绍他的新扫帚。

"……十秒钟内就从零到七十,不坏吧?要知道《飞天扫帚大全》上说,彗星290只有零到六十,而且还需要有一股顺风推着呢。"

赫敏正在十分恳切地跟卢平谈论她对小精灵权益的看法。

"我的意思是,这就跟狼人需要隔离一样,都是一派胡言,是不是?其根源都是巫师那种可怕的偏见,认为自己比别的生物优越……"

韦斯莱夫人和比尔又在争论那个老掉牙的问题:比尔的头发。

"……越来越没法收拾了,其实你长得挺精神的,如果头发短一点儿会好看得多,你说是不是呢,哈利?"

"哦——我不知道——"哈利说,没想到韦斯莱夫人居然来征求他的意见,有点儿惊慌。他偷偷地离开他们,朝弗雷德和乔治那边走去,他们正和蒙顿格斯一起挤在一个角落里。

蒙顿格斯一看见哈利就停住话头,但弗雷德眨眨眼睛,示意哈利过去。

"没关系,"他对蒙顿格斯说,"我们可以信任哈利,他是我们的资助人!"

"看看顿格给我们带来了什么,"乔治说着摊开手掌给哈利看,那上面是一堆枯干的黑豆荚般的东西,虽然一动不动,却发出轻微的哗啦哗啦的声音。

CHAPTER NINE The Woes of Mrs Weasley

'Venomous Tentacula seeds,' said George. 'We need them for the Skiving Snackboxes but they're a Class C Non-Tradeable Substance so we've been having a bit of trouble getting hold of them.'

'Ten Galleons the lot, then, Dung?' said Fred.

'Wiv all the trouble I went to to get 'em?' said Mundungus, his saggy, bloodshot eyes stretching even wider. 'I'm sorry, lads, but I'm not taking a Knut under twenty.'

'Dung likes his little joke,' Fred said to Harry.

'Yeah, his best one so far has been six Sickles for a bag of Knarl quills,' said George.

'Be careful,' Harry warned them quietly.

'What?' said Fred. 'Mum's busy cooing over Prefect Ron, we're OK.'

'But Moody could have his eye on you,' Harry pointed out.

Mundungus looked nervously over his shoulder.

'Good point, that,' he grunted. 'All right, lads, ten it is, if you'll take 'em quick.'

'Cheers, Harry!' said Fred delightedly, when Mundungus had emptied his pockets into the twins' outstretched hands and scuttled off towards the food. 'We'd better get these upstairs ...'

Harry watched them go, feeling slightly uneasy. It had just occurred to him that Mr and Mrs Weasley would want to know how Fred and George were financing their joke shop business when, as was inevitable, they finally found out about it. Giving the twins his Triwizard winnings had seemed a simple thing to do at the time, but what if it led to another family row and a Percy-like estrangement? Would Mrs Weasley still feel that Harry was as good as her son if she found out he had made it possible for Fred and George to start a career she thought quite unsuitable?

Standing where the twins had left him, with nothing but a guilty weight in the pit of his stomach for company, Harry caught the sound of his own name. Kingsley Shacklebolt's deep voice was audible even over the surrounding chatter.

'... why Dumbledore didn't make Potter a prefect?' said Kingsley.

'He'll have had his reasons,' replied Lupin.

第9章 韦斯莱夫人的烦恼

"毒触手的种子，"乔治说，"我们的速效逃课糖要用到它们，但这是一种C类禁止贸易物品，所以我们一直很难搞到。"

"这么些给十个加隆吧，顿格？"弗雷德说。

"这可是我费了九牛二虎之力才弄到的！"蒙顿格斯说，他那松弛的、充血的眼睛拉得更狭长了，"对不起，小伙子们，低于二十我绝不出手。"

"顿格就喜欢开点儿小玩笑。"弗雷德对哈利说。

"是啊，他最精彩的一个玩笑就是一袋刺佬儿尖刺要价六个西可。"乔治说。

"小心点儿。"哈利轻声提醒他们。

"怎么啦？"弗雷德说，"妈妈忙着跟级长罗恩情意绵绵地说悄悄话呢，我们没事儿的。"

"可是穆迪可能在用眼睛盯着你们。"哈利指出这一点。

蒙顿格斯紧张地扭头看了看。

"说得对。"他嘟哝道，"好吧，小伙子们，十个就十个吧，只要你们赶紧把它们弄走。"

"谢谢你了，哈利！"弗雷德高兴地说，蒙顿格斯已经把口袋里的东西都倒在双胞胎伸出来的手里，然后匆匆走过去取东西吃，"我们最好把这些东西拿到楼上去……"

哈利望着他们的背影，心里隐隐有些不安。他突然想到，韦斯莱先生和韦斯莱夫人最终肯定会发现弗雷德和乔治在做笑话店的生意，然后不可避免地就会想知道本钱从何而来。把三强争霸赛的奖金送给双胞胎，这在当时似乎是一件很简单的事情，但如果它又导致一场家庭风波，使亲人疏远，就像珀西那样呢？如果韦斯莱夫人发现是哈利使得弗雷德和乔治能够开展一种她认为很不合适的职业，她还会觉得哈利像她的亲生儿子一样好吗？

双胞胎走后，哈利独自站在那里，内心只有一种沉甸甸的负疚感。突然，他听见有人在说他的名字。金斯莱·沙克尔那低沉浑厚的声音，即使在周围的一片嘈杂声中也能听见。

"……邓布利多为什么不选波特当级长呢？"金斯莱问。

"他准有他自己的道理。"卢平回答。

CHAPTER NINE The Woes of Mrs Weasley

'But it would've shown confidence in him. It's what I'd've done,' persisted Kingsley, ''specially with the *Daily Prophet* having a go at him every few days ...'

Harry did not look round; he did not want Lupin or Kingsley to know he had heard. Though not remotely hungry, he followed Mundungus back towards the table. His pleasure in the party had evaporated as quickly as it had come; he wished he were upstairs in bed.

Mad-Eye Moody was sniffing at a chicken-leg with what remained of his nose; evidently he could not detect any trace of poison, because he then tore a strip off it with his teeth.

'... the handle's made of Spanish oak with anti-jinx varnish and in-built vibration control –' Ron was saying to Tonks.

Mrs Weasley yawned widely.

'Well, I think I'll sort out that Boggart before I turn in ... Arthur, I don't want this lot up too late, all right? Night, Harry, dear.'

She left the kitchen. Harry set down his plate and wondered whether he could follow her without attracting attention.

'You all right, Potter?' grunted Moody.

'Yeah, fine,' lied Harry.

Moody took a swig from his hipflask, his electric-blue eye staring sideways at Harry.

'Come here, I've got something that might interest you,' he said.

From an inner pocket of his robes Moody pulled a very tattered old wizarding photograph.

'Original Order of the Phoenix,' growled Moody. 'Found it last night when I was looking for my spare Invisibility Cloak, seeing as Podmore hasn't had the manners to return my best one ... thought people might like to see it.'

Harry took the photograph. A small crowd of people, some waving at him, others lifting their glasses, looked back up at him.

'There's me,' said Moody, unnecessarily pointing at himself. The Moody in the picture was unmistakeable, though his hair was slightly less grey and his nose was intact. 'And there's Dumbledore beside me, Dedalus Diggle on the other side ... that's Marlene McKinnon, she was killed two weeks after this was taken, they got her whole family. That's Frank and Alice Longbottom –'

第9章 韦斯莱夫人的烦恼

"但是那样会表现出对哈利的信任。换了我，我就会那么做，"金斯莱执意地说，"特别是在《预言家日报》三天两头地给他造谣……"

哈利没有转过头去。他不想让卢平和金斯莱知道他听见了。他尽管一点儿也不饿，但还是跟着蒙顿格斯回到了饭桌旁。他刚才突然产生的参加晚会的快乐又一下子消失得无影无踪。他真希望自己躺在楼上的床上。

疯眼汉穆迪用残缺不全的鼻子嗅了嗅一根鸡腿，显然他没有发现任何下毒的痕迹，因为他用牙齿扯下了一大块鸡肉。

"……扫帚把是用西班牙橡木做的，涂着防恶咒的清漆，还有内置的振动控制——"罗恩在对唐克斯说。

韦斯莱夫人打了个大大的哈欠。

"好了，我先去把那个博格特解决掉再上床睡觉……亚瑟，我不希望这些人闹得太晚，好吗？晚安，哈利，亲爱的。"

她说完就离开了厨房。哈利把盘子放在桌上，不知道能不能神不知鬼不觉地跟她一起离去。

"你没事吧，波特？"穆迪瓮声瓮气地问。

"没事呀，挺好的。"哈利没说实话。

穆迪对着他的弧形酒瓶喝了一大口，那只亮蓝色的魔眼斜过来望着哈利。

"来吧，我这儿有件东西，你可能会感兴趣。"他说。

穆迪从长袍里面的口袋掏出一张很破旧的魔法照片。

"最初的凤凰社，"穆迪声音低沉地说，"昨天晚上找我那件备用的隐形衣时发现的。看来波德摩不太懂规矩，不打算把我最好的那件隐形衣还给我了……我想可能有人愿意看看。"

哈利接过照片，上面有一小群人抬头望着他，有的朝他挥手致意，有的举起手里的酒杯。

"这是我。"穆迪指着自己说，其实这毫无必要。照片上的穆迪是不可能被认错的，尽管他那会儿头发不像现在这么白，鼻子也完好无损。"我旁边是邓布利多，另一边是德达洛·迪歌……这是马琳·麦金农，拍完这张照片两个星期后，她就被杀害了，他们还把她全家都抓了去。那是弗兰克·隆巴顿和艾丽斯·隆巴顿——"

CHAPTER NINE   The Woes of Mrs Weasley

Harry's stomach, already uncomfortable, clenched as he looked at Alice Longbottom; he knew her round, friendly face very well, even though he had never met her, because she was the image of her son, Neville.

'– poor devils,' growled Moody. 'Better dead than what happened to them … and that's Emmeline Vance, you've met her, and that there's Lupin, obviously … Benjy Fenwick, he copped it too, we only ever found bits of him … shift aside there,' he added, poking the picture, and the little photographic people edged sideways, so that those who were partially obscured could move to the front.

'That's Edgar Bones … brother of Amelia Bones, they got him and his family, too, he was a great wizard … Sturgis Podmore, blimey, he looks young … Caradoc Dearborn, vanished six months after this, we never found his body … Hagrid, of course, looks exactly the same as ever … Elphias Doge, you've met him, I'd forgotten he used to wear that stupid hat … Gideon Prewett, it took five Death Eaters to kill him and his brother Fabian, they fought like heroes … budge along, budge along …'

The little people in the photograph jostled among themselves and those hidden right at the back appeared at the forefront of the picture.

'That's Dumbledore's brother Aberforth, only time I ever met him, strange bloke … that's Dorcas Meadowes, Voldemort killed her personally … Sirius, when he still had short hair … and … there you go, thought that would interest you!'

Harry's heart turned over. His mother and father were beaming up at him, sitting on either side of a small, watery-eyed man whom Harry recognised at once as Wormtail, the one who had betrayed his parents' whereabouts to Voldemort and so helped to bring about their deaths.

'Eh?' said Moody.

Harry looked up into Moody's heavily scarred and pitted face. Evidently Moody was under the impression he had just given Harry a bit of a treat.

'Yeah,' said Harry, once again attempting to grin. 'Er … listen, I've just remembered, I haven't packed my …'

He was spared the trouble of inventing an object he had not packed. Sirius had just said, 'What's that you've got there, Mad-Eye?' and Moody had turned towards him. Harry crossed the kitchen, slipped through the door and up the stairs before anyone could call him back.

第9章 韦斯莱夫人的烦恼

哈利心里本来就不舒服，现在望着艾丽斯·隆巴顿，心里更是一阵发紧。他尽管从没见过她，却非常熟悉她那张圆圆的、充满友善的脸，因为她儿子纳威和她长得一模一样。

"——可怜的人，"穆迪粗声粗气地说，"死了也比遭那份罪强……这是爱米琳·万斯，你见过她的，这个显然是卢平……本吉·芬威克，他也遭遇了不幸，我们只找到了他的部分尸体……往旁边挪挪。"他用手碰碰照片，上面的小人儿都朝旁边移去，让那些本来被遮住的人挪到了前面。

"那是埃德加·博恩斯……阿米莉亚·博恩斯的哥哥，他们也抓走了他的全家，他是个了不起的巫师……斯多吉·波德摩，天哪，他看上去真年轻……卡拉多克·迪尔伯恩，照片拍完后六个月就失踪了，一直没有找到他的尸体……海格，这不用说了，看上去还是这副老样子……埃非亚斯·多吉，你见过的，我都忘记他以前老戴着那顶傻乎乎的帽子了……吉迪翁·普威特，出动了五个食死徒才把他和他弟弟费比安杀死，他们战斗得英勇顽强……往边上挪挪，往边上挪挪……"

照片上的小人儿挤在一起，让那些隐藏在后面的人出现在画面上。

"这是邓布利多的弟弟阿不福思，我只见过他那一次，是个奇怪的家伙……这是多卡斯·梅多斯，伏地魔亲手杀害了她……小天狼星，那时候他还留着短头发……还有……这里，我想你可能会有兴趣！"

哈利心里像打翻了五味瓶。他的妈妈和爸爸笑眯眯地望着他，他们俩中间坐着一个眼睛水汪汪的小个子男人，哈利一眼就认了出来，那是虫尾巴，就是他向伏地魔告发了哈利父母的下落，造成了他们俩的惨死。

"嗯？"穆迪说。

哈利抬头看着穆迪伤痕累累、坑坑洼洼的脸。显然，穆迪还以为自己给了哈利一件很稀罕的好东西呢。

"不错，"哈利说，又一次想勉强挤出一个笑容，"呃……对了，我刚想起来，我忘记收拾我的……"

他用不着绞尽脑汁编造一个他忘记收拾的东西了，因为小天狼星正好说道："你那儿是什么东西，疯眼汉？"穆迪转身朝那边望去。哈利赶紧走向厨房那头，不等有人来得及把他叫回去，就轻手轻脚地出了房门向楼上走去。

CHAPTER NINE The Woes of Mrs Weasley

He did not know why it had been such a shock; he had seen pictures of his parents before, after all, and he had met Wormtail ... but to have them sprung on him like that, when he was least expecting it ... no one would like that, he thought angrily ...

And then, to see them surrounded by all those other happy faces ... Benjy Fenwick, who had been found in bits, and Gideon Prewett, who had died like a hero, and the Longbottoms, who had been tortured into madness ... all waving happily out of the photograph forever more, not knowing that they were doomed ... well, Moody might find that interesting ... he, Harry, found it disturbing ...

Harry tiptoed up the stairs in the hall past the stuffed elf-heads, glad to be on his own again, but as he approached the first landing he heard noises. Someone was sobbing in the drawing room.

'Hello?' Harry said.

There was no answer but the sobbing continued. He climbed the remaining stairs two at a time, walked across the landing and opened the drawing-room door.

Someone was cowering against the dark wall, her wand in her hand, her whole body shaking with sobs. Sprawled on the dusty old carpet in a patch of moonlight, clearly dead, was Ron.

All the air seemed to vanish from Harry's lungs; he felt as though he were falling through the floor; his brain turned icy cold – Ron dead, no, it couldn't be –

But wait a moment, *it couldn't be* – Ron was downstairs –

'Mrs Weasley?' Harry croaked.

'*R – r – riddikulus!*' Mrs Weasley sobbed, pointing her shaking wand at Ron's body.

Crack.

Ron's body turned into Bill's, spread-eagled on his back, his eyes wide open and empty. Mrs Weasley sobbed harder than ever.

'*R – riddikulus!*' she sobbed again.

Crack.

Mr Weasley's body replaced Bill's, his glasses askew, a trickle of blood running down his face.

第9章 韦斯莱夫人的烦恼

哈利不知道他为什么感到如此震惊。其实他以前看见过爸爸妈妈的照片，还亲眼看见过虫尾巴……可是他们在他最不防备的时候那样突然地跳到了他面前……谁都不会喜欢的，他生气地想……

还有，看见他们周围所有那些愉快的面孔……本吉·芬威克，只找到尸体的一些残片；吉迪翁·普威特，像英雄一样勇敢战死；还有隆巴顿夫妇，被折磨成了疯子……他们都永远在照片上愉快地挥手，谁也不知道前面等着他们的厄运……唉，穆迪大概会觉得这很有趣……他，哈利，觉得这让人心神不安……

哈利踮着脚尖走上门厅的楼梯，走过那些挤在一起的家养小精灵的脑袋，他很高兴终于可以一个人清静一会儿了，可是就在他走近楼梯的第一个平台时，他听见了一个声音。有人在客厅里哭泣。

"你好？"哈利说。

没有人回答，哭泣声在继续。他一步两级地走完最后几级楼梯，走过平台，推开了客厅的门。

有一个人蜷缩在黑暗的墙边，手里拿着魔杖，哭得整个身体都在颤抖。而四肢伸展躺在灰扑扑的旧地毯上，躺在皎洁的月光下的，正是罗恩，显然已经死了。

哈利一下子觉得肺里的空气似乎都被吸空了，他觉得自己正朝地板下坠落，大脑里一片冰冷——罗恩死了，不，这不可能——

可是等一等，这不可能呀——罗恩在楼下呢——

"韦斯莱夫人？"哈利哑着嗓子说。

"滑—滑—滑稽滑稽！"韦斯莱夫人啜泣着说，用颤抖的魔杖指着罗恩的尸体。

啪！

罗恩的尸体变成了比尔的，伸展四肢仰面躺着，空洞失神的眼睛睁得大大的。韦斯莱夫人哭得比刚才更厉害了。

"滑—滑稽滑稽！"她又抽抽搭搭地说。

啪！

韦斯莱先生的尸体取代了比尔的，眼镜歪在一边，一道鲜血从脸上流淌下来。

CHAPTER NINE   The Woes of Mrs Weasley

'No!' Mrs Weasley moaned. 'No ... *riddikulus!* *Riddikulus!* *RIDDIKULUS!*'

Crack. Dead twins. *Crack.* Dead Percy. *Crack.* Dead Harry ...

'Mrs Weasley, just get out of here!' shouted Harry, staring down at his own dead body on the floor. 'Let someone else —'

'What's going on?'

Lupin had come running into the room, closely followed by Sirius, with Moody stumping along behind them. Lupin looked from Mrs Weasley to the dead Harry on the floor and seemed to understand in an instant. Pulling out his own wand, he said, very firmly and clearly:

'*Riddikulus!*'

Harry's body vanished. A silvery orb hung in the air over the spot where it had lain. Lupin waved his wand once more and the orb vanished in a puff of smoke.

'Oh – oh – oh!' gulped Mrs Weasley, and she broke into a storm of crying, her face in her hands.

'Molly,' said Lupin bleakly, walking over to her. 'Molly, don't ...'

Next second, she was sobbing her heart out on Lupin's shoulder.

'Molly, it was just a Boggart,' he said soothingly, patting her on the head. 'Just a stupid Boggart ...'

'I see them d – d – dead all the time!' Mrs Weasley moaned into his shoulder. 'All the t – t – time! I d – d – dream about it ...'

Sirius was staring at the patch of carpet where the Boggart, pretending to be Harry's body, had lain. Moody was looking at Harry, who avoided his gaze. He had a funny feeling Moody's magical eye had followed him all the way out of the kitchen.

'D – d – don't tell Arthur,' Mrs Weasley was gulping now, mopping her eyes frantically with her cuffs. 'I d – d – don't want him to know ... being silly ...'

Lupin handed her a handkerchief and she blew her nose.

'Harry, I'm so sorry. What must you think of me?' she said shakily. 'Not even able to get rid of a Boggart ...'

'Don't be stupid,' said Harry, trying to smile.

'I'm just s – s – so worried,' she said, tears spilling out of her eyes again. 'Half the f – f – family's in the Order, it'll b – b – be a miracle if we all come

第9章 韦斯莱夫人的烦恼

"不!"韦斯莱夫人呻吟道,"不……滑稽滑稽!滑稽滑稽!**滑稽滑稽**!"

啪!死去的双胞胎。啪!死去的珀西。啪!死去的哈利……

"韦斯莱夫人,赶紧离开这里!"哈利瞪着地板上他自己的尸体喊道,"让别人——"

"出什么事了?"

卢平跑进了房间,后面紧跟着小天狼星,穆迪拖着沉重的脚步也来了。卢平望望韦斯莱夫人,又望望地板上哈利的尸体,似乎一下子全明白了。他拔出自己的魔杖,清清楚楚、毫不含糊地说:

"滑稽滑稽!"

哈利的尸体不见了。一个银色的圆球悬浮在尸体刚才躺着的上空。卢平又挥了一下魔杖,圆球化成一股烟雾消失了。

"哦——哦——哦!"韦斯莱夫人抽噎着,然后突然用手捂住脸,号啕大哭。

"莫丽,"卢平忧郁地说,一边朝她走去,"莫丽,不要……"

一眨眼间,她扑在卢平的肩膀上,哭得伤心欲绝。

"莫丽,那只是一个博格特,"卢平拍着她的脑袋,安慰她道,"是一个愚蠢的博格特……"

"我总是看见他们死—死—死了!"韦斯莱夫人靠在他的肩膀上抽泣着说,"总是看—看见!做—做梦也梦见……"

小天狼星盯着刚才博格特装成哈利的尸体躺过的地方。穆迪看着哈利,哈利则躲避着他的目光。他有一种奇怪的感觉,似乎穆迪的那只魔眼一直追随着他走出了厨房。

"不—不—不要告诉亚瑟,"韦斯莱夫人这时忍住呜咽,用袖口使劲地擦着眼睛,"我不—不—不想让他知道……我这么傻……"

卢平递给她一块手帕,她擤了擤鼻子。

"哈利,真对不起。你会怎么看我呢?"她声音颤抖地说,"连一个博格特都对付不了……"

"别说傻话了。"哈利说,想勉强露出一点儿笑容。

"我只是太—太—太担心了,"她说,眼泪又从眼睛里扑簌簌地滚

CHAPTER NINE The Woes of Mrs Weasley

through this ... and P – P – Percy's not talking to us ... what if something d – d – dreadful happens and we've never m – m – made it up with him? And what's going to happen if Arthur and I get killed, who's g – g – going to look after Ron and Ginny?'

'Molly, that's enough,' said Lupin firmly. 'This isn't like last time. The Order is better prepared, we've got a head start, we know what Voldemort's up to –'

Mrs Weasley gave a little squeak of fright at the sound of the name.

'Oh, Molly, come on, it's about time you got used to hearing his name – look, I can't promise no one's going to get hurt, nobody can promise that, but we're much better off than we were last time. You weren't in the Order then, you don't understand. Last time we were outnumbered twenty to one by the Death Eaters and they were picking us off one by one ...'

Harry thought of the photograph again, of his parents' beaming faces. He knew Moody was still watching him.

'Don't worry about Percy,' said Sirius abruptly. 'He'll come round. It's only a matter of time before Voldemort moves into the open; once he does, the whole Ministry's going to be begging us to forgive them. And I'm not sure I'll be accepting their apology,' he added bitterly.

'And as for who's going to look after Ron and Ginny if you and Arthur died,' said Lupin, smiling slightly, 'what do you think we'd do, let them starve?'

Mrs Weasley smiled tremulously.

'Being silly,' she muttered again, mopping her eyes.

But Harry, closing his bedroom door behind him some ten minutes later, could not think Mrs Weasley silly. He could still see his parents beaming up at him from the tattered old photograph, unaware that their lives, like so many of those around them, were drawing to a close. The image of the Boggart posing as the corpse of each member of Mrs Weasley's family in turn kept flashing before his eyes.

Without warning, the scar on his forehead seared with pain again and his stomach churned horribly.

'Cut it out,' he said firmly, rubbing the scar as the pain receded.

'First sign of madness, talking to your own head,' said a sly voice from the

落下来,"家—家—家里一半的人都在凤凰社,除非出现奇迹我们才会全部从战争中活下来……珀—珀—珀西不跟我们说话了……如果发生了可—可—可怕的事情,我们永远没有机会跟—跟—跟他和解怎么办呢?如果亚瑟和我被杀害了,那可如何是好?谁会来照—照—照顾罗恩和金妮呢?"

"莫丽,够了。"卢平果断地说,"这和上次不一样。现在凤凰社的组织更加严密,我们有了一个有利的开端,知道伏地魔打算做什么——"

韦斯莱夫人听见那个名字,惊恐地发出一声尖叫。

"哦,莫丽,勇敢点儿,现在你应该习惯听到他的名字——听着,我没法保证不会有人受到伤害,谁也不可能保证这一点,但我们的情况比上次好得多。你那时候不在凤凰社里,你不明白。上次食死徒的人数是我们的二十倍,他们是把我们一个一个地干掉的……"

哈利又想起了那张照片,想起了他爸爸妈妈洋溢着欢笑的脸。他知道穆迪还在注视着他。

"不要担心珀西,"小天狼星突然说道,"他会回心转意的。伏地魔总有一天会公开亮相的,到那个时候,整个魔法部都会请求我们原谅他们。而我还不知道会不会接受他们的道歉呢。"他又尖刻地添上了最后一句。

"至于如果你和亚瑟遇害了,由谁来照顾罗恩和金妮,"卢平微微带笑地说,"你以为我们会怎么做,会让他们饿肚子吗?"

韦斯莱夫人颤抖着笑了笑。

"真是太傻了。"她又低声说了一句,擦了擦眼睛。

可是十分钟后,当哈利反手关上卧室的房门时,他无法认为韦斯莱夫人是在犯傻。他仍然能够看见爸爸妈妈从那张破烂的旧照片上笑眯眯地望着他,他们像周围的那么多人一样,浑然不知他们的生命就要终结。哈利眼前不断闪现着博格特轮番变出韦斯莱夫人家每个人的尸体的景象。

突然,他额头上的伤疤一阵剧痛,胃里也翻腾开了。

"停下!"他坚决地说,一边揉着伤疤,疼痛减轻了。

"疯狂的第一个迹象,就是跟自己的脑袋说话。"墙上那张空白画

CHAPTER NINE   The Woes of Mrs Weasley

empty picture on the wall.

Harry ignored it. He felt older than he had ever felt in his life and it seemed extraordinary to him that barely an hour ago he had been worried about a joke shop and who had got a prefect's badge.

第9章 韦斯莱夫人的烦恼

布里一个诡秘的声音说道。

哈利没去理它。他感到自己一下子成熟了很多，比以往任何时候都要成熟。而就在一个小时前，他还在担心笑话商店的事，担心谁得到了级长的徽章，这使他觉得不可思议。

CHAPTER TEN

Luna Lovegood

Harry had a troubled night's sleep. His parents wove in and out of his dreams, never speaking; Mrs Weasley sobbed over Kreacher's dead body, watched by Ron and Hermione, who were wearing crowns, and yet again Harry found himself walking down a corridor ending in a locked door. He awoke abruptly with his scar prickling to find Ron already dressed and talking to him.

'... better hurry up, Mum's going ballistic, she says we're going to miss the train ...'

There was a lot of commotion in the house. From what he heard as he dressed at top speed, Harry gathered that Fred and George had bewitched their trunks to fly downstairs to save the bother of carrying them, with the result that they had hurtled straight into Ginny and knocked her down two flights of stairs into the hall; Mrs Black and Mrs Weasley were both screaming at the top of their voices.

'– COULD HAVE DONE HER A SERIOUS INJURY, YOU IDIOTS –'

'– FILTHY HALF-BREEDS, BESMIRCHING THE HOUSE OF MY FATHERS –'

Hermione came hurrying into the room looking flustered, just as Harry was putting on his trainers. Hedwig was swaying on her shoulder, and she was carrying a squirming Crookshanks in her arms.

'Mum and Dad just sent Hedwig back.' The owl fluttered obligingly over and perched on top of her cage. 'Are you ready yet?'

'Nearly. Is Ginny all right?' Harry asked, shoving on his glasses.

'Mrs Weasley's patched her up,' said Hermione. 'But now Mad-Eye's complaining that we can't leave unless Sturgis Podmore's here, otherwise the guard will be one short.'

'Guard?' said Harry. 'We have to go to King's Cross with a guard?'

第10章

卢娜·洛夫古德

哈利这一夜睡得很不踏实。他的爸爸妈妈不停地在他的梦境里穿行，但从不说话。韦斯莱夫人对着克利切的尸体伤心哭泣，罗恩和赫敏头戴王冠在一旁看着。哈利发现自己又走在一条走廊上，走廊尽头是一扇紧锁的房门。他猛地惊醒过来，伤疤隐隐作痛。他发现罗恩已经穿好衣服，正跟他说话呢。

"……最好抓紧时间，妈妈要发脾气了，她说我们可能赶不上火车了……"

整座房子里一片混乱。哈利以最快的速度穿上衣服，听着外面的动静，似乎是弗雷德和乔治给他们的箱子施了魔法，让它们飞下楼去，省得自己搬，结果箱子径直撞向金妮，撞得她一连滚下两段楼梯，摔在门厅里。布莱克夫人和韦斯莱夫人同时声嘶力竭地尖叫起来。

"——弄不好会使她受重伤的。你们这两个白痴——"

"——肮脏的杂种，玷污我祖上的家宅——"

哈利正在穿软底运动鞋，赫敏匆匆跑进房间，一副紧张不安的样子。海德薇摇摇晃晃地立在她的肩膀上，她怀里还抱着动来动去的克鲁克山。

"爸爸妈妈刚把海德薇送回来。"猫头鹰很善解人意地扇动着翅膀飞了过来，落在自己的笼子上，"你准备好了吗？"

"差不多了。金妮没事儿吧？"哈利戴上眼镜问道。

"韦斯莱夫人给她包扎了一下。"赫敏说，"可是这会儿疯眼汉又抱怨说斯多吉·波德摩没来我们不能走，不然警卫就少了一个人。"

"警卫？"哈利说，"我们去国王十字车站还要警卫？"

CHAPTER TEN   Luna Lovegood

'*You* have to go to King's Cross with a guard,' Hermione corrected him.

'Why?' said Harry irritably. 'I thought Voldemort was supposed to be lying low, or are you telling me he's going to jump out from behind a dustbin to try and do me in?'

'I don't know, it's just what Mad-Eye says,' said Hermione distractedly, looking at her watch, 'but if we don't leave soon we're definitely going to miss the train ...'

'WILL YOU LOT GET DOWN HERE NOW, PLEASE!' Mrs Weasley bellowed and Hermione jumped as though scalded and hurried out of the room. Harry seized Hedwig, stuffed her unceremoniously into her cage, and set off downstairs after Hermione, dragging his trunk.

Mrs Black's portrait was howling with rage but nobody was bothering to close the curtains over her; all the noise in the hall was bound to rouse her again, anyway.

'Harry, you're to come with me and Tonks,' shouted Mrs Weasley – over the repeated screeches of '**MUDBLOODS! SCUM! CREATURES OF DIRT!**' – 'Leave your trunk and your owl, Alastor's going to deal with the luggage ... oh, for heaven's sake, Sirius, Dumbledore said no!'

A bear-like black dog had appeared at Harry's side as he was clambering over the various trunks cluttering the hall to get to Mrs Weasley.

'Oh honestly ...' said Mrs Weasley despairingly. 'Well, on your own head be it!'

She wrenched open the front door and stepped out into the weak September sunlight. Harry and the dog followed her. The door slammed behind them and Mrs Black's screeches were cut off instantly.

'Where's Tonks?' Harry said, looking round as they went down the stone steps of number twelve, which vanished the moment they reached the pavement.

'She's waiting for us just up here,' said Mrs Weasley stiffly, averting her eyes from the lolloping black dog beside Harry.

An old woman greeted them on the corner. She had tightly curled grey hair and wore a purple hat shaped like a pork pie.

'Wotcher, Harry,' she said, winking. 'Better hurry up, hadn't we, Molly?' she added, checking her watch.

'I know, I know,' moaned Mrs Weasley, lengthening her stride, 'but Mad-

第10章 卢娜·洛夫古德

"是你去国王十字车站需要警卫。"赫敏纠正他道。

"为什么？"哈利不耐烦地说，"我认为伏地魔现在正潜伏着等待时机呢，难道你要告诉我他会从一个垃圾箱后面跳出来，对我下毒手吗？"

"我不知道，反正疯眼汉是那么说的。"赫敏心不在焉地说，一边看了看手表，"如果不赶紧动身，我们就肯定赶不上火车了……"

"**拜托，你们都赶紧给我下来！**"韦斯莱夫人大吼一声，赫敏就像给开水烫了似的跳起来，一溜烟地跑出了屋子。哈利抓起海德薇，胡乱地塞进笼子，然后拖着箱子跟在赫敏后面往楼下走。

布莱克夫人的肖像在气愤地大嚷大叫，但没有人去拉上帷幔把她遮住。反正门厅里这么吵闹，肯定还会把她再次吵醒的。

"哈利，你跟着我和唐克斯，"韦斯莱夫人提高声音，盖过了那声嘶力竭、一遍遍重复"**泥巴种！败类！肮脏的渣滓！**"的叫骂声，"把你的箱子和猫头鹰放下，阿拉斯托会对付这些行李的……哦，看在老天的分上，小天狼星，邓布利多说过不行！"

就在哈利费力地跨过堆放在门厅里的大大小小的箱子，往韦斯莱夫人那儿移动时，一条熊一样大的黑狗出现在哈利身边。

"哦，说实在的……"韦斯莱夫人绝望地说，"好吧，后果由你自己负责！"

她一把拧开大门，走到外面九月微弱的阳光下。哈利和黑狗也跟了出来。门在他们身后重重地关上，布莱克夫人的尖叫声立刻被隔断了。

"唐克斯在哪儿？"哈利问，一边东张西望地和他们一起走下12号的台阶，刚来到人行道上，那座房子就消失了。

"她就在那边等着我们呢。"韦斯莱夫人板着脸说，目光躲着不去看那条蹦蹦跳跳走在哈利身边的黑狗。

街角处有一个老太太在跟他们打招呼。她有一头打着小卷儿的灰发，戴着一顶形状像猪肉馅饼的紫帽子。

"你好哇，哈利。"她眨了眨眼睛说。"我们得抓紧时间了，是不是，莫丽？"她看了看表。

"我知道，我知道，"韦斯莱夫人叹着气说，一边把步子迈得更大了，

CHAPTER TEN

Luna Lovegood

Eye wanted to wait for Sturgis ... if only Arthur could have got us cars from the Ministry again ... but Fudge won't let him borrow so much as an empty ink bottle these days ... *how* Muggles can stand travelling without magic ...'

But the great black dog gave a joyful bark and gambolled around them, snapping at pigeons and chasing its own tail. Harry couldn't help laughing. Sirius had been trapped inside for a very long time. Mrs Weasley pursed her lips in an almost Aunt Petunia-ish way.

It took them twenty minutes to reach King's Cross on foot and nothing more eventful happened during that time than Sirius scaring a couple of cats for Harry's entertainment. Once inside the station they lingered casually beside the barrier between platforms nine and ten until the coast was clear, then each of them leaned against it in turn and fell easily through on to platform nine and three-quarters, where the Hogwarts Express stood belching sooty steam over a platform packed with departing students and their families. Harry inhaled the familiar smell and felt his spirits soar ... he was really going back ...

'I hope the others make it in time,' said Mrs Weasley anxiously, staring behind her at the wrought-iron arch spanning the platform, through which new arrivals would come.

'Nice dog, Harry!' called a tall boy with dreadlocks.

'Thanks, Lee,' said Harry, grinning, as Sirius wagged his tail frantically.

'Oh good,' said Mrs Weasley, sounding relieved, 'here's Alastor with the luggage, look ...'

A porter's cap pulled low over his mismatched eyes, Moody came limping through the archway pushing a trolley loaded with their trunks.

'All OK,' he muttered to Mrs Weasley and Tonks, 'don't think we were followed ...'

Seconds later, Mr Weasley emerged on to the platform with Ron and Hermione. They had almost unloaded Moody's luggage trolley when Fred, George and Ginny turned up with Lupin.

'No trouble?' growled Moody.

'Nothing,' said Lupin.

'I'll still be reporting Sturgis to Dumbledore,' said Moody, 'that's the second time he's not turned up in a week. Getting as unreliable as

第10章 卢娜·洛夫古德

"可是疯眼汉还想等斯多吉呢……唉，如果亚瑟还能从部里给我们借到车子就好了……可是最近福吉连一个空墨水瓶都不肯借给他了……麻瓜们怎么受得了不靠魔法的旅行呢……"

可是大黑狗开心地大叫一声，围着他们跳跃嬉戏，假装扑过去咬鸽子，还绕着圈子追逐自己的尾巴。哈利忍不住哈哈大笑。小天狼星这么长时间一直被关在屋里可憋坏了。韦斯莱夫人噘起了嘴巴，那模样简直有点儿像佩妮姨妈。

他们步行了二十分钟才赶到国王十字车站，路上没有发生什么大事，只是小天狼星为了逗哈利开心，作势吓跑了一两只猫。一进车站，他们就假装若无其事地徘徊在第9和第10站台之间的隔墙边，等到四下里没有人了，才一个接一个地靠在墙上，神不知鬼不觉地穿越到 $9\frac{3}{4}$ 站台，只见霍格沃茨特快列车停在那里喷着黑色的蒸汽，站台上挤满了正在告别的学生和他们的家人。哈利大口呼吸着这熟悉的气味，感到心快活得像要飞起来一样……他真的要回学校了……

"真希望其他人能及时赶来。"韦斯莱夫人焦急地说，扭头望着横跨站台上方的锻铁拱门，待会儿后来的人将会从那里过来。

"这条狗真不赖，哈利！"一个梳着脏辫的高个子男孩大声说。

"谢谢你，李。"哈利咧嘴微笑着说，小天狼星在一边兴奋地摇着尾巴。

"哦，太好了，"韦斯莱夫人说，明显松了口气，"阿拉斯托带着行李过来了，看……"

一顶搬运工的帽子低低地扣在那两只不对称的眼睛上，穆迪推着一辆堆满箱子的手推车，一瘸一拐地穿过了拱门。

"一切正常，"他低声对韦斯莱夫人和唐克斯说，"看来我们没有被人跟踪……"

几秒钟后，韦斯莱先生带着罗恩和赫敏出现在站台上。他们把穆迪行李车上的箱子一件件搬下来，快要搬完时，弗雷德、乔治和金妮才跟卢平一起赶到了。

"没遇到麻烦吧？"穆迪粗声问道。

"没有。"卢平说。

"我还是要向邓布利多告斯多吉一状，"穆迪说，"这是他一星期里

CHAPTER TEN — Luna Lovegood

Mundungus.'

'Well, look after yourselves,' said Lupin, shaking hands all round. He reached Harry last and gave him a clap on the shoulder. 'You too, Harry. Be careful.'

'Yeah, keep your head down and your eyes peeled,' said Moody, shaking Harry's hand too. 'And don't forget, all of you – careful what you put in writing. If in doubt, don't put it in a letter at all.'

'It's been great meeting all of you,' said Tonks, hugging Hermione and Ginny. 'We'll see you soon, I expect.'

A warning whistle sounded; the students still on the platform started hurrying on to the train.

'Quick, quick,' said Mrs Weasley distractedly, hugging them at random and catching Harry twice. 'Write … be good … if you've forgotten anything we'll send it on … on to the train, now, hurry …'

For one brief moment, the great black dog reared on to its hind legs and placed its front paws on Harry's shoulders, but Mrs Weasley shoved Harry away towards the train door, hissing, 'For heaven's sake, act more like a dog, Sirius!'

'See you!' Harry called out of the open window as the train began to move, while Ron, Hermione and Ginny waved beside him. The figures of Tonks, Lupin, Moody and Mr and Mrs Weasley shrank rapidly but the black dog was bounding alongside the window, wagging its tail; blurred people on the platform were laughing to see it chasing the train, then they rounded a bend, and Sirius was gone.

'He shouldn't have come with us,' said Hermione in a worried voice.

'Oh, lighten up,' said Ron, 'he hasn't seen daylight for months, poor bloke.'

'Well,' said Fred, clapping his hands together, 'can't stand around chatting all day, we've got business to discuss with Lee. See you later,' and he and George disappeared down the corridor to the right.

The train was gathering still more speed, so that the houses outside the window flashed past, and they swayed where they stood.

'Shall we go and find a compartment, then?' Harry asked.

Ron and Hermione exchanged looks.

第10章　卢娜·洛夫古德

第二次不露面了。怎么变得像蒙顿格斯一样不可靠了。"

"好了，好好照顾你们自己。"卢平说着跟他们挨个儿握手。他最后来到哈利面前，拍了一下他的肩膀："你也是，哈利。要多加小心。"

"是啊，避免麻烦，提高警惕。"穆迪说着也跟哈利握了握手，"你们每个人都不要忘记——写信时千万不能什么都写。如果拿不准，就干脆别往信里写。"

"这次见到你们真是太好了。"唐克斯说着搂了搂赫敏和金妮，"我想我们很快就会再见面的。"

提醒大家上车的汽笛响起。站在站台上的学生们开始急急忙忙地登上火车。

"快点儿，快点儿，"韦斯莱夫人心烦意乱地说，胡乱地拥抱他们大家，两次把哈利抓过去搂了搂，"写信……听话……如果忘记了什么，我们会寄过去的……好了，上车吧，快点儿……"

刹那间，大黑狗靠两条后腿站了起来，把前爪搭在哈利的肩膀上，但韦斯莱夫人一把将哈利推向车门，一边压低声音说："看在老天的分儿上，小天狼星，你得更像一条狗的样子！"

"再见！"火车开动了，哈利从敞开的车窗向外喊道，罗恩、赫敏和金妮在他身边一个劲儿地挥手。唐克斯、卢平、穆迪、韦斯莱先生和韦斯莱夫人的身影很快地缩小了，只有那条大黑狗追着车窗奔跑，不住地摇晃着尾巴。站台上一掠而过的人们看到狗追火车，都被逗得哈哈大笑。接着火车拐过一个弯道，小天狼星不见了。

"他不应该跟我们一起来的。"赫敏用担心的语气说。

"哦，高兴点儿吧，"罗恩说，"他几个月没有看见阳光了，可怜的人哪。"

"好了，"弗雷德拍了一下手说，"总不能一整天都站在这里聊天吧，我们还有点儿事要跟李谈谈。待会儿见。"说完，他和乔治便从右边的过道上消失了。

火车行进的速度更快了，窗外的房屋呼呼地往后闪，他们原地站着直打晃儿。

"怎么样，我们去找间包厢吧？"哈利问。

罗恩和赫敏交换了一下目光。

CHAPTER TEN   Luna Lovegood

'Er,' said Ron.

'We're – well – Ron and I are supposed to go into the prefect carriage,' Hermione said awkwardly.

Ron wasn't looking at Harry; he seemed to have become intensely interested in the fingernails on his left hand.

'Oh,' said Harry. 'Right. Fine.'

'I don't think we'll have to stay there all journey,' said Hermione quickly. 'Our letters said we just get instructions from the Head Boy and Girl and then patrol the corridors from time to time.'

'Fine,' said Harry again. 'Well, I – I might see you later, then.'

'Yeah, definitely,' said Ron, casting a shifty, anxious look at Harry. 'It's a pain having to go down there, I'd rather – but we have to – I mean, I'm not enjoying it, I'm not Percy,' he finished defiantly.

'I know you're not,' said Harry and he grinned. But as Hermione and Ron dragged their trunks, Crookshanks and a caged Pigwidgeon off towards the engine end of the train, Harry felt an odd sense of loss. He had never travelled on the Hogwarts express without Ron.

'Come on,' Ginny told him, 'if we get a move on we'll be able to save them places.'

'Right,' said Harry, picking up Hedwig's cage in one hand and the handle of his trunk in the other. They struggled off down the corridor, peering through the glass-panelled doors into the compartments they passed, which were already full. Harry could not help noticing that a lot of people stared back at him with great interest and that several of them nudged their neighbours and pointed him out. After he had met this behaviour in five consecutive carriages he remembered that the *Daily Prophet* had been telling its readers all summer what a lying show-off he was. He wondered bleakly whether the people now staring and whispering believed the stories.

In the very last carriage they met Neville Longbottom, Harry's fellow fifth-year Gryffindor, his round face shining with the effort of pulling his trunk along and maintaining a one-handed grip on his struggling toad, Trevor.

'Hi, Harry,' he panted. 'Hi, Ginny ... everywhere's full ... I can't find a seat ...'

'What are you talking about?' said Ginny, who had squeezed past Neville

第10章　卢娜·洛夫古德

"嗯。"罗恩说。

"我们——嗯——罗恩和我应该到级长包厢去的。"赫敏尴尬地说。

罗恩没有望着哈利,他似乎突然对左手的指甲产生了十分浓厚的兴趣。

"噢,"哈利说,"行,好的。"

"我想我们不会一路上都待在那儿的,"赫敏很快地说,"信上说,我们只需去接受男生学生会主席和女生学生会主席的指示,然后时不时地在走廊上巡视一下。"

"好的,"哈利又说了一遍,"好吧,那么我——我们待会儿再见吧。"

"哎,没问题。"罗恩说着用惶恐不安、躲躲闪闪的目光扫了一眼哈利,"我真不愿意上那儿去,我情愿——可我们又不得不去——我是说,我根本就不喜欢去,我不是珀西。"他最后一句话说得斩钉截铁。

"我知道你不是。"哈利说着咧开嘴笑了。但是当赫敏和罗恩拖着箱子、抱着克鲁克山、拎着小猪的笼子朝火车头的方向走去时,哈利还是有了一种奇怪的失落感。以前每次乘坐霍格沃茨特快列车,他都是跟罗恩在一起的。

"走吧,"金妮对他说,"如果我们抓紧时间,还能为他们占到座位呢。"

"好吧。"哈利说。他一只手提起海德薇的笼子,另一只手抓住箱子把手。他们在过道里艰难地行走,透过玻璃门朝一间间包厢里张望,里面都已经坐满了人。哈利不由自主地注意到,许多人都怀着极大的兴趣盯着他看,有几个还用胳膊肘捅捅坐在旁边的人,对他指指点点。接连五节车厢都是这种情况,他这才想起《预言家日报》整个夏天都在告诉读者,他是怎样一个谎话连篇、特别爱卖弄的人。他郁闷地想,不知这些一边盯着他看、一边交头接耳的人是不是相信了那些谎言。

在最后一节车厢里,他们遇到了纳威·隆巴顿,他是哈利在格兰芬多五年级的同学。因为使劲拖着箱子,同时还要用一只手紧紧抓住他那只不断挣扎的蟾蜍莱福,他圆圆的脸上满是汗水。

"嘿,哈利,"他气喘吁吁地说,"嘿,金妮……到处都满了……我找不到座位……"

"你在说什么呀?"金妮从纳威身边挤过去,朝他身后的包厢里张

CHAPTER TEN   Luna Lovegood

to peer into the compartment behind him. 'There's room in this one, there's only Loony Lovegood in here –'

Neville mumbled something about not wanting to disturb anyone.

'Don't be silly,' said Ginny, laughing, 'she's all right.'

She slid the door open and pulled her trunk inside. Harry and Neville followed.

'Hi, Luna,' said Ginny, 'is it OK if we take these seats?'

The girl beside the window looked up. She had straggly, waist-length, dirty blonde hair, very pale eyebrows and protuberant eyes that gave her a permanently surprised look. Harry knew at once why Neville had chosen to pass this compartment by. The girl gave off an aura of distinct dottiness. Perhaps it was the fact that she had stuck her wand behind her left ear for safekeeping, or that she had chosen to wear a necklace of Butterbeer corks, or that she was reading a magazine upside-down. Her eyes ranged over Neville and came to rest on Harry. She nodded.

'Thanks,' said Ginny, smiling at her.

Harry and Neville stowed the three trunks and Hedwig's cage in the luggage rack and sat down. Luna watched them over her upside-down magazine, which was called The *Quibbler*. She did not seem to need to blink as much as normal humans. She stared and stared at Harry, who had taken the seat opposite her and now wished he hadn't.

'Had a good summer, Luna?' Ginny asked.

'Yes,' said Luna dreamily, without taking her eyes off Harry. 'Yes, it was quite enjoyable, you know. *You're* Harry Potter,' she added.

'I know I am,' said Harry.

Neville chuckled. Luna turned her pale eyes on him instead.

'And I don't know who you are.'

'I'm nobody,' said Neville hurriedly.

'No you're not,' said Ginny sharply. 'Neville Longbottom – Luna Lovegood. Luna's in my year, but in Ravenclaw.'

'*Wit beyond measure is man's greatest treasure*,' said Luna in a sing-song voice.

She raised her upside-down magazine high enough to hide her face and fell silent. Harry and Neville looked at each other with their eyebrows raised. Ginny suppressed a giggle.

第10章 卢娜·洛夫古德

望了一眼，说道，"这里面还有地方呢，只有疯姑娘洛夫古德一个人——"

纳威嘟哝了一句什么，似乎是不想去打扰别人。

"别傻了，"金妮大笑着说，"她没事儿的。"

她把门拉开，拖着箱子走进了包厢。哈利和纳威也跟了进去。

"你好，卢娜，"金妮说，"这些座位我们可以坐吗？"

坐在窗边的那个姑娘抬起了头。她长着一头乱蓬蓬、脏兮兮、长达腰际的金黄色头发，眉毛的颜色非常浅，两只眼睛向外凸出，这使她老有一种吃惊的表情。哈利立刻明白为什么纳威情愿放过这间包厢了。这姑娘身上明显透着一种疯疯癫癫的劲儿。这也许是因为她为了保险起见，居然把魔杖插在了左耳朵后面，或者是因为她居然戴着一串用黄油啤酒的软木塞串成的项链，或者是因为她读杂志时居然把杂志拿颠倒了。她的目光扫过纳威落在哈利身上。她点了点头。

"谢谢。"金妮说着对她微微一笑。

哈利和纳威把三个箱子和海德薇的笼子放在行李架上，然后坐了下来。卢娜从颠倒的杂志上望着他们，那本杂志的名字是"唱唱反调"。她似乎不像普通人那样需要经常眨眼睛，只是一个劲儿地盯着哈利看。哈利坐在她的对面，现在后悔不迭。

"暑假过得好吗，卢娜？"金妮问。

"是啊，"卢娜恍恍惚惚地说，眼睛仍然死死盯着哈利，"是啊，过得挺愉快的。你是哈利·波特。"她紧跟着说了一句。

"这我知道。"哈利说。

纳威咻咻地笑了。卢娜把浅色的眼睛转向了他。

"我不知道你是谁。"

"我谁也不是。"纳威赶紧说道。

"不，才不是呢，"金妮尖锐地说，"纳威·隆巴顿——这是卢娜·洛夫古德。卢娜和我同级，但是在拉文克劳。"

"过人的聪明才智是人类最大的财富。"卢娜用唱歌般的声音说。

她高高举起那本颠倒的杂志挡住自己的脸，不再出声了。哈利和纳威扬起眉毛互相望望。金妮强忍着不让自己咯咯笑出声来。

CHAPTER TEN   Luna Lovegood

The train rattled onwards, speeding them out into open country. It was an odd, unsettled sort of day; one moment the carriage was full of sunlight and the next they were passing beneath ominously grey clouds.

'Guess what I got for my birthday?' said Neville.

'Another Remembrall?' said Harry, remembering the marble-like device Neville's grandmother had sent him in an effort to improve his abysmal memory.

'No,' said Neville. 'I could do with one, though, I lost the old one ages ago ... no, look at this ...'

He dug the hand that was not keeping a firm grip on Trevor into his schoolbag and after a little bit of rummaging pulled out what appeared to be a small grey cactus in a pot, except that it was covered with what looked like boils rather than spines.

'*Mimbulus mimbletonia*,' he said proudly.

Harry stared at the thing. It was pulsating slightly, giving it the rather sinister look of some diseased internal organ.

'It's really, really rare,' said Neville, beaming. 'I don't know if there's one in the greenhouse at Hogwarts, even. I can't wait to show it to Professor Sprout. My Great Uncle Algie got it for me in Assyria. I'm going to see if I can breed from it.'

Harry knew that Neville's favourite subject was Herbology but for the life of him he could not see what he would want with this stunted little plant.

'Does it – er – do anything?' he asked.

'Loads of stuff!' said Neville proudly. 'It's got an amazing defensive mechanism. Here, hold Trevor for me ...'

He dumped the toad into Harry's lap and took a quill from his schoolbag. Luna Lovegood's popping eyes appeared over the top of her upside-down magazine again, to watch what Neville was doing. Neville held the *Mimbulus mimbletonia* up to his eyes, his tongue between his teeth, chose his spot, and gave the plant a sharp prod with the tip of his quill.

Liquid squirted from every boil on the plant; thick, stinking, dark green jets of it. They hit the ceiling, the windows, and spattered Luna Lovegood's magazine; Ginny, who had flung her arms up in front of her face just in time, merely looked as though she was wearing a slimy green hat, but Harry,

第10章 卢娜·洛夫古德

火车哐嘟哐嘟地往前开,把他们带到了空旷的乡村。这真是古怪的、变幻无常的一天。一会儿车厢里洒满阳光,一会儿又是天色阴沉,乌云密布。

"猜猜我生日得到了什么礼物?"纳威说。

"又是一个记忆球?"哈利说,他想起了纳威的奶奶为了提高纳威那糟糕透顶的记忆力,曾给他寄来的那个大理石般的玩意儿。

"不是,"纳威说,"我有一个就够了,不过那个旧的我已经丢了好久……不是,看看这个……"

他一只手紧紧攥着莱福,另一只手伸进书包翻找了一会儿,掏出一样东西,像是一棵栽在盆里的灰色小仙人掌,但上面不是长满了刺,而是布满一个个疖子般的东西。

"米布米宝。"他得意地说。

哈利瞪着那东西。它在微微地跳动,看上去像一个病变的内脏器官,让人感到不吉利。

"这是非常、非常稀罕的,"纳威满脸放光地说,"就连霍格沃茨的温室里都不一定有呢。我真想现在就拿给斯普劳特教授看看。这是我阿尔吉叔爷从亚述给我弄来的。我想看看我能不能培植它。"

哈利知道纳威最喜欢的一门课就是草药学,但是他怎么也弄不明白这种发育不良的小植物有什么用。

"它——嗯——它能做什么用吗?"他问。

"用处多着呢!"纳威骄傲地说,"它有一种惊人的自卫机制。看,替我拿着莱福……"

他把蟾蜍扔在哈利的膝盖上,从书包里拿出一支羽毛笔。卢娜·洛夫古德那双凸出的眼睛又从颠倒的杂志上露出来,注视着纳威的举动。纳威把舌尖含在牙齿间,把那盆米布米宝举到眼前,找准一个地方,用羽毛笔尖使劲捅了一下。

汁液从植物身上的每个疖子里喷射出来。一股股黏糊糊、臭烘烘的墨绿色汁液喷到了车厢的天花板上、窗户上,溅到卢娜·洛夫古德的杂志上。金妮幸好及时用胳膊挡住了脸,只是头上像戴了一顶黏糊糊的肮脏的绿帽子。哈利可就惨了,他两只手都忙着捉住莱福不让它

CHAPTER TEN   Luna Lovegood

whose hands had been busy preventing Trevor's escape, received a faceful. It smelled like rancid manure.

Neville, whose face and torso were also drenched, shook his head to get the worst out of his eyes.

'S – sorry,' he gasped. 'I haven't tried that before ... didn't realise it would be quite so ... don't worry, though, Stinksap's not poisonous,' he added nervously, as Harry spat a mouthful on to the floor.

At that precise moment the door of their compartment slid open.

'Oh ... hello, Harry,' said a nervous voice. 'Um ... bad time?'

Harry wiped the lenses of his glasses with his Trevor-free hand. A very pretty girl with long, shiny black hair was standing in the doorway smiling at him: Cho Chang, the Seeker on the Ravenclaw Quidditch team.

'Oh ... hi,' said Harry blankly.

'Um ...' said Cho. 'Well ... just thought I'd say hello ... bye then.'

Rather pink in the face, she closed the door and departed. Harry slumped back in his seat and groaned. He would have liked Cho to discover him sitting with a group of very cool people laughing their heads off at a joke he had just told; he would not have chosen to be sitting with Neville and Loony Lovegood, clutching a toad and dripping in Stinksap.

'Never mind,' said Ginny bracingly. 'Look, we can easily get rid of all this.' She pulled out her wand. '*Scourgify!*'

The Stinksap vanished.

'Sorry,' said Neville again, in a small voice.

Ron and Hermione did not turn up for nearly an hour, by which time the food trolley had already gone by. Harry, Ginny and Neville had finished their pumpkin pasties and were busy swapping Chocolate Frog Cards when the compartment door slid open and they walked in, accompanied by Crookshanks and a shrilly hooting Pigwidgeon in his cage.

'I'm starving,' said Ron, stowing Pigwidgeon next to Hedwig, grabbing a Chocolate Frog from Harry and throwing himself into the seat next to him. He ripped open the wrapper, bit off the Frog's head and leaned back with his eyes closed as though he had had a very exhausting morning.

'Well, there are two fifth-year prefects from each house,' said Hermione,

逃走，结果被喷了个满脸花。那气味就像恶臭难闻的大粪。

纳威的脸上和身上也都被喷湿了，他晃了晃脑袋，想把遭殃最厉害的眼睛里的汁液挤出来。

"对—对不起，"他喘着气说，"我以前没有试过……没想到会是这个样子，不过别担心，臭汁没有毒。"他看到哈利往地上吐了一口，不安地补充道。

不早不晚就在这个时候，他们包厢的门被拉开了。

"噢……你好，哈利，"一个怯生生的声音说，"嗯……我来得好像不是时候？"

哈利用没拿莱福的那只手擦了擦镜片。一个长得非常漂亮、一头长发乌黑油亮的姑娘正站在包厢门口，笑眯眯地望着他。是秋·张，拉文克劳魁地奇球队的找球手。

"噢……你好。"哈利不知所措地说。

"嗯……"秋说，"好吧……我就是想过来问声好……再见吧。"

她脸颊红红的，关上门走了。哈利垂头耷脑地倒在座位上，唉声叹气。他多么希望秋看见他和一群很酷的人坐在一起，他们被他讲的一个笑话逗得乐不可支。他真不愿意被她看见自己跟纳威和疯姑娘洛夫古德坐在一起，手里拿着一只癞蛤蟆，脸上淌着臭汁。

"没关系，"金妮安慰他说，"瞧，我们不费吹灰之力就能弄干净。"她抽出自己的魔杖，"清理一新！"

臭汁都消失了。

"对不起。"纳威又小声说了一遍。

罗恩和赫敏差不多一小时之后才过来。卖食品的手推车已经来过了，哈利、金妮和纳威吃完了南瓜馅饼，正忙着交换巧克力蛙的画片，这时包厢的门被推开，他们俩走了进来，跟他们在一起的还有克鲁克山和关在笼子里厉声尖叫的小猪。

"我饿惨了。"罗恩说着把小猪塞在海德薇旁边，从哈利手里抓过一块巧克力蛙，一屁股坐在哈利旁边的座位上。他撕开包装纸，一口咬掉了青蛙的脑袋，然后倒在椅背上，闭上了眼睛，似乎这一上午把他累坏了。

"是这样，每个学院的五年级都有两个级长，"赫敏说，她坐下时

looking thoroughly disgruntled as she took her seat. 'Boy and girl from each.'

'And guess who's a Slytherin prefect?' said Ron, still with his eyes closed.

'Malfoy,' replied Harry at once, certain his worst fear would be confirmed.

'Course,' said Ron bitterly, stuffing the rest of the frog into his mouth and taking another.

'And that complete *cow* Pansy Parkinson,' said Hermione viciously. 'How she got to be a prefect when she's thicker than a concussed troll ...'

'Who are Hufflepuff's?' Harry asked.

'Ernie Macmillan and Hannah Abbott,' said Ron thickly.

'And Anthony Goldstein and Padma Patil for Ravenclaw,' said Hermione.

'You went to the Yule Ball with Padma Patil,' said a vague voice.

Everyone turned to look at Luna Lovegood, who was gazing unblinkingly at Ron over the top of *The Quibbler*. He swallowed his mouthful of Frog.

'Yeah, I know I did,' he said, looking mildly surprised.

'She didn't enjoy it very much,' Luna informed him. 'She doesn't think you treated her very well, because you wouldn't dance with her. I don't think I'd have minded,' she added thoughtfully, 'I don't like dancing very much.'

She retreated behind *The Quibbler* again. Ron stared at the cover with his mouth hanging open for a few seconds, then looked around at Ginny for some kind of explanation, but Ginny had stuffed her knuckles in her mouth to stop herself giggling. Ron shook his head, bemused, then checked his watch.

'We're supposed to patrol the corridors every so often,' he told Harry and Neville, 'and we can give out punishments if people are misbehaving. I can't wait to get Crabbe and Goyle for something ...'

'You're not supposed to abuse your position, on!' said Hermione sharply.

'Yeah, right, because Malfoy won't abuse it at all,' said Ron sarcastically.

'So you're going to descend to his level?'

'No, I'm just going to make sure I get his mates before he gets mine.'

'For heaven's sake, Ron –'

'I'll make Goyle do lines, it'll kill him, he hates writing,' said Ron happily.

第 10 章 卢娜·洛夫古德

显得特别不高兴,"一男一女。"

"猜猜谁是斯莱特林的级长?"罗恩说,眼睛仍然闭着。

"马尔福。"哈利不假思索地回答,相信他最担心的事情会得到证实。

"没错。"罗恩苦闷地说,一边把青蛙的身体塞进嘴里,然后又拿了一块。

"还有那头十足的母牛潘西·帕金森,"赫敏尖刻地说,"她怎么能当级长呢,她比一个患了脑震荡的巨怪还要笨呢……"

"赫奇帕奇的是谁?"哈利问。

"厄尼·麦克米兰和汉娜·艾博。"罗恩含混不清地说。

"拉文克劳的是安东尼·戈德斯坦和帕德玛·佩蒂尔。"赫敏说。

"你和帕德玛·佩蒂尔一起参加过圣诞舞会呢。"一个朦胧的声音说。

大家都转过脸来望着卢娜·洛夫古德,她的眼睛从《唱唱反调》上方一眨不眨地盯着罗恩。罗恩赶紧把满嘴的巧克力蛙咽了下去。

"是啊,我知道的。"他说,显得有点儿吃惊。

"可是她玩得不太开心,"卢娜对他说,"她认为你对她不太好,因为你不肯跟她跳舞。我想我是不会在乎的,"她若有所思地又说道,"我不怎么喜欢跳舞。"

她又缩到《唱唱反调》后面去了。罗恩张大嘴巴呆呆地望着杂志封面,好几秒钟缓不过神来,随即转脸看看金妮,希望得到一些解释。可是金妮用手指关节堵着嘴,不让自己咯咯笑出声来。罗恩摇了摇头,整个儿给弄糊涂了,然后他看了看表。

"我们应该偶尔在过道里巡视巡视,"他对哈利和纳威说,"如果有人在做坏事,我们可以惩罚他们。我真想马上就抓住克拉布和高尔的什么把柄……"

"你不应该滥用职权,罗恩!"赫敏严厉地说。

"是啊,没错,因为马尔福是绝不会滥用职权的。"罗恩讽刺地说。

"难道你要把自己降低到他那个层次?"

"不,我只是要保证在他欺负我的朋友之前,先给他的朋友一点厉害瞧瞧。"

"看在老天的分儿上,罗恩——"

"我要罚高尔写句子,那会要了他的命,他最讨厌写字了。"罗恩

CHAPTER TEN — Luna Lovegood

He lowered his voice to Goyle's low grunt and, screwing up his face in a look of pained concentration, mimed writing in midair. '*I ... must ... not ... look ... like ... a ... baboon's ... backside.*'

Everyone laughed, but nobody laughed harder than Luna Lovegood. She let out a scream of mirth that caused Hedwig to wake up and flap her wings indignantly and Crookshanks to leap up into the luggage rack, hissing. Luna laughed so hard her magazine slipped out of her grasp, slid down her legs and on to the floor.

'That was *funny*!'

Her prominent eyes swam with tears as she gasped for breath, staring at Ron. Utterly nonplussed, he looked around at the others, who were now laughing at the expression on Ron's face and at the ludicrously prolonged laughter of Luna Lovegood, who was rocking backwards and forwards, clutching her sides.

'Are you taking the mickey?' said Ron, frowning at her.

'Baboon's ... backside!' she choked, holding her ribs.

Everyone else was watching Luna laughing, but Harry, glancing at the magazine on the floor, noticed something that made him dive for it. Upside-down it had been hard to tell what the picture on the front was, but Harry now realised it was a fairly bad cartoon of Cornelius Fudge; Harry only recognised him because of the lime-green bowler hat. One of Fudge's hands was clenched around a bag of gold; the other hand was throttling a goblin. The cartoon was captioned: *How Far Will Fudge Go to Gain Gringotts?*

Beneath this were listed the titles of other articles inside the magazine.

**Corruption in the Quidditch League:
HOW THE TORNADOS ARE TAKING CONTROL**

SECRETS OF THE ANCIENT RUNES REVEALED

SIRIUS BLACK: VILLAIN OR VICTIM?

'Can I have a look at this?' Harry asked Luna eagerly.

She nodded, still gazing at Ron, breathless with laughter.

开心地说。他放低声音,学着高尔粗声哑气的嗓音,把脸皱成一团,似乎在痛苦地集中注意力,假装在空气中写字:"我……绝……不……能……像……狒……狒……的……屁……股。"

大伙儿哈哈大笑,但是谁也没有卢娜·洛夫古德笑得那样厉害。她发出一串尖厉刺耳的狂笑,把海德薇从梦中惊醒了。它愤怒地扑扇着翅膀,吓得克鲁克山跳到行李架上,嘶嘶地叫着。卢娜笑得太厉害了,她手里的杂志掉下来,从腿上滑到了地板上。

"太好玩了!"

她急促地喘着气,一个劲儿地瞪着罗恩,两只凸出的眼睛里涌满了泪水。罗恩完全摸不着头脑,他疑惑地望望大家,而他们都被罗恩脸上的表情,还有卢娜·洛夫古德那没完没了的狂笑逗得开怀大笑。卢娜拼命捂着肚子,笑得前仰后合。

"你在嘲笑我吗?"罗恩冲她皱着眉头问道。

"狒狒的……屁股!"她按住肋骨,气喘吁吁地说。

其他人都在看卢娜狂笑,哈利却扫了一眼地上的那本杂志,突然注意到了什么,便伸手把杂志捡了起来。刚才颠倒着不容易看清封面上的图画,现在哈利看出那原来是一幅画得很糟糕的康奈利·福吉的漫画,哈利是由他头上那顶暗黄绿色的圆顶硬礼帽认出他来的。福吉一只手抓住一袋金子,另一只手掐着一个妖精的脖子。漫画上的说明文字是:福吉离霸占古灵阁还有多远?

紧接着下面列出了杂志里其他文章的标题:

魁地奇联盟里的腐败:龙卷风队如何掌握大权

古代如尼文揭秘

小天狼星布莱克:恶棍还是受害者?

"可以给我看看吗?"哈利急切地问卢娜。

她点点头,眼睛仍然盯着罗恩,笑得连气都喘不上来了。

Harry opened the magazine and scanned the index. Until this moment he had completely forgotten the magazine Kingsley had handed Mr Weasley to give to Sirius, but it must have been this edition of *The Quibbler*.

He found the page, and turned excitedly to the article.

This, too, was illustrated by a rather bad cartoon; in fact, Harry would not have known it was supposed to be Sirius if it hadn't been captioned. Sirius was standing on a pile of human bones with his wand out. The headline on the article said:

SIRUIS – BLACK AS HE'S PAINTED?
Notorious mass murderer or innocent singing sensation?

Harry had to read this first sentence several times before he was convinced that he had not misunderstood it. Since when had Sirius been a singing sensation?

> For fourteen years Sirius Black has been believed guilty of the mass murder of twelve innocent Muggles and one wizard. Black's audacious escape from Azkaban two years ago has led to the widest manhunt ever conducted by the Ministry of Magic. None of us has ever questioned that he deserves to be recaptured and handed back to the Dementors.
>
> BUT DOES HE?
>
> Startling new evidence has recently come to light that Sirius Black may not have committed the crimes for which he was sent to Azkaban. In fact, says Doris Purkiss, of 18 Acanthia Way, Little Norton, Black may not even have been present at the killings.
>
> 'What people don't realise is that Sirius Black is a false name,' says Mrs Purkiss. 'The man people believe to be Sirius Black is actually Stubby Boardman, lead singer of popular singing group The Hobgoblins, who retired from public life after being struck on the ear by a turnip at a concert in Little Norton Church Hall nearly fifteen years ago. I recognised him the moment I saw his picture in the paper. Now, Stubby couldn't possibly have

第10章 卢娜·洛夫古德

哈利打开杂志，扫了一眼目录。他已经把金斯莱委托韦斯莱先生转交给小天狼星的那本杂志忘了个一干二净，这会儿才又想起来，看来肯定就是这期的《唱唱反调》。

他找到页码，迫不及待地翻到那篇文章。

这一页也有一幅画得非常糟糕的漫画。实际上，如果没有说明文字，哈利简直认不出这个人就是小天狼星。画上的小天狼星站在一堆白骨上，手里举着魔杖，文章的标题是：

小天狼星——像画上的这么黑吗？
臭名昭著的杀人魔王
还是无辜的歌坛巨星？

哈利把这个句子读了好几遍，才确信没有弄错它的意思。小天狼星什么时候成了一位歌坛巨星？

十四年来，小天狼星布莱克一直被认为是个杀人魔王，杀害了十二个无辜的麻瓜和一名巫师。两年前布莱克胆大妄为地从阿兹卡班越狱逃跑，魔法部展开了前所未有的大范围搜捕。他应该被重新抓获，送回到摄魂怪手里，对此我们没有一个人提出质疑。

然而真是这样吗？

最近出现了令人惊诧的新证据，证明小天狼星布莱克也许并没有犯下他因之被送进阿兹卡班的那些罪行。小诺顿区刺叶路18号的多丽丝·珀基斯说，实际上，小天狼星可能根本就不在杀人现场。

"人们没有意识到，小天狼星布莱克是一个假名。"珀基斯夫人说，"人们以为是小天狼星布莱克的那个人，实际上是胖墩勃德曼，是流行歌唱组合淘气妖精的领唱，约十五年前在小诺顿区教堂大厅的一次音乐会上被一个萝卜打中耳朵后，就退出了公众生活。我在报纸上看到他的照片时一眼就认了出来。所以，胖墩勃德曼不可能犯下那些罪行，因为那天他正好和我在一起享受浪漫

CHAPTER TEN   Luna Lovegood

> committed those crimes, because on the day in question he happened to be enjoying a romantic candlelit dinner with me. I have written to the Minister for Magic and am expecting him to give Stubby, alias Sirius, a full pardon any day now.'

Harry finished reading and stared at the page in disbelief. Perhaps it was a joke, he thought, perhaps the magazine often printed spoof items. He flicked back a few pages and found the piece on Fudge.

> Cornelius Fudge, the Minister for Magic, denied that he had any plans to take over the running of the Wizarding Bank, Gringotts, when he was elected Minister for Magic five years ago. Fudge has always insisted that he wants nothing more than to 'co-operate peacefully' with the guardians of our gold.
> BUT DOES HE?
> Sources close to the Minister have recently disclosed that Fudge's dearest ambition is to seize control of the goblin gold supplies and that he will not hesitate to use force if need be.
> 'It wouldn't be the first time, either,' said a Ministry insider. 'Cornelius "Goblin-Crusher" Fudge, that's what his friends call him. If you could hear him when he thinks no one's listening, oh, he's always talking about the goblins he's had done in; he's had them drowned, he's had them dropped off buildings, he's had them poisoned, he's had them cooked in pies ...'

Harry did not read any further. Fudge might have many faults but Harry found it extremely hard to imagine him ordering goblins to be cooked in pies. He flicked through the rest of the magazine. Pausing every few pages, he read: an accusation that the Tutshill Tornados were winning the Quidditch League by a combination of blackmail, illegal broom-tampering and torture; an interview with a wizard who claimed to have flown to the moon on a Cleansweep Six and brought back a bag of moon frogs to prove it; and an article on ancient runes which at least explained why Luna had been reading *The Quibbler* upside-down. According to the magazine, if you turned the runes on their heads

第10章 卢娜·洛夫古德

的烛光晚宴。我已经给魔法部部长写了信,希望他能尽快给胖墩,又名小天狼星,彻底平反昭雪。"

哈利读完后,不敢相信地瞪着那篇文章。也许这是一个笑话,他想,也许杂志上经常刊登一些哗众取宠的笑料。他往后翻了几页,找到了关于福吉的那篇文章。

魔法部部长康奈利·福吉五年前当选部长时,曾经否认他有接管古灵阁巫师银行的打算。福吉总是一口咬定,他只想和我们的黄金保管者"和平合作"。

然而真是这样吗?

与部长密切接触的消息提供者最近透露,福吉最强烈的野心就是控制妖精的黄金储备,如果必要的话,他会毫不犹豫地动用武力。

"这也不会是第一次。"一位魔法部内部人士说,"他的朋友们都管他叫'妖精杀手'康奈利·福吉。但愿你能听见他在以为身旁没人时所说的话,哦,他总是在谈论他干掉的那些妖精。扔进水里淹死的,从楼上推下去摔死的,下毒药毒死的,还有做成馅饼烤熟的……"

哈利没有再读下去。福吉可能是有许多缺点,但哈利觉得很难想象他会命令别人把妖精做成馅饼,这太离奇了。他翻看杂志上的其他文章,偶尔停下来看两眼,他读到的内容有:有人指控塔特希尔龙卷风队是靠胁迫、非法对飞天扫帚做手脚、折磨对手等手段而赢得魁地奇联盟杯的;对一个巫师的采访,他宣称自己骑着一把横扫六星飞到了月亮上,并带回来一袋月亮上的青蛙作为证据;还有一篇文章讲的是古代如尼文,这至少解释了卢娜为什么一直颠倒着读《唱唱反调》。杂志上说,如果你把这些古代如尼文颠倒过来,就能看见它们其实是一个咒语,能把你仇敌的耳朵变成金橘。实际上,跟《唱唱反调》上的其他文章比起来,那篇提出小天狼星其实可能是淘气妖精领唱的文

CHAPTER TEN Luna Lovegood

they revealed a spell to make your enemy's ears turn into kumquats. In fact, compared to the rest of the articles in *The Quibbler*, the suggestion that Sirius might really be the lead singer of The Hobgoblins was quite sensible.

'Anything good in there?' asked Ron as Harry closed the magazine.

'Of course not,' said Hermione scathingly, before Harry could answer. '*The Quibbler's* rubbish, everyone knows that.'

'Excuse me,' said Luna; her voice had suddenly lost its dreamy quality. 'My father's the editor.'

'I – oh,' said Hermione, looking embarrassed. 'Well ... it's got some interesting ... I mean, it's quite ...'

'I'll have it back, thank you,' said Luna coldly, and leaning forwards she snatched it out of Harry's hands. Riffling through it to page fifty-seven, she turned it resolutely upside-down again and disappeared behind it, just as the compartment door opened for the third time.

Harry looked around; he had expected this, but that did not make the sight of Draco Malfoy smirking at him from between his cronies Crabbe and Goyle any more enjoyable.

'What?' he said aggressively, before Malfoy could open his mouth.

'Manners, Potter, or I'll have to give you a detention,' drawled Malfoy, whose sleek blond hair and pointed chin were just like his father's. 'You see, I, unlike you, have been made a prefect, which means that I, unlike you, have the power to hand out punishments.'

'Yeah,' said Harry, 'but you, unlike me, are a git, so get out and leave us alone.'

Ron, Hermione, Ginny and Neville laughed. Malfoy's lip curled.

'Tell me, how does it feel being second-best to Weasley, Potter?' he asked.

'Shut up, Malfoy,' said Hermione sharply.

'I seem to have touched a nerve,' said Malfoy, smirking. 'Well, just watch yourself, Potter, because I'll be *dogging* your footsteps in case you step out of line.'

'Get out!' said Hermione, standing up.

Sniggering, Malfoy gave Harry a last malicious look and departed, with Crabbe and Goyle lumbering along in his wake. Hermione slammed the compartment door behind them and turned to look at Harry, who knew at once that she, like him, had registered what Malfoy had said and been just as unnerved by it.

章还算是有点道理呢。

"上面有什么好东西吗?"罗恩看到哈利合上了杂志,问道。

"当然没有,"赫敏不等哈利回答,就尖刻地说,"《唱唱反调》是一堆垃圾,这是每个人都知道的。"

"对不起,"卢娜说,她的声音突然不再那么恍恍惚惚了,"我父亲是杂志主编。"

"我……哦,"赫敏显得非常尴尬地说,"是这样,有一些还是蛮有趣的……我的意思是,它还是很……"

"把它还给我吧,谢谢。"卢娜冷冷地说,探过身来一把从哈利手里夺过杂志,哗啦哗啦地翻到第五十七页,坚定不移地把它颠倒过来,把自己的脸挡在后面。就在这时,包厢的门第三次被拉开了。

哈利扭头一看,他其实早就预料到了,但此刻看到德拉科·马尔福在他两个死党克拉布和高尔的陪伴下,得意扬扬地冲自己冷笑时,他仍然感到很不愉快。

"怎么啦?"他不等马尔福开口,就挑衅地问道。

"注意礼貌,波特,不然我就让你关禁闭。"马尔福拖腔拖调地说,油光水滑的金黄色头发和尖尖的下巴跟他爸爸一模一样,"你看,我和你不同,我当上级长了,这就是说,我和你不同,我有权惩罚别人。"

"是吗,"哈利说,"可是你,和我不同,你是个饭桶,所以请你走开,别来打搅我们。"

罗恩、赫敏、金妮和纳威都哈哈大笑起来。马尔福的嘴唇扭曲了。

"告诉我,败在韦斯莱手下的滋味如何呀,波特?"他问。

"闭嘴,马尔福。"赫敏厉声说道。

"看来我触到痛处了。"马尔福得意地笑着说,"好吧,波特,你可要放规矩点儿,因为我会像一条猎狗一样跟着你,看你敢不敢越轨。"

"出去!"赫敏说着站了起来。

马尔福咻咻坏笑着,最后恶狠狠地朝哈利瞪了一眼,转身离开了,克拉布和高尔笨手笨脚地跟在后面。赫敏把包厢的门重重地关上,转脸望着哈利。哈利顿时就明白了,赫敏和他一样,也注意到了马尔福刚才说的话,并为此感到忧心忡忡。

CHAPTER TEN   Luna Lovegood

'Chuck us another Frog,' said Ron, who had clearly noticed nothing.

Harry could not talk freely in front of Neville and Luna. He exchanged another nervous look with Hermione, then stared out of the window.

He had thought Sirius coming with him to the station was a bit of a laugh, but suddenly it seemed reckless, if not downright dangerous ... Hermione had been right ... Sirius should not have come. What if Mr Malfoy had noticed the black dog and told Draco? What if he had deduced that the Weasleys, Lupin, Tonks and Moody knew where Sirius was hiding? Or had Malfoy's use of the word 'dogging' been a coincidence?

The weather remained undecided as they travelled further and further north. Rain spattered the windows in a half-hearted way, then the sun put in a feeble appearance before clouds drifted over it once more. When darkness fell and lamps came on inside the carriages, Luna rolled up *The Quibbler*, put it carefully away in her bag and took to staring at everyone in the compartment instead.

Harry was sitting with his forehead pressed against the train window, trying to get a first distant glimpse of Hogwarts, but it was a moonless night and the rain-streaked window was grimy.

'We'd better change,' said Hermione at last. She and Ron pinned their prefect badges carefully to their chests. Harry saw Ron checking his reflection in the black window.

At last, the train began to slow down and they heard the usual racket up and down it as everybody scrambled to get their luggage and pets assembled, ready to get off. As Ron and Hermione were supposed to supervise all this, they disappeared from the carriage again, leaving Harry and the others to look after Crookshanks and Pigwidgeon.

'I'll carry that owl, if you like,' said Luna to Harry, reaching out for Pigwidgeon as Neville stowed Trevor carefully in an inside pocket.

'Oh – er – thanks,' said Harry, handing her the cage and hoisting Hedwig's more securely into his arms.

They shuffled out of the compartment feeling the first sting of the night air on their faces as they joined the crowd in the corridor. Slowly, they moved towards the doors. Harry could smell the pine trees that lined the path down to the lake. He stepped down on to the platform and looked around, listening for the familiar call of 'firs'-years over 'ere ... firs'-years ...'

第10章 卢娜·洛夫古德

"再扔一只青蛙过来。"罗恩说,他显然什么也没留意。

当着纳威和卢娜的面,哈利不能敞开来说话。他又和赫敏交换了一下惶恐不安的眼神,然后转脸望着窗外。

他原来以为,小天狼星陪他到车站来只是一个玩笑之举,现在才发现这么做即便不是非常危险,也是不够谨慎……赫敏说得对……小天狼星是不应该来的。如果马尔福先生注意到了那条黑狗,并告诉了德拉科呢?如果他由此推断出韦斯莱夫妇、卢平、唐克斯和穆迪知道小天狼星藏在哪里呢?或者,马尔福刚才说"像一条猎狗一样跟着"这样的话只是一种巧合?

他们继续向北行进,天气还是变幻不定。雨点有一搭没一搭地敲打着车窗,然后太阳懒洋洋地探出脸来,很快云层飘过,又把它遮住了。夜幕降临,包厢里的灯亮了,卢娜卷起《唱唱反调》,小心地放进书包,然后转过脸来,目不转睛地盯着包厢里的每个人。

哈利坐在那里,将额头贴在车窗上,想远远地就能看见霍格沃茨,但这是一个没有月亮的夜晚,而且被雨水打湿的车窗上脏兮兮的。

"我们最好换衣服吧。"最后赫敏说道。她和罗恩仔细地把级长徽章戴在胸前。哈利看见罗恩对着漆黑的窗户照了照自己的模样。

终于,火车慢慢地减速了,他们又听见四下里一片纷乱嘈杂,因为每个人都忙着把行李和宠物归拢在一起,准备下车。罗恩和赫敏要监督秩序,就又从包厢里消失了,留下哈利和其他人照看克鲁克山和小猪。

"我来帮你提那只猫头鹰,如果你愿意的话?"卢娜对哈利说,伸手来接小猪,纳威在一旁小心地把莱福塞进长袍里面的口袋。

"哦——嗯——谢谢。"哈利说着把笼子递给了她,然后将海德薇更稳妥地抱在怀里。

他们拖着沉重的脚步走出包厢,汇入了过道里的人流,开始感觉到夜晚的空气吹在脸上的刺痛。他们慢慢地朝门口挪动,哈利可以闻到通向湖畔的小路两旁那一棵棵松树的清香。他下车来到站台上,环顾四周,竖起耳朵捕捉那熟悉的声音:"一年级新生上这儿来……一年级新生……"

CHAPTER TEN Luna Lovegood

But it did not come. Instead, a quite different voice, a brisk female one, was calling out, 'First-years line up over here, please! All first-years to me!'

A lantern came swinging towards Harry and by its light he saw the prominent chin and severe haircut of Professor Grubbly-Plank, the witch who had taken over Hagrid's Care of Magical Creatures lessons for a while the previous year.

'Where's Hagrid?' he said out loud.

'I don't know,' said Ginny, 'but we'd better get out of the way, we're blocking the door.'

'Oh, yeah ...'

Harry and Ginny became separated as they moved off along the platform and out through the station. Jostled by the crowd, Harry squinted through the darkness for a glimpse of Hagrid; he had to be here, Harry had been relying on it – seeing Hagrid again was one of the things he'd been looking forward to most. But there was no sign of him.

He can't have left, Harry told himself as he shuffled slowly through a narrow doorway on to the road outside with the rest of the crowd. *He's just got a cold or something* ...

He looked around for Ron or Hermione, wanting to know what they thought about the reappearance of Professor Grubbly-Plank, but neither of them was anywhere near him, so he allowed himself to be shunted forwards on to the dark rain-washed road outside Hogsmeade station.

Here stood the hundred or so horseless stagecoaches that always took the students above first year up to the castle. Harry glanced quickly at them, turned away to keep a lookout for Ron and Hermione, then did a double-take.

The coaches were no longer horseless. There were creatures standing between the carriage shafts. If he had had to give them a name, he supposed he would have called them horses, though there was something reptilian about them, too. They were completely fleshless, their black coats clinging to their skeletons, of which every bone was visible. Their heads were dragonish, and their pupil-less eyes white and staring. Wings sprouted from each wither – vast, black leathery wings that looked as though they ought to belong to giant bats. Standing still and quiet in the gloom, the creatures looked eerie and sinister. Harry could not understand why the coaches were being pulled by these horrible horses when they were quite capable of moving along by themselves.

第10章　卢娜·洛夫古德

可是他没有听见。取而代之的是一个完全陌生的声音，一个干脆利落的女声，正在大声喊着："请一年级新生上这儿排队！所有一年级新生都跟我来！"

一盏提灯摇摇晃晃地朝哈利这边移动，就着它的亮光，他看见了格拉普兰教授那突出的下巴和修剪得一丝不苟的头发，这位女巫前一年曾代替海格上过一段时间的保护神奇动物课。

"海格呢？"哈利大声问。

"我不知道，"金妮说，"但我们最好赶紧让开，我们把门都挡住了。"

"噢，好的……"

哈利和金妮顺着站台往车站外面走去，渐渐地两人分开了。哈利被人群推挤着往前走，一边眯起眼睛在黑暗中寻找海格的身影。海格不能不在这儿，哈利眼巴巴地盼着呢——再次见到海格是哈利内心最渴望的一件事。可是四下里都没有海格的影子。

他不可能离开，哈利一边想一边拖着沉重的脚步，和众人一起慢慢穿过狭窄的门道，来到外面的马路上。他可能只是患了感冒什么的……

他东张西望地寻找罗恩或赫敏，想知道他们对格拉普兰教授的再次出现有什么想法，可是他们俩都不在旁边，他只好由着自己被推向霍格莫德车站外那条被雨水冲刷过的黑乎乎的街道。

这里停着约一百辆没有马拉的马车，每年都是它们把一年级以上的学生送到城堡去的。哈利很快地扫了它们一眼，又转脸寻找罗恩和赫敏，接着他又回过头来细看。

马车前面不再是空的了。辕杆之间站着一些动物，如果硬要给它们一个名字的话，哈利觉得他会管它们叫马，尽管它们的模样有点儿类似爬行动物。它们身上一点肉也没有，黑色的毛皮紧紧地贴在骨架上，每一根骨头都清晰可见。它们的脑袋很像火龙的脑袋，没有瞳孔的眼睛白白的，目不转睛地瞪着。在肩骨间隆起的地方生出了翅膀——又大又黑的坚韧翅膀，看上去似乎应该属于巨大的蝙蝠。这些动物一动不动，静悄悄地站在夜色中，显得怪异而不吉利。哈利真不明白，这些马车明明自己就能行走，为什么还要用这些可怕的马来拉它们。

CHAPTER TEN Luna Lovegood

'Where's Pig?' said Ron's voice, right behind Harry.

'That Luna girl was carrying him,' said Harry, turning quickly, eager to consult Ron about Hagrid. 'Where d'you reckon –'

'– Hagrid is? I dunno,' said Ron, sounding worried. 'He'd better be OK ...'

A short distance away, Draco Malfoy, followed by a small gang of cronies including Crabbe, Goyle and Pansy Parkinson, was pushing some timid-looking second-years out of the way so that he and his friends could get a coach to themselves. Seconds later, Hermione emerged panting from the crowd.

'Malfoy was being absolutely foul to a first-year back there. I swear I'm going to report him, he's only had his badge three minutes and he's using it to bully people worse than ever ... where's Crookshanks?'

'Ginny's got him,' said Harry. 'There she is ...'

Ginny had just emerged from the crowd, clutching a squirming Crookshanks.

'Thanks,' said Hermione, relieving Ginny of the cat. 'Come on, let's get a carriage together before they all fill up ...'

'I haven't got Pig yet!' Ron said, but Hermione was already heading off towards the nearest unoccupied coach. Harry remained behind with Ron.

'What *are* those things, d'you reckon?' he asked Ron, nodding at the horrible horses as the other students surged past them.

'What things?'

'Those horse –'

Luna appeared holding Pigwidgeon's cage in her arms; the tiny owl was twittering excitedly as usual.

'Here you are,' she said. 'He's a sweet little owl, isn't he?'

'Er ... yeah ... he's all right,' said Ron gruffly. 'Well, come on then, let's get in ... what were you saying, Harry?'

'I was saying, what are those horse things?' Harry said, as he, Ron and Luna made for the carriage in which Hermione and Ginny were already sitting.

'What horse things?'

'The horse things pulling the carriages!' said Harry impatiently. They

第10章 卢娜·洛夫古德

"小猪呢?"罗恩的声音在哈利身后响起。

"那个叫卢娜的女生提着呢。"哈利说着急切地转过身来,想跟罗恩讨论一下海格的事,"你说,为什么不见——"

"——海格?不知道,"罗恩说,显得很是担忧,"他可别出什么事……"

在离他们不远的地方,德拉科·马尔福,后面跟着一小伙死党,包括克拉布、高尔和潘西·帕金森。马尔福正在把几个神情很胆怯的二年级同学推到一边,好让他和他的朋友们独占一辆马车。几秒钟后,赫敏气喘吁吁地从人群中钻了出来。

"马尔福刚才在那里对一个一年级新生态度非常恶劣。我发誓一定要告他一状,他戴上徽章还不满三分钟呢,就利用它变本加厉地欺负人……克鲁克山呢?"

"金妮抱着呢。"哈利说,"她来了……"

金妮刚从人群里闪身出来,紧紧抱着不断扭动的克鲁克山。

"谢谢。"赫敏说着把猫从金妮手里接了过来,"走吧,我们赶紧找一辆马车坐在一起,待会儿就没有地方了……"

"我还没有拿到小猪呢!"罗恩说,可是赫敏已经朝最近的一辆空马车走去。哈利陪罗恩留在原地。

"你看,那是些什么东西?"哈利问罗恩,并冲那些可怕的怪马点点头,其他学生蜂拥着从他们身边走过。

"什么东西?"

"那些马——"

卢娜怀里抱着小猪的笼子出现了。小猫头鹰像平常一样兴奋地吱吱乱叫。

"给你,"她说,"它真是一只可爱的小猫头鹰,是吧?"

"嗯……是啊……它挺好的。"罗恩粗声粗气地说,"好了,快走吧,我们赶紧进去……你刚才说什么,哈利?"

"我刚才说,那些像马一样的东西是什么?"哈利说着,一边和罗恩、卢娜一起朝赫敏和金妮已经坐上的那辆马车走去。

"什么像马一样的东西?"

"就是拉那些马车的像马一样的东西!"哈利不耐烦地说。他们离

CHAPTER TEN   Luna Lovegood

were, after all, about three feet from the nearest one; it was watching them with empty white eyes. Ron, however, gave Harry a perplexed look.

'What are you talking about?'

'I'm talking about – look!'

Harry grabbed Ron's arm and wheeled him about so that he was face to face with the winged horse. Ron stared straight at it for a second, then looked back at Harry.

'What am I supposed to be looking at?'

'At the – there, between the shafts! Harnessed to the coach! It's right there in front –'

But as Ron continued to look bemused, a strange thought occurred to Harry.

'Can't ... can't you see them?'

'See *what*?'

'Can't you see what's pulling the carriages?'

Ron looked seriously alarmed now.

'Are you feeling all right, Harry?'

'I ... yeah ...'

Harry felt utterly bewildered. The horse was there in front of him, gleaming solidly in the dim light issuing from the station windows behind them, vapour rising from its nostrils in the chilly night air. Yet, unless Ron was faking – and it was a very feeble joke if he was – Ron could not see it at all.

'Shall we get in, then?' said Ron uncertainly, looking at Harry as though worried about him.

'Yeah,' said Harry. 'Yeah, go on ...'

'It's all right,' said a dreamy voice from beside Harry as Ron vanished into the coach's dark interior. 'You're not going mad or anything. I can see them, too.'

'Can you?' said Harry desperately, turning to Luna. He could see the batwinged horses reflected in her wide silvery eyes.

'Oh, yes,' said Luna, 'I've been able to see them ever since my first day here. They've always pulled the carriages. Don't worry. You're just as sane as I am.'

Smiling faintly, she climbed into the musty interior of the carriage after Ron. Not altogether reassured, Harry followed her.

最近的那匹怪马大约只有两三步远了，它正用空洞的白眼睛注视着他们。可是罗恩困惑不解地看了哈利一眼。

"你在说什么呀？"

"我在说——你看！"

哈利抓住罗恩的胳膊，拖得他转过身来，面对那匹长着翅膀的怪马。罗恩直直地瞪眼看了一秒钟，然后转过脸来看着哈利。

"你叫我看什么呀？"

"看那个——那儿，就在辕杆之间！套在马车上的！就在你面前——"

可是罗恩还是一脸的迷惑，哈利突然产生了一个奇怪的想法。

"难道……难道你看不见它们？"

"看见什么？"

"难道你看不见拉马车的东西？"

这时候罗恩露出了非常惊愕的表情。

"你没有什么不对劲儿吧，哈利？"

"我……没事儿……"

哈利感到困惑极了。那匹马明明就在眼前，在他们身后车站窗户透出的朦胧灯光的映照下，实实在在地闪着光，鼻孔里喷出的气息在夜晚寒冷的空气中凝成了水汽。然而——除非罗恩是在装假——如果真是这样，这个玩笑可是太蹩脚了——罗恩居然根本看不见！

"我们进去吧，好吗？"罗恩忐忑不安地说，一边望着哈利，似乎很替他担心。

"好的，"哈利说，"好的，走吧……"

"没关系，"当罗恩钻进黑乎乎的马车车厢时，哈利身边一个恍恍惚惚的声音说道，"你并没有变疯什么的。我也能看见它们。"

"真的吗？"哈利迫切地问，转脸看着卢娜。他可以看见卢娜那双银白色的大眼睛里映出了那些长着蝙蝠翅膀的马。

"哦，是啊，"卢娜说，"我从第一天来这里就能看见它们。它们一直在拉马车。放心吧，你的头脑和我的一样清醒。"

她淡淡一笑，跟着罗恩钻进了发霉的马车车厢。哈利心头的疑虑并没有完全打消，但他还是跟着钻了进去。

CHAPTER ELEVEN

The Sorting Hat's New Song

Harry did not want to tell the others that he and Luna were having the same hallucination, if that was what it was, so he said nothing more about the horses as he sat down inside the carriage and slammed the door behind him. Nevertheless, he could not help watching the silhouettes of the horses moving beyond the window.

'Did everyone see that Grubbly-Plank woman?' asked Ginny. 'What's she doing back here? Hagrid can't have left, can he?'

'I'll be quite glad if he has,' said Luna, 'he isn't a very good teacher, is he?'

'Yes, he is!' said Harry, Ron and Ginny angrily.

Harry glared at Hermione. She cleared her throat and quickly said, 'Erm ... yes ... he's very good.'

'Well, we in Ravenclaw think he's a bit of a joke,' said Luna, unfazed.

'You've got a rubbish sense of humour then,' Ron snapped, as the wheels below them creaked into motion.

Luna did not seem perturbed by Ron's rudeness; on the contrary, she simply watched him for a while as though he were a mildly interesting television programme.

Rattling and swaying, the carriages moved in convoy up the road. When they passed between the tall stone pillars topped with winged boars on either side of the gates to the school grounds, Harry leaned forwards to try and see whether there were any lights on in Hagrid's cabin by the Forbidden Forest, but the grounds were in complete darkness. Hogwarts Castle, however, loomed ever closer: a towering mass of turrets, jet black against the dark sky, here and there a window blazing fiery bright above them.

The carriages jingled to a halt near the stone steps leading up to the oak

第 11 章

分院帽的新歌

哈利不想告诉别人,他和卢娜有了同样的幻觉——如果真是幻觉的话,所以他在车厢里坐下来,反手把门重重地关上,再也没有谈论那些马的事。然而,他忍不住去注视在窗外移动的那些马的侧影。

"你们大家都看见那个叫格拉普兰的女人了吧?"金妮问,"她又回这儿来做什么呢?海格不会离开吧?"

"海格走了我才高兴呢,"卢娜说,"他可不算一个好老师,对吧?"

"不,他是好老师!"哈利、罗恩和金妮气愤地说。

哈利不满地瞪着赫敏。赫敏清了清喉咙,赶紧说道:"嗯……是啊……他是很不错的。"

"得了吧,我们拉文克劳的同学都认为他是个荒唐可笑的人。"卢娜说,一副不管不顾、大大咧咧的劲儿。

"那说明你们的幽默感一塌糊涂。"罗恩不客气地回敬道,这时身下的车轮吱吱嘎嘎地开始转动了。

卢娜似乎并没有因罗恩的无礼而恼怒,相反,她盯着罗恩看了片刻,就好像他是一个还算有趣的电视节目。

马车排成一队,吱吱嘎嘎、摇摇晃晃地在路上行走着。他们经过通向学校场地的大门,大门两边高高的石柱顶上是带翅膀的野猪。这时哈利探着身子,想看看禁林旁边海格的小屋里有没有灯光,可是场地上一片漆黑。霍格沃茨城堡隐隐约约地越来越近:一座座高耸的塔楼在黑暗的夜空衬托下显得更加漆黑,偶尔可见一扇窗户在他们头顶上射出火红耀眼的光芒。

马车叮叮当当地停在了通往橡木大门的石阶旁,哈利第一个下了

CHAPTER ELEVEN The Sorting Hat's New Song

front doors and Harry got out of the carriage first. He turned again to look for lit windows down by the Forest, but there was definitely no sign of life within Hagrid's cabin. Unwillingly, because he had half hoped they would have vanished, he turned his eyes instead upon the strange, skeletal creatures standing quietly in the chill night air, their blank white eyes gleaming.

Harry had once before had the experience of seeing something that Ron could not, but that had been a reflection in a mirror, something much more insubstantial than a hundred very solid-looking beasts strong enough to pull a fleet of carriages. If Luna was to be believed, the beasts had always been there but invisible. Why, then, could Harry suddenly see them, and why could Ron not?

'Are you coming or what?' said Ron beside him.

'Oh ... yeah,' said Harry quickly and they joined the crowd hurrying up the stone steps into the castle.

The Entrance Hall was ablaze with torches and echoing with footsteps as the students crossed the flagged stone floor for the double doors to the right, leading to the Great Hall and the start-of-term feast.

The four long house tables in the Great Hall were filling up under the starless black ceiling, which was just like the sky they could glimpse through the high windows. Candles floated in midair all along the tables, illuminating the silvery ghosts who were dotted about the Hall and the faces of the students talking eagerly, exchanging summer news, shouting greetings at friends from other houses, eyeing one another's new haircuts and robes. Again, Harry noticed people putting their heads together to whisper as he passed; he gritted his teeth and tried to act as though he neither noticed nor cared.

Luna drifted away from them at the Ravenclaw table. The moment they reached Gryffindor's, Ginny was hailed by some fellow fourth-years and left to sit with them; Harry, Ron, Hermione and Neville found seats together about halfway down the table between Nearly Headless Nick, the Gryffindor house ghost, and Parvati Patil and Lavender Brown, the last two of whom gave Harry airy, overly-friendly greetings that made him quite sure they had stopped talking about him a split second before. He had more important things to worry about, however: he was looking over the students' heads to the staff table that ran along the top wall of the Hall.

车。他又转脸去望禁林那边有没有亮灯的窗户，然而海格的小屋里显然没有一点生命的迹象。哈利满不情愿地把目光转向那些皮包骨头的奇怪动物，心里隐约希望它们已经消失不见了，但它们仍然静静地站在夜晚寒冷的空气中，空洞的白眼睛闪闪发亮。

哈利看见的东西罗恩看不见，这种经历以前曾经有过一次，但那次只是镜子里的映像，比一百匹看上去实实在在、拉得动一队马车的牲畜要虚幻得多。如果卢娜的话是可信的，那么这些牲畜一直就存在，只是人们看不见而已。那么，为什么哈利突然能看见它们了，而罗恩却看不见呢？

"你到底走不走啊？"罗恩在他身边问道。

"噢……好的。"哈利赶紧说道，于是他们汇入人群，匆匆走上石阶，进入了城堡。

门厅被火把映照得红通通的，回响着学生们的脚步声。他们穿过石板铺的地面，向右边通往礼堂的两扇大门走去，开学宴会就在那里举行。

礼堂里摆着四张长长的学院餐桌，同学们纷纷就座，上面是没有星星的漆黑的天花板，与他们透过高高的窗户看见的外面天空一模一样。餐桌上空飘浮着一根根蜡烛，照亮了分散在礼堂里的那几个银白色的幽灵，照亮了同学们兴奋的面庞。他们在兴高采烈地谈话，交换暑假里的见闻，大声跟其他学院的朋友打招呼，互相审视着对方的新发型和新衣服。哈利又一次注意到，每当他走过时，人们都凑在一起交头接耳。他咬紧牙关，努力装出没看见、无所谓的样子。

卢娜离开他们坐到拉文克劳的桌子旁去了。他们刚走到格兰芬多的桌前，金妮就被几个四年级同学大呼小叫地拉过去坐了。哈利、罗恩、赫敏和纳威在桌子中央找到几个座位坐在一起，他们一边是格兰芬多学院的幽灵——差点没头的尼克，另一边是帕瓦蒂·佩蒂尔和拉文德·布朗。两个女生虚情假意、过分热情地跟哈利打招呼，这使哈利感觉到她们肯定一秒钟前还在议论自己。不过，他还有更重要的事情要操心呢。他的目光越过同学们的头顶，向礼堂前头的那张长长的教工桌子望去。

CHAPTER ELEVEN   The Sorting Hat's New Song

'He's not there.'

Ron and Hermione scanned the staff table too, though there was no real need; Hagrid's size made him instantly obvious in any line-up.

'He can't have left,' said Ron, sounding slightly anxious.

'Of course he hasn't,' said Harry firmly.

'You don't think he's … *hurt*, or anything, do you?' said Hermione uneasily.

'No,' said Harry at once.

'But where is he, then?'

There was a pause, then Harry said very quietly, so that Neville, Parvati and Lavender could not hear, 'Maybe he's not back yet. You know – from his mission – the thing he was doing over the summer for Dumbledore.'

'Yeah … yeah, that'll be it,' said Ron, sounding reassured, but Hermione bit her lip, looking up and down the staff table as though hoping for some conclusive explanation of Hagrid's absence.

'Who's *that*?' she said sharply, pointing towards the middle of the staff table.

Harry's eyes followed hers. They lit first upon Professor Dumbledore, sitting in his high-backed golden chair at the centre of the long staff table, wearing deep-purple robes scattered with silvery stars and a matching hat. Dumbledore's head was inclined towards the woman sitting next to him, who was talking into his ear. She looked, Harry thought, like somebody's maiden aunt: squat, with short, curly, mouse-brown hair in which she had placed a horrible pink Alice band that matched the fluffy pink cardigan she wore over her robes. Then she turned her face slightly to take a sip from her goblet and he saw, with a shock of recognition, a pallid, toadlike face and a pair of prominent, pouchy eyes.

'It's that Umbridge woman!'

'Who?' said Hermione.

'She was at my hearing, she works for Fudge!'

'Nice cardigan,' said Ron, smirking.

'She works for Fudge!' Hermione repeated, frowning. 'What on earth's she doing here, then?'

"他不在那儿。"

罗恩和赫敏的目光也在教工桌子上扫来扫去,其实这根本没有必要。海格的那副大块头,不管在哪个阵容里都会一下子凸显出来。

"他不可能离开的。"罗恩说,声音里微微透着担忧。

"当然不会。"哈利坚决地说。

"你们说他不会……受伤什么的吧,会吗?"赫敏不安地说。

"不会的。"哈利毫不迟疑地说。

"可是他去哪儿了呢?"

沉默了一会儿,哈利说话了,声音压得很低,以免让纳威、帕瓦蒂和拉文德听见:"也许他还没有回来呢。你们知道的——还没完成任务——就是他暑假里为邓布利多做的那件事情。"

"对……对,就是这样。"罗恩说,似乎一下子释然了,可是赫敏咬着嘴唇,目光来回扫视着教工桌子,似乎希望能为海格的缺席找到一个有说服力的解释。

"那是谁?"她尖声说,伸手指着教工桌子的中间。

哈利的目光随着她指的方向望去,先是落在了邓布利多教授身上。邓布利多坐在长长的教工桌子正中间的那把金色高背椅上,穿着布满银色星星的深紫色长袍,戴着一顶配套的帽子。邓布利多把头歪向了坐在他旁边的那个女人,她正对着他的耳朵说话。哈利觉得这女人看上去就像某个人的未婚的老姑妈,身材又矮又胖,留着一头拳曲的灰褐色短发,上面还戴着一个非常难看的粉红色大蝴蝶结,跟她罩在长袍外面的那件毛茸茸的粉红色开襟毛衣很相配。这时,她微微转过脸,端起高脚酒杯喝了一口,于是哈利看见了一张苍白的、癞蛤蟆似的脸,和一对眼皮松垂、眼珠凸出的眼睛。他一下子认出来了,非常震惊。

"就是那个姓乌姆里奇的女人!"

"谁?"赫敏说。

"她参加了对我的审问,她在福吉手下工作!"

"多漂亮的开襟毛衣啊!"罗恩假笑着说。

"她为福吉工作!"赫敏重复一遍,皱起了眉头,"那她到这里来做什么呢?"

CHAPTER ELEVEN   The Sorting Hat's New Song

'Dunno ...'

Hermione scanned the staff table, her eyes narrowed.

'No,' she muttered, 'no, surely not ...'

Harry did not understand what she was talking about but did not ask; his attention had been caught by Professor Grubbly-Plank who had just appeared behind the staff table; she worked her way along to the very end and took the seat that ought to have been Hagrid's. That meant the first-years must have crossed the lake and reached the castle, and sure enough, a few seconds later, the doors from the Entrance Hall opened. A long line of scared-looking first-years entered, led by Professor McGonagall, who was carrying a stool on which sat an ancient wizard's hat, heavily patched and darned with a wide rip near the frayed brim.

The buzz of talk in the Great Hall faded away. The first-years lined up in front of the staff table facing the rest of the students, and Professor McGonagall placed the stool carefully in front of them, then stood back.

The first-years' faces glowed palely in the candlelight. A small boy right in the middle of the row looked as though he was trembling. Harry recalled, fleetingly, how terrified he had felt when he had stood there, waiting for the unknown test that would determine to which house he belonged.

The whole school waited with bated breath. Then the rip near the hat's brim opened wide like a mouth and the Sorting Hat burst into song:

> *In times of old when I was new*
> *And Hogwarts barely started*
> *The founders of our noble school*
> *Thought never to be parted:*
> *United by a common goal,*
> *They had the selfsame yearning,*
> *To make the world's best magic school*
> *And pass along their learning.*
> *'Together we will build and teach!'*
> *The four good friends decided*
> *And never did they dream that they*
> *Might some day be divided,*

第11章 分院帽的新歌

"不知道……"

赫敏仔细看着教工桌子,眯起了眼睛。

"不,"她喃喃地说,"不会,肯定不会……"

哈利不明白赫敏在说什么,但也没有追问。他的注意力被刚出现在教工桌子后面的格拉普兰教授吸引住了。她走到桌子的最尽头,坐在了原本应该属于海格的座位上。这就是说,一年级新生肯定已经渡湖来到了城堡。果然,几秒钟后,通往大厅的门开了,长长的一队看上去惊魂未定的一年级新生由麦格教授领着走进了礼堂。麦格教授手里端着一个凳子,上面放了一顶古老的巫师帽,帽子上补丁摞补丁,磨损得起了毛边的帽檐旁有一道很宽的裂口。

礼堂里嗡嗡的谈话声渐渐平息了。一年级新生在教工桌子前排成一列,面对着其他年级的同学。麦格教授小心地把凳子放在他们前面,然后退到了后边。

一年级新生的脸在烛光的映照下闪着惨白的光。队伍中间的一个小男孩看上去似乎在瑟瑟发抖。哈利在一瞬间,想起当年他站在那里,等待那场将要决定他属于哪个学院的神秘测试时,心里曾是何等的忐忑不安。

全校的师生都屏住呼吸等待着。接着,帽檐旁的那道裂口像嘴一样张开了。分院帽大声唱起歌来:

> 很久以前我还是顶新帽,
> 那时霍格沃茨尚未建好,
> 高贵学堂的四位创建者,
> 以为他们永远不会分道扬镳。
> 同一个目标将他们相联,
> 彼此的愿望是那么一致:
> 要建成世上最好的魔法学校,
> 让他们的学识相传、延续。
> "我们将共同建校,共同教学!"
> 四位好友的主意十分坚决,
> 然而他们做梦也没有想到,
> 有朝一日他们会彼此分裂。

CHAPTER ELEVEN   The Sorting Hat's New Song

For were there such friends anywhere
As Slytherin and Gryffindor?
Unless it was the second pair
Of Hufflepuff and Ravenclaw?
So how could it have gone so wrong?
How could such friendships fail?
Why, I was there and so can tell
The whole sad, sorry tale.
Said Slytherin, 'We'll teach just those
Whose ancestry is purest.'
Said Ravenclaw, 'We'll teach those whose
Intelligence is surest.'
Said Gryffindor, 'We'll teach all those
With brave deeds to their name,'
Said Hufflepuff, 'I'll teach the lot,
And treat them just the same.'
These differences caused little strife
When first they came to light,
For each of the four founders had
A house in which they might
Take only those they wanted, so,
For instance, Slytherin
Took only pure-blood wizards
Of great cunning, just like him,
And only those of sharpest mind
Were taught by Ravenclaw
While the bravest and the boldest
Went to daring Gryffindor.
Good Hufflepuff, she took the rest,
And taught them all she knew,
Thus the houses and their founders
Retained friendships firm and true.
So Hogwarts worked in harmony

第11章 分院帽的新歌

这个世上还有什么朋友,
能比斯莱特林和格兰芬多更好?
除非你算上另一对挚友——
赫奇帕奇和拉文克劳?
这样的好事怎么会搞糟?
这样的友情怎么会一笔勾销?
唉,我亲眼目睹了这悲哀的一幕,
所以能在这里向大家细述。
斯莱特林说:"我们所教的学生,
他们的血统必须最最纯正。"
拉文克劳说:"我们所教的学生,
他们的智力必须高人一等。"
格兰芬多说:"我们所教的学生,
必须英勇无畏,奋不顾身。"
赫奇帕奇说:"我要教许多人,
并且对待他们一视同仁。"
这些分歧第一次露出端倪,
几乎没有引起什么纷争。
四位创建者每人拥有一个学院,
只招收他们各自想要的学生。
斯莱特林收的巫师如他本人,
诡计多端、血统纯正。
只有那些头脑最敏锐的后辈,
才能聆听拉文克劳的教诲。
若有谁大胆无畏、喜爱冒险,
便被勇敢的格兰芬多收进学院。
其余的都被好心的赫奇帕奇接收,
她把自己的全部本领向他们传授。
四个学院和它们的创建人,
就这样保持着牢固而真挚的友情。

CHAPTER ELEVEN   The Sorting Hat's New Song

For several happy years,
But then discord crept among us
Feeding on our faults and fears.
The houses that, like pillars four,
Had once held up our school,
Now turned upon each other and,
Divided, sought to rule.
And for a while it seemed the school
Must meet an early end,
What with duelling and with fighting
And the clash of friend on friend
And at last there came a morning
When old Slytherin departed
And though the fighting then died out
He left us quite downhearted.
And never since the founders four
Were whittled down to three
Have the houses been united
As they once were meant to be.
And now the Sorting Hat is here
And you all know the score:
I sort you into houses
Because that is what I'm for,
But this year I'll go further,
Listen closely to my song:
Though condemned I am to split you
Still I worry that it's wrong,
Though I must fulfil my duty
And must quarter every year
Still I wonder whether Sorting
May not bring the end I fear.

第11章 分院帽的新歌

在那许多愉快的岁月里,
霍格沃茨的教学十分和谐。
可是后来慢慢地出现了分裂,
并因我们的缺点和恐惧而愈演愈烈。
四个学院就像四根石柱,
曾将我们的学校牢牢撑住。
现在却互相反目,纠纷不断,
各个都想把大权独揽。
有那么一段时光,
学校眼看着就要夭亡。
无数的吵闹,无数的争斗,
昔日的好朋友反目成仇。
后来终于在某一天清晨,
老斯莱特林突然出走。
尽管那时纷争已经平息,
他还是让我们灰心不已。
四个创建者只剩下三个,
从此四个学院的情形,
再不像过去设想的那样
和睦相处,团结一心。
此刻分院帽就在你们面前,
你们都知道了事情的发展:
我把你们分进每个学院,
因为我的职责不容改变。
但是今年我要多说几句,
请你们把我的新歌仔细听取:
尽管我注定要使你们分裂,
但我担心这样做并不正确。
尽管我必须履行我的职责,
把每年的新生分成四份,
但我不知这样的分类,
会不会导致我所惧怕的崩溃。

CHAPTER ELEVEN The Sorting Hat's New Song

Oh, know the perils, read the signs,
The warning history shows,
For our Hogwarts is in danger
From external, deadly foes
And we must unite inside her
Or we'll crumble from within
I have told you, I have warned you ...
Let the Sorting now begin.

The Hat became motionless once more; applause broke out, though it was punctured, for the first time in Harry's memory, with muttering and whispers. All across the Great Hall students were exchanging remarks with their neighbours, and Harry, clapping along with everyone else, knew exactly what they were talking about.

'Branched out a bit this year, hasn't it?' said Ron, his eyebrows raised.

'Too right it has,' said Harry.

The Sorting Hat usually confined itself to describing the different qualities looked for by each of the four Hogwarts houses and its own role in Sorting them. Harry could not remember it ever trying to give the school advice before.

'I wonder if it's ever given warnings before?' said Hermione, sounding slightly anxious.

'Yes, indeed,' said Nearly Headless Nick knowledgeably, leaning across Neville towards her (Neville winced; it was very uncomfortable to have a ghost lean through you). 'The Hat feels itself honour-bound to give the school due warning whenever it feels –'

But Professor McGonagall, who was waiting to read out the list of first-years' names, was giving the whispering students the sort of look that scorches. Nearly Headless Nick placed a see-through finger to his lips and sat primly upright again as the muttering came to an abrupt end. With a last frowning look that swept the four house tables, Professor McGonagall lowered her eyes to her long piece of parchment and called out the first name.

'Abercrombie, Euan.'

第11章 分院帽的新歌

哦，知道危险，读懂征兆，
历史的教训给我们以警告，
我们的霍格沃茨面临着危难，
校外的仇敌正虎视眈眈。
我们的内部必须紧密团结，
不然一切就会从内部瓦解。
我已对你们直言相告，
我已为你们拉响警报……
现在让我们开始分院。

帽子说完又一动不动了。四下里响起了掌声，但其间夹杂着窃窃私语，这在哈利的记忆里还是头一次。在整个礼堂里，同学们都和坐在身边的人交头接耳，哈利和其他人一起拍着巴掌，心里很清楚他们在议论什么。

"今年有点跑题了，是不是？"罗恩扬起眉毛说。

"可不是吗。"哈利说。

通常，分院帽只描述霍格沃茨四个学院所看重的不同品质，以及它自己给学生分院的任务。哈利不记得它什么时候试图给学校提出忠告。

"不知道它以前有没有发出过警告？"赫敏说，声音微微显得有些不安。

"有过的，有过的，"差点没头的尼克知情地说，隔着纳威朝赫敏探过头来（纳威恐惧地退缩着———一个幽灵从你身体里穿过去，这是很不舒服的），"分院帽觉得自己在道义上有责任向学校提出适当的警告，如果它觉得——"

可是麦格教授正等着报出一年级新生的名单，这会儿用十分严厉的目光瞪着那些交头接耳的同学。差点没头的尼克用一根透明的手指压在嘴唇上，再次一本正经地坐得笔直，礼堂里的嗡嗡议论声戛然而止。麦格教授又皱着眉头扫了一眼四张桌子，然后垂眼望着手里那张长长的羊皮纸，大声报出第一个名字。

"尤安·阿伯克龙比。"

CHAPTER ELEVEN — The Sorting Hat's New Song

The terrified-looking boy Harry had noticed earlier stumbled forwards and put the Hat on his head; it was only prevented from falling right down to his shoulders by his very prominent ears. The Hat considered for a moment, then the rip near the brim opened again and shouted:

'*Gryffindor!*'

Harry clapped loudly with the rest of Gryffindor house as Euan Abercrombie staggered to their table and sat down, looking as though he would like very much to sink through the floor and never be looked at again.

Slowly, the long line of first-years thinned. In the pauses between the names and the Sorting Hat's decisions, Harry could hear Ron's stomach rumbling loudly. Finally, 'Zeller, Rose' was Sorted into Hufflepuff, and Professor McGonagall picked up the Hat and stool and marched them away as Professor Dumbledore rose to his feet.

Whatever his recent bitter feelings had been towards his Headmaster, Harry was somehow soothed to see Dumbledore standing before them all. Between the absence of Hagrid and the presence of those dragonish horses, he had felt that his return to Hogwarts, so long anticipated, was full of unexpected surprises, like jarring notes in a familiar song. But this, at least, was how it was supposed to be: their Headmaster rising to greet them all before the start-of-term feast.

'To our newcomers,' said Dumbledore in a ringing voice, his arms stretched wide and a beaming smile on his lips, 'welcome! To our old hands – welcome back! There is a time for speechmaking, but this is not it. Tuck in!'

There was an appreciative laugh and an outbreak of applause as Dumbledore sat down neatly and threw his long beard over his shoulder so as to keep it out of the way of his plate – for food had appeared out of nowhere, so that the five long tables were groaning under joints and pies and dishes of vegetables, bread and sauces and flagons of pumpkin juice.

'Excellent,' said Ron, with a kind of groan of longing, and he seized the nearest plate of chops and began piling them on to his plate, watched wistfully by Nearly Headless Nick.

'What were you saying before the Sorting?' Hermione asked the ghost.

'About the Hat giving warnings?'

'Oh, yes,' said Nick, who seemed glad of a reason to turn away from Ron,

第11章 分院帽的新歌

哈利刚才注意到的那个神色惊慌的小男孩跌跌撞撞地走上前,把帽子戴在了头上。幸亏有他那两只大得出奇的耳朵卡住,帽子才没有滑落到肩膀上。分院帽考虑了片刻,帽檐旁的裂口又张开了,大声宣布道:

"格兰芬多!"

哈利和格兰芬多的同学们一齐热烈鼓掌,尤安跟跟跄跄地走到他们的桌旁坐下来,看他那副神情,似乎巴不得地上有个洞让他钻进去,就再也没有人盯着他看了。

慢慢地,那支长长的一年级新生队伍一点点缩短了。在麦格教授报出名字和分院帽宣布分院结果之间的空隙,哈利可以听见罗恩的肚子咕咕直叫。最后,罗丝·泽勒被分进了赫奇帕奇,麦格教授拿起帽子和凳子大步走开了,这时邓布利多教授站了起来。

哈利最近对校长有过种种不满的情绪,但此刻看到邓布利多站在他们大家面前,他还是松了口气。海格不见了踪影,马车前面突然出现了那些像火龙一样的怪马,使哈利觉得他这次返回霍格沃茨,尽管是他梦寐以求的,却充满令他吃惊的意外,就像一首熟悉的歌曲里出现了不和谐的音符。但眼下的情形至少是正常的:在开学宴会开始前,他们的校长站起来问候大家。

"欢迎我们的新生,"邓布利多声音洪亮地说,他双臂张开,嘴上绽开灿烂的笑容,"欢迎!欢迎我们的老生——欢迎你们回来!演讲的时间多得是,但不是现在。痛痛快快地吃吧!"

礼堂里发出一片赞赏的笑声和热烈的鼓掌声,邓布利多端端正正地坐下来,把长长的胡子甩到肩膀上,不让它们挡着他的盘子——美味佳肴突然从天而降,五张长桌上一下子堆满了大块烤肉、馅饼、一盘盘的蔬菜、面包、果酱和一壶壶的南瓜汁,桌子因不堪重负而发出阵阵呻吟。

"太好了。"罗恩垂涎欲滴地叹了口气,抓起离他最近的一盘排骨,开始一块块地往自己盘子里堆,差点没头的尼克在一旁郁闷地看着他。

"分院之前你想说什么?"赫敏问幽灵,"就是关于帽子提出警告的事?"

"噢,对了,"尼克说,他似乎很高兴有理由把目光从罗恩身上挪开,

CHAPTER ELEVEN The Sorting Hat's New Song

who was now eating roast potatoes with almost indecent enthusiasm. 'Yes, I have heard the Hat give several warnings before, always at times when it detects periods of great danger for the school. And always, of course, its advice is the same: stand together, be strong from within.'

'Ow kunnit nofe skusin danger ifzat?' said Ron.

His mouth was so full Harry thought it was quite an achievement for him to make any noise at all.

'I beg your pardon?' said Nearly Headless Nick politely, while Hermione looked revolted. Ron gave an enormous swallow and said, 'How can it know if the school's in danger if it's a Hat?'

'I have no idea,' said Nearly Headless Nick. 'Of course, it lives in Dumbledore's office, so I daresay it picks things up there.'

'And it wants all the houses to be friends?' said Harry, looking over at the Slytherin table, where Draco Malfoy was holding court. 'Fat chance.'

'Well, now, you shouldn't take that attitude,' said Nick reprovingly. 'Peaceful co-operation, that's the key. We ghosts, though we belong to separate houses, maintain links of friendship. In spite of the competitiveness between Gryffindor and Slytherin, I would never dream of seeking an argument with the Bloody Baron.'

'Only because you're terrified of him,' said Ron.

Nearly Headless Nick looked highly affronted.

'Terrified? I hope I, Sir Nicholas de Mimsy-Porpington, have never been guilty of cowardice in my life! The noble blood that runs in my veins –'

'What blood?' asked Ron. 'Surely you haven't still got –?'

'It's a figure of speech!' said Nearly Headless Nick, now so annoyed his head was trembling ominously on his partially severed neck. 'I assume I am still allowed to enjoy the use of whichever words I like, even if the pleasures of eating and drinking are denied me! But I am quite used to students poking fun at my death, I assure you!'

'Nick, he wasn't really laughing at you!' said Hermione, throwing a furious look at Ron.

Unfortunately, Ron's mouth was packed to exploding point again and all he could manage was 'Node iddum eentup sechew,' which Nick did not seem to think constituted an adequate apology. Rising into the air, he straightened

第11章 分院帽的新歌

罗恩这会儿几乎是在狼吞虎咽地吃着烤土豆,"是啊,我以前好几次听过分院帽提出警告,总是在它感觉到学校面临巨大危险的时候。当然啦,它的忠告每次都是一样的:团结一致,保持内部的稳定。"

"托子系义等目子,左木为字套西较有危险呢?"罗恩说。

他嘴里塞得满满的,哈利觉得他能够发出声音来就已经很了不起了。

"对不起,你说什么?"差点没头的尼克很有礼貌地说,赫敏则露出一副厌恶的神情。罗恩使劲吞下嘴里的东西,说:"它只是一顶帽子,怎么会知道学校有危险呢?"

"我不知道。"差点没头的尼克说,"当然啦,它放在邓布利多的办公室里,所以我敢说它在那里听到了一些什么。"

"它希望四个学院的人都成为朋友?"哈利说,他朝斯莱特林的桌子望去,德拉科·马尔福正在那里侃侃而谈,"这种可能性很小啊。"

"哎,你不应该是这种态度。"尼克责备地说,"和平共处,共同合作,这才是关键。我们这些幽灵虽然属于不同的学院,但始终保持着亲密的友谊。格兰芬多和斯莱特林之间竞争这么激烈,我却做梦也没有想过找血人巴罗吵架。"

"那只是因为你害怕他。"罗恩说。

差点没头的尼克显出一副受了很大侮辱的样子。

"害怕?我相信我——尼古拉斯·德·敏西-波平顿爵士,在我的一生中从没有犯过胆怯的错误!我血管里流淌着高贵的血液——"

"什么血液?"罗恩问,"你肯定不会还有——?"

"那是一种修辞手法!"差点没头的尼克恼火极了,脑袋在割开一半的脖子上危险地颤动着,"我想,我仍然可以享受随心所欲地选择用词的自由,尽管我已不再拥有吃喝的乐趣!不过放心吧,我已经习惯了同学们拿我的死亡开玩笑!"

"尼克,他并不是真的在嘲笑你!"赫敏说,生气地白了罗恩一眼。

不幸的是,罗恩的嘴里又塞得快要爆炸了,他只能含糊不清地嘟哝一句"不是有意嘲笑你",而尼克似乎认为这句道歉过于轻描淡写。他一下子飞到空中,正了正插着羽毛的帽子,离开他们,飘向桌子的

CHAPTER ELEVEN The Sorting Hat's New Song

his feathered hat and swept away from them to the other end of the table, coming to rest between the Creevey brothers, Colin and Dennis.

'Well done, Ron,' snapped Hermione.

'What?' said Ron indignantly, having managed, finally, to swallow his food. 'I'm not allowed to ask a simple question?'

'Oh, forget it,' said Hermione irritably, and the pair of them spent the rest of the meal in huffy silence.

Harry was too used to their bickering to bother trying to reconcile them; he felt it was a better use of his time to eat his way steadily through his steak and kidney pie, then a large plateful of his favourite treacle tart.

When all the students had finished eating and the noise level in the Hall was starting to creep upwards again, Dumbledore got to his feet once more. Talking ceased immediately as all turned to face the Headmaster. Harry was feeling pleasantly drowsy now. His four-poster bed was waiting somewhere above, wonderfully warm and soft ...

'Well, now that we are all digesting another magnificent feast, I beg a few moments of your attention for the usual start-of-term notices,' said Dumbledore. 'First-years ought to know that the Forest in the grounds is out-of-bounds to students – and a few of our older students ought to know by now, too.' (Harry, Ron and Hermione exchanged smirks.)

'Mr Filch, the caretaker, has asked me, for what he tells me is the four-hundred-and-sixty-second time, to remind you all that magic is not permitted in corridors between classes, nor are a number of other things, all of which can be checked on the extensive list now fastened to Mr Filch's office door.

'We have had two changes in staffing this year. We are very pleased to welcome back Professor Grubbly-Plank, who will be taking Care of Magical Creatures lessons; we are also delighted to introduce Professor Umbridge, our new Defence Against the Dark Arts teacher.'

There was a round of polite but fairly unenthusiastic applause, during which Harry, Ron and Hermione exchanged slightly panicked looks; Dumbledore had not said for how long Grubbly-Plank would be teaching.

Dumbledore continued, 'Tryouts for the house Quidditch teams will take place on the –'

He broke off, looking enquiringly at Professor Umbridge. As she was

另一头，坐到克里维家的两兄弟——科林和丹尼斯中间去了。

"你干的好事，罗恩！"赫敏严厉地说。

"什么？"罗恩总算把满嘴的东西咽了下去，不服气地说，"我问一个简单的问题都不允许吗？"

"行了，别说啦。"赫敏没好气地说。在后来吃饭的时候，他们俩一直气鼓鼓地沉默着。

哈利对他们闹口角已经见怪不怪，认为犯不着去给他们调解。他觉得正好利用这个时间津津有味地享用他的牛排和腰子馅饼，接着是满满一大盘他最喜欢的糖浆水果馅饼。

同学们都吃饱喝足了，礼堂的声音渐渐嘈杂起来，这时邓布利多又一次站起身。说话声立刻停止了，大家都把脸转向了校长。哈利这会儿已经感到有点昏昏欲睡。他那张四柱床正在楼上某个地方等着他呢，那么温暖而柔软……

"好了，既然我们正在消化又一顿无比丰盛的美味，我请求大家安静一会儿，听我像往常一样讲讲新学期的注意事项。"邓布利多说，"一年级新生应该知道，场地里的禁林是学生不能进去的——这一点，我们的几位高年级同学现在也应该知道了。（哈利、罗恩和赫敏交换着调皮的笑容。）

"管理员费尔奇先生请求我，他还告诉我这已经是第四百六十二次了，请求我提醒你们大家，课间不许在走廊上施魔法，还有许多其他规定，都列在那张长长的单子上，贴在费尔奇先生办公室的门上。

"今年，我们的教师队伍有两个变动。我们很高兴地欢迎格拉普兰教授回来，她将教你们保护神奇动物课。我们同样高兴地介绍乌姆里奇教授，我们的黑魔法防御术课的新老师。"

礼堂里响起一片礼貌的但不很热情的掌声，哈利、罗恩和赫敏则交换了一个略微有些紧张的目光。邓布利多没有说格拉普兰要教多长时间。

邓布利多继续说道："学院魁地奇球队的选拔将于——"

他猛地顿住话头，询问地望着乌姆里奇教授。由于她站起来并不

CHAPTER ELEVEN The Sorting Hat's New Song

not much taller standing than sitting, there was a moment when nobody understood why Dumbledore had stopped talking, but then Professor Umbridge cleared her throat, '*Hem, hem,*' and it became clear that she had got to her feet and was intending to make a speech.

Dumbledore only looked taken aback for a moment, then he sat down smartly and looked alertly at Professor Umbridge as though he desired nothing better than to listen to her talk. Other members of staff were not as adept at hiding their surprise. Professor Sprout's eyebrows had disappeared into her flyaway hair and Professor McGonagall's mouth was as thin as Harry had ever seen it. No new teacher had ever interrupted Dumbledore before. Many of the students were smirking; this woman obviously did not know how things were done at Hogwarts.

'Thank you, Headmaster,' Professor Umbridge simpered, 'for those kind words of welcome.'

Her voice was high-pitched, breathy and little-girlish and, again, Harry felt a powerful rush of dislike that he could not explain to himself; all he knew was that he loathed everything about her, from her stupid voice to her fluffy pink cardigan. She gave another little throat-clearing cough ('*hem, hem*') and continued.

'Well, it is lovely to be back at Hogwarts, I must say!' She smiled, revealing very pointed teeth. 'And to see such happy little faces looking up at me!'

Harry glanced around. None of the faces he could see looked happy. On the contrary, they all looked rather taken-aback at being addressed as though they were five years old.

'I am very much looking forward to getting to know you all and I'm sure we'll be very good friends!'

Students exchanged looks at this; some of them were barely concealing grins.

'I'll be her friend as long as I don't have to borrow that cardigan,' Parvati whispered to Lavender, and both of them lapsed into silent giggles.

Professor Umbridge cleared her throat again ('*hem, hem*'), but when she continued, some of the breathiness had vanished from her voice. She sounded much more businesslike and now her words had a dull learned-by-heart sound to them.

'The Ministry of Magic has always considered the education of young

第11章 分院帽的新歌

比坐着的时候高出多少,所以一时间谁也不明白邓布利多为什么突然停住不说了,这时只听乌姆里奇教授清了清嗓子:"咳,咳。"大家才明白她已经站起来,正准备发表讲话呢。

邓布利多只是一刹那间显出惊讶的神情,接着就机敏地坐了下去,专注地望着乌姆里奇教授,似乎正迫不及待地想听她说话呢。其他教师则没有这样巧妙地掩饰他们的惊诧。斯普劳特教授的眉毛都快蹿到她飘拂的头发里去了,麦格教授把嘴巴抿得那么紧,是哈利从没见过的。以前还没有哪位新教师打断过邓布利多呢。许多学生都在暗暗发笑:这个女人显然不懂得霍格沃茨的规矩。

"谢谢你,校长,"乌姆里奇教授假笑着说,"谢谢你说了这么热情的欢迎辞。"

她的声音又高又尖,还带着气声,像小姑娘的声音,哈利又感到一种突如其来的强烈反感,他自己也不能解释这是为什么。他只知道他讨厌这个女人的一切,从她那假模假式的声音,到她身上那件毛茸茸的粉红色开襟毛衣。她又轻轻咳嗽几下清了清嗓子(咳,咳),继续往下说道:

"嗯,我必须说,能回到霍格沃茨真是太好了!"她咧嘴微笑着,露出嘴里很尖的牙齿,"看到这些愉快的小脸蛋朝上望着我,太好了!"

哈利朝周围看了看,他看到的面孔没有一张是愉快的。相反,他们都显得很吃惊,居然有人把他们当成五岁的小孩子。

"我迫切地希望早日认识你们大家,我相信我们会成为非常好的朋友!"

同学们听了这话,互相交换着目光。有些人几乎毫不掩饰地露出了一脸坏笑。

"我会跟她做朋友的,只要别让我借她那件开襟毛衣。"帕瓦蒂小声对拉文德说,两个人都不出声地咻咻笑了起来。

乌姆里奇教授又清了清嗓子(咳,咳),可是当她继续说话时,她声音里的一些气声不见了。现在她的声音变得一本正经得多,话也说得干巴巴的,好像那些话早就熟记在她心里似的。

"魔法部一向认为,教育年轻巫师是一项十分重要的事情。你们与

CHAPTER ELEVEN   The Sorting Hat's New Song

witches and wizards to be of vital importance. The rare gifts with which you were born may come to nothing if not nurtured and honed by careful instruction. The ancient skills unique to the wizarding community must be passed down the generations lest we lose them for ever. The treasure trove of magical knowledge amassed by our ancestors must be guarded, replenished and polished by those who have been called to the noble profession of teaching.'

Professor Umbridge paused here and made a little bow to her fellow staff members, none of whom bowed back to her. Professor McGonagall's dark eyebrows had contracted so that she looked positively hawklike, and Harry distinctly saw her exchange a significant glance with Professor Sprout as Umbridge gave another little *'hem, hem'* and went on with her speech.

'Every headmaster and headmistress of Hogwarts has brought something new to the weighty task of governing this historic school, and that is as it should be, for without progress there will be stagnation and decay. There again, progress for progress's sake must be discouraged, for our tried and tested traditions often require no tinkering. A balance, then, between old and new, between permanence and change, between tradition and innovation ...'

Harry found his attentiveness ebbing, as though his brain was slipping in and out of tune. The quiet that always filled the Hall when Dumbledore was speaking was breaking up as students put their heads together, whispering and giggling. Over on the Ravenclaw table Cho Chang was chatting animatedly with her friends. A few seats along from Cho, Luna Lovegood had got out *The Quibbler* again. Meanwhile, at the Hufflepuff table Ernie Macmillan was one of the few still staring at Professor Umbridge, but he was glassy-eyed and Harry was sure he was only pretending to listen in an attempt to live up to the new prefect's badge gleaming on his chest.

Professor Umbridge did not seem to notice the restlessness of her audience. Harry had the impression that a full-scale riot could have broken out under her nose and she would have ploughed on with her speech. The teachers, however, were still listening very attentively, and Hermione seemed to be drinking in every word Umbridge spoke, though, judging by her expression, they were not at all to her taste.

'... because some changes will be for the better, while others will come, in the fullness of time, to be recognised as errors of judgement. Meanwhile,

第 11 章 分院帽的新歌

生俱来的一些宝贵天赋,如果不在认真细致的指导下得到培养和锻炼,可能会白白浪费。魔法世界独有的古老的技艺,必须代代相传,不然就会消失殆尽。我们的祖先积累下的珍贵的魔法知识宝库,必须由那些有幸从事高贵的教育职业的人加以保护、补充和完善。"

说到这里,乌姆里奇教授停住话头,对着其他老师微微鞠了一躬,而他们谁也没有朝她回礼。麦格教授的两道黑眉毛紧紧拧在一起,使她看上去活像一只老鹰,而且哈利清清楚楚地看见,当乌姆里奇又轻轻"咳,咳"两下继续她的演讲时,麦格教授和斯普劳特教授交换了一个意味深长的眼神。

"霍格沃茨的历届校长,在肩负管理这所历史名校的重任时都有所创新,这是完全应该的,因为如果没有进步,就会停滞,就会衰败。然而同时,为进步而进步的做法是绝不应当受到鼓励的,我们的传统经过千锤百炼,往往并不需要拙劣的修正。要达到一种平衡,在旧与新之间,在恒久与变化之间,在传统与创新之间……"

哈利发现自己的注意力渐渐不集中了,似乎他的大脑开起了小差。邓布利多说话时四下里鸦雀无声,现在同学们都在交头接耳,窃窃私语,咯咯发笑,礼堂里一片嘈杂。在那边拉文克劳的桌上,秋·张正在兴高采烈地跟朋友们聊天。和她隔着几个座位的卢娜·洛夫古德又掏出了那本《唱唱反调》。与此同时,在赫奇帕奇的长桌上,厄尼·麦克米兰是仍然盯着乌姆里奇教授的为数不多的几个同学之一,但是他的目光呆滞无神,哈利可以肯定他只是在假装认真听讲,为的是不辜负他胸前那枚崭新的、闪闪发光的级长徽章。

乌姆里奇教授似乎没有注意到听众的坐立不安。哈利有一种感觉,即使她鼻子底下发生了一场大规模的暴动,她也会继续慢条斯理地演讲下去。然而教师们一个个听得都很仔细,赫敏似乎全神贯注地把乌姆里奇说的每一个字都听进去了,但从她的表情看,这些话她并不爱听。

"……因为有些变化取得了好的效果,而另一些变化到了适当的时候,就会被发现是决策失误。然而,有些旧的习惯将被保留,这是无可厚非的,而有些习惯已经陈旧过时,就必须抛弃。让我们不断前进,

CHAPTER ELEVEN   The Sorting Hat's New Song

some old habits will be retained, and rightly so, whereas others, outmoded and outworn, must be abandoned. Let us move forward, then, into a new era of openness, effectiveness and accountability, intent on preserving what ought to be preserved, perfecting what needs to be perfected, and pruning wherever we find practices that ought to be prohibited.'

She sat down. Dumbledore clapped. The staff followed his lead, though Harry noticed that several of them brought their hands together only once or twice before stopping. A few students joined in, but most had been taken unawares by the end of the speech, not having listened to more than a few words of it, and before they could start applauding properly, Dumbledore had stood up again.

'Thank you very much, Professor Umbridge, that was most illuminating,' he said, bowing to her. 'Now, as I was saying, Quidditch tryouts will be held ...'

'Yes, it certainly was illuminating,' said Hermione in a low voice.

'You're not telling me you enjoyed it?' Ron said quietly, turning a glazed face towards Hermione. 'That was about the dullest speech I've ever heard, and *I* grew up with Percy.'

'I said illuminating, not enjoyable,' said Hermione. 'It explained a lot.'

'Did it?' said Harry in surprise. 'Sounded like a load of waffle to me.'

'There was some important stuff hidden in the waffle,' said Hermione grimly.

'Was there?' said Ron blankly.

'How about: "progress for progress's sake must be discouraged"? How about: "pruning wherever we find practices that ought to be prohibited"?'

'Well, what does that mean?' said Ron impatiently.

'I'll tell you what it means,' said Hermione ominously. 'It means the Ministry's interfering at Hogwarts.'

There was a great clattering and banging all around them; Dumbledore had obviously just dismissed the school, because everyone was standing up ready to leave the Hall. Hermione jumped up, looking flustered.

'Ron, we're supposed to show the first-years where to go!'

'Oh yeah,' said Ron, who had obviously forgotten. 'Hey – hey, you lot! Midgets!'

'*Ron!*'

'Well, they are, they're titchy ...'

进入一个开明、高效和合乎情理的新时代,坚决保持应该保持的,完善需要完善的,摒弃那些我们必须禁止的。"

她坐了下去。邓布利多开始鼓掌,其他教师也跟着拍手,但哈利注意到他们有些人只拍了一两下就把手放下了。几个学生也一起鼓掌,但大多数学生只听了两三句就开了小差,这会儿根本没有意识到讲话已经结束,没等他们开始好好鼓掌,邓布利多就又站了起来。

"非常感谢你,乌姆里奇教授,你的讲话非常有启发性。"说着,他冲她欠了欠身,"好了,正如我刚才说的,魁地奇球队的选拔将于……"

"是啊,确实很有启发性。"赫敏压低声音说。

"你该不是说你听得津津有味吧?"罗恩小声问,把神情呆滞的脸转向赫敏,"这大概是我听过的最枯燥乏味的讲话了,而我还是在珀西身边长大的呢。"

"我说的是有启发性,不是有趣味性,"赫敏说,"它能说明许多问题。"

"是吗?"哈利惊讶地说,"在我听来像一大通废话。"

"废话里藏着一些重要的东西。"赫敏严肃地说。

"是吗?"罗恩茫然地问。

"什么叫'为进步而进步的做法是绝不应当受到鼓励的'?什么叫'摒弃那些我们必须禁止的'?"

"哎呀,到底是什么意思呢?"罗恩不耐烦地说。

"我来告诉你是什么意思吧,"赫敏咬着牙说,"这就说明魔法部在干预霍格沃茨。"

周围响起一片桌椅板凳的碰撞声,显然邓布利多已经宣布全校师生解散,因为大家都站起来准备离开礼堂了。赫敏一跃而起,显出很惊慌的样子。

"罗恩,我们应该去给一年级新生指路的!"

"哎呀,对了,"罗恩说,显然他已经把这件事忘得精光,"喂——喂,你们大家!小不点儿们!"

"罗恩!"

"咳,本来就是嘛,他们这么小……"

CHAPTER ELEVEN   The Sorting Hat's New Song

'I know, but you can't call them midgets! – First-years!' Hermione called commandingly along the table. 'This way, please!'

A group of new students walked shyly up the gap between the Gryffindor and Hufflepuff tables, all of them trying hard not to lead the group. They did indeed seem very small; Harry was sure he had not appeared that young when he had arrived here. He grinned at them. A blond boy next to Euan Abercrombie looked petrified; he nudged Euan and whispered something in his ear. Euan Abercrombie looked equally frightened and stole a horrified look at Harry, who felt the grin slide off his face like Stinksap.

'See you later,' he said to Ron and Hermione and he made his way out of the Great Hall alone, doing everything he could to ignore more whispering, staring and pointing as he passed. He kept his eyes fixed ahead as he wove his way through the crowd in the Entrance Hall, then he hurried up the marble staircase, took a couple of concealed short cuts and had soon left most of the crowds behind.

He had been stupid not to expect this, he thought angrily as he walked through the much emptier upstairs corridors. Of course everyone was staring at him; he had emerged from the Triwizard maze two months previously clutching the dead body of a fellow student and claiming to have seen Lord Voldemort return to power. There had not been time last term to explain himself before they'd all had to go home – even if he had felt up to giving the whole school a detailed account of the terrible events in that graveyard.

Harry had reached the end of the corridor to the Gryffindor common room and come to a halt in front of the portrait of the Fat Lady before he realised that he did not know the new password.

'Er ...' he said glumly, staring up at the Fat Lady, who smoothed the folds of her pink satin dress and looked sternly back at him.

'No password, no entrance,' she said loftily.

'Harry, I know it!' Someone panted up behind him and he turned to see Neville jogging towards him. 'Guess what it is? I'm actually going to be able to remember it for once –' He waved the stunted little cactus he had shown them on the train. '*Mimbulus mimbletonia!*'

'Correct,' said the Fat Lady, and her portrait swung open towards them like a door, revealing a circular hole in the wall behind, through which Harry and Neville now climbed.

第 11 章 分院帽的新歌

"我知道,但你也不能管他们叫小不点儿!——一年级新生!"赫敏很威严地冲着桌子那边喊,"请这边走!"

一群新生很害羞地从格兰芬多和赫奇帕奇桌子之间的过道走了过来,一个个都尽量缩在后面,不敢出头。他们看上去确实很小,哈利可以肯定,自己当初来这儿的时候肯定没有显得这么稚嫩。他咧嘴微笑地看着他们。尤安·阿伯克龙比旁边的一个金黄头发的男孩似乎被吓呆了,他用胳膊肘捅捅尤安,对着他的耳朵说了几句什么。尤安·阿伯克龙比也显出十分害怕的样子,偷偷地用惊恐的目光看了看哈利,哈利感觉到自己脸上的笑容像臭汁一样滑落了下来。

"待会儿见。"他对罗恩和赫敏说,然后独自朝礼堂外走去,一路上尽量不去注意人们盯视的目光,以及他们的悄声议论和指指点点。他目不斜视地穿过门厅里拥挤的人群,匆匆走上大理石楼梯,抄了两条隐蔽的近路,很快就把大多数人甩在了后面。

他真是昏了头,居然没有想到这点。他一边走在楼上清静得多的走廊上,一边这样气愤地想道。肯定每个人都要盯着他看的。他两个月前刚从三强争霸赛的迷宫里钻出来,怀里抱着一位同学的尸体,口口声声宣称说看见伏地魔卷土重来了。上学期,他没有来得及把事情解释清楚,大家就不得不放假回家了——尽管他当时有勇气想把那片墓地上发生的可怕事情原原本本地告诉全校师生。

哈利来到通向格兰芬多公共休息室的走廊尽头,在胖夫人的肖像前刹住脚步,这才想起他还不知道新的口令是什么。

"嗯……"他愁眉苦脸地抬头望着胖夫人,胖夫人抹平她那件粉红色丝绸衣服上的褶皱,用严厉的目光看着他。

"没有口令,就不能通过。"她傲慢地说。

"哈利,我知道!"身后有个人气喘吁吁地说,哈利转身看见纳威慢慢朝他跑来,"你猜是什么?我这次居然能记住了——"他挥动着他在火车上拿给他们看过的那盆发育不良的小仙人掌:"米布米宝!"

"对啦。"胖夫人说,她的肖像突然像门一样朝他们打开了,露出墙上的一个圆洞,哈利和纳威钻了进去。

CHAPTER ELEVEN The Sorting Hat's New Song

The Gryffindor common room looked as welcoming as ever, a cosy circular tower room full of dilapidated squashy armchairs and rickety old tables. A fire was crackling merrily in the grate and a few people were warming their hands by it before going up to their dormitories; on the other side of the room Fred and George Weasley were pinning something up on the noticeboard. Harry waved goodnight to them and headed straight for the door to the boys' dormitories; he was not in much of a mood for talking at the moment. Neville followed him.

Dean Thomas and Seamus Finnigan had reached the dormitory first and were in the process of covering the walls beside their beds with posters and photographs. They had been talking as Harry pushed open the door but stopped abruptly the moment they saw him. Harry wondered whether they had been talking about him, then whether he was being paranoid.

'Hi,' he said, moving across to his own trunk and opening it.

'Hey, Harry,' said Dean, who was putting on a pair of pyjamas in the West Ham colours. 'Good holiday?'

'Not bad,' muttered Harry, as a true account of his holiday would have taken most of the night to relate and he could not face it. 'You?'

'Yeah, it was OK,' chuckled Dean. 'Better than Seamus's, anyway, he was just telling me.'

'Why, what happened, Seamus?' Neville asked as he placed his *Mimbulus mimbletonia* tenderly on his bedside cabinet.

Seamus did not answer immediately; he was making rather a meal of ensuring that his poster of the Kenmare Kestrels Quidditch team was quite straight. Then he said, with his back still turned to Harry, 'Me mam didn't want me to come back.'

'What?' said Harry, pausing in the act of pulling off his robes.

'She didn't want me to come back to Hogwarts.'

Seamus turned away from his poster and pulled his own pyjamas out of his trunk, still not looking at Harry.

'But – why?' said Harry, astonished. He knew that Seamus's mother was a witch and could not understand, therefore, why she should have come over so Dursleyish.

Seamus did not answer until he had finished buttoning his pyjamas.

第11章 分院帽的新歌

格兰芬多公共休息室看上去像以前一样让人觉得愉快,这是塔楼中的一个圆形房间,摆满了已经磨破的、又松又软的扶手椅和摇摇晃晃的旧桌子。壁炉里噼噼啪啪地燃着旺火,几个人在那里把手烤热了再回楼上的宿舍。在房间的另一边,弗雷德和乔治·韦斯莱正把什么东西钉在布告栏里。哈利挥挥手祝他们晚安,就径直朝通向男生宿舍的那扇门走去。此刻他没有多少心情跟别人说话。纳威跟在他后面。

迪安·托马斯和西莫·斐尼甘已经先到了宿舍,正在往他们床边的墙上贴海报和照片。哈利把门推开时他们在说话,可是一看见他就突然停住不说了。哈利先是怀疑他们刚才是在议论他,接着又怀疑他自己有点疑神疑鬼。

"嘿。"他说,一边走到自己的箱子跟前,把它打开。

"你好,哈利,"迪安说,他正在穿一套和西汉姆联足球队队衣颜色相同的睡衣,"暑假过得好吗?"

"还行吧。"哈利含混地应付了一句。要原原本本地叙述他在暑假里的经历,恐怕说到下半夜都说不完,他没有精力这么做。"你呢?"

"啊,挺好的,"迪安轻轻笑着说,"反正比西莫强,他刚才正跟我说呢。"

"哟,出什么事了,西莫?"纳威一边把他的米布米宝小心翼翼地放在床头柜上,一边问道。

西莫没有马上回答。他正在格外细致地调整那张肯梅尔红隼魁地奇球队的海报,确保贴得端正。然后,他仍然背冲着哈利说道:"我妈本来不想让我来的。"

"什么?"哈利正在脱袍子,听了这话怔住了。

"她不想让我回霍格沃茨。"

西莫离开了那张海报,从箱子里拿出自己的睡衣,眼睛仍然没看哈利。

"可是——为什么呢?"哈利问,感到十分震惊。他知道西莫的母亲是个巫师,他不明白她怎么会变得像德思礼家的人一样了。

西莫没有马上回答,一直把睡衣上的纽扣都扣好了才说话。

'Well,' he said in a measured voice, 'I suppose ... because of you.'

'What d'you mean?' said Harry quickly.

His heart was beating rather fast. He felt vaguely as though something was closing in on him.

'Well,' said Seamus again, still avoiding Harry's eye, 'she ... er ... well, it's not just you, it's Dumbledore, too ...'

'She believes the *Daily Prophet*?' said Harry. 'She thinks I'm a liar and Dumbledore's an old fool?'

Seamus looked up at him.

'Yeah, something like that.'

Harry said nothing. He threw his wand down on to his bedside table, pulled off his robes, stuffed them angrily into his trunk and pulled on his pyjamas. He was sick of it; sick of being the person who is stared at and talked about all the time. If any of them knew, if any of them had the faintest idea what it felt like to be the one all these things had happened to ... Mrs Finnigan had no idea, the stupid woman, he thought savagely.

He got into bed and made to pull the hangings closed around him, but before he could do so, Seamus said, 'Look ... what *did* happen that night when ... you know, when ... with Cedric Diggory and all?'

Seamus sounded nervous and eager at the same time. Dean, who had been bending over his trunk trying to retrieve a slipper, went oddly still and Harry knew he was listening hard.

'What are you asking me for?' Harry retorted. 'Just read the *Daily Prophet* like your mother, why don't you? That'll tell you all you need to know.'

'Don't you have a go at my mother,' Seamus snapped.

'I'll have a go at anyone who calls me a liar,' said Harry.

'Don't talk to me like that!'

'I'll talk to you how I want,' said Harry, his temper rising so fast he snatched his wand back from his bedside table. 'If you've got a problem sharing a dormitory with me, go and ask McGonagall if you can be moved ... stop your mummy worrying –'

'Leave my mother out of this, Potter!'

'What's going on?'

第11章 分院帽的新歌

"嗯,"他斟词酌句地说,"我想大概是……因为你吧。"

"你这是什么意思?"哈利追问道。

他的心突然跳得很快,隐约感到似乎有什么东西正在朝他一步步逼近。

"嗯,"西莫又说道,仍然躲避着哈利的目光,"她……嗯……唉,也不光是因为你,还有邓布利多……"

"她相信了《预言家日报》?"哈利问,"她认为我是个骗子,邓布利多是个老糊涂?"

西莫抬头望着他。

"是啊,大概就是这个意思吧。"

哈利什么也没说。他把魔杖扔在床边的桌子上,脱下长袍,气呼呼地塞进箱子里,然后换上了睡衣。他感到厌倦,做一个总是被人盯着看、被人评头论足的人,实在让他感到厌倦。他们有谁明白,他们有谁哪怕只是明白那么一点点,这么多事情发生在一个人头上会是什么滋味……斐尼甘夫人不知道,这个愚蠢的女人,哈利恶狠狠地想。

他爬到床上,正要把帷帐拉上遮住自己,可是没等他这么做,西莫说话了:"哎……那天晚上……到底是怎么回事……你知道,就是……塞德里克·迪戈里和所有的事情?"

西莫的声音既紧张又充满好奇。迪安正弯腰从箱子里取一双拖鞋,听了这话,突然奇怪地僵住了,哈利知道他也在侧耳细听。

"你为什么还要问我?"哈利反驳道,"就像你妈妈那样读读《预言家日报》好了,为什么不呢?你需要知道的东西它都会告诉你的。"

"不许你对我妈妈说三道四。"西莫气愤地说。

"谁管我叫骗子,我就要对谁说三道四。"哈利说。

"不许你跟我这样说话!"

"我爱怎么跟你说话就怎么说话。"哈利说,他的火气噌噌地往上蹿,一把抓起床边桌子上的魔杖,"如果你觉得没法跟我住一个宿舍,就去问问麦格教授能不能让你搬出去……别再让你妈妈担心——"

"不许你再提我妈妈,波特!"

"出什么事了?"

CHAPTER ELEVEN — The Sorting Hat's New Song

Ron had appeared in the doorway. His wide eyes travelled from Harry, who was kneeling on his bed with his wand pointing at Seamus, to Seamus, who was standing there with his fists raised.

'He's having a go at my mother!' Seamus yelled.

'What?' said Ron. 'Harry wouldn't do that – we met your mother, we liked her ...'

'That's before she started believing every word the stinking *Daily Prophet* writes about me!' said Harry at the top of his voice.

'Oh,' said Ron, comprehension dawning across his freckled face. 'Oh ... right.'

'You know what?' said Seamus heatedly, casting Harry a venomous look. 'He's right, I don't want to share a dormitory with him any more, he's mad.'

'That's out of order, Seamus,' said Ron, whose ears were starting to glow red – always a danger sign.

'Out of order, am I?' shouted Seamus, who in contrast with Ron was going pale. 'You believe all the rubbish he's come out with about You-Know-Who, do you, you reckon he's telling the truth?'

'Yeah, I do!' said Ron angrily.

'Then you're mad, too,' said Seamus in disgust.

'Yeah? Well, unfortunately for you, pal, I'm also a prefect!' said Ron, jabbing himself in the chest with a finger. 'So unless you want detention, watch your mouth!'

Seamus looked for a few seconds as though detention would be a reasonable price to pay to say what was going through his mind; but with a noise of contempt he turned on his heel, vaulted into bed and pulled the hangings shut with such violence that they were ripped from the bed and fell in a dusty pile to the floor. Ron glared at Seamus, then looked at Dean and Neville.

'Anyone else's parents got a problem with Harry?' he said aggressively.

'My parents are Muggles, mate,' said Dean, shrugging. 'They don't know nothing about no deaths at Hogwarts, because I'm not stupid enough to tell them.'

'You don't know my mother, she'd weasel anything out of anyone!' Seamus snapped at him. 'Anyway, your parents don't get the *Daily Prophet*.

第11章 分院帽的新歌

罗恩出现在门口。他睁大眼睛望望跪在床上用魔杖指着西莫的哈利，又望望站在地上抡起两只拳头的西莫。

"他对我妈妈说三道四！"西莫大喊。

"什么？"罗恩说，"哈利不会那样做的——我们见过你妈妈，都很喜欢她……"

"那是在她开始相信垃圾《预言家日报》编派我的每一句话之前！"哈利直着嗓子吼道。

"噢，"罗恩说，布满雀斑的脸上显出恍然大悟的神情，"噢……是这样。"

"听我说，"西莫恶狠狠地白了哈利一眼，气极地说，"他说得对，我不想再跟他住在一个宿舍了，他疯了。"

"你太过分了，西莫。"罗恩说，他的耳朵开始红得发亮——一般来说，这是一个危险的信号。

"过分，我？"西莫喊道，他和罗恩正好相反，脸色越来越白，"你相信他编造的那些关于神秘人的胡言乱语，你认为他说的是实话？"

"是的，没错！"罗恩气愤地说。

"那你也疯了。"西莫厌恶地说。

"是吗？可是对你来说很不幸啊，哥们儿，我同时还是个级长！"罗恩用一根手指戳着自己的胸脯说，"所以，除非你想关禁闭，不然说话还是放规矩点！"

有那么几秒钟，似乎西莫觉得只要能把脑子里的想法一股脑儿吐出来，即使关禁闭也是值得的，可接着他轻蔑地哼了一声，原地一个转身，用手支撑着跳到床上，非常粗暴地拉上帷帐，结果用劲太大，把帷帐从床上扯了下来，落在地板上，灰扑扑的一大堆。罗恩严厉地瞪着西莫，然后转眼看着迪安和纳威。

"还有谁的父母对哈利有意见？"他咄咄逼人地问。

"我父母都是麻瓜，哥们儿，"迪安耸耸肩膀说，"他们根本不知道霍格沃茨有人死了，因为我才不会犯傻去告诉他们呢。"

"你不了解我妈妈，不管是谁都别想有什么事瞒过她！"西莫冲他嚷道，"而且，你父母反正也看不到《预言家日报》。他们还不知道我

CHAPTER ELEVEN   The Sorting Hat's New Song

They don't know our Headmaster's been sacked from the Wizengamot and the International Confederation of Wizards because he's losing his marbles –'

'My gran says that's rubbish,' piped up Neville. 'She says it's the *Daily Prophet* that's going downhill, not Dumbledore. She's cancelled our subscription. We believe Harry,' said Neville simply. He climbed into bed and pulled the covers up to his chin, looking owlishly over them at Seamus. 'My gran's always said You-Know-Who would come back one day. She says if Dumbledore says he's back, he's back.'

Harry felt a rush of gratitude towards Neville. Nobody else said anything. Seamus got out his wand, repaired the bed hangings and vanished behind them. Dean got into bed, rolled over and fell silent. Neville, who appeared to have nothing more to say either, was gazing fondly at his moonlit cactus.

Harry lay back on his pillows while Ron bustled around the next bed, putting his things away. He felt shaken by the argument with Seamus, whom he had always liked very much. How many more people were going to suggest that he was lying, or unhinged?

Had Dumbledore suffered like this all summer, as first the Wizengamot, then the International Confederation of Wizards had thrown him from their ranks? Was it anger at Harry, perhaps, that had stopped Dumbledore getting in touch with him for months? The two of them were in this together, after all; Dumbledore had believed Harry, announced his version of events to the whole school and then to the wider wizarding community. Anyone who thought Harry was a liar had to think that Dumbledore was, too, or else that Dumbledore had been hoodwinked …

They'll know we're right in the end, thought Harry miserably, as Ron got into bed and extinguished the last candle in the dormitory. But he wondered how many more attacks like Seamus's he would have to endure before that time came.

第11章 分院帽的新歌

们的校长已经被威森加摩和国际巫师联合会开除了，因为他正在失去理智——"

"我奶奶说那都是胡扯。"纳威尖声说起话来，"她说走下坡路的是《预言家日报》，不是邓布利多。她已经停止订这份报纸了。我们相信哈利。"纳威简单明确地说。他爬到床上，把被子一直拉到下巴上，两只眼睛越过其他人，严肃地望着西莫。"我奶奶总是说神秘人总有一天会回来的。她说，如果邓布利多说他回来了，那他肯定就是回来了。"

哈利心头涌起一股对纳威的感激之情。房间里谁也没有再说什么。西莫拿出他的魔杖，把床上的帷帐重新修好，藏到它后面去了。迪安也上了床，翻了个身，不再开口。纳威似乎也没有话要说了，非常慈爱地望着他那棵月光映照下的仙人掌。

哈利向后躺下，枕到枕头上，罗恩在旁边的床上窸窸窣窣地忙碌着收拾东西。与西莫的争吵使哈利感到心绪烦乱，他一直是非常喜欢西莫的呀。以后还会有多少人说他是骗子，说他精神失常呢？

是不是邓布利多整个暑假都在忍受这些？先被威森加摩开除，然后又被国际巫师联合会扫地出门？是不是邓布利多生哈利的气了，才好几个月一直没有跟他联系？不管怎么说，他们俩现在是拴在一起了。邓布利多相信了哈利，把他叙述的事情经过告诉了全校师生，之后又向范围更广的巫师界公布了。凡是认为哈利在说谎的人，都会认为邓布利多也是个骗子，或者认为邓布利多受了蒙蔽……

他们最后总会知道我们是对的，哈利愁闷地想，这时罗恩上了床，吹灭了宿舍里的最后一根蜡烛。可是哈利接着又想，在那个时候到来之前，他还要忍受多少像西莫这样的责难呢？

CHAPTER TWELVE

Professor Umbridge

Seamus dressed at top speed next morning and left the dormitory before Harry had even put on his socks.

'Does he think he'll turn into a nutter if he stays in a room with me too long?' asked Harry loudly, as the hem of Seamus's robes whipped out of sight.

'Don't worry about it, Harry,' Dean muttered, hoisting his schoolbag on to his shoulder, 'he's just ...'

But apparently he was unable to say exactly what Seamus was, and after a slightly awkward pause followed him out of the room.

Neville and Ron both gave Harry an it's-his-problem-not-yours look, but Harry was not much consoled. How much more of this would he have to take?

'What's the matter?' asked Hermione five minutes later, catching up with Harry and Ron halfway across the common room as they all headed towards breakfast. 'You look absolutely – Oh for heaven's sake.'

She was staring at the common-room noticeboard, where a large new sign had been put up.

GALLONS OF GALLEONS!

Pocket money failing to keep pace with your outgoings?

Like to earn a little extra **GOLD**?
Contact Fred and George Weasley,
Gryffindor common room,
for **SIMPLE, PART-TIME,
VIRTUALLY PAINLESS** jobs.

(We regret that ALL work is undertaken at applicant's own risk.)

第 12 章

乌姆里奇教授

第二天早晨,西莫飞快地穿好衣服,没等哈利穿上袜子就离开了宿舍。

"难道他以为跟我在一个房间里待得太久,他就会变成疯子吗?"西莫的衣摆一闪消失后,哈利大声问道。

"别把这事放在心上,哈利,"迪安低声嘟哝了一句,把书包背上肩头,"他只是……"

可是,他似乎说不出西莫到底是怎么回事,尴尬地顿了一下,便也跟着出了房间。

纳威和罗恩都用"这是他的问题,不怪你"的目光看着哈利,可是哈利并没有感到舒服多少。这样的情形,他还要忍受多久?

"出什么事了?"五分钟后,哈利和罗恩赶去吃早饭,刚走到公共休息室,赫敏追了上来,"你的脸色真是太——哦,我的天哪。"

她吃惊地望着公共休息室的布告栏,上面新贴了一张大启事。

大把大把的加隆!

零花钱不够应付开销吗?

想多挣一点儿金子吗?

请与格兰芬多公共休息室的弗雷德和乔治·韦斯莱联系,找一份简单的几乎毫无痛苦的课外临时工吧。

(很抱歉,所有的工作都由求职者自己承担风险。)

CHAPTER TWELVE Professor Umbridge

'They are the limit,' said Hermione grimly, taking down the sign, which Fred and George had pinned up over a poster giving the date of the first Hogsmeade weekend, which was to be in October. 'We'll have to talk to them, Ron.'

Ron looked positively alarmed.

'Why?'

'Because we're prefects!' said Hermione, as they climbed out through the portrait hole. 'It's up to us to stop this kind of thing!'

Ron said nothing; Harry could tell from his glum expression that the prospect of stopping Fred and George doing exactly what they liked was not one he found inviting.

'Anyway, what's up, Harry?' Hermione continued, as they walked down a flight of stairs lined with portraits of old witches and wizards, all of whom ignored them, being engrossed in their own conversation. 'You look really angry about something.'

'Seamus reckons Harry's lying about You-Know-Who,' said Ron succinctly, when Harry did not respond.

Hermione, who Harry had expected to react angrily on his behalf, sighed.

'Yes, Lavender thinks so too,' she said gloomily.

'Been having a nice little chat with her about whether or not I'm a lying, attention-seeking prat, have you?' Harry said loudly.

'No,' said Hermione calmly. 'I told her to keep her big fat mouth shut about you, actually. And it would be quite nice if you stopped jumping down our throats, Harry, because in case you haven't noticed, Ron and I are on your side.'

There was a short pause.

'Sorry,' said Harry in a low voice.

'That's quite all right,' said Hermione with dignity. Then she shook her head. 'Don't you remember what Dumbledore said at the last end-of-term feast?'

Harry and Ron both looked at her blankly and Hermione sighed again.

'About You-Know-Who. He said his "gift for spreading discord and enmity is very great. We can fight it only by showing an equally strong bond of friendship and trust –"'

'How do you remember stuff like that?' asked Ron, looking at her in admiration.

'I listen, Ron,' said Hermione, with a touch of asperity.

第12章 乌姆里奇教授

"他们太过分了。"赫敏板着脸说，一把将启事揭了下来，弗雷德和乔治是把启事钉在一张布告上的，布告上写着第一次到霍格莫德村过周末的日期是在十月份。"我们得跟他们谈谈了，罗恩。"

罗恩显得十分惊慌。

"为什么？"

"因为我们是级长！"赫敏说，这时他们三个从肖像洞口爬了出来，"得由我们来制止这样的事情！"

罗恩什么也没有说。哈利从他闷闷不乐的表情可以看出，他觉得要阻止弗雷德和乔治做他们喜欢的事情可不是什么美差。

"对了，出什么事了，哈利？"赫敏接着问道，他们走下一道楼梯，楼梯旁边挂着一排老巫师的肖像，一个个都忙着互相说话，顾不上理睬他们，"你好像为了什么事情很生气。"

"西莫认为哈利在神秘人的事情上说了谎话。"罗恩看到哈利没有回答，便简明扼要地说道。

哈利以为赫敏会站在他一边做出愤怒的反应，可她只是叹了口气。

"是啊，拉文德也是这样想的。"赫敏愁眉苦脸地说。

"你一直在跟她愉快地聊天，讨论我到底是不是个谎话连篇、爱出风头的傻瓜，是吗？"哈利大声说。

"不是，"赫敏心平气和地说，"实际上，我叫她闭上她那张大肥嘴，不许再对你说三道四。哈利，真希望你不要再对我们横加指责，因为我和罗恩是和你站在一边的，除非你没有注意到。"

短暂的静默。

"对不起。"哈利低声说。

"没关系，"赫敏端着架子说，接着又摇摇头，"你们不记得邓布利多在上学期结束的宴会上说的话了吗？"

哈利和罗恩傻乎乎地望着她，赫敏又叹了口气。

"关于神秘人的。邓布利多说他'制造冲突和敌意的手段十分高明。我们只有表现出同样牢不可破的友谊和信任——'"

"你怎么能记住这样的话？"罗恩钦佩地望着她问道。

"我仔细听了，罗恩。"赫敏略微有些粗暴地说。

CHAPTER TWELVE   Professor Umbridge

'So do I, but I still couldn't tell you exactly what –'

'The point,' Hermione pressed on loudly, 'is that this sort of thing is exactly what Dumbledore was talking about. You-Know-Who's only been back two months and we've already started fighting among ourselves. And the Sorting Hat's warning was the same: stand together, be united –'

'And Harry got it right last night,' retorted Ron. 'If that means we're supposed to get matey with the Slytherins – *fat chance.*'

'Well, I think it's a pity we're not trying for a bit of inter-house unity,' said Hermione crossly.

They had reached the foot of the marble staircase. A line of fourth-year Ravenclaws was crossing the Entrance Hall; they caught sight of Harry and hurried to form a tighter group, as though frightened he might attack stragglers.

'Yeah, we really ought to be trying to make friends with people like that,' said Harry sarcastically.

They followed the Ravenclaws into the Great Hall, all looking instinctively at the staff table as they entered. Professor Grubbly-Plank was chatting to Professor Sinistra, the Astronomy teacher, and Hagrid was once again conspicuous only by his absence. The enchanted ceiling above them echoed Harry's mood; it was a miserable rain-cloud grey.

'Dumbledore didn't even mention how long that Grubbly-Plank woman's staying,' he said, as they made their way across to the Gryffindor table.

'Maybe …' said Hermione thoughtfully.

'What?' said both Harry and Ron together.

'Well … maybe he didn't want to draw attention to Hagrid not being here.'

'What d'you mean, draw attention to it?' said Ron, half laughing. 'How could we not notice?'

Before Hermione could answer, a tall black girl with long braided hair had marched up to Harry.

'Hi, Angelina.'

'Hi,' she said briskly, 'good summer?' And without waiting for an answer, 'Listen, I've been made Gryffindor Quidditch Captain.'

'Nice one,' said Harry, grinning at her; he suspected Angelina's pep talks might not be as long-winded as Oliver Wood's had been, which could only be an improvement.

第12章 乌姆里奇教授

"我也听了呀,可是我还是说不出到底——"

"问题是,"赫敏很不客气地大声说,"这些才是邓布利多真正要说的话。神秘人回来才两个月,我们就已经开始自相争斗了。分院帽的警告也是同样的意思:团结一心——"

"哈利昨天晚上说得对,"罗恩反驳说,"如果这意味着我们要跟斯莱特林的人交朋友——可能性很小。"

"哎,我认为我们不能为学院之间的团结做出努力是非常遗憾的。"赫敏火气很冲地说。

他们来到大理石楼梯底下,拉文克劳的一群四年级学生正鱼贯穿过门厅。他们一看见哈利就赶紧凑成一堆,似乎唯恐哈利会对落在后面的人下毒手。

"是啊,我们确实应该努力跟那样的人交朋友。"哈利讽刺地说。

他们跟着拉文克劳的同学走进礼堂,一进门都不由自主地朝教工桌子望去。格拉普兰教授正跟天文学教师辛尼斯塔教授聊天,海格又一次因为缺席而格外引人注意。被施了魔法的天花板正好反映了哈利的情绪:灰蒙蒙的,一片愁云惨雾。

"邓布利多一句也没提那个姓格拉普兰的女人要在这儿待多久。"他说,这时他们正朝格兰芬多的桌子走去。

"也许……"赫敏若有所思地说。

"什么?"哈利和罗恩同时问道。

"噢……也许他不想让大家注意到海格不在。"

"你这是什么意思?不想让大家注意,"罗恩轻声笑了起来,"我们怎么可能不注意呢?"

赫敏还没来得及回答,一个梳着长辫子的黑皮肤高个子女孩大步走到哈利跟前。

"你好,安吉利娜。"

"你好,"她轻快地说,"暑假过得怎么样?"没等回答,她接着又说:"知道吗,我被选为格兰芬多魁地奇球队的队长了。"

"太好了。"哈利说,咧嘴朝她笑着。他猜想安吉利娜给球员们鼓劲时可能不像奥利弗·伍德那样啰嗦,这倒是一件好事。

'Yeah, well, we need a new Keeper now Oliver's left. Tryouts are on Friday at five o'clock and I want the whole team there, all right? Then we can see how the new person'll fit in.'

'OK,' said Harry.

Angelina smiled at him and departed.

'I'd forgotten Wood had left,' said Hermione vaguely as she sat down beside Ron and pulled a plate of toast towards her. 'I suppose that will make quite a difference to the team?'

'I s'pose,' said Harry, taking the bench opposite. 'He was a good Keeper ...'

'Still, it won't hurt to have some new blood, will it?' said Ron.

With a whoosh and a clatter, hundreds of owls came soaring in through the upper windows. They descended all over the Hall, bringing letters and packages to their owners and showering the breakfasters with droplets of water; it was clearly raining hard outside. Hedwig was nowhere to be seen, but Harry was hardly surprised; his only correspondent was Sirius, and he doubted Sirius would have anything new to tell him after only twenty-four hours apart. Hermione, however, had to move her orange juice aside quickly to make way for a large damp barn owl bearing a sodden *Daily Prophet* in its beak.

'What are you still getting that for?' said Harry irritably, thinking of Seamus as Hermione placed a Knut in the leather pouch on the owl's leg and it took off again. 'I'm not bothering ... load of rubbish.'

'It's best to know what the enemy is saying,' said Hermione darkly, and she unfurled the newspaper and disappeared behind it, not emerging until Harry and Ron had finished eating.

'Nothing,' she said simply, rolling up the newspaper and laying it down by her plate. 'Nothing about you or Dumbledore or anything.'

Professor McGonagall was now moving along the table handing out timetables.

'Look at today!' groaned Ron. 'History of Magic, double Potions, Divination and double Defence Against the Dark Arts ... Binns, Snape, Trelawney and that Umbridge woman all in one day! I wish Fred and George'd hurry up and get those Skiving Snackboxes sorted ...'

'Do mine ears deceive me?' said Fred, arriving with George and squeezing

第12章 乌姆里奇教授

"啊,对了,奥利弗走了,我们需要一个新的守门员。选拔将于星期五下午五点钟进行,我希望全体队员都能到场,行吗?这样我们可以看看那个新人能不能跟大家很好地配合。"

"好的。"哈利说。

安吉利娜朝他笑了笑走了。

"我忘记伍德已经走了,"赫敏在罗恩身边坐下,把一盘面包拖到面前,淡淡地说,"我想那会给球队带来很大的影响吧?"

"我想也是,"哈利在对面的板凳上坐了下来,"他是个出色的守门员……"

"不过,吸收一点新鲜血液也不坏呀,是不是?"罗恩说。

突然,嗖嗖嗖,咔啦咔啦咔啦,几百只猫头鹰从高处的窗口飞了进来。它们落到礼堂各处,把信件和包裹带给它们的主人,同时也把水珠洒在了吃早饭的人头上。显然,外面正在下着大雨。海德薇不见踪影,但哈利并不感到意外。给他写信的只有小天狼星,现在刚分别了二十四小时,估计小天狼星不会有什么新鲜事要告诉他。赫敏不得不手忙脚乱地把橘子汁挪到一边,给一只嘴里叼着一份湿漉漉的《预言家日报》的大谷仓猫头鹰腾出地方。

"你怎么还订那玩意儿?"哈利气恼地说,又想起了西莫,这时赫敏把一个纳特放进猫头鹰脚上的小皮钱袋,猫头鹰扑扇着翅膀飞走了,"我才不费那功夫……都是一堆垃圾。"

"最好了解一下敌人在说什么。"赫敏阴沉地说。她展开报纸,把自己挡在后面,一直到哈利和罗恩都吃完早饭了,才重新把脸露了出来。

"没有什么,"她简单地说,把报纸卷起来放在了盘子旁边,"没有说到你和邓布利多,什么都没有说。"

这时候,麦格教授顺着桌子挨个儿分发课程表。

"看看今天!"罗恩唉声叹气地说,"魔法史、两节魔药课、占卜课、两节黑魔法防御术课……宾斯、斯内普、特里劳妮,还有那个叫乌姆里奇的女人,都在这同一天里!我希望弗雷德和乔治加快速度,赶紧把那些速效逃课糖弄出来……"

"别是我的耳朵出毛病了吧?"弗雷德说,他和乔治刚来,挤坐在

CHAPTER TWELVE Professor Umbridge

on to the bench beside Harry. 'Hogwarts prefects surely don't wish to skive off lessons?'

'Look what we've got today,' said Ron grumpily, shoving his timetable under Fred's nose. 'That's the worst Monday I've ever seen.'

'Fair point, little bro,' said Fred, scanning the column. 'You can have a bit of Nosebleed Nougat cheap if you like.'

'Why's it cheap?' said Ron suspiciously.

'Because you'll keep bleeding till you shrivel up, we haven't got an antidote yet,' said George, helping himself to a kipper.

'Cheers,' said Ron moodily, pocketing his timetable, 'but I think I'll take the lessons.'

'And speaking of your Skiving Snackboxes,' said Hermione, eyeing Fred and George beadily, 'you can't advertise for testers on the Gryffindor noticeboard.'

'Says who?' said George, looking astonished.

'Says me,' said Hermione. 'And Ron.'

'Leave me out of it,' said Ron hastily.

Hermione glared at him. Fred and George sniggered.

'You'll be singing a different tune soon enough, Hermione,' said Fred, thickly buttering a crumpet. 'You're starting your fifth year, you'll be begging us for a Snackbox before long.'

'And why would starting fifth year mean I want a Skiving Snackbox?' asked Hermione.

'Fifth year's O.W.L. year,' said George.

'So?'

'So you've got your exams coming up, haven't you? They'll be keeping your noses so hard to that grindstone they'll be rubbed raw,' said Fred with satisfaction.

'Half our year had minor breakdowns coming up to O.W.L.s,' said George happily. 'Tears and tantrums ... Patricia Stimpson kept coming over faint ...'

'Kenneth Towler came out in boils, d'you remember?' said Fred reminiscently.

'That's 'cause you put Bulbadox powder in his pyjamas,' said George.

'Oh yeah,' said Fred, grinning. 'I'd forgotten ... hard to keep track

哈利旁边,"霍格沃茨的级长总不会想要逃课吧?"

"看看我们今天有多倒霉。"罗恩发着牢骚,把他的课程表塞到了弗雷德鼻子底下,"我还从没有碰到过这么糟糕的星期一呢。"

"说得对呀,老弟,"弗雷德一边浏览课程表一边说道,"如果你愿意,可以来点儿鼻血牛轧糖,便宜卖你。"

"为什么便宜?"罗恩怀疑地说。

"因为鼻血会一直流个不停,直到身体的血都流干。我们还没有研究出解药呢。"乔治说着开始吃一块熏鱼。

"谢谢啦,"罗恩闷闷不乐地说,把课程表装进了口袋,"我想我还是去上课吧。"

"说到你们的速效逃课糖,"赫敏严厉地瞪着弗雷德和乔治说,"你们不能在格兰芬多的布告栏上贴启事招聘试验者。"

"谁说的?"乔治说,一副很吃惊的样子。

"我说的,"赫敏说,"还有罗恩。"

"这事儿跟我可没关系。"罗恩赶紧说道。

赫敏气呼呼地瞪着他。弗雷德和乔治咻咻地笑。

"过不了多久,你就会改变腔调的,赫敏,"弗雷德说,一边往一块烤面饼上涂抹厚厚的黄油,"你们开始上五年级了,很快就会求着我们要逃课糖。"

"为什么上五年级就意味着我需要逃课糖呢?"赫敏问道。

"五年级是 O.W.L. 年。"乔治说。

"那又怎么样?"

"那就是说,你们就要面对考试了,是不是?考试会像一块砂轮使劲打磨你们的鼻子,会把鼻尖的皮都磨破。"弗雷德幸灾乐祸地说。

"就为了 O.W.L.,我们年级一半的同学都闹了点儿小毛病,"乔治兴高采烈地说,"哭鼻子抹泪啦,发脾气啦……帕翠霞·斯廷森动不动就晕倒……"

"肯尼思·托勒全身长满了疖子,你还记得吗?"弗雷德回忆道。

"那是因为你往他的睡衣里放了大泡粉。"乔治说。

"噢,对了,"弗雷德说着顽皮地笑了,"我忘记了……有时候真是

CHAPTER TWELVE   Professor Umbridge

sometimes, isn't it?'

'Anyway, it's a nightmare of a year, the fifth,' said George. 'If you care about exam results, anyway. Fred and I managed to keep our peckers up somehow.'

'Yeah ... you got, what was it, three O.W.L.s each?' said Ron.

'Yep,' said Fred unconcernedly. 'But we feel our futures lie outside the world of academic achievement.'

'We seriously debated whether we were going to bother coming back for our seventh year,' said George brightly, 'now that we've got –'

He broke off at a warning look from Harry, who knew George had been about to mention the Triwizard winnings he had given them.

'– now that we've got our O.W.L.s,' George said hastily. 'I mean, do we really need N.E.W.T.s? But we didn't think Mum could take us leaving school early, not on top of Percy turning out to be the world's biggest prat.'

'We're not going to waste our last year here, though,' said Fred, looking affectionately around at the Great Hall. 'We're going to use it to do a bit of market research, find out exactly what the average Hogwarts student requires from a joke shop, carefully evaluate the results of our research, then produce products to fit the demand.'

'But where are you going to get the gold to start a joke shop?' Hermione asked sceptically. 'You're going to need all the ingredients and materials – and premises too, I suppose ...'

Harry did not look at the twins. His face felt hot; he deliberately dropped his fork and dived down to retrieve it. He heard Fred say overhead, 'Ask us no questions and we'll tell you no lies, Hermione. C'mon, George, if we get there early we might be able to sell a few Extendable Ears before Herbology.'

Harry emerged from under the table to see Fred and George walking away, each carrying a stack of toast.

'What did that mean?' said Hermione, looking from Harry to Ron. '"Ask us no questions ..." Does that mean they've already got some gold to start a joke shop?'

'You know, I've been wondering about that,' said Ron, his brow furrowed. 'They bought me a new set of dress robes this summer and I couldn't understand where they got the Galleons ...'

第12章 乌姆里奇教授

很难记得清楚,是吧?"

"总之,五年级真是噩梦般的一年,"乔治说,"如果你们比较在乎考试成绩的话。还好,弗雷德和我总算精神头还不错。"

"是啊……你们后来每人通过了多少来着,三门 O.W.L.?"罗恩说。

"没错,"弗雷德漠不关心地说,"但我们觉得我们的前途是在学术成就之外。"

"我们严肃地讨论过还要不要回来上七年级,"乔治眉飞色舞地说,"既然我们已经有了——"

他看到哈利警告的目光,赶紧刹住口,哈利知道乔治要说到他送给他们的那笔三强争霸赛的奖金了。

"——既然我们现在已经有了 O.W.L. 证书,"乔治赶紧改口道,"我是说,难道我们真的需要 N.E.W.T. 证书吗?但是我们想妈妈肯定不会让我们提早离开学校的,现在珀西又变成了世界上最大的傻瓜,妈妈就更不会同意了。"

"不过我们不会浪费在这里的最后一年,"弗雷德说,一边留恋地环顾着礼堂,"我们要利用这一年时间做一些市场研究,弄清霍格沃茨的普通学生到底希望从笑话店里买到什么,认真鉴定我们的研究成果,然后生产出满足需要的产品。"

"可是你们从哪儿去弄开办笑话店的本钱呢?"赫敏怀疑地问,"你们需要所有的配料和原料——我想,还有店面……"

哈利没有看双胞胎,他感到脸上发烧,便故意把勺子掉在地上,然后俯身去捡。他听见弗雷德在他头顶上说:"别问我们,我们就不会编谎话骗你,赫敏。走吧,乔治,我们如果去得早,也许还能在草药课前卖掉几只伸缩耳呢。"

哈利从桌子底下钻出来,正好看见弗雷德和乔治走开的背影,每人手里拿着一摞面包。

"那是什么意思?"赫敏说,看看哈利,又看看罗恩,"'别问我们……'难道他们已经弄到了一些开办笑话店所需要的金子?"

"其实,我也一直在纳闷这件事呢。"罗恩紧锁着眉头说,"他们今年暑假给我买了一套新礼服长袍,我真不明白他们是从哪儿弄来的钱……"

CHAPTER TWELVE Professor Umbridge

Harry decided it was time to steer the conversation out of these dangerous waters.

'D'you reckon it's true this year's going to be really tough? Because of the exams?'

'Oh, yeah,' said Ron. 'Bound to be, isn't it? O.W.L.s are really important, affect the jobs you can apply for and everything. We get career advice, too, later this year, Bill told me. So you can choose what N.E.W.T.s you want to do next year.'

'D'you know what you want to do after Hogwarts?' Harry asked the other two, as they left the Great Hall shortly afterwards and set off towards their History of Magic classroom.

'Not really,' said Ron slowly. 'Except ... well ...'

He looked slightly sheepish.

'What?' Harry urged him.

'Well, it'd be cool to be an Auror,' said Ron in an off-hand voice.

'Yeah, it would,' said Harry fervently.

'But they're, like, the elite,' said Ron. 'You've got to be really good. What about you, Hermione?'

'I don't know,' she said. 'I think I'd like to do something really worthwhile.'

'An Auror's worthwhile!' said Harry.

'Yes, it is, but it's not the only worthwhile thing,' said Hermione thoughtfully, 'I mean, if I could take S.P.E.W. further ...'

Harry and Ron carefully avoided looking at each other.

History of Magic was by common consent the most boring subject ever devised by wizardkind. Professor Binns, their ghost teacher, had a wheezy, droning voice that was almost guaranteed to cause severe drowsiness within ten minutes, five in warm weather. He never varied the form of their lessons, but lectured them without pausing while they took notes, or rather, gazed sleepily into space. Harry and Ron had so far managed to scrape passes in this subject only by copying Hermione's notes before exams; she alone seemed able to resist the soporific power of Binns's voice.

Today, they suffered three quarters of an hour's droning on the subject of giant wars. Harry heard just enough within the first ten minutes to appreciate dimly that in another teacher's hands this subject might have been mildly

第12章 乌姆里奇教授

哈利认为必须赶紧转移话题,离开这片危险的水域。

"你们说,这个学年真的很够呛吗?因为那些考试?"

"噢,是的,"罗恩说,"那是肯定的,是吧?O.W.L.确实非常重要,影响到以后可以申请什么工作等等。这个学年的下学期我们还会得到求职方面的建议,比尔告诉我的。这样明年就可以挑选自己需要的 N.E.W.T. 科目了。"

"你知道你从霍格沃茨毕业后想做什么吗?"哈利问他们俩,这时他们已经离开礼堂,朝魔法史课的教室走去。

"还没想好,"罗恩慢吞吞地说,"除非……嗯……"

他显得有点儿不好意思。

"什么?"哈利催促道。

"嗯,当一个傲罗倒是蛮酷的。"罗恩用漫不经心的口吻说。

"是啊。"哈利热情高涨地说。

"可是傲罗差不多都是精英,"罗恩说,"必须非常出色才行呢。你呢,赫敏?"

"我不知道。"她说,"我想做一些真正有价值的事情。"

"当一个傲罗就很有价值!"哈利说。

"是的,但是有价值的事情并不止这一件,"赫敏若有所思地说,"我是说,如果我能进一步推动家养小精灵权益促进会……"

哈利和罗恩都小心地不去看对方的眼睛。

魔法史被公认为巫师界设计的最枯燥的一门课程。他们的幽灵老师宾斯教授说起话来呼哧带喘,拖腔拖调,几乎肯定能在十分钟内使人昏昏欲睡;如果天气炎热,五分钟就够了。他上课的形式一成不变,总是滔滔不绝地照本宣科,学生们就在底下做笔记,或者更准确地说,是在睡眼蒙眬地发愣。哈利和罗恩的这门功课一直勉强能够及格,多亏了在考试前照抄赫敏的笔记。似乎只有赫敏一个人能够抵挡住宾斯声音的催眠力量。

今天,他们忍受着宾斯教授拖着腔调讲述巨人战争的话题,足足忍受了四十五分钟。哈利刚听了十分钟,就隐约意识到如果换另一位老师,这个题目大概会比较引人入胜。接着他的大脑就走神了,在剩

CHAPTER TWELVE Professor Umbridge

interesting, but then his brain disengaged, and he spent the remaining thirty-five minutes playing hangman on a corner of his parchment with Ron, while Hermione shot them filthy looks out of the corner of her eye.

'How would it be,' she asked them coldly, as they left the classroom for break (Binns drifting away through the blackboard), 'if I refused to lend you my notes this year?'

'We'd fail our O.W.L.,' said Ron. 'If you want that on your conscience, Hermione ...'

'Well, you'd deserve it,' she snapped. 'You don't even try to listen to him, do you?'

'We do try,' said Ron. 'We just haven't got your brains or your memory or your concentration – you're just cleverer than we are – is it nice to rub it in?'

'Oh, don't give me that rubbish,' said Hermione, but she looked slightly mollified as she led the way out into the damp courtyard.

A fine misty drizzle was falling, so that the people standing in huddles around the yard looked blurred at the edges. Harry, Ron and Hermione chose a secluded corner under a heavily dripping balcony, turning up the collars of their robes against the chilly September air and talking about what Snape was likely to set them in the first lesson of the year. They had got as far as agreeing that it was likely to be something extremely difficult, just to catch them off guard after a two-month holiday, when someone walked around the corner towards them.

'Hello, Harry!'

It was Cho Chang and, what was more, she was on her own again. This was most unusual: Cho was almost always surrounded by a gang of giggling girls; Harry remembered the agony of trying to get her by herself to ask her to the Yule Ball.

'Hi,' said Harry, feeling his face grow hot. *At least you're not covered in Stinksap this time*, he told himself. Cho seemed to be thinking along the same lines.

'You got that stuff off, then?'

'Yeah,' said Harry, trying to grin as though the memory of their last meeting was funny as opposed to mortifying. 'So, did you ... er ... have a good summer?'

The moment he had said this he wished he hadn't – Cedric had been Cho's boyfriend and the memory of his death must have affected her holiday

第 12 章 乌姆里奇教授

下来的三十五分钟里,他和罗恩一直在他羊皮纸的一角玩刽子手游戏,赫敏不时用眼角的余光狠狠地瞪他们。

"如果我今年不把笔记借给你们,会怎么样呢?"他们离开教室去休息时(宾斯教授穿过黑板飘走了),赫敏冷冷地问他们。

"我们的魔法史 O.W.L. 就会不及格。"罗恩说,"如果你想受到良心的谴责,赫敏……"

"哼,那是你们活该,"她厉声反驳道,"你们根本就没有认真听他讲课,对吗?"

"我们努力来着,"罗恩说,"我们只是没有你那样的大脑,你那样的记性、那样好的注意力——你就是比我们聪明嘛——你就不要哪壶不开提哪壶了好不好?"

"哼,别给我灌这些迷魂汤。"赫敏说,但她的表情微微缓和了些,领头来到外面湿乎乎的院子里。

天上下着蒙蒙细雨,因此,三三两两挤在院子里的人们看上去轮廓有点儿模糊。哈利、罗恩和赫敏在一个不断滴水的阳台下找了个隐蔽的角落,竖起长袍的领子抵挡九月的寒风,一边谈论着在本学年的第一节魔药课上,斯内普会给他们布置什么作业。他们一致认为那大概是一件很难很难的任务,为的是在两个月的假期后给他们一个下马威。就在这时,有人绕过拐角朝他们走来。

"你好,哈利!"

是秋·张,更稀罕的是,她这次又是一个人。这真是不同寻常,秋几乎总是被一大帮叽叽咕咕的女生包围着。哈利还记得他曾经有过的痛苦:他千方百计想在秋独自一人时碰到她,好邀请她参加圣诞舞会。

"你好。"哈利说,感觉到自己的脸热得发烫。这次至少你身上没沾着臭汁,他对自己说。秋似乎也想到了同样的事情。

"看来,你把那玩意儿清除干净了?"

"是啊。"哈利说,竭力想露出点笑容,似乎他们上一次见面并不尴尬,而是挺好玩的,"那么,你……嗯……暑假过得好吗?"

话一出口,他就后悔不该这么问——塞德里克曾是秋的男朋友,他的死一定影响了秋在暑假里的心情,就像哈利自己也没有过好暑假

CHAPTER TWELVE   Professor Umbridge

almost as badly as it had affected Harry's. Something seemed to tauten in her face, but she said, 'Oh, it was all right, you know ...'

'Is that a Tornados badge?' Ron demanded suddenly, pointing to the front of Cho's robes, where a sky-blue badge emblazoned with a double gold 'T' was pinned. 'You don't support them, do you?'

'Yeah, I do,' said Cho.

'Have you always supported them, or just since they started winning the league?' said Ron, in what Harry considered an unnecessarily accusatory tone of voice.

'I've supported them since I was six,' said Cho coolly. 'Anyway ... see you, Harry.'

She walked away. Hermione waited until Cho was halfway across the courtyard before rounding on Ron.

'You are so tactless!'

'What? I only asked her if –'

'Couldn't you tell she wanted to talk to Harry on her own?'

'So? She could've done, I wasn't stopping –'

'Why on earth were you attacking her about her Quidditch team?'

'Attacking? I wasn't attacking her, I was only –'

'Who *cares* if she supports the Tornados?'

'Oh, come on, half the people you see wearing those badges only bought them last season –'

'But what does it *matter*?'

'It means they're not real fans, they're just jumping on the band-wagon –'

'That's the bell,' said Harry listlessly, because Ron and Hermione were bickering too loudly to hear it. They did not stop arguing all the way down to Snape's dungeon, which gave Harry plenty of time to reflect that between Neville and Ron he would be lucky ever to have two minutes of conversation with Cho that he could look back on without wanting to leave the country.

And yet, he thought, as they joined the queue lining up outside Snape's classroom door, she had chosen to come and talk to him, hadn't she? She had been Cedric's girlfriend; she could easily have hated Harry for coming out of the Triwizard maze alive when Cedric had died, yet she was talking to him in a perfectly friendly way, not as though she thought him mad, or a liar, or in some horrible way responsible for Cedric's death ... yes, she had

一样。秋的神色似乎微微紧了紧，但她说："噢，挺好的，你知道……"

"那是龙卷风队的徽章吗？"罗恩突然指着秋的长袍前襟问道，那里别着一枚天蓝色徽章，上面有两个鲜艳醒目的金色字母"T"，"你该不是支持他们吧？"

"我确实支持他们。"秋说。

"你是一直就支持他们呢，还是从他们赢得魁地奇联盟杯后才支持他们的？"罗恩问，用的是一种在哈利看来没有必要的指责口气。

"我从六岁起就支持他们了，"秋冷冷地说，"好吧……再见，哈利。"

她走开了。赫敏等到秋走到院子中间，便回过头来责骂罗恩。

"你太不懂事了！"

"什么？我不过问她是不是——"

"你难道看不出来，她是想跟哈利单独谈谈吗？"

"那又怎么样？她完全可以谈嘛，我又没有拦着她——"

"你凭什么对她支持的魁地奇球队横加指责？"

"指责？我没有指责她，我只是——"

"谁在乎她支持不支持龙卷风队？"

"哦，得啦，你看见那些人戴的徽章，一半都是上个赛季刚买的——"

"可那又有什么关系？"

"那就说明他们并不是真正的球迷，他们只是跟风，赶浪头——"

"上课铃响了。"哈利无精打采地说，罗恩和赫敏吵得太厉害了，没有听见铃声。他们在走向斯内普地下教室的一路上还在吵个不停。这使哈利有足够的时间想道，他身边有纳威和罗恩这两个人，不知这辈子还有没有运气，跟秋说上两分钟让他回忆起来不会无地自容的话。

当他们排在斯内普教室门外的队伍里时，他又想道，她是主动来跟我说话的，难道不是吗？她曾经是塞德里克的女朋友，本来是很有理由恨他的，因为他活着走出了三强争霸赛的迷宫，而塞德里克却死了，然而她却用十分友好的态度跟他说话，似乎并不认为他头脑不正常，谎话连篇，或对塞德里克的死负有某种可怕的责任……是的，她确实是主动来跟他说话，而且是两天里的第二次了……想到这里，哈利的

definitely chosen to come and talk to him, and that made the second time in two days ... and at this thought, Harry's spirits rose. Even the ominous sound of Snape's dungeon door creaking open did not puncture the small, hopeful bubble that seemed to have swelled in his chest. He filed into the classroom behind Ron and Hermione and followed them to their usual table at the back, ignoring the huffy, irritable noises now issuing from both of them.

'Settle down,' said Snape coldly, shutting the door behind him.

There was no real need for the call to order; the moment the class had heard the door close, quiet had fallen and all fidgeting stopped. Snape's mere presence was usually enough to ensure a class's silence.

'Before we begin today's lesson,' said Snape, sweeping over to his desk and staring around at them all, 'I think it appropriate to remind you that next June you will be sitting an important examination, during which you will prove how much you have learned about the composition and use of magical potions. Moronic though some of this class undoubtedly are, I expect you to scrape an "Acceptable" in your O.W.L., or suffer my ... displeasure.'

His gaze lingered this time on Neville, who gulped.

'After this year, of course, many of you will cease studying with me,' Snape went on. 'I take only the very best into my N.E.W.T. Potions class, which means that some of us will certainly be saying goodbye.'

His eyes rested on Harry and his lip curled. Harry glared back, feeling a grim pleasure at the idea that he would be able to give up Potions after fifth year.

'But we have another year to go before that happy moment of farewell,' said Snape softly, 'so, whether or not you are intending to attempt N.E.W.T., I advise all of you to concentrate your efforts upon maintaining the high pass level I have come to expect from my O.W.L. students.

'Today we will be mixing a potion that often comes up at Ordinary Wizarding Level: the Draught of Peace, a potion to calm anxiety and soothe agitation. Be warned: if you are too heavy-handed with the ingredients you will put the drinker into a heavy and sometimes irreversible sleep, so you will need to pay close attention to what you are doing.' On Harry's left, Hermione sat up a little straighter, her expression one of utmost attention. 'The ingredients and method –' Snape flicked his wand '– are on the

情绪欢悦起来,就连地下教室的门打开时发出的吱吱嘎嘎的阴森声音,也没有刺破那似乎在他内心深处膨胀起来的小小的希望泡泡。他跟在罗恩和赫敏后面走进教室,又跟着他们走向他们惯常坐的那张位于后排的桌子,假装没有听见他们俩发出的气呼呼的拌嘴声。

"安静。"斯内普冷冷地说,反手关上了教室的门。

其实他根本没有必要命令大家安静,全班同学一听见门关上了,立刻变得鸦雀无声,所有的小动作都停止了。一般来说,只要斯内普一出现,就足以让整个班级沉寂下来。

"在我们今天开始上课前,"斯内普快步走向讲台,严厉地望着他们大家说道,"我认为需要提醒你们一下,明年六月你们就要参加一项重要的考试了,那时你们将证明自己学到了多少魔药配制和使用方面的知识。尽管这个班上有几个人确实智力迟钝,但我希望你们在 O.W.L. 考试中都能够勉强'及格',不然我会……很生气。"

他的目光这次落在了纳威脸上,纳威吓得倒吸了一口冷气。

"当然啦,过了这一年,你们中间的许多人就不能再上我的课了,"斯内普继续说道,"我只挑选最优秀的学生进入我的 N.E.W.T. 魔药班,这就是说,我们跟有些人将不得不说再见了。"

他微微噘起了嘴,目光落在哈利脸上。哈利也毫不示弱地瞪着他,一想到过了五年级,他就可以放弃魔药课了,不由得感到一种恶狠狠的快意。

"但是在那愉快的告别时刻到来之前,我们还需要再坚持一年。"斯内普轻声细语地说,"因此,不管你们是否打算参加 N.E.W.T. 考试,我都建议你们大家集中精力学好功课,达到我要求我的 O.W.L. 学生们达到的较高的及格水平。

"今天,我们要配制一种普通巫师等级考试中经常出现的药剂:缓和剂,它能平息和舒缓烦躁焦虑的情绪。注意:如果放配料的时候马马虎虎,就会使服药者陷入一种死沉的,有时甚至是不可逆转的昏睡,所以你们需要格外注意自己的行为。"在哈利的左边,赫敏把身子坐得更直了一些,脸上是一副全神贯注的表情。"配料和配制方法——"斯内普一挥魔杖,"——在黑板上——"(黑板上果然出现了)"——你

blackboard –' (they appeared there) '– you will find everything you need –' he flicked his wand again '– in the store cupboard –' (the door of the said cupboard sprang open) '– you have an hour and a half … start.'

Just as Harry, Ron and Hermione had predicted, Snape could hardly have set them a more difficult, fiddly potion. The ingredients had to be added to the cauldron in precisely the right order and quantities; the mixture had to be stirred exactly the right number of times, firstly in clockwise, then in anti-clockwise directions; the heat of the flames on which it was simmering had to be lowered to exactly the right level for a specific number of minutes before the final ingredient was added.

'A light silver vapour should now be rising from your potion,' called Snape, with ten minutes left to go.

Harry, who was sweating profusely, looked desperately around the dungeon. His own cauldron was issuing copious amounts of dark grey steam; Ron's was spitting green sparks. Seamus was feverishly prodding the flames at the base of his cauldron with the tip of his wand, as they seemed to be going out. The surface of Hermione's potion, however, was a shimmering mist of silver vapour, and as Snape swept by he looked down his hooked nose at it without comment, which meant he could find nothing to criticise. At Harry's cauldron, however, Snape stopped, and looked down at it with a horrible smirk on his face.

'Potter, what is this supposed to be?'

The Slytherins at the front of the class all looked up eagerly; they loved hearing Snape taunt Harry.

'The Draught of Peace,' said Harry tensely.

'Tell me, Potter,' said Snape softly, 'can you read?'

Draco Malfoy laughed.

'Yes, I can,' said Harry, his fingers clenched tightly around his wand.

'Read the third line of the instructions for me, Potter.'

Harry squinted at the blackboard; it was not easy to make out the instructions through the haze of multi-coloured steam now filling the dungeon.

'"Add powdered moonstone, stir three times counter-clockwise, allow to simmer for seven minutes then add two drops of syrup of hellebore."'

们所需要的一切——"他又一挥魔杖,"——在储藏柜里——"(他所说的那个储藏柜的门一下子打开了)"——你们有一个半小时……开始吧。"

正像哈利、罗恩和赫敏所猜测的,斯内普布置他们配制的这种药剂是最难、最费手脚的一种。必须按照严格的顺序和分量将配料加进坩埚;必须将混合物搅拌到规定的次数,不能多也不能少,先是顺时针,然后是逆时针;坩埚沸腾时火苗的温度必须降至某个特定的标准,不能高也不能低,并保持一段特定的时间,然后才能加入最后一种配料。

"你们的药剂现在应该冒出一股淡淡的、银白色的蒸气。"还剩十分钟的时候斯内普说道。

哈利忙得大汗淋漓,绝望地抬头扫了一眼教室。他自己的坩埚冒出一团团深灰色的气体,罗恩的坩埚正喷溅着绿色的火花。西莫发了疯似的用魔杖尖去捅他坩埚下面的火苗,因为它们眼看就要熄灭了。赫敏的药剂倒是正冒出一股微微闪烁的银白色蒸气,当斯内普快步走过时,他鹰钩鼻上的眼睛低垂着看了看赫敏的坩埚,没有做任何评论,也就是说他挑不出任何毛病。可是,在哈利的坩埚旁,斯内普停下脚步,低头望着坩埚,脸上带着一种可怕的讥讽。

"波特,这是什么东西?"

教室前排的斯莱特林们都很感兴趣地抬起头来,他们最喜欢听斯内普挖苦哈利了。

"缓和剂。"哈利紧张地说。

"波特,告诉我,"斯内普轻声细语地说,"你认识字吗?"

德拉科·马尔福大声笑了起来。

"认识。"哈利说,手紧紧地攥住了魔杖。

"把操作说明的第三行念给我听听,波特。"

哈利眯眼望着黑板。现在地下教室里弥漫着各种颜色的蒸气,要看清黑板上的操作说明真不容易。

"加入月长石粉,逆时针搅拌三次,沸腾七分钟,再加入两滴嚏根草糖浆。"

CHAPTER TWELVE   Professor Umbridge

His heart sank. He had not added syrup of hellebore, but had proceeded straight to the fourth line of the instructions after allowing his potion to simmer for seven minutes.

'Did you do everything on the third line, Potter?'

'No,' said Harry very quietly.

'I beg your pardon?'

'No,' said Harry, more loudly. 'I forgot the hellebore.'

'I know you did, Potter, which means that this mess is utterly worthless. *Evanesco.*'

The contents of Harry's potion vanished; he was left standing foolishly beside an empty cauldron.

'Those of you who *have* managed to read the instructions, fill one flagon with a sample of your potion, label it clearly with your name and bring it up to my desk for testing,' said Snape. 'Homework: twelve inches of parchment on the properties of moonstone and its uses in potion-making, to be handed in on Thursday.'

While everyone around him filled their flagons, Harry cleared away his things, seething. His potion had been no worse than Ron's, which was now giving off a foul odour of bad eggs; or Neville's, which had achieved the consistency of just-mixed cement and which Neville was now having to gouge out of his cauldron; yet it was he, Harry, who would be receiving zero marks for the day's work. He stuffed his wand back into his bag and slumped down on to his seat, watching everyone else march up to Snape's desk with filled and corked flagons. When at long last the bell rang, Harry was first out of the dungeon and had already started his lunch by the time Ron and Hermione joined him in the Great Hall. The ceiling had turned an even murkier grey during the morning. Rain was lashing the high windows.

'That was really unfair,' said Hermione consolingly, sitting down next to Harry and helping herself to shepherd's pie. 'Your potion wasn't nearly as bad as Goyle's; when he put it in his flagon the whole thing shattered and set his robes on fire.'

'Yeah, well,' said Harry, glowering at his plate, 'since when has Snape ever been fair to me?'

Neither of the others answered; all three of them knew that Snape and Harry's mutual enmity had been absolute from the moment Harry had set foot in Hogwarts.

他的心往下一沉。他没有加嚏根草糖浆，他让药剂沸腾七分钟后，就直接执行第四条操作说明了。

"第三条里每一项你都做到了吗，波特？"

"没有。"哈利很小声地说。

"对不起，请你再说一遍。"

"没有，"哈利提高了声音说，"我忘记放嚏根草了。"

"我知道你忘记了，波特，这就意味着这一坩埚垃圾毫无用处。消失不见。"

哈利的药剂一下子消失了。他傻乎乎地站在一只空坩埚旁。

"凡是认真读了操作说明的同学，把你们的药剂样品装进一个大肚短颈瓶里，仔细标上自己的姓名，拿到我的讲台上接受检验。"斯内普说，"家庭作业：在羊皮纸上写十二英寸长的论文，论述月长石的特性及其在制药方面的用途，星期四交。"

哈利周围的同学都在往短颈瓶里装药剂，他把东西一样样收起来，心里气得不行。他的药剂并不比罗恩的差，罗恩的那一坩埚东西现在发出一股臭鸡蛋的气味；也不比纳威的差，纳威的药剂变得硬邦邦的，像刚刚搅拌好的水泥，纳威这会儿不得不使劲把它从坩埚里抠出来。然而偏偏是他，哈利，今天的作业得了零分。他把魔杖放回书包，一屁股坐在座位上，望着其他同学一个个拿着装满药剂、盖上软木塞的短颈瓶，走向斯内普的讲台。下课铃终于响了，哈利第一个冲出地下教室。他已经开始吃午饭了，罗恩和赫敏才来到礼堂。天花板比上午的时候更昏暗阴沉了，雨点啪啪地打着高处的窗户。

"那真是很不公平，"赫敏安慰他道，她坐在哈利身边，给自己拿了一块土豆泥肉馅饼，"你的药剂远不像高尔的那么糟糕，当他往瓶子里装的时候，那东西突然四下迸溅，把他的袍子都烧着了。"

"是啊，这也难怪，"哈利说，气呼呼地瞪着面前的盘子，"斯内普什么时候公平地对待过我啊？"

赫敏和罗恩谁也没有回答。三个人心里都清楚，斯内普和哈利之间的敌意，从哈利踏进霍格沃茨的那一刻起就已经根深蒂固了。

CHAPTER TWELVE Professor Umbridge

'I did think he might be a bit better this year,' said Hermione in a disappointed voice. 'I mean ... you know ...' she looked around carefully; there were half a dozen empty seats on either side of them and nobody was passing the table '... now he's in the Order and everything.'

'Poisonous toadstools don't change their spots,' said Ron sagely. 'Anyway, I've always thought Dumbledore was cracked to trust Snape. Where's the evidence he ever really stopped working for You-Know-Who?'

'I think Dumbledore's probably got plenty of evidence, even if he doesn't share it with you, Ron,' snapped Hermione.

'Oh, shut up, the pair of you,' said Harry heavily, as Ron opened his mouth to argue back. Hermione and Ron both froze, looking angry and offended. 'Can't you give it a rest?' said Harry. 'You're always having a go at each other, it's driving me mad.' And abandoning his shepherd's pie, he swung his schoolbag back over his shoulder and left them sitting there.

He walked up the marble staircase two steps at a time, past the many students hurrying towards lunch. The anger that had just flared so unexpectedly still blazed inside him, and the vision of Ron and Hermione's shocked faces afforded him a sense of deep satisfaction. *Serve them right, he thought, why can't they give it a rest ... bickering all the time ... it's enough to drive anyone up the wall ...*

He passed the large picture of Sir Cadogan the knight on a landing; Sir Cadogan drew his sword and brandished it fiercely at Harry, who ignored him.

'Come back, you scurvy dog! Stand fast and fight!' yelled Sir Cadogan in a muffled voice from behind his visor, but Harry merely walked on and when Sir Cadogan attempted to follow him by running into a neighbouring picture, he was rebuffed by its inhabitant, a large and angry-looking wolfhound.

Harry spent the rest of the lunch hour sitting alone underneath the trapdoor at the top of North Tower. Consequently, he was the first to ascend the silver ladder that led to Sybill Trelawney's classroom when the bell rang.

After Potions, Divination was Harry's least favourite class, which was due mainly to Professor Trelawney's habit of predicting his premature death every few lessons. A thin woman, heavily draped in shawls and glittering with strings of beads, she always reminded Harry of some kind of insect,

第12章 乌姆里奇教授

"我还以为他今年会有点儿好转呢,"赫敏用失望的口气说,"我的意思是……你们知道的……"她小心地望了望四周,他们两边都空着六七个座位,也没有人从桌子旁走过,"……现在他加入了凤凰社,还有所有的一切。"

"毒蘑菇是不会改变它们的斑点的,"罗恩一针见血地说,"反正,我一直认为邓布利多真是疯了,居然相信斯内普。有什么证据能证明他真的不再为神秘人工作了呢?"

"我认为邓布利多大概得到了足够的证据,不过他没有拿给你看,罗恩。"赫敏毫不客气地说。

"哦,闭嘴吧,你们两个。"罗恩张嘴正要反驳,哈利烦躁地说。赫敏和罗恩都怔住了,显得又生气又委屈。"你们就不能消停一会儿?"哈利说,"总是没完没了地斗来斗去,都快把我逼疯了。"说完,他扔下自己的土豆泥肉馅饼,把书包甩上肩头,扬长而去,留下两人坐在那里直发愣。

他一步两级地走上大理石楼梯,与许多匆匆忙忙赶去吃午饭的同学擦肩而过。刚才突然爆发的那股无名火,还在他心里熊熊燃烧着,想到罗恩和赫敏脸上惊愕的表情,他感到一种深深的快意。那是他们活该,他想道,他们为什么就不能安静点儿……总是一天到晚争争吵吵……换了谁都会被逼疯的……

在一处楼梯平台上,他从骑士卡多根爵士的大幅肖像前走过。卡多根爵士拔出宝剑,恶狠狠地朝哈利挥舞着,哈利根本不理睬他。

"回来,你这逃跑的懦夫!不许退缩,跟我战斗!"卡多根爵士从面罩后面用发闷的声音喊道,但哈利只顾继续往前走,卡多根爵士想来追他,于是跳进相邻的一幅画里,但住在画里的一条模样凶狠的大狼狗把他赶了回去。

在剩下来的午饭时间里,哈利一直独自坐在北塔楼顶上的活板门下。上课铃响起时,他便第一个爬上了通往西比尔·特里劳尼教室的银色梯子。

除了魔药课,占卜课是哈利最不喜欢的课程,这主要是因为特里劳尼教授有一个习惯,每过几堂课就要预言哈利会死于非命。特里劳

CHAPTER TWELVE   Professor Umbridge

with her glasses hugely magnifying her eyes. She was busy putting copies of battered leather-bound books on each of the spindly little tables with which her room was littered when Harry entered the room, but the light cast by the lamps covered by scarves and the low-burning, sickly-scented fire was so dim she appeared not to notice him as he took a seat in the shadows. The rest of the class arrived over the next five minutes. Ron emerged from the trapdoor, looked around carefully, spotted Harry and made directly for him, or as directly as he could while having to wend his way between tables, chairs and overstuffed pouffes.

'Hermione and me have stopped arguing,' he said, sitting down beside Harry.

'Good,' grunted Harry.

'But Hermione says she thinks it would be nice if you stopped taking out your temper on us,' said Ron.

'I'm not –'

'I'm just passing on the message,' said Ron, talking over him. 'But I reckon she's right. It's not our fault how Seamus and Snape treat you.'

'I never said it –'

'Good-day,' said Professor Trelawney in her usual misty, dreamy voice, and Harry broke off, again feeling both annoyed and slightly ashamed of himself. 'And welcome back to Divination. I have, of course, been following your fortunes most carefully over the holidays, and am delighted to see that you have all returned to Hogwarts safely – as, of course, I knew you would.

'You will find on the tables before you copies of *The Dream Oracle*, by Inigo Imago. Dream interpretation is a most important means of divining the future and one that may very probably be tested in your O.W.L. Not, of course, that I believe examination passes or failures are of the remotest importance when it comes to the sacred art of divination. If you have the Seeing Eye, certificates and grades matter very little. However, the Headmaster likes you to sit the examination, so …'

Her voice trailed away delicately, leaving them all in no doubt that Professor Trelawney considered her subject above such sordid matters as examinations.

'Turn, please, to the introduction and read what Imago has to say on the matter of dream interpretation. Then, divide into pairs. Use *The Dream Oracle*

尼教授是一个瘦巴巴的女人，裹着厚厚的披肩，戴着一串串闪闪发亮的珠子，她的眼镜把她的一双眼睛放大了好几倍，总使哈利联想起某种昆虫。哈利进屋时，她正忙着把一本本破破烂烂的皮革装订的书分发在每张桌子上，那些单薄的小桌子杂乱无章地摆放在教室里。盖着罩布的灯发出的光线，和散发出一股难闻气味的不太旺的炉火都十分昏暗。当哈利在阴影里找了一个座位坐下时，特里劳尼教授似乎没有看见他。接下来的五分钟里，班里的同学陆陆续续地来了。罗恩从活板门里探出头，仔细往四下里张望，看见了哈利，直接朝他走了过来，或者说是尽量直接走了过来，因为他必须小心地绕过那么多桌子、椅子和一只塞得鼓鼓囊囊的小坐垫。

"赫敏和我已经不吵了。"他说，在哈利身边坐了下来。

"很好。"哈利咕哝了一句。

"但赫敏说，她希望你不要动不动就朝我们发脾气。"罗恩说。

"我没有——"

"我只是传个话，"罗恩好言好语地劝说道，"但我认为她说得对。西莫和斯内普那么对待你又不是我们的错。"

"我从没有说过——"

"同学们好，"特里劳尼教授用她惯常那种模糊的、如梦似幻的声音说道，哈利赶紧闭了嘴，心里既恼火又有些羞愧。"欢迎你们回到占卜课上。当然啦，整个暑假我一直十分用心地关注着你们的命运，看到你们全都安然无恙地返回霍格沃茨，我非常高兴——因为，当然啦，我知道你们都会回来的。

"你们会发现在你们的桌子上有一本伊尼戈·英麦格写的《解梦指南》。解梦是占卜未来的一种十分重要的方法，也是你们的 O.W.L. 考试中很可能出现的一个题目。当然啦，我认为相比占卜这门神圣的艺术来说，能否通过考试实在是很不重要。只要你们有了慧眼，什么证书啦、等级啦，都是区区小事。不过，校长愿意让你们参加考试，所以……"

她的声音微妙地逐渐低了下去，使得同学们都确信，特里劳尼教授认为她这门课程要比考试之类的俗事重要得多。

"请把书翻到导论，读一读英麦格关于解梦问题的说法。然后，分

CHAPTER TWELVE   Professor Umbridge

to interpret each other's most recent dreams. Carry on.'

The one good thing to be said for this lesson was that it was not a double period. By the time they had all finished reading the introduction of the book, they had barely ten minutes left for dream interpretation. At the table next to Harry and Ron, Dean had paired up with Neville, who immediately embarked on a long-winded explanation of a nightmare involving a pair of giant scissors wearing his grandmother's best hat; Harry and Ron merely looked at each other glumly.

'I never remember my dreams,' said Ron, 'you say one.'

'You must remember one of them,' said Harry impatiently.

He was not going to share his dreams with anyone. He knew perfectly well what his regular nightmare about a graveyard meant, he did not need Ron or Professor Trelawney or the stupid *Dream Oracle* to tell him.

'Well, I dreamed I was playing Quidditch the other night,' said Ron, screwing up his face in an effort to remember. 'What d'you reckon that means?'

'Probably that you're going to be eaten by a giant marshmallow or something,' said Harry, turning the pages of *The Dream Oracle* without interest. It was very dull work looking up bits of dreams in the *Oracle* and Harry was not cheered up when Professor Trelawney set them the task of keeping a dream diary for a month as homework. When the bell went, he and Ron led the way back down the ladder, Ron grumbling loudly.

'D'you realise how much homework we've got already? Binns set us a foot-and-a-half-long essay on giant wars, Snape wants a foot on the use of moonstones, and now we've got a month's dream diary from Trelawney! Fred and George weren't wrong about O.W.L. year, were they? That Umbridge woman had better not give us any ...'

When they entered the Defence Against the Dark Arts classroom they found Professor Umbridge already seated at the teacher's desk, wearing the fluffy pink cardigan of the night before and the black velvet bow on top of her head. Harry was again reminded forcibly of a large fly perched unwisely on top of an even larger toad.

The class was quiet as it entered the room; Professor Umbridge was, as yet, an unknown quantity and nobody knew how strict a disciplinarian she was likely to be.

'Well, good afternoon!' she said, when finally the whole class had sat down.

成两人一组，用《解梦指南》来解释对方最近做过的梦。开始吧。"

这门课倒是有一个好处，它不是连上两节。等全班同学读完那本书的导论时，就只有十分钟时间让他们解释梦境了。在与哈利和罗恩相邻的桌子旁，迪安和纳威分在一组，纳威立刻就开始啰里啰嗦地解释一个噩梦，梦里有一把大剪刀嘎吱嘎吱地剪他奶奶最好的一顶帽子。哈利和罗恩只是愁眉苦脸地大眼瞪小眼。

"我做梦从来不记得。"罗恩说，"你说一个吧。"

"你总能想起一个的。"哈利不耐烦地说。

他不想把自己的梦说给任何人听。他心里很清楚他三天两头梦见一片墓地意味着什么，他不需要罗恩、特里劳尼教授或愚蠢的《解梦指南》来告诉他。

"好吧，那天夜里我梦见自己在打魁地奇球，"罗恩说，皱起眉头拼命回忆着，"你认为那意味着什么？"

"那大概意味着你要被一颗巨大的棉花糖吃掉之类的。"哈利兴味索然地翻看着《解梦指南》说道。在《解梦指南》里查找一个个梦境真是一件枯燥乏味的事情，后来特里劳尼教授布置他们记录下一个月里每天做的梦作为家庭作业，哈利听了更是闷闷不乐。下课铃响了，他和罗恩领头走下梯子，罗恩大声抱怨道：

"你知不知道我们已经有多少家庭作业了？宾斯叫我们写一篇一英尺半长的论文，谈巨人战争；斯内普要的论文是一英尺长，讲月长石的用途；现在特里劳尼又要我们记下一个月里每天做的梦！弗雷德和乔治说这个 O.W.L. 年日子难熬，看来确实这样，是不是？那个姓乌姆里奇的女人最好别再给我们……"

他们走进黑魔法防御术课的教室时，发现乌姆里奇教授已经坐在讲台后面了。她穿着前一天晚上穿的那件毛茸茸的粉红色开襟毛衣，头顶上戴着那个黑天鹅绒的蝴蝶结。哈利又一次强烈而鲜明地想到一只大苍蝇愚蠢地落在了一只更大的癞蛤蟆身上。

全班同学走进教室时都默不作声，乌姆里奇教授还是个未知数，谁也不知道她对课堂纪律的要求有多么严格。

"同学们，下午好！"全班同学都坐下后，她说道。

A few people mumbled 'good afternoon' in reply.

'Tut, tut,' said Professor Umbridge. '*That* won't do, now, will it? I should like you, please, to reply "Good afternoon, Professor Umbridge". One more time, please. Good afternoon, class!'

'Good afternoon, Professor Umbridge,' they chanted back at her.

'There, now,' said Professor Umbridge sweetly. 'That wasn't too difficult, was it? Wands away and quills out, please.'

Many of the class exchanged gloomy looks; the order 'wands away' had never yet been followed by a lesson they had found interesting. Harry shoved his wand back inside his bag and pulled out quill, ink and parchment. Professor Umbridge opened her handbag, extracted her own wand, which was an unusually short one, and tapped the blackboard sharply with it; words appeared on the board at once:

DEFENCE AGAINST THE DARK ARTS
A Return to Basic Principles

'Well now, your teaching in this subject has been rather disrupted and fragmented, hasn't it?' stated Professor Umbridge, turning to face the class with her hands clasped neatly in front of her. 'The constant changing of teachers, many of whom do not seem to have followed any Ministry-approved curriculum, has unfortunately resulted in your being far below the standard we would expect to see in your O.W.L. year.

'You will be pleased to know, however, that these problems are now to be rectified. We will be following a carefully structured, theory-centred, Ministry-approved course of defensive magic this year. Copy down the following, please.'

She rapped the blackboard again; the first message vanished and was replaced by the 'Course Aims'.

1. Understanding the principles underlying defensive magic.
2. Learning to recognise situations in which defensive magic can legally be used.
3. Placing the use of defensive magic in a context for practical use.

几个同学嘟哝着"下午好"作为回答。

"啧,啧,"乌姆里奇教授说,"这可不行,是不是?我希望你们这样回答:'下午好,乌姆里奇教授。'请再来一遍。同学们,下午好!"

"下午好,乌姆里奇教授。"他们异口同声地回答。

"这就对了,"乌姆里奇教授声音嗲嗲地说,"这并不太难,是不是?请收起魔杖,拿出羽毛笔。"

许多同学交换着郁闷的眼神。跟在"收起魔杖"这个命令后面的,从来都不是他们觉得有趣的课。哈利把他的魔杖塞进书包,拿出了羽毛笔、墨水和羊皮纸。乌姆里奇教授打开她的手提包,抽出一根短得出奇的魔杖,在黑板上使劲一敲,黑板上立刻出现了两行字:

黑魔法防御术
回归基本原理

"同学们,你们这门课的教学一直断断续续,不成系统,是不是?"乌姆里奇教授转身面对全班同学,两只手十指交叉,端端正正地放在胸前,然后说道,"教师不断更换,其中许多人似乎并没有遵照魔法部批准的课程标准进行授课,这不幸使你们现在远远没有达到 O.W.L. 年理应达到的水平。

"然而你们会很高兴地知道,这些问题即将得到改正。今年,我们要学习的是一门经过精心安排、以理论为中心、由魔法部批准的魔法防御术课程。请把这些话抄下来。"

她又敲了敲黑板,刚才那两行字消失了,取而代之的是"课程目标"。

1. 理解魔法防御术的基本原理。
2. 学会辨别可以合法使用魔法防御术的场合。
3. 在实际运用的背景下评定魔法防御术。

CHAPTER TWELVE   Professor Umbridge

For a couple of minutes the room was full of the sound of scratching quills on parchment. When everyone had copied down Professor Umbridge's three course aims she asked, 'Has everybody got a copy of *Defensive Magical Theory* by Wilbert Slinkhard?'

There was a dull murmur of assent throughout the class.

'I think we'll try that again,' said Professor Umbridge. 'When I ask you a question, I should like you to reply, "Yes, Professor Umbridge", or "No, Professor Umbridge". So: has everyone got a copy of *Defensive Magical Theory* by Wilbert Slinkhard?'

'Yes, Professor Umbridge,' rang through the room.

'Good,' said Professor Umbridge. 'I should like you to turn to page five and read "Chapter One, Basics for Beginners". There will be no need to talk.'

Professor Umbridge left the blackboard and settled herself in the chair behind the teacher's desk, observing them all with those pouchy toad's eyes. Harry turned to page five of his copy of *Defensive Magical Theory* and started to read.

It was desperately dull, quite as bad as listening to Professor Binns. He felt his concentration sliding away from him; he had soon read the same line half a dozen times without taking in more than the first few words. Several silent minutes passed. Next to him, Ron was absent-mindedly turning his quill over and over in his fingers, staring at the same spot on the page. Harry looked right and received a surprise to shake him out of his torpor. Hermione had not even opened her copy of *Defensive Magical Theory*. She was staring fixedly at Professor Umbridge with her hand in the air.

Harry could not remember Hermione ever neglecting to read when instructed to, or indeed resisting the temptation to open any book that came under her nose. He looked at her enquiringly, but she merely shook her head slightly to indicate that she was not about to answer questions, and continued to stare at Professor Umbridge, who was looking just as resolutely in another direction.

After several more minutes had passed, however, Harry was not the only one watching Hermione. The chapter they had been instructed to read was so tedious that more and more people were choosing to watch Hermione's mute attempt to catch Professor Umbridge's eye rather than struggle on with 'Basics for Beginners'.

第12章 乌姆里奇教授

教室里只听得羽毛笔在羊皮纸上写字的沙沙声，两三分钟后，当每个同学都把乌姆里奇教授的三个课程目标抄录下来后，她问道："是不是每位同学都有一本威尔伯特·斯林卡的《魔法防御理论》？"

班里响起一片喃喃表示肯定的声音。

"我认为我们还要再来一遍，"乌姆里奇教授说，"当我问你们一个问题时，我希望你们回答'是的，乌姆里奇教授'。或者'不，乌姆里奇教授'。再来一遍：是不是每位同学都有一本威尔伯特·斯林卡的《魔法防御理论》？"

"是的，乌姆里奇教授。"全班同学大声回答。

"很好。"乌姆里奇教授说，"我希望你们把书翻到第五页，读一读第一章，入门基础原理。读的时候不要交头接耳。"

乌姆里奇教授离开黑板，在讲台后面的椅子上坐了下来，用那两只癞蛤蟆似的鼓眼睛盯着大家。哈利把他那本《魔法防御理论》翻到第五页，开始读了起来。

内容十分枯燥，简直就跟听宾斯教授讲课一样毫无趣味。他感到自己的注意力一点点地减退了。很快，他就盯着一行文字看了六七遍，却只看懂了开头几个词。几分钟过去了，教室里鸦雀无声。在他旁边，罗恩心不在焉地把羽毛笔在手指上转来转去，眼睛呆呆地瞪着书上同一个地方。哈利把目光转向右边，猛地大吃一惊，一下子从麻木的状态中清醒过来。赫敏甚至没有打开她那本《魔法防御理论》。她眼睛一眨不眨地盯着乌姆里奇教授，一只手高高举起。

在哈利的记忆中，赫敏从来没在老师要求读书的时候不照着做，也从来没能抵挡住诱惑，不去翻开任何一本出现在她面前的书。哈利疑惑地看着她，但她只是微微摇了摇头，表示她现在不想回答问题，随即继续盯着乌姆里奇教授，而乌姆里奇教授的目光正同样坚定地望着别的方向。

又过了几分钟，注视着赫敏的可不止哈利一个人了。老师吩咐他们读的那一章实在太啰嗦乏味了，越来越多的同学都更愿意注视赫敏怎样不出声地吸引乌姆里奇教授的目光，而不愿再去吭哧吭哧地啃什么"入门基础原理"。

CHAPTER TWELVE Professor Umbridge

When more than half the class were staring at Hermione rather than at their books, Professor Umbridge seemed to decide that she could ignore the situation no longer.

'Did you want to ask something about the chapter, dear?' she asked Hermione, as though she had only just noticed her.

'Not about the chapter, no,' said Hermione.

'Well, we're reading just now,' said Professor Umbridge, showing her small pointed teeth. 'If you have other queries we can deal with them at the end of class.'

'I've got a query about your course aims,' said Hermione.

Professor Umbridge raised her eyebrows.

'And your name is?'

'Hermione Granger,' said Hermione.

'Well, Miss Granger, I think the course aims are perfectly clear if you read them through carefully,' said Professor Umbridge in a voice of determined sweetness.

'Well, I don't,' said Hermione bluntly. 'There's nothing written up there about *using* defensive spells.'

There was a short silence in which many members of the class turned their heads to frown at the three course aims still written on the blackboard.

'*Using* defensive spells?' Professor Umbridge repeated with a little laugh. 'Why, I can't imagine any situation arising in my classroom that would require you to use a defensive spell, Miss Granger. You surely aren't expecting to be attacked during class?'

'We're not going to use magic?' Ron exclaimed loudly.

'Students raise their hands when they wish to speak in my class, Mr –?'

'Weasley,' said Ron, thrusting his hand into the air.

Professor Umbridge, smiling still more widely, turned her back on him. Harry and Hermione immediately raised their hands too. Professor Umbridge's pouchy eyes lingered on Harry for a moment before she addressed Hermione.

'Yes, Miss Granger? You wanted to ask something else?'

'Yes,' said Hermione. 'Surely the whole point of Defence Against the Dark Arts is to practise defensive spells?'

第12章 乌姆里奇教授

后来，班上超过一半的同学都在盯着赫敏，而不是看着他们的课本，乌姆里奇教授似乎认为她再也不能对这种情况视而不见了。

"亲爱的，你是对这一章的内容有什么疑问吗？"她问赫敏，似乎刚刚注意到她。

"不，不是关于这一章的内容。"赫敏说。

"噢，我们现在是在读书，"乌姆里奇教授说，露出嘴里又小又尖的牙齿，"如果你有其他问题，我们可以下课再谈。"

"我对你的课程目标有一个疑问。"赫敏说。

乌姆里奇教授扬起了眉毛。

"你叫什么名字？"

"赫敏·格兰杰。"赫敏说。

"好吧，格兰杰小姐，我认为，这些课程目标写得非常清楚，只要你把它们从头到尾仔细读一遍。"乌姆里奇教授用坚定不移的嗲嗲的口吻说。

"可是，我不这么认为，"赫敏直言不讳地说，"那上面一个字也没有提到使用防御咒。"

一阵短暂的沉默，班里许多同学都扭过头去，皱着眉头看着仍然写在黑板上的三条课程目标。

"使用防御咒？"乌姆里奇教授轻声笑着重复道，"哎呀，我无法想象在我的课堂里会出现需要你们使用防御咒的情况，格兰杰小姐。你总不至于认为会在上课时受到攻击吧？"

"我们不使用魔法吗？"罗恩大声喊了一句。

"在我的班上，学生想讲话必须先举手，你是——"

"韦斯莱。"罗恩说着赶紧把手举了起来。

乌姆里奇教授笑得更慈祥了，但没有理会罗恩。哈利和赫敏马上也举起了手。乌姆里奇教授那双松泡泡的眼睛在哈利身上停留了一会儿，然后她对赫敏说：

"怎么，格兰杰小姐？你还有别的问题要问吗？"

"是的，"赫敏说，"黑魔法防御术的总体目标当然应该是练习防御咒，是吗？"

'Are you a Ministry-trained educational expert, Miss Granger?' asked Professor Umbridge, in her falsely sweet voice.

'No, but –'

'Well then, I'm afraid you are not qualified to decide what the "whole point" of any class is. Wizards much older and cleverer than you have devised our new programme of study. You will be learning about defensive spells in a secure, risk-free way –'

'What use is that?' said Harry loudly. 'If we're going to be attacked, it won't be in a –'

'*Hand*, Mr Potter!' sang Professor Umbridge.

Harry thrust his fist in the air. Again, Professor Umbridge promptly turned away from him, but now several other people had their hands up, too.

'And your name is?' Professor Umbridge said to Dean.

'Dean Thomas.'

'Well, Mr Thomas?'

'Well, it's like Harry said, isn't it?' said Dean. 'If we're going to be attacked, it won't be risk free.'

'I repeat,' said Professor Umbridge, smiling in a very irritating fashion at Dean, 'do you expect to be attacked during my classes?'

'No, but –'

Professor Umbridge talked over him. 'I do not wish to criticise the way things have been run in this school,' she said, an unconvincing smile stretching her wide mouth, 'but you have been exposed to some very irresponsible wizards in this class, very irresponsible indeed – not to mention,' she gave a nasty little laugh, 'extremely dangerous half-breeds.'

'If you mean Professor Lupin,' piped up Dean angrily, 'he was the best we ever –'

'*Hand*, Mr Thomas! As I was saying – you have been introduced to spells that have been complex, inappropriate to your age group and potentially lethal. You have been frightened into believing that you are likely to meet Dark attacks every other day –'

'No we haven't,' Hermione said, 'we just –'

'*Your hand is not up, Miss Granger!*'

第12章 乌姆里奇教授

"你是魔法部专门培训的教育专家吗,格兰杰小姐?"乌姆里奇教授用她那甜得发腻的假声音问。

"不是,但——"

"那好,我想你恐怕没有资格判断任何一门课的'总体目标'是什么。我们的最新学习计划,是由比你年长得多、聪明得多的巫师们设计制定的。你们将以一种安全的、没有风险的方式学习防御咒——"

"那有什么用呢?"哈利大声问,"如果我们受到攻击,那肯定不会是以一种——"

"举手,波特先生!"乌姆里奇教授用唱歌般的声音说。

哈利赶紧把手高高举起。乌姆里奇教授又故技重演,立刻转过脸去看别的地方,可是现在又有另外几个学生举起了手。

"你叫什么名字?"乌姆里奇教授问迪安。

"迪安·托马斯。"

"说吧,托马斯先生。"

"嗯,就像哈利说的那样,不是吗?"迪安说,"如果我们受到攻击,是不可能没有风险的。"

"我再说一遍,"乌姆里奇教授说,一边以那种特别令人恼火的方式朝迪安微笑着,"你认为在我的班上会受到攻击吗?"

"不会,可是——"

乌姆里奇教授的声音压过了迪安的声音。"我不愿意批评这个学校的一些办学方式,"她说,脸上堆起虚假的笑容,把那张阔嘴咧得更大了,"但是在这个班上你们接触了几位很不负责任的巫师,确实很不负责任——更不用说,"她发出一声刺耳的笑声,"还有特别危险的半人半兽。"

"如果你指的是卢平教授,"迪安气愤地说,"他可是我们遇到的最好的老师——"

"举手,托马斯先生!正如我刚才说的——他们给你们介绍的魔法都很复杂,不适合你们这个年龄段,而且具有极大的潜在危害。你们被吓得不轻,竟然以为自己三天两头就会遭到黑魔法的攻击——"

"不,我们没有,"赫敏说,"我们只是——"

"你没有举手,格兰杰小姐!"

CHAPTER TWELVE   Professor Umbridge

Hermione put up her hand. Professor Umbridge turned away from her.

'It is my understanding that my predecessor not only performed illegal curses in front of you, he actually performed them on you.'

'Well, he turned out to be a maniac, didn't he?' said Dean hotly. 'Mind you, we still learned loads.'

'*Your hand is not up, Mr Thomas!*' trilled Professor Umbridge. 'Now, it is the view of the Ministry that a theoretical knowledge will be more than sufficient to get you through your examination, which, after all, is what school is all about. And your name is?' she added, staring at Parvati, whose hand had just shot up.

'Parvati Patil, and isn't there a practical bit in our Defence Against the Dark Arts O.W.L.? Aren't we supposed to show that we can actually do the counter-curses and things?'

'As long as you have studied the theory hard enough, there is no reason why you should not be able to perform the spells under carefully controlled examination conditions,' said Professor Umbridge dismissively.

'Without ever practising them beforehand?' said Parvati incredulously. 'Are you telling us that the first time we'll get to do the spells will be during our exam?'

'I repeat, as long as you have studied the theory hard enough –'

'And what good's theory going to be in the real world?' said Harry loudly, his fist in the air again.

Professor Umbridge looked up.

'This is school, Mr Potter, not the real world,' she said softly.

'So we're not supposed to be prepared for what's waiting for us out there?'

'There is nothing waiting out there, Mr Potter.'

'Oh, yeah?' said Harry. His temper, which seemed to have been bubbling just beneath the surface all day, was reaching boiling point.

'Who do you imagine wants to attack children like yourselves?' enquired Professor Umbridge in a horribly honeyed voice.

'Hmm, let's think …' said Harry in a mock thoughtful voice. 'Maybe … *Lord Voldemort?*'

Ron gasped; Lavender Brown uttered a little scream; Neville slipped sideways off his stool. Professor Umbridge, however, did not flinch. She was

第12章 乌姆里奇教授

赫敏举起手,乌姆里奇教授转过脸去。

"据我所知,我的前任不仅在你们面前施用了非法的咒语,而且还在你们身上施用了这些咒语。"

"可是,后来发现他是个疯子嘛,是不是?"迪安气呼呼地说,"说实在的,我们仍然学到了不少东西呢。"

"你没有举手,托马斯先生!"乌姆里奇教授用颤颤的声音说,"好了,魔法部认为,理论知识足以帮助你们通过考试,说到底,让学生通过考试才是学校的宗旨所在。你叫什么名字?"她瞪着刚刚把手举起来的帕瓦蒂问道。

"帕瓦蒂·佩蒂尔。我们的黑魔法防御术课的考试里就没有一点实践性的内容吗?我们是不是应该显示出我们确实会施破解咒和其他魔法呢?"

"只要你们把理论学得非常扎实,就没有理由不会在严格控制的考试条件下施魔咒。"乌姆里奇教授轻蔑地说。

"事先不需要练习吗?"帕瓦蒂不敢相信地问,"难道你是在对我们说,我们第一次施那些魔咒就是在考试的时候吗?"

"我再说一遍,只要你们把理论学得非常扎实——"

"理论在现实世界里有什么用?"哈利又把拳头高高举起,大声问道。

乌姆里奇教授抬起目光。

"这是学校,波特先生,不是现实世界。"她轻声说。

"那么我们不需要做好准备,迎接等在外面的一切吗?"

"没有什么等在外面,波特先生。"

"哦,是吗?"哈利说。他的火气一整天都在内心暗暗翻腾,此刻已临近爆发点。

"你想象谁会来攻击你们这样的小孩子呢?"乌姆里奇教授用亲昵得可怕的声音问道。

"嗯,让我想想……"哈利用假装若有所思的口吻说,"也许……伏地魔?"

罗恩倒吸一口冷气,拉文德·布朗发出一声低低的尖叫,纳威一歪身从板凳上摔了下去,然而乌姆里奇教授却没有显出害怕的样子。

staring at Harry with a grimly satisfied expression on her face.

'Ten points from Gryffindor, Mr Potter.'

The classroom was silent and still. Everyone was staring at either Umbridge or Harry.

'Now, let me make a few things quite plain.'

Professor Umbridge stood up and leaned towards them, her stubby-fingered hands splayed on her desk.

'You have been told that a certain Dark wizard has returned from the dead –'

'He wasn't dead,' said Harry angrily, 'but yeah, he's returned!'

'Mr-Potter-you-have-already-lost-your-house-ten-points-do-not-make-matters-worse-for-yourself,' said Professor Umbridge in one breath without looking at him. 'As I was saying, you have been informed that a certain Dark wizard is at large once again. *This is a lie.*'

'It is NOT a lie!' said Harry. 'I saw him, I fought him!'

'Detention, Mr Potter!' said Professor Umbridge triumphantly. 'Tomorrow evening. Five o'clock. My office. I repeat, *this is a lie*. The Ministry of Magic guarantees that you are not in danger from any Dark wizard. If you are still worried, by all means come and see me outside class hours. If someone is alarming you with fibs about reborn Dark wizards, I would like to hear about it. I am here to help. I am your friend. And now, you will kindly continue your reading. Page five, "Basics for Beginners".'

Professor Umbridge sat down behind her desk. Harry, however, stood up. Everyone was staring at him; Seamus looked half scared, half fascinated.

'Harry, no!' Hermione whispered in a warning voice, tugging at his sleeve, but Harry jerked his arm out of her reach.

'So, according to you, Cedric Diggory dropped dead of his own accord, did he?' Harry asked, his voice shaking.

There was a collective intake of breath from the class, for none of them, apart from Ron and Hermione, had ever heard Harry talk about what had happened on the night Cedric had died. They stared avidly from Harry to Professor Umbridge, who had raised her eyes and was staring at him without a trace of a fake smile on her face.

'Cedric Diggory's death was a tragic accident,' she said coldly.

第12章 乌姆里奇教授

她只是盯着哈利,脸上露出一种恶狠狠的心满意足的表情。

"格兰芬多扣十分,波特先生。"

教室里一片沉默和寂静。大家要么盯着乌姆里奇,要么盯着哈利。

"好了,让我把几件事情弄弄清楚。"

乌姆里奇教授站了起来,身体朝前探着,两只手指短粗的手掌按在讲台上。

"有人告诉你们说,某个黑巫师死而复生了——"

"他没有死,"哈利生气地说,"但是没错,他回来了!"

"波特先生,你已经让你们学院丢了十分,别再把事情越弄越糟。"乌姆里奇教授一口气说完这句话,眼睛看也没看哈利,"正如我刚才说的,有人对你们说,某个黑巫师又出来活动了。这是无稽之谈。"

"这**不是**无稽之谈!"哈利说,"我看见他了,我跟他搏斗了!"

"关禁闭,波特先生!"乌姆里奇教授得意扬扬地说,"明天傍晚。五点钟。在我的办公室。我再说一遍,这是无稽之谈。魔法部保证你们不会遇到来自任何黑巫师的危险。如果你们仍然心存疑虑,请务必在课后来找我。如果有人用黑巫师死而复生的鬼话吓唬你们,我倒很愿意听一听。我随时准备帮助你们。我是你们的朋友。好了,请大家继续阅读第五页,入门基本原理。"

乌姆里奇教授在她的讲台后面坐下了。哈利却站了起来。同学们都呆呆地望着他,西莫看上去半是害怕半是好奇。

"哈利,不要!"赫敏小声警告道,拉了拉他的衣袖。但哈利一甩胳膊,不想让她够到。

"那么,照你的说法,塞德里克·迪戈里是自己死掉的喽?"哈利问,他的声音微微发颤。

全班同学同时倒吸了一口冷气,因为除了罗恩和赫敏,他们谁都没有听哈利谈论过塞德里克遇难那天夜里发生的事情。他们急切地望望哈利,又望望乌姆里奇教授,只见她抬起眼睛盯着哈利,脸上再也看不见一丝假笑了。

"塞德里克·迪戈里的死是一场不幸的事故。"她冷冷地说。

CHAPTER TWELVE   Professor Umbridge

'It was murder,' said Harry. He could feel himself shaking. He had hardly spoken to anyone about this, least of all thirty eagerly listening classmates. 'Voldemort killed him and you know it.'

Professor Umbridge's face was quite blank. For a moment, Harry thought she was going to scream at him. Then she said, in her softest, most sweetly girlish voice, 'Come here, Mr Potter, dear.'

He kicked his chair aside, strode around Ron and Hermione and up to the teacher's desk. He could feel the rest of the class holding its breath. He felt so angry he did not care what happened next.

Professor Umbridge pulled a small roll of pink parchment out of her handbag, stretched it out on the desk, dipped her quill into a bottle of ink and started scribbling, hunched over so that Harry could not see what she was writing. Nobody spoke. After a minute or so she rolled up the parchment and tapped it with her wand; it sealed itself seamlessly so that he could not open it.

'Take this to Professor McGonagall, dear,' said Professor Umbridge, holding out the note to him.

He took it from her without saying a word and left the room, not even looking back at Ron and Hermione, slamming the classroom door shut behind him. He walked very fast along the corridor, the note to McGonagall clutched tight in his hand, and turning a corner walked slap into Peeves the poltergeist, a wide-mouthed little man floating on his back in midair, juggling several ink-wells.

'Why, it's Potty Wee Potter!' cackled Peeves, allowing two of the inkwells to fall to the ground where they smashed and spattered the walls with ink; Harry jumped backwards out of the way with a snarl.

'Get out of it, Peeves.'

'Oooh, Crackpot's feeling cranky,' said Peeves, pursuing Harry along the corridor, leering as he zoomed along above him. 'What is it this time, my fine Potty friend? Hearing voices? Seeing visions? Speaking in –' Peeves blew a gigantic raspberry '– *tongues*?'

'I said, leave me ALONE!' Harry shouted, running down the nearest flight of stairs, but Peeves merely slid down the banister on his back beside him.

第12章 乌姆里奇教授

"是谋杀。"哈利说。他感觉到自己浑身发抖。他几乎没有跟任何人谈过这件事,更不用说当着三十个竖起耳朵聆听的同学的面。"伏地魔杀死了他,你明明知道。"

乌姆里奇教授的脸上毫无表情。有那么一刻,哈利还以为她要冲自己失声尖叫呢。可接着她用那种最最温柔、最最嗲声嗲气的小姑娘一般的声音说道:"过来,波特先生,亲爱的。"

哈利把椅子踢到一边,从罗恩和赫敏身边绕过,走向讲台。他可以感觉到全班同学都屏住了呼吸。他实在太气愤了,根本不在乎接下来会发生什么。

乌姆里奇教授从她的手提包里抽出一卷粉红色的羊皮纸,在讲台上摊平,用她的羽毛笔在墨水瓶里蘸了蘸,匆匆地写了起来。她身子俯在讲台上,因此哈利看不见她在写什么。谁也没有说话。过了一分钟左右,她卷起羊皮纸,用魔杖敲了一下,羊皮纸就自动牢牢地封死了,使哈利无法打开。

"亲爱的,把这个拿给麦格教授。"乌姆里奇教授说着把羊皮纸递给了哈利。

哈利一言不发,从她手里接过羊皮纸,也没有回头看一眼罗恩和赫敏就离开了教室,反手把门重重地关上了。他顺着走廊飞快地往前走,手里攥着给麦格教授的便条。转过一个拐角,他猛地撞上了恶作剧精灵皮皮鬼。他是个长着一张阔嘴巴的小个子男人,正平躺着悬在空中,像玩杂技一样抛接着几个墨水池。

"哎呀,是傻宝宝波特!"皮皮鬼咯咯笑着说,让两个墨水池落到地上摔得粉碎,墨水溅到了墙上。哈利赶紧往后一躲,大吼一声:

"滚开,皮皮鬼!"

"哎哟,怪人儿发怪脾气了。"皮皮鬼说,在走廊上追着哈利,在他上方往前飞,一边调皮地斜眼看着他,"这次又犯了什么事儿,我亲爱的傻宝宝朋友?脑子里听见声音啦?眼前有幻觉啦?又开始说——"皮皮鬼大声地嘘了一声,"——怪腔啦?"

"我说了,别来**烦**我!"哈利大喊一声,转身跑下离他最近的一道楼梯,但皮皮鬼平躺在他旁边的栏杆上也滑了下来。

> '*Oh, most think he's barking, the potty wee lad,*
> *But some are more kindly and think he's just sad,*
> *But Peevesy knows better and says that he's mad –*'

'SHUT UP!'

A door to his left flew open and Professor McGonagall emerged from her office looking grim and slightly harassed.

'What on *earth* are you shouting about, Potter?' she snapped, as Peeves cackled gleefully and zoomed out of sight. 'Why aren't you in class?'

'I've been sent to see you,' said Harry stiffly.

'Sent? What do you mean, *sent?*'

He held out the note from Professor Umbridge. Professor McGonagall took it from him, frowning, slit it open with a tap of her wand, stretched it out and began to read. Her eyes zoomed from side to side behind their square spectacles as she read what Umbridge had written, and with each line they became narrower.

'Come in here, Potter.'

He followed her inside her study. The door closed automatically behind him.

'Well?' said Professor McGonagall, rounding on him. 'Is this true?'

'Is what true?' Harry asked, rather more aggressively than he had intended. 'Professor?' he added, in an attempt to sound more polite.

'Is it true that you shouted at Professor Umbridge?'

'Yes,' said Harry.

'You called her a liar?'

'Yes.'

'You told her He Who Must Not Be Named is back?'

'Yes.'

Professor McGonagall sat down behind her desk, frowning at Harry. Then she said, 'Have a biscuit, Potter.'

'Have – what?'

'Have a biscuit,' she repeated impatiently, indicating a tartan tin lying on top of one of the piles of papers on her desk. 'And sit down.'

第12章 乌姆里奇教授

哦，好多人以为他脾气暴，波特波特傻宝宝，
有些人心肠不算坏，知道他只是太悲哀，
皮皮鬼心里最清楚，说他是发疯犯糊涂——

"闭嘴！"

他左边的一扇门突然打开，麦格教授从她的办公室里走了出来，神色严峻，微微透着疲惫。

"你到底在嚷嚷什么，波特？"她厉声问道，皮皮鬼开心地咯咯笑着，嗖的一下消失了，"你怎么不去上课？"

"我被打发来见你。"哈利生硬地说。

"打发？你这是什么意思，打发？"

哈利把乌姆里奇教授的便条递过去，麦格教授从他手里接过，皱着眉头，用魔杖一敲把封口撕开，展开读了起来。她读着乌姆里奇写的文字，眼睛在方方的镜片后面飞快地来回移动，每读完一行，眼睛就眯得更紧一些。

"进来，波特。"

哈利跟着麦格教授走进她的办公室。门在他身后自动关上了。

"怎么回事？"麦格教授突然厉声对他说，"这是真的吗？"

"什么是真的？"哈利问，语气咄咄逼人，他本来不想这样的。"教授？"他又找补了一句，努力使声音听上去礼貌一点儿。

"你真的冲乌姆里奇教授大吼大叫了？"

"是的。"哈利说。

"你说她是个骗子？"

"是的。"

"你告诉她那个连名字都不能提的人回来了？"

"是的。"

麦格教授在她的书桌后坐了下来，紧皱眉头望着哈利。然后她说："吃一块饼干吧，波特。"

"吃——什么？"

"吃一块饼干，"她不耐烦地又说了一遍，指着桌上一堆文件上的一个彩格图案的饼干盒，"坐下吧。"

CHAPTER TWELVE   Professor Umbridge

There had been a previous occasion when Harry, expecting to be caned by Professor McGonagall, had instead been appointed by her to the Gryffindor Quidditch team. He sank into a chair opposite her and helped himself to a Ginger Newt, feeling just as confused and wrong-footed as he had done on that occasion.

Professor McGonagall set down Professor Umbridge's note and looked very seriously at Harry.

'Potter, you need to be careful.'

Harry swallowed his mouthful of Ginger Newt and stared at her. Her tone of voice was not at all what he was used to; it was not brisk, crisp and stern; it was low and anxious and somehow much more human than usual.

'Misbehaviour in Dolores Umbridge's class could cost you much more than house points and a detention.'

'What do you –?'

'Potter, use your common sense,' snapped Professor McGonagall, with an abrupt return to her usual manner. 'You know where she comes from, you must know to whom she is reporting.'

The bell rang for the end of the lesson. Overhead and all around came the elephantine sounds of hundreds of students on the move.

'It says here she's given you detention every evening this week, starting tomorrow,' Professor McGonagall said, looking down at Umbridge's note again.

'Every evening this week!' Harry repeated, horrified. 'But, Professor, couldn't you –?'

'No, I couldn't,' said Professor McGonagall flatly.

'But –'

'She is your teacher and has every right to give you detention. You will go to her room at five o'clock tomorrow for the first one. Just remember: tread carefully around Dolores Umbridge.'

'But I was telling the truth!' said Harry, outraged. 'Voldemort is back, you know he is; Professor Dumbledore knows he is –'

'For heaven's sake, Potter!' said Professor McGonagall, straightening her glasses angrily (she had winced horribly when he had used Voldemort's name). 'Do you really think this is about truth or lies? It's about keeping your head down and your temper under control!'

第12章 乌姆里奇教授

以前曾经有过一次,哈利原以为要被麦格教授狠狠教训一顿,结果却被她选进了格兰芬多学院的魁地奇球队。此刻他坐在麦格教授对面的椅子上,自己拿了一块生姜蝶蛹饼干,感觉就像那次一样迷惑不解,不知所措。

麦格教授放下乌姆里奇教授的便条,非常严肃地望着哈利。

"波特,你需要小心哪。"

哈利咽下嘴里的生姜蝶蛹饼干,瞪着她。她的语气跟他以前所熟悉的完全不同。不再那么敏捷、干脆和严厉,而是低沉的、忧心忡忡的,似乎比平常更有人情味。

"在多洛雷斯·乌姆里奇的课上不守纪律,你付出的代价可能要比学院扣分和关禁闭严重得多。"

"你这是什么——"

"波特,用你的常识想一想,"麦格教授厉声地说,突然又恢复了她平常的腔调,"你知道她是什么来头,你一定知道她会去向谁汇报。"

下课铃响了。他们的头顶上和周围响起几百个学生同时走动的嘈杂声。

"这里写着,她这个星期每天晚上都要罚你关禁闭,从明天开始。"麦格教授又低头看了看乌姆里奇的便条,说道。

"这星期每天晚上!"哈利重复了一遍,简直被吓坏了,"可是,教授,难道你——"

"不行,我不能。"麦格教授断然地说。

"可是——"

"她是你的老师,她完全有权罚你关禁闭。你明天下午五点钟到她办公室去,开始第一次。记住:在多洛雷斯·乌姆里奇身边要千万留神。"

"可我说的是实话!"哈利愤愤不平地说,"伏地魔回来了,你知道的。邓布利多教授也知道他已经——"

"看在老天的分儿上,波特!"麦格教授生气地正了正眼镜,说道(刚才她听见哈利说出伏地魔的名字,脸部肌肉很厉害地抽搐了一下),"你真的以为问题在于说实话还是说谎话吗?问题在于你必须低着头做人,尽量不招惹麻烦,管好你自己的脾气!"

She stood up, nostrils wide and mouth very thin, and Harry stood up, too.

'Have another biscuit,' she said irritably, thrusting the tin at him.

'No, thanks,' said Harry coldly.

'Don't be ridiculous,' she snapped.

He took one.

'Thanks,' he said grudgingly.

'Didn't you listen to Dolores Umbridge's speech at the start-of-term feast, Potter?'

'Yeah,' said Harry. 'Yeah ... she said ... progress will be prohibited or ... well, it meant that ... that the Ministry of Magic is trying to interfere at Hogwarts.'

Professor McGonagall eyed him for a moment, then sniffed, walked around her desk and held open the door for him.

'Well, I'm glad you listen to Hermione Granger at any rate,' she said, pointing him out of her office.

她站了起来,鼻孔张得大大的,嘴唇抿得紧紧的,哈利也跟着站了起来。

"再吃一块饼干吧。"她烦躁地说,把饼干盒推给了哈利。

"不用了,谢谢。"哈利冷冷地回答。

"别犯傻啦。"她厉声道。

哈利拿了一块。

"谢谢。"他满不情愿地说。

"多洛雷斯·乌姆里奇在开学宴会上的讲话你没有听吗,波特?"

"听了,"哈利说,"听了……她说……进步将被禁止……嗯,这就说明……说明魔法部企图干涉霍格沃茨。"

麦格教授打量他片刻,然后从鼻子里哼了一声,绕过桌子,为他打开了房门。

"好吧,不管怎么说,我很高兴你至少听了赫敏·格兰杰的话。"她说,示意哈利离开她的办公室。

CHAPTER THIRTEEN

Detention with Dolores

Dinner in the Great Hall that night was not a pleasant experience for Harry. The news about his shouting match with Umbridge had travelled exceptionally fast even by Hogwarts' standards. He heard whispers all around him as he sat eating between Ron and Hermione. The funny thing was that none of the whisperers seemed to mind him overhearing what they were saying about him. On the contrary, it was as though they were hoping he would get angry and start shouting again, so that they could hear his story firsthand.

'He says he saw Cedric Diggory murdered ...'

'He reckons he duelled with You-Know-Who ...'

'Come off it ...'

'Who does he think he's kidding?'

'Pur-*lease* ...'

'What I don't get,' said Harry in a shaking voice, laying down his knife and fork (his hands were trembling too much to hold them steady), 'is why they all believed the story two months ago when Dumbledore told them ...'

'The thing is, Harry, I'm not sure they did,' said Hermione grimly. 'Oh, let's get out of here.'

She slammed down her own knife and fork; Ron looked longingly at his half-finished apple pie but followed suit. People stared at them all the way out of the Hall.

'What d'you mean, you're not sure they believed Dumbledore?' Harry asked Hermione when they reached the first-floor landing.

'Look, you don't understand what it was like after it happened,' said Hermione quietly. 'You arrived back in the middle of the lawn clutching

第 13 章

被多洛雷斯关禁闭

对哈利来说，那天晚上在礼堂吃晚饭可不是一次愉快的经历。他和乌姆里奇大吵一架的消息不胫而走，即使按霍格沃茨的标准衡量，这样的传播速度也是快得出奇。当他坐在罗恩和赫敏中间开始吃饭时，看见周围的人都在窃窃私语。有趣的是，那些交头接耳的人似乎谁也不在乎他会不会听见他们的议论。恰恰相反，他们好像巴不得他动怒，再次嚷嚷起来，这样他们就能亲耳听到他是怎么说的了。

"他说他看见塞德里克·迪戈里被杀害……"

"他以为自己跟神秘人决斗来着……"

"快别胡扯了……"

"他以为自己在蒙谁呢？"

"饶了我吧……"

"我不明白的是，"哈利放下手里的餐具，声音颤抖地说（他的手抖得太厉害，刀叉都拿不稳了），"两个月前邓布利多告诉他们这件事时，他们怎么就都相信了呢……"

"问题是，哈利，我不敢肯定他们当时是不是相信了。"赫敏神色严峻地说，"哦，我们快离开这儿吧。"

她重重地放下刀叉，罗恩恋恋不舍地看了看刚吃了一半的苹果馅饼，但还是照着做了。人们一直盯着他们走出了礼堂。

"你是什么意思，你不敢肯定他们是不是相信邓布利多？"他们来到二楼的楼梯平台时，哈利问赫敏。

"唉，其实你并不明白事情发生以后是什么情况。"赫敏轻声说，"你从草地中央回来了，怀里抱着塞德里克的尸体……我们谁都没有看见

CHAPTER THIRTEEN Detention with Dolores

Cedric's dead body ... none of us saw what happened in the maze ... we just had Dumbledore's word for it that You-Know-Who had come back and killed Cedric and fought you.'

'Which is the truth!' said Harry loudly.

'I know it is, Harry, so will you *please* stop biting my head off?' said Hermione wearily. 'It's just that before the truth could sink in, everyone went home for the summer, where they spent two months reading about how you're a nutcase and Dumbledore's going senile!'

Rain pounded on the windowpanes as they strode along the empty corridors back to Gryffindor Tower. Harry felt as though his first day had lasted a week, but he still had a mountain of homework to do before bed. A dull pounding pain was developing over his right eye. He glanced out of a rain-washed window at the dark grounds as they turned into the Fat Lady's corridor. There was still no light in Hagrid's cabin.

'*Mimbulus mimbletonia,*' said Hermione, before the Fat Lady could ask. The portrait swung open to reveal the hole behind it and the three of them scrambled through it.

The common room was almost empty; nearly everyone was still down at dinner. Crookshanks uncoiled himself from an armchair and trotted to meet them, purring loudly, and when Harry, Ron and Hermione took their three favourite chairs at the fireside he leapt lightly on to Hermione's lap and curled up there like a furry ginger cushion. Harry gazed into the flames, feeling drained and exhausted.

'*How* can Dumbledore have let this happen?' Hermione cried suddenly, making Harry and Ron jump; Crookshanks leapt off her, looking affronted. She pounded the arms of her chair in fury, so that bits of stuffing leaked out of the holes. 'How can he let that terrible woman teach us? And in our O.W.L. year, too!'

'Well, we've never had great Defence Against the Dark Arts teachers, have we?' said Harry. 'You know what it's like, Hagrid told us, nobody wants the job; they say it's jinxed.'

'Yes, but to employ someone who's actually refusing to let us do magic! *What's* Dumbledore playing at?'

'And she's trying to get people to spy for her,' said Ron darkly. 'Remember

第13章 被多洛雷斯关禁闭

迷宫里发生的一切……只是听邓布利多说神秘人回来了，杀死了塞德里克，还跟你展开了搏斗。"

"那是事实！"哈利大声说。

"我知道是事实，哈利，你能不能不要这样冲我大声嚷嚷？"赫敏疲倦地说，"实际上，大家还没完全理解这个事实，就都回家过暑假了。整整两个月的时间，他们读到的都是你是个疯子，邓布利多是个老糊涂！"

他们大步走在空荡荡的走廊上，返回格兰芬多的塔楼。雨水啪啪地敲打着窗户玻璃。哈利觉得这开学的第一天好像持续了一个星期，而他睡觉前还要完成那么一大堆家庭作业。他的右眼上方开始一跳一跳地疼。当他们拐进胖夫人的那条走廊时，他透过被雨水冲刷过的窗户望着外面黑黢黢的场地。海格的小屋里仍然没有灯光。

"米布米宝。"赫敏不等胖夫人开口发问就说道。肖像弹开，露出后面的洞口，他们三个爬了进去。

公共休息室里几乎空无一人，差不多所有的同学都还在下面吃晚饭。克鲁克山在一把扶手椅上舒展身体，小跑着过来迎接他们，发出很响的呼噜呼噜的喘息声。哈利、罗恩和赫敏在炉火旁他们最喜欢的三把椅子上坐定后，它轻盈地跳到赫敏的膝头，把身体蜷成一个毛茸茸的姜黄色坐垫。哈利望着火苗出神，感到极度疲倦，所有的精力都耗光了。

"邓布利多怎么能让这种事情发生呢？"赫敏突然嚷了起来，把哈利和罗恩吓了一跳。克鲁克山从她身上跳开，一副受到冒犯的样子。赫敏气愤地敲打着椅子的扶手，里面填塞的东西从破洞里漏了出来。"他怎么能让那个可怕的女人教我们呢？而且还在我们参加 O.W.L. 考试的这一年！"

"唉，我们的黑魔法防御术课从来就没有过像样的老师，是不是？"哈利说，"你知道是怎么回事，海格告诉过我们，谁也不愿意接这个活儿，他们说这份工作中了恶咒。"

"这倒也是，可是居然聘请了一位根本不让我们施魔法的人！邓布利多在玩什么把戏？"

"那女人还想让别人给她当密探。"罗恩郁闷地说，"记得吗，她说

CHAPTER THIRTEEN   Detention with Dolores

when she said she wanted us to come and tell her if we hear anyone saying You-Know-Who's back?'

'Of course she's here to spy on us all, that's obvious, why else would Fudge have wanted her to come?' snapped Hermione.

'Don't start arguing again,' said Harry wearily, as Ron opened his mouth to retaliate. 'Can't we just ... let's just do that homework, get it out of the way ...'

They collected their schoolbags from a corner and returned to the chairs by the fire. People were coming back from dinner now. Harry kept his face averted from the portrait hole, but could still sense the stares he was attracting.

'Shall we do Snape's stuff first?' said Ron, dipping his quill into his ink. '"*The properties ... of moonstone ... and its uses ... in potion-making ...*"' he muttered, writing the words across the top of his parchment as he spoke them. 'There.' He underlined the title, then looked up expectantly at Hermione.

'So, what are the properties of moonstone and its uses in potion-making?'

But Hermione was not listening; she was squinting over into the far corner of the room, where Fred, George and Lee Jordan were now sitting at the centre of a knot of innocent-looking first-years, all of whom were chewing something that seemed to have come out of a large paper bag that Fred was holding.

'No, I'm sorry, they've gone too far,' she said, standing up and looking positively furious. 'Come on, Ron.'

'I – what?' said Ron, plainly playing for time. 'No – come on, Hermione – we can't tell them off for giving out sweets.'

'You know perfectly well that those are bits of Nosebleed Nougat or – or Puking Pastilles or –'

'Fainting Fancies?' Harry suggested quietly.

One by one, as though hit over the head with an invisible mallet, the first-years were slumping unconscious in their seats; some slid right on to the floor, others merely hung over the arms of their chairs, their tongues lolling out. Most of the people watching were laughing; Hermione, however, squared her shoulders and marched directly over to where Fred and George now stood with clipboards, closely observing the unconscious first-years. Ron

第13章 被多洛雷斯关禁闭

如果我们听见有谁说神秘人回来了,她希望我们去向她汇报。"

"她来这儿当然就是为了刺探我们大家的,这还用说吗,不然福吉要她来做什么?"赫敏怒声说道。

"别再吵架了,"罗恩正想张嘴反驳,哈利疲倦地说,"我们能不能……能不能现在就做家庭作业,早做完早省心……"

他们从墙角拿来书包,回到炉火旁的椅子上。这时候同学们陆续吃完饭回来了。哈利侧着脸,尽量不去看肖像洞口,但仍然能感觉到大家都在盯着他。

"我们先写斯内普的那篇吧?"罗恩说着给他的羽毛笔蘸了蘸墨水,"月长石的……特性……以及它在……制药方面的……用途……"他低声嘟哝着,把这些字写在羊皮纸的最上面。"好了。"他在标题下面画了道横线,抬头满怀期待地望着赫敏。

"那么,月长石的特性以及它在制药方面的用途是什么呢?"

可是赫敏根本没听,她正眯起眼睛看着房间那头的角落,只见弗雷德、乔治和李·乔丹正坐在一群看上去天真幼稚的一年级新生中间,每个新生嘴里都在嚼着什么东西,看样子是从弗雷德手里提的那个大纸口袋里拿出来的。

"不行,对不起,他们实在太过分了。"赫敏说着腾地站起身,一副怒不可遏的样子,"来,罗恩。"

"我——干吗?"罗恩说,显然是在拖延时间,"不——算啦,赫敏——我们总不能因为他们发糖给别人吃,就训斥他们吧。"

"你心里很清楚,那些是鼻血牛轧糖,要么——要么就是吐吐糖,要么——"

"昏迷花糖?"哈利小声提醒道。

那些一年级新生就像被一把无形的大锤砸了一下脑袋,一个个在座位上昏了过去。有的扑通滑到了地上,有的只是瘫倒在椅子的扶手上,舌头伸得老长。在一旁观看的人多数都哈哈大笑起来,赫敏则挺起胸膛,大步流星地直冲弗雷德和乔治走去,这会儿他们正拿着带弹簧夹的写字板站在那里,仔细观察那些神志不清的一年级新生。罗恩的身体从椅子上抬起一半,迟疑地悬在那儿片刻,然后低声对哈利说:"她已经

435

CHAPTER THIRTEEN   Detention with Dolores

rose halfway out of his chair, hovered uncertainly for a moment or two, then muttered to Harry, 'She's got it under control,' before sinking as low in his chair as his lanky frame permitted.

'That's enough!' Hermione said forcefully to Fred and George, both of whom looked up in mild surprise.

'Yeah, you're right,' said George, nodding, 'this dosage looks strong enough, doesn't it?'

'I told you this morning, you can't test your rubbish on students!'

'We're paying them!' said Fred indignantly.

'I don't care, it could be dangerous!'

'Rubbish,' said Fred.

'Calm down, Hermione, they're fine!' said Lee reassuringly as he walked from first-year to first-year, inserting purple sweets into their open mouths.

'Yeah, look, they're coming round now,' said George.

A few of the first-years were indeed stirring. Several looked so shocked to find themselves lying on the floor, or dangling off their chairs, that Harry was sure Fred and George had not warned them what the sweets were going to do.

'Feel all right?' said George kindly to a small dark-haired girl lying at his feet.

'I – I think so,' she said shakily.

'Excellent,' said Fred happily, but the next second Hermione had snatched both his clipboard and the paper bag of Fainting Fancies from his hands.

'It is NOT excellent!'

'Course it is, they're alive, aren't they?' said Fred angrily.

'You can't do this, what if you made one of them really ill?'

'We're not going to make them ill, we've already tested them all on ourselves, this is just to see if everyone reacts the same –'

'If you don't stop doing it, I'm going to –'

'Put us in detention?' said Fred, in an I'd-like-to-see-you-try-it voice.

'Make us write lines?' said George, smirking.

Onlookers all over the room were laughing. Hermione drew herself up to

436

控制住了。"接着他把瘦长的身体尽量压得低低的,缩在椅子里。

"够了!"赫敏威严地对弗雷德和乔治说,他们俩都微微吃惊地抬起头来。

"是啊,你说得对,"乔治点点头说,"这个剂量看来是够劲儿了,是不是?"

"今天早晨我已经对你们说过了,不许在同学身上试验你们的这堆垃圾!"

"我们付钱给他们了!"弗雷德不服气地说。

"我不管,这可能很危险!"

"胡扯。"弗雷德说。

"冷静点儿,赫敏,不会有事儿的!"李·乔丹宽慰她说,一边在那些一年级新生中间走来走去,把紫色的糖果塞进他们张开的嘴巴里。

"是啊,你看,他们现在都醒过来了。"乔治说。

有几个新生确实开始动弹了。看到自己躺在地板上或瘫软在椅子上,显得非常震惊,因此哈利可以肯定,弗雷德和乔治事先并没有告诉他们这些糖是做什么用的。

"感觉还好吧?"乔治亲切地问躺在他脚下的一个黑头发的小个子女生。

"我——我想是吧。"女生颤抖着说。

"太棒了。"弗雷德高兴地说,可是紧接着赫敏就把他的写字板和那一袋昏迷花糖都夺了过去。

"根本**不是**太棒了!"

"当然是太棒了,他们都还活着,是不是?"弗雷德生气地说。

"你们不能这么做,万一害得他们中间有谁患上重病呢?"

"不会让他们得病的,这些糖我们已经在自己身上试验过了,现在只想看看是不是每个人的反应都一样——"

"如果你们不停止这么做,我就要——"

"罚我们关禁闭?"弗雷德说,声音里透着一种"我倒要看你敢不敢"的意思。

"罚我们写句子?"乔治嘲笑着说。

房间里在一旁观看的人都笑了起来。赫敏尽量把身体挺得笔直,

CHAPTER THIRTEEN   Detention with Dolores

her full height; her eyes were narrowed and her bushy hair seemed to crackle with electricity.

'No,' she said, her voice quivering with anger, 'but I will write to your mother.'

'You wouldn't,' said George, horrified, taking a step back from her.

'Oh, yes, I would,' said Hermione grimly. 'I can't stop you eating the stupid things yourselves, but you're not to give them to the first-years.'

Fred and George looked thunderstruck. It was clear that as far as they were concerned, Hermione's threat was way below the belt. With a last threatening look at them, she thrust Fred's clipboard and the bag of Fancies back into his arms, and stalked back to her chair by the fire.

Ron was now so low in his seat that his nose was roughly level with his knees.

'Thank you for your support, Ron,' Hermione said acidly.

'You handled it fine by yourself,' Ron mumbled.

Hermione stared down at her blank piece of parchment for a few seconds, then said edgily, 'Oh, it's no good, I can't concentrate now. I'm going to bed.'

She wrenched her bag open; Harry thought she was about to put her books away, but instead she pulled out two misshapen woolly objects, placed them carefully on a table by the fireplace, covered them with a few screwed-up bits of parchment and a broken quill and stood back to admire the effect.

'What in the name of Merlin are you doing?' said Ron, watching her as though fearful for her sanity.

'They're hats for house-elves,' she said briskly, now stuffing her books back into her bag. 'I did them over the summer. I'm a really slow knitter without magic but now I'm back at school I should be able to make lots more.'

'You're leaving out hats for the house-elves?' said Ron slowly. 'And you're covering them up with rubbish first?'

'Yes,' said Hermione defiantly, swinging her bag on to her back.

'That's not on,' said Ron angrily. 'You're trying to trick them into picking up the hats. You're setting them free when they might not want to be free.'

'Of course they want to be free!' said Hermione at once, though her face was turning pink. 'Don't you dare touch those hats, Ron!'

眯起眼睛，一头毛蓬蓬的头发似乎噼噼啪啪地闪着电光。

"不，"她说，声音因愤怒而微微发抖，"但我要写信给你们的妈妈。"

"你不会的。"乔治说，大惊失色地从她面前退后了一步。

"哦，会的，我会写的。"赫敏毫不含糊地说，"我无法阻止你们自己吃这些无聊的玩意儿，但你们不能把它们拿给一年级新生。"

弗雷德和乔治看样子完全被吓坏了。显然，在他们看来，赫敏的威胁是很阴险的一招。赫敏最后又狠狠地瞪了他们一眼，把弗雷德的写字板和那一袋花糖塞进他怀里，然后大步走回她炉火旁的椅子前。

这时候，罗恩在座位上把身体埋得低低的，鼻子差不多跟膝盖平行了。

"感谢你的支持，罗恩。"赫敏刻薄地说。

"你自己处理得很好嘛。"罗恩嘟哝了一句。

赫敏瞪着面前空白的羊皮纸，愣了几秒钟，然后烦躁地说："哦，没有用，我现在没法集中思想。我去睡觉了。"

她猛地打开书包，哈利以为她要把书本收起来，没想到她掏出了两件奇形怪状的羊毛织的东西，把它们小心地放在壁炉旁边的一张桌子上，并用几张皱巴巴的羊皮纸和一支破羽毛笔盖住，然后退后一步看看效果。

"我的天哪，你这到底是在做什么呀？"罗恩说，呆呆地望着她，好像怀疑她头脑是不是清醒。

"这些是给家养小精灵的帽子，"她轻快地说，现在才开始把书本塞进书包，"我暑假里织的。不用魔法，我织东西实在太慢了，现在回到了学校，应该能够再织出一大批了。"

"你要把帽子留给家养小精灵？"罗恩慢慢地问，"还用垃圾把它们先盖起来？"

"是的。"赫敏毫不示弱地说，把书包甩到了背后。

"那是行不通的，"罗恩气呼呼地说，"你不能欺骗他们捡起这些帽子。你给他们自由，他们也许并不想得到自由。"

"他们当然想得到自由！"赫敏不假思索地说，但脸色转成了粉红色，"你敢碰一碰那些帽子试试，罗恩！"

439

CHAPTER THIRTEEN   Detention with Dolores

She left. Ron waited until she had disappeared through the door to the girls' dormitories, then cleared the rubbish off the woolly hats.

'They should at least see what they're picking up,' he said firmly. 'Anyway ...' he rolled up the parchment on which he had written the title of Snape's essay, 'there's no point trying to finish this now, I can't do it without Hermione, I haven't got a clue what you're supposed to do with moonstones, have you?'

Harry shook his head, noticing as he did so that the ache in his right temple was getting worse. He thought of the long essay on giant wars and the pain stabbed at him sharply. Knowing perfectly well that when the morning came, he would regret not finishing his homework that night, he piled his books back into his bag.

'I'm going to bed too.'

He passed Seamus on the way to the door leading to the dormitories, but did not look at him. Harry had a fleeting impression that Seamus had opened his mouth to speak, but he sped up and reached the soothing peace of the stone spiral staircase without having to endure any more provocation.

The following day dawned just as leaden and rainy as the previous one. Hagrid was still absent from the staff table at breakfast.

'But on the plus side, no Snape today,' said Ron bracingly.

Hermione yawned widely and poured herself some coffee. She looked mildly pleased about something, and when Ron asked her what she had to be so happy about, she simply said, 'The hats have gone. Seems the house-elves do want freedom after all.'

'I wouldn't bet on it,' Ron told her cuttingly. 'They might not count as clothes. They didn't look anything like hats to me, more like woolly bladders.'

Hermione did not speak to him all morning.

Double Charms was succeeded by double Transfiguration. Professor Flitwick and Professor McGonagall both spent the first fifteen minutes of their lessons lecturing the class on the importance of O.W.L.s.

'What you must remember,' said little Professor Flitwick squeakily, perched as ever on a pile of books so that he could see over the top of his desk, 'is that these examinations may influence your futures for many years to come! If you have not already given serious thought to your careers, now is the time to

她走了。罗恩等她刚一出了通向女生宿舍的门，就把那些垃圾从羊毛帽子上拿掉了。

"至少应该让他们看清自己捡起来的是什么东西。"他坚决地说，"反正……"他卷起那张写着斯内普那篇论文标题的羊皮纸，"现在要把它写完是不可能的了。赫敏不在，我根本没法儿写，月长石到底有什么用，我真是一点儿也不知道。你呢？"

哈利摇了摇头，这才发现他的右边太阳穴疼得越来越厉害了。想起还要写那么长一篇关于巨人战争的文章，那疼痛更是如刀割一般。他知道明天早晨醒来，他肯定会后悔今天晚上没有完成家庭作业。他一边这么想着，一边把书本塞回书包里。

"我也去睡觉了。"

他走向通往男生宿舍的那扇门，正好与西莫擦肩而过，但看也没有看他。一闪念间，哈利仿佛觉得西莫张嘴想要说话，他赶紧加快脚步来到安静的、令人舒心的石头螺旋形楼梯上，不想再忍受别人的挑衅和刺激。

第二天早晨，天气和前一天一样灰蒙蒙的，细雨绵绵。吃早饭的时候，教工桌上还是不见海格的身影。

"可是从有利的方面看，斯内普今天也不在。"罗恩给他们打气说。

赫敏打了一个大大的哈欠，给自己倒了一些咖啡。她似乎在为什么事情暗暗高兴，后来罗恩问她到底为何开心成这样，她简单地说："帽子不见了。看来家养小精灵还是愿意得到自由的。"

"这我可说不准，"罗恩尖刻地对她说，"那些玩意儿大概根本就不能算衣物。在我看来，它们一点儿也不像帽子，倒更像是羊毛袋子。"

赫敏一上午都没跟他说话。

两节魔咒课后面接着是两节变形课。弗立维教授和麦格教授先后都用了十五分钟向全班同学强调 O.W.L. 考试的重要性。

"你们必须记住，"矮个子弗立维教授尖声尖气地说，他像往常一样站在一堆书上，这样才能从讲台上看到全班同学，"这些考试可能会影响到你们未来许多年的前途！如果你们还没有严肃认真地考虑过你

CHAPTER THIRTEEN   Detention with Dolores

do so. And in the meantime, I'm afraid, we shall be working harder than ever to ensure that you all do yourselves justice!'

They then spent over an hour revising Summoning Charms, which according to Professor Flitwick were bound to come up in their O.W.L., and he rounded off the lesson by setting them their largest ever amount of Charms homework.

It was the same, if not worse, in Transfiguration.

'You cannot pass an O.W.L.,' said Professor McGonagall grimly, 'without serious application, practice and study. I see no reason why everybody in this class should not achieve an O.W.L. in Transfiguration as long as they put in the work.' Neville made a sad little disbelieving noise. 'Yes, you too, Longbottom,' said Professor McGonagall. 'There's nothing wrong with your work except lack of confidence. So ... today we are starting Vanishing Spells. These are easier than Conjuring Spells, which you would not usually attempt until N.E.W.T. level, but they are still among the most difficult magic you will be tested on in your O.W.L.'

She was quite right; Harry found the Vanishing Spells horribly difficult. By the end of a double period neither he nor Ron had managed to vanish the snails on which they were practising, though Ron said hopefully he thought his looked a bit paler. Hermione, on the other hand, successfully vanished her snail on the third attempt, earning her a ten-point bonus for Gryffindor from Professor McGonagall. She was the only person not given homework; everybody else was told to practise the spell overnight, ready for a fresh attempt on their snails the following afternoon.

Now panicking slightly about the amount of homework they had to do, Harry and Ron spent their lunch hour in the library looking up the uses of moonstones in potion-making. Still angry about Ron's slur on her woolly hats, Hermione did not join them. By the time they reached Care of Magical Creatures in the afternoon, Harry's head was aching again.

The day had become cool and breezy, and as they walked down the sloping lawn towards Hagrid's cabin on the edge of the Forbidden Forest, they felt the occasional drop of rain on their faces. Professor Grubbly-Plank stood waiting for the class some ten yards from Hagrid's front door, a long trestle table in front of her laden with twigs. As Harry and Ron reached her, a loud shout of laughter sounded behind them; turning, they saw Draco Malfoy striding

们的职业，现在应该好好想想了。与此同时，为了保证你们都发挥出自己的水平，恐怕我们都要比以前更加努力才行！"

接着，他们花了一个多小时复习召唤咒，据弗立维教授说，这是他们的 O.W.L. 考试中肯定会有的内容。下课前，他布置的魔咒课作业数量比以往任何时候都多。

变形课的情况即使不是更糟，也好不到哪儿去。

"不经过认真的学习、实践和应用，"麦格教授严肃地说，"你们就不可能通过 O.W.L. 考试。我认为，只要投入了时间和精力，这个班上的所有同学都没有理由得不到变形课的 O.W.L. 合格证书。"纳威不敢相信地叹了口气。"没错，你也同样，隆巴顿。"麦格教授说，"你的操作没有任何错误，只是缺乏自信。因此……今天我们开始学习消失咒。消失咒要比你们一般在达到 N.E.W.T. 水平时才会练习的驱召咒简单一些，但它仍然是你们 O.W.L. 考试中会出现的最难的魔法之一。"

她说得很对。哈利发现消失咒难得要命。到两节课快结束时，他和罗恩谁都没能使他们用来练习的蜗牛消失，虽然罗恩不死心地说，他认为他那只蜗牛的颜色变浅了点儿。而赫敏刚试到第三次，就成功地使她的蜗牛消失了，因此从麦格教授那里为格兰芬多学院赢得了十分的奖励。只有她一个人不用做家庭作业，其他人都必须连夜练习这个咒语，准备第二天下午再在那些蜗牛身上尝试一番。

有这么多家庭作业要完成，哈利和罗恩有些慌神了。他们用午饭时间泡图书馆，查找月长石在制药方面的用途。赫敏还在为罗恩诋毁她的羊毛帽子而生气，没有跟他们一起去。下午，当他们去上保护神奇动物课时，哈利的脑袋又疼了起来。

天气阴冷，凉风习习，他们走下草坡、向禁林边上海格的小屋走去时，感到有零星的雨点落在他们脸上。格拉普兰教授站在海格小屋门前十米开外的地方等待同学们，她的面前有一张长长的搁板桌，上面放着许多细树枝。哈利和罗恩刚走到她身边，就听见身后传来一阵刺耳的笑声。回头一看，只见德拉科·马尔福大步朝他们走来，身边围着他那群形影不离的斯莱特林密友。显然他刚才说了什么特别好笑

CHAPTER THIRTEEN   Detention with Dolores

towards them, surrounded by his usual gang of Slytherin cronies. He had clearly just said something highly amusing, because Crabbe, Goyle, Pansy Parkinson and the rest continued to snigger heartily as they gathered around the trestle table and, judging by the way they all kept looking over at Harry, he was able to guess the subject of the joke without too much difficulty.

'Everyone here?' barked Professor Grubbly-Plank, once all the Slytherins and Gryffindors had arrived. 'Let's crack on then. Who can tell me what these things are called?'

She indicated the heap of twigs in front of her. Hermione's hand shot into the air. Behind her back, Malfoy did a buck-toothed imitation of her jumping up and down in eagerness to answer a question. Pansy Parkinson gave a shriek of laughter that turned almost at once into a scream, as the twigs on the table leapt into the air and revealed themselves to be what looked like tiny pixie-ish creatures made of wood, each with knobbly brown arms and legs, two twiglike fingers at the end of each hand and a funny flat, barklike face in which a pair of beetle-brown eyes glittered.

'Oooooh!' said Parvati and Lavender, thoroughly irritating Harry. Anyone would have thought Hagrid had never shown them impressive creatures; admittedly, the Flobberworms had been a bit dull, but the Salamanders and Hippogriffs had been interesting enough, and the Blast-Ended Skrewts perhaps too much so.

'Kindly keep your voices down, girls!' said Professor Grubbly-Plank sharply, scattering a handful of what looked like brown rice among the stick-creatures, who immediately fell upon the food. 'So – anyone know the names of these creatures? Miss Granger?'

'Bowtruckles,' said Hermione. 'They're tree-guardians, usually live in wand-trees.'

'Five points for Gryffindor,' said Professor Grubbly-Plank. 'Yes, these are Bowtruckles, and as Miss Granger rightly says, they generally live in trees whose wood is of wand quality. Anybody know what they eat?'

'Woodlice,' said Hermione promptly, which explained why what Harry had taken to be grains of brown rice were moving. 'But fairy eggs if they can get them.'

'Good girl, take another five points. So, whenever you need leaves or wood from a tree in which a Bowtruckle lodges, it is wise to have a gift of woodlice

的话,因为克拉布、高尔、潘西·帕金森和其他人围拢在搁板桌旁时,他们还忍不住开心地咯咯直笑,而且他们都不停地朝哈利这边看,因此哈利很容易就能猜出那个笑话说的是什么。

"人都来齐了吧?"格拉普兰教授看到斯莱特林和格兰芬多的同学都到了,便粗声粗气地问道,"我们开始吧。谁能告诉我这些东西叫什么名字?"

她指着面前的那一堆细树枝。赫敏腾地一下举起手。在她身后,马尔福龇着牙齿,学她上蹿下跳、急着回答问题的样子。潘西·帕金森发出一声刺耳的大笑,但几乎立刻就变成了一声尖叫,只见桌上的细树枝忽地蹿到空中,露出了它们的真面目,一个个像是木头做的小精灵,都长着褐色的、疙里疙瘩的腿和胳膊,每只手上有两根树枝般的手指,而每张扁平的、树皮般的滑稽面孔上,都有两只圆溜溜的褐色小眼睛在闪闪发亮。

"哎哟!"帕瓦蒂和拉文德说,这使哈利非常恼火。搞得谁都会以为海格从来没给他们看过什么有趣的动物。必须承认,弗洛伯毛虫确实有点儿乏味,但火蜥蜴和鹰头马身有翼兽还是挺有趣的,而炸尾螺或许有趣得过了头。

"姑娘们,请你们小声点儿!"格拉普兰教授严厉地说,抓了一把像是糙米一样的东西撒给那些枯枝般的动物,它们立刻扑上去吃了起来,"那么——有谁知道这些动物的名字?格兰杰小姐?"

"护树罗锅,"赫敏说,"它们是树木的保护神,通常生活在魔杖树上。"

"格兰芬多加五分。"格拉普兰教授说,"不错,这些动物是护树罗锅,格兰杰小姐说得很对,它们一般生活在枝干可以用来做魔杖的树上。有谁知道它们吃什么吗?"

"土鳖,"赫敏立刻答道,怪不得那些哈利以为是糙米的东西都在动个不停呢,"还有仙子蛋,如果它们能弄到的话。"

"好孩子,再加五分。所以,如果你们需要在护树罗锅栖息的树上采集树叶或木料,最好准备一些土鳖作为礼物,吸引它们的注意力,安抚它们的情绪。它们看上去没什么危险,但如果被惹急了,就会用

CHAPTER THIRTEEN   Detention with Dolores

ready to distract or placate it. They may not look dangerous, but if angered they will try to gouge at human eyes with their fingers, which, as you can see, are very sharp and not at all desirable near the eyeballs. So if you'd like to gather closer, take a few woodlice and a Bowtruckle – I have enough here for one between three – you can study them more closely. I want a sketch from each of you with all body-parts labelled by the end of the lesson.'

The class surged forwards around the trestle table. Harry deliberately circled around the back so that he ended up right next to Professor Grubbly-Plank.

'Where's Hagrid?' he asked her, while everyone else was choosing Bowtruckles.

'Never you mind,' said Professor Grubbly-Plank repressively, which had been her attitude last time Hagrid had failed to turn up for a class, too. Smirking all over his pointed face, Draco Malfoy leaned across Harry and seized the largest Bowtruckle.

'Maybe,' said Malfoy in an undertone, so that only Harry could hear him, 'the stupid great oaf's got himself badly injured.'

'Maybe you will if you don't shut up,' said Harry out of the side of his mouth.

'Maybe he's been messing with stuff that's too *big* for him, if you get my drift.'

Malfoy walked away, smirking over his shoulder at Harry, who felt suddenly sick. Did Malfoy know something? His father was a Death Eater after all; what if he had information about Hagrid's fate that had not yet reached the ears of the Order? He hurried back around the table to Ron and Hermione who were squatting on the grass some distance away and attempting to persuade a Bowtruckle to remain still long enough for them to draw it. Harry pulled out parchment and quill, crouched down beside the others and related in a whisper what Malfoy had just said.

'Dumbledore would know if something had happened to Hagrid,' said Hermione at once. 'It's just playing into Malfoy's hands to look worried; it tells him we don't know exactly what's going on. We've got to ignore him, Harry. Here, hold the Bowtruckle for a moment, just so I can draw its face ...'

'Yes,' came Malfoy's clear drawl from the group nearest them, 'Father was talking to the Minister just a couple of days ago, you know, and it sounds as though the Ministry's really determined to crack down on sub-standard teaching in this place. So even if that overgrown moron *does* show up again, he'll probably be sent packing straightaway.'

手指来挖人的眼睛。你们可以看到，它们的手指非常尖利，碰到人的眼球可不是好玩的。好了，如果你们愿意靠近一点，拿一些土鳖，领一只护树罗锅去——这里的护树罗锅够三个人分到一只——便可以更仔细地研究它们。我希望下课前每人完成一张草图，标出护树罗锅身体的每个部分。"

同学们都朝搁板桌拥去。哈利故意绕到后面，这样他正好站在了格拉普兰教授旁边。

"海格到哪儿去了？"趁其他人都在挑选护树罗锅时，哈利问她。

"不关你的事。"格拉普兰教授强硬地说，上一次海格没能来上课时，她也是这样的态度。德拉科·马尔福那张尖脸上堆满坏笑，他把身体探到哈利面前，抓住了那只最大的护树罗锅。

"说不定，"马尔福把声音压得很低，只有哈利一个人能听见，"那个愚蠢的傻大个儿受了重伤呢！"

"如果你不闭嘴，没准你才会受重伤！"哈利几乎不动嘴唇地说。

"说不定他正在摆弄他对付不了的大家伙呢，但愿你明白我的意思。"

马尔福走开了，一边还扭头朝哈利坏笑，哈利突然觉得一阵恶心。莫非马尔福真的知道一些情况？毕竟他父亲是一个食死徒啊。会不会他掌握了海格的下落，而凤凰社的人还没有听说呢？他匆忙绕过桌子，找到罗恩和赫敏，他们正蹲在不远处的草地上，试图说服护树罗锅安安稳稳地待一会儿，好让他们把它画下来。哈利掏出羊皮纸和羽毛笔，蹲在他们俩身边，小声地把马尔福刚才说的话告诉了他们。

"如果海格出了什么事，邓布利多一定会知道的。"赫敏立刻说道，"你要是显出担心的样子，就正好中了马尔福的圈套，他就会看出来我们不知道事情到底怎么样了。我们千万别去理睬他，哈利。来，抓住护树罗锅一会儿，让我把它的脸画下来……"

"没错，"从旁边那组人里传来马尔福清楚的、拖腔拖调的声音，"两天前我爸爸刚跟部长谈过话，听那意思，魔法部真的下决心要采取严厉措施，扭转这地方不规范的教学了。所以，即使那个傻大个儿真的又露面了，大概也会立马被打发回家的。"

CHAPTER THIRTEEN Detention with Dolores

'OUCH!'

Harry had gripped the Bowtruckle so hard that it had almost snapped, and it had just taken a great retaliatory swipe at his hand with its sharp fingers, leaving two long deep cuts there. Harry dropped it. Crabbe and Goyle, who had already been guffawing at the idea of Hagrid being sacked, laughed still harder as the Bowtruckle set off at full tilt towards the Forest, a little moving stick-man soon swallowed up among the tree roots. When the bell echoed distantly over the grounds, Harry rolled up his blood-stained Bowtruckle picture and marched off to Herbology with his hand wrapped in Hermione's handkerchief, and Malfoy's derisive laughter still ringing in his ears.

'If he calls Hagrid a moron one more time …' snarled Harry.

'Harry, don't go picking a row with Malfoy, don't forget, he's a prefect now, he could make life difficult for you …'

'Wow, I wonder what it'd be like to have a difficult life?' said Harry sarcastically. Ron laughed, but Hermione frowned. Together, they traipsed across the vegetable patch. The sky still appeared unable to make up its mind whether it wanted to rain or not.

'I just wish Hagrid would hurry up and get back, that's all,' said Harry in a low voice, as they reached the greenhouses. 'And *don't* say that Grubbly-Plank woman's a better teacher!' he added threateningly.

'I wasn't going to,' said Hermione calmly.

'Because she'll never be as good as Hagrid,' said Harry firmly, fully aware that he had just experienced an exemplary Care of Magical Creatures lesson and was thoroughly annoyed about it.

The door of the nearest greenhouse opened and some fourth-years spilled out of it, including Ginny.

'Hi,' she said brightly as she passed. A few seconds later, Luna Lovegood emerged, trailing behind the rest of the class, a smudge of earth on her nose, and her hair tied in a knot on the top of her head. When she saw Harry, her prominent eyes seemed to bulge excitedly and she made a beeline straight for him. Many of his classmates turned curiously to watch. Luna took a great breath and then said, without so much as a preliminary hello, 'I believe He Who Must Not Be Named is back and I believe you fought him and escaped

第13章 被多洛雷斯关禁闭

"哎哟！"

哈利把护树罗锅抓得太紧，几乎要把它折断了。护树罗锅挥起尖利的手指，报复性地在哈利手上狠狠抓了一下，哈利的手上留下两条又长又深的伤口。哈利丢下了护树罗锅。克拉布和高尔听说海格会被开除就已经在粗声大笑，现在笑得更厉害了。只见护树罗锅使出全身力气向禁林跑去，一个快速移动的棍棍小人儿很快就消失在树根间不见了。当场地那边远远传来下课的铃声时，哈利卷起那张血迹斑斑的护树罗锅草图，大步赶去上草药课，他手上包着赫敏的手帕，耳朵里还回响着马尔福讥讽的笑声。

"如果他再管海格叫傻大个儿……"哈利恶狠狠地说。

"哈利，别去跟马尔福吵架，别忘了，他现在是级长，他可以使你的日子变得非常难过……"

"哇，我倒想知道难过的日子是什么滋味。"哈利讽刺地说。罗恩笑了，但赫敏皱起了眉头。三个人拖着沉重的脚步穿过菜地。天空似乎仍然拿不定主意要不要下雨。

"我只希望海格赶紧把事情办完早点回来，就是这样。"他们来到温室时，哈利低声地说，"不许说格拉普兰那女人上课上得比他强！"他又威胁地说了一句。

"我本来就没想说。"赫敏平静地说。

"因为她永远也不会有海格那么好。"哈利斩钉截铁地说，其实他心里很清楚，他刚才经历的是一节保护神奇动物课的优秀示范课，他为此气恼得要命。

离他们最近的那间温室的门开了，一些四年级学生从里面拥了出来，其中就有金妮。

"嘿。"她走过时愉快地说。几秒钟后，卢娜·洛夫古德也出来了，落在全班其他同学的后面，鼻子上沾着一块泥土，头发在头顶上打成了一个结。她一看见哈利，那双向外凸起的眼睛似乎兴奋得鼓了出来。她直冲着哈利走过来。哈利班上的许多同学都好奇地转过脸来看着他们。卢娜深深地吸了口气，也没有先打一个招呼，就直通通地说道："我相信那个连名字都不能提的人回来了，我相信你跟他展开过搏斗，并

from him.'

'Er – right,' said Harry awkwardly. Luna was wearing what looked like a pair of orange radishes for earrings, a fact that Parvati and Lavender seemed to have noticed, as they were both giggling and pointing at her earlobes.

'You can laugh,' Luna said, her voice rising, apparently under the impression that Parvati and Lavender were laughing at what she had said rather than what she was wearing, 'but people used to believe there were no such things as the Blibbering Humdinger or the Crumple-Horned Snorkack!'

'Well, they were right, weren't they?' said Hermione impatiently. 'There *weren't* any such things as the Blibbering Humdinger or the Crumple-Horned Snorkack.'

Luna gave her a withering look and flounced away, radishes swinging madly. Parvati and Lavender were not the only ones hooting with laughter now.

'D'you mind not offending the only people who believe me?' Harry asked Hermione as they made their way into class.

'Oh, for heaven's sake, Harry, you can do better than *her*,' said Hermione. 'Ginny's told me all about her; apparently, she'll only believe in things as long as there's no proof at all. Well, I wouldn't expect anything else from someone whose father runs *The Quibbler*.'

Harry thought of the sinister winged horses he had seen on the night he had arrived and how Luna had said she could see them too. His spirits sank slightly. Had she been lying? But before he could devote much more thought to the matter, Ernie Macmillan had stepped up to him.

'I want you to know, Potter,' he said in a loud, carrying voice, 'that it's not only weirdos who support you. I personally believe you one hundred per cent. My family have always stood firm behind Dumbledore, and so do I.'

'Er – thanks very much, Ernie,' said Harry, taken aback but pleased. Ernie might be pompous on occasions like this, but Harry was in a mood to deeply appreciate a vote of confidence from somebody who did not have radishes dangling from their ears. Ernie's words had certainly wiped the smile from Lavender Brown's face and as he turned to talk to Ron and Hermione, Harry caught Seamus's expression, which looked both confused and defiant.

To nobody's surprise, Professor Sprout started their lesson by lecturing

逃脱了他的魔爪。"

"呃——是的。"哈利尴尬地说。卢娜戴着一对橘红色水萝卜样的耳坠,帕瓦蒂和拉文德看来注意到了这点,她们俩咯咯笑着,用手指着她的耳垂。

"你们可以笑,"卢娜说,声音提高了,显然她以为帕瓦蒂和拉文德是在笑她刚才说的话,而不是笑她戴的东西,"可是人们以前还以为世界上没有泡泡鼻涕怪和弯角鼾兽之类的东西呢!"

"对啊,他们没有错啊,是不是?"赫敏不耐烦地说,"世界上确实没有泡泡鼻涕怪和弯角鼾兽之类的东西呀。"

卢娜咄咄逼人地瞪了赫敏一眼,猛一转身走开了,两个水萝卜剧烈地晃荡着。这时尖声大笑的可不止帕瓦蒂和拉文德两个人了。

"就这么几个相信我的人,你能不能别惹他们生气?"他们走进教室时,哈利对赫敏说。

"哦,看在上天的分儿上,哈利,你总不至于把希望寄托在她身上吧。"赫敏说,"金妮把她所有的事情都告诉我了。显然,她只相信那些毫无根据的事情。唉,我就知道,她父亲办着《唱唱反调》,她还能好到哪儿去呢?"

哈利想起了他到校那天晚上看见的那些不吉利的带翅膀的怪马,想起卢娜当时说她也能看见它们,他的心微微往下一沉。难道她在说谎?可是没等哈利进一步深想这个问题,厄尼·麦克米兰走到了他的面前。

"我希望你知道,波特,"他用响亮的、传得很远的声音说道,"并不是只有怪人才支持你。我个人百分之百地相信你。我们全家始终坚决拥护邓布利多,我也是这样。"

"哦——非常感谢,厄尼。"哈利说,他很吃惊,同时也很高兴。厄尼这么做也许有点儿哗众取宠,但是以哈利当时的心情,能够得到一个耳朵上没挂胡萝卜的人投来的信任的一票,他真是由衷地感激。厄尼的话无疑使拉文德·布朗脸上的笑容一扫而光;当哈利转身跟罗恩和赫敏说话时,他瞥见了西莫的表情,看上去又困惑又不服气。

不出大家所料,斯普劳特教授一上课就向他们强调 O.W.L. 的重要

CHAPTER THIRTEEN — Detention with Dolores

them about the importance of O.W.L.s. Harry wished all the teachers would stop doing this; he was starting to get an anxious, twisted feeling in his stomach every time he remembered how much homework he had to do, a feeling that worsened dramatically when Professor Sprout gave them yet another essay at the end of class. Tired and smelling strongly of dragon dung, Professor Sprout's preferred type of fertiliser, the Gryffindors trooped back up to the castle, none of them talking very much; it had been another long day.

As Harry was starving, and he had his first detention with Umbridge at five o'clock, he headed straight for dinner without dropping off his bag in Gryffindor Tower so that he could bolt something down before facing whatever she had in store for him. He had barely reached the entrance of the Great Hall, however, when a loud and angry voice yelled, 'Oi, Potter!'

'What now?' he muttered wearily, turning to face Angelina Johnson, who looked as though she was in a towering temper.

'I'll tell you *what now*,' she said, marching straight up to him and poking him hard in the chest with her finger. 'How come you've landed yourself in detention for five o'clock on Friday?'

'What?' said Harry. 'Why ... oh yeah, Keeper tryouts!'

'*Now* he remembers!' snarled Angelina. 'Didn't I tell you I wanted to do a tryout with the *whole team*, and find someone who *fitted in with everyone?* Didn't I tell you I'd booked the Quidditch pitch specially? And now you've decided you're not going to be there!'

'I didn't decide not to be there!' said Harry, stung by the injustice of these words. 'I got detention from that Umbridge woman, just because I told her the truth about You-Know-Who.'

'Well, you can just go straight to her and ask her to let you off on Friday,' said Angelina fiercely, 'and I don't care how you do it. Tell her You-Know-Who's a figment of your imagination if you like, just *make sure you're there!*'

She stormed away.

'You know what?' Harry said to Ron and Hermione as they entered the Great Hall. 'I think we'd better check with Puddlemere United whether Oliver Wood's been killed during a training session, because Angelina seems to be channelling his spirit.'

'What d'you reckon are the odds of Umbridge letting you off on Friday?'

第13章 被多洛雷斯关禁闭

性。哈利真希望所有的老师都别再谈这件事了。每当他想起有那么多家庭作业要做,就感到焦躁不安,心里一阵阵发紧。下课时斯普劳特教授又布置他们写一篇论文,哈利的这种感觉顿时变得更强烈了。格兰芬多的同学们一个个精疲力竭,身上散发着浓浓的火龙粪味儿——这是斯普劳特教授最喜欢的一种肥料——排着队返回城堡,谁也没有心思多说话。这又是特别累人的一天。

哈利饿坏了,五点钟他还要到乌姆里奇那里去关第一次禁闭。他来不及把书包送到格兰芬多塔楼,就直接赶去吃晚饭,这样可以匆匆忙忙吃点东西,再去面对乌姆里奇为他准备的不知什么差使。然而,他刚来到礼堂门口,就听见一个愤怒的声音高喊道:"喂,波特!"

"又怎么了?"他疲惫地嘀咕道,一转身看见了安吉利娜·约翰逊,看她那样子好像马上就要大发雷霆了。

"我来告诉你又怎么了,"她说,几步冲到他面前,用手指使劲戳着哈利的胸口,"你怎么在星期五下午五点钟给自己弄了个关禁闭?"

"什么?"哈利说,"哎呀……对了,选拔守门员!"

"这会儿倒想起来了!"安吉利娜吼叫着说,"我不是告诉过你,我希望全队球员都参加选拔,找到一个能跟每个队员都配合默契的人吗?我不是告诉过你,我已经特地定好了魁地奇球场吗?现在你又决定不去参加了!"

"我没有决定不去参加!"哈利说,觉得被这些不公平的话刺伤了,"是那个叫乌姆里奇的女人罚我关禁闭,就因为我跟她说了关于神秘人的实话。"

"好吧,你可以直接去找她,请她星期五放你一马,"安吉利娜情绪激动地说,"我不管你怎么做。如果你愿意,不妨告诉她神秘人是你凭空想象出来的,只要保证你能够到场就行!"

她气势汹汹地走了。

"你们知道吗?"罗恩和赫敏走进礼堂时,哈利对他们说,"我想我们最好去找普德米尔联队核实一下,奥利弗·伍德是不是在训练期间不幸去世了,因为他的灵魂好像附在安吉利娜身上了。"

"你认为乌姆里奇有多少可能会在星期五放你一马呢?"他们在格

CHAPTER THIRTEEN   Detention with Dolores

said Ron sceptically, as they sat down at the Gryffindor table.

'Less than zero,' said Harry glumly, tipping lamb chops on to his plate and starting to eat. 'Better try, though, hadn't I? I'll offer to do two more detentions or something, I dunno …' He swallowed a mouthful of potato and added, 'I hope she doesn't keep me too long this evening. You realise we've got to write three essays, practise Vanishing Spells for McGonagall, work out a counter-charm for Flitwick, finish the Bowtruckle drawing and start that stupid dream diary for Trelawney?'

Ron moaned and for some reason glanced up at the ceiling.

'*And* it looks like it's going to rain.'

'What's that got to do with our homework?' said Hermione, her eyebrows raised.

'Nothing,' said Ron at once, his ears reddening.

At five to five Harry bade the other two goodbye and set off for Umbridge's office on the third floor. When he knocked on the door she called, 'Come in,' in a sugary voice. He entered cautiously, looking around.

He had known this office under three of its previous occupants. In the days when Gilderoy Lockhart had lived here it had been plastered in beaming portraits of himself. When Lupin had occupied it, it was likely you would meet some fascinating Dark creature in a cage or tank if you came to call. In the impostor Moody's days it had been packed with various instruments and artefacts for the detection of wrongdoing and concealment.

Now, however, it looked totally unrecognisable. The surfaces had all been draped in lacy covers and cloths. There were several vases full of dried flowers, each one residing on its own doily, and on one of the walls was a collection of ornamental plates, each decorated with a large technicoloured kitten wearing a different bow around its neck. These were so foul that Harry stared at them, transfixed, until Professor Umbridge spoke again.

'Good evening, Mr Potter.'

Harry started and looked around. He had not noticed her at first because she was wearing a luridly flowered set of robes that blended only too well with the tablecloth on the desk behind her.

'Evening, Professor Umbridge,' Harry said stiffly.

'Well, sit down,' she said, pointing towards a small table draped in lace

第13章 被多洛雷斯关禁闭

兰芬多的桌旁坐下来时,罗恩怀疑地说。

"一点儿也没有,"哈利郁闷地说,一边把小羊排倒进自己的盘子里吃了起来,"不过最好还是试一试,对吗?我可以提出增加两次关禁闭什么的……"他咽下一大口土豆,接着说道,"希望她今天晚上别把我留得太晚。你们知道吗,我们要写三篇论文,给麦格练习消失咒,给弗立维设计一个破解咒,把护树罗锅的草图画完,还要开始给特里劳尼写那无聊的做梦日记!"

罗恩叹了口气,不知为什么抬头扫了一眼天花板。

"而且看样子天要下雨了。"

"那跟我们的家庭作业有什么关系吗?"赫敏扬起眉毛问。

"没什么。"罗恩赶紧说道,耳朵变得通红。

五点差五分的时候,哈利告别了他们俩,朝四楼乌姆里奇的办公室走去。他敲了敲门,只听一个甜得发腻的声音喊道:"进来。"哈利小心翼翼地走了进去,四下张望。

前面三位主人住在这里的时候,哈利曾经很熟悉这间办公室。在吉德罗·洛哈特居住的那些日子,墙上到处贴着他本人笑容满面的照片。卢平住进来后,每次进来找他,都有可能见到某些非常有趣的黑魔法生物,关在笼子里或水箱里。而冒牌的穆迪住在这里的时候,房间里堆满了各种各样的器具和手工制品,用来探测别人的不轨行为和伪装。

此刻,这个房间简直完全认不出来了。所有的东西上都盖着带花边的罩布和台布。还有几个插满干花的花瓶,每个都放在单独的小垫子上。一面墙上挂着一组装饰性的盘子,每个盘子上都有一只色彩鲜艳的小猫,各自脖子上戴着一个不同的蝴蝶结。这些东西太令人恶心了,哈利简直被吓住了,只顾呆呆地望着它们,这时乌姆里奇教授又说话了。

"晚上好,波特先生。"

哈利吓得急忙回过头来。他一开始没有注意到她,因为她穿着一件艳俗的印花长袍,颜色同她身后书桌上的桌布融在一起,简直分不出来。

"晚上好,乌姆里奇教授。"哈利不自然地说。

"好吧,坐下吧。"她说,指着一张垂着花边的小桌子。她已经在

CHAPTER THIRTEEN — Detention with Dolores

beside which she had drawn up a straight-backed chair. A piece of blank parchment lay on the table, apparently waiting for him.

'Er,' said Harry, without moving. 'Professor Umbridge. Er – before we start, I – I wanted to ask you a ... a favour.'

Her bulging eyes narrowed.

'Oh, yes?'

'Well, I'm ... I'm in the Gryffindor Quidditch team. And I was supposed to be at the tryouts for the new Keeper at five o'clock on Friday and I was – was wondering whether I could skip detention that night and do it – do it another night ... instead ...'

He knew long before he reached the end of his sentence that it was no good.

'Oh, no,' said Umbridge, smiling so widely that she looked as though she had just swallowed a particularly juicy fly. 'Oh, no, no, no. This is your punishment for spreading evil, nasty, attention-seeking stories, Mr Potter, and punishments certainly cannot be adjusted to suit the guilty one's convenience. No, you will come here at five o'clock tomorrow, and the next day, and on Friday too, and you will do your detentions as planned. I think it rather a good thing that you are missing something you really want to do. It ought to reinforce the lesson I am trying to teach you.'

Harry felt the blood surge to his head and heard a thumping noise in his ears. So he told 'evil, nasty, attention-seeking stories', did he?

She was watching him with her head slightly to one side, still smiling widely, as though she knew exactly what he was thinking and was waiting to see whether he would start shouting again. With a massive effort, Harry looked away from her, dropped his schoolbag beside the straight-backed chair and sat down.

'There,' said Umbridge sweetly, 'we're getting better at controlling our temper already, aren't we? Now, you are going to be doing some lines for me, Mr Potter. No, not with your quill,' she added, as Harry bent down to open his bag. 'You're going to be using a rather special one of mine. Here you are.'

She handed him a long, thin black quill with an unusually sharp point.

'I want you to write, *I must not tell lies*,' she told him softly.

'How many times?' Harry asked, with a creditable imitation of politeness.

'Oh, as long as it takes for the message to *sink in*,' said Umbridge sweetly.

第13章 被多洛雷斯关禁闭

旁边放了一把直背椅，桌上有一张空白的羊皮纸，显然是为哈利准备的。

"嗯，"哈利没有动弹，说道，"乌姆里奇教授，嗯——在我们开始前，我——我想请求你——……—件事。"

那双向外凸出的眼睛眯了起来。

"哦，什么？"

"是这样，我……我是格兰芬多魁地奇球队的队员。我应该在星期五下午五点钟参加新守门员的选拔，我——我不知道那天晚上能不能不来关禁闭，另外——另外找一个晚上再补上……"

他不等把话说完，心里就知道不会有用的。

"哦，不行。"乌姆里奇说，咧开大嘴笑得那么肉麻，好像刚吞下了一只特别美味多汁的苍蝇，"哦，不行，不行，不行。这是对你散布邪恶、卑鄙、哗众取宠的谎言的惩罚。波特先生，惩罚当然不能为满足有过失者的方便而随意调整。不行，明天、后天，还有星期五，你都必须在下午五点钟到这里来，按计划关禁闭。我认为，你错过一些你特别喜欢的活动，这其实倒是一件好事。它应该能强化我打算给你的教训。"

哈利感到血一下子冲上了脑袋，耳朵里嗡嗡作响。听她的意思，他是散布了"邪恶、卑鄙、哗众取宠的谎言"？

她微微偏着脑袋注视着哈利，脸上仍然挂着肉麻的微笑，似乎很清楚哈利心里在想什么，正等着看他会不会再次发作，大喊大叫。哈利费了很大的努力，转开目光不去看她，把书包扔在那把直背椅旁边坐了下来。

"不错，"乌姆里奇娇滴滴地说，"我们已经比较能够控制自己的情绪了，是不是？现在，你要为我写几个句子，波特先生。不，不是用你的羽毛笔，"看见哈利弯腰去打开书包，她赶紧补充道，"你要用的是我的一支很不同寻常的笔。给。"

她递给哈利一支细细长长、笔尖特别尖利的黑色羽毛笔。

"我要你写：我不可以说谎。"她语调轻柔地对哈利说。

"写多少遍？"哈利问，也做出一副值得称赞的彬彬有礼的样子。

"哦，一直写到这句话刻在你心里。"乌姆里奇嗲声嗲气地说，"开

CHAPTER THIRTEEN   Detention with Dolores

'Off you go.'

She moved over to her desk, sat down and bent over a stack of parchment that looked like essays for marking. Harry raised the sharp black quill, then realised what was missing.

'You haven't given me any ink,' he said.

'Oh, you won't need ink,' said Professor Umbridge, with the merest suggestion of a laugh in her voice.

Harry placed the point of the quill on the paper and wrote:

I must not tell lies.

He let out a gasp of pain. The words had appeared on the parchment in what appeared to be shining red ink. At the same time, the words had appeared on the back of Harry's right hand, cut into his skin as though traced there by a scalpel – yet even as he stared at the shining cut, the skin healed over again, leaving the place where it had been slightly redder than before but quite smooth.

Harry looked round at Umbridge. She was watching him, her wide, toadlike mouth stretched in a smile.

'Yes?'

'Nothing,' said Harry quietly.

He looked back at the parchment, placed the quill on it once more, wrote *I must not tell lies*, and felt the searing pain on the back of his hand for a second time; once again, the words had been cut into his skin; once again, they healed over seconds later.

And on it went. Again and again Harry wrote the words on the parchment in what he soon came to realise was not ink, but his own blood. And, again and again, the words were cut into the back of his hand, healed, and reappeared the next time he set quill to parchment.

Darkness fell outside Umbridge's window. Harry did not ask when he would be allowed to stop. He did not even check his watch. He knew she was watching him for signs of weakness and he was not going to show any, not even if he had to sit there all night, cutting open his own hand with this quill …

第13章 被多洛雷斯关禁闭

始写吧。"

她走到自己的书桌旁坐了下来，埋头对付一堆羊皮纸，看样子像是一批等待批改的论文。哈利举起尖利的黑色羽毛笔，这才发现缺少了什么。

"你没有给我墨水。"他说。

"哦，你不需要墨水的。"乌姆里奇教授说，声音里带着一点浅浅的笑意。

哈利把羽毛笔的笔尖落在纸上，写道：

我不可以说谎。

他疼得倒抽了一口冷气。出现在羊皮纸上的字，看上去是用鲜红的墨水写成的。与此同时，这行字出现在了哈利右手的手背上，而且深深陷进了皮肉里，像是用解剖刀刻上去的一样——然而，就在他眼睁睁地瞪着这些红艳艳的伤口时，皮肤又愈合了，刚才有字的地方只比以前稍微红了一点儿，但摸上去很光滑。

哈利扭头去看乌姆里奇。她正注视着他，那张癞蛤蟆似的阔嘴咧成了一个微笑。

"怎么啦？"

"没什么。"哈利轻声说。

他低头望着羊皮纸，再一次把笔尖落在上面，写下我不可以说谎。他又一次感到手背上烧灼般的疼痛，那些字又一次刻进他的皮肤，几秒钟后，伤口又一次愈合了。

就这样，哈利一遍又一遍地把这行字写在羊皮纸上。他很快就发现，他用的不是墨水，而是他自己的鲜血。一遍又一遍地，这些字刻进了他的手背，然后愈合，然后，当他再把笔尖落在羊皮纸上时，这些字又会再一次出现。

乌姆里奇办公室的窗外，夜幕渐渐降临了。哈利没有问她什么时候可以停止。他甚至没有看看表上几点钟了。他知道乌姆里奇在注视他，看他有没有服软的迹象，他不想显露出一丝一毫的软弱，即使他要在这里坐一整夜，用这支羽毛笔把自己的手深深地割开……

459

CHAPTER THIRTEEN — Detention with Dolores

'Come here,' she said, after what seemed hours.

He stood up. His hand was stinging painfully. When he looked down at it he saw that the cut had healed, but that the skin there was red raw.

'Hand,' she said.

He extended it. She took it in her own. Harry repressed a shudder as she touched him with her thick, stubby fingers on which she wore a number of ugly old rings.

'Tut, tut, I don't seem to have made much of an impression yet,' she said, smiling. 'Well, we'll just have to try again tomorrow evening, won't we? You may go.'

Harry left her office without a word. The school was quite deserted; it was surely past midnight. He walked slowly up the corridor, then, when he had turned the corner and was sure she would not hear him, broke into a run.

He had not had time to practise Vanishing Spells, had not written a single dream in his dream diary and had not finished the drawing of the Bowtruckle, nor had he written his essays. He skipped breakfast next morning to scribble down a couple of made-up dreams for Divination, their first lesson, and was surprised to find a dishevelled Ron keeping him company.

'How come you didn't do it last night?' Harry asked, as Ron stared wildly around the common room for inspiration. Ron, who had been fast asleep when Harry got back to the dormitory, muttered something about 'doing other stuff', bent low over his parchment and scrawled a few words.

'That'll have to do,' he said, slamming the diary shut. 'I've said I dreamed I was buying a new pair of shoes, she can't make anything weird out of that, can she?'

They hurried off to North Tower together.

'How was detention with Umbridge, anyway? What did she make you do?'

Harry hesitated for a fraction of a second, then said, 'Lines.'

'That's not too bad, then, eh?' said Ron.

'Nope,' said Harry.

'Hey – I forgot – did she let you off for Friday?'

第13章 被多洛雷斯关禁闭

"过来。"过了似乎好几个小时之后,乌姆里奇说道。

哈利站了起来。他的手火辣辣地疼。他低头一看,发现伤口虽然愈合了,但那里的皮肤红红的,露着嫩肉。

"手。"乌姆里奇说。

哈利把手伸了出去。她把它握在自己的手里。当她用肥厚短粗、戴着一大堆丑陋的老式戒指的手指触摸哈利的手时,哈利拼命克制住一阵战栗。

"啧啧,看来我还没有给你留下一个深刻的烙印。"她笑容可掬地说,"没关系,我们明天晚上还得再试一试,对不对?你可以走了。"

哈利一言不发地离开了她的办公室。学校里几乎空无一人,时间肯定已经过了半夜。他慢慢地走过走廊,当他拐了个弯、确信乌姆里奇不会听见时,便撒腿跑了起来。

他没有时间练习消失咒,做梦日记里一个梦也没有记,护树罗锅的草图还没有画完,那么多篇论文一篇也没有写。第二天早上,他没吃早饭,匆匆忙忙地编了两个梦,草草写下来,准备拿到上午第一节的占卜课上交差。他吃惊地发现罗恩衣冠不整,蓬头垢面,也在临时抱佛脚。

"你昨天晚上怎么没做呢?"哈利问道,罗恩漫无目的地在公共休息室里东张西望,寻找灵感。昨夜哈利回到宿舍时,罗恩已经沉沉地睡着了。听了哈利的问话,他嘀咕了一句,像是"干别的事情了",然后埋头在羊皮纸上划拉了几行字。

"这肯定能对付了,"他啪地合上日记本说道,"我说我梦见自己在买一双新鞋,这下子她总编派不出离奇的算命鬼话了吧?"

他们一起匆匆赶往北塔楼。

"对了,在乌姆里奇那里关禁闭怎么样?她叫你做什么了?"

哈利迟疑了一刹那,说:"写句子。"

"那倒不算太糟糕,是吧?"罗恩说。

"是啊。"哈利说。

"哟——我忘记了——她准了你星期五的假吗?"

CHAPTER THIRTEEN Detention with Dolores

'No,' said Harry.

Ron groaned sympathetically.

It was another bad day for Harry; he was one of the worst in Transfiguration, not having practised Vanishing Spells at all. He had to give up his lunch hour to complete the picture of the Bowtruckle and, meanwhile, Professors McGonagall, Grubbly-Plank and Sinistra gave them yet more homework, which he had no prospect of finishing that evening because of his second detention with Umbridge. To cap it all, Angelina Johnson tracked him down at dinner again and, on learning that he would not be able to attend Friday's Keeper tryouts, told him she was not at all impressed by his attitude and that she expected players who wished to remain on the team to put training before their other commitments.

'I'm in detention!' Harry yelled after her as she stalked away. 'D'you think I'd rather be stuck in a room with that old toad or playing Quidditch?'

'At least it's only lines,' said Hermione consolingly, as Harry sank back on to his bench and looked down at his steak and kidney pie, which he no longer fancied very much. 'It's not as if it's a dreadful punishment, really ...'

Harry opened his mouth, closed it again and nodded. He was not really sure why he was not telling Ron and Hermione exactly what was happening in Umbridge's room: he only knew that he did not want to see their looks of horror; that would make the whole thing seem worse and therefore more difficult to face. He also felt dimly that this was between himself and Umbridge, a private battle of wills, and he was not going to give her the satisfaction of hearing that he had complained about it.

'I can't believe how much homework we've got,' said Ron miserably.

'Well, why didn't you do any last night?' Hermione asked him. 'Where were you, anyway?'

'I was ... I fancied a walk,' said Ron shiftily.

Harry had the distinct impression that he was not alone in concealing things at the moment.

The second detention was just as bad as the previous one. The skin on the back of Harry's hand became irritated more quickly now and was soon red and inflamed. Harry thought it unlikely that it would keep healing as effectively for

第13章 被多洛雷斯关禁闭

"没有。"哈利说。

罗恩同情地呻吟了一声。

对哈利来说,这又是很难熬的一天。变形课上他是表现最差的几个人之一,因为他根本就没有练习消失咒。午饭时间他不得不放弃休息,把护树罗锅的那张草图画完。这还不算,麦格、格拉普兰和辛尼斯塔教授又给他们布置了一大堆家庭作业,他根本不可能在当天晚上完成,因为还要到乌姆里奇那里去关第二次禁闭。更糟糕的是,安吉利娜·约翰逊在吃晚饭时又找到他,听说他不能参加星期五选拔守门员的训练后,告诉他说,她对他的态度很不满意,她希望每个打算留在球队的人都把训练放在一切活动的首位。

"我在关禁闭!"她昂首挺胸地走开时,哈利冲着她的背影嚷道,"你以为我不愿意去打魁地奇球,情愿跟那个老癞蛤蟆关在一间屋里吗?"

"还好,只是写写句子,"赫敏安慰他道,哈利一屁股坐在板凳上,低头望着面前的牛排腰子馅饼,他现在已经没有多少胃口了,"看起来倒不算是很可怕的惩罚……"

哈利张了张嘴又闭上了,随即点了点头。他也不明白自己为什么不想把乌姆里奇办公室里发生的一切告诉罗恩和赫敏。他只知道不想看到他们脸上惊恐的表情,那只会使事情显得更糟,因而也就更难面对。他还隐隐约约地感到,这是他和乌姆里奇之间的事情,是一场私底下的意志较量,他不想让她听到他在抱怨而感到快意。

"真不敢相信我们有这么多家庭作业要做。"罗恩烦恼地说。

"那你昨天晚上干吗什么都不做呢?"赫敏问他,"你到底上哪儿去了?"

"我……我当时想散散步。"罗恩闪烁其词地说。

哈利有一个很清楚的感觉:此刻隐瞒真相的不止他一个人。

第二次关禁闭和第一次同样痛苦难熬。哈利手背上的皮肤现在变得更敏感,很快就变红了,像着了火一样疼。哈利觉得过不了多久,伤口就不会那样有效地愈合了。过不了多久,那些字就会深深刻进他

CHAPTER THIRTEEN — Detention with Dolores

long. Soon the cut would remain etched into his hand and Umbridge would, perhaps, be satisfied. He let no gasp of pain escape him, however, and from the moment of entering the room to the moment of his dismissal, again past midnight, he said nothing but 'good evening' and 'goodnight'.

His homework situation, however, was now desperate, and when he returned to the Gryffindor common room he did not, though exhausted, go to bed, but opened his books and began Snape's moonstone essay. It was half past two by the time he had finished it. He knew he had done a poor job, but there was no help for it; unless he had something to give in he would be in detention with Snape next. He then dashed off answers to the questions Professor McGonagall had set them, cobbled together something on the proper handling of Bowtruckles for Professor Grubbly-Plank, and staggered up to bed, where he fell fully clothed on top of the covers and fell asleep immediately.

Thursday passed in a haze of tiredness. Ron seemed very sleepy too, though Harry could not see why he should be. Harry's third detention passed in the same way as the previous two, except that after two hours the words *I must not tell lies* did not fade from the back of Harry's hand, but remained scratched there, oozing droplets of blood. The pause in the pointed quill's scratching made Professor Umbridge look up.

'Ah,' she said softly, moving around her desk to examine his hand herself. 'Good. That ought to serve as a reminder to you, oughtn't it? You may leave for tonight.'

'Do I still have to come back tomorrow?' said Harry, picking up his schoolbag with his left hand rather than his smarting right one.

'Oh yes,' said Professor Umbridge, smiling as widely as before. 'Yes, I think we can etch the message a little deeper with another evening's work.'

Harry had never before considered the possibility that there might be another teacher in the world he hated more than Snape, but as he walked back towards Gryffindor Tower he had to admit he had found a strong contender. She's evil, he thought, as he climbed a staircase to the seventh floor, she's an evil, twisted, mad old –

'Ron?'

He had reached the top of the stairs, turned right and almost walked into Ron, who was lurking behind a statue of Lachlan the Lanky, clutching

的手背，乌姆里奇大概就会满意了。不过，哈利拼命忍着不发出疼痛的喘息，而且，从他走进办公室直到乌姆里奇放他离去——又是午夜之后，他只说了两句话，"晚上好"和"晚安"。

他的家庭作业已经到了不堪收拾的地步，因此他返回格兰芬多公共休息室后，尽管累得一点力气也没有了，但并没有上床睡觉，而是打开书本，开始写斯内普布置的那篇关于月长石的论文。写完时已经是两点半了。他知道写得很糟糕，但也没有办法，他必须交点东西上去，不然接下来就要被斯内普关禁闭了。接着，他匆匆回答了麦格教授给他们布置的几个问题，又拼凑了一些怎样恰当地对付护树罗锅的东西，准备拿去应付格拉普兰教授，然后才跟跟跄跄地上床睡觉，连衣服也没脱，一头倒在被子上，立刻就沉沉地睡着了。

星期四是在昏昏沉沉的疲劳中度过的。罗恩看上去也是一脸困倦，哈利真不明白他为什么会这样。哈利的第三次关禁闭跟前两次没有什么两样，只是过了两个小时后，哈利手背上的我不可以说谎便不再消失，一道道红红的划痕留在那里，冒出细细的血珠。乌姆里奇教授听不到羽毛笔尖的沙沙响声，便抬起头来。

"啊，"她温柔地说，绕过她的书桌过来查看哈利的手，"很好。这应该可以时时提醒你了，是不是？你今晚可以走了。"

"明天还要来吗？"哈利问，用左手拎起书包，因为右手疼痛难忍。

"哦，是的，"乌姆里奇教授说，笑得还像以前一样肉麻，"是的，我想再有一夜的努力，我们就可以把这句话刻得更深一些。"

哈利以前认为，他不可能恨世界上的哪个老师比恨斯内普更厉害，可是当他走回格兰芬多的塔楼时，他不得不承认斯内普找到了一位强有力的竞争对手。这个女人是歹毒的，他一边爬上通往八楼的楼梯一边想着，她是一个邪恶、变态、疯狂的老——

"罗恩？"

他走到楼梯顶上，向右一转，差点儿撞到了罗恩身上。罗恩鬼鬼祟祟地藏在瘦子拉克伦的雕像后面，手里抓着他的飞天扫帚。罗恩看

CHAPTER THIRTEEN   Detention with Dolores

his broomstick. He gave a great leap of surprise when he saw Harry and attempted to hide his new Cleansweep Eleven behind his back.

'What are you doing?'

'Er – nothing. What are *you* doing?'

Harry frowned at him.

'Come on, you can tell me! What are you hiding here for?'

'I'm – I'm hiding from Fred and George, if you must know,' said Ron. 'They just went past with a bunch of first-years, I bet they're testing stuff on them again. I mean, they can't do it in the common room now, can they, not with Hermione there.'

He was talking in a very fast, feverish way.

'But what have you got your broom for, you haven't been flying, have you?' Harry asked.

'I – well – well, OK, I'll tell you, but don't laugh, all right?' Ron said defensively, turning redder with every second. 'I – I thought I'd try out for Gryffindor Keeper now I've got a decent broom. There. Go on. Laugh.'

'I'm not laughing,' said Harry. Ron blinked. 'It's a brilliant idea! It'd be really cool if you got on the team! I've never seen you play Keeper, are you good?'

'I'm not bad,' said Ron, who looked immensely relieved at Harry's reaction. 'Charlie, Fred and George always made me Keep for them when they were training during the holidays.'

'So you've been practising tonight?'

'Every evening since Tuesday … just on my own, though. I've been trying to bewitch Quaffles to fly at me, but it hasn't been easy and I don't know how much use it'll be.' Ron looked nervous and anxious. 'Fred and George are going to laugh themselves stupid when I turn up for the tryouts. They haven't stopped taking the mickey out of me since I got made a prefect.'

'I wish I was going to be there,' said Harry bitterly, as they set off together towards the common room.

'Yeah, so do – Harry, what's that on the back of your hand?'

Harry, who had just scratched his nose with his free right hand, tried to hide it, but had as much success as Ron with his Cleansweep.

见哈利时惊得跳了起来,赶紧把他那崭新的横扫十一星藏到背后。

"你在做什么?"

"呃——没什么。你在做什么?"

哈利朝他皱起眉头。

"行了,快告诉我吧!你藏在这里搞什么鬼?"

"我——我在躲弗雷德和乔治,如果你一定要知道的话。"罗恩说,"他们刚和一群一年级新生从这里走过去,我敢说他们又在新生身上试验那些玩意儿了。我是说,现在只要有赫敏在,他们就不敢在公共休息室里做这件事了,对吧。"

他慌乱地、滔滔不绝地说。

"可是你拿着你的飞天扫帚做什么?你该不是在飞吧,嗯?"哈利问。

"我——嗯——嗯,好吧,我告诉你,可是不许笑话我,好吗?"罗恩提防地说,脸红得越来越厉害了,"我——我想,既然我有了一把体面的飞天扫帚,不妨去试试参加格兰芬多守门员的选拔。就是这样。好了,你笑吧。"

"我不会笑的。"哈利说。罗恩眨了眨眼睛。"这个主意太棒了!如果你能进入球队,真是再好不过了!我还没有见过你当守门员呢,你技术怎么样?"

"不算坏吧,"罗恩说,看到哈利的反应,他似乎大松了一口气,"查理、弗雷德和乔治在假期里练球时,总是叫我当守门员。"

"这么说,你今晚一直在练习?"

"每天晚上都在练,从星期二开始……不过就我一个人。我一直想给鬼飞球施魔法,让它们朝我飞来,可是不太容易,我不知道这会有多少用。"罗恩显得很紧张和焦虑,"弗雷德和乔治看到我也来参加选拔,肯定会笑掉大牙的。自从我被选为级长后,他们就一直不停止地嘲笑我。"

"真希望到时候我也能去。"哈利苦涩地说,他们一起朝公共休息室走去。

"是啊,我也——哈利,你的手背上是什么?"

哈利刚才用没拎书包的右手挠了挠鼻子,现在想藏起来,已经来不及了,就像罗恩想藏他的扫帚一样没有成功。

CHAPTER THIRTEEN Detention with Dolores

'It's just a cut – it's nothing – it's –'

But Ron had grabbed Harry's forearm and pulled the back of Harry's hand up level with his eyes. There was a pause, during which he stared at the words carved into the skin, then, looking sick, he released Harry.

'I thought you said she was just giving you lines?'

Harry hesitated, but after all, Ron had been honest with him, so he told Ron the truth about the hours he had been spending in Umbridge's office.

'The old hag!' Ron said in a revolted whisper as they came to a halt in front of the Fat Lady, who was dozing peacefully with her head against her frame. 'She's sick! Go to McGonagall, say something!'

'No,' said Harry at once. 'I'm not giving her the satisfaction of knowing she's got to me.'

'*Got to you*? You can't let her get away with this!'

'I don't know how much power McGonagall's got over her,' said Harry.

'Dumbledore, then, tell Dumbledore!'

'No,' said Harry flatly.

'Why not?'

'He's got enough on his mind,' said Harry, but that was not the true reason. He was not going to go to Dumbledore for help when Dumbledore had not spoken to him once since June.

'Well, I reckon you should –' Ron began, but he was interrupted by the Fat Lady, who had been watching them sleepily and now burst out, 'Are you going to give me the password or will I have to stay awake all night waiting for you to finish your conversation?'

Friday dawned sullen and sodden as the rest of the week. Though Harry automatically glanced towards the staff table when he entered the Great Hall, it was without any real hope of seeing Hagrid, and he turned his mind immediately to his more pressing problems, such as the mountainous pile of homework he had to do and the prospect of yet another detention with Umbridge.

Two things sustained Harry that day. One was the thought that it was almost the weekend; the other was that, dreadful though his final detention

"只是划伤了——没有什么——没有——"

可是罗恩一把抓住哈利的胳膊,把哈利的手背拉到他的眼前。他呆呆地望着刻进皮肤里的那一行字,片刻之后,他显出恶心要吐的样子,放开了哈利。

"我记得你说她只是罚你写句子呀?"

哈利迟疑着,可毕竟罗恩已经对他说了实话,于是他把在乌姆里奇办公室里几个小时的遭遇如实地告诉了罗恩。

"那个老女妖!"罗恩厌恶地低声说道,他们在胖夫人面前停下脚步,胖夫人正把脑袋靠在相框上,恬静地打着瞌睡,"她不正常!去找麦格说说这个情况!"

"不,"哈利不假思索地说,"我不想让她知道她弄得我心烦意乱,她会感到得意的。"

"弄得你心烦意乱?你不能让她白白地这么做!"

"我不知道麦格有多大权力能够管束她。"哈利说。

"邓布利多,那就告诉邓布利多!"

"不。"哈利斩钉截铁地说。

"为什么不?"

"他需要考虑的事情太多了。"哈利说,其实这不是真正的原因。他不想到邓布利多那里寻求帮助,因为邓布利多从六月份起就没有跟他说过一次话。

"那么,我想你应该——"罗恩话没说完,就被胖夫人打断了,她刚才一直睡眼蒙眬地望着他们,这会儿忍不住嚷了起来,"你们到底给不给我口令,还是要我整夜在这里醒着,等你们两个把话说完?"

星期五早晨,天色还是和这星期的前几天一样阴沉而潮湿。哈利走进礼堂时,尽管还是习惯性地朝教工桌子扫了一眼,但实际上已经对看到海格不抱什么希望了。他立刻就把思路转到一些更迫在眉睫的事情上,比如必须完成的堆积如山的家庭作业,还有必须再到乌姆里奇那里去关一次禁闭。

那天有两件事情给了哈利一些力量。一是他想到马上就要到周末

CHAPTER THIRTEEN   Detention with Dolores

with Umbridge was sure to be, he had a distant view of the Quidditch pitch from her window and might, with luck, be able to see something of Ron's tryout. These were rather feeble rays of light, it was true, but Harry was grateful for anything that might lighten his present darkness; he had never had a worse first week of term at Hogwarts.

At five o'clock that evening he knocked on Professor Umbridge's office door for what he sincerely hoped would be the final time, and was told to enter. The blank parchment lay ready for him on the lace-covered table, the pointed black quill beside it.

'You know what to do, Mr Potter,' said Umbridge, smiling sweetly at him.

Harry picked up the quill and glanced through the window. If he just shifted his chair an inch or so to the right ... on the pretext of shifting himself closer to the table, he managed it. He now had a distant view of the Gryffindor Quidditch team soaring up and down the pitch, while half a dozen black figures stood at the foot of the three high goalposts, apparently awaiting their turn to Keep. It was impossible to tell which one was Ron at this distance.

I must not tell lies, Harry wrote. The cut in the back of his right hand opened and began to bleed afresh.

I must not tell lies. The cut dug deeper, stinging and smarting.

I must not tell lies. Blood trickled down his wrist.

He chanced another glance out of the window. Whoever was defending the goalposts now was doing a very poor job indeed. Katie Bell scored twice in the few seconds Harry dared to watch. Hoping very much that the Keeper wasn't Ron, he dropped his eyes back to the parchment dotted with blood.

I must not tell lies.

I must not tell lies.

He looked up whenever he thought he could risk it; when he could hear the scratching of Umbridge's quill or the opening of a desk drawer. The third person to try out was pretty good, the fourth was terrible, the fifth dodged a Bludger exceptionally well but then fumbled an easy save. The sky was darkening, and Harry doubted he would be able to see the sixth and seventh people at all.

了，二是尽管最后一次到乌姆里奇那里关禁闭肯定会很恐怖，但从她办公室的窗户能远远地看见魁地奇球场，如果运气好，说不定还能多少看见一点罗恩的选拔情况呢。当然，这些都是十分渺茫的希望之光，可是哈利目前的处境一片黑暗，但凡有什么事情能带来一点点光亮，他都会感到欣慰。他在霍格沃茨还从没经历过比这更糟糕的开学第一个星期呢。

那天傍晚五点钟，哈利敲响了乌姆里奇教授办公室的门——他满心希望这是最后一次。乌姆里奇喊他进去，在铺着花边的桌子上，那张空白羊皮纸已经在等着他了，旁边放着那支尖利的黑色羽毛笔。

"你知道该怎么做，波特先生。"乌姆里奇说，一边嗲兮兮地冲他笑着。

哈利拿起羽毛笔，朝窗外望了一眼。只要把椅子再往右边挪一两寸……他假装往桌子跟前挪了挪，做到了这点。现在他能远远地看见格兰芬多魁地奇球队的队员们在球场上飞来飞去的身影了，三根高高的球门柱底下站着六七个黑乎乎的人影，显然在等着当守门员。离得太远了，不可能看清哪一个是罗恩。

我不可以说谎，哈利写道。他右手背上的伤口裂开了，再次流出鲜血。

我不可以说谎。伤口陷得更深，火辣辣地剧痛。

我不可以说谎。鲜血顺着手腕流淌下来。

他冒险又朝窗外望了一眼。现在防守球门柱的不知是谁，表现糟糕透了。在哈利鼓足勇气偷看的几秒钟内，凯蒂·贝尔就连进了两球。他垂下目光，重新望着血迹斑斑的羊皮纸，真希望那个守门员不是罗恩。

我不可以说谎。

我不可以说谎。

他只要觉得有机会就抬头往窗外看，只要能听见乌姆里奇的羽毛笔写字的声音，或听见她打开书桌抽屉的声音。第三个参加选拔的人很不错，第四个非常差劲，第五个特别漂亮地躲过了一个游走球，却把一个很容易接住的球漏进了球门。天色越来越黑，哈利心想恐怕不可能看见第六和第七个候选人了。

CHAPTER THIRTEEN   Detention with Dolores

I must not tell lies.

I must not tell lies.

The parchment was now shining with drops of blood from the back of his hand, which was searing with pain. When he next looked up, night had fallen and the Quidditch pitch was no longer visible.

'Let's see if you've got the message yet, shall we?' said Umbridge's soft voice half an hour later.

She moved towards him, stretching out her short ringed fingers for his arm. And then, as she took hold of him to examine the words now cut into his skin, pain seared, not across the back of his hand, but across the scar on his forehead. At the same time, he had a most peculiar sensation somewhere around his midriff.

He wrenched his arm out of her grip and leapt to his feet, staring at her. She looked back at him, a smile stretching her wide, slack mouth.

'Yes, it hurts, doesn't it?' she said softly.

He did not answer. His heart was thumping very hard and fast. Was she talking about his hand or did she know what he had just felt in his forehead?

'Well, I think I've made my point, Mr Potter. You may go.'

He caught up his schoolbag and left the room as quickly as he could.

Stay calm, he told himself, as he sprinted up the stairs. *Stay calm, it doesn't necessarily mean what you think it means* ...

'*Mimbulus mimbletonia!*' he gasped at the Fat Lady, who swung forwards once more.

A roar of sound greeted him. Ron came running towards him, beaming all over his face and slopping Butterbeer down his front from the goblet he was clutching.

'Harry, I did it, I'm in, I'm Keeper!'

'What? Oh – brilliant!' said Harry, trying to smile naturally, while his heart continued to race and his hand throbbed and bled.

'Have a Butterbeer.' Ron pressed a bottle on him. 'I can't believe it – where's Hermione gone?'

'She's there,' said Fred, who was also swigging Butterbeer, and pointed to an armchair by the fire. Hermione was dozing in it, her drink tipping

第13章 被多洛雷斯关禁闭

我不可以说谎。

我不可以说谎。

羊皮纸上满是从他手背上流出的殷红的鲜血,他的手背疼得像着了火一般。当他再次抬头看时,夜幕已经降临,他再也看不清魁地奇球场上的情形了。

"让我们看看你有没有吃透这句话,好吗?"半小时后,乌姆里奇柔声细语地说。

她朝哈利走来,伸出她短粗的、戴着戒指的手指来抓他的胳膊。当她抓住哈利、仔细查看那些深深刻进他皮肉的文字时,哈利感到一阵烧灼般的剧痛,但不是手背在痛,而是他额头上的伤疤在痛。与此同时,他上腹部的什么地方还产生了一种十分异样的感觉。

哈利把胳膊从她手里挣脱出来,腾地站起身,直直地瞪着她。她也望着他,脸上的笑容把那张松泡泡的阔嘴抻得大大的。

"是啊,很疼,是不是?"她温柔地问。

哈利没有回答。怦怦怦,他的心跳得很响很快。乌姆里奇是在说他的手,还是她知道他刚才额头上的感觉呢?

"好吧,我认为我的目的达到了,波特先生。你可以走了。"

哈利拎起书包,尽快离开了房间。

保持冷静,他一边三步并作两步地奔上楼梯一边对自己说。保持冷静,不一定就是你认为的那样……

"米布米宝!"他气喘吁吁地对胖夫人说,肖像又一次打开了。

迎接他的是一片喧闹。罗恩迎面朝他跑来,满脸笑开了花,手里端着高脚酒杯,黄油啤酒洒得胸前都是。

"哈利,我成功了,我入选了,我是守门员了!"

"什么?哦——太棒了!"哈利说,努力使自己笑得自然一些,而他的心还在怦怦地狂跳,手还在突突地阵痛,还在流血。

"喝一点黄油啤酒吧,"罗恩塞给他一个酒瓶,"我真不敢相信——赫敏去哪儿了?"

"她在那儿。"也在大口喝着黄油啤酒的弗雷德说,指了指炉火旁的一把扶手椅。赫敏正坐在椅子上打瞌睡,手里的酒杯歪向一边,眼

CHAPTER THIRTEEN   Detention with Dolores

precariously in her hand.

'Well, she said she was pleased when I told her,' said Ron, looking slightly put out.

'Let her sleep,' said George hastily. It was a few moments before Harry noticed that several of the first-years gathered around them bore unmistakeable signs of recent nosebleeds.

'Come here, Ron, and see if Oliver's old robes fit you,' called Katie Bell, 'we can take off his name and put yours on instead ...'

As Ron moved away, Angelina came striding up to Harry.

'Sorry I was a bit short with you earlier, Potter,' she said abruptly. 'It's stressful this managing lark, you know, I'm starting to think I was a bit hard on Wood sometimes.' She was watching Ron over the rim of her goblet with a slight frown on her face.

'Look, I know he's your best mate, but he's not fabulous,' she said bluntly. 'I think with a bit of training he'll be all right, though. He comes from a family of good Quidditch players. I'm banking on him turning out to have a bit more talent than he showed today, to be honest. Vicky Frobisher and Geoffrey Hooper both flew better this evening, but Hooper's a real whiner, he's always moaning about something or other, and Vicky's involved in all sorts of societies. She admitted herself that if training clashed with her Charms Club she'd put Charms first. Anyway, we're having a practice session at two o'clock tomorrow, so just make sure you're there this time. And do me a favour and help Ron as much as you can, OK?'

He nodded, and Angelina strolled back to Alicia Spinnet. Harry moved over to sit next to Hermione, who awoke with a jerk as he put down his bag.

'Oh, Harry, it's you ... good about Ron, isn't it?' she said blearily. 'I'm just so – so – so tired,' she yawned. 'I was up until one o'clock making more hats. They're disappearing like mad!'

And sure enough, now that he looked, Harry saw that there were woolly hats concealed all around the room where unwary elves might accidentally pick them up.

'Great,' said Harry distractedly; if he did not tell somebody soon, he would burst. 'Listen, Hermione, I was just up in Umbridge's office and she touched my arm ...'

第 13 章　被多洛雷斯关禁闭

看就要洒出来了。

"嗯，刚才我把消息告诉她时，她还说她很高兴呢。"罗恩说，显得有点不高兴。

"让她睡吧。"乔治赶忙说道。过了一会儿，哈利才注意到周围那几个一年级新生脸上毫无疑问都带着刚流过鼻血的痕迹。

"来吧，罗恩，看看奥利弗的旧袍子你穿上合适不合适。"凯蒂·贝尔大声说，"我们可以把他的名字摘掉，换上你的……"

罗恩走了过去，安吉利娜大步走到哈利面前。

"对不起，我先前对你有些粗暴，波特。"她突然说，"当一个头儿压力太大了，你知道。我现在开始觉得我之前对伍德的态度有点儿不太公平。"她的目光越过高脚酒杯的边缘望着罗恩，微微蹙起了眉头。

"是这样，我知道他是你最好的朋友，但他不是最理想的，"她直率地说，"不过我认为经过一些训练，他应该没有问题。他家里出过一批出色的魁地奇球员。说实在话，我希望他以后能表现得比今天更有天分。维基·弗罗比舍和杰弗里·胡珀今晚都飞得比他好，可是胡珀动不动就哼哼唧唧，总是为一些鸡毛蒜皮的事没完没了地抱怨，维基的社团活动太多了。她自己也承认，如果训练和她的魔咒俱乐部相冲突，她会把魔咒俱乐部放在第一位。不管怎么说，我们明天下午两点钟有一场训练，这次你可一定要去。还要拜托你一件事，尽量多帮助帮助罗恩，好吗？"

哈利点了点头，安吉利娜慢慢走回去找艾丽娅·斯平内特了。哈利过去坐在赫敏身边，他刚放下书包，赫敏就猛地惊醒过来。

"哦，哈利，是你……罗恩真棒，是吗？"她睡眼惺忪地说。"我只是太——太——太累了，"她打了个哈欠，"我一点钟才睡觉，一直在织帽子。它们一眨眼就被拿光了！"

果然，哈利仔细一看，发现房间里到处藏着羊毛帽子，让毫无防备的小精灵可以无意中捡拾起来。

"太好了。"哈利心不在焉地说，如果再不马上找人说说，他就要憋得爆炸了，"听着，赫敏，我刚才在乌姆里奇的办公室里，她碰了我的胳膊……"

475

CHAPTER THIRTEEN Detention with Dolores

Hermione listened closely. When Harry had finished, she said slowly, 'You're worried You-Know-Who's controlling her like he controlled Quirrell?'

'Well,' said Harry, dropping his voice, 'it's a possibility, isn't it?'

'I suppose so,' said Hermione, though she sounded unconvinced. 'But I don't think he can be *possessing* her the way he possessed Quirrell, I mean, he's properly alive again now, isn't he, he's got his own body, he wouldn't need to share someone else's. He could have her under the Imperius Curse, I suppose …'

Harry watched Fred, George and Lee Jordan juggling empty Butterbeer bottles for a moment. Then Hermione said, 'But last year your scar hurt when nobody was touching you, and didn't Dumbledore say it had to do with what You-Know-Who was feeling at the time? I mean, maybe this hasn't got anything to do with Umbridge at all, maybe it's just coincidence it happened while you were with her?'

'She's evil,' said Harry flatly. 'Twisted.'

'She's horrible, yes, but … Harry, I think you ought to tell Dumbledore your scar hurt.'

It was the second time in two days he had been advised to go to Dumbledore and his answer to Hermione was just the same as his answer to Ron.

'I'm not bothering him with this. Like you just said, it's not a big deal. It's been hurting on and off all summer – it was just a bit worse tonight, that's all –'

'Harry, I'm sure Dumbledore would *want* to be bothered by this –'

'Yeah,' said Harry, before he could stop himself, 'that's the only bit of me Dumbledore cares about, isn't it, my scar?'

'Don't say that, it's not true!'

'I think I'll write and tell Sirius about it, see what he thinks –'

'Harry, you can't put something like that in a letter!' said Hermione, looking alarmed. 'Don't you remember, Moody told us to be careful what we put in writing! We just can't guarantee owls aren't being intercepted any more!'

'All right, all right, I won't tell him, then!' said Harry irritably. He got to his feet. 'I'm going to bed. Tell Ron for me, will you?'

第13章 被多洛雷斯关禁闭

赫敏专注地听着。哈利讲完后，她慢慢地说："你担心神秘人控制了她，就像当年控制奇洛一样？"

"是啊，"哈利压低声音说，"有这种可能，是不是？"

"我想也是，"赫敏说，不过听她的语气，似乎并不完全相信，"但我认为神秘人不可能再像支配奇洛那样支配她。我的意思是，神秘人现在已经活过来了，是不是，他有了自己的身体，不需要再去霸占别人的肉体。我想，他大概对乌姆里奇施了夺魂咒……"

哈利望着弗雷德、乔治和李·乔丹抛接黄油啤酒的空瓶子，一时间没有说话。然后赫敏又说道："去年，没有人碰你，你的伤疤也会疼起来，邓布利多不是说这与神秘人当时的感觉有关吗？我的意思是，说不定这跟乌姆里奇根本没有什么关系，发生这样的事时你正好跟她在一起，也许只是巧合而已？"

"她是魔鬼，"哈利斩钉截铁地说，"变态。"

"她确实很可怕，没错，但是……哈利，我认为你最好去告诉邓布利多你的伤疤又疼了。"

这是两天里第二次有人建议他去找邓布利多，他对赫敏的回答跟对罗恩的回答完全一样。

"我不想用这件事去打扰他。就像你刚才说的，这不是什么大不了的事。整个暑假都在断断续续地疼——只是今晚疼得更厉害一点儿，没什么——"

"哈利，我相信邓布利多愿意被这件事打扰——"

"是啊，"哈利没来得及控制住自己，脱口说道，"这是邓布利多唯一关心我的地方，是不是，我的伤疤？"

"别这么说，不是这样的！"

"我想，我还是写信把这件事告诉小天狼星吧，看看他怎么想——"

"哈利，你不能在信里谈这样的事情！"赫敏说，显得很惊慌，"你不记得啦，穆迪告诉我们写信时千万要小心！我们不能保证猫头鹰不会被人半路截走！"

"好吧，好吧，那我就不告诉他！"哈利烦躁地说。他站了起来。"我要去睡觉了。替我告诉罗恩一声，好吗？"

CHAPTER THIRTEEN   Detention with Dolores

'Oh no,' said Hermione, looking relieved, 'if you're going that means I can go too, without being rude. I'm absolutely exhausted and I want to make some more hats tomorrow. Listen, you can help me if you like, it's quite fun, I'm getting better, I can do patterns and bobbles and all sorts of things now.'

Harry looked into her face, which was shining with glee, and tried to look as though he was vaguely tempted by this offer.

'Er ... no, I don't think I will, thanks,' he said. 'Er – not tomorrow. I've got loads of homework to do ...'

And he traipsed off to the boys' stairs, leaving her looking slightly disappointed.

第13章 被多洛雷斯关禁闭

"哦,不行,"赫敏显出松了口气的样子,说道,"既然你要走了,就说明我也可以离开而不显得失礼了。我真是累坏了,明天还想再织一些帽子。对了,如果你愿意,可以帮我一起织,很好玩的,现在我的技术越来越好了,还能织出图案、小毛球和各种花样呢。"

哈利仔细望着赫敏的脸,发现那上面闪烁着喜悦的光芒,他竭力显出对她提出的建议有点儿动心的样子。

"呃……不,我恐怕不能,谢谢。"他说,"呃——明天不行。我有一大堆家庭作业要做呢……"

他拖着疲惫的脚步走向男生宿舍的楼梯,赫敏被撇在那里,显得有些失望。

CHAPTER FOURTEEN

Percy and Padfoot

Harry was first to wake up in his dormitory next morning. He lay for a moment watching dust swirl in the ray of sunlight coming through the gap in his four-poster's hangings, and savoured the thought that it was Saturday. The first week of term seemed to have dragged on for ever, like one gigantic History of Magic lesson.

Judging by the sleepy silence and the freshly minted look of that beam of sunlight, it was just after daybreak. He pulled open the curtains around his bed, got up and started to dress. The only sound apart from the distant twittering of birds was the slow, deep breathing of his fellow Gryffindors. He opened his schoolbag carefully, pulled out parchment and quill and headed out of the dormitory for the common room.

Making straight for his favourite squashy old armchair beside the now extinct fire, Harry settled himself down comfortably and unrolled his parchment while looking around the room. The detritus of crumpled-up bits of parchment, old Gobstones, empty ingredient jars and sweet wrappers that usually covered the common room at the end of each day was gone, as were all Hermione's elf hats. Wondering vaguely how many elves had now been set free whether they wanted to be or not, Harry uncorked his ink bottle, dipped his quill into it, then held it suspended an inch above the smooth yellowish surface of his parchment, thinking hard ... but after a minute or so he found himself staring into the empty grate, at a complete loss for what to say.

He could now appreciate how hard it had been for Ron and Hermione to write him letters over the summer. How was he supposed to tell Sirius everything that had happened over the past week and pose all the questions he was burning to ask without giving potential letter-thieves a lot of information he did not want them to have?

第 14 章

珀西和大脚板

第二天早晨,哈利是宿舍里第一个醒来的。他在床上躺了一会儿,望着灰尘在四柱床帷帐缝隙中透进来的那缕阳光中飞旋起舞,喜滋滋地想起了今天是星期六。新学期的第一个星期太漫长了,似乎永远熬不到尽头,就像一堂没完没了的魔法史课。

四下里是一片熟睡中的寂静,那一缕阳光仿佛是刚刚打造出来的,看来天色刚刚放亮。哈利拉开床周围的帘子,开始起床穿衣服。除了远处小鸟叽叽喳喳的啁啾,唯一的声音就是他那些格兰芬多同学缓慢、均匀的呼吸声。他小心翼翼地打开书包,拿出羊皮纸和羽毛笔,离开宿舍朝公共休息室走去。

哈利径直走向已经熄灭的炉火旁他最喜欢的那把松软的旧扶手椅,舒舒服服地坐下来,展开羊皮纸,一边打量着房间里的情景。平常一天下来,公共休息室里总是散了一地的羊皮纸团、破旧的高布石、空原料罐和糖纸,现在这些垃圾都不见了,同样不见的还有赫敏织的那些家养小精灵的帽子。哈利心不在焉地想,不知道现在有多少小精灵自愿或不自愿地被释放了。他这么想着,打开了墨水瓶的盖子,把羽毛笔伸进去蘸了蘸,然后让笔尖悬在光滑、泛黄的羊皮纸面上一英寸的地方,苦苦思索着……一两分钟后,他发现自己盯着空空的壁炉发呆,根本不知道该写些什么。

他现在才理解罗恩和赫敏暑假里给他写信有多么难了。怎么才能把刚过去的这一星期发生的每一件事都告诉小天狼星,并提出他迫不及待想问的所有问题,同时又不能让潜在的偷信贼得到许多他不想让他们知道的情报呢?

CHAPTER FOURTEEN   Percy and Padfoot

He sat quite motionless for a while, gazing into the fireplace, then, finally coming to a decision, he dipped his quill into the ink bottle once more and set it resolutely on the parchment.

> *Dear Snuffles,*
>
> *Hope you're OK, the first week back here's been terrible, I'm really glad it's the weekend.*
>
> *We've got a new Defence Against the Dark Arts teacher, Professor Umbridge. She's nearly as nice as your mum. I'm writing because that thing I wrote to you about last summer happened again last night when I was doing a detention with Umbridge.*
>
> *We're all missing our biggest friend, we hope he'll be back soon.*
>
> *Please write back quickly.*
>
> *Best,*
>
> *Harry*

Harry reread the letter several times, trying to see it from the point of view of an outsider. He could not see how they would know what he was talking about – or who he was talking to – just from reading this letter. He did hope Sirius would pick up the hint about Hagrid and tell them when he might be back. Harry did not want to ask directly in case it drew too much attention to what Hagrid might be up to while he was not at Hogwarts.

Considering it was a very short letter, it had taken a long time to write; sunlight had crept halfway across the room while he had been working on it and he could now hear distant sounds of movement from the dormitories above. Sealing the parchment carefully, he climbed through the portrait hole and headed off for the Owlery.

'I would *not* go that way if I were you,' said Nearly Headless Nick, drifting disconcertingly through a wall just ahead of Harry as he walked down the passage. 'Peeves is planning an amusing joke on the next person to pass the bust of Paracelsus halfway down the corridor.'

'Does it involve Paracelsus falling on top of the person's head?' asked Harry.

'Funnily enough, it *does*,' said Nearly Headless Nick in a bored voice.

第14章 珀西和大脚板

他一动不动地坐了一会儿，眼睛出神地望着壁炉，然后他终于拿定了主意，又把羽毛笔在墨水瓶里蘸了蘸，果断地在羊皮纸上写了起来。

亲爱的伤风：

希望你一切都好，回到这里的第一个星期糟糕极了，我真高兴终于到了周末。

我们有了一位新的黑魔法防御术课老师，乌姆里奇教授。她差不多像你妈妈一样好。我今天写信给你，是因为去年夏天我写信告诉你的那件事昨晚又出现了，当时我正在乌姆里奇那里关禁闭。

我们都很想念我们的那位最大的朋友，希望他能很快回来。

请尽快回信。

祝顺利。

哈　利

哈利把信读了好几遍，竭力从一个局外人的角度来审视它。他觉得，光靠读这封信，局外人决不会明白他在说什么——或在跟谁说话。他真希望小天狼星能够读懂关于海格的暗示，并告诉他们海格大概什么时候才能回来。哈利不想直接地问，担心会引起别人的过多注意，怀疑海格不在霍格沃茨会去做什么。

这封信很短，相比之下所花的时间就很长了。在他写信的工夫，阳光已经慢慢照到屋子中间，现在他能隐约听见楼上宿舍里的动静了。他小心地把羊皮纸封好，爬过肖像洞口，直奔猫头鹰棚屋去了。

"如果我是你，才不会走那条路呢。"哈利走在过道里时，差点没头的尼克突然从他面前的墙里飘了出来，惊得他不知所措，"皮皮鬼正在搞一个滑稽的玩笑，要捉弄下一个从走廊中间帕拉瑟胸像前面走过的人呢。"

"是不是让帕拉瑟掉在那个人的头顶上？"哈利问。

"太有趣了，确实如此，"差点没头的尼克用厌烦的声音说，"皮皮鬼从来玩不出什么巧妙精细的把戏。我得赶紧去找血人巴罗……他大

CHAPTER FOURTEEN Percy and Padfoot

'Subtlety has never been Peeves's strong point. I'm off to try and find the Bloody Baron ... he might be able to put a stop to it ... see you, Harry ...'

'Yeah, bye,' said Harry and instead of turning right, he turned left, taking a longer but safer route up to the Owlery. His spirits rose as he walked past window after window showing brilliantly blue sky; he had training later, he would be back on the Quidditch pitch at last.

Something brushed his ankles. He looked down and saw the caretaker's skeletal grey cat, Mrs Norris, slinking past him. She turned lamplike yellow eyes on him for a moment before disappearing behind a statue of Wilfred the Wistful.

'I'm not doing anything wrong,' Harry called after her. She had the unmistakeable air of a cat that was off to report to her boss, yet Harry could not see why; he was perfectly entitled to walk up to the Owlery on a Saturday morning.

The sun was high in the sky now and when Harry entered the Owlery the glassless windows dazzled his eyes; thick silvery beams of sunlight crisscrossed the circular room in which hundreds of owls nestled on rafters, a little restless in the early-morning light, some clearly just returned from hunting. The straw-covered floor crunched a little as he stepped across tiny animal bones, craning his neck for a sight of Hedwig.

'There you are,' he said, spotting her somewhere near the very top of the vaulted ceiling. 'Get down here, I've got a letter for you.'

With a low hoot she stretched her great white wings and soared down on to his shoulder.

'Right, I know this says Snuffles on the outside,' he told her, giving her the letter to clasp in her beak and, without knowing exactly why, whispering, 'but it's for Sirius, OK?'

She blinked her amber eyes once and he took that to mean that she understood.

'Safe flight, then,' said Harry and he carried her to one of the windows; with a moment's pressure on his arm, Hedwig took off into the blindingly bright sky. He watched her until she became a tiny black speck and vanished, then switched his gaze to Hagrid's hut, clearly visible from this window, and just as clearly uninhabited, the chimney smokeless, the curtains drawn.

第14章 珀西和大脚板

概能够制止这件事……再见,哈利……"

"好的,再见。"哈利没有向右转,而是向左转,走了一条较远但更安全的路去猫头鹰棚屋。他走过一个又一个窗口,都能看到外面蔚蓝明亮的天空,他的心情越来越好。他待会儿还要参加训练,终于又能回到魁地奇球场了。

什么东西蹭了他的脚脖子一下。他低头一看,只见管理员的那只骨瘦如柴的灰猫洛丽丝夫人悄没声儿地走了过去。它用两只灯泡般的黄眼睛盯着哈利看了片刻,然后钻到忧郁的威尔福雕像后面不见了。

"我没做什么坏事。"哈利冲着它身后喊道。看它那样子,无疑是一只急急忙忙去找主人汇报的猫,而哈利不明白这是为什么。他完全有资格在一个星期六早晨到猫头鹰棚屋去呀。

现在太阳已经高高地挂在天空,哈利走进棚屋时,没有玻璃的窗户晃得他睁不开眼睛。一道道银白色的阳光纵横交错地照进这个圆形房间,几百只猫头鹰栖息在栖木上,在早晨的光线中显得有点儿焦躁不安,有几只显然刚从外面捕食回来。哈利伸长脖子寻找海德薇的身影时,脚下踩着细碎的动物骨头,铺着稻草的地面发出嘎吱嘎吱的响声。

"你在这儿。"他说,在靠近拱形天花板最顶部的地方看见了海德薇,"下来吧,我有一封信给你。"

海德薇低低地叫了一声,展开巨大的白色翅膀飞下来落在他的肩头。

"是的,我知道外面写的是'伤风',"哈利对它说,一边把信拿给它用嘴叼住,然后他也不知道为什么,又压低声音说,"但是给小天狼星的,明白吗?"

海德薇眨了一下琥珀色的眼睛,哈利知道这表示它听明白了。

"那就祝你一路平安。"哈利说,带着它来到一扇窗口。海德薇用力蹬了一下他的胳膊,腾身跃起,飞到了外面明晃晃的晴朗天空中。哈利一直注视着它,直到它变成了一个小黑点,彻底消失不见。然后他把目光转向海格的小屋,从这扇窗户正好可以看得很清楚,然而烟囱没有冒烟,窗帘拉得紧紧的,很明显仍然没有住人。

CHAPTER FOURTEEN Percy and Padfoot

The treetops of the Forbidden Forest swayed in a light breeze. Harry watched them, savouring the fresh air on his face, thinking about Quidditch later ... then he saw it. A great, reptilian winged horse, just like the ones pulling the Hogwarts carriages, with leathery black wings spread wide like a pterodactyl's, rose up out of the trees like a grotesque, giant bird. It soared in a great circle, then plunged back into the trees. The whole thing had happened so quickly, Harry could hardly believe what he had seen, except that his heart was hammering madly.

The Owlery door opened behind him. He leapt in shock and, turning quickly, saw Cho Chang holding a letter and a parcel in her hands.

'Hi,' said Harry automatically.

'Oh ... hi,' she said breathlessly. 'I didn't think anyone would be up here this early ... I only remembered five minutes ago, it's my mum's birthday.'

She held up the parcel.

'Right,' said Harry. His brain seemed to have jammed. He wanted to say something funny and interesting, but the memory of that terrible winged horse was fresh in his mind.

'Nice day,' he said, gesturing to the windows. His insides seemed to shrivel with embarrassment. The weather. He was talking about the *weather* ...

'Yeah,' said Cho, looking around for a suitable owl. 'Good Quidditch conditions. I haven't been out all week, have you?'

'No,' said Harry.

Cho had selected one of the school barn owls. She coaxed it down on to her arm where it held out an obliging leg so that she could attach the parcel.

'Hey, has Gryffindor got a new Keeper yet?' she asked.

'Yeah,' said Harry. 'It's my friend Ron Weasley, d'you know him?'

'The Tornados-hater?' said Cho rather coolly. 'Is he any good?'

'Yeah,' said Harry, 'I think so. I didn't see his tryout, though, I was in detention.'

Cho looked up, the parcel only half attached to the owl's legs.

'That Umbridge woman's foul,' she said in a low voice. 'Putting you in detention just because you told the truth about how – how – how he died. Everyone heard about it, it was all over the school. You were really brave standing up to her like that.'

第14章 珀西和大脚板

禁林的树梢在微风中轻轻摇摆，哈利望着它们，享受着新鲜空气吹拂在脸上的愉快感觉，心里想着待会儿的魁地奇球训练……就在这时，他看见了它——一匹巨大的、爬行动物般的、带翅膀的马，跟那天拉着霍格沃茨马车的那些怪马一模一样。只见它像翼手龙一般将坚韧的黑色翅膀充分展开，忽地从树丛中飞了出来，如同一只奇异的巨鸟。它盘旋了一大圈，又忽地一头扎进树丛。整个事情发生得太快了，哈利简直不敢相信他看到的情景，只知道自己的心像打鼓一样怦怦狂跳。

身后猫头鹰棚屋的门开了。他吃惊地跳了起来，猛一转身，看见秋·张手里拿着一封信和一个包裹。

"你好。"哈利下意识地说。

"噢……你好。"秋气喘吁吁地说，"我没想到这么早就有人上来了……五分钟前我才想起今天是我妈妈的生日。"

她举起手里的包裹。

"噢。"哈利说。他脑子里似乎一片混乱。他很想说几句好玩的、风趣的话，但脑海里闪过的却是刚才那匹可怕的长着翅膀的怪马。

"天气真不错。"他说着指了指窗外。他的五脏六腑似乎都因尴尬而缩成了一团。天气。他居然在谈天气……

"是啊。"秋说，一边东张西望寻找一只合适的猫头鹰，"正好适合打魁地奇球。我整个一星期都没出去，你呢？"

"也没有。"哈利说。

秋选中了学校的一只谷仓猫头鹰。她轻声唤它落到她的胳膊上，猫头鹰落定后顺从地伸出一只脚，让秋把包裹系在上面。

"对了，格兰芬多找到新的守门员了吗？"她问。

"找到了，"哈利说，"是我的朋友罗恩·韦斯莱，你认识他吗？"

"就是那个讨厌龙卷风队的人？"秋很冷淡地说，"他怎么样？"

"不错，"哈利说，"我想是的。不过我没有去看他的选拔，我被关禁闭了。"

秋抬起头，包裹在猫头鹰腿上只系好了一半。

"那个姓乌姆里奇的女人真讨厌，"她低声说，"就因为你讲了——讲了——讲了他遇难的实情，她就关你的禁闭。大家都听说了这件事，整个学校都传遍了。你能那样跟她针锋相对，真是很勇敢。"

CHAPTER FOURTEEN   Percy and Padfoot

Harry's insides reinflated so rapidly he felt as though he might actually float a few inches off the dropping-strewn floor. Who cared about a stupid flying horse; Cho thought he had been really brave. For a moment, he considered accidentally-on-purpose showing her his cut hand as he helped her tie her parcel on to her owl ... but the very instant this thrilling thought occurred, the Owlery door opened again.

Filch the caretaker came wheezing into the room. There were purple patches on his sunken, veined cheeks, his jowls were aquiver and his thin grey hair dishevelled; he had obviously run here. Mrs Norris came trotting at his heels, gazing up at the owls overhead and mewing hungrily. There was a restless shifting of wings from above and a large brown owl snapped his beak in a menacing fashion.

'Aha!' said Filch, taking a flat-footed step towards Harry, his pouchy cheeks trembling with anger. 'I've had a tip-off that you are intending to place a massive order for Dungbombs!'

Harry folded his arms and stared at the caretaker.

'Who told you I was ordering Dungbombs?'

Cho was looking from Harry to Filch, also frowning; the barn owl on her arm, tired of standing on one leg, gave an admonitory hoot but she ignored it.

'I have my sources,' said Filch in a self-satisfied hiss. 'Now hand over whatever it is you're sending.'

Feeling immensely thankful that he had not dawdled in posting off the letter, Harry said, 'I can't, it's gone.'

'*Gone?*' said Filch, his face contorting with rage.

'Gone,' said Harry calmly.

Filch opened his mouth furiously, mouthed for a few seconds, then raked Harry's robes with his eyes.

'How do I know you haven't got it in your pocket?'

'Because –'

'I saw him send it,' said Cho angrily.

Filch rounded on her.

'You saw him –?'

'That's right, I saw him,' she said fiercely.

第14章 珀西和大脚板

哈利的五脏六腑又一下子膨胀起来，速度之快，使他感到自己能从落满鸟粪的地面上腾起好几英寸。谁还在乎一匹愚蠢的飞马呢，秋认为他真是很勇敢。一闪念间，他甚至想趁着帮秋往猫头鹰腿上系包裹的机会，故意假装不小心地让她看见他受伤的手背……可是这个激动人心的想法刚一冒头，猫头鹰棚屋的门又被推开了。

管理员费尔奇呼哧呼哧地走了进来。他那塌陷的、脉络纵横的面颊上满是紫色的斑点，下巴上的垂肉抖个不停，稀疏的花白头发乱糟糟的。显然他是一路跑来的。洛丽丝夫人小跑着跟在他脚后，盯着头顶上的那些猫头鹰，饥饿地喵喵叫着。上面传来一片不安地扇动翅膀的声音，一只很大的棕色猫头鹰气势汹汹地把嘴咂得嗒嗒响。

"啊哈！"费尔奇说，拖着脚朝哈利跨近一步，皮肉松弛的面颊气得直抖，"我得到了一个情报，你打算订购大批的粪弹！"

哈利抱起双臂，瞪着管理员。

"谁对你说我订购了粪弹？"

秋望望哈利，又望望费尔奇，也皱起了眉头。她胳膊上的那只谷仓猫头鹰用一条腿站累了，提醒地叫了一声，但秋没有理会。

"我有我的情报来源。"费尔奇洋洋自得地咬着牙说，"现在把你要送的东西交出来。"

哈利暗自庆幸自己没有拖延就把信寄走了，他说："交不出来，已经走了。"

"走了？"费尔奇说，气得五官都变了形。

"走了。"哈利平静地说。

费尔奇恼怒地张开嘴，嘴唇无声地开合了几秒钟，然后用眼睛扫视着哈利的长袍。

"我怎么知道你没有装在口袋里呢？"

"因为——"

"我看见他寄出去的。"秋气愤地说。

费尔奇立刻把矛头对准了秋·张。

"你看见他——？"

"不错，我看见的。"秋激动地说。

CHAPTER FOURTEEN Percy and Padfoot

There was a moment's pause in which Filch glared at Cho and Cho glared right back, then the caretaker turned and shuffled back towards the door. He stopped with his hand on the handle and looked back at Harry.

'If I get so much as a whiff of a Dungbomb ...'

He stumped off down the stairs. Mrs Norris cast a last longing look at the owls and followed him.

Harry and Cho looked at each other.

'Thanks,' Harry said.

'No problem,' said Cho, finally fixing the parcel to the barn owl's other leg, her face slightly pink. 'You *weren't* ordering Dungbombs, were you?'

'No,' said Harry.

'I wonder why he thought you were, then?' she said as she carried the owl to the window.

Harry shrugged. He was quite as mystified by that as she was, though oddly it was not bothering him very much at the moment.

They left the Owlery together. At the entrance of a corridor that led towards the west wing of the castle, Cho said, 'I'm going this way. Well, I'll ... I'll see you around, Harry.'

'Yeah ... see you.'

She smiled at him and departed. Harry walked on, feeling quietly elated. He had managed to have an entire conversation with her and not embarrassed himself once ... *you were really brave standing up to her like that ...* Cho had called him brave ... she did not hate him for being alive ...

Of course, she had preferred Cedric, he knew that ... though if he'd only asked her to the Ball before Cedric had, things might have turned out differently ... she had seemed sincerely sorry that she'd had to refuse when Harry asked her ...

'Morning,' Harry said brightly to Ron and Hermione as he joined them at the Gryffindor table in the Great Hall.

'What are you looking so pleased about?' said Ron, eyeing Harry in surprise.

'Erm ... Quidditch later,' said Harry happily, pulling a large platter of bacon and eggs towards him.

'Oh ... yeah ...' said Ron. He put down the piece of toast he was eating

第14章 珀西和大脚板

片刻的静默，费尔奇瞪着秋，秋也瞪着费尔奇。然后管理员一转身，拖着脚朝门口走去。他的手停在门把手上，扭头望着哈利。

"如果我闻到有粪弹的味儿……"

他嘟嘟囔囔地走下楼梯。洛丽丝夫人恋恋不舍地看了那些猫头鹰最后一眼，跟着他下去了。

哈利和秋互相对望着。

"谢谢。"哈利说。

"没什么。"秋说，这才终于把包裹系在谷仓猫头鹰的另一条腿上，脸上微微泛着红晕，"你刚刚不是在订购粪弹吧？"

"不是。"哈利说。

"真奇怪，那他怎么以为你订了？"她一边说一边抱着猫头鹰走向窗口。

哈利耸了耸肩膀。他和秋一样，也觉得这件事蹊跷得很，然而奇怪的是，他此刻并没有怎么把它放在心上。

他们一起离开了猫头鹰棚屋。走到一条通往城堡西侧的走廊口时，秋说："我要从这边走了。嗯，我……我们再见吧，哈利。"

"好的……再见。"

秋朝他嫣然一笑，走了。哈利继续往前走，心里暗暗地一阵狂喜。他总算跟秋有了一次完整的对话，并且没有让自己出丑……你能那样跟她针锋相对，真是很勇敢……秋说他勇敢……秋并没有因为他活着而恨他……

当然啦，她更喜欢塞德里克，哈利知道……不过，如果他抢在塞德里克之前邀请她参加圣诞舞会，事情可能会完全不同……当哈利向她发出邀请时，她似乎是真心为自己不得不拒绝哈利而感到遗憾……

"早上好。"哈利来到礼堂，来到格兰芬多桌子旁罗恩和赫敏的身边，兴高采烈地对他们说。

"你这么开心，有什么喜事啊？"罗恩吃惊地打量着哈利，问道。

"唔……待会儿要打魁地奇球嘛。"哈利高兴地说，把一大盘熏咸肉和鸡蛋拖到自己面前。

"噢……是啊……"罗恩说。他放下吃了一半的面包，喝了一大口

491

CHAPTER FOURTEEN   Percy and Padfoot

and took a large swig of pumpkin juice. Then he said, 'Listen ... you don't fancy going out a bit earlier with me, do you? Just to – er – give me some practice before training? So I can, you know, get my eye in a bit.'

'Yeah, OK,' said Harry.

'Look, I don't think you should,' said Hermione seriously. 'You're both really behind on homework as it –'

But she broke off; the morning post was arriving and, as usual, the *Daily Prophet* was soaring towards her in the beak of a screech owl, which landed perilously close to the sugar bowl and held out a leg. Hermione pushed a Knut into its leather pouch, took the newspaper, and scanned the front page critically as the owl took off.

'Anything interesting?' said Ron. Harry grinned, knowing Ron was keen to keep her off the subject of homework.

'No,' she sighed, 'just some guff about the bass player in the Weird Sisters getting married.'

Hermione opened the paper and disappeared behind it. Harry devoted himself to another helping of eggs and bacon. Ron was staring up at the high windows, looking slightly preoccupied.

'Wait a moment,' said Hermione suddenly. 'Oh no ... Sirius!'

'What's happened?' said Harry, snatching at the paper so violently it ripped down the middle, with him and Hermione each holding one half.

'"*The Ministry of Magic has received a tip-off from a reliable source that Sirius Black, notorious mass murderer ... blah blah blah ... is currently hiding in London!*"' Hermione read from her half in an anguished whisper.

'Lucius Malfoy, I'll bet anything,' said Harry in a low, furious voice. 'He did recognise Sirius on the platform ...'

'What?' said Ron, looking alarmed. 'You didn't say –'

'Shh!' said the other two.

'... "*Ministry warns wizarding community that Black is very dangerous ... killed thirteen people ... broke out of Azkaban ...*" the usual rubbish,' Hermione concluded, laying down her half of the paper and looking fearfully at Harry and Ron. 'Well, he just won't be able to leave the house again, that's all,' she whispered. 'Dumbledore did warn him not to.'

第14章 珀西和大脚板

南瓜汁，然后说："听着……你愿意早一点儿跟我一起出去吗？就是——呃——在训练前陪我练习练习？这样，你知道的，我就能多少找到点儿球感了。"

"行啊。"哈利说。

"慢着，我认为你们不应该这么做，"赫敏严肃地说，"你们俩都落下了一大堆家庭作业——"

可是她突然停住了话头。早晨的邮件来了，像平常一样，一只长耳猫头鹰叼着《预言家日报》朝她飞来，看着很危险地落在糖碗旁边，伸出了一条腿。赫敏把一个纳特塞进它的皮钱袋，拿过报纸，目光犀利地浏览着第一版，那只猫头鹰抖抖翅膀飞走了。

"有什么有趣的内容吗？"罗恩问。哈利咧嘴笑了，知道罗恩是急于把赫敏从家庭作业的话题上引开。

"没有，"她叹了口气，"都是关于古怪姐妹演唱组里那个贝斯手结婚的无聊八卦。"

赫敏展开报纸，把自己挡在了后面。哈利又津津有味地吃了一份鸡蛋和熏咸肉。罗恩呆呆地望着高处的窗户，看上去好像忧心忡忡的样子。

"等一等，"赫敏突然说道，"哦，糟糕……小天狼星！"

"出什么事了？"哈利一把抓过报纸，他用力太大，把报纸撕成了两半，他和赫敏各拿着一半。

"魔法部从消息可靠人士那里获悉，小天狼星布莱克，那个臭名昭著的杀人魔王……目前就藏在伦敦！"赫敏忧心忡忡地小声读着她那一半报纸。

"准是卢修斯·马尔福，我敢打赌，"哈利压低声音气愤地说，"他在站台上确实认出了小天狼星……"

"什么？"罗恩显得很惊慌地说，"你该不是说——"

"嘘！"另外两个同时说。

"……魔法部提醒巫师界，布莱克十分危险……杀害了十三个人……从阿兹卡班越狱出逃……又是惯常的那一套废话。"赫敏总结道，放下她那一半报纸，忧虑地望着哈利和罗恩，"得，他又一步也不能离开房子了。"她小声说，"邓布利多确实提醒过他不要出门的。"

493

CHAPTER FOURTEEN Percy and Padfoot

Harry looked down glumly at the bit of the *Prophet* he had torn off. Most of the page was devoted to an advertisement for Madam Malkin's Robes for All Occasions, which was apparently having a sale.

'Hey!' he said, flattening it down so Hermione and Ron could see it. 'Look at this!'

'I've got all the robes I want,' said Ron.

'No,' said Harry. 'Look ... this little piece here ...'

Ron and Hermione bent closer to read it; the item was barely an inch long and placed right at the bottom of a column. It was headlined:

TRESPASS AT MINISTRY

Sturgis Podmore, 38, of number two, Laburnum Gardens, Clapham, has appeared in front of the Wizengamot charged with trespass and attempted robbery at the Ministry of Magic on 31st August. Podmore was arrested by Ministry of Magic watchwizard Eric Munch, who found him attempting to force his way through a top-security door at one o'clock in the morning. Podmore, who refused to speak in his own defence, was convicted on both charges and sentenced to six months in Azkaban.

'Sturgis Podmore?' said Ron slowly. 'He's that bloke who looks like his head's been thatched, isn't he? He's one of the Ord—'

'Ron, *shh*!' said Hermione, casting a terrified look around them.

'Six months in Azkaban!' whispered Harry, shocked. 'Just for trying to get through a door!'

'Don't be silly, it wasn't just for trying to get through a door. What on earth was he doing at the Ministry of Magic at one o'clock in the morning?' breathed Hermione.

'D'you reckon he was doing something for the Order?' Ron muttered.

'Wait a moment ...' said Harry slowly. 'Sturgis was supposed to come and see us off, remember?'

The other two looked at him.

'Yeah, he was supposed to be part of our guard going to King's Cross,

第14章 珀西和大脚板

哈利愁眉苦脸地望着他撕下来的那一半《预言家日报》。那一版的大部分版面都被一则摩金夫人长袍专卖店的广告占据了，似乎是在搞减价大甩卖。

"嘿！"他说，把报纸摊在桌上，让赫敏和罗恩也能看见，"看看这个！"

"我各种袍子都有了。"罗恩说。

"不是，"哈利说，"看……这里的这篇小文章……"

罗恩和赫敏低头细看。那篇文章还不到一英寸长，在那一栏的最下面，内容是：

非法侵入魔法部

斯多吉·波德摩，现年三十八岁，家住克拉彭区金莲花公园2号，日前在威森加摩接受审判，被控于八月三十一日非法侵入魔法部并企图实施抢劫。波德摩被魔法部的警卫埃里克·芒奇抓获，芒奇发现他在凌晨一点企图闯过一道一级保密门。波德摩拒绝为自己辩护，被判两项指控成立，在阿兹卡班监禁六个月。

"斯多吉·波德摩？"罗恩慢慢地说，"就是那个脑袋上像顶着一堆稻草的家伙，是吗？他是凤凰社的——"

"罗恩，嘘！"赫敏说，一边惊恐地望望四周。

"在阿兹卡班监禁六个月！"哈利十分震惊，低声说道，"就因为企图闯过一道门！"

"别傻了，不会只是因为企图闯过一道门。他凌晨一点钟跑到魔法部去做什么呢？"赫敏压低声音说。

"你们说，他会不会是在给凤凰社做事呢？"罗恩小声而含混不清地问。

"等一下……"哈利慢慢地说，"斯多吉那天是应该来送我们的，记得吗？"

另外两人都看着他。

"是啊，他应该是护送我们去国王十字车站的警卫之一，记得吗？

remember? And Moody was all annoyed because he didn't turn up; so he couldn't have been on a job for them, could he?'

'Well, maybe they didn't expect him to get caught,' said Hermione.

'It could be a frame-up!' Ron exclaimed excitedly. 'No – listen!' he went on, dropping his voice dramatically at the threatening look on Hermione's face. 'The Ministry suspects he's one of Dumbledore's lot so – I dunno – they *lured* him to the Ministry, and he wasn't trying to get through a door at all! Maybe they've just made something up to get him!'

There was a pause while Harry and Hermione considered this. Harry thought it seemed far-fetched. Hermione, on the other hand, looked rather impressed.

'Do you know, I wouldn't be at all surprised if that were true.'

She folded up her half of the newspaper thoughtfully. As Harry laid down his knife and fork, she seemed to come out of a reverie.

'Right, well, I think we should tackle that essay for Sprout on self-fertilising shrubs first and if we're lucky we'll be able to start McGonagall's Inanimatus Conjurus Spell before lunch ...'

Harry felt a small twinge of guilt at the thought of the pile of homework awaiting him upstairs, but the sky was a clear, exhilarating blue, and he had not been on his Firebolt all week ...

'I mean, we can do it tonight,' said Ron, as he and Harry walked down the sloping lawns towards the Quidditch pitch, their broomsticks over their shoulders, and with Hermione's dire warnings that they would fail all their O.W.L.s still ringing in their ears. 'And we've got tomorrow. She gets too worked up about work, that's her trouble ...' There was a pause and he added, in a slightly more anxious tone, 'D'you think she meant it when she said we weren't copying from her?'

'Yeah, I do,' said Harry. 'Still, this is important, too, we've got to practise if we want to stay on the Quidditch team ...'

'Yeah, that's right,' said Ron, in a heartened tone. 'And we have got plenty of time to do it all ...'

As they approached the Quidditch pitch, Harry glanced over to his right to where the trees of the Forbidden Forest were swaying darkly. Nothing flew out of them; the sky was empty but for a few distant owls fluttering around

第14章 珀西和大脚板

就因为他没有露面,穆迪恼火得要命。所以他不可能是在为他们办事,对吗?"

"那,也许他们没想到他会被捕。"赫敏说。

"这也许是诬陷!"罗恩激动地嚷了起来,"不——你们听着!"看到赫敏脸上威胁的表情,他夸张地突然降低声音,继续说道:"魔法部怀疑他是邓布利多一伙的,所以——我也说不好——他们就把他引诱到魔法部,他根本就没有企图闯过一道门!他们没准是在故意编造一些借口,好把他抓起来!"

哈利和赫敏沉默了片刻,思索着他的话。哈利认为这似乎有点牵强附会,但赫敏却显得很感兴趣。

"知道吗,如果真是这样,我一点儿也不会感到吃惊。"

她若有所思地叠着她那半张报纸。当哈利放下手中的刀叉时,她仿佛突然从沉思中惊醒过来。

"啊,对了,我想,我们应该先写斯普劳特布置的那篇自株传粉灌木的论文,如果顺利的话,还可以在午饭前开始练习麦格教授的非动物驱召咒……"

哈利想到楼上等着他的那一大堆家庭作业,心里有点儿负罪感,可是外面的天空那样清澈、蔚蓝,令人心旷神怡,而他已经一整个星期没有骑他的火弩箭了……

"我是说,我们可以今天晚上再做。"罗恩说,这时他和哈利走下草坡,直奔魁地奇球场。他们肩膀上扛着飞天扫帚,耳边依然回响着赫敏严厉的警告,说他们的O.W.L.考试肯定会门门不及格。"还有明天呢。她太把功课放在心上了,那是她的毛病……"顿了一下,他又用微微有些不安的声音说,"她说不让我们抄她的,你认为她真的会说到做到吗?"

"是啊,我想会的,"哈利说,"但是这个也很重要啊,如果我们想留在魁地奇球队里,就必须多多练习……"

"是啊,没错,"罗恩说,语气一下子振作起来,"我们有的是时间做这些事……"

他们走近魁地奇球场时,哈利朝右边望去,远处禁林里的树木黑黢黢的,随风微微摇摆。不见有东西从里面飞出来,天空中什么也没有,

CHAPTER FOURTEEN Percy and Padfoot

the Owlery tower. He had enough to worry about; the flying horse wasn't doing him any harm; he pushed it out of his mind.

They collected balls from the cupboard in the changing room and set to work, Ron guarding the three tall goalposts, Harry playing Chaser and trying to get the Quaffle past Ron. Harry thought Ron was pretty good; he blocked three-quarters of the goals Harry attempted to put past him and played better the longer they practised. After a couple of hours they returned to the castle for lunch – during which Hermione made it quite clear she thought they were irresponsible – then returned to the Quidditch pitch for the real training session. All their teammates but Angelina were already in the changing room when they entered.

'All right, Ron?' said George, winking at him.

'Yeah,' said Ron, who had become quieter and quieter all the way down to the pitch.

'Ready to show us all up, Ickle Prefect?' said Fred, emerging tousle-haired from the neck of his Quidditch robes, a slightly malicious grin on his face.

'Shut up,' said Ron, stony-faced, pulling on his own team robes for the first time. They fitted him well considering they had been Oliver Wood's, who was rather broader in the shoulder.

'OK, everyone,' said Angelina, entering from the Captain's office, already changed. 'Let's get to it; Alicia and Fred, if you can just bring out the ball crate for us. Oh, and there are a couple of people out there watching but I want you to just ignore them, all right?'

Something in her would-be casual voice made Harry think he might know who the uninvited spectators were, and sure enough, when they left the changing room for the bright sunlight of the pitch it was to a storm of catcalls and jeers from the Slytherin Quidditch team and assorted hangers-on, who were grouped halfway up the empty stands and whose voices echoed loudly around the stadium.

'What's that Weasley's riding?' Malfoy called in his sneering drawl. 'Why would anyone put a flying charm on a mouldy old log like that?'

Crabbe, Goyle and Pansy Parkinson guffawed and shrieked with laughter. Ron mounted his broom and kicked off from the ground and Harry followed him, watching his ears turn red from behind.

第14章 珀西和大脚板

只有几只猫头鹰远远地在猫头鹰棚屋周围盘旋。他需要操心的事情已经够多了,那匹飞马并没有对他造成什么伤害。于是,他把它从脑子里赶了出去。

他们在更衣室的橱柜里拿了球开始练习,罗恩守住那三根球门柱,哈利充当追球手,想办法让鬼飞球突破罗恩的封锁。哈利认为罗恩的表现相当不错,哈利试图破门进球,但他进攻的球四分之三都被罗恩挡了出来,而且罗恩的状态越来越好。两个小时后,他们返回城堡吃午饭——饭桌上赫敏明确地告诉他们,她认为他们没有责任感——然后他们又回到魁地奇球场,开始真正的训练。他们走进更衣室时,除了安吉利娜,其他队友都已经到了。

"怎么样,罗恩?"乔治说,冲他眨了眨眼睛。

"还好。"罗恩说,在走向球场的一路上,他的话越来越少。

"准备在我们面前露一手,小不点儿级长?"弗雷德说,毛蓬蓬的脑袋从魁地奇袍的领口钻出来,脸上带着一丝坏笑。

"闭嘴。"罗恩板着脸说,第一次穿上了他自己的队服。袍子穿在他身上还挺合适,要知道这以前可是奥利弗·伍德的袍子,伍德的肩膀比罗恩的宽得多。

"好了,诸位,"安吉利娜从队长办公室走进来,已经换好了衣服,"我们开始吧。艾丽娅,弗雷德,劳驾你们帮大家把球箱子搬出去。噢,外面有几个人在观看,我希望你们只当没看见,好吗?"

她的语气故意显得很随便,哈利觉得自己已经猜到那些不请自来的观众是谁了。果然,当他们离开更衣室来到外面阳光灿烂的球场时,突然听到一阵尖叫声和嘲笑声,是斯莱特林魁地奇球队的队员和一些五花八门的追随者,他们聚集在空荡荡的看台中央,声音在露天球场周围响亮地回荡着。

"那个韦斯莱骑的是什么玩意儿?"马尔福用他冷嘲热讽、拖腔拖调的声音说,"怎么居然有人给那么一根发霉的破木头念飞行咒呢?"

克拉布、高尔和潘西·帕金森粗声大笑,尖声狂叫。罗恩骑上自己的飞天扫帚,蹬离了地面。哈利跟着他,从后面看见他的两只耳朵越来越红。

CHAPTER FOURTEEN   Percy and Padfoot

'Ignore them,' he said, accelerating to catch up with Ron, 'we'll see who's laughing after we play them ...'

'Exactly the attitude I want, Harry,' said Angelina approvingly, soaring around them with the Quaffle under her arm and slowing to hover on the spot in front of her airborne team. 'OK, everyone, we're going to start with some passes just to warm up, the whole team please –'

'Hey, Johnson, what's with that hairstyle, anyway?' shrieked Pansy Parkinson from below. 'Why would anyone want to look like they've got worms coming out of their head?'

Angelina swept her long braided hair out of her face and continued calmly, 'Spread out, then, and let's see what we can do ...'

Harry reversed away from the others to the far side of the pitch. Ron fell back towards the opposite goal. Angelina raised the Quaffle with one hand and threw it hard to Fred, who passed to George, who passed to Harry, who passed to Ron, who dropped it.

The Slytherins, led by Malfoy, roared and screamed with laughter. Ron, who had pelted towards the ground to catch the Quaffle before it landed, pulled out of the dive untidily, so that he slipped sideways on his broom, and returned to playing height, blushing. Harry saw Fred and George exchange looks, but uncharacteristically neither of them said anything, for which he was grateful.

'Pass it on, Ron,' called Angelina, as though nothing had happened.

Ron threw the Quaffle to Alicia, who passed back to Harry, who passed to George ...

'Hey, Potter, how's your scar feeling?' called Malfoy. 'Sure you don't need a lie down? It must be, what, a whole week since you were in the hospital wing, that's a record for you, isn't it?'

George passed to Angelina; she reverse-passed to Harry, who had not been expecting it, but caught it in the very tips of his fingers and passed it quickly to Ron, who lunged for it and missed by inches.

'Come on now, Ron,' said Angelina crossly, as he dived for the ground again, chasing the Quaffle. 'Pay attention.'

It would have been hard to say whether Ron's face or the Quaffle was a deeper scarlet when he again returned to playing height. Malfoy and the rest of the Slytherin team were howling with laughter.

第14章 珀西和大脚板

"别理他们，"他一边说一边加快速度追上罗恩，"等到跟他们比赛完，我们就会看到谁在笑了……"

"我要的就是这个态度，哈利。"安吉利娜赞许地说。她胳膊底下夹着一只鬼飞球，飞着绕过他们，然后放慢速度，在半空中停在她的队员们前面。"好了，诸位，我们先传几个球热热身，所有队员注意——"

"喂，约翰逊，你那个发型是怎么回事呀？"潘西·帕金森在下面尖声尖气地问，"怎么居然有人愿意让自己看上去像是脑袋里钻出蚯蚓来呢？"

安吉利娜把挡在脸前的长辫子甩到脑后，继续平静地说："现在散开，看看我们做得怎么样……"

哈利一转身离开了其他人，来到球场的那一端。罗恩退向对面的球门。安吉利娜一只手举起鬼飞球，使劲朝弗雷德扔去，弗雷德传给乔治，乔治传给哈利，哈利再传给罗恩，罗恩没有接住。

那些斯莱特林们由马尔福打头，又是笑又是叫。罗恩猛地冲向地面，好赶在鬼飞球落地前把它抓住。他停止俯冲时的动作拖泥带水，差点从飞天扫帚上滑下去，然后他满脸通红地重新升到传球高度。哈利看见弗雷德和乔治交换了一下眼色，但破天荒第一次他们谁也没说什么，哈利感到松了口气。

"继续传，罗恩。"安吉利娜说，只当什么事也没发生。

罗恩把鬼飞球扔给艾丽娅，艾丽娅又传给哈利，哈利传给乔治……

"喂，波特，你的伤疤感觉怎么样？"马尔福喊道，"你真的不需要躺下来休息休息吗？你肯定有整整一星期没上医院了吧，这次可是破纪录了，是吧？"

乔治把球传给了安吉利娜，安吉利娜回手传给了哈利，哈利没想到会传给自己，但还是用手指尖把球接住了，飞快地传给罗恩，罗恩扑过去接球，差几英寸没接住。

"别这样，罗恩，"安吉利娜看到罗恩又俯冲到地面去追鬼飞球，恼火地说，"多留点儿神！"

当罗恩重新升到传球高度时，很难说清是他的脸还是鬼飞球红得更厉害。马尔福和斯莱特林球队的其他球员爆发出一阵哄笑。

CHAPTER FOURTEEN   Percy and Padfoot

On his third attempt, Ron caught the Quaffle; perhaps out of relief he passed it on so enthusiastically that it soared straight through Katie's outstretched hands and hit her hard in the face.

'Sorry!' Ron groaned, zooming forwards to see whether he had done any damage.

'Get back in position, she's fine!' barked Angelina. 'But as you're passing to a teammate, do try not to knock her off her broom, won't you? We've got Bludgers for that!'

Katie's nose was bleeding. Down below, the Slytherins were stamping their feet and jeering. Fred and George converged on Katie.

'Here, take this,' Fred told her, handing her something small and purple from out of his pocket, 'it'll clear it up in no time.'

'All right,' called Angelina, 'Fred, George, go and get your bats and a Bludger. Ron, get up to the goalposts. Harry, release the Snitch when I say so. We're going to aim for Ron's goal, obviously.'

Harry zoomed off after the twins to fetch the Snitch.

'Ron's making a right pig's ear of things, isn't he?' muttered George, as the three of them landed at the crate containing the balls and opened it to extract one of the Bludgers and the Snitch.

'He's just nervous,' said Harry, 'he was fine when I was practising with him this morning.'

'Yeah, well, I hope he hasn't peaked too soon,' said Fred gloomily.

They returned to the air. When Angelina blew her whistle, Harry released the Snitch and Fred and George let fly the Bludger. From that moment on, Harry was barely aware of what the others were doing. It was his job to recapture the tiny fluttering golden ball that was worth a hundred and fifty points to the Seeker's team and doing so required enormous speed and skill. He accelerated, rolling and swerving in and out of the Chasers, the warm autumn air whipping his face, and the distant yells of the Slytherins so much meaningless roaring in his ears ... but too soon, the whistle brought him to a halt again.

'Stop – *stop* – STOP!' screamed Angelina. 'Ron – you're not covering your middle post!'

Harry looked round at Ron, who was hovering in front of the left-hand hoop, leaving the other two completely unprotected.

'Oh ... sorry ...'

第14章 珀西和大脚板

第三次，罗恩接住了鬼飞球。也许是因为松了口气，他传球出去时太激动了，球直接飞过凯蒂张开的双手，重重地撞在她脸上。

"对不起！"罗恩呻吟着说，嗖地飞过去看凯蒂伤得重不重。

"回到原位，她没事！"安吉利娜吼道，"但你是传球给队友，别想着把她从飞天扫帚上打下去，行吗？这件事有游走球来做呢！"

凯蒂的鼻子流血了。下面的斯莱特林们又是跺脚又是嘲笑。弗雷德和乔治向凯蒂靠拢过去。

"给，把这个吃了，"弗雷德从口袋里掏出一个紫色的小东西递给她，说道，"血很快就会止住的。"

"好吧，"安吉利娜说，"弗雷德、乔治，去拿你们的球棒和一只游走球来。罗恩，快到球门柱那儿去。哈利，一听到我的命令，就把金色飞贼放出来。我们要开始进攻罗恩的球门了。"

哈利跟着双胞胎飞下去取金色飞贼。

"罗恩把事情弄得一团糟，是吧？"乔治低声说，他们三个降落在装球的箱子旁边，打开箱子取出了一只游走球和那只金色飞贼。

"他只是太紧张了。"哈利说，"今天上午我陪他练习时，他挺好的。"

"哦，但愿他不会这么快就过了高峰期。"弗雷德担忧地说。

他们回到空中。安吉利娜一吹哨子，哈利放开金色飞贼，弗雷德和乔治松手让游走球飞了出去。从那一刻起，哈利就不太知道其他人在做什么了。他的任务是抓住那只振翅飞翔的小金球，那可以给自己的球队净挣一百五十分呢。要做到这点，需要有过人的速度和精湛的技巧。他加快速度，在追球手们之间灵巧地蹿进蹿出，温暖的秋风吹拂着他的脸，远处斯莱特林们的叫嚷在他耳边回响，但已经不再有任何意义……可是没过一会儿，哨声吹响，他只好又停住了。

"停下——停下——**停下**！"安吉利娜尖叫道，"罗恩——你没有守住中间！"

哈利转脸去看罗恩，只见他盘旋在左边的圆环前，另外两个圆环完全无人防守。

"哦……对不起……"

CHAPTER FOURTEEN   Percy and Padfoot

'You keep shifting around while you're watching the Chasers!' said Angelina. 'Either stay in centre position until you have to move to defend a hoop, or else circle the hoops, but don't drift vaguely off to one side, that's how you let in the last three goals!'

'Sorry ...' Ron repeated, his red face shining like a beacon against the bright blue sky.

'And Katie, can't you do something about that nosebleed?'

'It's just getting worse!' said Katie thickly, attempting to stem the flow with her sleeve.

Harry glanced round at Fred, who was looking anxious and checking his pockets. He saw Fred pull out something purple, examine it for a second and then look round at Katie, evidently horror-struck.

'Well, let's try again,' said Angelina. She was ignoring the Slytherins, who had now set up a chant of '*Gryffindor are losers, Gryffindor are losers,*' but there was a certain rigidity about her seat on the broom nevertheless.

This time they had been flying for barely three minutes when Angelina's whistle sounded. Harry, who had just sighted the Snitch circling the opposite goalpost, pulled up feeling distinctly aggrieved.

'What now?' he said impatiently to Alicia, who was nearest.

'Katie,' she said shortly.

Harry turned and saw Angelina, Fred and George all flying as fast as they could towards Katie. Harry and Alicia sped towards her, too. It was plain that Angelina had stopped training just in time; Katie was now chalk white and covered in blood.

'She needs the hospital wing,' said Angelina.

'We'll take her,' said Fred. 'She – er – might have swallowed a Blood Blisterpod by mistake –'

'Well, there's no point continuing with no Beaters and a Chaser gone,' said Angelina glumly as Fred and George zoomed off towards the castle supporting Katie between them. 'Come on, let's go and get changed.'

The Slytherins continued to chant as they trailed back into the changing rooms.

'How was practice?' asked Hermione rather coolly half an hour later, as Harry and Ron climbed through the portrait hole into the Gryffindor

第14章 珀西和大脚板

"你得一边盯着追球手,一边不停地挪来挪去!"安吉利娜说,"要么守在中间,等必须防守某个圆环时再移动,要么就绕着三个圆环盘旋,千万不能莫名其妙地移到一边去,刚才那三个球就是这样漏进去的!"

"对不起……"罗恩又说了一遍,他的脸在蔚蓝色天空的衬托下,像烽火一样红得发亮。

"还有凯蒂,你就不能想点办法止住鼻血吗?"

"越来越厉害了!"凯蒂声音发闷地说,一边用袖子堵住不断流出的鲜血。

哈利扭头去看弗雷德,只见他神色慌张,正在检查自己的口袋。哈利看见弗雷德掏出一个紫色的东西,仔细看了一秒钟,然后回过头去看着凯蒂,显然被吓坏了。

"好了,我们再试一试。"安吉利娜说。斯莱特林们正在齐声合唱"格兰芬多输惨了,格兰芬多输惨了",安吉利娜假装没有听见,但她骑在扫帚上的姿势显然有点儿僵硬。

这次他们刚飞了不到三分钟,安吉利娜的哨子就又响了。哈利刚看见金色飞贼在对面球门柱周围飞速盘旋,但也只好停下来,心里明显感到很懊丧。

"又怎么啦?"他不耐烦地问离他最近的艾丽娅。

"凯蒂。"艾丽娅简洁地回答。

哈利一转脸,看见安吉利娜、弗雷德和乔治都拼命朝凯蒂飞去。哈利和艾丽娅也迅速赶了过去。看来安吉利娜停止训练的命令下得还算及时,凯蒂的脸色白得像一张纸,身上血迹斑斑。

"她需要上医院。"安吉利娜说。

"我们送她去吧。"弗雷德说,"她——呃——大概是误吃了一颗血崩豆——"

"唉,少了击球手和一个追球手,再继续训练也没有什么意思了。"安吉利娜板着脸说,弗雷德和乔治一左一右搀扶着凯蒂朝城堡急匆匆地冲过去,"走吧,我们去换衣服。"

他们没精打采地走回更衣室,斯莱特林们还在大声唱个不停。

"训练怎么样?"半小时后哈利和罗恩从肖像洞口钻进格兰芬多公

CHAPTER FOURTEEN — Percy and Padfoot

common room.

'It was –' Harry began.

'Completely lousy,' said Ron in a hollow voice, sinking into a chair beside Hermione. She looked up at Ron and her frostiness seemed to melt.

'Well, it was only your first one,' she said consolingly, 'it's bound to take time to –'

'Who said it was me who made it lousy?' snapped Ron.

'No one,' said Hermione, looking taken aback, 'I thought –'

'You thought I was bound to be rubbish?'

'No, of course I didn't! Look, you said it was lousy so I just –'

'I'm going to get started on some homework,' said Ron angrily and stomped off to the staircase to the boys' dormitories and vanished from sight. Hermione turned to Harry.

'*Was* he lousy?'

'No,' said Harry loyally.

Hermione raised her eyebrows.

'Well, I suppose he could've played better,' Harry muttered, 'but it was only the first training session, like you said …'

Neither Harry nor Ron seemed to make much headway with their homework that night. Harry knew Ron was too preoccupied with how badly he had performed at Quidditch practice and he himself was having difficulty in getting the '*Gryffindor are losers*' chant out of his head.

They spent the whole of Sunday in the common room, buried in their books while the room around them filled up, then emptied. It was another clear, fine day and most of their fellow Gryffindors spent the day out in the grounds, enjoying what might well be some of the last sunshine that year. By the evening, Harry felt as though somebody had been beating his brain against the inside of his skull.

'You know, we probably should try and get more homework done during the week,' Harry muttered to Ron, as they finally laid aside Professor McGonagall's long essay on the Inanimatus Conjurus Spell and turned miserably to Professor Sinistra's equally long and difficult essay about Jupiter's many moons.

'Yeah,' said Ron, rubbing slightly bloodshot eyes and throwing his fifth spoiled bit of parchment into the fire beside them. 'Listen … shall we just ask Hermione if we can have a look at what she's done?'

第14章 珀西和大脚板

共休息室，赫敏很冷淡地问道。

"还算——"哈利刚想说话。

"完全搞砸了。"罗恩声音空洞地说，一屁股坐在赫敏旁边的椅子上。赫敏抬头看了看罗恩，冷淡的态度似乎缓和了些。

"没关系，你这是第一次参加训练，"她安慰道，"肯定需要时间——"

"谁说是我把训练搞砸的？"罗恩没好气地问。

"没有谁呀，"赫敏，看上去大吃了一惊，"我以为——"

"你以为我注定就是废物吗？"

"不，我当然不是这样想的！瞧，你说训练搞砸了，所以我就——"

"我要去做家庭作业了，"罗恩气呼呼地说，重重地走向通往男生宿舍的楼梯，身体一闪消失了。赫敏转向哈利。

"是他搞砸的吗？"

"不是。"哈利忠诚地维护朋友。

赫敏扬起眉毛。

"唉，我认为他可以表现得更好一些，"哈利喃喃地说，"但就像你说的，这只是第一次训练……"

那天晚上，哈利和罗恩在家庭作业上都没有取得多少进展。哈利知道罗恩尽想着他在魁地奇球训练时的糟糕表现，他自己也很难把"格兰芬多输惨了"的歌声从脑子里赶走。

整个星期天，他们都待在公共休息室里，埋头书本。房间里先是挤满了人，然后又都走空了。这又是晴朗宜人的一天，格兰芬多的大多数同学都在外面的场地上享受着也许是今年的最后一点阳光。到了晚上，哈利觉得仿佛有人在他的脑壳里使劲敲打他的脑袋。

"我们平时确实应该尽量多做掉一些作业。"哈利低声对罗恩说，他们终于结束了麦格教授的那篇关于非动物驱召咒的长篇论文，开始苦巴巴地对付辛尼斯塔教授那篇同样难、同样长的论文，是关于木星的许多卫星的。

"是啊，"罗恩说着揉了揉微微充血的眼睛，把第五张作废的羊皮纸扔进了旁边的炉火里，"哎……我们要不去问问赫敏，能不能让我们看看她写的论文？"

507

CHAPTER FOURTEEN   Percy and Padfoot

Harry glanced over at her; she was sitting with Crookshanks on her lap and chatting merrily to Ginny as a pair of knitting needles flashed in midair in front of her, now knitting a pair of shapeless elf socks.

'No,' he said heavily, 'you know she won't let us.'

And so they worked on while the sky outside the windows became steadily darker. Slowly, the crowd in the common room began to thin again. At half past eleven, Hermione wandered over to them, yawning.

'Nearly done?'

'No,' said Ron shortly.

'Jupiter's biggest moon is Ganymede, not Callisto,' she said, pointing over Ron's shoulder at a line in his Astronomy essay, 'and it's Io that's got the volcanoes.'

'Thanks,' snarled Ron, scratching out the offending sentences.

'Sorry, I only –'

'Yeah, well, if you've just come over here to criticise –'

'Ron –'

'I haven't got time to listen to a sermon, all right, Hermione, I'm up to my neck in it here –'

'No – look!'

Hermione was pointing to the nearest window. Harry and Ron both looked over. A handsome screech owl was standing on the window sill, gazing into the room at Ron.

'Isn't that Hermes?' said Hermione, sounding amazed.

'Blimey, it is!' said Ron quietly, throwing down his quill and getting to his feet. 'What's Percy writing to me for?'

He crossed to the window and opened it; Hermes flew inside, landed on Ron's essay and held out a leg to which a letter was attached. Ron took the letter off it and the owl departed at once, leaving inky footprints across Ron's drawing of the moon Io.

'That's definitely Percy's handwriting,' said Ron, sinking back into his chair and staring at the words on the outside of the scroll: *Ronald Weasley, Gryffindor House, Hogwarts.* He looked up at the other two. 'What d'you reckon?'

'Open it!' said Hermione eagerly, and Harry nodded.

第14章 珀西和大脚板

哈利朝赫敏望去。她正坐在那里跟金妮愉快地聊天，克鲁克山蜷缩在她的腿上，两根织针悬在她面前来回穿梭，她正在织一双怪模怪样的小精灵袜子。

"不行，"哈利语气沉重地说，"你知道她不会让我们看的。"

于是他们继续绞尽脑汁地想啊写啊，窗外的天空越来越黑。渐渐地，公共休息室里的人又开始变得稀少起来。到了十一点半，赫敏打着哈欠朝他们走来。

"快做完了吧？"

"没有。"罗恩没好气地说。

"木星最大的卫星是木卫三，不是木卫四，"她从罗恩身后指着他那篇天文学论文中的一行文字说道，"有火山的应该是木卫一。"

"谢谢。"罗恩凶巴巴地说，把那个写错的句子重重划去了。

"对不起，我只是——"

"是啊，如果你只是到这里来挑毛病的——"

"罗恩——"

"我没有时间听你唠唠叨叨地教训人，好吗，赫敏，我这里已经忙得不可开交了——"

"不——快看！"

赫敏指着离他们最近的那扇窗户。哈利和罗恩都抬头看去。一只漂亮的长耳猫头鹰站在窗台上，瞪大眼睛看着屋里的罗恩。

"这是赫梅斯吗？"赫敏问，显得很惊愕。

"天哪，正是它！"罗恩小声说，扔下羽毛笔，站了起来，"珀西怎么会给我写信呢？"

罗恩走过去打开窗户，赫梅斯飞了进来，落在他的论文上，伸出一条腿，上面系着一封信。罗恩把信解了下来，猫头鹰立刻就飞走了，在罗恩画的木卫一上留下沾着墨水的脚印。

"没错，这肯定是珀西的笔迹。"罗恩说，一屁股坐回椅子上，瞪着羊皮纸卷外的几行字：霍格沃茨，格兰芬多学院，罗恩·韦斯莱。他抬头望着哈利和赫敏："你们怎么看？"

"打开！"赫敏急切地说，哈利点点头。

CHAPTER FOURTEEN   Percy and Padfoot

Ron unrolled the scroll and began to read. The further down the parchment his eyes travelled, the more pronounced became his scowl. When he had finished reading, he looked disgusted. He thrust the letter at Harry and Hermione, who leaned towards each other to read it together:

> Dear Ron,
>
> I have only just heard (from no less a person than the Minister for Magic himself, who has it from your new teacher, Professor Umbridge) that you have become a Hogwarts prefect.
>
> I was most pleasantly surprised when I heard this news and must firstly offer my congratulations. I must admit that I have always been afraid that you would take what we might call the 'Fred and George' route, rather than following in my footsteps, so you can imagine my feelings on hearing you have stopped flouting authority and have decided to shoulder some real responsibility.
>
> But I want to give you more than congratulations, Ron, I want to give you some advice, which is why I am sending this at night rather than by the usual morning post. Hopefully, you will be able to read this away from prying eyes and avoid awkward questions.
>
> From something the Minister let slip when telling me you are now a prefect, I gather that you are still seeing a lot of Harry Potter. I must tell you, Ron, that nothing could put you in danger of losing your badge more than continued fraternisation with that boy. Yes, I am sure you are surprised to hear this – no doubt you will say that Potter has always been Dumbledore's favourite – but I feel bound to tell you that Dumbledore may not be in charge at Hogwarts much longer and the people who count have a very different – and probably more accurate – view of Potter's behaviour. I shall say no more here, but if you look at the *Daily Prophet* tomorrow you will get a good idea of the way the wind is blowing – and see if you can spot yours truly!
>
> Seriously, Ron, you do not want to be tarred with the same brush as Potter, it could be very damaging to your future prospects, and I am talking here about life after school, too. As you must be aware, given that our father escorted him to court, Potter had a disciplinary hearing this summer in front of the whole Wizengamot and he did not come out of it looking too good. He got off on a mere technicality, if you ask me, and many of the people I've spoken

第14章 珀西和大脚板

罗恩打开羊皮纸卷看了起来。他的目光顺着羊皮纸一行一行地扫下去，眉头皱得越来越紧。看完信后，他脸上一副厌恶的神情。他把信塞给哈利和赫敏，他们俩凑在一起同时看了起来。

亲爱的罗恩：

我刚听说（从魔法部部长本人那里获悉，他是听你们的新老师乌姆里奇教授说的）你已经成为霍格沃茨的一名级长了。

听到这个消息，我非常高兴和意外，在此先表示对你的祝贺。我必须承认，我一直担心你会走上我们所谓的"弗雷德和乔治"的道路，而不是跟随我的足迹，因此你可以想象，当我听说你终于不再藐视权威，并决心真正肩负起一些责任时，我心里是何等的快慰。

但是，罗恩，我想要给你的不仅仅是祝贺，我还想给你一些忠告，因此我是在夜里寄这封信的，而不是通过平常的早晨邮件递送。我希望你能避开别人的刺探读这封信，避免遇到令人尴尬的提问。

部长告诉我你被选为级长时漏了点口风，我听出你现在还经常跟哈利·波特泡在一起。我必须告诉你，罗恩，如果你继续和那个男孩打得火热，就极有危险丢掉你的级长徽章。是的，我相信你听了这话会感到吃惊——你无疑会说波特一直是邓布利多的得意门生——可是我觉得我有必要告诉你，邓布利多在霍格沃茨当权的日子可能不会很长了，权威人士对波特的行为有着截然不同——也许更加准确——的看法。我这里不便多说，但如果你看了明天的《预言家日报》，便会清楚地明白现在的风向——就看你是不是能够确定自己的立场！

严肃地说，罗恩，你不应该与波特成为一路货色，这可能对你的前途十分不利，我说的还有走出校门以后的人生。你肯定知道，是我们的父亲陪波特去法庭的，他今年夏天受到整个威森加摩的审问，而他是由于侥幸才逃脱了罪责。我个人认为，他是钻了空子才勉强脱身，与我交谈过的许多人都仍然相信他

CHAPTER FOURTEEN   Percy and Padfoot

to remain convinced of his guilt.

It may be that you are afraid to sever ties with Potter – I know that he can be unbalanced and, for all I know, violent – but if you have any worries about this, or have spotted anything else in Potter's behaviour that is troubling you, I urge you to speak to Dolores Umbridge, a truly delightful woman who I know will be only too happy to advise you.

This leads me to my other bit of advice. As I have hinted above, Dumbledore's regime at Hogwarts may soon be over. Your loyalty, Ron, should be not to him, but to the school and the Ministry. I am very sorry to hear that, so far, Professor Umbridge is encountering very little co-operation from staff as she strives to make those necessary changes within Hogwarts that the Ministry so ardently desires (although she should find this easier from next week – again, see the *Daily Prophet* tomorrow!). I shall say only this – a student who shows himself willing to help Professor Umbridge now may be very well-placed for Head Boyship in a couple of years!

I am sorry that I was unable to see more of you over the summer. It pains me to criticise our parents, but I am afraid I can no longer live under their roof while they remain mixed up with the dangerous crowd around Dumbledore. (If you are writing to Mother at any point, you might tell her that a certain Sturgis Podmore, who is a great friend of Dumbledore's, has recently been sent to Azkaban for trespass at the Ministry. Perhaps that will open their eyes to the kind of petty criminals with whom they are currently rubbing shoulders.) I count myself very lucky to have escaped the stigma of association with such people – the Minister really could not be more gracious to me – and I do hope, Ron, that you will not allow family ties to blind you to the misguided nature of our parents' beliefs and actions, either. I sincerely hope that, in time, they will realise how mistaken they were and I shall, of course, be ready to accept a full apology when that day comes.

Please think over what I have said most carefully, particularly the bit about Harry Potter, and congratulations again on becoming prefect.

Your brother,

Percy

第14章 珀西和大脚板

是有罪的。

也许你不敢与波特断绝关系——我知道他可能已精神错乱，而且据我所知，还有暴力倾向——如果你确实有这方面的顾虑，或发现波特的举止还有令你感到不安的地方，我恳请你找多洛雷斯·乌姆里奇谈谈，她是一位十分可爱随和的女人，我知道她一定很乐意给你一些忠告。

说到这里，我不妨再给你一点告诫。正如我前面提到过的，邓布利多在霍格沃茨掌权的日子可能很快就要结束了。罗恩，你不应该效忠于他，而应该效忠于学校和魔法部。我十分遗憾地听说，迄今为止，乌姆里奇教授努力在霍格沃茨贯彻魔法部极力倡导的变革时，居然很少得到其他教员的支持合作。（不过她下个星期就会发现工作更容易开展了——同样请看明天的《预言家日报》！）我只想说明一点——如果某个学生眼下表现出愿意协助乌姆里奇教授，两年后便很可能成为男生学生会主席！

很遗憾我暑假里未能经常看见你。我很不愿意批评我们的父母，但如果他们继续跟邓布利多周围那帮危险人物混在一起，我恐怕再也不能与他们生活在同一个屋檐下了。（如果你什么时候给母亲写信，不妨告诉她说，有一个叫斯多吉·波德摩的人，是邓布利多的密友，最近因非法侵入魔法部而被送进了阿兹卡班。也许这会使他们看清他们目前交往的都是怎样一些下三烂的罪犯。）我认为自己十分幸运地及时摆脱了与这帮人为伍的耻辱——部长对我真是宽宏大量——因此我真心希望，罗恩，你也不要让亲情蒙蔽了双眼，看不清我们父母的信仰和行为的错误性质。我真诚地希望，他们总有一天会认识到自己错了。当然，当那一天到来时，我将很愿意接受他们由衷的道歉。

请十分慎重地考虑我说的话，特别是关于哈利·波特的那些，再次祝贺你当选级长。

你的哥哥

珀　西

CHAPTER FOURTEEN Percy and Padfoot

Harry looked up at Ron.

'Well,' he said, trying to sound as though he found the whole thing a joke, 'if you want to – er – what is it?' – he checked Percy's letter – 'Oh yeah – "sever ties" with me, I swear I won't get violent.'

'Give it back,' said Ron, holding out his hand. 'He is –' Ron said jerkily, tearing Percy's letter in half 'the world's –' he tore it into quarters 'biggest –' he tore it into eighths '*git*.' He threw the pieces into the fire.

'Come on, we've got to get this finished sometime before dawn,' he said briskly to Harry, pulling Professor Sinistra's essay back towards him.

Hermione was looking at Ron with an odd expression on her face.

'Oh, give them here,' she said abruptly.

'What?' said Ron.

'Give them to me, I'll look through them and correct them,' she said.

'Are you serious? Ah, Hermione, you're a life-saver,' said Ron, 'what can I –?'

'What you can say is, "We promise we'll never leave our homework this late again,"' she said, holding out both hands for their essays, but she looked slightly amused all the same.

'Thanks a million, Hermione,' said Harry weakly, passing over his essay and sinking back into his armchair, rubbing his eyes.

It was now past midnight and the common room was deserted but for the three of them and Crookshanks. The only sound was that of Hermione's quill scratching out sentences here and there on their essays and the ruffle of pages as she checked various facts in the reference books strewn across the table. Harry was exhausted. He also felt an odd, sick, empty feeling in his stomach that had nothing to do with tiredness and everything to do with the letter now curling blackly in the heart of the fire.

He knew that half the people inside Hogwarts thought him strange, even mad; he knew that the *Daily Prophet* had been making snide allusions to him for months, but there was something about seeing it written down like that in Percy's writing, about knowing that Percy was advising Ron to drop him and even to tell tales about him to Umbridge, that made his situation real to him as nothing else had. He had known Percy for four years, had stayed in his house during the summer holidays, shared a tent with him during

第14章 珀西和大脚板

哈利抬头看着罗恩。

"嗯,"他说,努力使声音听上去似乎他觉得整件事都非常可笑,"如果你想——呃——怎么说来着?"——他看了看珀西的信——"噢,对了——跟我'断绝关系',我发誓我绝不会有暴力倾向。"

"把信还给我,"罗恩伸出手说,"他是——"罗恩冲动地说,一把将珀西的信撕成两半,"世界上——"他将信撕成四片,"最大的——"他将信撕成八片,"傻瓜。"他把碎纸片扔进了炉火。

"来吧,我们得在天亮前把这东西写完。"他轻快地对哈利说,把辛尼斯塔教授的论文又拉到面前。

赫敏望着罗恩,脸上的表情有些古怪。

"哦,把它们拿过来。"她突然说道。

"什么?"罗恩说。

"把它们给我,我看一遍,修改一下。"她说。

"你说的是真的?啊,赫敏,你真是一个救命恩人,"罗恩说,"我该说什么——"

"你只要说:'我们保证再也不把家庭作业拖到这么晚了。'"赫敏伸出两只手接过他们的论文,但她看上去还是挺愉快的。

"万分感谢,赫敏。"哈利疲倦地说,把论文递了过去,瘫坐在他的扶手椅上揉着眼睛。

时间已过午夜,公共休息室里空荡荡的,只有他们三个和克鲁克山。四下里一片寂静,只听见赫敏的羽毛笔在他们的论文上这里那里划去一些句子的声音,还有她查找摊在桌上的那些参考书、核实一些细节时翻动书页的声音。哈利累极了。他还感到内心有一种空落落的、不舒服的异样感觉,这感觉跟疲劳没有关系,而跟此刻在炉火里卷成黑色灰烬的那封信大有关系。

他知道霍格沃茨校内一半的人都认为他很古怪,甚至疯狂。他知道《预言家日报》几个月来一直在别有用心地提及他,但是此刻看见珀西信里白纸黑字地写着那样的话,得知珀西建议罗恩与他断绝关系,甚至到乌姆里奇那里去告他的状,他才第一次真真切切地认识到自己的处境。他已经认识珀西四年了,暑假曾住在他们家里,魁地奇球世

CHAPTER FOURTEEN — Percy and Padfoot

the Quidditch World Cup, had even been awarded full marks by him in the second task of the Triwizard Tournament last year, yet now, Percy thought him unbalanced and possibly violent.

And with a surge of sympathy for his godfather, Harry thought Sirius was probably the only person he knew who could really understand how he felt at the moment, because Sirius was in the same situation. Nearly everyone in the wizarding world thought Sirius a dangerous murderer and a great Voldemort supporter and he had had to live with that knowledge for fourteen years ...

Harry blinked. He had just seen something in the fire that could not have been there. It had flashed into sight and vanished immediately. No ... it could not have been ... he had imagined it because he had been thinking about Sirius ...

'OK, write that down,' Hermione said to Ron, pushing his essay and a sheet covered in her own writing back to Ron, 'then add this conclusion I've written for you.'

'Hermione, you are honestly the most wonderful person I've ever met,' said Ron weakly, 'and if I'm ever rude to you again –'

'– I'll know you're back to normal,' said Hermione. 'Harry, yours is OK except for this bit at the end, I think you must have misheard Professor Sinistra, Europa's covered in ice, not mice – Harry?'

Harry had slid off his chair on to his knees and was now crouching on the singed and threadbare hearthrug, gazing into the flames.

'Er – Harry?' said Ron uncertainly. 'Why are you down there?'

'Because I've just seen Sirius's head in the fire,' said Harry.

He spoke quite calmly; after all, he had seen Sirius's head in this very fire the previous year and talked to it, too; nevertheless, he could not be sure that he had really seen it this time ... it had vanished so quickly ...

'Sirius's head?' Hermione repeated. 'You mean like when he wanted to talk to you during the Triwizard Tournament? But he wouldn't do that now, it would be too – *Sirius!*'

She gasped, gazing at the fire; Ron dropped his quill. There in the middle of the dancing flames sat Sirius's head, long dark hair falling around his grinning face.

第14章 珀西和大脚板

界杯赛时还跟他合住一个帐篷,甚至在上学期的三强争霸赛的第二个项目中,还从他那里得到过满分,然而现在,珀西认为他精神错乱,还可能有暴力倾向。

哈利心头油然涌起一阵对教父的同情,他想,在他认识的人当中,也许只有小天狼星一个人能够真正理解他目前的感受,因为小天狼星的处境和他一样。巫师界里几乎人人都认为小天狼星是一个危险的杀人犯,是伏地魔的得力拥护者,小天狼星曾不得不顶着这样的罪名生活了十四年……

哈利眨了眨眼睛。他刚才在炉火里看到一样东西,一样绝不可能在那里出现的东西。它突然闪现,又立刻消失了。不……不可能……一定是他的幻觉,因为他正在想着小天狼星……

"好了,把这个抄一遍,"赫敏对罗恩说,把他的论文和一张她写满文字的纸推给罗恩,"再加上我给你写的这个结尾。"

"赫敏,你真是我有生以来遇见的最好的人,"罗恩有气无力地说,"如果我再敢对你耍态度——"

"——我就知道你又恢复正常了。"赫敏说,"哈利,你的没问题,只是最后这里,我想你肯定是把辛尼斯塔教授的话听错了,木卫二上覆盖着冰雪,而不是老鼠——哈利?"

哈利已经从椅子上滑下去跪在地上,此时正俯身趴在壁炉前布满焦痕和绽线的地毯上,直瞪瞪地望着火苗。

"哦——哈利?"罗恩不安地问,"你在那下面做什么?"

"我刚才在火里看见小天狼星的脑袋了。"哈利说。

他说得很平静。毕竟,他上学期就在这个壁炉里看见过小天狼星的脑袋,而且还跟它说过话。但他不能肯定这次是不是真的看见了……它刚才消失得太快了……

"小天狼星的脑袋?"赫敏重复了一遍,"你是说就像三强争霸赛期间他想跟你说话时那样?可是他现在不会那么做的,那太——小天狼星!"

她倒吸了一口气,盯着炉火。罗恩丢下手里的羽毛笔。在跳动的火苗中央,赫然出现了小天狼星的脑袋,长长的黑发垂落在笑嘻嘻的脸庞周围。

CHAPTER FOURTEEN   Percy and Padfoot

'I was starting to think you'd go to bed before everyone else had disappeared,' he said. 'I've been checking every hour.'

'You've been popping into the fire every hour?' Harry said, half laughing.

'Just for a few seconds to check if the coast was clear.'

'But what if you'd been seen?' said Hermione anxiously.

'Well, I think a girl – first-year, by the look of her – might've got a glimpse of me earlier, but don't worry,' Sirius said hastily, as Hermione clapped a hand to her mouth, 'I was gone the moment she looked back at me and I'll bet she just thought I was an oddly-shaped log or something.'

'But, Sirius, this is taking an awful risk –' Hermione began.

'You sound like Molly,' said Sirius. 'This was the only way I could come up with of answering Harry's letter without resorting to a code – and codes are breakable.'

At the mention of Harry's letter, Hermione and Ron both turned to stare at him.

'You didn't say you'd written to Sirius!' said Hermione accusingly.

'I forgot,' said Harry, which was perfectly true; his meeting with Cho in the Owlery had driven everything before it out of his mind. 'Don't look at me like that, Hermione, there was no way anyone would have got secret information out of it, was there, Sirius?'

'No, it was very good,' said Sirius, smiling. 'Anyway, we'd better be quick, just in case we're disturbed – your scar.'

'What about –?' Ron began, but Hermione interrupted him.

'We'll tell you afterwards. Go on, Sirius.'

'Well, I know it can't be fun when it hurts, but we don't think it's anything to really worry about. It kept aching all last year, didn't it?'

'Yeah, and Dumbledore said it happened whenever Voldemort was feeling a powerful emotion,' said Harry, ignoring, as usual, Ron and Hermione's winces. 'So maybe he was just, I dunno, really angry or something the night I had that detention.'

'Well, now he's back it's bound to hurt more often,' said Sirius.

'So you don't think it had anything to do with Umbridge touching me when I was in detention with her?' Harry asked.

第14章 珀西和大脚板

"我还以为你们会在其他人走光之前就上床睡觉呢。"他说,"我每小时都过来看看。"

"你每小时都在炉火里冒一下脑袋?"哈利轻声笑着说。

"只有几秒钟,看看这里是不是安全了。"

"但如果你被人看见了怎么办呢?"赫敏担忧地说。

"是啊,我觉得刚才有个女生——看她的样子,好像是个一年级新生——大概看见我了。不过别担心,"小天狼星看到赫敏一只手捂住嘴巴,赶紧说道,"等她定睛细看时,我已经不见了,我敢说她肯定以为我只是一截奇形怪状的木头什么的。"

"可是,小天狼星,这样做太冒险了——"赫敏说。

"你说起话来像莫丽。"小天狼星说,"我只有用这个办法才能过来回答哈利信上的问题,而不用靠密码——密码是可以被人破译的。"

听到提及哈利的信,赫敏和罗恩都转头望着他。

"你没说过你给小天狼星写了信!"赫敏责怪地说。

"我忘记了。"哈利说,这是千真万确的。他和秋在猫头鹰棚屋的邂逅,使他把之前发生的所有事情都忘了个精光。"别用那种眼光看着我,赫敏,谁也不可能从信里得到秘密情报。是吧,小天狼星?"

"是的,确实写得很巧妙。"小天狼星微笑着说,"好了,我们最好抓紧时间,以免被人打断——先说你的伤疤。"

"关于那个——"罗恩话没说完就被赫敏打断了。

"我们待会儿再告诉你。继续说吧,小天狼星。"

"好吧,我知道伤疤疼起来可不是好玩的,但我们认为这其实没什么可担忧的。它去年也经常疼,不是吗?"

"是啊,邓布利多说每当伏地魔有强烈的情绪波动时,我的伤疤就会疼,"哈利说,他像平常一样假装没有看见罗恩和赫敏脸上的恐惧表情,"所以,我关禁闭的那天晚上,他大概正好——也许是特别生气什么的吧。"

"是啊,现在他回来了,伤疤肯定会疼得更频繁了。"小天狼星说。

"那么,你认为这跟我在乌姆里奇那里关禁闭时她碰我并没有什么关系?"哈利问。

'I doubt it,' said Sirius. 'I know her by reputation and I'm sure she's no Death Eater –'

'She's foul enough to be one,' said Harry darkly, and Ron and Hermione nodded vigorously in agreement.

'Yes, but the world isn't split into good people and Death Eaters,' said Sirius with a wry smile. 'I know she's a nasty piece of work, though – you should hear Remus talk about her.'

'Does Lupin know her?' asked Harry quickly, remembering Umbridge's comments about dangerous half-breeds during her first lesson.

'No,' said Sirius, 'but she drafted a bit of anti-werewolf legislation two years ago that makes it almost impossible for him to get a job.'

Harry remembered how much shabbier Lupin looked these days and his dislike of Umbridge deepened even further.

'What's she got against werewolves?' said Hermione angrily.

'Scared of them, I expect,' said Sirius, smiling at her indignation. 'Apparently, she loathes part-humans; she campaigned to have merpeople rounded up and tagged last year, too. Imagine wasting your time and energy persecuting merpeople when there are little toerags like Kreacher on the loose.'

Ron laughed but Hermione looked upset.

'Sirius!' she said reproachfully. 'Honestly, if you made a bit of an effort with Kreacher, I'm sure he'd respond. After all, you are the only member of his family he's got left, and Professor Dumbledore said –'

'So, what are Umbridge's lessons like?' Sirius interrupted. 'Is she training you all to kill half-breeds?'

'No,' said Harry, ignoring Hermione's affronted look at being cut off in her defence of Kreacher. 'She's not letting us use magic at all!'

'All we do is read the stupid textbook,' said Ron.

'Ah, well, that figures,' said Sirius. 'Our information from inside the Ministry is that Fudge doesn't want you trained in combat.'

'*Trained in combat!*' repeated Harry incredulously. 'What does he think we're doing here, forming some sort of wizard army?'

第14章 珀西和大脚板

"我想没有关系。"小天狼星说,"我通过别人的评价对她有了解,我相信她不是食死徒——"

"她坏成这样,完全有资格当食死徒。"哈利面色阴沉地说,罗恩和赫敏拼命点头表示赞同。

"不错,但世界上并不是只有好人和食死徒。"小天狼星面带苦笑说道,"不过我知道她是个讨厌的家伙——你们真该听听莱姆斯是怎么说她的。"

"卢平也认识她?"哈利马上问道,想起了乌姆里奇在第一节课上谈到危险的半人半兽时的评论。

"不认识,"小天狼星说,"但乌姆里奇两年前起草了一个反狼人的法律,害得卢平简直没办法找到工作。"

哈利想起卢平这些日子显得更落魄了许多,内心对乌姆里奇的厌恶又加深了几分。

"她跟狼人有什么仇?"赫敏气愤地说。

"我想是害怕他们吧。"小天狼星说,笑眯眯地看着赫敏动怒的样子,"显然,她仇恨半人类,去年她还到处奔走游说,要把人鱼驱拢在一起,打上标签。想想吧,克利切那样的讨厌鬼还在到处乱跑,却浪费时间和精力去迫害人鱼。"

罗恩哈哈大笑,赫敏却显得很恼火。

"小天狼星!"她责备地说,"说老实话,如果你在克利切身上多下些功夫,我相信他不会无动于衷。毕竟,你是他从属的家庭里的最后一位成员,邓布利多教授说——"

"那么,乌姆里奇的课怎么样?"小天狼星打断了她,"她是不是训练你们大家去杀害半人半兽?"

"没有,"哈利说,假装没有看见赫敏为克利切辩护时被突然打断的恼火神情,"她根本不让我们使用魔法!"

"我们光是念那本愚蠢的教科书。"罗恩说。

"啊,那并不奇怪。"小天狼星说,"我们从魔法部内部得到情报,福吉不想让你们进行格斗训练。"

"格斗训练!"哈利不敢相信地说道,"他以为我们在这里做什么,组织一支巫师军队吗?"

CHAPTER FOURTEEN   Percy and Padfoot

'That's exactly what he thinks you're doing,' said Sirius, 'or, rather, that's exactly what he's afraid Dumbledore's doing – forming his own private army, with which he will be able to take on the Ministry of Magic.'

There was a pause at this, then Ron said, 'That's the most stupid thing I've ever heard, including all the stuff that Luna Lovegood comes out with.'

'So we're being prevented from learning Defence Against the Dark Arts because Fudge is scared we'll use spells against the Ministry?' said Hermione, looking furious.

'Yep,' said Sirius. 'Fudge thinks Dumbledore will stop at nothing to seize power. He's getting more paranoid about Dumbledore by the day. It's a matter of time before he has Dumbledore arrested on some trumped-up charge.'

This reminded Harry of Percy's letter.

'D'you know if there's going to be anything about Dumbledore in the *Daily Prophet* tomorrow? Ron's brother Percy reckons there will be –'

'I don't know,' said Sirius, 'I haven't seen anyone from the Order all weekend, they're all busy. It's just been Kreacher and me here ...'

There was a definite note of bitterness in Sirius's voice.

'So you haven't had any news about Hagrid, either?'

'Ah ...' said Sirius, 'well, he was supposed to be back by now, no one's sure what's happened to him.' Then, seeing their stricken faces, he added quickly, 'But Dumbledore's not worried, so don't you three get yourselves in a state; I'm sure Hagrid's fine.'

'But if he was supposed to be back by now ...' said Hermione in a small, anxious voice.

'Madame Maxime was with him, we've been in touch with her and she says they got separated on the journey home – but there's nothing to suggest he's hurt or – well, nothing to suggest he's not perfectly OK.'

Unconvinced, Harry, Ron and Hermione exchanged worried looks.

'Listen, don't go asking too many questions about Hagrid,' said Sirius hastily, 'it'll just draw even more attention to the fact that he's not back and I know Dumbledore doesn't want that. Hagrid's tough, he'll be OK.' And when they did not appear cheered by this, Sirius added, 'When's your next Hogsmeade weekend, anyway? I was thinking, we got away with the dog

第14章 珀西和大脚板

"这正是他以为你们在做的事情,"小天狼星说,"或者说得更准确些,这正是他害怕邓布利多在做的事情——组织一支自己的秘密部队,然后就可以用它跟魔法部较量了。"

听了这话,大家静默了片刻,然后罗恩说:"我还从来没听说过这么愚蠢的话呢,就连卢娜·洛夫古德的那些疯话也没这么傻。"

"那么,就因为福吉害怕我们用咒语对付魔法部,就不让我们学习黑魔法防御术啦?"赫敏说,一脸气冲冲的样子。

"是啊,"小天狼星说,"福吉认为邓布利多会不择手段地篡权夺位。他对邓布利多的疑心一天比一天重。总有一天他会捏造莫须有的罪名把邓布利多抓起来的。"

这使哈利想起了珀西的信。

"你知道明天的《预言家日报》上会有关于邓布利多的内容吗?罗恩的哥哥珀西认为会有——"

"我不知道,"小天狼星说,"我整个周末都没有看见凤凰社的人,他们一个个忙得要命。一直只有我和克利切在那儿……"

小天狼星的声音里明显透着痛苦。

"那么你也不知道海格的任何消息,是吗?"

"啊……"小天狼星说,"其实,他现在应该回来了,谁也说不准他发生了什么事情。"他看到他们愁眉苦脸的表情,又赶紧补充道,"可是邓布利多并不担心,所以你们三个也不要焦急不安。我相信海格不会有事的。"

"可是,如果说他现在应该回来了……"赫敏用焦虑的声音轻轻说。

"马克西姆女士当时跟他在一起,我们一直跟马克西姆保持着联系,她说他们在回家的路上分开了——但这并不表明海格受了伤或者——是啊,并不表明他不是安然无恙。"

哈利、罗恩和赫敏并没有完全信服,他们担忧地交换着目光。

"听着,不要太多打听海格的事,"小天狼星急忙说道,"这会使别人更注意到他没有回来,我知道邓布利多不愿意那样。海格很厉害,他一定不会有事的。"看到他们听了这话并没有高兴起来,小天狼星又说:"对了,你们下次什么时候到霍格莫德村过周末?我一直在想,上

disguise at the station, didn't we? I thought I could –'

'NO!' said Harry and Hermione together, very loudly.

'Sirius, didn't you see the *Daily Prophet*?' said Hermione anxiously.

'Oh, that,' said Sirius, grinning, 'they're always guessing where I am, they haven't really got a clue –'

'Yeah, but we think this time they have,' said Harry. 'Something Malfoy said on the train made us think he knew it was you, and his father was on the platform, Sirius – you know, Lucius Malfoy – so don't come up here, whatever you do. If Malfoy recognises you again –'

'All right, all right, I've got the point,' said Sirius. He looked most displeased. 'Just an idea, thought you might like to get together.'

'I would, I just don't want you chucked back in Azkaban!' said Harry.

There was a pause in which Sirius looked out of the fire at Harry, a crease between his sunken eyes.

'You're less like your father than I thought,' he said finally, a definite coolness in his voice. 'The risk would've been what made it fun for James.'

'Look –'

'Well, I'd better get going, I can hear Kreacher coming down the stairs,' said Sirius, but Harry was sure he was lying. 'I'll write to tell you a time I can make it back into the fire, then, shall I? If you can stand to risk it?'

There was a tiny *pop*, and the place where Sirius's head had been was flickering flame once more.

第14章 珀西和大脚板

次我在火车站装狗装得很成功,是不是?我想我可以——"

"不!"哈利和赫敏同时说,声音很响。

"小天狼星,你没有看《预言家日报》吗?"赫敏忧心忡忡地问。

"噢,那个,"小天狼星咧嘴笑着说,"他们总是猜测我在哪儿,但并没有真的搞到什么线索——"

"不,我们认为这次他们发现了线索。"哈利说,"马尔福在火车上说了一句话,使我们觉得他知道那条狗就是你,当时他父亲就在站台上——你知道的,小天狼星,就是卢修斯·马尔福——所以千万千万别再上这儿来了。如果马尔福再认出你来——"

"好吧,好吧,我明白了,"小天狼星说,显得很不高兴,"我只是一时兴起,以为你们大概愿意一起聚聚。"

"我愿意啊,只是不愿意你再被关进阿兹卡班!"哈利说。

片刻的静默,小天狼星从炉火里望着哈利,凹陷的眼睛中间有一道深纹。

"你不如我想的那样像你父亲,"他最后说道,声音里明显透着冷淡,"对詹姆来说,只有冒险才是有趣的。"

"可是——"

"好了,我得走了,我听见克利切下楼来了。"小天狼星说,但哈利可以肯定他在说谎,"那么我写信告诉你我什么时候能再回到炉火里,好吗?不知你敢不敢冒这个险?"

随着噗的一声轻响,小天狼星的脑袋不见了,那里重又闪烁着跳动的火苗。

CHAPTER FIFTEEN

The Hogwarts High Inquisitor

They had expected to have to comb Hermione's *Daily Prophet* carefully next morning to find the article Percy had mentioned in his letter. However, the departing delivery owl had barely cleared the top of the milk jug when Hermione let out a huge gasp and flattened the newspaper to reveal a large photograph of Dolores Umbridge, smiling widely and blinking slowly at them from beneath the headline.

MINISTRY SEEKS EDUCATIONAL REFORM
DOLORES UMBRIDGE APPOINTED
FIRST EVER HIGH INQUISITOR

'Umbridge – "High Inquisitor"?' said Harry darkly, his half-eaten piece of toast slipping from his fingers. 'What does *that* mean?'

Hermione read aloud:

> *'In a surprise move last night the Ministry of Magic passed new legislation giving itself an unprecedented level of control at Hogwarts School of Witchcraft and Wizardry.*
>
> *'"The Minister has been growing uneasy about goings-on at Hogwarts for some time," said Junior Assistant to the Minister, Percy Weasley. "He is now responding to concerns voiced by anxious parents, who feel the school may be moving in a direction they do not approve of."*
>
> *'This is not the first time in recent weeks that the Minister, Cornelius Fudge, has used new laws to effect improvements at the wizarding school. As recently as 30th August, Educational Decree Number Twenty-two was passed, to ensure*

第 15 章

霍格沃茨的高级调查官

他们本来以为第二天早晨要在赫敏的《预言家日报》上仔细搜寻，才能找到珀西信里提到的那篇文章。然而，送信的猫头鹰刚从牛奶罐上飞开，赫敏就猛地吸了口冷气。她展开报纸，露出一幅多洛雷斯·乌姆里奇的大照片。她满脸笑容，朝他们一下一下地眨着眼睛，上面是标题：

魔法部寻求教育改革
多洛雷斯·乌姆里奇被任命为
第一任高级调查官

"乌姆里奇——高级调查官？"哈利阴沉地说，吃了一半的面包片从他指间滑落，"这是什么意思？"

赫敏大声念道：

> 昨晚魔法部出人意料地通过了一项新的法令，使其对霍格沃茨魔法学校的控制达到了前所未有的程度。
>
> "一段时间以来，部长对霍格沃茨的现状日益感到不安。"部长初级助理珀西·韦斯莱说，"他是听了家长们的担忧之后采取的行动，忧心忡忡的家长们觉得学校似乎正朝着一个他们很不赞成的方向发展。"
>
> 在最近几个星期，部长康奈利·福吉已经不是第一次采用新的法令对魔法学校实施改进。就在不久前的八月三十日通过了《第

CHAPTER FIFTEEN   The Hogwarts High Inquisitor

that, in the event of the current Headmaster being unable to provide a candidate for a teaching post, the Ministry should select an appropriate person.

"'That's how Dolores Umbridge came to be appointed to the teaching staff at Hogwarts," said Weasley last night. "Dumbledore couldn't find anyone so the Minister put in Umbridge, and of course, she's been an immediate success —'"

'She's been a WHAT?' said Harry loudly.

'Wait, there's more,' said Hermione grimly.

"'— an immediate success, totally revolutionising the teaching of Defence Against the Dark Arts and providing the Minister with on-the-ground feedback about what's really happening at Hogwarts."

'It is this last function that the Ministry has now formalised with the passing of Educational Decree Number Twenty-three, which creates the new position of Hogwarts High Inquisitor.

"'This is an exciting new phase in the Minister's plan to get to grips with what some are calling the falling standards at Hogwarts," said Weasley. "The Inquisitor will have powers to inspect her fellow educators and make sure that they are coming up to scratch. Professor Umbridge has been offered this position in addition to her own teaching post and we are delighted to say that she has accepted."

'The Ministry's new moves have received enthusiastic support from parents of students at Hogwarts.

"'I feel much easier in my mind now that I know Dumbledore is being subjected to fair and objective evaluation," said Mr Lucius Malfoy, 41, speaking from his Wiltshire mansion last night. "Many of us with our children's best interests at heart have been concerned about some of Dumbledore's eccentric decisions in the last few years and are glad to know that the Ministry is keeping an eye on the situation."

'Among those eccentric decisions are undoubtedly the controversial staff appointments previously described in this newspaper, which have included the employment of werewolf Remus Lupin, half-giant Rubeus Hagrid and delusional ex-Auror, "Mad-Eye" Moody.

'Rumours abound, of course, that Albus Dumbledore, once Supreme Mugwump of the International Confederation of Wizards and Chief Warlock of the Wizengamot, is no longer up to the task of managing the prestigious school of Hogwarts.

第15章 霍格沃茨的高级调查官

二十二号教育令》，确保如果目前的校长不能提供某一教职的候选人，将由魔法部推荐一个合适的人选。

"多洛雷斯·乌姆里奇就是这样被任命为霍格沃茨的教师的，"韦斯莱昨晚说，"邓布利多找不到人，部长就指派了乌姆里奇，不用说，她立刻就大获成功——"

"她立刻就**什么**？"哈利大声说。
"等等，还没完呢。"赫敏板着脸说。

"——立刻就大获成功，使黑魔法防御术课发生了突破性变革，并及时向部长提供了霍格沃茨真实状况的现场反馈信息。"

最近这次临时行动因魔法部《第二十三号教育令》的通过而正式生效，同时产生了霍格沃茨高级调查官这一新的职位。

"在部长试图控制所谓霍格沃茨教育水平下降趋势的计划中，这是一个令人激动的新阶段。"韦斯莱说，"调查官将有权审查她的教员同事，确保他们都能达到标准。乌姆里奇教授在其教职之外被授予这一职位，我们很高兴地告诉大家她已经欣然接受。"

魔法部的这些新措施得到了霍格沃茨学生家长的热烈支持。

"现在知道邓布利多将得到公正而客观的评估，我总算安心多了。"现年四十一岁的卢修斯·马尔福先生昨晚在他威尔特郡的宅邸里说，"我们许多关心自己孩子切身利益的人最近几年一直为邓布利多的古怪决策忧心忡忡，现在得知魔法部正在密切注意这一局面，感到十分欣慰。"

那些古怪决策，无疑包括任用有争议的教职员工，对此本报已有过评述，譬如雇用狼人莱姆斯·卢平，二分之一混血统巨人鲁伯·海格，以及有妄想症的前傲罗"疯眼汉"穆迪。

当然人们还纷纷传言，阿不思·邓布利多，一度曾是国际巫师联合会的会长和威森加摩的首席魔法师，现已不再能够承担管理霍格沃茨这所名校的重任。

CHAPTER FIFTEEN The Hogwarts High Inquisitor

'"I think the appointment of the Inquisitor is a first step towards ensuring that Hogwarts has a headmaster in whom we can all repose our confidence," said a Ministry insider last night.

'Wizengamot elders Griselda Marchbanks and Tiberius Ogden have resigned in protest at the introduction of the post of Inquisitor to Hogwarts.

'"Hogwarts is a school, not an outpost of Cornelius Fudge's office," said Madam Marchbanks. "This is a further disgusting attempt to discredit Albus Dumbledore."

'(For a full account of Madam Marchbanks's alleged links to subversive goblin groups, turn to page seventeen.)'

Hermione finished reading and looked across the table at the other two.

'So now we know how we ended up with Umbridge! Fudge passed this "Educational Decree" and forced her on us! And now he's given her the power to inspect the other teachers!' Hermione was breathing fast and her eyes were very bright. 'I can't believe this. It's *outrageous*!'

'I know it is,' said Harry. He looked down at his right hand, clenched on the table-top, and saw the faint white outline of the words Umbridge had forced him to cut into his skin.

But a grin was unfurling on Ron's face.

'What?' said Harry and Hermione together, staring at him.

'Oh, I can't wait to see McGonagall inspected,' said Ron happily. 'Umbridge won't know what's hit her.'

'Well, come on,' said Hermione, jumping up, 'we'd better get going, if she's inspecting Binns's class we don't want to be late ...'

But Professor Umbridge was not inspecting their History of Magic lesson, which was just as dull as the previous Monday, nor was she in Snape's dungeon when they arrived for double Potions, where Harry's moonstone essay was handed back to him with a large, spiky black 'D' scrawled in an upper corner.

'I have awarded you the grades you would have received if you presented this work in your O.W.L.,' said Snape with a smirk, as he swept among them, passing back their homework. 'This should give you a realistic idea of what to expect in the examination.'

第15章 霍格沃茨的高级调查官

"我认为,任命一位调查官,是保证霍格沃茨拥有一位我们都能信任的校长的第一步。"一位魔法部内部人士昨晚说。

威森加摩的元老格丝尔达·玛奇班和提贝卢斯·奥格登因抗议给霍格沃茨委派调查官而辞职。

"霍格沃茨是一所学校,不是康奈利·福吉办公室的外派驻地。"玛奇班夫人说,"这是企图进一步败坏阿不思·邓布利多的名声,是令人厌恶的行为。"

(关于玛奇班夫人被指控暗中勾结妖精颠覆集团的详细报道,请见本报第十七版。)

赫敏念完了,隔着桌子看着哈利和罗恩。

"现在总算知道怎么会给我们弄来个乌姆里奇了!福吉通过这个'教育令'硬把她派到了我们这里!现在福吉又给她权力审查其他教师!"赫敏呼吸急促,两只眼睛炯炯发亮,"我真不敢相信。这简直是无耻!"

"我知道是无耻。"哈利说。他低眼望着放在桌上紧握的右手,看见乌姆里奇逼他刻进皮肤里的那句话还留着的泛白的淡淡痕迹。

可是罗恩脸上绽开了一个调皮的微笑。

"怎么啦?"哈利和赫敏瞪着他同时问道。

"哦,我迫不及待地想看到麦格教授被审查,"罗恩开心地说,"乌姆里奇挨了打都不会知道是怎么回事。"

"哎呀,快点吧,"赫敏说着一跃而起,"我们得走了,如果她要检查宾斯的课,我们可不能迟到……"

然而乌姆里奇教授并没有检查他们的魔法史课,这节课仍然跟上个星期一那样枯燥乏味。后来他们赶去上两节魔药课时,乌姆里奇也不在斯内普的地下教室里。哈利那篇月长石的论文发下来了,顶上一角草草地批着一个又长又尖的黑黑的"D"。

"如果你们在 O.W.L. 考试中交出这样的东西,我给你们的这个成绩就是你们将会得到的。"斯内普讥笑着说,一边快步走在全班同学中间,把家庭作业发还给他们,"这应该使你们对考试中会出现什么内容有一个清醒的认识。"

CHAPTER FIFTEEN   The Hogwarts High Inquisitor

Snape reached the front of the class and turned to face them.

'The general standard of this homework was abysmal. Most of you would have failed had this been your examination. I expect to see a great deal more effort for this week's essay on the various varieties of venom antidotes, or I shall have to start handing out detentions to those dunces who get a "D".'

He smirked as Malfoy sniggered and said in a carrying whisper, 'Some people got a "*D*"? Ha!'

Harry realised that Hermione was looking sideways to see what grade he had received; he slid his moonstone essay back into his bag as quickly as possible, feeling that he would rather keep that information private.

Determined not to give Snape an excuse to fail him this lesson, Harry read and reread every line of instructions on the blackboard at least three times before acting on them. His Strengthening Solution was not precisely the clear turquoise shade of Hermione's but it was at least blue rather than pink, like Neville's, and he delivered a flask of it to Snape's desk at the end of the lesson with a feeling of mingled defiance and relief.

'Well, that wasn't as bad as last week, was it?' said Hermione, as they climbed the steps out of the dungeon and made their way across the Entrance Hall towards lunch. 'And the homework didn't go too badly, either, did it?'

When neither Ron nor Harry answered, she pressed on, 'I mean, all right, I didn't expect the top grade, not if he's marking to O.W.L. standard, but a pass is quite encouraging at this stage, wouldn't you say?'

Harry made a non-committal noise in his throat.

'Of course, a lot can happen between now and the exam, we've got plenty of time to improve, but the grades we're getting now are a sort of baseline, aren't they? Something we can build on ...'

They sat down together at the Gryffindor table.

'Obviously, I'd have been *thrilled* if I'd got an "O" –'

'Hermione,' said Ron sharply, 'if you want to know what grades we got, ask.'

'I don't – I didn't mean – well, if you want to tell me –'

'I got a "P",' said Ron, ladling soup into his bowl. 'Happy?'

'Well, that's nothing to be ashamed of,' said Fred, who had just arrived at the table with George and Lee Jordan and was sitting down on Harry's right. 'Nothing wrong with a good healthy "P".'

第15章 霍格沃茨的高级调查官

斯内普走到教室前面，转身朝着同学们。

"这次家庭作业的总体水平糟糕透了。如果是考试，你们大多数人都不会及格。我希望，在本星期关于各种不同类型的解毒剂的论文中，你们能够多下一些功夫，不然我就不得不让那些得了'D'的笨蛋关禁闭了。"

他满脸讥笑，马尔福轻轻地嗤笑几声，用虽然很小，但传得很远的声音说："还有人得了'D'？哈！"

哈利意识到赫敏侧脸望过来，想看看他得到了什么成绩。他赶紧把那篇月长石的论文塞进书包，他觉得宁愿不让别人知道这件事。

哈利拿定主意，这节课绝不再让斯内普抓到把柄，判他不及格。他把黑板上的每行说明反复看了至少三遍才开始操作。他配制出来的增强剂虽然不像赫敏的那样是清澈的碧绿色，但至少是蓝色的，而不像纳威的那样是粉红色的。下课时，他怀着一种示威和宽慰混杂的心情，装了一瓶样品送到斯内普的讲台上。

"还好，不像上星期那么糟糕了，是不是？"赫敏说，这时他们离开地下教室走上阶梯，穿过门厅去吃午饭，"家庭作业也不算太坏，是不是？"

看到罗恩和哈利都没有回答，她又继续说道："我是说，我并不指望得到最高成绩，因为他是按照 O.W.L. 考试的标准给我们打分的，但在这个阶段能及格就很令人鼓舞了，你们说不是吗？"

哈利喉咙里发出一点含糊的声音。

"当然啦，从现在开始到考试，还会出现很多变化，我们有足够的时间提高和进步，但现在得到的成绩就像是一个起点线，是不是？我们可以在此基础上……"

他们一起在格兰芬多桌旁坐了下来。

"不用说，如果我得到一个'O'，肯定会兴奋得要命——"

"赫敏，"罗恩尖刻地说，"如果你想知道我们得了什么成绩，就直接问好了。"

"我不——我不是这意思——不过，如果你们愿意告诉我——"

"我得了个'P'，"罗恩一边说一边把汤舀进自己碗里，"高兴了吧？"

"唉，这没有什么可丢脸的，"弗雷德说，他刚和乔治、李·乔丹一起来到桌旁，坐在了哈利右边，"一个健康又精神的'P'，没有什么不好。"

CHAPTER FIFTEEN   The Hogwarts High Inquisitor

'But,' said Hermione, 'doesn't "P" stand for ...'

'"Poor", yeah,' said Lee Jordan. 'Still, better than "D", isn't it? "Dreadful"?'

Harry felt his face grow warm and faked a small coughing fit over his roll. When he emerged from this he was sorry to find that Hermione was still in full flow about O.W.L. grades.

'So top grade's "O" for "Outstanding",' she was saying, 'and then there's "A" –'

'No, "E",' George corrected her, '"E" for "Exceeds Expectations". And I've always thought Fred and I should've got "E" in everything, because we exceeded expectations just by turning up for the exams.'

They all laughed except Hermione, who ploughed on, 'So, after "E" it's "A" for "Acceptable", and that's the last pass grade, isn't it?'

'Yep,' said Fred, dunking an entire roll in his soup, transferring it to his mouth and swallowing it whole.

'Then you get "P" for "Poor"–' Ron raised both his arms in mock celebration – 'and "D" for "Dreadful".'

'And then "T",' George reminded him.

'"T"?' asked Hermione, looking appalled. 'even lower than a "D"? What on earth does "T" stand for?'

'"Troll",' said George promptly.

Harry laughed again, though he was not sure whether or not George was joking. He imagined trying to conceal from Hermione that he had received 'T's in all his O.W.L.s and immediately resolved to work harder from now on.

'You lot had an inspected lesson yet?' Fred asked them.

'No,' said Hermione at once. 'Have you?'

'Just now, before lunch,' said George. 'Charms.'

'What was it like?' Harry and Hermione asked together.

Fred shrugged.

'Not that bad. Umbridge just lurked in the corner making notes on a clipboard. You know what Flitwick's like, he treated her like a guest, didn't seem to bother him at all. She didn't say much. Asked Alicia a couple of questions about what the classes are normally like, Alicia told her they were

"可是,"赫敏说,"'P'不是代表……"

"'差',没错,"李·乔丹说,"但还是比'D'强啊,对不对?'D'是'糟透了'?"

哈利觉得脸上一阵发烧,假装被面包卷呛着了,咳嗽了几声。等他缓过劲来,发现赫敏还在大谈特谈O.W.L.考试评分等级的事,不禁十分懊丧。

"最高成绩'O'代表'优秀',"只听她说道,"然后是'A'——"

"不,是'E',"乔治纠正她说,"'E'代表'超出预期'。我总是觉得,弗雷德和我每门功课都应该得到'E',因为我们来参加考试就是超出预期了。"

他们都大笑起来,只有赫敏没笑,她不屈不挠地探讨着这个话题:"那么,'E'后面是'A',代表'及格',那是最低的及格线,是不是?"

"没错。"弗雷德说,把整个面包卷在汤里浸了浸,塞进嘴里,一口吞了下去。

"那么,'P'就是'差'——"罗恩举起双臂,假装庆祝,"——然后是'D',代表'糟透了'。"

"后面还有'T'呢。"乔治提醒他。

"'T'?"赫敏问,显然吓了一跳,"比'D'还要低吗?'T'代表的是什么呢?"

"'巨怪'。"乔治不假思索地说。

哈利又笑了起来,尽管他不能肯定乔治是不是在开玩笑。他想象着自己拼命瞒着赫敏,不让她知道他在O.W.L.考试中每门功课都得了"T"的情景,便立刻下定决心,从现在起一定要用功学习。

"你们的课被检查过吗?"弗雷德问他们。

"没有。"赫敏立刻说,"你们呢?"

"就在刚才,吃饭之前,"乔治说,"是魔咒课。"

"怎么样啊?"哈利和赫敏同时问。

弗雷德耸了耸肩膀。

"还不算坏。乌姆里奇只是缩在墙角,在写字板上不停地做笔记。你们知道弗立维的脾气,他把乌姆里奇当成一个客人,似乎根本没把这事放在心上。乌姆里奇没说多少话。问了艾丽娅几个问题,打听平

CHAPTER FIFTEEN The Hogwarts High Inquisitor

really good, that was it.'

'I can't see old Flitwick getting marked down,' said George, 'he usually gets everyone through their exams all right.'

'Who've you got this afternoon?' Fred asked Harry.

'Trelawney –'

'A "T" if ever I saw one.'

'– and Umbridge herself.'

'Well, be a good boy and keep your temper with Umbridge today,' said George. 'Angelina'll do her nut if you miss any more Quidditch practices.'

But Harry did not have to wait for Defence Against the Dark Arts to meet Professor Umbridge. He was pulling out his dream diary in a seat at the very back of the shadowy Divination room when Ron elbowed him in the ribs and, looking round, he saw Professor Umbridge emerging through the trapdoor in the floor. The class, which had been talking cheerily, fell silent at once. The abrupt fall in the noise level made Professor Trelawney, who had been wafting about handing out copies of *The Dream Oracle*, look round.

'Good afternoon, Professor Trelawney,' said Professor Umbridge with her wide smile. 'You received my note, I trust? Giving the time and date of your inspection?'

Professor Trelawney nodded curtly and, looking very disgruntled, turned her back on Professor Umbridge and continued to give out books. Still smiling, Professor Umbridge grasped the back of the nearest armchair and pulled it to the front of the class so that it was a few inches behind Professor Trelawney's seat. She then sat down, took her clipboard from her flowery bag and looked up expectantly, waiting for the class to begin.

Professor Trelawney pulled her shawls tight about her with slightly trembling hands and surveyed the class through her hugely magnifying lenses.

'We shall be continuing our study of prophetic dreams today,' she said in a brave attempt at her usual mystic tones, though her voice shook slightly. 'Divide into pairs, please, and interpret each other's latest night-time visions with the aid of the *Oracle*.'

She made as though to sweep back to her seat, saw Professor Umbridge sitting right beside it, and immediately veered left towards Parvati and Lavender, who were already deep in discussion about Parvati's most recent dream.

常上课是什么样的。艾丽娅回答说课上得非常好,就是这些。"

"我认为弗立维的分数不会低,"乔治说,"他总是让每个人都能通过考试。"

"你们今天下午是谁的课?"弗雷德问哈利。

"特里劳尼——"

"要是我见过一个'T',那就是她了。"

"——还有乌姆里奇本人。"

"啊,今天你要表现得规矩一点儿,在乌姆里奇面前管住自己的脾气。"乔治说,"如果你再错过魁地奇球训练,安吉利娜肯定要气得发疯了。"

可是哈利不用等到上黑魔法防御术课才能见到乌姆里奇教授。在昏暗的占卜课教室最后排的座位上,哈利正要抽出他的做梦日记,罗恩用胳膊肘捅了捅他。他转脸一看,只见乌姆里奇教授从地板上的活板门里钻了出来。正在说说笑笑的同学们顿时沉默了,正在走来走去分发《解梦指南》的特里劳尼教授听见教室里的声音突然低了下去,便回过头来。

"下午好,特里劳尼教授,"乌姆里奇教授又是那种满脸堆笑的样子,"我相信你一定收到我的通知了?上面写着检查你上课的日期和时间。"

特里劳尼教授板着脸点点头,显得很不高兴,转身背朝乌姆里奇教授,继续发课本。乌姆里奇教授仍然满脸是笑,抓住离她最近的那把扶手椅的椅背,把椅子拉到教室前面,放在特里劳尼教授座位后面几英寸的地方。然后她坐下来,从花里胡哨的包里掏出写字板,满怀期待地抬起头,等着开始上课。

特里劳尼教授用微微发抖的双手紧了紧身上裹的披肩,透过那副把眼睛放大了好多倍的大眼镜审视着全班同学。

"今天我们继续学习有预示性的梦,"她勇敢地用平常那种神秘莫测的语气说话,然而声音有些微微发抖,"请同学们分成两人一组,在《解梦指南》的帮助下,互相解释对方最近在梦里看到的情景。"

她刚要快步走回自己的座位,突然看见乌姆里奇教授就坐在那旁边,便立刻向左一转,朝帕瓦蒂和拉文德走去,她们俩已经在专心讨论帕瓦蒂最近做的一个梦了。

CHAPTER FIFTEEN   The Hogwarts High Inquisitor

Harry opened his copy of *The Dream Oracle*, watching Umbridge covertly. She was already making notes on her clipboard. After a few minutes she got to her feet and began to pace the room in Trelawney's wake, listening to her conversations with students and posing questions here and there. Harry bent his head hurriedly over his book.

'Think of a dream, quick,' he told Ron, 'in case the old toad comes our way.'

'I did it last time,' Ron protested, 'it's your turn, you tell me one.'

'Oh, I dunno ...' said Harry desperately, who could not remember dreaming anything at all over the last few days. 'Let's say I dreamed I was ... drowning Snape in my cauldron. Yeah, that'll do ...'

Ron chortled as he opened his *Dream Oracle*.

'OK, we've got to add your age to the date you had the dream, the number of letters in the subject ... would that be "drowning" or "cauldron" or "Snape"?'

'It doesn't matter, pick any of them,' said Harry, chancing a glance behind him. Professor Umbridge was now standing at Professor Trelawney's shoulder making notes while the Divination teacher questioned Neville about his dream diary.

'What night did you dream this again?' Ron said, immersed in calculations.

'I dunno, last night, whenever you like,' Harry told him, trying to listen to what Umbridge was saying to Professor Trelawney. They were only a table away from him and Ron now. Professor Umbridge was making another note on her clipboard and Professor Trelawney was looking extremely put out.

'Now,' said Umbridge, looking up at Trelawney, 'you've been in this post how long, exactly?'

Professor Trelawney scowled at her, arms crossed and shoulders hunched as though wishing to protect herself as much as possible from the indignity of the inspection. After a slight pause in which she seemed to decide that the question was not so offensive that she could reasonably ignore it, she said in a deeply resentful tone, 'Nearly sixteen years.'

'Quite a period,' said Professor Umbridge, making a note on her clipboard. 'So it was Professor Dumbledore who appointed you?'

'That's right,' said Professor Trelawney shortly.

第 15 章　霍格沃茨的高级调查官

哈利打开他那本《解梦指南》，一边偷偷地注视着乌姆里奇。她已经在写字板上记着什么了。几分钟后，她站起来，开始跟着特里劳尼在教室里走来走去，听特里劳尼跟同学们对话，并不时地提出一两个问题。哈利赶紧埋头书本上。

"快想一个梦出来，"他对罗恩说，"说不定那个老癞蛤蟆要往这边来了。"

"我上次说过了，"罗恩抗议道，"这次该你了，你对我说一个吧。"

"唉，我不知道……"哈利焦急地说，他一点儿也想不起最近几天做过什么梦，"我就说我梦见……把斯内普放在我的坩埚里淹死了。行，这个准行……"

罗恩乐得咯咯直笑，翻开了他的那本《解梦指南》。

"好吧，我们要用你的年龄加上你做梦那天的日期，还有主题词的字母个数……主题词是'淹死'，还是'坩埚'，还是'斯内普'呢？"

"没关系，随便挑一个吧。"哈利说着冒险朝后面扫了一眼。乌姆里奇教授就站在特里劳尼教授身后，当占卜课老师询问纳威做梦日记写得怎样时，乌姆里奇在写字板上记个不停。

"你哪天夜里做了这个梦？"罗恩一边埋头计算一边问道。

"不知道，昨天夜里吧，你说哪天就哪天。"哈利对他说，一边拼命想听清乌姆里奇在对特里劳尼教授说什么。她们现在跟他和罗恩只隔着一张桌子，乌姆里奇教授又在写字板上记了几笔，特里劳尼教授显得十分恼怒。

"那么，"乌姆里奇抬头看着特里劳尼，说道，"你在这个岗位上多长时间了，确切地说？"

特里劳尼教授狠狠地瞪着她，交叉双臂，耸起肩膀，似乎想尽量保护自己，不受这种粗暴无礼的调查的伤害。她微微顿了一下，大概断定这个问题并不那么唐突，她没有理由对它置之不理，便用十分愠怒的口吻说："差不多十六年了。"

"时间不短了。"乌姆里奇教授说着又在她的写字板上记了几笔，"这么说是邓布利多教授任用你的？"

"没错。"特里劳尼教授干脆利落地说。

539

CHAPTER FIFTEEN The Hogwarts High Inquisitor

Professor Umbridge made another note.

'And you are a great-great-granddaughter of the celebrated Seer Cassandra Trelawney?'

'Yes,' said Professor Trelawney, holding her head a little higher.

Another note on the clipboard.

'But I think – correct me if I am mistaken – that you are the first in your family since Cassandra to be possessed of Second Sight?'

'These things often skip – er – three generations,' said Professor Trelawney.

Professor Umbridge's toadlike smile widened.

'Of course,' she said sweetly, making yet another note. 'Well, if you could just predict something for me, then?' And she looked up enquiringly, still smiling.

Professor Trelawney stiffened as though unable to believe her ears. 'I don't understand you,' she said, clutching convulsively at the shawl around her scrawny neck.

'I'd like you to make a prediction for me,' said Professor Umbridge very clearly.

Harry and Ron were not the only people now watching and listening sneakily from behind their books. Most of the class were staring transfixed at Professor Trelawney as she drew herself up to her full height, her beads and bangles clinking.

'The Inner Eye does not See upon command!' she said in scandalised tones.

'I see,' said Professor Umbridge softly, making yet another note on her clipboard.

'I – but – but ... *wait*!' said Professor Trelawney suddenly, in an attempt at her usual ethereal voice, though the mystical effect was ruined somewhat by the way it was shaking with anger. 'I ... I think I *do* see something ... something that concerns *you* ... why, I sense something ... something *dark* ... some grave peril ...'

Professor Trelawney pointed a shaking finger at Professor Umbridge who continued to smile blandly at her, eyebrows raised.

'I am afraid ... I am afraid that you are in grave danger!' Professor Trelawney finished dramatically.

There was a pause. Professor Umbridge's eyebrows were still raised.

'Right,' she said softly, scribbling on her clipboard once more. 'Well, if that's really the best you can do ...'

第15章 霍格沃茨的高级调查官

乌姆里奇教授又记了几笔。

"你是大名鼎鼎的先知卡珊德拉·特里劳尼的玄孙女?"

"是的。"特里劳尼教授说,把头昂得更高了一点。

写字板上又记下了几笔。

"可是我认为——如果我说错了你可以纠正——自卡珊德拉之后,你是你们家族里第一个具有第二视觉的人?"

"这些事情经常隔代——呃——隔三代遗传的。"特里劳尼教授说。

乌姆里奇教授那癞蛤蟆似的嘴笑得更大了。

"当然。"她娇滴滴地说,又记了几笔,"好吧,不知你是否可以为我预言点什么,嗯?"她询问地抬起头,依旧满脸堆笑。

特里劳尼教授浑身一下子绷紧了,似乎无法相信自己的耳朵。"我不明白你的意思。"她说,战栗地抓住围在瘦削的脖子上的披肩。

"我希望你能为我做一个预言。"乌姆里奇教授清清楚楚地说。

现在,从课本后面偷看和偷听的人可不止哈利和罗恩两个了。教室里大多数同学都呆呆地望着特里劳尼教授,只见她把身体挺得笔直,那些珠子和手镯叮叮当当响个不停。

"天目是不会受命而看的!"她用愤慨的语气说。

"明白了。"乌姆里奇教授轻轻说,又在她的写字板上记了几笔。

"我——可是——可是……等一等!"特里劳尼教授突然说,她试图用平常那种虚无缥缈的声音说话,但由于气得全身发抖,破坏了那种声音的神秘效果,"我……我觉得我确实看见了什么……是关于你的……啊,我感觉到了某种东西……某种黑色的东西……某种极其危险的……"

特里劳尼教授用颤抖的手指指着乌姆里奇教授,乌姆里奇教授的脸上还是那样和蔼可亲地笑着,两根眉毛扬了起来。

"恐怕……恐怕你会遇到可怕的危险!"特里劳尼教授戏剧性地结束了她的话。

一阵静默。乌姆里奇教授的眉毛仍然扬着。

"好吧,"她轻轻地说,又在写字板上草草划拉了几笔,"好吧,如果你充其量只能做到这点……"

CHAPTER FIFTEEN The Hogwarts High Inquisitor

She turned away, leaving Professor Trelawney standing rooted to the spot, her chest heaving. Harry caught Ron's eye and knew that Ron was thinking exactly the same as he was: they both knew that Professor Trelawney was an old fraud, but on the other hand, they loathed Umbridge so much that they felt very much on Trelawney's side – until she swooped down on them a few seconds later, that is.

'Well?' she said, snapping her long fingers under Harry's nose, uncharacteristically brisk. 'Let me see the start you've made on your dream diary, please.'

And by the time she had interpreted Harry's dreams at the top of her voice (all of which, even the ones that involved eating porridge, apparently foretold a gruesome and early death), he was feeling much less sympathetic towards her. All the while, Professor Umbridge stood a few feet away, making notes on that clipboard, and when the bell rang she descended the silver ladder first and was waiting for them all when they reached their Defence Against the Dark Arts lesson ten minutes later.

She was humming and smiling to herself when they entered the room. Harry and Ron told Hermione, who had been in Arithmancy, exactly what had happened in Divination while they all took out their copies of *Defensive Magical Theory*, but before Hermione could ask any questions Professor Umbridge had called them all to order and silence fell.

'Wands away,' she instructed them all with a smile, and those people who had been hopeful enough to take them out, sadly returned them to their bags. 'As we finished Chapter One last lesson, I would like you all to turn to page nineteen today and commence "Chapter Two, Common Defensive Theories and their Derivation". There will be no need to talk.'

Still smiling her wide, self-satisfied smile, she sat down at her desk. The class gave an audible sigh as it turned, as one, to page nineteen. Harry wondered dully whether there were enough chapters in the book to keep them reading through all this year's lessons and was on the point of checking the contents page when he noticed that Hermione had her hand in the air again.

Professor Umbridge had noticed, too, and what was more, she seemed to have worked out a strategy for just such an eventuality. Instead of trying to pretend she had not noticed Hermione she got to her feet and walked around the front row of desks until they were face to face, then she bent down and whispered, so that the rest of the class could not hear, 'What is it this time, Miss Granger?'

第 15 章 霍格沃茨的高级调查官

她转身走开了，特里劳尼教授呆呆地站在原地，胸脯剧烈地起伏着。哈利和罗恩对了一下眼神，知道罗恩心里的想法跟他完全一样。他们都知道特里劳尼教授是个大骗子，但另一方面，他们太憎恨乌姆里奇了，觉得情愿偏向特里劳尼一边——然而几秒钟后她突然对他们发难，他们就不这么想了。

"怎么样？"特里劳尼教授说，把长长的手指猛地戳到哈利鼻子底下，动作是一反常态地敏捷，"请让我看看你的做梦日记的开头几篇。"

当她用最高的嗓门解释完哈利的那些梦（所有的梦，包括关于喝粥的梦，都明显预示着可怕的早夭），哈利觉得对她的同情减少了许多。这个时候，乌姆里奇教授一直站在几步开外，在那写字板上记个不停。下课铃响了，她第一个下了银色的梯子。当他们十分钟后赶去上黑魔法防御术课时，她又在那儿等着大家了。

他们走进教室时，她在那里自己笑眯眯地哼着小曲儿。赫敏刚才去上算术占卜课了，哈利和罗恩一边拿出他们的《魔法防御理论》课本，一边把占卜课上发生的事情都告诉了她。没等赫敏来得及提问，乌姆里奇教授就命令大家安静下来。教室里立刻鸦雀无声。

"收起魔杖。"她笑容可掬地吩咐大家，那些抱有一线希望把魔杖拿出来的同学，只好失望地又把它们放回书包，"上节课我们学完了第一章，今天我希望你们都把书翻到第十九页，开始读第二章，普通防御理论及其起源。看书时不要讲话。"

她咧着大嘴，沾沾自喜地微笑着，在讲台后面坐了下来。全班同学整齐划一地把书翻到了第十九页，发出一片清晰可闻的叹气声。哈利闷闷不乐地想，不知这本书有没有那么多章节，够他们整个一学年在课上阅读。他正在查看目录，突然发现赫敏又把手举了起来。

乌姆里奇教授也注意到了，而且，她似乎已经对可能发生这样的事情想好了对策。她不再假装没有看见赫敏，而是站起来绕过前排课桌，面对面地站在赫敏跟前，然后弯下腰压低声音，不让全班同学听见她说话。"这次又怎么啦，格兰杰小姐？"

CHAPTER FIFTEEN   The Hogwarts High Inquisitor

'I've already read Chapter Two,' said Hermione.

'Well then, proceed to Chapter Three.'

'I've read that too. I've read the whole book.'

Professor Umbridge blinked but recovered her poise almost instantly.

'Well, then, you should be able to tell me what Slinkhard says about counter-jinxes in Chapter fifteen.'

'He says that counter-jinxes are improperly named,' said Hermione promptly. 'He says "counter-jinx" is just a name people give their jinxes when they want to make them sound more acceptable.'

Professor Umbridge raised her eyebrows and Harry knew she was impressed, against her will.

'But I disagree,' Hermione continued.

Professor Umbridge's eyebrows rose a little higher and her gaze became distinctly colder.

'You disagree?'

'Yes, I do,' said Hermione, who, unlike Umbridge, was not whispering, but speaking in a clear, carrying voice that had by now attracted the attention of the rest of the class. 'Mr Slinkhard doesn't like jinxes, does he? But I think they can be very useful when they're used defensively.'

'Oh, you do, do you?' said Professor Umbridge, forgetting to whisper and straightening up. 'Well, I'm afraid it is Mr Slinkhard's opinion, and not yours, that matters within this classroom, Miss Granger.'

'But –' Hermione began.

'That is enough,' said Professor Umbridge. She walked back to the front of the class and stood before them, all the jauntiness she had shown at the beginning of the lesson gone. 'Miss Granger, I am going to take five points from Gryffindor house.'

There was an outbreak of muttering at this.

'What for?' said Harry angrily.

'Don't you get involved!' Hermione whispered urgently to him.

'For disrupting my class with pointless interruptions,' said Professor Umbridge smoothly. 'I am here to teach you using a Ministry-approved method that does not include inviting students to give their opinions on matters about which they understand very little. Your previous teachers in this subject

"第二章我已经读过了。"赫敏说。

"那好,接着读第三章。"

"那一章我也读过了。我把整本书都读完了。"

乌姆里奇教授眨眨眼睛,但几乎立刻就恢复了镇定。

"那好,你应该能够告诉我,在第十五章里,斯林卡关于反恶咒是怎么说的。"

"他说反恶咒这个词不恰当。"赫敏不假思索地说,"他说'反恶咒'这个词实际上是人们用来称呼他们的恶咒的,他们想使那些恶咒听上去更容易被人接受。"

乌姆里奇教授扬起眉毛,哈利知道她尽管不乐意,却也不由得心服口服。

"但我不同意。"赫敏继续说。

乌姆里奇教授的眉毛扬得更高了一些,目光明显变冷了。

"你不同意?"

"是的,不同意。"赫敏说,她不像乌姆里奇那样悄声耳语,而是用清晰的、传得很远的声音说话,把全班同学的注意力都吸引了过来,"斯林卡先生不喜欢恶咒,是吗?但我认为当恶咒用于防御时,会非常管用的。"

"哦,你是这么认为的?"乌姆里奇教授说,忘记了压低声音,并且站直了身体,"恐怕在这个教室里真正重要的是斯林卡先生的观点,而不是你的观点,格兰杰小姐。"

"可是——"赫敏刚要说话。

"够了。"乌姆里奇教授说。她走到教室前面,对着全班同学,刚开始上课时那种喜气洋洋的劲头一下子不见了。"格兰杰小姐,我要给格兰芬多学院扣掉五分。"

听了这话,教室里响起一片窃窃私语。

"为什么?"哈利气愤地问。

"你别掺和进来!"赫敏焦急地小声对他说。

"因为用毫无意义的打岔扰乱我的课堂纪律。"乌姆里奇教授流利地说,"我在这里教课采用的是魔法部批准的方法,不包括鼓励学生对

CHAPTER FIFTEEN The Hogwarts High Inquisitor

may have allowed you more licence, but as none of them – with the possible exception of Professor Quirrell, who did at least appear to have restricted himself to age-appropriate subjects – would have passed a Ministry inspection –'

'Yeah, Quirrell was a great teacher,' said Harry loudly, 'there was just that minor drawback of him having Lord Voldemort sticking out of the back of his head.'

This pronouncement was followed by one of the loudest silences Harry had ever heard. Then –

'I think another week's detentions would do you some good, Mr Potter,' said Umbridge sleekly.

The cut on the back of Harry's hand had barely healed and, by the following morning, it was bleeding again. He did not complain during the evening's detention; he was determined not to give Umbridge the satisfaction; over and over again he wrote *I must not tell lies* and not a sound escaped his lips, though the cut deepened with every letter.

The very worst part of this second week's worth of detentions was, just as George had predicted, Angelina's reaction. She cornered him just as he arrived at the Gryffindor table for breakfast on Tuesday and shouted so loudly that Professor McGonagall came sweeping down upon the pair of them from the staff table.

'Miss Johnson, how *dare* you make such a racket in the Great Hall! five points from Gryffindor!'

'But Professor – he's gone and landed himself in detention *again* –'

'What's this, Potter?' said Professor McGonagall sharply, rounding on Harry. 'Detention? from whom?'

'From Professor Umbridge,' muttered Harry, not meeting Professor McGonagall's beady, square-framed eyes.

'Are you telling me,' she said, lowering her voice so that the group of curious Ravenclaws behind them could not hear, 'that after the warning I gave you last Monday you lost your temper in Professor Umbridge's class again?'

'Yes,' Harry muttered, speaking to the floor.

'Potter, you must get a grip on yourself! You are heading for serious

第15章 霍格沃茨的高级调查官

他们不很理解的事情发表自己的观点。以前教你们这门课的老师也许给了你们更多的自由，但他们没有一个人能够通过魔法部的调查——大概奇洛教授除外，至少他似乎只教授适合你们这个年龄的内容——"

"是啊，奇洛真是个了不起的好老师，"哈利大声说，"只是有一点小小的美中不足，他让伏地魔粘在他的后脑勺上了。"

这句话一出口，教室里一片沉默，哈利从没听见过这样掷地有声的沉默。接着——

"我认为再关一个星期的禁闭会对你有点帮助，波特先生。"乌姆里奇圆滑地说。

哈利手背上的伤口没有完全愈合，第二天早晨又流血了。晚上关禁闭时他没有叫一声痛，他打定主意不让乌姆里奇感到得意。他一遍又一遍地写我不可以说谎，不让一点声音从嘴唇间漏出来，尽管每写一个字母伤口就刻得更深。

正像乔治所预言的，哈利第二个星期关禁闭，最糟糕的后果就是安吉利娜的反应。星期二早上哈利刚到格兰芬多桌旁准备吃早饭，安吉利娜就堵住他，冲他大发脾气，声音嚷得那么响，使得麦格教授离开教工桌子，飞快地朝他们走来。

"约翰逊小姐，你怎么敢在礼堂里这样大吵大嚷！格兰芬多扣掉五分！"

"可是教授——他又弄得自己被关禁闭了——"

"怎么回事，波特？"麦格教授转过身来对着哈利严厉地问，"关禁闭？谁关你禁闭？"

"乌姆里奇教授。"哈利低声说，不敢去看麦格教授方框眼镜后面那双犀利的眼睛。

"难道你是说，"她放低声音，不让他们后面那群好奇的拉文克劳们听见，"我上个星期一警告过你之后，你又在乌姆里奇教授的课堂上发了脾气？"

"是的。"哈利对着地板小声说。

"波特，你必须管住自己！你会碰到大麻烦的！格兰芬多再扣掉

CHAPTER FIFTEEN   The Hogwarts High Inquisitor

trouble! Another five points from Gryffindor!'

'But – what –? Professor, no!' Harry said, furious at this injustice, 'I'm already being punished by *her*, why do you have to take points as well?'

'Because detentions do not appear to have any effect on you whatsoever!' said Professor McGonagall tartly. 'No, not another word of complaint, Potter! And as for you, Miss Johnson, you will confine your shouting matches to the Quidditch pitch in future or risk losing the team captaincy!'

Professor McGonagall strode back towards the staff table. Angelina gave Harry a look of deepest disgust and stalked away, upon which he flung himself on to the bench beside Ron, fuming.

'She's taken points off Gryffindor because I'm having my hand sliced open every night! How is that fair, *how*?'

'I know, mate,' said Ron sympathetically, tipping bacon on to Harry's plate, 'she's bang out of order.'

Hermione, however, merely rustled the pages of her *Daily Prophet* and said nothing.

'You think McGonagall was right, do you?' said Harry angrily to the picture of Cornelius Fudge obscuring Hermione's face.

'I wish she hadn't taken points from you, but I think she's right to warn you not to lose your temper with Umbridge,' said Hermione's voice, while Fudge gesticulated forcefully from the front page, clearly giving some kind of speech.

Harry did not speak to Hermione all through Charms, but when they entered Transfiguration he forgot about being cross with her. Professor Umbridge and her clipboard were sitting in a corner and the sight of her drove the memory of breakfast right out of his head.

'Excellent,' whispered Ron, as they sat down in their usual seats. 'Let's see Umbridge get what she deserves.'

Professor McGonagall marched into the room without giving the slightest indication that she knew Professor Umbridge was there.

'That will do,' she said and silence fell immediately. 'Mr Finnigan, kindly come here and hand back the homework – Miss Brown, please take this box of mice – don't be silly, girl, they won't hurt you – and hand one to each student –'

'*Hem, hem*,' said Professor Umbridge, employing the same silly little cough

第15章 霍格沃茨的高级调查官

五分！"

"可是——什么——？教授，不！"哈利被这种不公平的处理惹火了，说道，"我已经被她惩罚了，你为什么还要扣分？"

"因为关禁闭似乎对你并不起任何作用！"麦格教授尖刻地说，"行了，不许再抱怨一个字，波特！至于你，约翰逊小姐，今后你只许在魁地奇球场上大叫大嚷，不然就有可能丢掉队长的职务！"

麦格教授大步流星地走回教工桌子。安吉利娜怒不可遏地瞪了哈利一眼，昂首挺胸地走了，哈利一屁股坐在罗恩身边的板凳上，气得不行。

"她扣了格兰芬多的分数，就因为我每天晚上手背都被割开！这样公平吗，公平吗？"

"我知道，哥们儿，"罗恩同情地说，把熏咸肉倒进哈利的盘子里，"她肯定有毛病了。"

赫敏却只是翻着她的《预言家日报》，什么也没说。

"你认为麦格做得对，是吗？"哈利气愤地对着遮住赫敏面孔的康奈利·福吉的照片说。

"我也不希望她给你扣分，但我认为她提醒你别对乌姆里奇发脾气是对的。"说话的是赫敏的声音，眼前却是福吉在报纸的头版上有力地打着手势，显然他正在发表什么讲话。

整个魔咒课上，哈利没有跟赫敏说话，但当他们走进变形课教室时，他一下子忘记了跟赫敏生气的事。乌姆里奇教授拿着她的写字板，赫然坐在一个角落里。哈利一看见她，就把吃早饭时的不快抛到了脑后。

"太好了，"他们在惯常的座位上坐下时，罗恩小声说，"让我们看看乌姆里奇怎么自作自受吧。"

麦格教授大步走进教室，从她的神情看，似乎根本不知道乌姆里奇教授的存在。

"好了，"她说，教室里立刻安静下来，"斐尼甘先生，请过来把家庭作业发下去——布朗小姐，请把这盒老鼠拿去——别那么傻，姑娘，它们不会咬你的——给每个同学分一只——"

"咳，咳。"乌姆里奇教授发出咳嗽声，还是她开学第一天晚上用

CHAPTER FIFTEEN The Hogwarts High Inquisitor

she had used to interrupt Dumbledore on the first night of term. Professor McGonagall ignored her. Seamus handed back Harry's essay; Harry took it without looking at him and saw, to his relief, that he had managed an 'A'.

'Right then, everyone, listen closely – Dean Thomas, if you do that to the mouse again I shall put you in detention – most of you have now successfully Vanished your snails and even those who were left with a certain amount of shell have got the gist of the spell. Today, we shall be –'

'*Hem, hem,*' said Professor Umbridge.

'*Yes?*' said Professor McGonagall, turning round, her eyebrows so close together they seemed to form one long, severe line.

'I was just wondering, Professor, whether you received my note telling you of the date and time of your inspec–'

'Obviously I received it, or I would have asked you what you are doing in my classroom,' said Professor McGonagall, turning her back firmly on Professor Umbridge. Many of the students exchanged looks of glee. 'As I was saying: today, we shall be practising the altogether more difficult Vanishment of mice. Now, the Vanishing Spell –'

'*Hem, hem.*'

'I wonder,' said Professor McGonagall in cold fury, turning on Professor Umbridge, 'how you expect to gain an idea of my usual teaching methods if you continue to interrupt me? You see, I do not generally permit people to talk when I am talking.'

Professor Umbridge looked as though she had just been slapped in the face. She did not speak, but straightened the parchment on her clipboard and began scribbling furiously.

Looking supremely unconcerned, Professor McGonagall addressed the class once more.

'As I was saying: the Vanishing Spell becomes more difficult with the complexity of the animal to be Vanished. The snail, as an invertebrate, does not present much of a challenge; the mouse, as a mammal, offers a much greater one. This is not, therefore, magic you can accomplish with your mind on your dinner. So – you know the incantation, let me see what you can do ...'

'How she can lecture me about not losing my temper with Umbridge!' Harry muttered to Ron under his breath, but he was grinning – his anger with Professor McGonagall had quite evaporated.

第15章 霍格沃茨的高级调查官

来打断邓布利多的那种愚蠢的轻咳。麦格教授假装没有听见。西莫把哈利的论文发还给他。哈利没有看他，接过论文，看到自己总算得到了一个"A"，不禁松了口气。

"好了，同学们，请仔细听好——迪安·托马斯，如果你再那样折腾那只老鼠，我就关你的禁闭——现在，大多数同学都能顺利地念消失咒让蜗牛消失了，就连那些还留下一点儿蜗牛壳的同学也都掌握了这个咒语的要点。今天，我们要——"

"咳，咳。"乌姆里奇教授发出咳嗽声。

"怎么啦？"麦格教授说着转过身去，两根眉毛聚在一起，似乎形成了一根长长的、令人生畏的直线。

"教授，我只想知道你有没有收到我的便条，上面通知了检查你上课情况的日期和时——"

"我显然是收到了，不然我就会问你跑到我的教室里来做什么了。"麦格教授说着又果断地转身背对乌姆里奇教授。许多同学交换着喜悦的目光。"正如我刚才说的：今天，我们要练习更难的老鼠消失咒。好，消失咒——"

"咳，咳。"

"我不明白，"麦格教授转身冲着乌姆里奇教授，带着怒气冷冷地说，"如果你不停地打断我，又怎么能够了解我平常的教学方法呢？你要知道，我说话时一般是不允许别人说话的。"

乌姆里奇教授看上去像被人扇了一记耳光。她没有说话，而是正了正写字板上的羊皮纸，恼羞成怒地草草写了起来。

麦格教授一副无所谓的样子，再一次对全班同学说道：

"我刚才说到：消失咒，随着需要消失的动物越来越复杂，它也越来越难掌握。蜗牛是一种无脊椎动物，挑战性不是很大，而老鼠是一种哺乳动物，要求就高得多了。这可不是你们脑子里惦记着晚饭就能完成的魔法。好了——咒语你们已经知道了，让我看看你们做得怎么样……"

"她还教训我不该对乌姆里奇发脾气呢！"哈利压低声音对罗恩说，但脸上带着调皮的笑容——他对麦格教授的怨气一下子烟消云散了。

CHAPTER FIFTEEN   The Hogwarts High Inquisitor

Professor Umbridge did not follow Professor McGonagall around the class as she had followed Professor Trelawney; perhaps she realised Professor McGonagall would not permit it. She did, however, take many more notes while sitting in her corner, and when Professor McGonagall finally told them all to pack away, she rose with a grim expression on her face.

'Well, it's a start,' said Ron, holding up a long wriggling mouse-tail and dropping it back into the box Lavender was passing around.

As they filed out of the classroom, Harry saw Professor Umbridge approach the teacher's desk; he nudged Ron, who nudged Hermione in turn, and the three of them deliberately fell back to eavesdrop.

'How long have you been teaching at Hogwarts?' Professor Umbridge asked.

'Thirty-nine years this December,' said Professor McGonagall brusquely, snapping her bag shut.

Professor Umbridge made a note.

'Very well,' she said, 'you will receive the results of your inspection in ten days' time.'

'I can hardly wait,' said Professor McGonagall, in a coldly indifferent voice, and she strode off towards the door. 'Hurry up, you three,' she added, sweeping Harry, Ron and Hermione before her.

Harry could not help giving her a faint smile and could have sworn he received one in return.

He had thought that the next time he would see Umbridge would be in his detention that evening, but he was wrong. When they walked down the lawns towards the Forest for Care of Magical Creatures, they found her and her clipboard waiting for them beside Professor Grubbly-Plank.

'You do not usually take this class, is that correct?' Harry heard her ask as they arrived at the trestle table where the group of captive Bowtruckles were scrabbling around for woodlice like so many living twigs.

'Quite correct,' said Professor Grubbly-Plank, hands behind her back and bouncing on the balls of her feet. 'I am a substitute teacher standing in for Professor Hagrid.'

Harry exchanged uneasy looks with Ron and Hermione. Malfoy was whispering with Crabbe and Goyle; he would surely love this opportunity to tell tales on Hagrid to a member of the Ministry.

第15章 霍格沃茨的高级调查官

乌姆里奇教授没有像在特里劳尼教授的课堂上那样，跟着麦格教授在教室里走来走去，也许她意识到麦格教授不会准许。她只是坐在角落里，往写字板上记了又记，当麦格教授最后叫全班同学收拾东西下课时，她站了起来，一张脸板得吓人。

"嘿，至少成功了一部分。"罗恩说着，拎起一根长长的、不断扭动的老鼠尾巴，扔进拉文德传递过来的盒子里。

同学们鱼贯走出教室，哈利看见乌姆里奇教授朝讲台走去。他捅了捅罗恩，罗恩又捅了捅赫敏，三个人故意落在后面偷听。

"你在霍格沃茨任教多长时间了？"乌姆里奇教授问。

"到今年十二月就满三十九年了。"麦格教授生硬地回答，啪的一声合上了提包。

乌姆里奇教授记了几笔。

"很好，"她说，"你将在十天之内收到对你的调查结果。"

"我迫不及待。"麦格教授用极其冷漠的口吻说，然后大步朝门口走来，"快点儿，你们三个。"她说，扫了一眼她前面的哈利、罗恩和赫敏。

哈利忍不住朝她露出一个淡淡的微笑，并且可以肯定麦格教授也对他笑了笑。

他以为要等到晚上关禁闭时才会再次看见乌姆里奇呢，可是他错了。当他们顺着草地去上保护神奇动物课时，他发现乌姆里奇正抱着她的写字板站在格拉普兰教授身边等着他们呢。

"你平常不教这门课，是不是？"哈利听见她这么问，这时他们来到长条搁板桌旁，那堆被捕获的护树罗锅正你争我夺地抢吃土鳖，就像无数根有生命的树枝。

"非常正确，"格拉普兰教授说，两只手背在身后，一下一下地踮着脚尖，"我是代课教师，临时代替海格教授。"

哈利和罗恩、赫敏交换着不安的目光。马尔福在对克拉布和高尔窃窃私语。他肯定巴不得利用这个机会向一位魔法部官员散布关于海格的流言蜚语。

CHAPTER FIFTEEN The Hogwarts High Inquisitor

'Hmm,' said Professor Umbridge, dropping her voice, though Harry could still hear her quite clearly. 'I wonder – the Headmaster seems strangely reluctant to give me any information on the matter – can *you* tell me what is causing Professor Hagrid's very extended leave of absence?'

Harry saw Malfoy look up eagerly.

''Fraid I can't,' said Professor Grubbly-Plank breezily. 'Don't know anything more about it than you do. Got an owl from Dumbledore, would I like a couple of weeks' teaching work. I accepted. That's as much as I know. Well ... shall I get started then?'

'Yes, please do,' said Professor Umbridge, scribbling on her clipboard.

Umbridge took a different tack in this class and wandered amongst the students, questioning them on magical creatures. Most people were able to answer well and Harry's spirits lifted somewhat; at least the class was not letting Hagrid down.

'Overall,' said Professor Umbridge, returning to Professor Grubbly-Plank's side after a lengthy interrogation of Dean Thomas, 'how do you, as a temporary member of staff – an objective outsider, I suppose you might say – how do you find Hogwarts? Do you feel you receive enough support from the school management?'

'Oh, yes, Dumbledore's excellent,' said Professor Grubbly-Plank heartily. 'Yes, I'm very happy with the way things are run, very happy indeed.'

Looking politely incredulous, Umbridge made a tiny note on her clipboard and went on, 'And what are you planning to cover with this class this year – assuming, of course, that Professor Hagrid does not return?'

'Oh, I'll take them through the creatures that most often come up in O.W.L.,' said Professor Grubbly-Plank. 'Not much left to do – they've studied unicorns and Nifflers, I thought we'd cover Porlocks and Kneazles, make sure they can recognise Crups and Knarls, you know ...'

'Well, *you* seem to know what you're doing, at any rate,' said Professor Umbridge, making a very obvious tick on her clipboard. Harry did not like the emphasis she put on '*you*' and liked it even less when she put her next question to Goyle. 'Now, I hear there have been injuries in this class?'

Goyle gave a stupid grin. Malfoy hastened to answer the question.

'That was me,' he said. 'I was slashed by a Hippogriff.'

第15章 霍格沃茨的高级调查官

"唔,"乌姆里奇教授放低了声音,但哈利仍然能很清楚地听见她说的话,"我不明白——校长似乎很奇怪地不愿意向我提供这件事的任何情况——你能不能告诉我,是什么原因使海格教授这么长时间没来上课?"

哈利看见马尔福急切地抬起头来。

"恐怕不能,"格拉普兰教授语调轻松地说,"我知道的并不比你多。只收到过猫头鹰捎来的邓布利多的信,问我愿不愿意代两个星期的课。我接受了。我所知道的就只有这么多。好了……我可以开始了吗?"

"好吧,请开始吧。"乌姆里奇教授说,在写字板上唰唰地写着。

乌姆里奇这节课采取了一种不同的方法,她在同学们中间走来走去,询问他们关于神奇动物的知识。大多数同学都能答得很好,哈利的心情稍微好了点儿。至少全班同学在关键时候没有给海格丢脸。

"总的来说,"乌姆里奇教授在盘问了迪安·托马斯很长时间之后,回到格拉普兰教授身边,"作为一个临时代课教师——或者不如说,一个客观的局外人——你认为霍格沃茨怎么样?你觉得你从学校的管理人员那里得到了足够的支持吗?"

"哦,是的,邓布利多很出色,"格拉普兰教授由衷地说,"我对这里的办学方式非常满意,确实非常满意。"

乌姆里奇显得怀疑但不失礼貌,她在写字板上记了一笔,继续问道:"你打算这一学年给这个班的学生教些什么呢——当然啦,假设海格教授不回来的话?"

"哦,我要把O.W.L.考试中经常会出现的动物都教给他们,"格拉普兰教授说,"剩下来的不多了——他们已经学了独角兽和嗅嗅,我想我们还要学习庞洛克和猫狸子,确保他们能够辨认燕尾狗和刺佬儿,你知道……"

"看来,至少你似乎知道自己在做什么。"乌姆里奇教授说,很明显地在写字板上打了个钩儿。哈利不喜欢她格外强调那个"你"字,更不喜欢她接着又向高尔发问:"对了,我听说这门课上曾有同学受过伤?"

高尔傻乎乎地咧嘴笑了。马尔福急不可耐地抢着回答。

"是我,"他说,"我被一头鹰头马身有翼兽划伤了。"

CHAPTER FIFTEEN The Hogwarts High Inquisitor

'A Hippogriff?' said Professor Umbridge, now scribbling frantically.

'Only because he was too stupid to listen to what Hagrid told him to do,' said Harry angrily.

Both Ron and Hermione groaned. Professor Umbridge turned her head slowly in Harry's direction.

'Another night's detention, I think,' she said softly. 'Well, thank you very much, Professor Grubbly-Plank, I think that's all I need here. You will be receiving the results of your inspection within ten days.'

'Jolly good,' said Professor Grubbly-Plank, and Professor Umbridge set off back across the lawn to the castle.

It was nearly midnight when Harry left Umbridge's office that night, his hand now bleeding so severely that it was staining the scarf he had wrapped around it. He expected the common room to be empty when he returned, but Ron and Hermione had sat up waiting for him. He was pleased to see them, especially as Hermione was disposed to be sympathetic rather than critical.

'Here,' she said anxiously, pushing a small bowl of yellow liquid towards him, 'soak your hand in that, it's a solution of strained and pickled Murtlap tentacles, it should help.'

Harry placed his bleeding, aching hand into the bowl and experienced a wonderful feeling of relief. Crookshanks curled around his legs, purring loudly, then leapt into his lap and settled down.

'Thanks,' he said gratefully, scratching behind Crookshanks's ears with his left hand.

'I still reckon you should complain about this,' said Ron in a low voice.

'No,' said Harry flatly.

'McGonagall would go nuts if she knew –'

'Yeah, she probably would,' said Harry. 'And how long do you reckon it'd take Umbridge to pass another decree saying anyone who complains about the High Inquisitor gets sacked immediately?'

Ron opened his mouth to retort but nothing came out and, after a moment, he closed it again, defeated.

'She's an awful woman,' said Hermione in a small voice. '*Awful.* You know, I was just saying to Ron when you came in ... we've got to do something about her.'

第15章 霍格沃茨的高级调查官

"鹰头马身有翼兽?"乌姆里奇教授说,一边在纸上飞快地写着。
"那只是因为他自己太傻,不听海格的吩咐。"哈利生气地说。
罗恩和赫敏都唉声叹气。乌姆里奇教授慢慢地把头转向哈利这边。
"我想,再关你一晚上禁闭吧。"她温柔地说,"好了,非常感谢,格拉普兰教授,我想我不再需要别的了。你将在十天之内收到对你的调查结果。"
"好极了。"格拉普兰教授说,乌姆里奇教授拔腿穿过草地朝城堡走去。

那天夜里,当哈利离开乌姆里奇的办公室时,已经差不多半夜了,他的手在不停地流血,包手的围巾上沾满了血迹。他以为回去时公共休息室里不会有人了,没想到罗恩和赫敏都坐在那里等他呢。他看见他们非常高兴,特别是赫敏表现出的是同情,而不是批评。
"给,"她焦急地说,把一小碗黄色的液体推到哈利面前,"把你的手浸在里面,这是一种经过过滤和酸洗的莫特拉鼠触角的汁液,应该能管点用。"
哈利把疼痛流血的手浸在碗里,疼痛一下子就减轻了,他顿时感到舒服极了。克鲁克山绕着他的腿蜷缩起来,大声地呼噜呼噜叫着,然后跳到他的膝头趴下来。
"谢谢。"哈利感激地说,用左手挠了挠克鲁克山的耳朵根。
"我仍然觉得你应该去说说这件事。"罗恩低声说。
"不。"哈利断然地说。
"麦格如果知道了,准会气得发疯——"
"是啊,她大概会的。"哈利说,"可谁知道过多久乌姆里奇又会通过另一条法令,规定凡是对高级调查官有意见的人都要被立即开除?"
罗恩张了张嘴想反驳,但什么也没说出来,愣了一会儿,又把嘴合上了,一副垂头丧气的样子。
"她是个可怕的女人,"赫敏小声说,"可怕。你知道吗,你进来的时候我正在跟罗恩说……我们必须对她采取一点行动了。"

CHAPTER FIFTEEN — The Hogwarts High Inquisitor

'I suggested poison,' said Ron grimly.

'No ... I mean, something about what a dreadful teacher she is, and how we're not going to learn any Defence from her at all,' said Hermione.

'Well, what can we do about that?' said Ron, yawning. ''S too late, isn't it? She's got the job, she's here to stay. Fudge'll make sure of that.'

'Well,' said Hermione tentatively. 'You know, I was thinking today ...' she shot a slightly nervous look at Harry and then plunged on, 'I was thinking that – maybe the time's come when we should just – just do it ourselves.'

'Do what ourselves?' said Harry suspiciously, still floating his hand in the essence of Murtlap tentacles.

'Well – learn Defence Against the Dark Arts ourselves,' said Hermione.

'Come off it,' groaned Ron. 'You want us to do extra work? D'you realise Harry and I are behind on homework again and it's only the second week?'

'But this is much more important than homework!' said Hermione.

Harry and Ron goggled at her.

'I didn't think there was anything in the universe more important than homework!' said Ron.

'Don't be silly, of course there is,' said Hermione, and Harry saw, with an ominous feeling, that her face was suddenly alight with the kind of fervour that S.P.E.W. usually inspired in her. 'It's about preparing ourselves, like Harry said in Umbridge's first lesson, for what's waiting for us out there. It's about making sure we really can defend ourselves. If we don't learn anything for a whole year –'

'We can't do much by ourselves,' said Ron in a defeated voice. 'I mean, all right, we can go and look jinxes up in the library and try and practise them, I suppose –'

'No, I agree, we've gone past the stage where we can just learn things out of books,' said Hermione. 'We need a teacher, a proper one, who can show us how to use the spells and correct us if we're going wrong.'

'If you're talking about Lupin ...' Harry began.

'No, no, I'm not talking about Lupin,' said Hermione. 'He's too busy with the Order and, anyway, the most we could see him is during Hogsmeade weekends and that's not nearly often enough.'

'Who, then?' said Harry, frowning at her.

"我建议下毒。"罗恩一本正经地说。

"不……我的意思是,我们刚才在说她是一个多么糟糕的老师,从她那里根本学不到什么黑魔法防御知识。"赫敏说。

"唉,那我们能有什么办法呢。"罗恩打了个哈欠说,"已经来不及了,是不是?她得到了这份工作,注定要在这里待下去。福吉会保证这一点的。"

"嗯,"赫敏犹豫不决地说,"是这样,我今天在想……"她有点紧张地望了哈利一眼,然后继续说道,"我在想——也许我们应该索性——索性自己来做了。"

"自己来做什么?"哈利怀疑地问,他的手仍然泡在莫特拉鼠触角的汁液里。

"嗯——我们自己学习黑魔法防御术。"赫敏说。

"别胡扯了,"罗恩抱怨道,"你还要增加我们的负担?难道你不知道,我和哈利又落下了一堆家庭作业,现在才第二个星期呢?"

"可是这比家庭作业重要得多!"赫敏说。

哈利和罗恩瞪大眼睛看着她。

"我以为世界上再也没有什么比家庭作业更重要的了!"罗恩说。

"别说傻话,当然有。"赫敏说,哈利看到她脸上突然容光焕发,就像平常她对S.P.E.W.表现出来的狂热激情一样,他不由得产生了一种不祥的感觉,"我的意思是,就像哈利在乌姆里奇的第一节课上说的,我们要做好准备,去对付外面将会等待我们的一切。我是说,我们要确保真的能够保护自己。如果整整一年什么也学不到——"

"我们自己做不了什么,"罗恩用一种心灰意冷的口吻说,"我是说,不错,我们可以到图书馆从书里找到一些恶咒自己练习,我想——"

"不,我认为我们已经过了只从书本上学习知识的阶段了。"赫敏说,"我们需要一个老师,一个合适的老师,他可以教我们怎样使用咒语,如果我们做得不对,还可以纠正我们。"

"如果你是在说卢平……"哈利话没说完。

"不,不,我不是在说他,"赫敏说,"他整天忙着凤凰社的事,而且,我们最多能在去霍格莫德村过周末时看见他,这个次数是远远不够的。"

"那么是谁呢?"哈利朝她皱起眉头。

CHAPTER FIFTEEN The Hogwarts High Inquisitor

Hermione heaved a very deep sigh.

'Isn't it obvious?' she said. 'I'm talking about *you*, Harry.'

There was a moment's silence. A light night breeze rattled the windowpanes behind Ron, and the fire guttered.

'About me what?' said Harry.

'I'm talking about *you* teaching us Defence Against the Dark Arts.'

Harry stared at her. Then he turned to Ron, ready to exchange the exasperated looks they sometimes shared when Hermione elaborated on far-fetched schemes like S.P.E.W. To Harry's consternation, however, Ron did not look exasperated.

He was frowning slightly, apparently thinking. Then he said, 'That's an idea.'

'What's an idea?' said Harry.

'You,' said Ron. 'Teaching us to do it.'

'But ...'

Harry was grinning now, sure the pair of them were pulling his leg.

'But I'm not a teacher, I can't –'

'Harry, you're the best in the year at Defence Against the Dark Arts,' said Hermione.

'Me?' said Harry, now grinning more broadly than ever. 'No I'm not, you've beaten me in every test –'

'Actually, I haven't,' said Hermione coolly. 'You beat me in our third year – the only year we both sat the test and had a teacher who actually knew the subject. But I'm not talking about test results, Harry. Think what you've *done*!'

'How d'you mean?'

'You know what, I'm not sure I want someone this stupid teaching me,' Ron said to Hermione, smirking slightly. He turned to Harry.

'Let's think,' he said, pulling a face like Goyle concentrating. 'Uh ... first year – you saved the Philosopher's Stone from You-Know-Who.'

'But that was luck,' said Harry, 'it wasn't skill –'

'Second year,' Ron interrupted, 'you killed the Basilisk and destroyed Riddle.'

'Yeah, but if Fawkes hadn't turned up, I –'

'Third year,' said Ron, louder still, 'you fought off about a hundred Dementors at once –'

赫敏深深地吐了一口气。

"你还看不出来吗？"她说，"我说的是你，哈利。"

片刻的沉默。夜晚的微风吹得罗恩身后的窗户嘎嘎作响，炉子里的火已经熄灭了。

"我怎么啦？"哈利说。

"我是说让你教我们黑魔法防御术。"

哈利呆呆地瞪着赫敏，然后转向罗恩，想和罗恩交换一下气恼的眼神。有时赫敏滔滔不绝地阐述S.P.E.W.之类的荒唐计划时，他们常会这样交换眼神。然而令哈利惊愕的是，罗恩的表情并不气恼。

罗恩微微蹙起眉头，显然是在思考。然后他说："这倒是个主意。"

"什么是个主意？"哈利说。

"你呀，"罗恩说，"教我们大家学魔法。"

"可是……"

哈利脸上露出了笑容，这两个人肯定是在跟他开玩笑呢。

"可我不是老师，我不能——"

"哈利，你是全年级在黑魔法防御术方面最出色的。"赫敏说。

"我？"哈利说，笑得比先前更开心了，"我才不是呢，你每次考试成绩都比我好——"

"实际上不是的，"赫敏冷静地说，"三年级的时候你就超过了我——只有那一年我们俩都考了试，而且当时遇到了一位真正懂行的老师。但我这里讲的不是考试成绩，哈利。想想你做的那些事情！"

"什么意思？"

"要我说，我倒不敢肯定我真想要一个这么傻的人来教我呢。"罗恩微微嘲笑地对赫敏说。然后他转向哈利。

"让我想想，"他说，一边学着高尔拼命动脑筋时拉长脸的样子，"啊……第一年——你从神秘人那里保住了魔法石。"

"可那是凭运气，"哈利说，"不是凭技能——"

"第二年，"罗恩打断了他，"你杀死了蛇怪，消灭了里德尔。"

"是啊，但如果当时福克斯不出现，我——"

"第三年，"罗恩的声音更高了，"你一下子击退了一百个摄魂怪——"

CHAPTER FIFTEEN — The Hogwarts High Inquisitor

'You know that was a fluke, if the Time-Turner hadn't –'

'Last year,' Ron said, almost shouting now, 'you fought off You-Know-Who *again* –'

'Listen to me!' said Harry, almost angrily, because Ron and Hermione were both smirking now. 'Just listen to me, all right? It sounds great when you say it like that, but all that stuff was luck – I didn't know what I was doing half the time, I didn't plan any of it, I just did whatever I could think of, and I nearly always had help –'

Ron and Hermione were still smirking and Harry felt his temper rise; he wasn't even sure why he was feeling so angry.

'Don't sit there grinning like you know better than I do, I was there, wasn't I?' he said heatedly. 'I know what went on, all right? And I didn't get through any of that because I was brilliant at Defence Against the Dark Arts, I got through it all because – because help came at the right time, or because I guessed right – but I just blundered through it all, I didn't have a clue what I was doing – STOP LAUGHING!'

The bowl of Murtlap essence fell to the floor and smashed. He became aware that he was on his feet, though he couldn't remember standing up. Crookshanks streaked away under a sofa. Ron and Hermione's smiles had vanished.

'*You don't know what it's like!* You – neither of you – you've never had to face him, have you? You think it's just memorising a bunch of spells and throwing them at him, like you're in class or something? The whole time you know there's nothing between you and dying except your own – your own brain or guts or whatever – like you can think straight when you know you're about a nanosecond from being murdered, or tortured, or watching your friends die – they've never taught us that in their classes, what it's like to deal with things like that – and you two sit there acting like I'm a clever little boy to be standing here, alive, like Diggory was stupid, like he messed up – you just don't get it, that could just as easily have been me, it would have been if Voldemort hadn't needed me –'

'We weren't saying anything like that, mate,' said Ron, looking aghast. 'We weren't having a go at Diggory, we didn't – you've got the wrong end of the –'

第15章 霍格沃茨的高级调查官

"你知道那是侥幸,如果时间转换器没有——"

"去年,"罗恩简直是在大喊大叫了,"你又一次摆脱了神秘人的魔爪——"

"听我说!"哈利几乎是气愤地说,因为现在罗恩和赫敏都在那儿发笑了,"先听我说,好吗?这些事情说起来挺了不起的,可凭的全都是运气——我一半的时间都不知道自己在做什么,根本就不是计划好的,我只是凭着感觉行事,而且差不多总是能得到帮助——"

罗恩和赫敏还在那儿发笑,哈利觉得火气上来了。他自己也不明白为什么这么生气。

"别一脸坏笑地坐在那儿,好像你们知道得比我还清楚,当时在场的是我,不是吗?"他激动地说,"我知道是怎么回事,好吗?我每次能够死里逃生,并不是因为我在黑魔法防御术方面多么出色,我能够侥幸逃脱都是因为——因为我总能够及时得到帮助,或者因为我的感觉还算准确——但每次我都是糊里糊涂地过来的,我根本不知道自己在做什么——**别笑啦**!"

那碗莫特拉鼠触角的汁液掉在地上,碗摔得粉碎。他这才发现自己站了起来,却不记得是怎么站起来的。克鲁克山溜进了沙发底下。罗恩和赫敏脸上的笑容不见了。

"你们根本不知道那是什么滋味!你们——你们谁都没有面对过他,是不是?你们以为那只是背诵一大堆咒语朝他们扔过去,就像你们在课堂上那样?那些时候,你明知道在你和死亡之间没有任何东西,除了你自己——你自己的智慧,或勇气,或其他什么——你明知道自己转眼间就会被人杀害,或遭受折磨,或眼睁睁地看着朋友死去,还怎么能够正常地思考,他们从没有在课堂上告诉过我们,应对那样的情况是什么感觉——而你们俩坐在这里摆出这副样子,就好像我是一个聪明的男孩,所以才活着站在这里,就好像塞德里克是个傻瓜,把事情弄糟了——你们根本不明白,那个人很有可能就是我,如果不是因为伏地魔需要我——"

"我们没有说过那样的话,哥们儿,"罗恩说,显然被吓坏了,"我们没有对迪戈里说三道四,没有——你完全理解错了——"

CHAPTER FIFTEEN   The Hogwarts High Inquisitor

He looked helplessly at Hermione, whose face was stricken.

'Harry,' she said timidly, 'don't you see? This ... this is exactly why we need you ... we need to know what it's r-really like ... facing him ... facing V-Voldemort.'

It was the first time she had ever said Voldemort's name and it was this, more than anything else, that calmed Harry. Still breathing hard, he sank back into his chair, becoming aware as he did so that his hand was throbbing horribly again. He wished he had not smashed the bowl of Murtlap essence.

'Well ... think about it,' said Hermione quietly. 'Please?'

Harry could not think of anything to say. He was feeling ashamed of his outburst already. He nodded, hardly aware of what he was agreeing to.

Hermione stood up.

'Well, I'm off to bed,' she said, in a voice that was clearly as natural as she could make it. 'Erm ... night.'

Ron had got to his feet, too.

'Coming?' he said awkwardly to Harry.

'Yeah,' said Harry. 'In ... in a minute. I'll just clear this up.'

He indicated the smashed bowl on the floor. Ron nodded and left.

'*Reparo*,' Harry muttered, pointing his wand at the broken pieces of china. They flew back together, good as new, but there was no returning the Murtlap essence to the bowl.

He was suddenly so tired he was tempted to sink back into his armchair and sleep there, but instead he forced himself to his feet and followed Ron upstairs. His restless night was punctuated once more by dreams of long corridors and locked doors and he awoke next day with his scar prickling again.

第 15 章 霍格沃茨的高级调查官

他求助地望着赫敏,赫敏也是一脸的惊慌。

"哈利,"她战战兢兢地说,"你不明白吗?正因为……因为这个我们才需要你……我们需要知道那是什……什么感觉……面对着伏—伏地魔。"

这是赫敏第一次说出伏地魔的名字,也正是这一点使哈利的心情平静了下来。他仍然急促地喘着气,重新坐到了椅子上,这时才意识到他的手又在一跳一跳地剧痛。他真后悔不该打碎那碗莫特拉鼠触角的汁液。

"怎么样……好好考虑考虑,"赫敏小声地说,"好吗?"

哈利不知道该说什么。他已经为刚才的大发雷霆感到羞愧了。他点点头,其实并不清楚他同意的是什么。

赫敏站了起来。

"好吧,我要去睡觉了。"她说,显然在尽量使自己的声音自然一些,"唔……晚安。"

罗恩也站起身来。

"走吧?"他有点尴尬地对哈利说。

"好的,"哈利说,"过……过一会儿吧,我把这里收拾收拾。"

他指着地上的碎碗。罗恩点点头离开了。

"恢复如初。"哈利用魔杖指着那些碎瓷片,低声说道。碎片立刻拼拢在一起,瓷碗又完好如初,可是里面的莫特拉鼠触角的汁液再也回不来了。

他突然感到无比的疲倦,真想倒在扶手椅上睡一觉,但还是强迫自己站起来,跟在罗恩后面上了楼。夜里他睡得很不踏实,总是梦见那些长长的走廊和紧锁的房门。第二天早晨醒来时,他额头上的伤疤又开始刺痛了。

CHAPTER SIXTEEN

In the Hog's Head

Hermione made no mention of Harry giving Defence Against the Dark Arts lessons for two whole weeks after her original suggestion. Harry's detentions with Umbridge were finally over (he doubted whether the words now etched into the back of his hand would ever fade entirely); Ron had had four more Quidditch practices and not been shouted at during the last two; and all three of them had managed to Vanish their mice in Transfiguration (Hermione had actually progressed to Vanishing kittens), before the subject was broached again, on a wild, blustery evening at the end of September, when the three of them were sitting in the library, looking up potion ingredients for Snape.

'I was wondering,' Hermione said suddenly, 'whether you'd thought any more about Defence Against the Dark Arts, Harry.'

'Course I have,' said Harry grumpily, 'can't forget it, can we, with that hag teaching us –'

'I meant the idea Ron and I had –' Ron cast her an alarmed, threatening kind of look. She frowned at him, '– Oh, all right, the idea I had, then – about you teaching us.'

Harry did not answer at once. He pretended to be perusing a page of *Asiatic Anti-Venoms*, because he did not want to say what was in his mind.

He had given the matter a great deal of thought over the past fortnight. Sometimes it seemed an insane idea, just as it had on the night Hermione had proposed it, but at others, he had found himself thinking about the spells that had served him best in his various encounters with Dark creatures and Death Eaters – found himself, in fact, subconsciously planning lessons ...

'Well,' he said slowly, when he could no longer pretend to find *Asiatic Anti-*

第 16 章

在猪头酒吧

自从第一次提出让哈利讲授黑魔法防御术课的建议之后,赫敏整整两个星期没有再提这件事。哈利在乌姆里奇那里的关禁闭终于结束了(他怀疑那行已深深刻进他手背的文字恐怕永远不会完全消失了),罗恩又参加了四次魁地奇球训练,最后两次没有受到大声呵斥。在变形课上,他们三个都成功地念咒让老鼠消失了(实际上赫敏已经更进一步,在练习让小猫消失的咒语了)。然后,在九月底一个狂风大作的夜晚,他们三个坐在图书馆里,为斯内普查找魔药成分时,这个话题又被提了出来。

"我很想知道,"赫敏突然说道,"你有没有再考虑过黑魔法防御术的事,哈利。"

"当然考虑过,"哈利没好气地说,"怎么能忘记呢,有那个女妖在教我们——"

"我指的是我和罗恩的那个主意——"罗恩用惊恐的、带有威胁的目光瞪了赫敏一眼,赫敏朝罗恩皱起眉头,"——哦,好吧,就说是我的那个主意吧——由你来教我们。"

哈利没有马上回答。他在假装仔细阅读《亚洲抗毒大全》中的一页,不想把脑子里的想法说出来。

在刚刚过去的两个星期里,他对这件事情考虑了很多。有时觉得这是一个荒唐的念头,就像赫敏刚提出来的那天晚上一样,有时却发现自己在思索他与黑魔法生物和食死徒的各种交锋中,最起作用的那些咒语——发现自己实际上是在潜意识中备课……

"嗯,"他不能再假装对《亚洲抗毒大全》感兴趣了,于是慢悠悠地说,

CHAPTER SIXTEEN In the Hog's Head

Venoms interesting, 'yeah, I – I've thought about it a bit.'

'And?' said Hermione eagerly.

'I dunno,' said Harry, playing for time. He looked up at Ron.

'I thought it was a good idea from the start,' said Ron, who seemed keener to join in this conversation now that he was sure Harry was not going to start shouting again.

Harry shifted uncomfortably in his chair.

'You did listen to what I said about a load of it being luck, didn't you?'

'Yes, Harry,' said Hermione gently, 'but all the same, there's no point pretending that you're not good at Defence Against the Dark Arts, because you are. You were the only person last year who could throw off the Imperius Curse completely, you can produce a Patronus, you can do all sorts of stuff that full-grown wizards can't, Viktor always said –'

Ron looked round at her so fast he appeared to crick his neck. Rubbing it, he said, 'Yeah? What did Vicky say?'

'Ho ho,' said Hermione in a bored voice. 'He said Harry knew how to do stuff even he didn't, and he was in the final year at Durmstrang.'

Ron was looking at Hermione suspiciously.

'You're not still in contact with him, are you?'

'So what if I am?' said Hermione coolly, though her face was a little pink. 'I can have a pen-pal if I –'

'He didn't only want to be your pen-pal,' said Ron accusingly.

Hermione shook her head exasperatedly and, ignoring Ron, who was continuing to watch her, said to Harry, 'Well, what do you think? Will you teach us?'

'Just you and Ron, yeah?'

'Well,' said Hermione, looking a mite anxious again. 'Well ... now, don't fly off the handle again, Harry, please ... but I really think you ought to teach anyone who wants to learn. I mean, we're talking about defending ourselves against V-Voldemort. Oh, don't be pathetic, Ron. It doesn't seem fair if we don't offer the chance to other people.'

Harry considered this for a moment, then said, 'Yeah, but I doubt anyone except you two would want to be taught by me. I'm a nutter, remember?'

'Well, I think you might be surprised how many people would be interested

第16章 在猪头酒吧

"是啊，我——我是想过一点儿。"

"怎么样？"赫敏急切地说。

"我也说不好。"哈利拖延着时间。他抬头看着罗恩。

"我从一开始就觉得这是一个好主意。"罗恩说，他看到哈利肯定不会再嚷嚷了，便似乎比较热心参与这场谈话了。

哈利局促地在椅子上动来动去。

"你们听我说了那一切全靠运气，是不是？"

"是的，哈利，"赫敏温和地说，"可是，你假装在黑魔法防御术方面不出色是没有用的，因为你确实很出色。去年，只有你一个人能彻底摆脱夺魂咒，你能变出一个守护神，你能做到各种就连成年巫师也做不到的事情，威克多尔以前总是说——"

罗恩猛地把头转向她，速度太快，似乎把脖子都拧痛了。他一边揉着脖子一边说："什么？威基说什么啦？"

"呵呵，"赫敏用腻烦的口吻说，"他说哈利会的魔法就连他也不会，而他当时已在德姆斯特朗上最后一年级了。"

罗恩怀疑地打量着赫敏。

"你该不会还跟他保持联系吧？"

"是又怎么样？"赫敏冷冷地说，但她的脸微微有些泛红，"我也可以有一个笔友嘛——"

"他可不只是想做你的笔友。"罗恩指责地说。

赫敏气恼地摇了摇头，没理睬继续注视着她的罗恩，对哈利说道："那么，你是怎么想的呢？你会教我们吗？"

"就教你和罗恩，是吗？"

"嗯，"赫敏说，看上去又有一点不安，"嗯……你听了可千万别再发脾气，哈利，求求你了……但我确实认为，只要有谁想学，你都应该教他们。我是说，我们是在谈论如何保护自己，抵抗伏—伏地魔。哦，别那么厌，罗恩。如果我们不给其他人提供机会，似乎不太公平。"

哈利考虑了片刻，然后说道："是啊，但我怀疑除了你们俩，还有谁会愿意我去教他们呢。别忘了我是一个疯子！"

"嘿，我想，当你知道竟然有那么多人有兴趣听你讲一讲时，你恐

CHAPTER SIXTEEN   In the Hog's Head

in hearing what you've got to say,' said Hermione seriously. 'Look,' she leaned towards him – Ron, who was still watching her with a frown on his face, leaned forwards to listen too – 'you know the first weekend in October's a Hogsmeade weekend? How would it be if we tell anyone who's interested to meet us in the village and we can talk it over?'

'Why do we have to do it outside school?' said Ron.

'Because,' said Hermione, returning to the diagram of the Chinese Chomping Cabbage she was copying, 'I don't think Umbridge would be very happy if she found out what we were up to.'

Harry had been looking forward to the weekend trip into Hogsmeade, but there was one thing worrying him. Sirius had maintained a stony silence since he had appeared in the fire at the beginning of September; Harry knew they had made him angry by saying they didn't want him to come – but he still worried from time to time that Sirius might throw caution to the winds and turn up anyway. What were they going to do if the great black dog came bounding up the street towards them in Hogsmeade, perhaps under the nose of Draco Malfoy?

'Well, you can't blame him for wanting to get out and about,' said Ron, when Harry discussed his fears with him and Hermione. 'I mean, he's been on the run for over two years, hasn't he, and I know that can't have been a laugh, but at least he was free, wasn't he? And now he's just shut up all the time with that ghastly elf.'

Hermione scowled at Ron, but otherwise ignored the slight on Kreacher.

'The trouble is,' she said to Harry, 'until V–Voldemort – oh, for heaven's sake, Ron – comes out into the open, Sirius is going to have to stay hidden, isn't he? I mean, the stupid Ministry isn't going to realise Sirius is innocent until they accept that Dumbledore's been telling the truth about him all along. And once the fools start catching real Death Eaters again, it'll be obvious Sirius isn't one ... I mean, he hasn't got the Mark, for one thing.'

'I don't reckon he'd be stupid enough to turn up,' said Ron bracingly. 'Dumbledore'd go mad if he did and Sirius listens to Dumbledore even if he doesn't like what he hears.'

When Harry continued to look worried, Hermione said, 'Listen, Ron and

怕会感到吃惊的。"赫敏认真地说。"瞧，"她朝哈利探过身——罗恩仍然皱着眉头注视着她，这时也凑上前来听——"知道十月的第一个周末我们要去霍格莫德吗？我们不妨叫每个感兴趣的人在村里跟我们见见面，好好议一议这件事，怎么样？"

"为什么一定要弄到校外去呢？"罗恩问。

"因为，"赫敏说，一边低头继续抄写那张中国咬人甘蓝的图表，"如果乌姆里奇发现了我们要做的事情，她肯定不会很高兴的。"

哈利一直盼望着到霍格莫德村去过周末，但是有一件事让他很担心。小天狼星自从九月初在炉火中出现过一次之后，这么长时间都没有音讯。哈利知道，他们当时说不想让他再来，一定惹得他很不高兴——但是哈利有时仍然担心小天狼星会不顾一切，鲁莽行事，出现在村子里。如果到了霍格莫德村，一条大黑狗在路上冲他们奔来，说不定就在德拉科·马尔福的鼻子底下，那可怎么办呢？

"我说，你不能怪他想出来散散心。"当哈利把他的担忧告诉罗恩和赫敏时，罗恩说道，"我是说，他在外面逃跑了两年多，是不是，虽然那并不是什么好玩的事，但至少那时候他是自由的，是不是？现在却整天跟那个可怕的小精灵关在一起。"

赫敏气呼呼地瞪着罗恩，但她对罗恩这样贬损克利切并没有作更多的表示。

"问题是，"她对哈利说，"在伏—伏地魔——哦，看在老天的分儿上，别这样，罗恩——在他公开出现之前，小天狼星不得不一直隐藏着，是不是？我是说，愚蠢的魔法部先要承认邓布利多说的关于伏地魔的话都是真的，才会意识到小天狼星是无辜的。一旦那些傻瓜又开始捉拿真正的食死徒时，大家便会看出小天狼星不是食死徒了……我是说，至少他没有标记呀。"

"我认为他不会傻乎乎地跑到这里来的。"罗恩安慰他们道，"如果他这么做，邓布利多肯定会气得发疯，而小天狼星很听邓布利多的话，尽管他并不喜欢那些意见。"

看到哈利还是一脸的担忧，赫敏说："听着，我和罗恩一直在试探

CHAPTER SIXTEEN In the Hog's Head

I have been sounding out people who we thought might want to learn some proper Defence Against the Dark Arts, and there are a couple who seem interested. We've told them to meet us in Hogsmeade.'

'Right,' said Harry vaguely, his mind still on Sirius.

'Don't worry, Harry,' Hermione said quietly. 'You've got enough on your plate without Sirius, too.'

She was quite right, of course, he was barely keeping up with his homework, though he was doing much better now that he was no longer spending every evening in detention with Umbridge. Ron was even further behind with his work than Harry, because while they both had Quidditch practice twice a week, Ron also had his prefect duties. However, Hermione, who was taking more subjects than either of them, had not only finished all her homework but was also finding time to knit more elf clothes. Harry had to admit that she was getting better; it was now almost always possible to distinguish between the hats and the socks.

The morning of the Hogsmeade visit dawned bright but windy. After breakfast they queued up in front of Filch, who matched their names to the long list of students who had permission from their parents or guardian to visit the village. With a slight pang, Harry remembered that if it hadn't been for Sirius, he would not have been going at all.

When Harry reached Filch, the caretaker gave a great sniff as though trying to detect a whiff of something from Harry. Then he gave a curt nod that set his jowls aquiver again and Harry walked on, out on to the stone steps and the cold, sunlit day.

'Er – why was Filch sniffing you?' asked Ron, as he, Harry and Hermione set off at a brisk pace down the wide drive to the gates.

'I suppose he was checking for the smell of Dungbombs,' said Harry with a small laugh. 'I forgot to tell you …'

And he recounted the story of sending his letter to Sirius and Filch bursting in seconds later, demanding to see the letter. To his slight surprise, Hermione found this story highly interesting, much more, indeed, than he did himself.

'He said he was tipped off you were ordering Dungbombs? But who tipped him off?'

'I dunno,' said Harry, shrugging. 'Maybe Malfoy, he'd think it was a laugh.'

第16章 在猪头酒吧

那些我们认为可能想学习一些正规的黑魔法防御术的人,其中两三个似乎很感兴趣。我们叫他们在霍格莫德村跟我们碰面。"

"好的。"哈利淡淡地说,心里还在想着小天狼星。

"不要担心,哈利,"赫敏轻声说,"你要做的事情已经够多的了,别老惦记着小天狼星了。"

她说得当然很对,哈利的家庭作业只是勉强能按时完成,不过现在不用每天晚上到乌姆里奇那里关禁闭了,他觉得轻松了不少。罗恩的功课落得比哈利还要多,因为他们俩都要参加每星期两次的魁地奇球训练,罗恩还要履行级长的职责。而赫敏呢,她选的科目比他们俩都多,却不仅做完了所有的家庭作业,还能找到时间给小精灵织衣服。哈利不得不承认她的手艺越来越好,现在几乎可以分得出哪些是帽子,哪些是袜子了。

到霍格莫德村去的那天早晨,天气晴朗,但是有风。吃过早饭,他们在费尔奇面前排起了长队,他要对着那张长长的名单核对他们的名字,名单上列的是得到家长或监护人允许,可以拜访霍格莫德村的同学。哈利突然揪心地想到,如果不是小天狼星,他根本就去不成。

哈利走到费尔奇面前时,管理员使劲嗅了嗅鼻子,似乎想从哈利身上闻出什么东西的气味。然后他草草点了下头,下巴上的垂肉又颤抖起来,哈利继续往前走,来到石阶上,来到寒冷的阳光灿烂的户外。

"呃——费尔奇为什么使劲嗅你?"罗恩问,这时候,他、哈利和赫敏正迈着轻快的脚步,走在通往大门的宽阔车道上。

"我猜他是想闻闻有没有粪弹的气味吧,"哈利轻声笑着说,"我忘记告诉你们了……"

他把给小天狼星寄信、费尔奇几秒钟后冲进来要求看信的事原原本本地讲给他们听。使他微微感到吃惊的是,赫敏对这件事非常感兴趣,甚至比哈利自己还要感兴趣得多。

"他说他得到情报,你在订购粪弹?那么是谁向他提供情报的呢?"

"不知道,"哈利耸了耸肩膀说,"大概是马尔福吧,他会觉得这很有趣。"

CHAPTER SIXTEEN   In the Hog's Head

They walked between the tall stone pillars topped with winged boars and turned left on to the road into the village, the wind whipping their hair into their eyes.

'Malfoy?' said Hermione, sceptically. 'Well … yes … maybe …'

And she remained deep in thought all the way into the outskirts of Hogsmeade.

'Where are we going, anyway?' Harry asked. 'The Three Broomsticks?'

'Oh – no,' said Hermione, coming out of her reverie, 'no, it's always packed and really noisy. I've told the others to meet us in the Hog's Head, that other pub, you know the one, it's not on the main road. I think it's a bit … you know … *dodgy* … but students don't normally go in there, so I don't think we'll be overheard.'

They walked down the main street past Zonko's Wizarding Joke Shop, where they were not surprised to see Fred, George and Lee Jordan, past the post office, from which owls issued at regular intervals, and turned up a side-street at the top of which stood a small inn. A battered wooden sign hung from a rusty bracket over the door, with a picture on it of a wild boar's severed head, leaking blood on to the white cloth around it. The sign creaked in the wind as they approached. All three of them hesitated outside the door.

'Well, come on,' said Hermione, slightly nervously. Harry led the way inside.

It was not at all like the Three Broomsticks, whose large bar gave an impression of gleaming warmth and cleanliness. The Hog's Head bar comprised one small, dingy and very dirty room that smelled strongly of something that might have been goats. The bay windows were so encrusted with grime that very little daylight could permeate the room, which was lit instead with the stubs of candles sitting on rough wooden tables. The floor seemed at first glance to be compressed earth, though as Harry stepped on to it he realised that there was stone beneath what seemed to be the accumulated filth of centuries.

Harry remembered Hagrid mentioning this pub in his first year: 'Yeh get a lot o' funny folk in the Hog's Head,' he had said, explaining how he had won a dragon's egg from a hooded stranger there. At the time Harry had wondered why Hagrid had not found it odd that the stranger kept his face hidden throughout their encounter; now he saw that keeping your face hidden was something of a fashion in the Hog's Head. There was a man at the bar whose whole head was wrapped in dirty grey bandages, though he was still managing to gulp endless glasses of some smoking, fiery substance through a slit over his

第16章 在猪头酒吧

他们从顶上立着带翅膀野猪的高高石柱之间穿过，向左拐到通往村子的路上，风把他们的头发吹得挡住了眼睛。

"马尔福？"赫敏表示怀疑地说，"嗯……是啊……有可能……"

然后，在快到霍格莫德村的一路上，她一直在沉思默想。

"我们到底上哪儿去呀？"哈利问，"三把扫帚吗？"

"哦——不是，"赫敏从沉思中惊醒过来，说道，"不是，那里总是挤满了人，嘈杂得厉害。我叫其他人在猪头酒吧跟我们碰头，就是另外一家酒吧，你们知道的，不在大路上。我也觉得这有点儿……怎么说呢……有些破败……但同学们一般不上那儿去，所以我想我们不会被人偷听到。"

他们顺着大路往前走，经过佐科笑话店——不出所料，他们在这里看见了弗雷德、乔治和李·乔丹，经过邮局——每过一会儿就有一些猫头鹰从里面飞出来，然后他们拐进旁边的一条小路，顶端有一家小酒吧。破破烂烂的木头招牌悬挂在门上锈迹斑斑的支架上，上面画着一个被砍下来的野猪头，血迹渗透了包着它的白布。他们走近时，招牌被风吹得吱吱嘎嘎作响。他们三人在门外迟疑着。

"走，进去吧。"赫敏说，显得有点儿紧张。哈利领头走了进去。

里面与三把扫帚酒吧完全不一样，那儿的大吧台总使人感到明亮、干净而温暖。猪头酒吧只有一间又小又暗、非常肮脏的屋子，散发着一股浓浓的羊膻味。几扇凸窗上积着厚厚的污垢，光线几乎透不进来，只有粗糙的木头桌子上点着一些蜡烛头。哈利第一眼望去，以为地面是压实的泥地，可是踩在上面才发现，原本是石头铺的地面上积了几个世纪的污秽。

哈利想起一年级时海格提到过这家酒吧："猪头酒吧里有许多古怪的家伙。"他这么说，解释他是怎么从酒吧里一个戴兜帽的陌生人手里赢得一只火龙蛋的。当时哈利还纳闷，在他们交往时那人始终把脸挡得严严实实，海格为什么不觉得奇怪呢。现在他才发现，猪头酒吧里似乎很流行把脸隐藏起来。吧台那儿有一个人，整个脑袋都裹在脏兮兮的灰色绷带里，却仍然能一杯接一杯地把一种冒烟的、燃着火苗的东西从嘴上一道绷带的缝隙中灌进去。窗边的一张桌子旁坐着两个戴

mouth; two figures shrouded in hoods sat at a table in one of the windows; Harry might have thought them Dementors if they had not been talking in strong Yorkshire accents, and in a shadowy corner beside the fireplace sat a witch with a thick, black veil that fell to her toes. They could just see the tip of her nose because it caused the veil to protrude slightly.

'I don't know about this, Hermione,' Harry muttered, as they crossed to the bar. He was looking particularly at the heavily veiled witch. 'Has it occurred to you Umbridge might be under that?'

Hermione cast an appraising eye over the veiled figure.

'Umbridge is shorter than that woman,' she said quietly. 'And anyway, even if Umbridge does come in here there's nothing she can do to stop us, Harry, because I've double- and triple-checked the school rules. We're not out of bounds; I specifically asked Professor Flitwick whether students were allowed to come in the Hog's Head, and he said yes, but he advised me strongly to bring our own glasses. And I've looked up everything I can think of about study groups and homework groups and they're definitely allowed. I just don't think it's a good idea if we *parade* what we're doing.'

'No,' said Harry drily, 'especially as it's not exactly a homework group you're planning, is it?'

The barman sidled towards them out of a back room. He was a grumpy-looking old man with a great deal of long grey hair and beard. He was tall and thin and looked vaguely familiar to Harry.

'What?' he grunted.

'Three Butterbeers, please,' said Hermione.

The man reached beneath the counter and pulled up three very dusty, very dirty bottles, which he slammed on the bar.

'Six Sickles,' he said.

'I'll get them,' said Harry quickly, passing over the silver. The barman's eyes travelled over Harry, resting for a fraction of a second on his scar. Then he turned away and deposited Harry's money in an ancient wooden till whose drawer slid open automatically to receive it. Harry, Ron and Hermione retreated to the furthest table from the bar and sat down, looking around. The man in the dirty grey bandages rapped the counter with his knuckles and received another smoking drink from the barman.

第16章 在猪头酒吧

兜帽的人影,若不是他们用很浓重的约克郡口音在说话,哈利简直以为他们是摄魂怪。在壁炉旁一个阴暗的角落里坐着一个女巫,厚厚的黑色纱巾一直垂到她的双脚。他们只能看见她的鼻尖,因为它把纱巾顶得微微突起。

"我觉得不大对劲儿,赫敏。"他们朝吧台走去时,哈利低声说。他格外注意地望着那个全身裹纱巾的女巫。"你有没有想到那里面会是乌姆里奇呢?"

赫敏掂量着朝那裹纱巾的身影扫了一眼。

"乌姆里奇比这个女人矮,"她悄声说,"而且,就算乌姆里奇上这儿来了,她也不能阻止我们,哈利,因为我把学校的规章制度反复看了两三遍。我们没有越轨。我还专门问过弗立维教授,学生可不可以进猪头酒吧,他说可以,但他一再建议我要自己带上杯子。我查遍了我能想到的组织学习小组和作业小组的规定,它们都是在绝对被允许的范围内的。我只是觉得我们做这件事不应该过分张扬。"

"是的,"哈利干巴巴地说,"特别是你筹划的实际上并不是一个作业小组,对吗?"

酒吧老板侧身从一个后门闪出,朝他们迎上来。他是个看上去脾气暴躁的老头儿,长着一大堆长长的灰色头发和胡子。他个子又高又瘦,哈利隐约感觉似乎在哪儿见过他。

"要什么?"他嘟哝着问。

"请来三瓶黄油啤酒。"赫敏说。

那人弯腰从柜台底下掏出三只布满灰尘、肮脏透顶的瓶子,重重地放在吧台上。

"六个西可。"他说。

"我来付。"哈利赶紧说道,把银币递了过去。酒吧老板的目光移向哈利,在他的伤疤上停留了一刹那。然后他移开目光,把哈利给他的钱放进一只古老的木头钱柜,抽屉自动滑开,把钱吞了进去。哈利、罗恩和赫敏退到离吧台最远的一张桌旁坐了下来,东张西望。那个裹着脏兮兮的灰色绷带的男人用指关节敲打着柜台,又从酒吧老板那儿得到了一杯冒烟的饮料。

CHAPTER SIXTEEN In the Hog's Head

'You know what?' Ron murmured, looking over at the bar with enthusiasm. 'We could order anything we liked in here. I bet that bloke would sell us anything, he wouldn't care. I've always wanted to try Firewhisky –'

'You – are – a – *prefect*,' snarled Hermione.

'Oh,' said Ron, the smile fading from his face. 'Yeah ...'

'So, who did you say is supposed to be meeting us?' Harry asked, wrenching open the rusty top of his Butterbeer and taking a swig.

'Just a couple of people,' Hermione repeated, checking her watch and looking anxiously towards the door. 'I told them to be here about now and I'm sure they all know where it is – oh, look, this might be them now.'

The door of the pub had opened. A thick band of dusty sunlight split the room in two for a moment and then vanished, blocked by the incoming rush of a crowd of people.

First came Neville with Dean and Lavender, who were closely followed by Parvati and Padma Patil with (Harry's stomach did a backflip) Cho and one of her usually-giggling girlfriends, then (on her own and looking so dreamy she might have walked in by accident) Luna Lovegood; then Katie Bell, Alicia Spinnet and Angelina Johnson, Colin and Dennis Creevey, Ernie Macmillan, Justin Finch-Fletchley, Hannah Abbott, a Hufflepuff girl with a long plait down her back whose name Harry did not know; three Ravenclaw boys he was pretty sure were called Anthony Goldstein, Michael Corner and Terry Boot then Ginny, followed by a tall skinny blond boy with an upturned nose whom Harry recognised vaguely as being a member of the Hufflepuff Quidditch team and, bringing up the rear, Fred and George Weasley with their friend Lee Jordan, all three of whom were carrying large paper bags crammed with Zonko's merchandise.

'A couple of people?' said Harry hoarsely to Hermione. '*A couple of people?*'

'Yes, well, the idea seemed quite popular,' said Hermione happily. 'Ron, do you want to pull up some more chairs?'

The barman had frozen in the act of wiping out a glass with a rag so filthy it looked as though it had never been washed. Possibly, he had never seen his pub so full.

'Hi,' said Fred, reaching the bar first and counting his companions quickly, 'could we have ... twenty-five Butterbeers, please?'

第16章 在猪头酒吧

"你猜怎么着?"罗恩怀着极大的热情望着吧台,喃喃地说,"在这里我们可以想点什么就点什么。我敢说那家伙肯定会什么都卖给我们的,他才不管那么多呢。我一直想尝尝火焰威士忌——"

"你——是——个——级长。"赫敏恶狠狠地说。

"噢,"罗恩说,脸上的笑容隐去了,"是啊……"

"那么,你说谁会来跟我们碰头呢?"哈利问,一边拧开他那瓶黄油啤酒的锈迹斑斑的瓶盖,喝了一大口。

"就那么三两个人,"赫敏说着看了看表,焦急地朝门口张望,"我叫他们差不多这个时候到,估计他们肯定都知道在什么地方——哦,看,这大概就是他们了。"

酒吧的门开了,一道粗粗的、弥漫着灰尘的阳光把屋子一分为二,转眼又消失了,是被拥进来的一大帮人挡住了。

首先进来的是纳威、迪安和拉文德,后面紧跟着帕瓦蒂和帕德玛·佩蒂尔,还有(哈利内心抽搐了一下)秋和她那帮叽叽喳喳的女友中的一个,然后是(独自一人,神情恍惚,仿佛是不经意间走进来的)卢娜·洛夫古德,再后面是凯蒂·贝尔、艾丽娅·斯平内特和安吉利娜·约翰逊、科林和丹尼斯·克里维兄弟俩、厄尼·麦克米兰、贾斯廷·芬列里、汉娜·艾博,还有一个哈利叫不出名字的赫奇帕奇女生,一根长长的辫子拖在背上,三个拉文克劳男生,哈利可以肯定他们叫安东尼·戈德斯坦、迈克尔·科纳和泰瑞·布特,还有金妮,后面跟着一个瘦瘦高高、长着一个翘鼻子的黄头发男生,哈利模模糊糊记得他是赫奇帕奇魁地奇球队的队员,走在最后的是弗雷德、乔治和他们的朋友李·乔丹,三个人怀里都抱着大纸袋,里面装满了在佐科笑话店买的东西。

"三两个人?"哈利声音嘶哑地对赫敏说,"三两个人?"

"是啊,不错,看来这个主意很得人心。"赫敏高兴地说,"罗恩,你是不是再搬几把椅子过来?"

酒吧老板正在用一块脏得像是从来没洗过的破布擦一只玻璃杯,看到这情景不禁呆住了。他的酒吧大概从没来过这么多人。

"嘿,"弗雷德说,抢先走到吧台旁,迅速数了数他的同伴,"劳驾,能不能给我们来……二十五瓶黄油啤酒?"

CHAPTER SIXTEEN In the Hog's Head

The barman glared at him for a moment, then, throwing down his rag irritably as though he had been interrupted in something very important, he started passing up dusty Butterbeers from under the bar.

'Cheers,' said Fred, handing them out. 'Cough up, everyone, I haven't got enough gold for all of these ...'

Harry watched numbly as the large chattering group took their beers from Fred and rummaged in their robes to find coins. He could not imagine what all these people had turned up for until the horrible thought occurred to him that they might be expecting some kind of speech, at which he rounded on Hermione.

'What have you been telling people?' he said in a low voice. 'What are they expecting?'

'I've told you, they just want to hear what you've got to say,' said Hermione soothingly; but Harry continued to look at her so furiously that she added quickly, 'you don't have to do anything yet, I'll speak to them first.'

'Hi, Harry,' said Neville, beaming and taking a seat opposite him.

Harry tried to smile back, but did not speak; his mouth was exceptionally dry. Cho had just smiled at him and sat down on Ron's right. Her friend, who had curly reddish-blonde hair, did not smile, but gave Harry a thoroughly mistrustful look which plainly told him that, given her way, she would not be here at all.

In twos and threes the new arrivals settled around Harry, Ron and Hermione, some looking rather excited, others curious, Luna Lovegood gazing dreamily into space. When everybody had pulled up a chair, the chatter died out. Every eye was upon Harry.

'Er,' said Hermione, her voice slightly higher than usual out of nerves. 'Well – er – hi.'

The group focused its attention on her instead, though eyes continued to dart back regularly to Harry.

'Well ... erm ... well, you know why you're here. Erm ... well, Harry here had the idea – I mean' (Harry had thrown her a sharp look) 'I had the idea – that it might be good if people who wanted to study Defence Against the Dark Arts – and I mean, really study it, you know, not the rubbish that Umbridge is doing with us –' (Hermione's voice became suddenly much

第16章 在猪头酒吧

酒吧老板瞪了他片刻,然后恼怒地把破布扔下,似乎正在做一件非常重要的事情被打断了,他开始从吧台下面拿出一瓶瓶灰扑扑的黄油啤酒。

"谢谢!"弗雷德说着把啤酒传给大家,"每个人都出点钱吧,我可买不起这么多啤酒……"

哈利麻木地望着这一大帮叽叽喳喳的人从弗雷德手中接过啤酒,然后在袍子里摸索着寻找硬币。他想象不出这么多人是来做什么的,接着他突然产生了一个可怕的想法:他们大概想听人演讲,于是他恼怒地转向赫敏。

"你对别人是怎么说的?"他压低声音问,"他们想听到什么?"

"我已经告诉过你了,他们只是想听你讲讲你要说的话。"赫敏安慰他道,见哈利还是怒气冲冲地看着她,她便赶紧补充道,"现在还不需要你做什么,我先对他们说几句。"

"嘿,哈利。"纳威绽开满脸笑容,在哈利对面坐了下来。

哈利勉强对他报以微笑,但什么也没说。他嘴里突然变得特别干。秋刚才对他嫣然一笑,坐在了罗恩右边。她的朋友,就是那个长着一头淡红金色鬈发的女生,却没笑,而是用完全不信任的眼光看了看哈利,似乎准确无误地告诉他,若依着她自己的意思,是根本不会上这儿来的。

这些新来的人三三两两地围着哈利、罗恩和赫敏坐了下来,有的显得很兴奋,有的则充满好奇,卢娜·洛夫古德恍恍惚惚地独自发呆。每个人都在椅子上坐定了,说话声也渐渐平静下来。大家的目光都盯在哈利身上。

"嗯,"赫敏说,因为紧张,她的声音比平常略高一些,"嗯——呃——大家好。"

这伙人把注意力转向了赫敏,但目光仍然不时地扫到哈利身上。

"是这样……嗯……咳,你们都知道为什么要上这儿来。嗯……是这样,哈利想出一个主意——我是说——"(哈利狠狠地瞪了她一眼)"——我想出一个主意——如果有谁愿意学习黑魔法防御术——我是说,学到真本事,而不是那个乌姆里奇教给我们的那堆垃圾——"(赫

CHAPTER SIXTEEN   In the Hog's Head

stronger and more confident) '– because nobody could call that Defence Against the Dark Arts –' ('Hear, hear,' said Anthony Goldstein, and Hermione looked heartened) '– Well, I thought it would be good if we, well, took matters into our own hands.'

She paused, looked sideways at Harry, and went on, 'And by that I mean learning how to defend ourselves properly, not just in theory but doing the real spells –'

'You want to pass your Defence Against the Dark Arts O.W.L. too, though, I bet?' said Michael Corner.

'Of course I do,' said Hermione at once. 'But more than that, I want to be properly trained in defence because ... because ...' she took a great breath and finished, 'because Lord Voldemort is back.'

The reaction was immediate and predictable. Cho's friend shrieked and slopped Butterbeer down herself; Terry Boot gave a kind of involuntary twitch; Padma Patil shuddered, and Neville gave an odd yelp that he managed to turn into a cough. All of them, however, looked fixedly, even eagerly, at Harry.

'Well ... that's the plan, anyway,' said Hermione. 'If you want to join us, we need to decide how we're going to –'

'Where's the proof You-Know-Who's back?' said the blond Hufflepuff player in a rather aggressive voice.

'Well, Dumbledore believes it –' Hermione began.

'You mean, Dumbledore believes *him*,' said the blond boy, nodding at Harry.

'Who are *you*?' said Ron, rather rudely.

'Zacharias Smith,' said the boy, 'and I think we've got the right to know exactly what makes him say You-Know-Who's back.'

'Look,' said Hermione, intervening swiftly, 'that's really not what this meeting was supposed to be about –'

'It's OK, Hermione,' said Harry.

It had just dawned on him why there were so many people there. He thought Hermione should have seen this coming. Some of these people – maybe even most of them – had turned up in the hopes of hearing Harry's story firsthand.

第16章 在猪头酒吧

敏的声音突然变得坚定和理直气壮了许多)"——谁也不会管那玩意儿叫黑魔法防御术——"("说得好,说得好!"安东尼·戈德斯坦说,赫敏似乎很受鼓舞)"——我想,我们不妨,嗯,自己解决问题。"

她顿了顿,侧脸看看哈利,继续说道:"我的意思是学会如何有效地保护自己,不仅是学理论,还要练习真正的魔咒——"

"但是我想,你肯定也需要通过黑魔法防御术课的O.W.L.考试吧?"迈克尔·科纳说。

"当然是的,"赫敏立刻说道,"但是比那更重要的是,我想在防御术方面得到正规的训练,因为……因为……"她深深吸了口气才把话说完,"因为伏地魔回来了。"

大家的反应立竿见影,不出所料。秋的女友尖叫一声,把黄油啤酒泼洒在自己身上;泰瑞·布特不由自主地抽搐了一下;帕德玛·佩蒂尔打了个寒战;纳威发出一声怪叫,又及时把它转化为咳嗽。但他们都眼巴巴地,甚至是迫切地望着哈利。

"嗯……计划就是这样,"赫敏说,"如果你们想加入,我们需要决定一下今后怎么——"

"有什么证据证明神秘人回来了?"那个黄头发赫奇帕奇球员用咄咄逼人的口气问。

"噢,邓布利多相信——"赫敏话没说完。

"你是想说,邓布利多相信他。"黄头发的男孩说着冲哈利点了点头。

"你是谁?"罗恩很不礼貌地问。

"扎卡赖斯·史密斯。"那男孩说,"我认为我们有权知道他究竟为什么要说神秘人回来了。"

"注意,"赫敏敏捷地插进来说,"这其实并不是这次聚会所要讨论的——"

"没关系,赫敏。"哈利说。

他这才明白为什么会来这么多人。他认为赫敏本应该看清这一点。这帮人中有一些——甚至是大多数——之所以来,是想亲耳听听哈利编了哪些谎话。

CHAPTER SIXTEEN   In the Hog's Head

'What makes me say You-Know-Who's back?' he asked, looking Zacharias straight in the face. 'I saw him. But Dumbledore told the whole school what happened last year, and if you didn't believe him, you won't believe me, and I'm not wasting an afternoon trying to convince anyone.'

The whole group seemed to have held its breath while Harry spoke. Harry had the impression that even the barman was listening. He was wiping the same glass with the filthy rag, making it steadily dirtier.

Zacharias said dismissively, 'All Dumbledore told us last year was that Cedric Diggory got killed by You-Know-Who and that you brought Diggory's body back to Hogwarts. He didn't give us details, he didn't tell us exactly how Diggory got murdered, I think we'd all like to know –'

'If you've come to hear exactly what it looks like when Voldemort murders someone I can't help you,' Harry said. His temper, always so close to the surface these days, was rising again. He did not take his eyes from Zacharias Smith's aggressive face, and was determined not to look at Cho. 'I don't want to talk about Cedric Diggory, all right? So if that's what you're here for, you might as well clear out.'

He cast an angry look in Hermione's direction. This was, he felt, all her fault; she had decided to display him like some sort of freak and of course they had all turned up to see just how wild his story was. But none of them left their seats, not even Zacharias Smith, though he continued to gaze intently at Harry.

'So,' said Hermione, her voice very high-pitched again. 'So … like I was saying … if you want to learn some defence, then we need to work out how we're going to do it, how often we're going to meet and where we're going to –'

'Is it true,' interrupted the girl with the long plait down her back, looking at Harry, 'that you can produce a Patronus?'

There was a murmur of interest around the group at this.

'Yeah,' said Harry slightly defensively.

'A corporeal Patronus?'

The phrase stirred something in Harry's memory.

'Er – you don't know Madam Bones, do you?' he asked.

The girl smiled.

第16章 在猪头酒吧

"我为什么要说神秘人回来了?"他直视着扎卡赖斯的脸问道,"因为我看见他了。邓布利多上学年结束时已经对全校同学讲了事情的经过,如果你不相信他,那么你也不会相信我,我不想浪费一下午时间说服别人相信我。"

哈利说话时,大家似乎都屏住了呼吸。哈利感觉到就连酒吧老板也在听。他不停地用那块肮脏的破布擦着同一只玻璃杯,把它擦得更脏了。

扎卡赖斯轻蔑地说:"上学期邓布利多只告诉我们塞德里克·迪戈里被神秘人杀死了,你把迪戈里的尸体带回到霍格沃茨。他没有告诉我们具体的细节,他没有告诉我们迪戈里究竟是怎么被害的,我认为我们都很想知道——"

"如果你来是想听听伏地魔杀人是什么情形,我可没法帮助你。"哈利说。他的火气这些日子总是接近临界点,现在又噌噌地往上蹿了。他眼睛仍然盯着扎卡赖斯·史密斯那张咄咄逼人的脸,并打定主意不去看秋。"我不想谈论塞德里克·迪戈里,明白吗?如果你上这儿来就是为了这个,你现在就可以走了。"

他气呼呼地朝赫敏那边瞪了一眼。他觉得这一切都怪她,是她决定把他当个怪物一样拿出来展览的,不用问,他们都是想来看看他编的那些谎话到底有多离奇。然而,他们没有一个人离开座位,就连扎卡赖斯也不例外,尽管他仍然毫不示弱地盯着哈利。

"所以,"赫敏说,她的声音又变得尖细,"所以……就像我刚才说的……如果你们想学习一些防御术,我们就需要筹划一下该怎么做,多长时间碰一次面,在什么地方碰面——"

"那是真的吗,"那个背后拖着一根长辫子的女生望着哈利,打断了赫敏的话,"你真的能变出一个守护神吗?"

听了这话,大伙儿很感兴趣地低声议论起来。

"是啊。"哈利有点提防地说。

"一个实体守护神?"

这句话使哈利想起了什么。

"呃——你不认识博恩斯女士吧?"他问。

那女生笑了。

CHAPTER SIXTEEN In the Hog's Head

'She's my auntie,' she said. 'I'm Susan Bones. She told me about your hearing. So – is it really true? You make a stag Patronus?'

'Yes,' said Harry.

'Blimey, Harry!' said Lee, looking deeply impressed. 'I never knew that!'

'Mum told Ron not to spread it around,' said Fred, grinning at Harry. 'She said you got enough attention as it was.'

'She's not wrong,' mumbled Harry, and a couple of people laughed.

The veiled witch sitting alone shifted very slightly in her seat.

'And did you kill a Basilisk with that sword in Dumbledore's office?' demanded Terry Boot. 'That's what one of the portraits on the wall told me when I was in there last year ...'

'Er – yeah, I did, yeah,' said Harry.

Justin Finch-Fletchley whistled; the Creevey brothers exchanged awestruck looks and Lavender Brown said 'Wow!' softly. Harry was feeling slightly hot around the collar now; he was determinedly looking anywhere but at Cho.

'And in our first year,' said Neville to the group at large, 'he saved that Philological Stone –'

'Philosopher's,' hissed Hermione.

'Yes, that – from You-Know-Who,' finished Neville.

Hannah Abbott's eyes were as round as Galleons.

'And that's not to mention,' said Cho (Harry's eyes snapped across to her; she was looking at him, smiling; his stomach did another somersault) 'all the tasks he had to get through in the Triwizard Tournament last year – getting past dragons and merpeople and Acromantula and things ...'

There was a murmur of impressed agreement around the table. Harry's insides were squirming. He was trying to arrange his face so that he did not look too pleased with himself. The fact that Cho had just praised him made it much, much harder for him to say the thing he had sworn to himself he would tell them.

'Look,' he said, and everyone fell silent at once, 'I ... I don't want to sound like I'm trying to be modest or anything, but ... I had a lot of help with all that stuff ...'

'Not with the dragon, you didn't,' said Michael Corner at once. 'That was a seriously cool bit of flying ...'

'Yeah, well –' said Harry, feeling it would be churlish to disagree.

"她是我姑姑,"她说,"我叫苏珊·博恩斯。我姑姑对我说了你受审的事。那么——这是真的喽?你能变出一头牡鹿守护神?"

"是的。"哈利说。

"天啊,哈利!"李说,显出十分钦佩的样子,"我以前从不知道!"

"妈妈叫罗恩不要四处张扬,"弗雷德朝哈利咧嘴笑着说,"她说你受到的注意已经够多的了。"

"她说得没错。"哈利低声说,有几个人大声笑了起来。

裹纱巾的女巫在座位上不易察觉地动了动。

"你用邓布利多办公室的那把剑杀死了蛇怪?"泰瑞·布特问道,"那是去年墙上的一幅肖像告诉我的……"

"嗯——是的,确实是这样。"哈利说。

贾斯廷·芬列里吹了声口哨,克里维兄弟俩交换了一个震惊的目光,拉文德·布朗轻轻叫了一声:"哇!"哈利觉得他衣领周围开始有点发热了。他下定决心就是不去看秋。

"我们上一年级的时候,"纳威对大伙儿说,"他抢出了那颗魔术石——"

"是魔法石。"赫敏小声地纠正他。

"噢,对——是从神秘人手中。"纳威把话说完。

汉娜·艾博的眼睛瞪得像金加隆那么圆。

"更不用说,"秋说(哈利猛地将目光转向她,她面带微笑看着他,他的内心又是一阵翻腾),"上学期他在三强争霸赛里所完成的那些项目——穿越火龙、人鱼和巨蜘蛛等等……"

桌旁响起一片表示钦佩和赞同的喃喃声。哈利内心一阵悸动。他拼命调整自己的面部表情,不要显出太得意的样子。秋这样赞扬他,使得他刚才发誓要对他们说的话现在很难说得出口了。

"其实,"他说,大家立刻安静了下来,"我……我不想表现得故作谦虚什么的,可是……所有那些事情我都得到过许多帮助……"

"穿越火龙那次你没有得到帮助,"迈克尔·科纳立刻说,"你当时飞起来的样子真够酷的……"

"是啊,嗯——"哈利说,觉得再表示反对就会显得无礼了。

CHAPTER SIXTEEN   In the Hog's Head

'And nobody helped you get rid of those Dementors this summer,' said Susan Bones.

'No,' said Harry, 'no, OK, I know I did bits of it without help, but the point I'm trying to make is –'

'Are you trying to weasel out of showing us any of this stuff?' said Zacharias Smith.

'Here's an idea,' said Ron loudly, before Harry could speak, 'why don't you shut your mouth?'

Perhaps the word 'weasel' had affected Ron particularly strongly. In any case, he was now looking at Zacharias as though he would like nothing better than to thump him. Zacharias flushed.

'Well, we've all turned up to learn from him and now he's telling us he can't really do any of it,' he said.

'That's not what he said,' snarled Fred.

'Would you like us to clean out your ears for you?' enquired George, pulling a long and lethal-looking metal instrument from inside one of the Zonko's bags.

'Or any part of your body, really, we're not fussy where we stick this,' said Fred.

'Yes, well,' said Hermione hastily, 'moving on ... the point is, are we agreed we want to take lessons from Harry?'

There was a murmur of general agreement. Zacharias folded his arms and said nothing, though perhaps this was because he was too busy keeping an eye on the instrument in Fred's hand.

'Right,' said Hermione, looking relieved that something had at last been settled. 'Well, then, the next question is how often we do it. I really don't think there's any point in meeting less than once a week –'

'Hang on,' said Angelina, 'we need to make sure this doesn't clash with our Quidditch practice.'

'No,' said Cho, 'nor with ours.'

'Nor ours,' added Zacharias Smith.

'I'm sure we can find a night that suits everyone,' said Hermione, slightly impatiently, 'but you know, this is rather important, we're talking about learning to defend ourselves against V-Voldemort's Death Eaters –'

第16章 在猪头酒吧

"今年夏天你摆脱那些摄魂怪时也没有人帮助你。"苏珊·博恩斯说。

"是的,"哈利说,"是的,对,我知道我做的有些事情没有得到帮助,但我想要说明的是——"

"你该不是在耍滑头,不想把这些魔法展示给我们看吧?"扎卡赖斯·史密斯说。

"我有一个主意,"罗恩不等哈利说话就大声说,"你干吗不闭上你的嘴呢?"

也许"耍滑头"这个词特别令罗恩反感。反正,他此刻狠狠地瞪着扎卡赖斯,似乎恨不得上去揍他一顿。扎卡赖斯脸红了。

"我们都是来跟他学东西的,可是他却说他实际上什么都不会。"他说。

"他不是这么说的。"弗雷德气呼呼地说。

"你是不是要我们帮你洗洗耳朵呀?"乔治问道,从一只佐科笑话店的购物袋里掏出一个长长的、看着怪可怕的金属玩意儿。

"或者你身体上随便什么部位,我们才不管把它插在哪儿呢。"弗雷德说。

"好了,好了,"赫敏赶紧说道,"言归正传……关键是,我们一致同意让哈利给我们上课吗?"

大家喃喃地表示赞同。扎卡赖斯抱着双臂什么也没说,不过这也许是因为他正紧张地盯着弗雷德手里的东西。

"好的。"赫敏说,显得松了口气,总算有一件事情定下来了,"那么,第二个问题是,我们多长时间上一次课。我想,少于一星期一次恐怕没有什么用——"

"慢着,"安吉利娜说,"一定要保证这跟我们的魁地奇球训练不相冲突。"

"对,"秋说,"也不能跟我们的相冲突。"

"还有我们的。"扎卡赖斯·史密斯说。

"我相信我们能找到一个适合所有人的晚上,"赫敏说,略微有些不耐烦,"但是你们知道,这是很重要的,我们谈论的是学点本事保护自己,抵抗伏—伏地魔的食死徒——"

CHAPTER SIXTEEN In the Hog's Head

'Well said!' barked Ernie Macmillan, who Harry had been expecting to speak long before this. 'Personally, I think this is really important, possibly more important than anything else we'll do this year, even with our O.W.L.s coming up!'

He looked around impressively, as though waiting for people to cry 'Surely not!' When nobody spoke, he went on, 'I, personally, am at a loss to see why the Ministry has foisted such a useless teacher on us at this critical period. Obviously, they are in denial about the return of You-Know-Who, but to give us a teacher who is trying to actively prevent us from using defensive spells –'

'We think the reason Umbridge doesn't want us trained in Defence Against the Dark Arts,' said Hermione, 'is that she's got some ... some mad idea that Dumbledore could use the students in the school as a kind of private army. She thinks he'd mobilise us against the Ministry.'

Nearly everybody looked stunned at this news; everybody except Luna Lovegood, who piped up, 'Well, that makes sense. After all, Cornelius Fudge has got his own private army.'

'What?' said Harry, completely thrown by this unexpected piece of information.

'Yes, he's got an army of Heliopaths,' said Luna solemnly.

'No, he hasn't,' snapped Hermione.

'Yes, he has,' said Luna.

'What are Heliopaths?' asked Neville, looking blank.

'They're spirits of fire,' said Luna, her protuberant eyes widening so that she looked madder than ever, 'great tall flaming creatures that gallop across the ground burning everything in front of –'

'They don't exist, Neville,' said Hermione tartly.

'Oh, yes, they do!' said Luna angrily.

'I'm sorry, but where's the proof of that?' snapped Hermione.

'There are plenty of eye-witness accounts. Just because you're so narrow-minded you need to have everything shoved under your nose before you –'

'*Hem, hem*,' said Ginny, in such a good imitation of Professor Umbridge that several people looked around in alarm and then laughed. 'Weren't we trying to decide how often we're going to meet and have defence lessons?'

第16章 在猪头酒吧

"说得好!"厄尼·麦克米兰大声喊道,哈利本以为他早就会开口说话的,"我个人认为,这确实非常重要,大概比我们今年要做的其他任何事情都重要,甚至包括即将到来的O.W.L.考试!"

他威严地扫视大家一眼,似乎等着有人大声说"那可不对!"看到没有人开口,他继续说:"我个人十分纳闷,为什么在这样一个至关重要的时期,魔法部给我们塞进来那样一个根本没用的老师。显然,他们拒绝相信神秘人已经回来了,但也不至于给我们派来这么个千方百计阻止我们使用防御咒的老师——"

"我们认为,乌姆里奇之所以不让我们练习黑魔法防御术,"赫敏说,"是因为她脑子里有一些……一些荒唐的想法,以为邓布利多会利用学校的学生组成一支秘密军队。她以为邓布利多会鼓动我们去对抗魔法部。"

听到这个消息,几乎每个人都惊得目瞪口呆,只有卢娜·洛夫古德例外,她尖声道:"是的,这也说得通。毕竟康奈利·福吉就有自己的秘密军队。"

"什么?"哈利说,完全被这个意想不到的信息惊呆了。

"是的,他有一支黑利奥帕组成的军队。"卢娜一本正经地说。

"不可能。"赫敏不客气地说。

"千真万确。"卢娜说。

"黑利奥帕是什么?"纳威问,显得很茫然。

"它们是火精灵,"卢娜说,凸出的眼睛睁得大大的,使她显得比平常更加疯狂,"是浑身冒火的庞然大物,在大地上飞奔而过,能把面前的一切烧得精光——"

"它们根本不存在,纳威。"赫敏尖刻地说。

"哦,存在!"卢娜生气地说。

"对不起,请问有什么证据呢?"赫敏厉声地问。

"有大量目击者的报道。就因为你这么孤陋寡闻,需要所有的东西都塞到你的鼻子底下才会——"

"咳,咳,"金妮惟妙惟肖地模仿着乌姆里奇教授,几个人吃惊地东张西望,然后哈哈大笑起来,"刚才我们不是要决定多长时间聚会一次上防御课的吗?"

CHAPTER SIXTEEN In the Hog's Head

'Yes,' said Hermione at once, 'yes, we were, you're right, Ginny.'

'Well, once a week sounds cool,' said Lee Jordan.

'As long as –' began Angelina.

'Yes, yes, we know about the Quidditch,' said Hermione in a tense voice. 'Well, the other thing to decide is where we're going to meet ...'

This was rather more difficult; the whole group fell silent.

'Library?' suggested Katie Bell after a few moments.

'I can't see Madam Pince being too chuffed with us doing jinxes in the library,' said Harry.

'Maybe an unused classroom?' said Dean.

'Yeah,' said Ron, 'McGonagall might let us have hers, she did when Harry was practising for the Triwizard.'

But Harry was pretty certain that McGonagall would not be so accommodating this time. For all that Hermione had said about study and homework groups being allowed, he had the distinct feeling that this one might be considered a lot more rebellious.

'Right, well, we'll try to find somewhere,' said Hermione. 'We'll send a message round to everybody when we've got a time and a place for the first meeting.'

She rummaged in her bag and produced parchment and a quill, then hesitated, rather as though she was steeling herself to say something.

'I – I think everybody should write their name down, just so we know who was here. But I also think,' she took a deep breath, 'that we all ought to agree not to shout about what we're doing. So if you sign, you're agreeing not to tell Umbridge or anybody else what we're up to.'

Fred reached out for the parchment and cheerfully wrote his signature, but Harry noticed at once that several people looked less than happy at the prospect of putting their names on the list.

'Er ...' said Zacharias slowly, not taking the parchment that George was trying to pass to him, 'well ... I'm sure Ernie will tell me when the meeting is.'

But Ernie was looking rather hesitant about signing, too. Hermione raised her eyebrows at him.

'I – well, we are *prefects*,' Ernie burst out. 'And if this list was found ... well, I mean to say ... you said yourself, if Umbridge finds out –'

592

"对啊,"赫敏立刻说道,"对啊,你说得对,金妮。"

"我说,一星期一次再好不过了。"李·乔丹说。

"只要——"安吉利娜刚想说话。

"是的,是的,我们知道还有魁地奇球。"赫敏用紧张的口气说,"还有一件事情需要决定,就是我们在什么地方聚会……"

这个问题比较复杂,大家都陷入了沉默。

"图书馆?"片刻之后凯蒂·贝尔建议道。

"我们在图书馆里练习恶咒,平斯女士恐怕不会太高兴。"哈利说。

"要么找一间不用的教室?"迪安说。

"是啊,"罗恩说,"麦格大概会让我们用她的教室呢,上回哈利为三强争霸赛训练时,她就是这么做的。"

然而哈利可以肯定,麦格这次不会这么通融了。尽管赫敏说学习小组和作业小组是允许的,但哈利心里很清楚,别人会认为他们这个小组大逆不道。

"这样吧,我们想办法找一个地方,"赫敏说,"等确定了第一次聚会的时间和地点,就发消息通知大家。"

她在包里翻找了一阵,拿出羊皮纸和一支羽毛笔,然后迟疑着,似乎在下决心强迫自己把话说出来。

"我——我想让每个人把自己的名字写下来,这样就知道今天来的都有谁了。我同时还认为,"她深深吸了口气,"我们应该一致同意不把我们要做的事情张扬出去。所以你们一旦签了名,就表示同意不把我们的事情告诉乌姆里奇或其他任何人。"

弗雷德伸手接过羊皮纸,欣然地在上面签了自己的名字,可是哈利立刻注意到,有几个人听说要把他们的名字写在名单上,显得不太高兴。

"呃……"扎卡赖斯慢吞吞地说,没有接乔治递过去的羊皮纸,"嗯……我想厄尼肯定会告诉我什么时候聚会的。"

可是厄尼对于签名也显得很犹豫。赫敏对他扬起了眉毛。

"我……嗯,我们是级长,"厄尼脱口而出,"如果名单被别人发现了……嗯,我的意思是……你自己也说了,如果被乌姆里奇发现了——"

CHAPTER SIXTEEN — In the Hog's Head

'You just said this group was the most important thing you'd do this year,' Harry reminded him.

'I – yes,' said Ernie, 'yes, I do believe that, it's just –'

'Ernie, do you really think I'd leave that list lying around?' said Hermione testily.

'No. No, of course not,' said Ernie, looking slightly less anxious. 'I – yes, of course I'll sign.'

Nobody raised objections after Ernie, though Harry saw Cho's friend give her a rather reproachful look before adding her own name. When the last person – Zacharias – had signed, Hermione took the parchment back and slipped it carefully into her bag. There was an odd feeling in the group now. It was as though they had just signed some kind of contract.

'Well, time's ticking on,' said Fred briskly, getting to his feet. 'George, Lee and I have got items of a sensitive nature to purchase, we'll be seeing you all later.'

In twos and threes the rest of the group took their leave, too. Cho made rather a business of fastening the catch on her bag before leaving, her long dark curtain of hair swinging forwards to hide her face, but her friend stood beside her, arms folded, clicking her tongue, so that Cho had little choice but to leave with her. As her friend ushered her through the door, Cho looked back and waved at Harry.

'Well, I think that went quite well,' said Hermione happily, as she, Harry and Ron walked out of the Hog's Head into the bright sunlight a few moments later. Harry and Ron were clutching their bottles of Butterbeer.

'That Zacharias bloke's a wart,' said Ron, who was glowering after the figure of Smith, just discernible in the distance.

'I don't like him much, either,' admitted Hermione, 'but he overheard me talking to Ernie and Hannah at the Hufflepuff table and he seemed really interested in coming, so what could I say? But the more people the better really – I mean, Michael Corner and his friends wouldn't have come if he hadn't been going out with Ginny –'

Ron, who had been draining the last few drops from his Butterbeer bottle, gagged and sprayed Butterbeer down his front.

'He's WHAT?' spluttered Ron, outraged, his ears now resembling curls of raw beef. 'She's going out with – my sister's going – what d'you mean,

第16章 在猪头酒吧

"你刚才还说参加这个小组是你今年要做的最重要的事情。"哈利提醒他。

"我——是的,"厄尼说,"是的,这点我相信,只是——"

"厄尼,你真的以为我会把这张名单到处乱扔吗?"赫敏恼火地说。

"不,不,当然不是,"厄尼说,显得稍稍不那么担心了,"我——好吧,我当然要签名。"

在厄尼之后,没有人再提出反对,不过哈利看见秋的女友朝她责备地白了一眼,才签上了自己的名字。当最后一个人——扎卡赖斯——也把名字签上后,赫敏把羊皮纸收回去仔细放进书包。现在小组里有了一种奇怪的感觉。似乎大家刚刚签了一份契约。

"好了,时间过得真快。"弗雷德大大咧咧地说,一边站了起来,"乔治、李和我还要去买一些高度机密的东西,我们待会儿见!"

其他人也三三两两地起身告辞。秋在离开前磨磨蹭蹭地系着书包上的搭扣,长长的、瀑布般的黑发飘到前面挡住了她的脸,但她的女友站在她旁边,抱着双臂,不耐烦地咂着舌头,秋别无选择,只好和她一起走了。就在女友陪她走出门时,秋回过脸,冲哈利挥了挥手。

"我觉得进行得还算顺利。"片刻之后,赫敏和哈利、罗恩一起走出猪头酒吧,来到阳光灿烂的户外,她高兴地说。哈利和罗恩手里还攥着各自的那瓶黄油啤酒。

"那个叫扎卡赖斯的家伙是个讨厌鬼。"罗恩说,怒气冲冲地瞪着远处隐约可见的扎卡赖斯的背影。

"我也不太喜欢他,"赫敏承认道,"但那天我在赫奇帕奇桌上跟厄尼和汉娜说话时,被他听见了,他似乎特别感兴趣地要来,我能说什么呢?不过确实是人来得越多越好——我是说,迈克尔·科纳如果不是在跟金妮谈恋爱,他和他那些朋友是不会来的——"

罗恩正把瓶里最后几滴黄油啤酒倒进嘴里,听了这话,一下子呛住了,啤酒洒在了胸前。

"他**在什么**?"罗恩气急败坏地问,两只耳朵活像两个生牛肉卷,"她在谈恋爱——我的妹妹在谈恋爱——你说什么,在跟迈克尔·科纳谈

CHAPTER SIXTEEN — In the Hog's Head

Michael Corner?'

'Well, that's why he and his friends came, I think — well, they're obviously interested in learning defence, but if Ginny hadn't told Michael what was going on —'

'When did this — when did she —?'

'They met at the Yule Ball and got together at the end of last year,' said Hermione composedly. They had turned into the High Street and she paused outside Scrivenshaft's Quill Shop, where there was a handsome display of pheasant feather quills in the window. 'Hmm ... I could do with a new quill.'

She turned into the shop. Harry and Ron followed her.

'Which one was Michael Corner?' Ron demanded furiously.

'The dark one,' said Hermione.

'I didn't like him,' said Ron at once.

'Big surprise,' said Hermione under her breath.

'But,' said Ron, following Hermione along a row of quills in copper pots, 'I thought Ginny fancied Harry!'

Hermione looked at him rather pityingly and shook her head.

'Ginny *used* to fancy Harry, but she gave up on him months ago. Not that she doesn't *like* you, of course,' she added kindly to Harry while she examined a long black and gold quill.

Harry, whose head was still full of Cho's parting wave, did not find this subject quite as interesting as Ron, who was positively quivering with indignation, but it did bring something home to him that until now he had not really registered.

'So that's why she talks now?' he asked Hermione. 'She never used to talk in front of me.'

'Exactly,' said Hermione. 'Yes, I think I'll have this one ...'

She went up to the counter and handed over fifteen Sickles and two Knuts, with Ron still breathing down her neck.

'Ron,' she said severely as she turned and trod on his feet, 'this is exactly why Ginny hasn't told you she's seeing Michael, she knew you'd take it badly. So don't *harp on* about it, for heaven's sake.'

恋爱？"

"是啊，我想正因为这个，科纳和他那些朋友才会来的——是啊，他们显然对学习防御术很感兴趣，但如果金妮没有告诉迈克尔是怎么回事——"

"什么时候开始——她什么时候——"

"去年年底，他们在圣诞舞会上遇见的，后来就开始约会。"赫敏镇静地说。他们拐上大路，她在文人居羽毛笔店外停住脚步，橱窗里陈列着许多讨人喜欢的野鸡羽毛笔，摆放得非常漂亮。"唔……我想买一支新笔。"

她转身进了商店。哈利和罗恩也跟了进去。

"迈克尔·科纳是哪个家伙？"罗恩气呼呼地问。

"黑皮肤的那个。"赫敏说。

"我不喜欢他。"罗恩不假思索地说。

"真让我吃惊。"赫敏压低声音说。

"可是，"罗恩说，跟着赫敏走过一排排插在铜钵里的羽毛笔，"我还以为金妮喜欢哈利呢！"

赫敏十分同情地看着他，摇了摇头。

"金妮以前是喜欢哈利，但几个月前她放弃了。当然啦，她并不是不喜欢你。"她好心地对哈利补充一句，一边仔细检查一支长长的、黑色和金色相间的羽毛笔。

哈利脑子里还满是秋离开时朝他挥手的情景，对这个话题不像罗恩那么感兴趣，罗恩简直是气得发抖了。但哈利确实想起了一些他在此之前没怎么注意的情况。

"怪不得她现在开始说话了，是吗？"他问赫敏，"她以前在我面前从不说话的。"

"对极了。"赫敏说，"好吧，我想我就要这一支了……"

她走向柜台，递过去十五个西可和两个纳特，罗恩仍然对着她的脖子呼哧呼哧地喘粗气。

"罗恩，"赫敏转身踩了下他的脚，严厉地说，"金妮正是因为这个才没有告诉你她在跟迈克尔谈恋爱的，她就知道你会一听就炸。所以，看在老天的分儿上，别再对这件事唠叨个没完了。"

CHAPTER SIXTEEN In the Hog's Head

'What d'you mean? Who's taking anything badly? I'm not going to harp on about anything ...' Ron continued to chunter under his breath all the way down the street.

Hermione rolled her eyes at Harry and then said in an undertone, while Ron was still muttering imprecations about Michael Corner, 'And talking about Michael and Ginny ... what about Cho and you?'

'What d'you mean?' said Harry quickly.

It was as though boiling water was rising rapidly inside him; a burning sensation that was causing his face to smart in the cold – had he been that obvious?

'Well,' said Hermione, smiling slightly, 'she just couldn't keep her eyes off you, could she?'

Harry had never before appreciated just how beautiful the village of Hogsmeade was.

第16章 在猪头酒吧

"你这话是什么意思?谁一听就炸?我才不会为什么事唠叨个没完呢……"罗恩走在街上,还一直在不出声地嘀咕。

赫敏冲哈利翻了翻眼睛,然后趁罗恩仍在低声咒骂迈克尔·科纳的工夫低声说:"说起迈克尔和金妮……你和秋怎么样啦?"

"你这是什么意思?"哈利赶紧问道。

似乎有一股沸腾的热水在身体里迅速奔涌,带给他一种火辣辣的感觉,使他的脸在寒风中感到刺痛——他表现得那么明显吗?

"嘿,"赫敏微微带笑说,"她简直就不能把目光从你身上挪开,是不是?"

哈利从没有发现霍格莫德村竟是这样美丽。

CHAPTER SEVENTEEN

Educational Decree Number Twenty-Four

Harry felt happier for the rest of the weekend than he had done all term. He and Ron spent much of Sunday catching up with all their homework again, and although this could hardly be called fun, the last burst of autumn sunshine persisted, so rather than sitting hunched over tables in the common room they took their work outside and lounged in the shade of a large beech tree on the edge of the lake. Hermione, who of course was up to date with all her work, brought more wool outside with her and bewitched her knitting needles so that they flashed and clicked in midair beside her, producing more hats and scarves.

Knowing they were doing something to resist Umbridge and the Ministry, and that he was a key part of the rebellion, gave Harry a feeling of immense satisfaction. He kept reliving Saturday's meeting in his mind: all those people, coming to him to learn Defence Against the Dark Arts ... and the looks on their faces as they had heard some of the things he had done ... and Cho praising his performance in the Triwizard Tournament – knowing all those people did not think him a lying weirdo, but someone to be admired, buoyed him up so much that he was still cheerful on Monday morning, despite the imminent prospect of all his least favourite classes.

He and Ron headed downstairs from their dormitory, discussing Angelina's idea that they were to work on a new move called the Sloth Grip Roll during that night's Quidditch practice, and not until they were halfway across the sunlit common room did they notice the addition to the room that had already attracted the attention of a small group of people.

A large sign had been affixed to the Gryffindor noticeboard, so large it covered everything else on it – the lists of second-hand spellbooks for sale, the regular reminders of school rules from Argus Filch, the Quidditch team training timetable, the offers to barter certain Chocolate Frog Cards for others, the Weasleys' latest

第 17 章

第二十四号教育令

这个周末余下的时光，哈利觉得整个学期都没这么开心。他和罗恩星期天又花了不少时间赶家庭作业，虽然这很难说是乐趣，但秋天最后的灿烂阳光依旧照耀着，所以他们没有伏在公共休息室的书桌前，而是把作业拿到外面，坐在湖边一棵大山毛榉树底下。赫敏的功课当然都按时做完了，她又带了些毛线出来，对织针施了魔法，让它们在她身边咔嗒咔嗒地飞舞，织出更多的帽子和围巾。

想到他们在反抗乌姆里奇和魔法部，自己是反叛的关键人物，哈利感到极大的满足。他不断地在脑子里重温星期六的聚会：那么多人来向他学习黑魔法防御术……他们听了他的事迹之后的表情……秋赞扬他在三强争霸赛中的表现……大家没有把他当成说谎的怪物，而是当成钦佩的对象，这使他情绪高涨，直到星期一早晨还很兴奋，尽管还要上所有他最不喜欢的课。

他和罗恩一起走下宿舍楼梯，一边讨论着安吉利娜的主意：在当晚的魁地奇比赛中练习新招术：树懒抱树滚。走到阳光明亮的公共休息室中间，他们才发现屋里多了点东西，它已经吸引了一小群人的注意。

格兰芬多的布告栏上贴了一张大告示，大得盖住了布告栏上其他的一切——售卖二手咒语书的单子、阿格斯·费尔奇定期提醒的校规、魁地奇球队训练日程、交换巧克力蛙画片的条子、韦斯莱兄弟找人做试验的新广告、到霍格莫德村过周末的日期，还有失物招领启事。新

CHAPTER SEVENTEEN — Educational Decree Number Twenty-Four

advertisement for testers, the dates of the Hogsmeade weekends and the lost and found notices. The new sign was printed in large black letters and there was a highly official-looking seal at the bottom beside a neat and curly signature.

BY ORDER OF THE HIGH INQUISITOR OF HOGWARTS
All student organisations, societies, teams, groups
and clubs are henceforth disbanded.

An organisation, society, team, group or club is hereby
defined as a regular meeting of three or more students.

Permission to re-form may be sought from the
High Inquisitor (Professor Umbridge).

No student organisation, society, team, group or club
may exist without the knowledge and approval of
the High Inquisitor.

Any student found to have formed, or to belong to, an
organisation, society, team, group or club that has not been
approved by the High Inquisitor will be expelled.

The above is in accordance with
Educational Decree Number Twenty-four.

Signed:

Dolores Jane Umbridge,
High Inquisitor

M.O.M.

Harry and Ron read the notice over the heads of some anxious-looking second-years.

'Does this mean they're going to shut down the Gobstones Club?' one of them asked his friend.

'I reckon you'll be OK with Gobstones,' Ron said darkly, making the second-year jump. 'I don't think we're going to be as lucky, though, do you?' he asked Harry as the second-years hurried away.

第17章 第二十四号教育令

告示上印着大黑体字，底下有一个看上去很正式的印章，旁边是工整的花体签名。

霍格沃茨高级调查官令

兹解散一切学生组织、协会、团队或俱乐部。

组织、协会、团队和俱乐部的定义是三名或三名以上学生的定期集会。

可向高级调查官（乌姆里奇教授）请求重组。

未经高级调查官批准，不得存在任何学生组织、协会、团队或俱乐部。

如发现有学生未经高级调查官批准而组建或参加任何组织、协会、团队或俱乐部，立即开除。

以上条例符合《第二十四号教育令》。

签名：
高级调查官
多洛雷斯·简·乌姆里奇

M.O.M.

哈利和罗恩越过一些二年级学生的头顶读着告示，那几人显得有些担忧。

"他们会关掉高布石俱乐部吗？"其中一个问他的朋友。

"我想你们的高布石没事。"罗恩阴沉地说，把那二年级学生吓了一跳，二年级学生急忙走了。"但我们可能不会那么幸运，你觉得呢？"他问哈利。

CHAPTER SEVENTEEN   Educational Decree Number Twenty-Four

Harry was reading the notice through again. The happiness that had filled him since Saturday was gone. His insides were pulsing with rage.

'This isn't a coincidence,' he said, his hands forming fists. 'She knows.'

'She can't,' said Ron at once.

'There were people listening in that pub. And let's face it, we don't know how many of the people who turned up we can trust ... any of them could have run off and told Umbridge ...'

And he had thought they believed him, thought they even admired him ...

'Zacharias Smith!' said Ron at once, punching a fist into his hand. 'Or – I thought that Michael Corner had a really shifty look, too –'

'I wonder if Hermione's seen this yet?' Harry said, looking round at the door to the girls' dormitories.

'Let's go and tell her,' said Ron. He bounded forwards, pulled open the door and set off up the spiral staircase.

He was on the sixth stair when there was a loud, wailing, klaxon-like sound and the steps melted together to make a long, smooth stone slide like a helter-skelter. There was a brief moment when Ron tried to keep running, arms working madly like windmills, then he toppled over backwards and shot down the newly created slide, coming to rest on his back at Harry's feet.

'Er – I don't think we're allowed in the girls' dormitories,' said Harry, pulling Ron to his feet and trying not to laugh.

Two fourth-year girls came zooming gleefully down the stone slide.

'Oooh, who tried to get upstairs?' they giggled happily, leaping to their feet and ogling Harry and Ron.

'Me,' said Ron, who was still rather dishevelled. 'I didn't realise that would happen. It's not fair!' he added to Harry, as the girls headed off for the portrait hole, still giggling madly. 'Hermione's allowed in our dormitory, how come we're not allowed –?'

'Well, it's an old-fashioned rule,' said Hermione, who had just slid neatly on to a rug in front of them and was now getting to her feet, 'but it says in *Hogwarts: A History*, that the founders thought boys were less trustworthy than girls. Anyway, why were you trying to get in there?'

'To see you – look at this!' said Ron, dragging her over to the noticeboard.

Hermione's eyes slid rapidly down the notice. Her expression became stony.

'Someone must have blabbed to her!' Ron said angrily.

'They can't have done,' said Hermione in a low voice.

第 17 章 第二十四号教育令

哈利重新读着告示,星期六以来的满心快乐消失了,他现在满腔怒火。

"这不是巧合,"他攥着拳头说,"她知道了。"

"不可能。"罗恩马上说。

"酒吧里人多耳杂。正视事实吧,我们不知道在场的有多少人可以信任……任何人都可能跑去向乌姆里奇告密……"

而他还以为他们相信他,甚至钦佩他……

"扎卡赖斯·史密斯!"罗恩一拳砸在掌心里,"要么就是——我觉得那个迈克尔·科纳也有些鬼鬼祟祟——"

"不知道赫敏看了这个没有?"哈利扭头望望通往女生宿舍的门。

"我们去告诉她。"罗恩说。他一个箭步跳过去,拉开门冲上了螺旋形的楼梯。

他跑到第六级的时候出了事故。在一阵高音汽笛般的响声中,楼梯融化了,变成一条长长的、光溜溜的石滑梯。一刹那间,罗恩还想往前跑,胳膊像风车一样乱舞,然后他向后一倒,顺着新生成的滑梯倒栽下来,躺在哈利的脚下。

"哦——我想我们是不能进入女生宿舍的。"哈利忍着笑把罗恩拉了起来。

两个四年级女生开心地从石滑梯上滑下。

"哦,谁想上楼?"她们咯咯笑着跳起来,眼睛盯着哈利和罗恩。

"我,"罗恩说,他的衣服还乱着,"我没想到会这样。这不公平!"他对哈利说,两个女生朝肖像洞口走去,还在咯咯疯笑,"赫敏可以进我们宿舍,为什么不许我们——?"

"这是一条古板的规矩,"赫敏说,她刚轻轻巧巧地滑到他们面前的地毯上,正在站起身来,"可是《霍格沃茨:一段校史》说学校创始人认为男孩没有女孩可靠。好啦,你们为什么想进去?"

"找你啊——你看!"罗恩把她拽到布告栏前。

赫敏的目光顺着告示迅速下移,面容凝重起来。

"一定有人告密了!"罗恩愤然道。

"不可能。"赫敏低声说。

CHAPTER SEVENTEEN   Educational Decree Number Twenty-Four

'You're so naive,' said Ron, 'you think just because you're all honourable and trustworthy –'

'No, they can't have done, because I put a jinx on that piece of parchment we all signed,' said Hermione grimly. 'Believe me, if anyone's run off and told Umbridge, we'll know exactly who they are and they will really regret it.'

'What'll happen to them?' said Ron eagerly.

'Well, put it this way,' said Hermione, 'it'll make Eloise Midgeon's acne look like a couple of cute freckles. Come on, let's get down to breakfast and see what the others think ... I wonder whether this has been put up in all the houses?'

It was immediately apparent on entering the Great Hall that Umbridge's sign had not only appeared in Gryffindor Tower. There was a peculiar intensity about the chatter and an extra measure of movement in the Hall as people scurried up and down their tables conferring on what they had read. Harry, Ron and Hermione had barely taken their seats when Neville, Dean, Fred, George and Ginny descended upon them.

'Did you see it?'

'D'you reckon she knows?'

'What are we going to do?'

They were all looking at Harry. He glanced around to make sure there were no teachers near them.

'We're going to do it anyway, of course,' he said quietly.

'Knew you'd say that,' said George, beaming and thumping Harry on the arm.

'The prefects as well?' said Fred, looking quizzically at Ron and Hermione.

'Of course,' said Hermione coolly.

'Here come Ernie and Hannah Abbott,' said Ron, looking over his shoulder. '*And* those Ravenclaw blokes and Smith ... and no one looks very spotty.'

Hermione looked alarmed.

'Never mind spots, the idiots can't come over here now, it'll look really suspicious – sit down!' she mouthed to Ernie and Hannah, gesturing frantically to them to rejoin the Hufflepuff table. 'Later! We'll – talk – to – you – *later!*'

'I'll tell Michael,' said Ginny impatiently, swinging herself off her bench, 'the fool, honestly ...'

She hurried off towards the Ravenclaw table; Harry watched her go. Cho was sitting not far away, talking to the curly-haired friend she had brought along to the Hog's Head. Would Umbridge's notice scare her off meeting

第17章 第二十四号教育令

"你太天真了，"罗恩说，"你以为就因为你是正直可靠的——"

"不，不可能，因为我在我们签字的那张羊皮纸上加了一个咒语。"赫敏严肃地说，"相信我，如果有人去向乌姆里奇告密，我们准能知道，而且他们会后悔不迭的。"

"他们会怎么样？"罗恩急切地问。

"这么说吧，它会让爱洛伊丝·米德根的青春痘看上去像几颗可爱的雀斑。"赫敏说，"走，我们去吃早饭，看看别人是怎么想的……是不是所有的学院都贴了？"

一进礼堂，他们就看出乌姆里奇的告示不仅贴在格兰芬多楼内。礼堂里有一种特殊的紧张气氛，叽叽喳喳，异常纷乱，人们跑来跑去谈论着看到的消息。哈利、罗恩和赫敏刚坐下，纳威、迪安、弗雷德、乔治、金妮就冲了过来。

"你们看到了吗？"

"你认为她知道了吗？"

"我们怎么办？"

他们都看着哈利。哈利朝四周扫了一眼，确保附近没有教师。

"我们当然还是要干。"他小声说道。

"就知道你会这么说。"乔治眉开眼笑，重重地一拍哈利的胳膊。

"级长们也参加吗？"弗雷德满怀疑问地望着罗恩和赫敏。

"当然。"赫敏冷静地说。

"厄尼和汉娜·艾博过来了，"罗恩回头看着，"还有拉文克劳的那些小子和史密斯……谁也没长出多少粉刺。"

赫敏神色惊慌。

"别管粉刺了，那些傻瓜现在不能过来，会引起怀疑的——坐下！"她用口型对厄尼和汉娜说，使劲打手势让他们坐回赫奇帕奇餐桌旁，"等会儿！我们——等会儿——再聊！"

"我去告诉迈克尔，"金妮不耐烦地说，一甩腿跳下凳子，"这个笨蛋，真是……"

她快步走向拉文克劳的餐桌，哈利望着她。秋坐在不远处，正跟她带到猪头酒吧的那个鬈发女朋友聊天。乌姆里奇的告示会不会吓得

CHAPTER SEVENTEEN   Educational Decree Number Twenty-Four

them again?

But the full repercussions of the sign were not felt until they were leaving the Great Hall for History of Magic.

'Harry! *Ron!*'

It was Angelina and she was hurrying towards them looking perfectly desperate.

'It's OK,' said Harry quietly, when she was near enough to hear him. 'We're still going to –'

'You realise she's including Quidditch in this?' Angelina said over him. 'We have to go and ask permission to re-form the Gryffindor team!'

'*What?*' said Harry.

'No way,' said Ron, appalled.

'You read the sign, it mentions teams too! So listen, Harry ... I am saying this for the last time ... please, please don't lose your temper with Umbridge again or she might not let us play any more!'

'OK, OK,' said Harry, for Angelina looked as though she was on the verge of tears. 'Don't worry, I'll behave myself ...'

'Bet Umbridge is in History of Magic,' said Ron grimly, as they set off for Binns's lesson. 'She hasn't inspected Binns yet ... bet you anything she's there ...'

But he was wrong; the only teacher present when they entered was Professor Binns, floating an inch or so above his chair as usual and preparing to continue his monotonous drone on giant wars. Harry did not even attempt to follow what he was saying today; he doodled idly on his parchment ignoring Hermione's frequent glares and nudges, until a particularly painful poke in the ribs made him look up angrily.

'*What?*'

She pointed at the window. Harry looked round. Hedwig was perched on the narrow window ledge, gazing through the thick glass at him, a letter tied to her leg. Harry could not understand it; they had just had breakfast, why on earth hadn't she delivered the letter then, as usual? Many of his classmates were pointing out Hedwig to each other, too.

'Oh, I've always loved that owl, she's so beautiful,' Harry heard Lavender sigh to Parvati.

He glanced round at Professor Binns who continued to read his notes, serenely unaware that the class's attention was even less focused upon him than

第17章 第二十四号教育令

她不敢来聚会呢？

可是，直到他们离开礼堂去上魔法史课时，才感受到告示的全面影响。

"哈利！罗恩！"

是安吉利娜，她匆匆走来，一脸的绝望。

"没事，"等她走近了，哈利小声说，"我们还会——"

"你发现她把魁地奇球也包括在内了吗？"安吉利娜盖过他的声音说，"我们得去请求重组格兰芬多球队！"

"什么？"哈利说。

"不可能。"罗恩震惊地叫道。

"你们读了告示，上面提到团队！听着，哈利……我说最后一遍……求你，求你不要再跟乌姆里奇闹脾气，不然她可能再也不让我们比赛了！"

"好，好，"哈利说，因为安吉利娜好像快要哭出来了，"别担心，我会注意的……"

"我敢打赌乌姆里奇在魔法史课上，"他们赶着去上课时，罗恩阴郁地说，"她还没有检察过宾斯的课……我可以拿身家性命打赌她在那儿……"

可是他错了，课堂上只有一位教师，就是宾斯教授。他像往常一样飘在他的座椅上方一英寸处，准备继续他那关于巨人战争的嗡嗡说教。哈利甚至没有试图去听他今天讲的内容，他在羊皮纸上信手涂画，不理睬赫敏多次的瞪眼和推搡，直到肋部挨了特疼的一戳才恼火地抬起头来。

"干什么？"

赫敏指指窗外。哈利扭头一看，海德薇栖在窄窄的窗台上，透过厚厚的玻璃看着他，脚上系着一封信。哈利不明白，他们刚吃过早餐，它为什么不像往常一样在那时送信呢？许多同学也在指点着海德薇。

"哦，我一直喜欢那只猫头鹰，它真漂亮。"哈利听见拉文德对帕瓦蒂赞叹说。

CHAPTER SEVENTEEN   Educational Decree Number Twenty-Four

usual. Harry slipped quietly off his chair, crouched down and hurried along the row to the window, where he slid the catch and opened it very slowly.

He had expected Hedwig to hold out her leg so that he could remove the letter and then fly off to the Owlery, but the moment the window was open wide enough she hopped inside, hooting dolefully. He closed the window with an anxious glance at Professor Binns, crouched low again and sped back to his seat with Hedwig on his shoulder. He regained his seat, transferred Hedwig to his lap and made to remove the letter tied to her leg.

Only then did he realise that Hedwig's feathers were oddly ruffled; some were bent the wrong way, and she was holding one of her wings at an odd angle.

'She's hurt!' Harry whispered, bending his head low over her. Hermione and Ron leaned in closer; Hermione even put down her quill. 'Look – there's something wrong with her wing –'

Hedwig was quivering; when Harry made to touch the wing she gave a little jump, all her feathers on end as though she was inflating herself, and gazed at him reproachfully.

'Professor Binns,' said Harry loudly, and everyone in the class turned to look at him. 'I'm not feeling well.'

Professor Binns raised his eyes from his notes, looking amazed, as always, to find the room in front of him full of people.

'Not feeling well?' he repeated hazily.

'Not at all well,' said Harry firmly, getting to his feet with Hedwig concealed behind his back. 'I think I need to go to the hospital wing.'

'Yes,' said Professor Binns, clearly very much wrong-footed. 'Yes ... yes, hospital wing ... well, off you go, then, Perkins ...'

Once outside the room, Harry returned Hedwig to his shoulder and hurried off up the corridor, pausing to think only when he was out of sight of Binns's door. His first choice of somebody to cure Hedwig would have been Hagrid, of course, but as he had no idea where Hagrid was his only remaining option was to find Professor Grubbly-Plank and hope she would help.

He peered out of a window at the blustery, overcast grounds. There was no sign of her anywhere near Hagrid's cabin; if she was not teaching, she was probably in the staff room. He set off downstairs, Hedwig hooting feebly as she swayed on his shoulder.

Two stone gargoyles flanked the staff-room door. As Harry approached, one of them croaked, 'You should be in class, Sonny Jim.'

第17章 第二十四号教育令

他瞟了一眼讲台，宾斯教授继续安详地念着讲义，没发觉全班的注意力比平常更不集中在他身上。哈利悄悄溜下座位，猫着腰沿着座位快步走到窗前，拨开窗钩，慢慢地打开窗户。

他以为海德薇会伸脚让他把信取下，然后飞回猫头鹰棚屋，可是窗户一开到足够宽，它就跳了进来，哀哀直叫。哈利关上窗，担心地瞥了一眼宾斯教授，猫腰溜回座位，海德薇蹲在他的肩头。他坐下后，把海德薇放到腿上，开始取它脚上的信。

这时他才发现海德薇的羽毛异常蓬乱，有的倒折着，一只翅膀弯成一个奇怪的角度。

"它受伤了。"哈利小声说，头低垂在海德薇的身体上方。赫敏和罗恩凑过来，赫敏甚至放下了她的羽毛笔。"看——它的翅膀不对劲——"

海德薇在颤抖，哈利碰到它的翅膀时，它惊跳了一下，羽毛全部竖了起来，好像充了气一般，它责怪地看着哈利。

"宾斯教授，"哈利大声说，全班都回过头来，"我不舒服。"

宾斯教授从讲义上抬起眼睛，像往常一样似乎很惊讶地发现屋子里坐满了人。

"不舒服？"他恍惚地重复道。

"很不舒服，"哈利坚定地说，把海德薇藏在身后站了起来，"我想我需要去校医院。"

"对，"宾斯教授显然有些手足无措，"对……对，校医院……好，那你去吧，珀金斯……"

一出教室，哈利就把海德薇放回肩头，顺着走廊疾行，直到看不见宾斯的门才停下来思考。他想到的给海德薇疗伤的第一人选当然是海格，但是不知道海格在哪儿，现在唯一的选择只有去找格拉普兰教授，希望她能帮忙。

他透过窗户朝狂风大作、阴云笼罩的场地上张望。海格的小屋附近看不到格拉普兰教授的踪影，如果没在上课，她可能在教工休息室。哈利往楼下跑去，海德薇在他肩上摇晃起来，微弱地鸣叫。

教工休息室门口立着一对滴水嘴石兽，哈利走近时，其中一只声音沙哑地说："你该在教室里，年轻人。"

CHAPTER SEVENTEEN   Educational Decree Number Twenty-Four

'This is urgent,' said Harry curtly.

'Ooooh, *urgent*, is it?' said the other gargoyle in a high-pitched voice. 'Well, that's put us in our place, hasn't it?'

Harry knocked. He heard footsteps, then the door opened and he found himself face to face with Professor McGonagall.

'You haven't been given another detention!' she said at once, her square spectacles flashing alarmingly.

'No, Professor!' said Harry hastily.

'Well then, why are you out of class?'

'It's *urgent*, apparently,' said the second gargoyle snidely.

'I'm looking for Professor Grubbly-Plank,' Harry explained. 'It's my owl, she's injured.'

'Injured owl, did you say?'

Professor Grubbly-Plank appeared at Professor McGonagall's shoulder, smoking a pipe and holding a copy of the *Daily Prophet*.

'Yes,' said Harry, lifting Hedwig carefully off his shoulder, 'she turned up after the other post owls and her wing's all funny, look –'

Professor Grubbly-Plank stuck her pipe firmly between her teeth and took Hedwig from Harry while Professor McGonagall watched.

'Hmm,' said Professor Grubbly-Plank, her pipe waggling slightly as she talked. 'Looks like something's attacked her. Can't think what would have done it, though. Thestrals will sometimes go for birds, of course, but Hagrid's got the Hogwarts Thestrals well-trained not to touch owls.'

Harry neither knew nor cared what Thestrals were; he just wanted to know that Hedwig was going to be all right. Professor McGonagall, however, looked sharply at Harry and said, 'Do you know how far this owl's travelled, Potter?'

'Er,' said Harry. 'From London, I think.'

He met her eyes briefly and knew, by the way her eyebrows had joined in the middle, that she understood 'London' to mean 'number twelve, Grimmauld Place'.

Professor Grubbly-Plank pulled a monocle out of the inside of her robes and screwed it into her eye to examine Hedwig's wing closely. 'I should be able to sort this out if you leave her with me, Potter,' she said, 'she shouldn't be flying long distances for a few days, in any case.'

'Er – right – thanks,' said Harry, just as the bell rang for break.

第 17 章　第二十四号教育令

"情况紧急。"哈利简短地答道。

"哦,情况紧急,是吗?"另一只石兽尖声说,"这下我们可没话说了,对不对?"

哈利敲敲门,脚步声响起,门开了,站在他面前的是麦格教授。

"你不会又被关禁闭了吧!"她一见哈利就说,方眼镜片闪着危险的光。

"没有,教授!"哈利急忙说。

"那你为什么没上课?"

"显然是情况紧急。"第二只石兽讥讽地说。

"我想找格拉普兰教授,"哈利解释道,"我的猫头鹰受伤了。"

"受伤的猫头鹰?"

格拉普兰教授出现在麦格教授身旁,吸着烟斗,手拿一份《预言家日报》。

"是的,"哈利小心地把海德薇从肩上举了起来,"它比其他猫头鹰到得都晚,而且它的翅膀有问题,看——"

格拉普兰教授把烟斗紧紧地咬在嘴里,从哈利手中接过海德薇,麦格教授在一旁看着。

"嗯,"格拉普兰教授说,嘴里的烟斗一动一动的,"看来它遭到了袭击,可是想不出会是什么东西……当然,夜骐有时会袭击鸟类,但霍格沃茨的夜骐已经被海格训练过,不会袭击猫头鹰……"

哈利既不知道也不关心夜骐是什么,他只想弄清海德薇有没有事。但麦格教授锐利地看着哈利说:"你知道这只猫头鹰飞了多远吗,波特?"

"嗯,"哈利说,"是从伦敦飞过来的吧,我想。"

他匆匆接触到麦格教授的目光,从她眉心拧起的样子看出,她明白"伦敦"代表着"格里莫广场12号"。

格拉普兰教授从袍子里掏出一只镜片,安到她的眼睛上,仔细检查海德薇的翅膀。"如果你把它留在我这儿,我应该可以把这些伤治好,波特。"她说,"反正它这几天不应做长途飞行。"

"呃——好的——谢谢。"哈利说,这时下课铃响了。

CHAPTER SEVENTEEN   Educational Decree Number Twenty-Four

'No problem,' said Professor Grubbly-Plank gruffly, turning back into the staff room.

'Just a moment, Wilhelmina!' said Professor McGonagall. 'Potter's letter!'

'Oh yeah!' said Harry, who had momentarily forgotten the scroll tied to Hedwig's leg. Professor Grubbly-Plank handed it over and then disappeared into the staff room carrying Hedwig, who was staring at Harry as though unable to believe he would give her away like this. Feeling slightly guilty, he turned to go, but Professor McGonagall called him back.

'Potter!'

'Yes, Professor?'

She glanced up and down the corridor; there were students coming from both directions.

'Bear in mind,' she said quickly and quietly, her eyes on the scroll in his hand, 'that channels of communication in and out of Hogwarts may be being watched, won't you?'

'I –' said Harry, but the flood of students rolling along the corridor was almost upon him. Professor McGonagall gave him a curt nod and retreated into the staff room, leaving Harry to be swept out into the courtyard with the crowd. He spotted Ron and Hermione already standing in a sheltered corner, their cloak collars turned up against the wind. Harry slit open the scroll as he hurried towards them and found five words in Sirius's handwriting:

Today, same time, same place.

'Is Hedwig OK?' asked Hermione anxiously, the moment he was within earshot.

'Where did you take her?' asked Ron.

'To Grubbly-Plank,' said Harry. 'And I met McGonagall ... listen ...'

And he told them what Professor McGonagall had said. To his surprise, neither of the others looked shocked. On the contrary, they exchanged significant looks.

'What?' said Harry, looking from Ron to Hermione and back again.

'Well, I was just saying to Ron ... what if someone had tried to intercept Hedwig? I mean, she's never been hurt on a flight before, has she?'

'Who's the letter from, anyway?' asked Ron, taking the note from Harry.

'Snuffles,' said Harry quietly.

'"Same time, same place?" Does he mean the fire in the common room?'

第17章 第二十四号教育令

"没什么。"格拉普兰教授粗声说道,转身走进了教师办公室。

"等会儿,威尔米娜!"麦格教授叫道,"波特的信!"

"哦,对了!"哈利说,他一时忘了系在海德薇脚上的纸卷。格拉普兰教授把它递了过来,带着海德薇消失在屋内。海德薇一直盯着哈利,似乎不能相信他会这样把自己交出去。哈利有点内疚地转身离开,但麦格教授把他叫住了。

"波特!"

"是,教授?"

麦格教授朝走廊上看看,两头都有学生走来。

"记住,"她小声急促地说,眼睛望着哈利手里的纸卷,"霍格沃茨内外的通信渠道可能被监视了,知道吗?"

"我——"哈利说,但走廊上的人流几乎已涌到他身边。麦格教授简单地对他点点头,退回屋里,哈利被人群裹挟着走到外面的院子里,看到罗恩和赫敏已经站在一个有遮盖的角落,斗篷领子竖着挡风。哈利快步向他们走去,一边撕开纸卷,看到了小天狼星的字迹:

今天,老时间,老地方。

"海德薇没事吧?"他一走近,赫敏就焦急地问。

"你把它弄哪儿去了?"罗恩问。

"交给了格拉普兰,"哈利说,"我还碰到了麦格……听着……"

他转述了麦格教授的话,令他奇怪的是,两人都没显得震惊,而是意味深长地交换了一下眼色。

"怎么?"哈利来回地看着罗恩和赫敏。

"我刚才还对罗恩讲……会不会有人拦截了海德薇?它以前从没在飞行中受过伤,是不是?"

"到底是谁的信?"罗恩把纸条抓了过去。

"伤风的。"哈利小声说。

"老时间,老地方?他是不是指公共休息室的壁炉?"

CHAPTER SEVENTEEN Educational Decree Number Twenty-Four

'Obviously,' said Hermione, also reading the note. She looked uneasy. 'I just hope nobody else has read this ...'

'But it was still sealed and everything,' said Harry, trying to convince himself as much as her. 'And nobody would understand what it meant if they didn't know where we'd spoken to him before, would they?'

'I don't know,' said Hermione anxiously, hitching her bag back over her shoulder as the bell rang again, 'it wouldn't be exactly difficult to reseal the scroll by magic ... and if anyone's watching the Floo Network ... but I don't really see how we can warn him not to come without *that* being intercepted, too!'

They trudged down the stone steps to the dungeons for Potions, all three of them lost in thought, but as they reached the bottom of the steps they were recalled to themselves by the voice of Draco Malfoy, who was standing just outside Snape's classroom door, waving around an official-looking piece of parchment and talking much louder than was necessary so that they could hear every word.

'Yeah, Umbridge gave the Slytherin Quidditch team permission to continue playing straightaway, I went to ask her first thing this morning. Well, it was pretty much automatic, I mean, she knows my father really well, he's always popping in and out of the Ministry ... it'll be interesting to see whether Gryffindor are allowed to keep playing, won't it?'

'Don't rise,' Hermione whispered imploringly to Harry and Ron, who were both watching Malfoy, faces set and fists clenched. 'It's what he wants.'

'I mean,' said Malfoy, raising his voice a little more, his grey eyes glittering malevolently in Harry and Ron's direction, 'if it's a question of influence with the Ministry, I don't think they've got much chance ... from what my father says, they've been looking for an excuse to sack Arthur Weasley for years ... and as for Potter ... my father says it's a matter of time before the Ministry has him carted off to St Mungo's ... apparently they've got a special ward for people whose brains have been addled by magic.'

Malfoy made a grotesque face, his mouth sagging open and his eyes rolling. Crabbe and Goyle gave their usual grunts of laughter; Pansy Parkinson shrieked with glee.

Something collided hard with Harry's shoulder, knocking him sideways. A split second later he realised that Neville had just charged past him, heading straight for Malfoy.

'Neville, *no!*'

Harry leapt forward and seized the back of Neville's robes; Neville struggled frantically, his fists flailing, trying desperately to get at Malfoy who

"显然是的,"赫敏也在看着纸条,表情有点不安,"但愿没人看过这信……"

"信还封得好好的,"哈利说,试图安慰她,也是想说服自己,"而且没人看得懂,除非他们知道我们上次在哪儿跟他说过话,是不是?"

"我没把握,"赫敏担忧地说,把书包甩到肩上,因为铃声又响了,"用魔法重新封上纸卷并不是很难……要是再有人监视飞路网……可是我不知道用什么方式警告他才能不被拦截!"

他们沉重地走下地下教室的石阶去上魔药课,三人都在沉思,可是下到底层时,他们被德拉科·马尔福的声音唤醒了。他正站在斯内普教室门外,挥舞着一张公文样的羊皮纸,提高了嗓门在嚷嚷,他们听得清清楚楚。

"没错,乌姆里奇马上就批准了斯莱特林魁地奇球队继续活动,我今天一早去问她的。嘿,这事办起来简直毫不费劲。跟你说吧,她和我爸爸很熟,我爸爸经常出入魔法部……格兰芬多能不能继续活动就有的瞧了,是不是?"

"别发火,"赫敏恳求地对哈利和罗恩说,他们俩都瞪着马尔福,脸色铁青,握着拳头,"他就想激怒你们……"

"我是说,"马尔福又提高了一些嗓门,灰眼睛恶意地朝哈利和罗恩这边闪着,"如果这事要论在魔法部的影响力,我觉得他们没什么机会……据我爸爸说,部里这些年一直在找理由撤掉亚瑟·韦斯莱……至于波特嘛……我爸说部里把他送到圣芒戈去只是迟早的事……他们好像有个特殊病房,专收脑子被魔法搞坏的人……"

马尔福扮出一副怪相,嘴拉得老长,眼珠转来转去。克拉布和高尔像往常一样咯咯傻笑,潘西·帕金森兴奋地尖叫。

什么东西猛地撞到哈利肩上,把他撞到了一边。他刹那间意识到纳威从他身边冲了过去,直奔马尔福。

"纳威,不要!"

哈利一个箭步,抓住纳威袍子的后摆,纳威疯狂地挣扎,挥着拳头,

CHAPTER SEVENTEEN   Educational Decree Number Twenty-Four

looked, for a moment, extremely shocked.

'Help me!' Harry flung at Ron, managing to get an arm around Neville's neck and dragging him backwards, away from the Slytherins. Crabbe and Goyle were flexing their arms as they stepped in front of Malfoy, ready for the fight. Ron seized Neville's arms, and together he and Harry succeeded in dragging Neville back into the Gryffindor line. Neville's face was scarlet; the pressure Harry was exerting on his throat rendered him quite incomprehensible, but odd words spluttered from his mouth.

'Not ... funny ... don't ... Mungo's ... show ... him ...'

The dungeon door opened. Snape appeared there. His black eyes swept up the Gryffindor line to the point where Harry and Ron were wrestling with Neville.

'Fighting, Potter, Weasley, Longbottom?' Snape said in his cold, sneering voice. 'Ten points from Gryffindor. Release Longbottom, Potter, or it will be detention. Inside, all of you.'

Harry let go of Neville, who stood panting and glaring at him.

'I had to stop you,' Harry gasped, picking up his bag. 'Crabbe and Goyle would've torn you apart.'

Neville said nothing; he merely snatched up his own bag and stalked off into the dungeon.

'What in the name of Merlin,' said Ron slowly, as they followed Neville, 'was *that* about?'

Harry did not answer. He knew exactly why the subject of people who were in St Mungo's because of magical damage to their brains was highly distressing to Neville, but he had sworn to Dumbledore that he would not tell anyone Neville's secret. Even Neville did not know Harry knew.

Harry, Ron and Hermione took their usual seats at the back of the class, pulled out parchment, quills and their copies of *One Thousand Magical Herbs and Fungi*. The class around them was whispering about what Neville had just done, but when Snape closed the dungeon door with an echoing bang, everybody immediately fell silent.

'You will notice,' said Snape, in his low, sneering voice, 'that we have a guest with us today.'

He gestured towards the dim corner of the dungeon and Harry saw Professor Umbridge sitting there, clipboard on her knee. He glanced sideways at Ron and Hermione, his eyebrows raised. Snape and Umbridge, the two teachers he hated most. It was hard to decide which one he wanted

第17章 第二十四号教育令

拼命想去揍马尔福。马尔福一时显得惊骇万分。

"帮帮我！"哈利对罗恩喊道，他一只胳膊搂住纳威的脖子，把他往后拖离斯莱特林那帮人。克拉布和高尔现在也活动起了胳膊，护在马尔福身前，准备打架。罗恩急忙上前抓住纳威的手臂，和哈利一起把他拖回格兰芬多这边。纳威脸涨得通红，哈利加在他脖子上的力量使他话语不清，但他嘴里还是蹦出了一些字眼。

"不是……开玩笑……不要……芒戈……教训……他……"

地下教室的门开了，斯内普站在那儿，他的黑眼珠扫向格兰芬多这边，看到哈利、罗恩和纳威扭在一起。

"打架，波特、韦斯莱、隆巴顿？"斯内普用他那冷冰冰的、讥讽的语调说，"格兰芬多扣十分。放开隆巴顿，波特，不然就关禁闭。全部进教室。"

哈利放开手，纳威站在那儿喘着气，对他怒目而视。

"我必须拦着你，"哈利气喘吁吁地说，一边捡起书包，"克拉布和高尔会把你撕碎的。"

纳威没说话，抓起自己的书包，大步走进地下教室。

"看在老天的分上，"他们跟在纳威后面，罗恩迟钝地说，"这是怎么回事？"

哈利没有回答，他了解为什么纳威最听不得脑子被魔法搞坏而进圣芒戈的话，但他对邓布利多发过誓，不把纳威的秘密告诉任何人。就连纳威也不知道哈利是知情者。

哈利、罗恩和赫敏在教室后排的老位子上坐下来，抽出羊皮纸、羽毛笔和《千种神奇药草及蕈类》课本。周围的同学都在交头接耳地议论纳威刚才的行为，但当斯内普关上地下教室的门，发出重重的回响时，全班顿时肃静下来。

"大家会发现，"斯内普用低沉、讥讽的语调说，"我们今天有一位客人。"

他朝昏暗的角落一指，哈利看见乌姆里奇教授坐在那儿，腿上放着写字板。他瞟瞟罗恩和赫敏，扬了扬眉毛。斯内普和乌姆里奇，他

619

CHAPTER SEVENTEEN   Educational Decree Number Twenty-Four

to triumph over the other.

'We are continuing with our Strengthening Solution today. You will find your mixtures as you left them last lesson; if correctly made they should have matured well over the weekend – instructions –' he waved his wand again '– on the board. Carry on.'

Professor Umbridge spent the first half-hour of the lesson making notes in her corner. Harry was very interested in hearing her question Snape; so interested, that he was becoming careless with his potion again.

'Salamander blood, Harry!' Hermione moaned, grabbing his wrist to prevent him adding the wrong ingredient for the third time, 'not pomegranate juice!'

'Right,' said Harry vaguely, putting down the bottle and continuing to watch the corner. Umbridge had just got to her feet. 'Ha,' he said softly, as she strode between two lines of desks towards Snape, who was bending over Dean Thomas's cauldron.

'Well, the class seem fairly advanced for their level,' she said briskly to Snape's back. 'Though I would question whether it is advisable to teach them a potion like the Strengthening Solution. I think the Ministry would prefer it if that was removed from the syllabus.'

Snape straightened up slowly and turned to look at her.

'Now ... how long have you been teaching at Hogwarts?' she asked, her quill poised over her clipboard.

'Fourteen years,' Snape replied. His expression was unfathomable. His eyes on Snape, Harry added a few drops to his potion; it hissed menacingly and turned from turquoise to orange.

'You applied first for the Defence Against the Dark Arts post, I believe?' Professor Umbridge asked Snape.

'Yes,' said Snape quietly.

'But you were unsuccessful?'

Snape's lip curled.

'Obviously.'

Professor Umbridge scribbled on her clipboard.

'And you have applied regularly for the Defence Against the Dark Arts post since you first joined the school, I believe?'

'Yes,' said Snape quietly, barely moving his lips. He looked very angry.

第17章 第二十四号教育令

最讨厌的两个老师……他难以决定自己希望谁占上风。

"今天继续配增强剂，你们会看到自己上节课留下的混合液，如果配得对，周末的时候应该已经充分发酵了。操作方法——"他又挥起魔杖，"——在黑板上。开始。"

乌姆里奇教授前半个小时都在角落里记笔记。哈利一心想听她向斯内普提问，以至于配药时又粗心大意了。

"火蜥蜴血，哈利！"赫敏叫道，抓着他的手腕，不让他第三次加错成分，"不是石榴汁！"

"好的。"哈利心不在焉地说，放下瓶子，继续注视着角落里，乌姆里奇刚刚站起来。"哈。"他轻声说。只见乌姆里奇从两排桌子间走向斯内普，斯内普正在俯身查看迪安·托马斯的坩埚。

"哎呀，这个班看来学得相当深嘛，"乌姆里奇轻快地对着斯内普的后背说，"但我怀疑教他们增强剂这样的药剂是否可取。我想部里会希望把它从课程中删掉。"

斯内普缓缓直起腰，转身看着她。

"那么……你在霍格沃茨教课有多久了？"乌姆里奇问，羽毛笔做好了在写字板上记录的准备。

"十四年。"斯内普的表情深不可测。哈利紧紧盯着他，加了几滴液体，药水发出可怕的嘶嘶声，由青绿变成了橘黄。

"你先申请任教黑魔法防御术课，是不是？"乌姆里奇教授问斯内普。

"是的。"斯内普低声说。

"但没申请到？"

斯内普撇着嘴。

"显而易见。"

乌姆里奇教授在写字板上刷刷地写着。

"你进校以来多次申请任教黑魔法防御术课，是不是？"

"是的。"斯内普低声说，嘴唇几乎不动。他看上去很恼火。

CHAPTER SEVENTEEN   Educational Decree Number Twenty-Four

'Do you have any idea why Dumbledore has consistently refused to appoint you?' asked Umbridge.

'I suggest you ask him,' said Snape jerkily.

'Oh, I shall,' said Professor Umbridge, with a sweet smile.

'I suppose this is relevant?' Snape asked, his black eyes narrowed.

'Oh yes,' said Professor Umbridge, 'yes, the Ministry wants a thorough understanding of teachers' – er – backgrounds.'

She turned away, walked over to Pansy Parkinson and began questioning her about the lessons. Snape looked round at Harry and their eyes met for a second. Harry hastily dropped his gaze to his potion, which was now congealing foully and giving off a strong smell of burned rubber.

'No marks again, then, Potter,' said Snape maliciously, emptying Harry's cauldron with a wave of his wand. 'You will write me an essay on the correct composition of this potion, indicating how and why you went wrong, to be handed in next lesson, do you understand?'

'Yes,' said Harry furiously. Snape had already given them homework and he had Quidditch practice this evening; this would mean another couple of sleepless nights. It did not seem possible that he had awoken that morning feeling very happy. All he felt now was a fervent desire for this day to end.

'Maybe I'll skive off Divination,' he said glumly, as they stood in the courtyard after lunch, the wind whipping at the hems of robes and brims of hats. 'I'll pretend to be ill and do Snape's essay instead, then I won't have to stay up half the night.'

'You can't skive off Divination,' said Hermione severely.

'Hark who's talking, you walked out of Divination, you hate Trelawney!' said Ron indignantly.

'I don't *hate* her,' said Hermione loftily. 'I just think she's an absolutely appalling teacher and a real old fraud. But Harry's already missed History of Magic and I don't think he ought to miss anything else today!'

There was too much truth in this to ignore, so half an hour later Harry took his seat in the hot, overperfumed atmosphere of the Divination classroom, feeling angry at everybody. Professor Trelawney was yet again handing out copies of *The Dream Oracle*. Harry thought he'd surely be much better employed doing Snape's punishment essay than sitting here trying to find meaning in a lot of made-up dreams.

It seemed, however, that he was not the only person in Divination who was in

"你知道邓布利多为什么屡次拒绝用你吗?"乌姆里奇问。

"我建议你去问他。"斯内普生硬地答道。

"我会的。"乌姆里奇教授笑容可掬地说。

"这有关系吗?"斯内普问,他的黑眼睛眯缝起来。

"有啊,"乌姆里奇教授说,"部里希望全面了解教师的——呃——背景。"

她转身走开,踱到潘西·帕金森身边,开始向她询问课程情况。斯内普回头看看哈利,两人视线短暂相交,哈利急忙垂眼看他的药水,它现在已经凝结成污浊不堪的一体,发出橡胶烧煳了的冲鼻气味。

"又是零分,波特。"斯内普恶狠狠地说,魔杖一挥清空了哈利的坩埚,"你给我写一篇这种药剂正确配制的文章,注明你错在哪儿,为什么错,下节课交上来,听懂了吗?"

"听懂了。"哈利愤怒地说。斯内普已经给他们布置了作业,今晚还有魁地奇球训练,这意味着他又得熬两个通宵。简直不能相信他今天早上醒来还感觉非常快乐呢,他现在只盼着这一天赶快结束。

"我也许要逃占卜课了,"午饭后他们又站在院子里时,他沮丧地说,风掀着他的袍摆和帽檐,"装病赶写斯内普的文章,免得熬夜……"

"你不能逃占卜课。"赫敏正色说。

"听听谁在说话,你自己走出了占卜课的课堂,你恨特里劳尼!"罗恩打抱不平。

"我不恨她,"赫敏高傲地说,"我只觉得她是个糟糕的老师,一个彻头彻尾的老骗子……但哈利已经少上了魔法史课,我觉得他今天不应该再缺课了!"

这话中的实情不容忽视,所以半小时后,哈利坐到了占卜课那热烘烘、散发着一股腻人香水味的课堂上,生着所有人的气。特里劳尼教授又在发《解梦指南》的课本,与其坐在这里琢磨一堆编造的梦,还不如写斯内普罚做的文章呢。

然而,他不是占卜课上唯一一个没好气的人。特里劳尼把一本《解

a temper. Professor Trelawney slammed a copy of the *Oracle* down on the table between Harry and Ron and swept away, her lips pursed; she threw the next copy of the *Oracle* at Seamus and Dean, narrowly avoiding Seamus's head, and thrust the final one into Neville's chest with such force that he slipped off his pouffe.

'Well, carry on!' said Professor Trelawney loudly, her voice high-pitched and somewhat hysterical, 'you know what to do! Or am I such a sub-standard teacher that you have never learned how to open a book?'

The class stared perplexedly at her, then at each other. Harry, however, thought he knew what was the matter. As Professor Trelawney flounced back to the high-backed teacher's chair, her magnified eyes full of angry tears, he leaned his head closer to Ron's and muttered, 'I think she's got the results of her inspection back.'

'Professor?' said Parvati Patil in a hushed voice (she and Lavender had always rather admired Professor Trelawney). 'Professor, is there anything – er – wrong?'

'Wrong!' cried Professor Trelawney in a voice throbbing with emotion. 'Certainly not! I have been insulted, certainly ... insinuations have been made against me ... unfounded accusations levelled ... but no, there is nothing wrong, certainly not!'

She took a great shuddering breath and looked away from Parvati, angry tears spilling from under her glasses.

'I say nothing,' she choked, 'of sixteen years of devoted service ... it has passed, apparently, unnoticed ... but I shall not be insulted, no, I shall not!'

'But, Professor, who's insulting you?' asked Parvati timidly.

'The Establishment!' said Professor Trelawney, in a deep, dramatic, wavering voice. 'Yes, those with eyes too clouded by the mundane to See as I See, to Know as I Know ... of course, we Seers have always been feared, always persecuted ... it is – alas – our fate.'

She gulped, dabbed at her wet cheeks with the end of her shawl, then she pulled a small embroidered handkerchief from her sleeve, and blew her nose very hard with a sound like Peeves blowing a raspberry.

Ron sniggered. Lavender shot him a disgusted look.

'Professor,' said Parvati, 'do you mean ... is it something Professor Umbridge –?'

'Do not speak to me about that woman!' cried Professor Trelawney, leaping to her feet, her beads rattling and her spectacles flashing. 'Kindly continue with your work!'

第17章 第二十四号教育令

梦指南》掼在哈利和罗恩的桌子上,嘟着嘴大步走开,把下一本《解梦指南》朝西莫和迪安扔去,差点砸到了西莫的脑袋,又把最后一本塞到纳威胸前,推得他从凳子上滑了下去。

"好了,开始吧!"特里劳尼教授大声说,声音尖得有点歇斯底里,"你们知道该干什么!难道我教得有那么差劲,你们都没学会打开课本吗?"

同学们困惑地看着她,接着面面相觑。但哈利认为他知道是怎么回事。特里劳尼教授怒冲冲地走回高背教师椅,被镜片放大的眼睛里盈满愤怒的泪水。哈利把脑袋凑向罗恩,小声说:"我想她收到调查结果了。"

"教授?"帕瓦蒂·佩蒂尔小声问(她和拉文德一直相当钦佩特里劳尼教授),"教授,有什么——不对吗?"

"不对!"特里劳尼教授叫了起来,声音激动得直发抖,"当然没有!我受了侮辱……含沙射影……毫无根据的指责……但是没有不对,当然没有……"

她颤抖地深吸了一口气,扭过脸去,愤怒的泪水从眼镜下涌了出来。

"且不提,"她哽咽道,"我十六年兢兢业业……显然没人注意……但我不应该受到侮辱,不应该!"

"可是教授,谁在侮辱您呢?"帕瓦蒂怯怯地问。

"当权者!"特里劳尼教授用戏剧般的低沉颤抖的声音说,"那些眼睛被世俗蒙蔽,不能见我所见、知我所知的人……当然,我们这些先知总是让人害怕,总是受迫害……这是——唉——我们的命……"

她哽噎了,用披肩角擦擦湿漉漉的面颊,从袖子里抽出一块小绣花手帕,使劲地擤鼻子,声音就像皮皮鬼发出的呸呸声。

罗恩偷偷地笑。拉文德鄙夷地瞪了他一眼。

"教授,"帕瓦蒂说,"您说的……是不是乌姆里奇教授……?"

"别跟我提那个女人!"特里劳尼教授大喊一声,跳了起来,身上的珠子哗啦哗啦响,眼镜片一闪一闪,"请你们做作业吧!"

CHAPTER SEVENTEEN   Educational Decree Number Twenty-Four

And she spent the rest of the lesson striding among them, tears still leaking from behind her glasses, muttering what sounded like threats under her breath.

'... may well choose to leave ... the indignity of it ... on probation ... we shall see ... how she dares ...'

'You and Umbridge have got something in common,' Harry told Hermione quietly when they met again in Defence Against the Dark Arts. 'She obviously reckons Trelawney's an old fraud, too ... looks like she's put her on probation.'

Umbridge entered the room as he spoke, wearing her black velvet bow and an expression of great smugness.

'Good afternoon, class.'

'Good afternoon, Professor Umbridge,' they chanted drearily.

'Wands away, please.'

But there was no answering flurry of movement this time; nobody had bothered to take out their wands.

'Please turn to page thirty-four of *Defensive Magical Theory* and read the third chapter, entitled "The Case for Non-Offensive Responses to Magical Attack". There will be –'

'– no need to talk,' Harry, Ron and Hermione said together, under their breaths.

'*No* Quidditch practice,' said Angelina in hollow tones when Harry, Ron and Hermione entered the common room after dinner that night.

'But I kept my temper!' said Harry, horrified. 'I didn't say anything to her, Angelina, I swear, I –'

'I know, I know,' said Angelina miserably. 'She just said she needed a bit of time to consider.'

'Consider what?' said Ron angrily. 'She's given the Slytherins permission, why not us?'

But Harry could imagine how much Umbridge was enjoying holding the threat of no Gryffindor Quidditch team over their heads and could easily understand why she would not want to relinquish that weapon over them too soon.

'Well,' said Hermione, 'look on the bright side – at least now you'll have time to do Snape's essay!'

'That's a bright side, is it?' snapped Harry, while Ron stared incredulously at Hermione. 'No Quidditch practice, and extra Potions?'

Harry slumped down into a chair, dragged his Potions essay reluctantly

第17章 第二十四号教育令

余下的时间里,她在班上走来走去,眼镜后还有泪水滴下,并不时地喃喃自语,好像在威胁谁。

"……干脆辞职算了……这种耻辱……留用察看……走着瞧……她怎么敢……"

"你和乌姆里奇有一点相同,"他们在黑魔法防御术课上会合时,哈利悄悄对赫敏说,"她显然也认为特里劳尼是个老骗子……好像让她留用察看了。"

说话间乌姆里奇走进了教室,戴着她的黑天鹅绒蝴蝶结,踌躇满志。

"下午好,同学们。"

"下午好,乌姆里奇教授。"大家拖腔拖调地说。

"请收起魔杖……"

但这次没有一片忙乱,因为根本没人把魔杖拿出来。

"请翻到《魔法防御理论》第三十四页,读第三章对魔法袭击采取非进攻性反应的理由,看书时——"

"——请不要讲话。"哈利、罗恩和赫敏在嗓子眼里说。

"没有魁地奇球训练了。"晚饭后哈利、罗恩和赫敏走进公共休息室时,安吉利娜声音空洞地说。

"可是我很克制呀!"哈利说,显得十分震惊,"我没对她说什么,安吉利娜,我发誓——"

"我知道,我知道,"安吉利娜痛苦地说,"她只说她还要考虑考虑。"

"考虑什么?"罗恩愤然说道,"她批准了斯莱特林,凭什么不批准我们?"

但是哈利能想象出来,乌姆里奇多么喜欢把格兰芬多魁地奇球队当作悬在他们头上的威胁,她当然不愿意过早放弃这个武器。

"算啦,"赫敏说,"往好的方面想吧——至少你有时间写斯内普的文章了!"

"这是好的方面?"哈利抢白道,罗恩难以置信地望着赫敏,"没有魁地奇球训练,魔药课又罚作业!"

哈利跌坐在椅子上,不情愿地从书包里抽出魔药课的论文开始

CHAPTER SEVENTEEN   Educational Decree Number Twenty-Four

from his bag and set to work. It was very hard to concentrate; even though he knew Sirius was not due in the fire until much later, he could not help glancing into the flames every few minutes just in case. There was also an incredible amount of noise in the room: Fred and George appeared finally to have perfected one type of Skiving Snackbox, which they were taking turns to demonstrate to a cheering and whooping crowd.

First, Fred would take a bite out of the orange end of a chew, at which he would vomit spectacularly into a bucket they had placed in front of them. Then he would force down the purple end of the chew, at which the vomiting would immediately cease. Lee Jordan, who was assisting the demonstration, was lazily Vanishing the vomit at regular intervals with the same Vanishing Spell Snape kept using on Harry's potions.

What with the regular sounds of retching, cheering and the sound of Fred and George taking advance orders from the crowd, Harry was finding it exceptionally difficult to focus on the correct method for Strengthening Solution. Hermione was not helping matters; the cheers and the sound of vomit hitting the bottom of Fred and George's bucket were punctuated by her loud and disapproving sniffs, which Harry found, if anything, more distracting.

'Just go and stop them, then!' he said irritably, after crossing out the wrong weight of powdered griffin claw for the fourth time.

'I can't, they're not *technically* doing anything wrong,' said Hermione through gritted teeth. 'They're quite within their rights to eat the foul things themselves and I can't find a rule that says the other idiots aren't entitled to buy them, not unless they're proven to be dangerous in some way and it doesn't look as though they are.'

She, Harry and Ron watched George projectile-vomit into the bucket, gulp down the rest of the chew and straighten up, beaming with his arms wide to protracted applause.

'You know, I don't get why Fred and George only got three O.W.L.s each,' said Harry, watching as Fred, George and Lee collected gold from the eager crowd. 'They really know their stuff.'

'Oh, they only know flashy stuff that's of no real use to anyone,' said Hermione disparagingly.

'No real use?' said Ron in a strained voice. 'Hermione, they've made about twenty-six Galleons already.'

It was a long while before the crowd around the Weasley twins dispersed, then Fred, Lee and George sat up counting their takings even longer, so it was well past midnight when Harry, Ron and Hermione finally had the

第17章 第二十四号教育令

写。他很难集中思想，尽管他知道小天狼星在火中现身还早，但还是忍不住过几分钟就朝火里看看，以防万一。屋子里吵得要命：弗雷德和乔治好像终于完善了一种速效逃课糖，正在轮流向起哄喝彩的人群演示。

弗雷德先咬口香糖橘黄色的一头，马上大口呕吐起来，吐进他们摆在面前的桶里，然后又强咽下紫色的一头，呕吐立刻停止。每过一阵子，李·乔丹便懒洋洋地清空呕吐物，用的是斯内普常对哈利的药水使用的消失咒。

呕吐声、喝彩声、人们纷纷向弗雷德和乔治订货的声音，使哈利简直没法集中思想写增强剂的正确配方。赫敏也不帮忙，欢呼声和呕吐物落到桶底的声音中夹杂着赫敏不满的大声冷笑，哈利觉得这更让人分神。

"去阻止他们好了！"他烦躁地说，第四次划去写错的狮身鹰首兽爪粉的分量。

"我不能，他们技术上没有犯任何错误。"赫敏咬着牙说，"吃脏东西是他们自己的权利，我也找不到一条规定说别的傻瓜不能买它，除非能证明它有危险，可看上去并没有……"

她和哈利、罗恩看着乔治把呕吐物喷射到桶里，吞下剩下的糖，直起身来微笑着张开手臂，博得长长的喝彩。

"我不明白弗雷德和乔治为什么都只得了三门O.W.L.证书，"哈利看着弗雷德、乔治和李从热切的人群中收金币，"他们学得不错嘛……"

"哦，他们只会一些没用的花哨东西。"赫敏轻蔑地说。

"没用？"罗恩怪叫道，"赫敏，他们已经收了二十六个加隆了。"

韦斯莱兄弟周围的人群很晚才散去，然后弗雷德、李和乔治又坐在那里数钱，午夜过后很久，哈利、罗恩和赫敏总算可以享有公共休息室的清静了。弗雷德终于炫耀地摇着他的钱盒子，关上了通往男生

common room to themselves. At long last, Fred had closed the doorway to the boys' dormitories behind him, rattling his box of Galleons ostentatiously so that Hermione scowled. Harry, who was making very little progress with his Potions essay, decided to give it up for the night. As he put his books away, Ron, who was dozing lightly in an armchair, gave a muffled grunt, awoke, and looked blearily into the fire.

'Sirius!' he said.

Harry whipped round. Sirius's untidy dark head was sitting in the fire again.

'Hi,' he said, grinning.

'Hi,' chorused Harry, Ron and Hermione, all three kneeling down on the hearthrug. Crookshanks purred loudly and approached the fire, trying, despite the heat, to put his face close to Sirius's.

'How're things?' said Sirius.

'Not that good,' said Harry, as Hermione pulled Crookshanks back to stop him singeing his whiskers. 'The Ministry's forced through another decree, which means we're not allowed to have Quidditch teams –'

'Or secret Defence Against the Dark Arts groups?' said Sirius.

There was a short pause.

'How did you know about that?' Harry demanded.

'You want to choose your meeting places more carefully,' said Sirius, grinning still more broadly. 'The Hog's Head, I ask you.'

'Well, it was better than the Three Broomsticks!' said Hermione defensively. 'That's always packed with people –'

'Which means you'd have been harder to overhear,' said Sirius. 'You've got a lot to learn, Hermione.'

'Who overheard us?' Harry demanded.

'Mundungus, of course,' said Sirius, and when they all looked puzzled he laughed. 'He was the witch under the veil.'

'That was Mundungus?' Harry said, stunned. 'What was he doing in the Hog's Head?'

'What do you think he was doing?' said Sirius impatiently. 'Keeping an eye on you, of course.'

'I'm still being followed?' asked Harry angrily.

'Yeah, you are,' said Sirius, 'and just as well, isn't it, if the first thing you're going to do on your weekend off is organise an illegal defence group.'

But he looked neither angry nor worried. On the contrary, he was looking at Harry with distinct pride.

宿舍的门，惹得赫敏皱起眉头。哈利的魔药课论文没写几个字，他决定今晚放弃了。他收拾书本的时候，在扶手椅上打瞌睡的罗恩哼了一声醒过来，迷糊地望向火焰。

"小天狼星！"他叫道。

哈利迅速转身，小天狼星那乱蓬蓬的黑脑袋又出现在火中。

"你们好！"他笑嘻嘻地说。

"你好！"哈利、罗恩和赫敏同声说，三人都跪到壁炉前的地毯上。克鲁克山喵喵叫着凑近炉火，不顾灼热，把脸凑近小天狼星。

"情况怎么样？"小天狼星问。

"不大好，"哈利说，赫敏把克鲁克山拉了回来，免得它烤焦胡须，"部里又出了个法令，意味着我们不能有魁地奇球队了——"

"——还有秘密黑魔法防御小组？"小天狼星说。

片刻沉默。

"你怎么知道的？"哈利问。

"你们选聚会地点时要更谨慎些，"小天狼星的嘴咧得更开了，"猪头酒吧，你们怎么想的……"

"总比三把扫帚强吧！"赫敏辩解道，"那儿总是挤满了人——"

"——那才不容易偷听呀，"小天狼星说，"你要学的东西还很多，赫敏。"

"谁偷听了我们？"哈利问。

"当然是蒙顿格斯，"小天狼星说，看到三人疑惑的样子，他笑了起来，"就是那个披着长纱巾的女巫。"

"那是蒙顿格斯？"哈利问，不觉惊呆了，"他在猪头酒吧干什么？"

"你说他在干什么？"小天狼星不耐烦地说，"自然是盯着你们了。"

"还有人在跟踪我？"哈利愤怒地问。

"对，是这样，"小天狼星说，"而且很有必要，是不是？如果你周末放假做的第一件事就是组织一个非法的防御小组。"

但他看上去既不生气也不着急，相反，他望着哈利的目光中带着明显的自豪。

CHAPTER SEVENTEEN   Educational Decree Number Twenty-Four

'Why was Dung hiding from us?' asked Ron, sounding disappointed. 'We'd've liked to've seen him.'

'He was banned from the Hog's Head twenty years ago,' said Sirius, 'and that barman's got a long memory. We lost Moody's spare Invisibility Cloak when Sturgis was arrested, so Dung's been dressing as a witch a lot lately ... anyway ... first of all, Ron – I've sworn to pass on a message from your mother.'

'Oh yeah?' said Ron, sounding apprehensive.

'She says on no account whatsoever are you to take part in an illegal secret Defence Against the Dark Arts group. She says you'll be expelled for sure and your future will be ruined. She says there will be plenty of time to learn how to defend yourself later and that you are too young to be worrying about that right now. She also' (Sirius's eyes turned to the other two) 'advises Harry and Hermione not to proceed with the group, though she accepts that she has no authority over either of them and simply begs them to remember that she has their best interests at heart. She would have written all this to you, but if the owl had been intercepted you'd all have been in real trouble, and she can't say it for herself because she's on duty tonight.'

'On duty doing what?' said Ron quickly.

'Never you mind, just stuff for the Order,' said Sirius. 'So it's fallen to me to be the messenger and make sure you tell her I passed it all on, because I don't think she trusts me to.'

There was another pause in which Crookshanks, mewing, attempted to paw Sirius's head, and Ron fiddled with a hole in the hearthrug.

'So, you want me to say I'm not going to take part in the Defence group?' he muttered finally.

'Me? Certainly not!' said Sirius, looking surprised. 'I think it's an excellent idea!'

'You do?' said Harry, his heart lifting.

'Of course I do!' said Sirius. 'D'you think your father and I would've lain down and taken orders from an old hag like Umbridge?'

'But – last term all you did was tell me to be careful and not take risks –'

'Last year, all the evidence was that someone inside Hogwarts was trying to kill you, Harry!' said Sirius impatiently. 'This year, we know there's someone outside Hogwarts who'd like to kill us all, so I think learning to defend yourselves properly is a very good idea!'

'And if we do get expelled?' Hermione asked, a quizzical look on her face.

'Hermione, this whole thing was your idea!' said Harry, staring at her.

第 17 章 第二十四号教育令

"顿格为什么躲着我们？"罗恩失望地问，"我们愿意见到他。"

"他二十年前被禁止进猪头酒吧，那个酒吧老板记性好极了。"小天狼星说，"斯多吉被捕时我们丢掉了穆迪的备用隐形斗篷，所以顿格近来经常扮成女巫……好了……首先，罗恩——我向你妈妈发了誓要转达她的口信。"

"啊？说吧。"罗恩有些害怕。

"她叫你无论如何不要参加非法的秘密黑魔法防御小组。她说你肯定会被开除，毁了你的前程。她说以后有的是时间学着保护自己，你现在想那些还太早。她也——"小天狼星的目光转向了另外两人，"——劝哈利和赫敏不要搞这个小组，虽然她承认自己没有资格这样要求你们，但她只求你们记得，她是为你们好。她本想写信，但如果猫头鹰被抓，你们就倒霉了，她也不能自己来说，因为她今晚值班。"

"值什么班？"罗恩忙问。

"别担心，只是凤凰社的事，所以我就当了信使，别忘了告诉她我把口信带到了，因为我感觉她不大信任我。"

又是一阵沉默，克鲁克山喵喵地想去抓小天狼星的脑袋，罗恩抠着地毯上的一个小洞。

"这么说，你是想让我表态不参加防御小组？"哈利终于开口喃喃地问道。

"我？当然不是！"小天狼星惊讶地说，"我觉得这是个好主意！"

"真的？"哈利说，一下子振奋起来。

"当然啦！"小天狼星说，"你想你爸爸和我会乖乖地听乌姆里奇那老女妖的命令吗？"

"可是——上学期你总叫我小心，别冒险——"

"上学期各种迹象表明霍格沃茨校内有人想杀你，哈利！"小天狼星不耐烦地说，"这学期我们知道霍格沃茨校外有人想把我们都干掉，所以我想学习自卫是很好的主意！"

"如果真被开除了呢？"赫敏的脸上带着疑问。

"赫敏，这件事可都是你的主意！"哈利瞪着她说。

CHAPTER SEVENTEEN   Educational Decree Number Twenty-Four

'I know it was. I just wondered what Sirius thought,' she said, shrugging.

'Well, better expelled and able to defend yourselves than sitting safely in school without a clue,' said Sirius.

'Hear, hear,' said Harry and Ron enthusiastically.

'So,' said Sirius, 'how are you organising this group? Where are you meeting?'

'Well, that's a bit of a problem now,' said Harry. 'Dunno where we're going to be able to go.'

'How about the Shrieking Shack?' suggested Sirius.

'Hey, that's an idea!' said Ron excitedly, but Hermione made a sceptical noise and all three of them looked at her, Sirius's head turning in the flames.

'Well, Sirius, it's just that there were only four of you meeting in the Shrieking Shack when you were at school,' said Hermione, 'and all of you could transform into animals and I suppose you could all have squeezed under a single Invisibility Cloak if you'd wanted to. But there are twenty-eight of us and none of us is an Animagus, so we wouldn't need so much an Invisibility Cloak as an Invisibility Marquee –'

'Fair point,' said Sirius, looking slightly crestfallen. 'Well, I'm sure you'll come up with somewhere. There used to be a pretty roomy secret passageway behind that big mirror on the fourth floor, you might have enough space to practise jinxes in there.'

'Fred and George told me it's blocked,' said Harry, shaking his head. 'Caved in or something.'

'Oh …' said Sirius, frowning. 'Well, I'll have a think and get back to –'

He broke off. His face was suddenly tense, alarmed. He turned sideways, apparently looking into the solid brick wall of the fireplace.

'Sirius?' said Harry anxiously.

But he had vanished. Harry gaped at the flames for a moment, then turned to look at Ron and Hermione.

'Why did he –?'

Hermione gave a horrified gasp and leapt to her feet, still staring at the fire.

A hand had appeared amongst the flames, groping as though to catch hold of something; a stubby, short-fingered hand covered in ugly old-fashioned rings.

The three of them ran for it. At the door of the boys' dormitory Harry looked back. Umbridge's hand was still making snatching movements amongst the flames, as though she knew exactly where Sirius's hair had been moments before and was determined to seize it.

第17章　第二十四号教育令

"我知道……我只是想听听小天狼星的看法。"她耸耸肩说。

"宁可为自卫而被开除，也比安全地坐在学校里两眼一抹黑强。"小天狼星说。

"好哇，好哇。"哈利和罗恩热烈地欢呼。

"那么，你们如何组织这个小组？在哪儿聚会？"

"现在有点麻烦，"哈利说，"不知道能去哪儿……"

"尖叫棚屋怎么样？"小天狼星提议道。

"嘿，这主意不错！"罗恩兴奋地说，但赫敏发出了怀疑的声音，三人都一起看着她，小天狼星的脑袋在火里转动着。

"小天狼星，你在学校那会儿，只有你们四个人在尖叫棚屋碰头，"赫敏说，"你们都能变成动物，而且我想如果愿意的话，你们可以挤进一件隐形衣里。可是我们有二十八个人，都不会变动物，我们需要的不是一件隐形衣，而是一顶隐形大帐篷——"

"言之有理。"小天狼星说，看上去有点气馁，"我想你们会找到一个地方的……五楼的大镜子后面以前有一个挺大的秘密通道，够你们练习魔咒的——"

"弗雷德和乔治说给堵上了，"哈利摇摇头说，"好像是塌了。"

"哦……"小天狼星皱眉道，"好吧，我想想再——"

他的话音断了，脸色突然变得紧张而惊恐。他转过头，似乎在朝壁炉的砖墙里看。

"小天狼星？"哈利担心地说。

可是他已经消失了。哈利对着火苗愣了片刻，转身看着罗恩和赫敏。

"他怎么——？"

赫敏惊叫一声，跳了起来，眼睛还盯着火里。

火里出现了一只手，摸索着像要抓住什么东西，一只五指短粗的手，戴满难看的老式戒指……

三人吓得撒腿就跑，在男生宿舍门口哈利回头看了一眼。乌姆里奇的手还在火焰中乱抓，好像她知道小天狼星的头刚才就在那里，决心要抓住它似的。

CHAPTER EIGHTEEN

Dumbledore's Army

'Umbridge has been reading your mail, Harry. There's no other explanation.'

'You think Umbridge attacked Hedwig?' he said, outraged.

'I'm almost certain of it,' said Hermione grimly. 'Watch your frog, it's escaping.'

Harry pointed his wand at the bullfrog that had been hopping hopefully towards the other side of the table – '*Accio!*' – and it zoomed gloomily back into his hand.

Charms was always one of the best lessons in which to enjoy a private chat; there was generally so much movement and activity that the danger of being overheard was very slight. Today, with the room full of croaking bullfrogs and cawing ravens, and with a heavy downpour of rain clattering and pounding against the classroom windows, Harry, Ron and Hermione's whispered discussion about how Umbridge had nearly caught Sirius went quite unnoticed.

'I've been suspecting this ever since Filch accused you of ordering Dungbombs, because it seemed such a stupid lie,' Hermione whispered. 'I mean, once your letter had been read it would have been quite clear you *weren't* ordering them, so you wouldn't have been in trouble at all – it's a bit of a feeble joke, isn't it? But then I thought, what if somebody just wanted an excuse to read your mail? Well then, it would be a perfect way for Umbridge to manage it – tip off Filch, let him do the dirty work and confiscate the letter, then either find a way of stealing it from him or else demand to see it – I don't think Filch would object, when's he ever stuck up for a student's rights? Harry, you're squashing your frog.'

Harry looked down; he was indeed squeezing his bullfrog so tightly its eyes were popping; he replaced it hastily upon the desk.

第18章

邓布利多军

"乌姆里奇看了你的信,哈利,没有别的解释。"

"你认为乌姆里奇攻击了海德薇?"他愤怒地问。

"我几乎可以肯定。"赫敏神情严峻地说,"注意你的牛蛙,它要跑了。"

哈利用魔杖指着满怀希望地朝桌子另一头蹦去的牛蛙——"牛蛙飞来!"——牛蛙沮丧地落回了他的手里。

魔咒课永远是最适合讲悄悄话的课之一:教室里一般都很热闹,被别人听见的可能性很小。今天,教室里满是呱呱叫的牛蛙和嘎嘎叫的乌鸦,外面倾盆大雨敲打着窗户,哈利、罗恩和赫敏的窃窃私语根本没人听见,他们议论着乌姆里奇怎么会差点抓到了小天狼星。

"自从费尔奇说你订了粪弹,我就一直有这种怀疑,因为那显然是个愚蠢的谎话。"赫敏小声说,"只要看了你的信,就会很清楚你没订,所以你不应该有麻烦——那是一个无聊的玩笑,不是吗?但后来我想,要是有人就想找借口看你的信呢?那样,对乌姆里奇可是个好办法——告诉费尔奇,让他做恶人没收那封信,然后从他那儿偷去,或直接要求看信——我不认为费尔奇会拒绝,他什么时候维护过学生的权利?哈利,你要把你的牛蛙捏死了。"

哈利低头一看,牛蛙被他攥得太紧,眼睛都突出来了,他忙把它放到桌上。

CHAPTER EIGHTEEN   Dumbledore's Army

'It was a very, very close call last night,' said Hermione. 'I just wonder if Umbridge knows how close it was. *Silencio.*'

The bullfrog on which she was practising her Silencing Charm was struck dumb mid-croak and glared at her reproachfully.

'If she'd caught Snuffles –'

Harry finished the sentence for her.

'– He'd probably be back in Azkaban this morning.' He waved his wand without really concentrating; his bullfrog swelled like a green balloon and emitted a high-pitched whistle.

'*Silencio!*' said Hermione hastily, pointing her wand at Harry's frog, which deflated silently before them. 'Well, he mustn't do it again, that's all. I just don't know how we're going to let him know. We can't send him an owl.'

'I don't reckon he'll risk it again,' said Ron. 'He's not stupid, he knows she nearly got him. *Silencio.*'

The large and ugly raven in front of him let out a derisive caw.

'*Silencio. SILENCIO!*'

The raven cawed more loudly.

'It's the way you're moving your wand,' said Hermione, watching Ron critically, 'you don't want to wave it, it's more a sharp *jab*.'

'Ravens are harder than frogs,' said Ron testily.

'Fine, let's swap,' said Hermione, seizing Ron's raven and replacing it with her own fat bullfrog. '*Silencio!*' The raven continued to open and close its sharp beak, but no sound came out.

'Very good, Miss Granger!' said Professor Flitwick's squeaky little voice, making Harry, Ron and Hermione all jump. 'Now, let me see you try, Mr Weasley.'

'Wha–? Oh – oh, right,' said Ron, very flustered. 'Er – *silencio!*'

He jabbed at the bullfrog so hard he poked it in the eye: the frog gave a deafening croak and leapt off the desk.

It came as no surprise to any of them that Harry and Ron were given additional practice of the Silencing Charm for homework.

They were allowed to remain inside over break due to the downpour outside. They found seats in a noisy and overcrowded classroom on the first floor in which Peeves was floating dreamily up near the chandelier, occasionally blowing an ink pellet at the top of somebody's head. They had

第18章 邓布利多军

"昨晚可真够险的。"赫敏说,"我在想乌姆里奇知不知道她只是差一点儿。无声无息!"

她用来练无声无息咒的牛蛙叫到一半突然哑了,责备地看着她。

"如果她抓到了伤风——"

哈利接着替她把话讲完。

"——伤风今早可能就回到阿兹卡班了。"哈利心不在焉地挥挥魔杖,他的牛蛙鼓成了一个绿气球,发出一声尖叫。

"无声无息!"赫敏急忙用魔杖指着哈利的牛蛙说,牛蛙无声地瘪了下来,"反正,他不能再这么来了。可是我不知道怎么告诉他。不能让猫头鹰送信了。"

"我想他不会再冒险了。"罗恩说,"他又不笨,他知道自己差点被她抓到。无声无息!"

他面前那只丑陋的大乌鸦嘲笑地呱呱大叫。

"无声无息!**无声无息!**"

乌鸦叫得更响了。

"你的魔杖动得不对,"赫敏用批评的眼光看着罗恩,"不要挥舞,应该迅速一刺。"

"乌鸦比牛蛙难。"罗恩咬着牙说。

"好,我们交换。"赫敏抓过罗恩的乌鸦换掉了她那只肥牛蛙,"无声无息!"乌鸦的尖嘴还在一张一合,但没有了声音。

"很好,格兰杰小姐!"弗立维教授尖细的嗓门说,三人吓了一跳,"现在我来看你练习,韦斯莱先生!"

"什——?噢——噢,好的,"罗恩慌张地说,"呃——无声无息!"

他刺得用力过猛,戳到了牛蛙的眼睛,牛蛙发出一声震耳欲聋的大叫,从桌上蹦了下去。

结果不出他们所料,哈利和罗恩的家庭作业中增加了无声无息咒练习。

因为下雨,课间休息可以留在室内。他们在二楼一间闹哄哄、挤满了人的教室里找了个座位,皮皮鬼在吊灯旁梦幻般地飘着,时而朝

CHAPTER EIGHTEEN   Dumbledore's Army

barely sat down when Angelina came struggling towards them through the groups of gossiping students.

'I've got permission!' she said. 'To re-form the Quidditch team!'

'*Excellent!*' said Ron and Harry together.

'Yeah,' said Angelina, beaming. 'I went to McGonagall and I *think* she might have appealed to Dumbledore. Anyway, Umbridge had to give in. Ha! So I want you down at the pitch at seven o'clock tonight, all right, because we've got to make up time. You realise we're only three weeks away from our first match?'

She squeezed away from them, narrowly dodged an ink pellet from Peeves, which hit a nearby first-year instead, and vanished from sight.

Ron's smile slipped slightly as he looked out of the window, which was now opaque with hammering rain.

'Hope this clears up. What's up with you, Hermione?'

She, too, was gazing at the window, but not as though she really saw it. Her eyes were unfocused and there was a frown on her face.

'Just thinking ...' she said, still frowning at the rain-washed window.

'About Siri– Snuffles?' said Harry.

'No ... not exactly ...' said Hermione slowly. 'More ... wondering ... I suppose we're doing the right thing ... I think ... aren't we?'

Harry and Ron looked at each other.

'Well, that clears that up,' said Ron. 'It would've been really annoying if you hadn't explained yourself properly.'

Hermione looked at him as though she had only just realised he was there.

'I was just wondering,' she said, her voice stronger now, 'whether we're doing the right thing, starting this Defence Against the Dark Arts group.'

'What?' said Harry and Ron together.

'Hermione, it was your idea in the first place!' said Ron indignantly.

'I know,' said Hermione, twisting her fingers together. 'But after talking to Snuffles ...'

'But he's all for it,' said Harry.

'Yes,' said Hermione, staring at the window again. 'Yes, that's what made me think maybe it wasn't a good idea after all ...'

Peeves floated over them on his stomach, peashooter at the ready;

第18章 邓布利多军

某人头顶上吹一滴墨珠。他们刚坐下,安吉利娜就从一堆堆聊天的学生中挤了过来。

"我得到批准了!"她说,"重组魁地奇球队!"

"太棒了!"罗恩和哈利一齐说。

"是啊,"安吉利娜满面春风地说,"我找了麦格教授,我想她可能去求邓布利多了——总之,乌姆里奇只好让步。哈!所以我请你们今晚七点到球场,行吗,我们得补时间。你们意识到离第一场比赛只有三星期了吗?"

她从他们身边挤过去,勉强躲过了皮皮鬼吹出的墨珠,墨珠落到了旁边一个一年级新生的身上,她的身影随之消失。

罗恩看看窗外,笑容在慢慢地消失,窗玻璃被大雨打得一片模糊。"但愿天会放晴……你怎么了,赫敏?"

赫敏也望着窗户,但好像对一切视而不见。她目光茫然,眉头微锁。

"我在想……"她依然皱眉望着雨打的窗户。

"想小天——'伤风'?"哈利问。

"不……不完全是……"赫敏慢吞吞地说,"我是想……我们是在做正确的事……是吗?"

哈利和罗恩对视了一下。

"哦,你说得可真明白,"罗恩说,"你要是说得不清不楚就该让人心烦了。"

赫敏看着他,好像刚刚发现他在那儿似的。

"我只是在想,"她的声音有力了一点,"我们做得是不是正确,组织黑魔法防御小组。"

"什么?"哈利和罗恩齐声说。

"赫敏,这一开始可是你的主意啊!"罗恩抱怨道。

"我知道,"赫敏绞着手说,"但是跟伤风谈过之后……"

"可他很赞成!"哈利说。

"对,"赫敏又望着窗户说,"对,正是这样我才觉得也许不是个好主意……"

皮皮鬼俯身飘到他们头上,用豆子枪瞄准他们,三人下意识地举

641

automatically all three of them lifted their bags to cover their heads until he had passed.

'Let's get this straight,' said Harry angrily, as they put their bags back on the floor, 'Sirius agrees with us, so you don't think we should do it any more?'

Hermione looked tense and rather miserable. Now staring at her own hands, she said, 'Do you honestly trust his judgement?'

'Yes, I do!' said Harry at once. 'He's always given us great advice!'

An ink pellet whizzed past them, striking Katie Bell squarely in the ear. Hermione watched Katie leap to her feet and start throwing things at Peeves; it was a few moments before Hermione spoke again and it sounded as though she was choosing her words very carefully.

'You don't think he has become ... sort of ... reckless ... since he's been cooped up in Grimmauld Place? You don't think he's ... kind of ... living through us?'

'What d'you mean, "living through us"?' Harry retorted.

'I mean ... well, I think he'd love to be forming secret Defence societies right under the nose of someone from the Ministry ... I think he's really frustrated at how little he can do where he is ... so I think he's keen to kind of ... egg us on.'

Ron looked utterly perplexed.

'Sirius is right,' he said, 'you *do* sound just like my mother.'

Hermione bit her lip and did not answer. The bell rang just as Peeves swooped down on Katie and emptied an entire ink bottle over her head.

The weather did not improve as the day wore on, so that at seven o'clock that evening, when Harry and Ron went down to the Quidditch pitch for practice, they were soaked through within minutes, their feet slipping and sliding on the sodden grass. The sky was a deep, thundery grey and it was a relief to gain the warmth and light of the changing rooms, even if they knew the respite was only temporary. They found Fred and George debating whether to use one of their own Skiving Snackboxes to get out of flying.

'... but I bet she'd know what we'd done,' Fred said out of the corner of his mouth. 'If only I hadn't offered to sell her some Puking Pastilles yesterday.'

'We could try the Fever Fudge,' George muttered, 'no one's seen that yet –'

起书包挡着脑袋，直到他过去。

"有话直说吧，"他们把书包放回地上时，哈利恼火地说，"小天狼星支持我们，结果你倒觉得我们不应该干下去了？"

赫敏显得紧张而难过。她看着自己的手说："你真相信他的判断吗？"

"我相信！"哈利马上说，"他总给我们出好点子！"

一滴墨珠从他们身旁飞过，正中凯蒂·贝尔的耳朵。赫敏看着凯蒂跳起来朝皮皮鬼扔东西。过了好一会儿赫敏才开口，她好像在斟词酌句。

"你不觉得他自从被困在格里莫广场之后，变得……有点……鲁莽了吗？你不觉得他……好像在……通过我们生活吗？"

"你说什么，'通过我们生活'？"哈利质问道。

"我是说……嗯，我想他愿意在部里派来的人眼皮底下搞一个秘密防御小组……他待在那个地方什么也干不了，一定憋得慌……所以我想他会积极地……怂恿我们。"

罗恩看上去完全被搞糊涂了。

"小天狼星说得对，"他说，"你说话真像我妈妈。"

赫敏咬着嘴唇没有答腔。上课铃响了，皮皮鬼向凯蒂俯冲过去，把一瓶墨水全倒在了她头上。

天气并没有好转，晚上七点钟哈利和罗恩去魁地奇球场训练时，几分钟就被淋得透湿，脚在湿漉漉的草地上直打滑。天空灰沉沉的，雷声阵阵。进到温暖明亮的更衣室里真是舒了口气，但他们知道这轻松只是暂时的。他们发现弗雷德和乔治正在讨论要不要用一种速效逃课糖来躲避飞行。

"……可是我打赌她会知道的，"弗雷德咧嘴说，"我昨天要是没向她兜售吐吐糖就好了。"

"我们可以用发烧糖，"乔治悄声说，"没人看到过——"

CHAPTER EIGHTEEN   Dumbledore's Army

'Does it work?' enquired Ron hopefully, as the hammering of rain on the roof intensified and wind howled around the building.

'Well, yeah,' said Fred, 'your temperature'll go right up.'

'But you get these massive pus-filled boils, too,' said George, 'and we haven't worked out how to get rid of them yet.'

'I can't see any boils,' said Ron, staring at the twins.

'No, well, you wouldn't,' said Fred darkly, 'they're not in a place we generally display to the public.'

'But they make sitting on a broom a right pain in the –'

'All right, everyone, listen up,' said Angelina loudly, emerging from the Captain's office. 'I know it's not ideal weather, but there's a chance we'll be playing Slytherin in conditions like this so it's a good idea to work out how we're going to cope with them. Harry, didn't you do something to your glasses to stop the rain fogging them up when we played Hufflepuff in that storm?'

'Hermione did it,' said Harry. He pulled out his wand, tapped his glasses and said, '*Impervius!*'

'I think we all ought to try that,' said Angelina. 'If we could just keep the rain off our faces it would really help visibility – all together, come on – *Impervius*! OK. Let's go.'

They all stowed their wands back in the inside pockets of their robes, shouldered their brooms and followed Angelina out of the changing rooms.

They squelched through the deepening mud to the middle of the pitch; visibility was still very poor even with the Impervius Charm; light was fading fast and curtains of rain were sweeping the grounds.

'All right, on my whistle,' shouted Angelina.

Harry kicked off from the ground, spraying mud in all directions, and shot upwards, the wind pulling him slightly off course. He had no idea how he was going to see the Snitch in this weather; he was having enough difficulty seeing the one Bludger with which they were practising; a minute into the practice it almost unseated him and he had to use the Sloth Grip Roll to avoid it. Unfortunately, Angelina did not see this. In fact, she did not appear to be able to see anything; none of them had a clue what the others were doing. The wind was picking up; even at a distance Harry could hear the swishing, pounding sounds of the rain pummelling the surface of the lake.

Angelina kept them at it for nearly an hour before conceding defeat. She led her sodden and disgruntled team back into the changing rooms, insisting that the practice had not been a waste of time, though without any real

"灵吗?"罗恩满怀希望地问,屋顶上雨敲得更响了,狂风绕着屋子呼啸。

"还行,"弗雷德说,"你的体温会一下子升上去——"

"但也会长一些大脓包,"乔治说,"我们还没想出消除它们的办法。"

"我看不到脓包啊。"罗恩打量着这对双胞胎兄弟。

"你是看不到,"弗雷德阴沉地说,"它们不长在我们通常露在外面的部位。"

"可是会使你坐在扫帚上简直像——"

"好了,大家听我说。"安吉利娜从队长办公室走出来大声说,"我知道天气不理想,但我们很可能在这种条件下跟斯莱特林队比赛,所以最好练练怎么对付。哈利,我们在那场暴雨中跟赫奇帕奇比赛,你不是用了点法子就使雨水不蒙住眼镜了吗?"

"是赫敏做的。"哈利说,他抽出魔杖,敲了敲眼镜说,"防水防湿!"

"我想我们都应该试一试,"安吉利娜说,"只要不让雨打到脸上,视线就清楚多了——大家一起来——防水防湿!好,我们走吧。"

他们都把魔杖收进袍子里面的口袋里,扛起飞天扫帚,跟着安吉利娜出了更衣室。

一行人踏着越来越厚的泥泞走到球场中央,虽然有防水防湿咒,但能见度还是很低,光线迅速减弱,雨帘狂扫场地。

"好,听我口哨。"安吉利娜喊道。

哈利双脚一蹬腾空而起,泥水四溅,风吹得他有一点偏斜。他不知道在这种天气怎么能看到飞贼,光是看他们练习用的游走球就够费劲的了。开场一分钟游走球就差点把他撞下了飞天扫帚,他不得不用树懒抱树滚来躲避。可惜安吉利娜没看见,事实上,她好像什么都看不见,他们都不知道别人在干什么。风越来越猛,哈利甚至能听到远处雨水啪啪抽打湖面的声音。

安吉利娜让他们练了近一个小时才作罢。她把落汤鸡一般、发着牢骚的队员带回更衣室,坚持说这次训练不是浪费时间,不过她的语

CHAPTER EIGHTEEN Dumbledore's Army

conviction in her voice. Fred and George were looking particularly annoyed; both were bandy-legged and winced with every movement. Harry could hear them complaining in low voices as he towelled his hair dry.

'I think a few of mine have ruptured,' said Fred in a hollow voice.

'Mine haven't,' said George, wincing, 'they're throbbing like mad ... feel bigger if anything.'

'OUCH!' said Harry.

He pressed the towel to his face, his eyes screwed tight with pain. The scar on his forehead had seared again, more painfully than it had in weeks.

'What's up?' said several voices.

Harry emerged from behind his towel; the changing room was blurred because he was not wearing his glasses, but he could still tell that everyone's face was turned towards him.

'Nothing,' he muttered, 'I – poked myself in the eye, that's all.'

But he gave Ron a significant look and the two of them hung back as the rest of the team filed back outside, muffled in their cloaks, their hats pulled low over their ears.

'What happened?' said Ron, the moment Alicia had disappeared through the door. 'Was it your scar?'

Harry nodded.

'But ...' looking scared, Ron strode across to the window and stared out into the rain, 'he – he can't be near us now, can he?'

'No,' Harry muttered, sinking on to a bench and rubbing his forehead. 'He's probably miles away. It hurt because ... he's ... angry.'

Harry had not meant to say that at all, and heard the words as though a stranger had spoken them – yet knew at once that they were true. He did not know how he knew it, but he did; Voldemort, wherever he was, whatever he was doing, was in a towering temper.

'Did you see him?' said Ron, looking horrified. 'Did you ... get a vision, or something?'

Harry sat quite still, staring at his feet, allowing his mind and his memory to relax in the aftermath of the pain.

A confused tangle of shapes, a howling rush of voices ...

'He wants something done, and it's not happening fast enough,' he said.

Again, he felt surprised to hear the words coming out of his mouth, and yet was quite certain they were true.

调也显得底气不足。弗雷德和乔治特别窝火，两人都变成了罗圈腿，每走一步都龇牙咧嘴。哈利用毛巾擦时听到他们在小声抱怨。

"我的有几个可能破了。"弗雷德声音沉闷地说。

"我的还没有，"乔治从牙缝里挤出声音说，"胀得厉害……好像又大了……"

"哎哟！"哈利叫了一声。

他用毛巾捂住脸，疼得双眼紧闭。他前额的伤疤又灼痛起来，好几个星期没这么痛了。

"怎么了？"几个声音同时问道。

哈利拿开毛巾，更衣室模糊一片，因为他没戴眼镜，但他能感觉到大家的脸都朝着他。

"没什么，"他咕哝道，"我——不小心碰到眼睛了，没事。"

他对罗恩使了个眼色，当队员们裹上斗篷、拉低了帽檐、鱼贯出去时，他们俩留了下来。

"怎么回事？"艾丽娅一从门口消失，罗恩就问，"是你的伤疤吗？"

哈利点点头。

"可是……"罗恩惊疑地走到窗前，朝雨中看了看，"他——他现在不可能离我们很近，是不是？"

"是啊，"哈利低声说，一屁股坐到凳子上，揉着额头，"他也许在千里之外。我疼是因为……他……发怒了。"

哈利根本没想这么说，这话在他听来像出自一个陌生人之口——但他马上意识到这是真情。他也不知道这意识从何而来，但他的确知道，伏地魔，无论在哪里或在做什么，都正在大发脾气。

"你看到他了吗？"罗恩恐惧地说，"你……是不是看到了幻象？"

哈利静静地坐着，盯着自己的脚，让思想与记忆在余痛中放松……纷乱的影像，喧嚣的声音……

"他想办一件事，但办得不够快。"

他又一次惊奇地听到自己说出这句话，但很清楚它是实情。

CHAPTER EIGHTEEN   Dumbledore's Army

'But ... how do you know?' said Ron.

Harry shook his head and covered his eyes with his hands, pressing down upon them with his palms. Little stars erupted in them. He felt Ron sit down on the bench beside him and knew Ron was staring at him.

'Is this what it was about last time?' said Ron in a hushed voice. 'When your scar hurt in Umbridge's office? You-Know-Who was angry?'

Harry shook his head.

'What is it, then?'

Harry was thinking himself back. He had been looking into Umbridge's face ... his scar had hurt ... and he had had that odd feeling in his stomach ... a strange, leaping feeling ... a *happy* feeling ... but of course, he had not recognised it for what it was, as he had been feeling so miserable himself ...

'Last time, it was because he was pleased,' he said. 'Really pleased. He thought ... something good was going to happen. And the night before we came back to Hogwarts ...' he thought back to the moment when his scar had hurt so badly in his and Ron's bedroom in Grimmauld Place ... 'he was furious ...'

He looked round at Ron, who was gaping at him.

'You could take over from Trelawney, mate,' he said in an awed voice.

'I'm not making prophecies,' said Harry.

'No, you know what you're doing?' Ron said, sounding both scared and impressed. 'Harry, *you're reading You-Know-Who's mind*!'

'No,' said Harry, shaking his head. 'It's more like ... his mood, I suppose. I'm just getting flashes of what mood he's in. Dumbledore said something like this was happening last year. He said that when Voldemort was near me, or when he was feeling hatred, I could tell. Well, now I'm feeling it when he's pleased, too ...'

There was a pause. The wind and rain lashed at the building.

'You've got to tell someone,' said Ron.

'I told Sirius last time.'

'Well, tell him about this time!'

'Can't, can I?' said Harry grimly. 'Umbridge is watching the owls and the fires, remember?'

'Well then, Dumbledore.'

第18章 邓布利多军

"可是……你怎么知道的？"罗恩问。

哈利摇摇头，用手紧紧地按住眼睛，眼前迸出无数的星星。他感到罗恩在他身边坐了下来，知道罗恩在盯着他。

"上次是这样吗？"罗恩屏着气问，"在乌姆里奇办公室里你伤疤疼的那次，神秘人也是在发怒吗？"

哈利摇摇头。

"那次是什么？"

哈利回忆着。他在看乌姆里奇的脸……伤疤痛起来……他腹部有一种异样的感觉……一种奇怪的、跳跃的感觉……高兴的感觉……当然，他当时没有分辨出来，因为他自己是那么痛苦……

"上次是因为他很高兴，真的高兴。他想到……有件好事要发生。我们回霍格沃茨前的那一夜……"他回忆起在格里莫广场他和罗恩的卧室里，伤疤疼得特别厉害的那次，"他在大发雷霆……"

他转过头，见罗恩目瞪口呆地盯着他。

"你可以代替特里劳尼了，哥们儿。"罗恩钦佩地说。

"我没有预言。"哈利说。

"不，你知道你在做什么吗？"罗恩的语气中充满敬畏，"哈利，你在读神秘人的思想！"

"不，"哈利摇头道，"我想那只是……他的情绪。我只是对他的情绪有一些闪电般的感觉……邓布利多去年说过会发生这种情况……他说当伏地魔靠近我，或当他感到仇恨时，我就会有感应。现在他高兴时我也有感应了……"

片刻的沉默，风雨抽打着房屋。

"你得告诉什么人。"罗恩说。

"我上次告诉小天狼星了。"

"那好，这次也告诉他！"

"不行吧？"哈利沉重地说，"乌姆里奇在监视猫头鹰和炉火，你忘了吗？"

"那就邓布利多——"

'I've just told you, he already knows,' said Harry shortly, getting to his feet, taking his cloak off his peg and swinging it around him. 'There's no point telling him again.'

Ron did up the fastening of his own cloak, watching Harry thoughtfully.

'Dumbledore'd want to know,' he said.

Harry shrugged.

'C'mon ... we've still got Silencing Charms to practise.'

They hurried back through the dark grounds, sliding and stumbling up the muddy lawns, not talking. Harry was thinking hard. What was it that Voldemort wanted done that was not happening quickly enough?

'... *he's got other plans ... plans he can put into operation very quietly indeed ... stuff he can only get by stealth ... like a weapon. Something he didn't have last time.*'

Harry had not thought about those words in weeks; he had been too absorbed in what was going on at Hogwarts, too busy dwelling on the ongoing battles with Umbridge, the injustice of all the Ministry interference ... but now they came back to him and made him wonder ... Voldemort's anger would make sense if he was no nearer to laying hands on the *weapon*, whatever it was. Had the Order thwarted him, stopped him from seizing it? Where was it kept? Who had it now?

'*Mimbulus mimbletonia*,' said Ron's voice and Harry came back to his senses just in time to clamber through the portrait hole into the common room.

It appeared that Hermione had gone to bed early, leaving Crookshanks curled in a nearby chair and an assortment of knobbly knitted elf hats lying on a table by the fire. Harry was rather grateful that she was not around, because he did not much want to discuss his scar hurting and have her urge him to go to Dumbledore, too. Ron kept throwing him anxious glances, but Harry pulled out his Charms books and set to work on finishing his essay, though he was only pretending to concentrate and by the time Ron said he was going up to bed, too, he had written hardly anything.

Midnight came and went while Harry was reading and rereading a passage about the uses of scurvy-grass, lovage and sneezewort and not taking in a word of it.

> *These plantes are moste efficacious in the inflaming of the braine, and are therefore much used in Confusing and Befuddlement Draughts, where the wizard is desirous of producing hot-headedness and recklessness...*

第18章 邓布利多军

"我告诉过你,他已经知道了。"哈利站起来,从挂钩上摘下他的斗篷披到身上,"再告诉他没有意义。"

罗恩系上斗篷,若有所思地望着哈利。

"邓布利多会想知道的。"他说。

哈利耸耸肩。

"走吧,我们还要练无声无息咒呢……"

他们匆匆穿过黑暗的场地,在泥泞的草坪上一步一滑地前进,谁也没有说话。哈利在努力思考。伏地魔想办而办得不够快的事是什么呢?

"……他还有其他计划……他可以神不知鬼不觉地实施的计划……某种只有偷偷摸摸才能得到的东西……比如一件武器。他以前没有的东西。"

哈利几星期来都没有琢磨过这些话,他一心只关注着霍格沃茨的情况,与乌姆里奇的斗争,魔法部的不公正干预……但现在这些话又回到他脑子里,引起了他的思考……如果是因为迟迟搞不到那件武器——不管它是什么,伏地魔的怒气就可以解释了。是不是凤凰社阻挠了他?武器藏在哪儿?目前在谁的手里?

"米布米宝。"罗恩的声音说,哈利回过神来,刚刚来得及从肖像洞口钻进公共休息室。

赫敏好像早就睡了,克鲁克山蜷缩在一旁的椅子上,赫敏织出的各种疙里疙瘩的小精灵帽留在炉旁的桌子上。哈利有些庆幸赫敏不在,他不太想讨论伤疤疼的事,赫敏也会催他去找邓布利多。罗恩老是担心地看着他,但哈利抽出魔药学课本,开始写他的论文,其实只是假装集中思想。到罗恩也去睡觉时,他还没写多少。

夜阑人静,哈利反复读着一段关于坏血草、独活草和喷嚏草用途的文字,却一点也没读进去。

这些植物最易造成脑炎,多用于迷乱药中,致人急躁鲁莽……

CHAPTER EIGHTEEN — Dumbledore's Army

... Hermione said Sirius was becoming reckless cooped up in Grimmauld Place ...

... *moste efficacious in the inflaming of the braine, and are therefore much used* ...

... the *Daily Prophet* would think his brain was inflamed if they found out that he knew what Voldemort was feeling ...

... *therefore much used in Confusing and Befuddlement Draughts* ...

... confusing was the word, all right; *why* did he know what Voldemort was feeling? What was this weird connection between them, which Dumbledore had never been able to explain satisfactorily?

... *where the wizard is desirous* ...

... how Harry would like to sleep ...

... *of producing hot-headedness* ...

... it was warm and comfortable in his armchair before the fire, with the rain still beating heavily on the windowpanes, Crookshanks purring, and the crackling of the flames ...

The book slipped from Harry's slack grip and landed with a dull thud on the hearthrug. His head lolled sideways ...

He was walking once more along a windowless corridor, his footsteps echoing in the silence. As the door at the end of the passage loomed larger, his heart beat fast with excitement ... if he could only open it ... enter beyond ...

He stretched out his hand ... his fingertips were inches from it ...

'Harry Potter, sir!'

He awoke with a start. The candles had all been extinguished in the common room, but there was something moving close by.

'Whozair?' said Harry, sitting upright in his chair. The fire was almost out,

第18章 邓布利多军

……赫敏说小天狼星被困在格里莫广场后变得鲁莽……

……最易造成脑炎,多用于……

……如果发现他能知道伏地魔的感觉,《预言家日报》会认为他得了脑炎……

……多用于迷乱药中……

……迷乱……没错……,他为什么能知道伏地魔的感觉呢?他们之间这种奇怪的联系是什么呢?邓布利多一直没有做出令人满意的解释。

……致人……

他真想睡觉……

……急躁鲁莽……

……壁炉前的扶手椅温暖舒适,雨还在敲打窗户,克鲁克山呜呜地叫着,炉火噼啪作响……

课本从哈利手中滑落,掉在地毯上,发出一声闷响,他的脑袋歪到了一边……

他又走在一条没有窗户的走廊里,脚步声在寂静中回响。走廊尽头那扇门越来越近,他的心跳兴奋地加快……要是能够推开它……走进去……

他伸出手……手指离它只有几英寸了……

"哈利·波特,先生!"

他惊醒过来。公共休息室的蜡烛都已熄灭,但近旁有个东西在动。"谁?"哈利坐直了身体,炉火几乎燃尽,屋里很暗。

CHAPTER EIGHTEEN   Dumbledore's Army

the room very dark.

'Dobby has your owl, sir!' said a squeaky voice.

'Dobby?' said Harry thickly, peering through the gloom towards the source of the voice.

Dobby the house-elf was standing beside the table on which Hermione had left half a dozen of her knitted hats. His large, pointed ears were now sticking out from beneath what looked like all the hats Hermione had ever knitted; he was wearing one on top of the other, so that his head seemed elongated by two or three feet, and on the very topmost bobble sat Hedwig, hooting serenely and obviously cured.

'Dobby volunteered to return Harry Potter's owl,' said the elf squeakily, with a look of positive adoration on his face, 'Professor Grubbly-Plank says she is all well now, sir.' He sank into a deep bow so that his pencil-like nose brushed the threadbare surface of the hearthrug and Hedwig gave an indignant hoot and fluttered on to the arm of Harry's chair.

'Thanks, Dobby!' said Harry, stroking Hedwig's head and blinking hard, trying to rid himself of the image of the door in his dream ... it had been very vivid. Looking back at Dobby, he noticed that the elf was also wearing several scarves and innumerable socks, so that his feet looked far too big for his body.

'Er ... have you been taking *all* the clothes Hermione's been leaving out?'

'Oh, no, sir,' said Dobby happily. 'Dobby has been taking some for Winky, too, sir.'

'Yeah, how is Winky?' asked Harry.

Dobby's ears drooped slightly.

'Winky is still drinking lots, sir,' he said sadly, his enormous round green eyes, large as tennis balls, downcast. 'She still does not care for clothes, Harry Potter. Nor do the other house-elves. None of them will clean Gryffindor Tower any more, not with the hats and socks hidden everywhere, they finds them insulting, sir. Dobby does it all himself, sir, but Dobby does not mind, sir, for he always hopes to meet Harry Potter and tonight, sir, he has got his wish!' Dobby sank into a deep bow again. 'But Harry Potter does not seem happy,' Dobby went on, straightening up again and looking timidly at Harry. 'Dobby heard him muttering in his sleep. Was Harry Potter having bad dreams?'

'Not really bad,' said Harry, yawning and rubbing his eyes. 'I've had worse.'

The elf surveyed Harry out of his vast, orb-like eyes. Then he said very seriously, his ears drooping, 'Dobby wishes he could help Harry Potter, for

第18章 邓布利多军

"多比把您的猫头鹰带来了，先生！"一个尖细的声音说。

"多比？"哈利麻木地应了一声，在黑暗中朝声音的方向望去。

家养小精灵多比站在赫敏留下六七顶小花帽的桌边，那对尖尖的大耳朵中间像是戴着赫敏织过的所有帽子，一顶压一顶，使他的脑袋似乎变长了两三英尺，最顶上蹲着海德薇，平静地叫着，显然已经痊愈。

"多比自告奋勇来送回哈利·波特的猫头鹰！"小精灵尖声尖气地说，脸上充满崇敬，"格拉普兰教授说它已经好了，先生！"他深鞠一躬，铅笔尖般的鼻子擦到了破旧的地毯，海德薇不满地叫了一声，飞到哈利的椅子扶手上。

"谢谢，多比！"哈利抚摸着海德薇的脑袋，使劲眨着眼睛，想除去梦中所见的那扇门的影像……它是那么鲜明……他仔细一瞧多比，发现这小精灵还围着几条围巾，穿着不知多少双袜子，使他的脚看上去大得不成比例。

"呃……你拿了赫敏放在这里的全部衣服吗？"

"哦，不是，先生，"多比愉快地说，"多比还拿了些给闪闪，先生。"

"噢，闪闪怎么样？"哈利问。

多比的耳朵微微耷拉了下来。

"闪闪还是酗酒，先生。"他难过地说，网球那么大的绿眼睛垂了下去，"她还是不在意穿什么衣服，哈利·波特。其他家养小精灵也无所谓。他们都不肯打扫格兰芬多塔楼了，帽子和袜子藏得到处都是，他们觉得那是侮辱。都是多比一个人在搞卫生，先生，但多比不介意，先生，因为他总希望遇见哈利·波特，今晚他如愿以偿了，先生！"多比又深鞠一躬。"但哈利·波特好像不高兴，"多比直起腰，怯怯地望着哈利，"多比听到他说梦话了。哈利·波特做了噩梦吗？"

"还好，"哈利打了个哈欠，揉揉眼睛，"我做过更可怕的。"

小精灵用他那大大的、圆圆的眼睛端详着哈利，然后耷拉下耳朵，特别认真地说："多比想帮助哈利·波特，因为哈利·波特解放了多比，

Harry Potter set Dobby free and Dobby is much, much happier now.'

Harry smiled.

'You can't help me, Dobby, but thanks for the offer.'

He bent and picked up his Potions book. He'd have to try to finish the essay tomorrow. He closed the book and as he did so the firelight illuminated the thin white scars on the back of his hand – the result of his detentions with Umbridge ...

'Wait a moment – there *is* something you can do for me, Dobby,' said Harry slowly.

The elf looked round, beaming.

'Name it, Harry Potter, sir!'

'I need to find a place where twenty-eight people can practise Defence Against the Dark Arts without being discovered by any of the teachers. Especially,' Harry clenched his hand on the book, so that the scars shone pearly white, 'Professor Umbridge.'

He expected the elf's smile to vanish, his ears to droop; he expected him to say it was impossible, or else that he would try to find somewhere, but his hopes were not high. What he had not expected was for Dobby to give a little skip, his ears waggling cheerfully, and clap his hands together.

'Dobby knows the perfect place, sir!' he said happily. 'Dobby heard tell of it from the other house-elves when he came to Hogwarts, sir. It is known by us as the Come and Go room, sir, or else as the Room of Requirement!'

'Why?' said Harry curiously.

'Because it is a room that a person can only enter,' said Dobby seriously, 'when they have real need of it. Sometimes it is there, and sometimes it is not, but when it appears, it is always equipped for the seeker's needs. Dobby has used it, sir,' said the elf, dropping his voice and looking guilty, 'when Winky has been very drunk; he has hidden her in the Room of Requirement and he has found antidotes to Butterbeer there, and a nice elf-sized bed to settle her on while she sleeps it off, sir ... and Dobby knows Mr Filch has found extra cleaning materials there when he has run short, sir, and –'

'And if you really needed a bathroom,' said Harry, suddenly remembering something Dumbledore had said at the Yule Ball the previous Christmas, 'would it fill itself with chamber pots?'

'Dobby expects so, sir,' said Dobby, nodding earnestly. 'It is a most amazing room, sir.'

第18章 邓布利多军

多比现在比从前快乐了好多好多。"

哈利笑了。

"你帮不了我的,多比,但是谢谢你。"

他俯身捡起魔药学课本,只能明天拼命赶了。他合上书时,炉火照亮了手背上那道白色的伤疤,那是被乌姆里奇关禁闭的结果。

"等一等——有一件事你可以帮我,多比。"哈利慢慢地说。

小精灵看了过来,喜笑颜开。

"说吧,哈利·波特,先生!"

"我需要一个地方,能让二十八个人练习黑魔法防御术而不被老师们发现,尤其是,"哈利攥紧课本,伤疤发出白色光泽,"乌姆里奇教授。"

他以为小精灵的笑容会消失,耳朵会耷拉下来;他以为多比会说这不可能,或者说他会努力,但希望不大。可是他没想到,多比轻轻一跳,耳朵愉快地摆动起来,两手一拍。

"多比知道一个绝妙的地方,先生!"他高兴地说,"多比来霍格沃茨时听其他小精灵提到过,我们叫它'来去屋',先生,或'有求必应屋'!"

"为什么?"哈利好奇地问。

"因为这间屋子只有当一个人真正需要它时才能进得去。"多比严肃地说,"它时有时无,当它出现时,总是布置得符合求助者的需要。多比用过它,先生。"小精灵的声音低了下去,面有愧色,"闪闪醉得厉害时,多比就把她藏在有求必应屋里,他发现那儿有黄油啤酒的醒酒药,还有一个符合小精灵尺寸的床可以让闪闪睡觉,先生……多比还知道,费尔奇先生工具不够时在那儿找到过备用的清洁用具,先生,还有——"

"还有,如果你需要一个厕所,"哈利问,突然想起邓布利多在去年圣诞舞会上说过的话,"它会备有很多便壶吗?"

"多比认为会的,先生,"多比认真地点头道,"那是一间非常奇妙的屋子,先生。"

CHAPTER EIGHTEEN — Dumbledore's Army

'How many people know about it?' said Harry, sitting up straighter in his chair.

'Very few, sir. Mostly people stumbles across it when they needs it, sir, but often they never finds it again, for they do not know that it is always there waiting to be called into service, sir.'

'It sounds brilliant,' said Harry, his heart racing. 'It sounds perfect, Dobby. When can you show me where it is?'

'Any time, Harry Potter, sir,' said Dobby, looking delighted at Harry's enthusiasm. 'We could go now, if you like!'

For a moment Harry was tempted to go with Dobby. He was halfway out of his seat, intending to hurry upstairs for his Invisibility Cloak when, not for the first time, a voice very much like Hermione's whispered in his ear: *reckless*. It was, after all, very late, and he was exhausted.

'Not tonight, Dobby,' said Harry reluctantly, sinking back into his chair. 'This is really important ... I don't want to blow it, it'll need proper planning. Listen, can you just tell me exactly where this Room of Requirement is, and how to get in there?'

Their robes billowed and swirled around them as they splashed across the flooded vegetable patch to double Herbology, where they could hardly hear what Professor Sprout was saying over the hammering of raindrops hard as hailstones on the greenhouse roof. The afternoon's Care of Magical Creatures lesson was to be relocated from the storm-swept grounds to a free classroom on the ground floor and, to their intense relief, Angelina had sought out her team at lunch to tell them that Quidditch practice was cancelled.

'Good,' said Harry quietly, when she told him, 'because we've found somewhere to have our first Defence meeting. Tonight, eight o'clock, seventh floor opposite that tapestry of Barnabas the Barmy being clubbed by those trolls. Can you tell Katie and Alicia?'

She looked slightly taken aback but promised to tell the others. Harry returned hungrily to his sausages and mash. When he looked up to take a drink of pumpkin juice, he found Hermione watching him.

'What?' he said thickly.

'Well ... it's just that Dobby's plans aren't always that safe. Don't you remember when he lost you all the bones in your arm?'

'This room isn't just some mad idea of Dobby's; Dumbledore knows about

第18章 邓布利多军

"有多少人知道它?"哈利坐直了身体。

"很少,先生。人们通常在需要时才会偶然闯进去,但以后就再也找不着它了,因为他们不知道它一直在那儿听候需要,先生。"

"听起来很棒,"哈利说,心跳加快了,"听起来妙极了,多比。你什么时候能带我去看看?"

"什么时候都行,哈利·波特,先生,"看到哈利热切的样子,多比显得很高兴,"如果您愿意,现在就可以去。"

哈利很想马上就去,他正要站起来,打算跑上楼去拿隐形衣,然而(不是第一次),一个很像赫敏的声音在他耳边说:鲁莽。时间毕竟太晚,他已精疲力竭。

"今晚算了,多比,"哈利不情愿地说,又坐回到椅子上,"这件事很重要……我不想办砸,需要周密地计划……你能不能告诉我这个有求必应屋在哪儿,怎么进去?"

他们溅着水花穿过淹了水的菜地去上两节草药课,袍子被吹得鼓鼓的,在风中飘舞。雨点像冰雹一样打着温室的屋顶,几乎听不到斯普劳特教授在说什么。下午的保护神奇动物课从风雨肆虐的户外转移到了一楼的一个空教室里。午饭时安吉利娜跟队员们说魁地奇球训练取消了,大家如释重负。

"正好,"哈利小声说,"因为我们找到了防御小组第一次集会的地方。今晚八点钟,在八楼,巨怪棒打傻巴拿巴的挂毯对面。你能通知凯蒂和艾丽娅吗?"

安吉利娜似乎有些吃惊,但答应通知其他人。哈利继续狼吞虎咽地吃着他的香肠和土豆泥。当他抬起头来喝南瓜汁时,发现赫敏正看着他。

"怎么啦?"他含混地问。

"嗯……多比的计划并不总是那么安全。你不记得是他让你失去了手臂里所有的骨头吗?"

"这间屋子不只是多比的胡思乱想,邓布利多也知道,他在圣诞舞

CHAPTER EIGHTEEN — Dumbledore's Army

it, too, he mentioned it to me at the Yule Ball.'

Hermione's expression cleared.

'Dumbledore told you about it?'

'Just in passing,' said Harry, shrugging.

'Oh, well, that's all right then,' said Hermione briskly and raised no more objections.

Together with Ron they had spent most of the day seeking out those people who had signed their names to the list in the Hog's Head and telling them where to meet that evening. Somewhat to Harry's disappointment, it was Ginny who managed to find Cho Chang and her friend first; however, by the end of dinner he was confident that the news had been passed to every one of the twenty-five people who had turned up in the Hog's Head.

At half past seven Harry, Ron and Hermione left the Gryffindor common room, Harry clutching a certain piece of aged parchment in his hand. Fifth-years were allowed to be out in the corridors until nine o'clock, but all three of them kept looking around nervously as they made their way along the seventh floor.

'Hold it,' Harry warned, unfolding the piece of parchment at the top of the last staircase, tapping it with his wand and muttering, '*I solemnly swear that I am up to no good.*'

A map of Hogwarts appeared on the blank surface of the parchment. Tiny black moving dots, labelled with names, showed where various people were.

'Filch is on the second floor,' said Harry, holding the map close to his eyes, 'and Mrs Norris is on the fourth.'

'And Umbridge?' said Hermione anxiously.

'In her office,' said Harry, pointing. 'OK, let's go.'

They hurried along the corridor to the place Dobby had described to Harry, a stretch of blank wall opposite an enormous tapestry depicting Barnabas the Barmy's foolish attempt to train trolls for the ballet.

'OK,' said Harry quietly, while a moth-eaten troll paused in his relentless clubbing of the would-be ballet teacher to watch them. 'Dobby said to walk past this bit of wall three times, concentrating hard on what we need.'

They did so, turning sharply at the window just beyond the blank stretch of wall, then at the man-sized vase on its other side. Ron had screwed up his eyes in concentration; Hermione was whispering something under her breath; Harry's fists were clenched as he stared ahead of him.

We need somewhere to learn to fight ... he thought. *Just give us a place to practise ... somewhere they can't find us ...*

第18章 邓布利多军

会上跟我提起过。"

赫敏脸色晴朗起来。

"邓布利多跟你说过？"

"顺便提了一句。"哈利耸耸肩。

"噢，那就好。"赫敏轻快地说，没有再提出异议。

他们和罗恩一整天都在分头找在猪头酒吧签名的人，通知晚上开会。哈利有些失望，金妮在他之前找到了秋·张和她的朋友。晚饭结束时，他确信上次去猪头酒吧的二十五个人都得到了消息。

七点半，哈利、罗恩和赫敏离开了格兰芬多的公共休息室，哈利手里握着一片古旧的羊皮纸。虽然五年级学生可以在走廊上待到九点，但当他们三人走向八楼时，还是紧张地左顾右盼。

"等等。"在最后一段楼梯顶上哈利警告地说。他展开羊皮纸，用魔杖敲敲它，轻轻念道："我庄严宣誓我不干好事。"

空白的羊皮纸上出现了一幅霍格沃茨地图，移动的黑点上标着名字，显示出在霍格沃茨的所有人的位置。

"费尔奇在三楼，"哈利把活点地图举到眼前仔细看着，"洛丽丝夫人在五楼。"

"乌姆里奇呢？"赫敏担心地问。

"在她的办公室里。"哈利指着乌姆里奇的位置说，"好，走吧。"

他们迅速穿过走廊，来到多比描述的地方，即画着傻巴拿巴试图教巨怪跳芭蕾舞的巨幅挂毯前，对面是一段白墙。

"到了。"哈利低声说，一个被虫蛀的巨怪停止了痛打这个试图成为芭蕾舞教师的人，扭头注视着他们，"多比说要三次走过这段墙，集中精神想我们需要什么。"

他们照此而行，走到白墙一端的窗户处向后转，走到另一端一人高的花瓶处再折回。罗恩眯着眼集中思想，赫敏小声念念有词，哈利双手握拳目视前方。

我们需要一个学习搏斗的地方……他想，给我们一个练习的场所……不会被发现……

CHAPTER EIGHTEEN   Dumbledore's Army

'Harry!' said Hermione sharply, as they wheeled around after their third walk past.

A highly polished door had appeared in the wall. Ron was staring at it, looking slightly wary. Harry reached out, seized the brass handle, pulled open the door and led the way into a spacious room lit with flickering torches like those that illuminated the dungeons eight floors below.

The walls were lined with wooden bookcases and instead of chairs there were large silk cushions on the floor. A set of shelves at the far end of the room carried a range of instruments such as Sneakoscopes, Secrecy Sensors and a large, cracked Foe-Glass that Harry was sure had hung, the previous year, in the fake Moody's office.

'These will be good when we're practising Stunning,' said Ron enthusiastically, prodding one of the cushions with his foot.

'And just look at these books!' said Hermione excitedly, running a finger along the spines of the large leather-bound tomes. '*A Compendium of Common Curses and their Counter-Actions ... The Dark Arts Outsmarted ... Self-Defensive Spellwork ...* wow ...' She looked around at Harry, her face glowing, and he saw that the presence of hundreds of books had finally convinced Hermione that what they were doing was right. 'Harry, this is wonderful, there's everything we need here!'

And without further ado she slid *Jinxes for the Jinxed* from its shelf, sank on to the nearest cushion and began to read.

There was a gentle knock on the door. Harry looked round. Ginny, Neville, Lavender, Parvati and Dean had arrived.

'Whoa,' said Dean, staring around, impressed. 'What is this place?'

Harry began to explain, but before he had finished more people had arrived and he had to start all over again. By the time eight o'clock arrived, every cushion was occupied. Harry moved across to the door and turned the key protruding from the lock; it clicked in a satisfyingly loud way and everybody fell silent, looking at him. Hermione carefully marked her page of *Jinxes for the Jinxed* and set the book aside.

'Well,' said Harry, slightly nervously. 'This is the place we've found for practice sessions, and you've – er – obviously found it OK.'

'It's fantastic!' said Cho, and several people murmured their agreement.

'It's bizarre,' said Fred, frowning around at it. 'We once hid from Filch in here, remember, George? But it was just a broom cupboard then.'

第18章 邓布利多军

"哈利！"他们第三次转身时，赫敏突然说。

墙上出现了一扇非常光滑的门。罗恩盯着它，心存戒备。哈利伸手握住铜把手，拉开了门，带头走进一间宽敞的屋子，里面像八层楼下面的地下教室里一样点着摇曳的火把。

墙边是一溜木书架，地上没有椅子，但放着缎面的大坐垫。屋子另一头的架子上摆着窥镜、探密器等各种仪器，还有一面有裂缝的大照妖镜，哈利确信就是去年挂在假穆迪办公室里的那面。

"这些练昏迷咒的时候有用。"罗恩用脚踢踢坐垫，兴奋地说。

"看这些书！"赫敏激动地伸出一根手指，从一排排皮面大厚书的书脊上划过，"《普通咒语及解招》……《智胜黑魔法》……《自卫咒语集》……哇……"她回头望着哈利，脸上放光，哈利看出，这几百本书终于让赫敏相信他们的行动是对的了，"哈利，太棒了，我们要的东西应有尽有。"

她立刻从书架上抽出《以毒攻毒集》，坐到最近的垫子上读了起来。

轻轻的敲门声响起，哈利转身一看，金妮、纳威、帕瓦蒂和迪安到了。

"哇，"迪安环顾四周，惊叹道，"这是什么地方？"

哈利开始解释，可是没等他说完，又有人进来了，他只好从头讲起。八点钟时，每个垫子上都坐了人。哈利走到门口，转动锁上的钥匙，发出令人满意的咔嗒一声，大家都安静下来看着他。赫敏仔细地在《以毒攻毒集》的书页上加上标记，把书放到了一边。

"嗯，"哈利有点紧张，"这就是我们找到的练习场所，大家——哦——显然觉得还不错——"

"太妙了！"秋说，有几人小声附和。

"真怪，"弗雷德皱眉打量着四周，"我们在这儿躲过费尔奇，乔治，你还记得吗？可那次它只是个扫帚间……"

CHAPTER EIGHTEEN   Dumbledore's Army

'Hey, Harry, what's this stuff?' asked Dean from the rear of the room, indicating the Sneakoscopes and the Foe-Glass.

'Dark detectors,' said Harry, stepping between the cushions to reach them. 'Basically they all show when Dark wizards or enemies are around, but you don't want to rely on them too much, they can be fooled ...'

He gazed for a moment into the cracked Foe-Glass; shadowy figures were moving around inside it, though none was recognisable. He turned his back on it.

'Well, I've been thinking about the sort of stuff we ought to do first and – er –' He noticed a raised hand. 'What, Hermione?'

'I think we ought to elect a leader,' said Hermione.

'Harry's leader,' said Cho at once, looking at Hermione as though she were mad.

Harry's stomach did yet another back-flip.

'Yes, but I think we ought to vote on it properly,' said Hermione, unperturbed. 'It makes it formal and it gives him authority. So – everyone who thinks Harry ought to be our leader?'

Everybody put up their hand, even Zacharias Smith, though he did it very half-heartedly.

'Er – right, thanks,' said Harry, who could feel his face burning. 'And – *what*, Hermione?'

'I also think we ought to have a name,' she said brightly, her hand still in the air. 'It would promote a feeling of team spirit and unity, don't you think?'

'Can we be the Anti-Umbridge League?' said Angelina hopefully.

'Or the Ministry of Magic are Morons Group?' suggested Fred.

'I was thinking,' said Hermione, frowning at Fred, 'more of a name that didn't tell everyone what we were up to, so we can refer to it safely outside meetings.'

'The Defence Association?' said Cho. 'The DA for short, so nobody knows what we're talking about?'

'Yeah, the DA's good,' said Ginny. 'Only let's make it stand for Dumbledore's Army, because that's the Ministry's worst fear, isn't it?'

There was a good deal of appreciative murmuring and laughter at this.

'All in favour of the DA?' said Hermione bossily, kneeling up on her cushion to count. 'That's a majority – motion passed!'

She pinned the piece of parchment with all of their signatures on it on to the wall and wrote across the top in large letters:

第18章 邓布利多军

"喂,哈利,这是什么?"迪安在后排指着窥镜和照妖镜问。

"黑魔法探测器,"哈利从垫子间走了过去,"一般都用来显示附近有没有黑巫师或敌人活动,但不要太依赖这些仪器,它们可能会受到干扰……"

他朝裂了缝的照妖镜里看了一会儿,有隐约的人影在晃动,但都看不真切。他没再理会它。

"好,我一直在考虑我们首先该干什么——呃——"他发现一只手举了起来,"什么事,赫敏?"

"我想我们应该选一个领导。"赫敏说。

"哈利就是领导。"秋马上说,看她的眼光,好像赫敏疯了似的。

哈利心头又是一跳。

"没错,但我想我们应该正式选举,"赫敏镇静地说,"这样可以正式授权给他。所以——谁觉得哈利应该做我们的领导?"

全体举手,连扎卡赖斯·史密斯也举手了,尽管有点勉强。

"啊——谢谢。"哈利觉得脸上发烧,"还有——什么,赫敏?"

"我还觉得我们应该有个名称,"她清晰地说,手还举在空中,"这可以促进团结,加强集体精神,是不是?"

"叫'反乌姆里奇联盟'行吗?"安吉利娜期待地问。

"或者叫'魔法部是笨蛋小组'?"弗雷德提议。

"我想,"赫敏皱眉望着弗雷德说,"这个名称最好让人看不出我们是干什么的,这样我们可以在外面安全地提到它。"

"防御协会?"秋说,"简称 D.A.,谁也不知道我们在说什么。"

"嘿,D.A. 不错,"金妮说,"但我们把全名叫作'邓布利多军'吧,那可是魔法部最害怕的,对吧?"

一片低低的赞许声和笑声。

"都同意 D.A. 吗?"赫敏像主持人似的问,一边跪起来数人头,"大多数——动议通过了。"

她把签着所有人名字的羊皮纸钉到墙上,在顶端用大字通栏写道:

CHAPTER EIGHTEEN — Dumbledore's Army

DUMBLEDORE'S ARMY

'Right,' said Harry, when she had sat down again, 'shall we get practising then? I was thinking, the first thing we should do is *Expelliarmus*, you know, the Disarming Charm. I know it's pretty basic but I've found it really useful –'

'Oh, *please*,' said Zacharias Smith, rolling his eyes and folding his arms. 'I don't think *Expelliarmus* is exactly going to help us against You-Know-Who, do you?'

'I've used it against him,' said Harry quietly. 'It saved my life in June.'

Smith opened his mouth stupidly. The rest of the room was very quiet.

'But if you think it's beneath you, you can leave,' Harry said.

Smith did not move. Nor did anybody else.

'OK,' said Harry, his mouth slightly drier than usual with all these eyes upon him, 'I reckon we should all divide into pairs and practise.'

It felt very odd to be issuing instructions, but not nearly as odd as seeing them followed. Everybody got to their feet at once and divided up. Predictably, Neville was left partnerless.

'You can practise with me,' Harry told him. 'Right – on the count of three, then – one, two, three –'

The room was suddenly full of shouts of *Expelliarmus*. Wands flew in all directions; missed spells hit books on shelves and sent them flying into the air. Harry was too quick for Neville, whose wand went spinning out of his hand, hit the ceiling in a shower of sparks and landed with a clatter on top of a bookshelf, from which Harry retrieved it with a Summoning Charm. Glancing around, he thought he had been right to suggest they practise the basics first; there was a lot of shoddy spellwork going on; many people were not succeeding in Disarming their opponents at all, but merely causing them to jump backwards a few paces or wince as their feeble spell whooshed over them.

'*Expelliarmus!*' said Neville, and Harry, caught unawares, felt his wand fly out of his hand.

'I DID IT!' said Neville gleefully. 'I've never done it before – I DID IT!'

'Good one!' said Harry encouragingly, deciding not to point out that in a real duel Neville's opponent was unlikely to be staring in the opposite direction with his wand held loosely at his side. 'Listen, Neville, can you take

第18章 邓布利多军

邓布利多军

"很好,"她坐下之后哈利说,"我们开始练习吧?我想第一个要练的是除你武器,大家知道,就是缴械咒。我知道这比较基础,但我觉得它确实有用——"

"哦,拜托,"扎卡赖斯·史密斯抱着胳膊,翻了翻白眼说,"我想除你武器对神秘人不起作用吧?"

"我对他用过,"哈利平静地说,"就在六月份,它救了我的命。"

史密斯呆呆地张着嘴巴,屋里鸦雀无声。

"但如果你不屑于练它,可以离开。"哈利说。

史密斯没有动。其他人也都没动。

"好,"这么多的目光集中在哈利身上,他的嘴有点发干,"我想我们应该分成两人一组进行练习。"

发指示的感觉很怪,而看到指示被执行的感觉更怪。大家立刻站起来两两结对。可以想见,纳威落了单。

"你可以跟我练。"哈利对他说,"好——听我数到三——一、二、三——"

屋里顿时响起一片除你武器的叫喊声,魔杖四处乱飞,打偏了的咒语击中架子上的书籍,一本本的书飞到了空中。哈利身手快,纳威的魔杖旋转着飞出去,撞到天花板上,火星四溅,然后当啷一声落到书架顶上,哈利用召唤咒把它收了回来。他看看周围,感到从基本功练起是对的。许多咒语用得乱七八糟,不少人根本不能解除对手的武器,只能逼着他们往后跳几步或畏缩一下,无力的咒语从他们头上呼啸飞过。

"除你武器!"纳威喝道,哈利猝不及防,魔杖脱手飞出。

"**我成功了!**"纳威欢喜地说,"以前从来没有——**我成功了!**"

"不错!"哈利鼓励地说,决定不指出在真正搏斗时,对手不可能看着别处,魔杖松松握在一边,"纳威,你能不能轮流跟罗恩和赫敏练

CHAPTER EIGHTEEN   Dumbledore's Army

it in turns to practise with Ron and Hermione for a couple of minutes so I can walk around and see how the rest are doing?'

Harry moved off into the middle of the room. Something very odd was happening to Zacharias Smith. Every time he opened his mouth to disarm Anthony Goldstein, his own wand would fly out of his hand, yet Anthony did not seem to be making a sound. Harry did not have to look far to solve the mystery: Fred and George were several feet from Smith and taking it in turns to point their wands at his back.

'Sorry, Harry,' said George hastily, when Harry caught his eye. 'Couldn't resist.'

Harry walked around the other pairs, trying to correct those who were doing the spell wrong. Ginny was teamed with Michael Corner; she was doing very well, whereas Michael was either very bad or unwilling to jinx her. Ernie Macmillan was flourishing his wand unnecessarily, giving his partner time to get in under his guard; the Creevey brothers were enthusiastic but erratic and mainly responsible for all the books leaping off the shelves around them; Luna Lovegood was similarly patchy, occasionally sending Justin Finch-Fletchley's wand spinning out of his hand, at other times merely causing his hair to stand on end.

'OK, stop!' Harry shouted. *'Stop! STOP!'*

I need a whistle, he thought, and immediately spotted one lying on top of the nearest row of books. He caught it up and blew hard. Everyone lowered their wands.

'That wasn't bad,' said Harry, 'but there's definite room for improvement.' Zacharias Smith glared at him. 'Let's try again.'

He moved off around the room again, stopping here and there to make suggestions. Slowly, the general performance improved. He avoided going near Cho and her friend for a while, but after walking twice around every other pair in the room felt he could not ignore them any longer.

'Oh no,' said Cho rather wildly as he approached. *'Expelliarmious!* I mean, *Expellimellius!* I – oh, sorry, Marietta!'

Her curly-haired friend's sleeve had caught fire; Marietta extinguished it with her own wand and glared at Harry as though it was his fault.

'You made me nervous, I was doing all right before then!' Cho told Harry ruefully.

'That was quite good,' Harry lied, but when she raised her eyebrows he said, 'Well, no, it was lousy, but I know you can do it properly, I was watching from over there.'

She laughed. Her friend Marietta looked at them rather sourly and turned away.

第18章 邓布利多军

一会儿,我随便走走,看看大家练得怎么样。"

哈利走到屋子中央,扎卡赖斯·史密斯出了很奇怪的情况,每次他张嘴要解除安东尼·戈德斯坦的武器时,自己的魔杖却飞了出去,而安东尼好像并没有发声。但哈利没多久就解开了谜团,弗雷德和乔治离史密斯不远,两人轮流用魔杖指着他的后背。

"对不起,哈利,"看到哈利的目光,乔治忙说,"没忍住。"

哈利走了一圈,努力纠正做错的人。金妮和迈克尔·科纳一组,她做得很好,迈克尔要么是水平很差,要么是不肯对金妮念这个咒语。厄尼·麦克米兰不必要地挥舞着魔杖,使得对方有时间进行防御。克里维兄弟很热情,但技术不稳定,附近架子上飞起的书大都是他们的功劳。卢娜·洛夫古德也是反复无常,有时能让贾斯廷·芬列里的魔杖旋转着飞出,其他时候则只是让他的头发竖了起来。

"好了,停!"哈利喊道,"停!**停**!"

我需要一个哨子,他这样一想,便马上在最近的一排书上发现了一个。他抓起哨子使劲一吹。大家都垂下了魔杖。

"练得不错,"哈利说,"但还有应该改进的地方。"扎卡赖斯·史密斯瞪着他。"我们再来……"

他又开始在屋里巡视,不时停下来提提意见。大家的技术渐渐改善。他起先避免走近秋和她的朋友,但巡视两圈之后,他觉得不能再忽略她们了。

"哦,"他走近时,秋慌乱地说,"除你武衣!不是,除你火器!不——哦,对不起,玛丽埃塔!"

她那鬈发朋友的袖子着火了。玛丽埃塔用自己的魔杖把火扑灭,然后瞪着哈利,好像是他的错似的。

"你让我紧张了,我原来做得挺好的!"秋懊丧地说。

"很不错,"哈利撒谎道,但看到秋扬起眉毛,忙又改口说,"哦,不,很糟糕,但我知道你能做好,我在那边看到……"

秋笑了起来。玛丽埃塔酸溜溜地看着他们俩,扭身走了。

CHAPTER EIGHTEEN — Dumbledore's Army

'Don't mind her,' Cho muttered. 'She doesn't really want to be here but I made her come with me. Her parents have forbidden her to do anything that might upset Umbridge. You see – her mum works for the Ministry.'

'What about your parents?' asked Harry.

'Well, they've forbidden me to get on the wrong side of Umbridge, too,' said Cho, drawing herself up proudly. 'But if they think I'm not going to fight You-Know-Who after what happened to Cedric –'

She broke off, looking rather confused, and an awkward silence fell between them; Terry Boot's wand went whizzing past Harry's ear and hit Alicia Spinnet hard on the nose.

'Well, my dad is very supportive of any anti-Ministry action!' said Luna Lovegood proudly from just behind Harry; evidently she had been eavesdropping on his conversation while Justin finch-fletchley attempted to disentangle himself from the robes that had flown up over his head. 'He's always saying he'd believe anything of Fudge; I mean, the number of goblins Fudge has had assassinated! And of course he uses the Department of Mysteries to develop terrible poisons, which he secretly feeds to anybody who disagrees with him. And then there's his Umgubular Slashkilter –'

'Don't ask,' Harry muttered to Cho as she opened her mouth, looking puzzled. She giggled.

'Hey, Harry,' Hermione called from the other end of the room, 'have you checked the time?'

He looked down at his watch and was shocked to see it was already ten past nine, which meant they needed to get back to their common rooms immediately or risk being caught and punished by Filch for being out of bounds. He blew his whistle; everybody stopped shouting '*Expelliarmus*' and the last couple of wands clattered to the floor.

'Well, that was pretty good,' said Harry, 'but we've overrun, we'd better leave it here. Same time, same place next week?'

'Sooner!' said Dean Thomas eagerly and many people nodded in agreement.

Angelina, however, said quickly, 'The Quidditch season's about to start, we need team practices too!'

'Let's say next Wednesday night, then,' said Harry, 'we can decide on additional meetings then. Come on, we'd better get going.'

He pulled out the Marauder's Map again and checked it carefully for signs of teachers on the seventh floor. He let them all leave in threes and fours,

第18章 邓布利多军

"别管她，"秋小声说，"她不大想来，是我拖她来的。她父母不许她做触犯乌姆里奇的事情，你知道——她妈妈在部里工作。"

"那你父母呢？"哈利问。

"他们也不让我跟乌姆里奇作对，"秋说，骄傲地挺直了身躯，"但如果他们以为在塞德里克的事之后，我还会不抵抗神秘人——"

她没有说下去，神情显得有些迷茫，两人尴尬地沉默了一阵子。泰瑞·布特的魔杖从哈利耳边呼啸而过，重重地打在艾丽娅·斯平内特的鼻子上。

"我爸爸非常支持反魔法部的行动！"卢娜·洛夫古德在哈利身后自豪地说。她显然偷听了他们的谈话，贾斯廷·芬列里在努力挣脱裹到他头上的袍子。"他总说他相信福吉什么事都干得出来，我是说，看看他派人暗杀了多少妖精！当然，福吉还利用神秘事务司研制可怕的毒药，偷偷地对跟他有分歧的人下药。还有他的阿古巴什吉特——"

"别问。"看到秋困惑地张开嘴巴，哈利说。秋笑了。

"嘿，哈利，"赫敏在屋子另一头喊道，"你看时间了吗？"

哈利低头一看手表，吃了一惊——已经九点十分，他们必须马上回公共休息室了，否则可能会被费尔奇抓到，因为触犯校规受到严惩。他一吹哨子，大家停止了叫嚷"除你武器"，最后几根魔杖噼里啪啦地落到了地上。

"非常好，"哈利说，"但我们超过时间了，就到这里吧。下星期同一时间，同一地点？"

"早点更好！"迪安·托马斯急切地说，不少人点头赞同。

但安吉利娜忙说："魁地奇赛季要开始了，球队也要训练！"

"那就下星期三晚上吧，"哈利说，"到时候再决定其他集会时间……好，我们最好赶快走……"

他又抽出活点地图，仔细查看八楼有没有教师。他让大家三四个人结伴走，然后担心地看着他们的小黑点是否安全回到了宿舍：赫奇

671

CHAPTER EIGHTEEN   Dumbledore's Army

watching their tiny dots anxiously to see that they returned safely to their dormitories: the Hufflepuffs to the basement corridor that also led to the kitchens; the Ravenclaws to a tower on the west side of the castle, and the Gryffindors along the corridor to the Fat Lady's portrait.

'That was really, really good, Harry,' said Hermione, when finally it was just her, Harry and Ron who were left.

'Yeah, it was!' said Ron enthusiastically, as they slipped out of the door and watched it melt back into stone behind them. 'Did you see me disarm Hermione, Harry?'

'Only once,' said Hermione, stung. 'I got you loads more than you got me –'

'I did not only get you once, I got you at least three times –'

'Well, if you're counting the one where you tripped over your own feet and knocked the wand out of my hand –'

They argued all the way back to the common room, but Harry was not listening to them. He had one eye on the Marauder's Map, but he was also thinking of Cho saying he made her nervous.

第18章 邓布利多军

帕奇的回到了那条也通向厨房地下室的走廊，拉文克劳的回到了城堡西面的塔楼，格兰芬多的沿八楼走廊回到了胖夫人肖像前。

"真是太棒了，哈利。"赫敏说，屋里只剩下了她、哈利和罗恩。

"是啊！"罗恩热烈地说，他们溜出门去，看着那扇门在身后重新变成石头，"哈利，你看到我让赫敏的魔杖脱手了吗？"

"只有一次。"赫敏像被刺了一下，"我胜你的次数多得多——"

"不止一次，我胜了你至少三次——"

"哼，如果你算上自己绊了一跤，把我魔杖撞掉的那次——"

他们一路吵回了公共休息室，但哈利没有听，他还在看活点地图，同时回想着秋说的他让她紧张的那句话。

CHAPTER NINETEEN

The Lion and the Serpent

Harry felt as though he were carrying some kind of talisman inside his chest over the following two weeks, a glowing secret that supported him through Umbridge's classes and even made it possible for him to smile blandly as he looked into her horrible bulging eyes. He and the DA were resisting her under her very nose, doing the very thing she and the Ministry most feared, and whenever he was supposed to be reading Wilbert Slinkhard's book during her lessons he dwelled instead on satisfying memories of their most recent meetings, remembering how Neville had successfully disarmed Hermione, how Colin Creevey had mastered the Impediment Jinx after three meetings' hard effort, how Parvati Patil had produced such a good Reductor Curse that she had reduced the table carrying all the Sneakoscopes to dust.

He was finding it almost impossible to fix a regular night of the week for the DA meetings, as they had to accommodate three separate teams' Quidditch practices, which were often rearranged due to bad weather conditions; but Harry was not sorry about this; he had a feeling that it was probably better to keep the timing of their meetings unpredictable. If anyone was watching them, it would be hard to make out a pattern.

Hermione soon devised a very clever method of communicating the time and date of the next meeting to all the members in case they needed to change it at short notice, because it would look suspicious if people from different Houses were seen crossing the Great Hall to talk to each other too often. She gave each of the members of the DA a fake Galleon (Ron became very excited when he first saw the basket and was convinced she was actually giving out gold).

'You see the numerals around the edge of the coins?' Hermione said, holding one up for examination at the end of their fourth meeting. The coin gleamed fat and yellow in the light from the torches. 'On real Galleons that's just a serial

第 19 章

狮子与蛇

此后的两个星期中,哈利觉得他胸口好像戴着护身符,一个热乎乎的秘密支撑着他上完了乌姆里奇的课,甚至使他能看着乌姆里奇可怕的癫蛤蟆眼温和地微笑。他和 D.A. 在乌姆里奇的眼皮底下抵抗她,做着她和魔法部最害怕的事情。每当她的课上要读威尔伯特·斯林卡的书时,哈利就去回忆最近集会的满意片段:纳威如何解除了赫敏的武器,科林·克里维如何在三次集会之后终于掌握了障碍咒,帕瓦蒂·佩蒂尔如何成功地运用粉碎咒把摆满窥镜的桌子变成了尘土。

哈利发现几乎无法把 D.A. 的集会固定在一星期的某个晚上,因为要避开三支魁地奇球队的训练,而且训练时间常因天气情况而变更。但哈利并不烦恼,他觉得集会时间不固定或许更好。如果有人监视他们的话,倒不容易找到规律。

赫敏很快想出了一种很聪明的方式,用来在临时变更的情况下通知所有成员下次集会的时间。因为如果不同学院的人频繁地在礼堂里穿梭交谈,容易引起怀疑。她给每个成员一枚假加隆(罗恩第一次看到篮子时很兴奋,以为赫敏真的在发金币呢)。

"看到硬币边缘的数字了吗?"第四次集会结束时,赫敏举起一枚硬币给大家看。硬币在火把的照耀下发出黄灿灿的光芒,"在真加隆上它只是一个编号,代表铸成这枚硬币的妖精。但这些假币上的数字会变动,显示下次集会的时间。改时间时硬币会发热,如果你把它放在

CHAPTER NINETEEN   The Lion and the Serpent

number referring to the goblin who cast the coin. On these fake coins, though, the numbers will change to reflect the time and date of the next meeting. The coins will grow hot when the date changes, so if you're carrying them in a pocket you'll be able to feel them. We take one each, and when Harry sets the date of the next meeting he'll change the numbers on *his* coin, and because I've put a Protean Charm on them, they'll all change to mimic his.'

A blank silence greeted Hermione's words. She looked around at all the faces upturned to her, rather disconcerted.

'Well – I thought it was a good idea,' she said uncertainly, 'I mean, even if Umbridge asked us to turn out our pockets, there's nothing fishy about carrying a Galleon, is there? But ... well, if you don't want to use them –'

'You can do a Protean Charm?' said Terry Boot.

'Yes,' said Hermione.

'But that's ... that's N.E.W.T. standard, that is,' he said weakly.

'Oh,' said Hermione, trying to look modest. 'Oh ... well ... yes, I suppose it is.'

'How come you're not in Ravenclaw?' he demanded, staring at Hermione with something close to wonder. 'With brains like yours?'

'Well, the Sorting Hat did seriously consider putting me in Ravenclaw during my Sorting,' said Hermione brightly, 'but it decided on Gryffindor in the end. So, does that mean we're using the Galleons?'

There was a murmur of assent and everybody moved forwards to collect one from the basket. Harry looked sideways at Hermione.

'You know what these remind me of?'

'No, what's that?'

'The Death Eaters' scars. Voldemort touches one of them, and all their scars burn, and they know they've got to join him.'

'Well ... yes,' said Hermione quietly, 'that is where I got the idea ... but you'll notice I decided to engrave the date on bits of metal rather than on our members' skin.'

'Yeah ... I prefer your way,' said Harry, grinning, as he slipped his Galleon into his pocket. 'I suppose the only danger with these is that we might accidentally spend them.'

'Fat chance,' said Ron, who was examining his own fake Galleon with a slightly mournful air, 'I haven't got any real Galleons to confuse it with.'

As the first Quidditch match of the season, Gryffindor versus Slytherin,

676

第19章 狮子与蛇

口袋里，就会感觉到。我们每人拿一枚，哈利确定了下次集会时间，就修改他硬币上的数字，大家的硬币都会有同样变化，因为我给它们施了一个变化咒。"

赫敏说完后众人默不作声，她看看一张张仰望着她的面孔，有些发窘。

"嗯——我以为是个好主意，"她没把握地说，"我想，就算乌姆里奇要翻我们的口袋，带一个加隆也没什么可疑的，是不是？可是……好吧，如果你们不想用……"

"你会施变化咒？"泰瑞·布特问。

"会啊。"赫敏说。

"可那是……那是 N.E.W.T. 水平啊。"泰瑞弱弱地说。

"哦，"赫敏努力显得谦虚一些，"哦……啊……是，我想是的……"

"你怎么没在拉文克劳？"泰瑞惊奇地望着赫敏问道，"你有这样的脑子？"

"分院帽是正经考虑过要把我放到拉文克劳的，"赫敏轻松地说，"可最后决定了格兰芬多。那么，我们就用这些加隆啦？"

一片赞同声，每个人上前从篮里拿了一枚金币。哈利斜睨着赫敏。

"你知道这让我想起了什么吗？"

"不知道，什么呀？"

"食死徒的伤疤。伏地魔碰到其中一个人的伤疤，所有人的伤疤都会痛，他们就知道该去找他了。"

"对……"赫敏轻声说，"我就是受了这个启发……但你会发现我决定把时间刻在金属上，而不是成员的皮肤上……"

"嗯……我喜欢你的方式，"哈利笑着把他的加隆揣进了口袋里，"我想唯一的危险是我们可能会不小心把它给花了。"

"机会不大，"罗恩有点悲哀地看着他的假币说，"我没有真加隆跟它混在一起。"

随着本赛季的第一场魁地奇球赛——格兰芬多队与斯莱特林队交

CHAPTER NINETEEN   The Lion and the Serpent

drew nearer, their DA meetings were put on hold because Angelina insisted on almost daily practices. The fact that the Quidditch Cup had not been held for so long added considerably to the interest and excitement surrounding the forthcoming game; the Ravenclaws and Hufflepuffs were taking a lively interest in the outcome, for they, of course, would be playing both teams over the coming year; and the Heads of House of the competing teams, though they attempted to disguise it under a decent pretence of sportsmanship, were determined to see their own side victorious. Harry realised how much Professor McGonagall cared about beating Slytherin when she abstained from giving them homework in the week leading up to the match.

'I think you've got enough to be getting on with at the moment,' she said loftily. Nobody could quite believe their ears until she looked directly at Harry and Ron and said grimly, 'I've become accustomed to seeing the Quidditch Cup in my study, boys, and I really don't want to have to hand it over to Professor Snape, so use the extra time to practise, won't you?'

Snape was no less obviously partisan; he had booked the Quidditch pitch for Slytherin practice so often that the Gryffindors had difficulty getting on it to play. He was also turning a deaf ear to the many reports of Slytherin attempts to hex Gryffindor players in the corridors. When Alicia Spinnet turned up in the hospital wing with her eyebrows growing so thick and fast they obscured her vision and obstructed her mouth, Snape insisted that she must have attempted a Hair-thickening Charm on herself and refused to listen to the fourteen eye-witnesses who insisted they had seen the Slytherin Keeper, Miles Bletchley, hit her from behind with a jinx while she worked in the library.

Harry felt optimistic about Gryffindor's chances; they had, after all, never lost to Malfoy's team. Admittedly, Ron was still not performing to Wood's standard, but he was working extremely hard to improve. His greatest weakness was a tendency to lose confidence after he'd made a blunder; if he let in one goal he became flustered and was therefore likely to miss more. On the other hand, Harry had seen Ron make some truly spectacular saves when he was on form; during one memorable practice he had hung one-handed from his broom and kicked the Quaffle so hard away from the goalhoop that it soared the length of the pitch and through the centre hoop at the other end; the rest of the team felt this save compared favourably with one made recently by Barry Ryan, the Irish International Keeper, against Poland's top Chaser, Ladislaw Zamojski. Even Fred had said that Ron might yet make him and George proud, and that they were seriously considering admitting he was related to them, something they assured him they had been trying to deny for four years.

第19章 狮子与蛇

锋的临近，D.A.的集会暂停了，因为安吉利娜坚持几乎每天训练。魁地奇杯已经长期没有赛事，更增加了人们对这场球赛的兴趣和热情。拉文克劳与赫奇帕奇非常关心比赛结果，因为他们来年要跟这两个队较量。两个学院的院长虽然表面上装得洒脱，很有体育精神的样子，却暗下决心要看到己方取胜。哈利看出麦格教授多么希望他们打败斯莱特林，她在比赛前一星期免除了他们的家庭作业。

"我想你们这一段够忙的了。"她高傲地说，大家都不敢相信自己的耳朵，直到她望着哈利和罗恩严肃地说，"同学们，我已经看惯了魁地奇杯摆在我的书房里，实在不想把它交给斯内普教授，所以请用这多出的时间加强训练，行不行？"

斯内普的偏向也是明摆着的：他老是为斯莱特林队预租球场，使得格兰芬多队很难找到场地训练。他还对多起斯莱特林学生企图在走廊里用魔法坑害格兰芬多球员的报告置若罔闻。当艾丽娅·斯平内特眉毛长得挡住了眼睛和嘴巴、被送进校医院时，斯内普一口咬定是她自己用了生发咒，而不肯听十四个目击者的证词，他们明明看到斯莱特林队守门员迈尔斯·布莱奇在图书馆里从背后对艾丽娅施了魔法。

哈利对格兰芬多队感到乐观，毕竟，他们以前从没有输给过马尔福的球队。不可否认，罗恩的球技还没达到伍德的水平，但他正在刻苦提高。他最大的弱点是犯了错误就会失去信心，一个球没守住，他就心烦意乱，结果丢球更多。但是，哈利也见过罗恩状态好时真正精彩的救球：在一次难忘的训练中，罗恩单手吊在扫帚上，把鬼飞球从球门边大力踢开，使它一直飞到球场另一端，穿过了对方球门中间的圆环。其他队员都认为这个救球，比前不久爱尔兰国家队守门员巴里·瑞安对波兰最好的追球手拉迪斯洛·扎莫斯基的那一球更精彩。就连弗雷德都说，罗恩也许还会让他和乔治感到自豪，他们在认真考虑承认和罗恩有亲戚关系，他告诉罗恩他们四年来一直想否认这一点。

CHAPTER NINETEEN   The Lion and the Serpent

The only thing really worrying Harry was how much Ron was allowing the tactics of the Slytherin team to upset him before they even got on to the pitch. Harry, of course, had endured their snide comments for over four years, so whispers of, 'Hey, Potty, I heard Warrington's sworn to knock you off your broom on Saturday', far from chilling his blood, made him laugh. 'Warrington's aim's so pathetic I'd be more worried if he was aiming for the person next to me,' he retorted, which made Ron and Hermione laugh and wiped the smirk off Pansy Parkinson's face.

But Ron had never endured a relentless campaign of insults, jeers and intimidation. When Slytherins, some of them seventh-years and considerably larger than he was, muttered as they passed in the corridors, 'Got your bed booked in the hospital wing, Weasley?' he didn't laugh, but turned a delicate shade of green. When Draco Malfoy imitated Ron dropping the Quaffle (which he did whenever they came within sight of each other), Ron's ears glowed red and his hands shook so badly that he was likely to drop whatever he was holding at the time, too.

October extinguished itself in a rush of howling winds and driving rain and November arrived, cold as frozen iron, with hard frosts every morning and icy draughts that bit at exposed hands and faces. The skies and the ceiling of the Great Hall turned a pale, pearly grey, the mountains around Hogwarts were snowcapped, and the temperature in the castle dropped so low that many students wore their thick protective dragonskin gloves in the corridors between lessons.

The morning of the match dawned bright and cold. When Harry awoke he looked round at Ron's bed and saw him sitting bolt upright, his arms around his knees, staring fixedly into space.

'You all right?' said Harry.

Ron nodded but did not speak. Harry was reminded forcibly of the time Ron had accidentally put a Slug-vomiting Charm on himself; he looked just as pale and sweaty as he had done then, not to mention as reluctant to open his mouth.

'You just need some breakfast,' Harry said bracingly. 'C'mon.'

The Great Hall was filling up fast when they arrived, the talk louder and the mood more exuberant than usual. As they passed the Slytherin table there was an upsurge of noise. Harry looked round and saw that, in addition to the usual green and silver scarves and hats, every one of them was wearing

第19章 狮子与蛇

唯一真正让哈利担心的是，罗恩在进球场之前就会被斯莱特林队的战术搞得慌了神。哈利当然已经听惯了他们四年多来对他的恶言恶语，所以像"嘿，傻宝宝波特，我听到沃林顿发誓说星期六要把你从扫帚上撞下去"这样的话根本不会让他胆战心惊，只会让他笑笑而已。"沃林顿的准头那么差，如果他要撞的是我旁边的那个人，我会更担心一些。"他的反驳让罗恩和赫敏哈哈大笑，潘西·帕金森脸上得意的笑容消失了。

但罗恩没有经受过这种侮辱、讥讽和恫吓的无情攻势。当一些斯莱特林的学生（其中有比他块头大得多的七年级学生）在他们从走廊里走过时低声说："在校医院订好床位了吗，韦斯莱？"罗恩没有笑，而是脸色有点发绿。当德拉科·马尔福模仿罗恩漏接鬼飞球（每次他们见面时，他都会这么做）时，罗恩耳根通红，双手发抖，手上拿着什么都会掉。

十月在狂风暴雨中结束，十一月来临了，寒如冻铁，每天早晨都是一层坚霜，冰冷的风割着露在外面的手和面颊。天空和礼堂的天花板变成了淡淡的苍灰色，霍格沃茨周围的群山戴上了雪帽，城堡里的气温下降了那么多，课间在走廊上时，许多学生都戴着厚厚的火龙皮手套。

比赛那天的清晨，天气晴朗而寒冷。哈利醒过来看看罗恩的床，只见他坐得笔直，手臂抱着膝盖，目光呆滞。

"你没事吧？"哈利问。

罗恩点点头，但没有说话。哈利不禁想起罗恩不慎对自己施了吐鼻涕虫咒的情景，此刻他看上去和当时一样，面色苍白，汗津津的，而且同样不肯张嘴。

"你需要吃点早饭，"哈利鼓励地说，"走。"

他们走进礼堂时，里面的人正迅速多起来，说话声比往常更响，气氛也更热烈。他们走过斯莱特林餐桌时，听见了一阵喧哗。哈利环顾左右，看到每个人不仅和平时一样穿戴着银绿相间的围巾和帽子，还多戴了一枚皇冠状的银徽章。不知什么原因，他们中的许多人都一

CHAPTER NINETEEN   The Lion and the Serpent

a silver badge in the shape of what seemed to be a crown. For some reason many of them waved at Ron, laughing uproariously. Harry tried to see what was written on the badges as he walked by, but he was too concerned to get Ron past their table quickly to linger long enough to read them.

They received a rousing welcome at the Gryffindor table, where everyone was wearing red and gold, but far from raising Ron's spirits the cheers seemed to sap the last of his morale; he collapsed on to the nearest bench looking as though he were facing his final meal.

'I must've been mental to do this,' he said in a croaky whisper. '*Mental.*'

'Don't be thick,' said Harry firmly, passing him a choice of cereals, 'you're going to be fine. It's normal to be nervous.'

'I'm rubbish,' croaked Ron. 'I'm lousy. I can't play to save my life. What was I thinking?'

'Get a grip,' said Harry sternly. 'Look at that save you made with your foot the other day, even Fred and George said it was brilliant.'

Ron turned a tortured face to Harry.

'That was an accident,' he whispered miserably. 'I didn't mean to do it – I slipped off my broom when none of you were looking and when I was trying to get back on I kicked the Quaffle by accident.'

'Well,' said Harry, recovering quickly from this unpleasant surprise, 'a few more accidents like that and the game's in the bag, isn't it?'

Hermione and Ginny sat down opposite them wearing red and gold scarves, gloves and rosettes.

'How're you feeling?' Ginny asked Ron, who was now staring into the dregs of milk at the bottom of his empty cereal bowl as though seriously considering attempting to drown himself in them.

'He's just nervous,' said Harry.

'Well, that's a good sign, I never feel you perform as well in exams if you're not a bit nervous,' said Hermione heartily.

'Hello,' said a vague and dreamy voice from behind them. Harry looked up: Luna Lovegood had drifted over from the Ravenclaw table. Many people were staring at her and a few were openly laughing and pointing; she had managed to procure a hat shaped like a life-size lion's head, which was perched precariously on her head.

'I'm supporting Gryffindor,' said Luna, pointing unnecessarily at her hat. 'Look what it does ...'

第19章 狮子与蛇

边朝罗恩挥手,一边放声大笑。哈利想看清徽章上是什么字,但他急于带罗恩赶快走过这张餐桌,没来得及细看。

他们在格兰芬多的餐桌旁受到了热烈欢迎,这里的每个人都是金红相间的围巾和帽子。可是欢呼声不仅没使罗恩振作起来,反倒似乎吸走了他最后的一点士气。他颓然坐到最近的一张凳子上,好像面前是他的断头饭。

"我这么做准是疯了,"他声音沙哑地低声说,"疯了。"

"别胡说,"哈利严厉地说,递给他一些麦片,"你没问题,紧张是正常的。"

"我是废物,"罗恩说,"我没用,我根本打不了球。我是怎么想的?"

"别泄气,"哈利坚定地说,"看看你那天用脚救的那个球,连弗雷德和乔治都说精彩——"

罗恩痛苦地看着哈利。

"那是意外,"他可怜巴巴地小声说,"是撞上的——当时我从扫帚上滑了下去,你们都没看见,我正想法爬上去时,碰巧踢到了鬼飞球。"

"哦,"哈利迅速从这个扫兴的意外中恢复过来,"再来几次这样的意外,我们就赢定了,是不是?"

赫敏和金妮坐在他们对面,戴着金红相间的围巾、手套,还有玫瑰形的徽章。

"你感觉怎么样?"金妮问罗恩,罗恩正盯着空了的麦片碗底剩下的牛奶,像在认真考虑是否要把自己溺死在里面。

"他只是有些紧张。"哈利说。

"那是好现象,我发现一点不紧张时考试就考不好。"赫敏热情地说。

"你们好。"一个梦呓般的声音在他们身后说。哈利抬起头来:卢娜·洛夫古德从拉文克劳餐桌旁溜达过来。许多人在看着她,有的公然笑着对她指指点点。她搞了一顶狮头形状的帽子,有真狮子头那么大,摇摇欲坠地戴在头上。

"我支持格兰芬多,"卢娜不必要地指着她的帽子说,"看它会干什么……"

CHAPTER NINETEEN   The Lion and the Serpent

She reached up and tapped the hat with her wand. It opened its mouth wide and gave an extremely realistic roar that made everyone in the vicinity jump.

'It's good, isn't it?' said Luna happily. 'I wanted to have it chewing up a serpent to represent Slytherin, you know, but there wasn't time. Anyway ... good luck, Ronald!'

She drifted away. They had not quite recovered from the shock of Luna's hat before Angelina came hurrying towards them, accompanied by Katie and Alicia, whose eyebrows had mercifully been returned to normal by Madam Pomfrey.

'When you're ready,' she said, 'we're going to go straight down to the pitch, check out conditions and change.'

'We'll be there in a bit,' Harry assured her. 'Ron's just got to have some breakfast.'

It became clear after ten minutes, however, that Ron was not capable of eating anything more and Harry thought it best to get him down to the changing rooms. As they rose from the table, Hermione got up, too, and taking Harry's arm she drew him to one side.

'Don't let Ron see what's on those Slytherins' badges,' she whispered urgently.

Harry looked questioningly at her, but she shook her head warningly; Ron had just ambled over to them, looking lost and desperate.

'Good luck, Ron,' said Hermione, standing on tiptoe and kissing him on the cheek. 'And you, Harry –'

Ron seemed to come to himself slightly as they walked back across the Great Hall. He touched the spot on his face where Hermione had kissed him, looking puzzled, as though he was not quite sure what had just happened. He seemed too distracted to notice much around him, but Harry cast a curious glance at the crown-shaped badges as they passed the Slytherin table, and this time he made out the words etched on to them:

Weasley is our King

第19章 狮子与蛇

她伸手用魔杖敲了敲帽子,狮头张开大嘴,发出一声逼真的狮吼,把周围人都吓了一跳。

"不错吧?"卢娜快活地说,"我本来想让它咀嚼一条象征斯莱特林的蛇,可是来不及了。不管怎样……祝你好运,罗恩!"

她飘然而去。大家还没从她那顶帽子的惊吓中恢复过来,只见安吉利娜带着凯蒂和艾丽娅匆匆走来,艾丽娅的眉毛总算被庞弗雷女士变回正常了。

"大家准备好之后,"安吉利娜说,"我们就直接去球场,查看情况,换衣服。"

"我们一会儿就去,"哈利向她保证,"罗恩要吃点早饭。"

十分钟后,罗恩显然什么也吃不下了,哈利觉得最好还是带他去更衣室。他们起身时,赫敏也站了起来,她抓住哈利的胳膊,把他拉到一边。

"别让罗恩看到斯莱特林徽章上的字。"她急切地说。

哈利询问地望着她,但她警告地摇摇头。罗恩已经慢慢走了过来,表情茫然而绝望。

"祝你好运,罗恩,"赫敏踮起脚亲了亲他的面颊,"还有你,哈利——"

穿过礼堂时,罗恩似乎清醒了一些,摸着面颊上被赫敏亲过的地方,显得有些困惑,仿佛不明白发生了什么。他似乎已经注意不到周围的事情。但哈利走过斯莱特林餐桌时,好奇地瞥了一眼那些皇冠状的徽章,这次他看清了上面刻的字:

韦斯莱是我们的王

Weasley is our King

CHAPTER NINETEEN   The Lion and the Serpent

With an unpleasant feeling that this could mean nothing good, he hurried Ron across the Entrance Hall, down the stone steps and out into the icy air.

The frosty grass crunched under their feet as they hurried down the sloping lawns towards the stadium. There was no wind at all and the sky was a uniform pearly white, which meant that visibility would be good without the drawback of direct sunlight in the eyes. Harry pointed out these encouraging factors to Ron as they walked, but he was not sure that Ron was listening.

Angelina had changed already and was talking to the rest of the team when they entered. Harry and Ron pulled on their robes (Ron attempted to do his up back-to-front for several minutes before Alicia took pity on him and went to help), then sat down to listen to the prematch talk while the babble of voices outside grew steadily louder as the crowd came pouring out of the castle towards the pitch.

'OK, I've only just found out the final line-up for Slytherin,' said Angelina, consulting a piece of parchment. 'Last year's Beaters, Derrick and Bole, have left, but it looks as though Montague's replaced them with the usual gorillas, rather than anyone who can fly particularly well. They're two blokes called Crabbe and Goyle, I don't know much about them –'

'We do,' said Harry and Ron together.

'Well, they don't look bright enough to tell one end of a broom from the other,' said Angelina, pocketing her parchment, 'but then I was always surprised Derrick and Bole managed to find their way on to the pitch without signposts.'

'Crabbe and Goyle are in the same mould,' Harry assured her.

They could hear hundreds of footsteps mounting the banked benches of the spectators' stands. Some people were singing, though Harry could not make out the words. He was starting to feel nervous, but he knew his butterflies were as nothing compared to Ron's, who was clutching his stomach and staring straight ahead again, his jaw set and his complexion pale grey.

'It's time,' said Angelina in a hushed voice, looking at her watch. 'C'mon everyone ... good luck.'

The team rose, shouldered their brooms and marched in single file out of the changing room and into the dazzling sky. A roar of sound greeted them in which Harry could still hear singing, though it was muffled by the cheers and whistles.

The Slytherin team was standing waiting for them. They, too, were wearing those silver crown-shaped badges. The new Captain, Montague,

第19章 狮子与蛇

他感到这不会是什么好话,便赶快带着罗恩穿过门厅,下了石阶,走入寒冷的空气中。

结霜的草地在脚下嘎吱嘎吱地响,他们匆匆走下斜坡,赶往体育场。没有风,天空是均匀的珠白色,这意味着能见度较好,不会有阳光刺眼。哈利一边走一边向罗恩指出这些有利条件,但搞不清罗恩听到了没有。

安吉利娜已经换好衣服,正在对其他队员讲话。哈利和罗恩套上球袍(罗恩一开始穿反了,半天也穿不上去,几分钟后艾丽娅动了恻隐之心,过来帮了一把),坐下来听赛前训话,外面的人声越来越响,人们从城堡拥向了球场。

"我看到了斯莱特林的最后阵容,"安吉利娜看着一张羊皮纸说,"去年的击球手德里克和博尔走了,但蒙太好像新找了两只普通的大猩猩,而不是飞行高手。这两人叫克拉布和高尔,我不大了解他们——"

"我们了解。"哈利和罗恩一起说。

"他们好像连扫帚的头尾都分不清。"安吉利娜收起羊皮纸说,"不过话说回来,我一直奇怪德里克和博尔不靠路标是怎么找到球场的。"

"克拉布和高尔也是一路货。"哈利安慰她说。

他们听到无数双脚登上看台的声音。有人在唱歌,但哈利听不清歌词。他开始感到紧张,但知道他的不安与罗恩的相比微不足道。罗恩捂着肚子,目光又变得呆滞了,表情僵硬,脸色灰白。

"到时间了,"安吉利娜看看表,小声说,"走吧……祝我们好运。"

队员们站了起来,扛起飞天扫帚,列队走出更衣室,飞到炫目的天空中,受到雷鸣般的欢迎,哈利还能听到歌声,尽管被欢呼声和口哨声所掩盖。

斯莱特林队员已经站在那里,也戴着皇冠状的银徽章。新队长蒙太身材与达力相仿,粗大的前臂像带毛的火腿。他身后是几乎同样粗壮的克拉布和高尔,他们俩蠢笨地眨着眼睛,挥舞着新发的球棒。马

CHAPTER NINETEEN   The Lion and the Serpent

was built along the same lines as Dudley Dursley, with massive forearms like hairy hams. Behind him lurked Crabbe and Goyle, almost as large, blinking stupidly, swinging their new Beaters' bats. Malfoy stood to one side, the sunlight gleaming on his white-blond head. He caught Harry's eye and smirked, tapping the crown-shaped badge on his chest.

'Captains, shake hands,' ordered the referee Madam Hooch, as Angelina and Montague reached each other. Harry could tell that Montague was trying to crush Angelina's fingers, though she did not wince. 'Mount your brooms ...'

Madam Hooch placed her whistle in her mouth and blew.

The balls were released and the fourteen players shot upwards. Out of the corner of his eye Harry saw Ron streak off towards the goalhoops. Harry zoomed higher, dodging a Bludger, and set off on a wide lap of the pitch, gazing around for a glint of gold; on the other side of the stadium, Draco Malfoy was doing exactly the same.

'And it's Johnson – Johnson with the Quaffle, what a player that girl is, I've been saying it for years but she still won't go out with me –'

'JORDAN!' yelled Professor McGonagall.

'– just a fun fact, Professor, adds a bit of interest – and she's ducked Warrington, she's passed Montague, she's – ouch – been hit from behind by a Bludger from Crabbe ... Montague catches the Quaffle, Montague heading back up the pitch and – nice Bludger there from George Weasley, that's a Bludger to the head for Montague, he drops the Quaffle, caught by Katie Bell, Katie Bell of Gryffindor reverse-passes to Alicia Spinnet and Spinnet's away –'

Lee Jordan's commentary rang through the stadium and Harry listened as hard as he could through the wind whistling in his ears and the din of the crowd, all yelling and booing and singing.

'– dodges Warrington, avoids a Bludger – close call, Alicia – and the crowd are loving this, just listen to them, what's that they're singing?'

And as Lee paused to listen, the song rose loud and clear from the sea of green and silver in the Slytherin section of the stands:

> *'Weasley cannot save a thing,*
> *He cannot block a single ring,*
> *That's why Slytherins all sing:*
> *Weasley is our King.*

尔福站在旁边,阳光照在他淡金色的头发上闪闪发亮。他捕捉到了哈利的目光,拍拍胸口的银徽章,得意地笑了。

"双方队长握手。"裁判霍琦女士喊道,安吉利娜和蒙太走到了一起。哈利看得出蒙太想捏断安吉利娜的手指,但安吉利娜没有畏缩。"骑上扫帚……"

霍琦女士把哨子塞进嘴里用力一吹。

开球了,十四名球员腾空而起,哈利用眼角的余光看见罗恩直奔球门的圆环。哈利急速上升,躲开了一个游走球,开始绕着大圈飞行,四下寻找一点金光。在运动场的另一端,德拉科·马尔福也是如此。

"约翰逊,约翰逊抢到了鬼飞球,这姑娘打得真好,这话我都说好几年了,她还不肯跟我约会——"

"**乔丹**!"麦格教授喊道。

"开个玩笑,教授,加一点作料——她躲过了沃林顿,闪过了蒙太,她——哎哟——她被身后来的游走球击中了,克拉布打来的……蒙太抓住了鬼飞球,蒙太带球往回冲——乔治·韦斯莱打出一个漂亮的游走球,奔着蒙太的头部飞去,蒙太丢掉了鬼飞球,被凯蒂·贝尔抓起,格兰芬多的凯蒂·贝尔反传给艾丽娅·斯平内特,斯平内特马上——"

李·乔丹的解说在球场上回响,哈利竭力聆听,耳边是呼啸的风声和观众的喧嚣,他们在高声喊叫,喝倒彩,唱歌。

"躲过了沃林顿,避开一个游走球——好悬哪,艾丽娅——观众喜欢这个,听听这声音,他们在唱什么?"

李·乔丹停下来听时,歌声响亮地从看台上斯莱特林那一片银绿相间的海洋中扬起:

> 韦斯莱那个小傻样,
> 他一个球也不会挡,
> 斯莱特林人放声唱:
> 韦斯莱是我们的王。

CHAPTER NINETEEN   The Lion and the Serpent

> *'Weasley was born in a bin*
> *He always lets the Quaffle in*
> *Weasley will make sure we win*
> *Weasley is our King.'*

'– and Alicia passes back to Angelina!' Lee shouted, and as Harry swerved, his insides boiling at what he had just heard, he knew Lee was trying to drown out the words of the song. 'Come on now, Angelina – looks like she's got just the Keeper to beat! – SHE SHOOTS – SHE – aaaah …'

Bletchley, the Slytherin Keeper, had saved the goal; he threw the Quaffle to Warrington who sped off with it, zigzagging in between Alicia and Katie; the singing from below grew louder and louder as he drew nearer and nearer Ron.

> *'Weasley is our King,*
> *Weasley is our King,*
> *He always lets the Quaffle in*
> *Weasley is our King.'*

Harry could not help himself: abandoning his search for the Snitch, he turned his Firebolt towards Ron, a lone figure at the far end of the pitch, hovering before the three goalhoops while the massive Warrington pelted towards him.

'– and it's Warrington with the Quaffle, Warrington heading for goal, he's out of Bludger range with just the Keeper ahead –'

A great swell of song rose from the Slytherin stands below:

> *'Weasley cannot save a thing,*
> *He cannot block a single ring …'*

'– so it's the first test for new Gryffindor Keeper Weasley, brother of Beaters Fred and George, and a promising new talent on the team – come on, Ron!'

> 韦斯莱生在垃圾箱，
> 他总把球往门里放，
> 韦斯莱保我赢这场，
> 韦斯莱是我们的王。

"——艾丽娅把球回传给安吉利娜！"李叫道。哈利拨转方向，感到五脏六腑都在翻腾，他知道李·乔丹努力想把歌声盖过去。"加油，安吉利娜——看来她只有守门员要对付了！——她射门了——她——啊……"

斯莱特林队守门员布莱奇把球扑住了，他把鬼飞球抛给沃林顿，沃林顿带球疾驰，绕过了艾丽娅和凯蒂。他离罗恩越来越近，下面的歌声也越来越响——

> 韦斯莱是我们的王，
> 韦斯莱是我们的王，
> 他总把球往门里放，
> 韦斯莱是我们的王。

哈利无法控制自己，他顾不上寻找金色飞贼，掉转火弩箭注视着罗恩，球场另一头那个孤单的身影守在三个球门圆环前，魁梧的沃林顿在向他飞驰。

"——沃林顿拿到了鬼飞球，沃林顿朝球门冲去，游走球追不上他了，前面只有守门员——"

斯莱特林的看台上的歌声突然嘹亮起来：

> 韦斯莱那个小傻样，
> 他一个球也不会挡……

"——现在是对格兰芬多的新守门员韦斯莱的第一个考验，他是击球手弗雷德和乔治的弟弟，球队的后起之秀——加油，罗恩！"

CHAPTER NINETEEN   The Lion and the Serpent

But the scream of delight came from the Slytherins' end: Ron had dived wildly, his arms wide, and the Quaffle had soared between them straight through Ron's central hoop.

'Slytherin score!' came Lee's voice amid the cheering and booing from the crowds below, 'so that's ten–nil to Slytherin – bad luck, Ron.'

The Slytherins sang even louder:

*'WEASLEY WAS BORN IN A BIN
HE ALWAYS LETS THE QUAFFLE IN ...'*

'– and Gryffindor back in possession and it's Katie Bell tanking up the pitch –' cried Lee valiantly, though the singing was now so deafening that he could hardly make himself heard above it.

*'WEASLEY WILL MAKE SURE WE WIN
WEASLEY IS OUR KING ...'*

'Harry, WHAT ARE YOU DOING?' screamed Angelina, soaring past him to keep up with Katie. 'GET GOING!'

Harry realised he had been stationary in midair for over a minute, watching the progress of the match without sparing a thought for the whereabouts of the Snitch; horrified, he went into a dive and started circling the pitch again, staring around, trying to ignore the chorus now thundering through the stadium:

*'WEASLEY IS OUR KING,
WEASLEY IS OUR KING ...'*

There was no sign of the Snitch anywhere he looked; Malfoy was still circling the stadium just as he was. They passed one another midway around the pitch, going in opposite directions, and Harry heard Malfoy singing loudly:

'WEASLEY WAS BORN IN A BIN ...'

'– and it's Warrington again,' bellowed Lee, 'who passes to Pucey, Pucey's

第19章 狮子与蛇

但欢呼声从斯莱特林那一方发出：罗恩张着胳膊一扑，鬼飞球从他腋下飞过，径直穿入中间的那个圆环。

"斯莱特林得分！"李的声音在看台上的观众发出的喝彩声和嘘声中响起，"十比零，斯莱特林领先——罗恩运气不佳……"

斯莱特林的人唱得更响了：

> 韦斯莱生在垃圾箱，
> 他总把球往门里放……

"——格兰芬多又控制了球，凯蒂·贝尔在场上飞驰——"李·乔丹英勇地喊道，尽管歌声现已震耳欲聋，他的声音几乎听不见了。

> 韦斯莱保我赢这场，
> 韦斯莱是我们的王……

"哈利，你在干什么？"安吉利娜尖叫着从他身边飞过，去追赶凯蒂，"动起来！"

哈利发现自己在空中静止了一分多钟，只顾观看比赛战况，想都没想要去寻找飞贼。他吓了一跳，急忙俯冲，又开始绕球场兜圈子，瞪大眼睛搜寻，努力不去理会现已响彻全场的合唱：

> 韦斯莱是我们的王，
> 韦斯莱是我们的王……

不见飞贼的踪影，马尔福也和哈利一样在兜圈子。他们擦肩而过，哈利听到马尔福高声唱着：

> 韦斯莱生在垃圾箱……

"——又是沃林顿，"李·乔丹高吼，"传给了普塞，普塞越过了斯

CHAPTER NINETEEN   The Lion and the Serpent

off past Spinnet, come on now, Angelina, you can take him – turns out you can't – but nice Bludger from Fred Weasley, I mean, George Weasley, oh, who cares, one of them, anyway, and Warrington drops the Quaffle and Katie Bell – er – drops it, too – so that's Montague with the Quaffle, Slytherin Captain Montague takes the Quaffle and he's off up the pitch, come on now, Gryffindor, block him!'

Harry zoomed around the end of the stadium behind the Slytherin goalhoops, willing himself not to look at what was going on at Ron's end. As he sped past the Slytherin Keeper, he heard Bletchley singing along with the crowd below:

'WEASLEY CANNOT SAVE A THING ...'

'– and Pucey's dodged Alicia again and he's heading straight for goal, stop it, Ron!'

Harry did not have to look to see what had happened: there was a terrible groan from the Gryffindor end, coupled with fresh screams and applause from the Slytherins. Looking down, Harry saw the pug-faced Pansy Parkinson right at the front of the stands, her back to the pitch as she conducted the Slytherin supporters who were roaring:

*'THAT'S WHY SLYTHERINS ALL SING
WEASLEY IS OUR KING.'*

But twenty–nil was nothing, there was still time for Gryffindor to catch up or catch the Snitch. A few goals and they would be in the lead as usual, Harry assured himself, bobbing and weaving through the other players in pursuit of something shiny that turned out to be Montague's watchstrap.

But Ron let in two more goals. There was an edge of panic in Harry's desire to find the Snitch now. If he could just get it soon and finish the game quickly.

'– and Katie Bell of Gryffindor dodges Pucey, ducks Montague, nice swerve, Katie, and she throws to Johnson, Angelina Johnson takes the Quaffle, she's past Warrington, she's heading for goal, come on now, Angelina – GRYFFINDOR SCORE! It's forty–ten, forty–ten to Slytherin and Pucey has the Quaffle ...'

Harry could hear Luna's ludicrous lion hat roaring amidst the Gryffindor cheers and felt heartened; only thirty points in it, that was nothing, they could

第 19 章 狮子与蛇

平内特，安吉利娜加油，你能追上他——结果并没能——但弗雷德·韦斯莱打出了一个漂亮的游走球，不，是乔治·韦斯莱，咳，管他呢，反正是他们俩中的一个。沃林顿丢掉了鬼飞球，凯蒂·贝尔——呃——也丢掉了……现在是蒙太拿到了鬼飞球，斯莱特林的队长蒙太拿到了鬼飞球，正朝前场冲去，格兰芬多加油，拦住他！"

哈利从斯莱特林的球门后面绕过，强迫自己不去看罗恩那头的情况。越过斯莱特林的守门员时，他听到布莱奇和下面的人一起唱着：

韦斯莱那个小傻样……

"——普塞又躲过了艾丽娅，直奔球门而去，扑住它，罗恩！"
哈利不用看就知道发生了什么：格兰芬多一方发出痛苦的呻吟，而斯莱特林们爆发出尖叫声和鼓掌声。哈利向下望去，看到脸长得像狮子狗的潘西·帕金森背对球场站在看台前，指挥着斯莱特林的啦啦队高唱：

**斯莱特林人放声唱，
韦斯莱是我们的王。**

但二十比零不算什么，格兰芬多还有时间追上比分或抓住飞贼，只要进几个球，他们就又能像以往一样领先了，哈利安慰着自己。他在其他球员之间上下穿行，追着一个亮闪闪的东西，不料却是蒙太的表带……

可是罗恩又让对方进了两个球。哈利寻找飞贼的动机里有了惶恐的成分。他只盼着快点找到它，结束这场比赛……

"——格兰芬多的凯蒂·贝尔带球晃过普塞，又躲开了蒙太，好身法，凯蒂，她把球传给约翰逊。安吉利娜·约翰逊接住鬼飞球，甩掉了沃林顿，冲向球门。加油，安吉利娜——**格兰芬多得分**！四十比十，斯莱特林四十比十领先，普塞得到了鬼飞球……"

哈利听见卢娜那顶滑稽的狮子帽在格兰芬多的欢呼声中咆哮，深受鼓舞，只差三十分，没什么，很容易追平。哈利躲开克拉布向他径

695

CHAPTER NINETEEN The Lion and the Serpent

pull back easily. Harry ducked a Bludger that Crabbe had sent rocketing in his direction and resumed his frantic scouring of the pitch for the Snitch, keeping one eye on Malfoy in case he showed signs of having spotted it, but Malfoy, like him, was continuing to soar around the stadium, searching fruitlessly ...

'– Pucey throws to Warrington, Warrington to Montague, Montague back to Pucey – Johnson intervenes, Johnson takes the Quaffle, Johnson to Bell, this looks good – I mean bad – Bell's hit by a Bludger from Goyle of Slytherin and it's Pucey in possession again ...'

'WEASLEY WAS BORN IN A BIN
HE ALWAYS LETS THE QUAFFLE IN
WEASLEY WILL MAKE SURE WE WIN ...'

But Harry had seen it at last: the tiny fluttering Golden Snitch was hovering feet from the ground at the Slytherin end of the pitch.

He dived ...

In a matter of seconds, Malfoy was streaking out of the sky on Harry's left, a green and silver blur lying flat on his broom ...

The Snitch skirted the foot of one of the goalhoops and scooted off towards the other side of the stands; its change of direction suited Malfoy, who was nearer; Harry pulled his Firebolt around, he and Malfoy were now neck and neck ...

Feet from the ground, Harry lifted his right hand from his broom, stretching towards the Snitch ... to his right, Malfoy's arm extended too, was reaching, groping ...

It was over in two breathless, desperate, windswept seconds – Harry's fingers closed around the tiny, struggling ball – Malfoy's fingernails scrabbled the back of Harry's hand hopelessly – Harry pulled his broom upwards, holding the struggling ball in his hand and the Gryffindor spectators screamed their approval ...

They were saved, it did not matter that Ron had let in those goals, nobody would remember as long as Gryffindor had won –

WHAM.

A Bludger hit Harry squarely in the small of the back and he flew forwards off his broom. Luckily he was only five or six feet above the ground,

第19章 狮子与蛇

直射来的一个游走球,继续在场中疯狂地搜索金色飞贼,一边留意着马尔福是否发现了它,但马尔福和他一样绕场奔驰,一无所获……

"——普塞传给沃林顿,沃林顿传给蒙太,蒙太又传给普塞——约翰逊抢断,约翰逊拿到了鬼飞球,传给贝尔,看上去不错——不好——贝尔被斯莱特林队员高尔打出的游走球击中,普塞又拿到了球……"

**韦斯莱生在垃圾箱,
他总把球往门里放,
韦斯莱保我赢这场——**

哈利终于看到了,小小的、忽闪忽闪的金色飞贼,正在斯莱特林那端的球场上方几英尺处盘旋。

他俯冲过去……

一刹那间,马尔福从哈利左边冲出,一道银绿相间的身影伏在扫帚上……

飞贼绕过球门圆环的柱脚,向看台另一侧飞去,这一转向对马尔福十分有利,他离得更近。哈利拨转火弩箭,他和马尔福现在并驾齐驱……

离地面几英尺时,哈利右手放开扫帚把,伸向飞贼……在他右边,马尔福的手臂也伸了出去,抓够着……

在风声呼啸的千钧一发之际,一切都结束了——哈利的手指握住了小小的、挣扎着的金球——马尔福的指甲绝望地抓向了哈利的手背——哈利一拨飞天扫帚腾空升起,手里攥着还在挣扎的小球,格兰芬多的支持者高声叫好……

他们得救了,虽然罗恩放进了那么多球,但只要格兰芬多获胜,没人会记得——

砰!

一个游走球正中哈利的后腰,他从扫帚上飞了出去,幸好他抓飞贼时俯冲而下,离地面只有五六英尺了,但还是被打得喘不过气来,

697

CHAPTER NINETEEN   The Lion and the Serpent

having dived so low to catch the Snitch, but he was winded all the same as he landed flat on his back on the frozen pitch. He heard Madam Hooch's shrill whistle, an uproar in the stands compounded of catcalls, angry yells and jeering, a thud, then Angelina's frantic voice.

'Are you all right?'

'Course I am,' said Harry grimly, taking her hand and allowing her to pull him to his feet. Madam Hooch was zooming towards one of the Slytherin players above him, though he could not see who it was from this angle.

'It was that thug Crabbe,' said Angelina angrily, 'he whacked the Bludger at you the moment he saw you'd got the Snitch – but we won, Harry, we won!'

Harry heard a snort from behind him and turned around, still holding the Snitch tightly in his hand: Draco Malfoy had landed close by. White-faced with fury, he was still managing to sneer.

'Saved Weasley's neck, haven't you?' he said to Harry. 'I've never seen a worse Keeper ... but then he was *born in a bin* ... did you like my lyrics, Potter?'

Harry didn't answer. He turned away to meet the rest of the team who were now landing one by one, yelling and punching the air in triumph; all except Ron, who had dismounted from his broom over by the goalposts and seemed to be making his way slowly back to the changing rooms alone.

'We wanted to write another couple of verses!' Malfoy called, as Katie and Alicia hugged Harry. 'But we couldn't find rhymes for fat and ugly – we wanted to sing about his mother, see –'

'Talk about sour grapes,' said Angelina, casting Malfoy a disgusted look.

'– we couldn't fit in *useless loser* either – for his father, you know –'

Fred and George had realised what Malfoy was talking about. Halfway through shaking Harry's hand, they stiffened, looking round at Malfoy.

'Leave it!' said Angelina at once, taking Fred by the arm. 'Leave it, Fred, let him yell, he's just sore he lost, the jumped-up little –'

'– but you like the Weasleys, don't you, Potter?' said Malfoy, sneering. 'Spend holidays there and everything, don't you? Can't see how you stand the stink, but I suppose when you've been dragged up by Muggles, even the Weasleys' hovel smells OK –'

Harry grabbed hold of George. Meanwhile, it was taking the combined efforts of Angelina, Alicia and Katie to stop Fred leaping on Malfoy, who was

第19章 狮子与蛇

仰面摔倒在冻硬的球场上。他听见霍琦女士尖厉的哨声,看台上哗然大乱,混杂着嘘声、嘲笑声和愤怒的叫喊声,嗵的一声,接着是安吉利娜焦急的声音。

"你没事吧?"

"当然。"哈利咬牙说,抓住安吉利娜的手,让她把自己拉起来。霍琦女士向哈利上方的一个斯莱特林队员冲去,从哈利的角度看不出那人是谁。

"是那个暴徒,克拉布!"安吉利娜气愤地说,"他一看你抓到了飞贼,就把游走球狠狠地向你打来——但我们赢了,哈利,我们赢了!"

哈利听到背后一声冷笑,他转过身去,手里仍紧攥着飞贼:德拉科·马尔福降落在旁边,气得脸色发白,但嘴角还带着一丝嘲讽。

"救了韦斯莱一命,是不是?"他对哈利说,"我从没见过这么臭的守门员……可他是生在垃圾箱嘛……你喜欢我的歌词吗,波特?"

哈利没有回答,走开去迎接他的队友,他们陆续降落,得意扬扬地呐喊欢呼,挥着拳头。只有罗恩除外,他在球门柱那边下了扫帚,一个人慢慢地走回了更衣室。

"我们还想多写几行歌词!"马尔福嚷道,凯蒂和艾丽娅正在和哈利拥抱,"可是又肥又丑不好押韵——我们想唱唱他的老妈——"

"酸葡萄。"安吉利娜厌恶地瞪了马尔福一眼。

"——没用的废物也不好押韵——他爸爸——"

弗雷德和乔治意识到马尔福在说什么。两兄弟正在和哈利握手,他们僵住了,回头看着马尔福。

"别理他,"安吉利娜赶忙拉住弗雷德的胳膊说,"别理他,弗雷德,让他喊去,他只是输了球眼红,这个没教养的小——"

"——可你喜欢韦斯莱家,是不是,波特?"马尔福讥笑道,"还在那儿度假,是不是?不知你怎么受得了那股臭味,不过我想你是被麻瓜带大的,韦斯莱家的土窝闻起来就不错了——"

哈利抓住了乔治,安吉利娜、艾丽娅和凯蒂三个人才拖住了弗雷德,不让他扑向马尔福。马尔福放肆地笑着。哈利扭头找霍琦女士,但她

699

CHAPTER NINETEEN   The Lion and the Serpent

laughing openly. Harry looked around for Madam Hooch, but she was still berating Crabbe for his illegal Bludger attack.

'Or perhaps,' said Malfoy, leering as he backed away, 'you can remember what *your* mother's house stank like, Potter, and Weasley's pigsty reminds you of it –'

Harry was not aware of releasing George, all he knew was that a second later both of them were sprinting towards Malfoy. He had completely forgotten that all the teachers were watching: all he wanted to do was cause Malfoy as much pain as possible; with no time to draw out his wand, he merely drew back the fist clutching the Snitch and sank it as hard as he could into Malfoy's stomach –

'Harry! HARRY! GEORGE! *NO!*'

He could hear girls' voices screaming, Malfoy yelling, George swearing, a whistle blowing and the bellowing of the crowd around him, but he did not care. Not until somebody in the vicinity yelled '*Impedimenta!*' and he was knocked over backwards by the force of the spell, did he abandon the attempt to punch every inch of Malfoy he could reach.

'What do you think you're doing?' screamed Madam Hooch, as Harry leapt to his feet. It seemed to have been her who had hit him with the Impediment Jinx; she was holding her whistle in one hand and a wand in the other; her broom lay abandoned several feet away. Malfoy was curled up on the ground, whimpering and moaning, his nose bloody; George was sporting a swollen lip; Fred was still being forcibly restrained by the three Chasers, and Crabbe was cackling in the background. 'I've never seen behaviour like it – back up to the castle, both of you, and straight to your Head of House's office! Go! *Now!*'

Harry and George marched off the pitch, both panting, neither saying a word to the other. The howling and jeering of the crowd grew fainter and fainter until they reached the Entrance Hall, where they could hear nothing except the sound of their own footsteps. Harry became aware that something was still struggling in his right hand, the knuckles of which he had bruised against Malfoy's jaw. Looking down, he saw the Snitch's silver wings protruding from between his fingers, struggling for release.

They had barely reached the door of Professor McGonagall's office when she came marching along the corridor behind them. She was wearing a Gryffindor scarf, but tore it from her throat with shaking hands as she strode towards them, looking livid.

'In!' she said furiously, pointing to the door. Harry and George entered.

第19章 狮子与蛇

还在斥责克拉布犯规击球。

"也可能是，"马尔福一边朝后退，一边斜睨着眼睛说，"你记得你妈妈家的臭味，韦斯莱家的猪圈让你想起——"

哈利没意识到他松开了乔治，只知道一秒钟后他们俩一起扑向了马尔福。哈利完全忘了所有老师都在观看，只想让马尔福越痛越好。没时间拔魔杖，他抡起攥着飞贼的拳头，使出浑身力气朝马尔福的肚子上揍去。

"哈利！**哈利！乔治！住手！**"

他听到女孩子的尖叫、马尔福的惨叫、乔治的诅咒，还有吹哨声和周围人的叫嚷声，但他不予理会，直到旁边有人断喝："障碍重重！"咒语的一股力量把他向后撞倒，他才停止了狠揍他够得到的每一寸马尔福的身体……

"你们在干什么？"霍琦女士喊道，哈利跳了起来。看来是霍琦女士用障碍咒击中了哈利。她一手举着哨子，一手拿着魔杖，她的飞天扫帚躺在几英尺外。马尔福蜷缩在地上呻吟号叫，鼻子流着血。乔治嘴唇肿了，弗雷德还在被三个追球手扭着，克拉布在后面咯咯地笑。"我从没见过这种行为——回城堡去，你们两个，直接去院长办公室！快去！"

哈利和乔治大步离开了球场，两人都气喘吁吁，一句话也不说。人群的喧哗渐渐远去，他们走到门厅时，只能听见他们自己的脚步声了。哈利发觉他的右手中还有东西在挣扎。他低下头，看到飞贼的银色翅膀从他的指缝间钻出来，想要挣脱出去。他的指关节都被马尔福的下巴磕伤了。

刚到麦格教授办公室的门口，就见她大步从他们身后的走廊走来。她戴着格兰芬多的围巾，但走向他们时，她用颤抖的双手把围巾从脖子上扯了下来，脸色铁青。

"进去！"她指着门厉声说。哈利和乔治进去之后，她走到办公桌

701

CHAPTER NINETEEN   The Lion and the Serpent

She strode around behind her desk and faced them, quivering with rage as she threw the Gryffindor scarf aside on to the floor.

'*Well?*' she said. 'I have never seen such a disgraceful exhibition. Two on one! explain yourselves!'

'Malfoy provoked us,' said Harry stiffly.

'Provoked you?' shouted Professor McGonagall, slamming a fist on to her desk so that her tartan tin slid sideways off it and burst open, littering the floor with Ginger Newts. 'He'd just lost, hadn't he? Of course he wanted to provoke you! But what on earth he can have said that justified what you two –'

'He insulted my parents,' snarled George. 'And Harry's mother.'

'But instead of leaving it to Madam Hooch to sort out, you two decided to give an exhibition of Muggle duelling, did you?' bellowed Professor McGonagall. 'Have you any idea what you've –?'

'*Hem, hem.*'

Harry and George both spun round. Dolores Umbridge was standing in the doorway wrapped in a green tweed cloak that greatly enhanced her resemblance to a giant toad, and was smiling in the horrible, sickly, ominous way that Harry had come to associate with imminent misery.

'May I help, Professor McGonagall?' asked Professor Umbridge in her most poisonously sweet voice.

Blood rushed into Professor McGonagall's face.

'Help?' she repeated, in a constricted voice. 'What do you mean, *help?*'

Professor Umbridge moved forwards into the office, still smiling her sickly smile.

'Why, I thought you might be grateful for a little extra authority.'

Harry would not have been surprised to see sparks fly from Professor McGonagall's nostrils.

'You thought wrong,' she said, turning her back on Umbridge. 'Now, you two had better listen closely. I do not care what provocation Malfoy offered you, I do not care if he insulted every family member you possess, your behaviour was disgusting and I am giving each of you a week's worth of detentions! Do not look at me like that, Potter, you deserve it! And if either of you ever –'

'*Hem, hem.*'

Professor McGonagall closed her eyes as though praying for patience as she turned her face towards Professor Umbridge again.

'*Yes?*'

第19章 狮子与蛇

后面，面向他们，把格兰芬多的围巾扔到地上，气得浑身发抖。

"真行啊？"她说，"我从没见过这样丢人的表演。两个打一个！你们自己解释吧！"

"是马尔福挑衅。"哈利僵硬地说。

"挑衅？"麦格教授吼道，猛地一捶桌子，她的彩格饼干盒滑到地上震开了，生姜蝾螈饼干撒了一地，"他刚输了球，是不是，他当然想挑衅你们！可他究竟能说什么，至于让你们两个——"

"他侮辱我的父母，"乔治大叫，"还有哈利的母亲。"

"可是你们没有让霍琦女士来解决，而是决定展示麻瓜的斗殴方式，是吗？"麦格教授吼道，"你们知不知道自己——？"

"咳，咳。"

乔治和哈利一齐转过身去，多洛雷斯·乌姆里奇站在门口，裹着一件绿花呢斗篷，使她更像一只大癞蛤蟆。她脸上挂着那种令人恶心的、阴森森的可怕笑容，哈利已经习惯把它与灾难联系在一起。

"需要我帮忙吗，麦格教授？"乌姆里奇用她骨子里最毒的甜腻声音问。

麦格教授脸上血色上涌。

"帮忙？"她努力压低声音说，"你是什么意思，帮忙？"

乌姆里奇教授走进了办公室，依然令人恶心地笑着。

"哦，我以为你会感激多一点点官方支持呢。"

就算看到麦格教授鼻孔里冒出火星，哈利也不会奇怪。

"你想错了。"她说，没理睬乌姆里奇，"现在，你们两个听仔细。我不管马尔福如何挑衅，哪怕他侮辱了你们的每一位亲属。你们的行为令人厌恶，我罚你们每人关禁闭一星期！别那样看着我，波特，你们活该！如果你们哪一个——"

"咳，咳。"

麦格教授闭上眼睛，似乎在祈求耐心，她再次转向乌姆里奇教授。

"什么事？"

CHAPTER NINETEEN The Lion and the Serpent

'I think they deserve rather more than detentions,' said Umbridge, smiling still more broadly.

Professor McGonagall's eyes flew open.

'But unfortunately,' she said, with an attempt at a reciprocal smile that made her look as though she had lockjaw, 'it is what I think that counts, as they are in my House, Dolores.'

'Well, *actually*, Minerva,' simpered Professor Umbridge, 'I think you'll find that what I think *does* count. Now, where is it? Cornelius just sent it ... I mean,' she gave a false little laugh as she rummaged in her handbag, 'the *Minister* just sent it ... ah yes ...'

She had pulled out a piece of parchment which she now unfurled, clearing her throat fussily before starting to read what it said.

'*Hem, hem* ... "Educational Decree Number Twenty-five".'

'Not another one!' exclaimed Professor McGonagall violently.

'Well, yes,' said Umbridge, still smiling. 'As a matter of fact, Minerva, it was you who made me see that we *needed* a further amendment ... you remember how you overrode me, when I was unwilling to allow the Gryffindor Quidditch team to re-form? How you took the case to Dumbledore, who insisted that the team be allowed to play? Well, now, I couldn't have that. I contacted the Minister at once, and he quite agreed with me that the High Inquisitor has to have the power to strip pupils of privileges, or she – that is to say, I – would have less authority than common teachers! And you see now, don't you, Minerva, how right I was in attempting to stop the Gryffindor team re-forming? *Dreadful* tempers ... anyway, I was reading out our amendment ... *hem, hem* ... "the High Inquisitor will henceforth have supreme authority over all punishments, sanctions and removal of privileges pertaining to the students of Hogwarts, and the power to alter such punishments, sanctions and removals of privileges as may have been ordered by other staff members. Signed, Cornelius Fudge, Minister for Magic, Order of Merlin First Class, etc., etc."'

She rolled up the parchment and put it back into her handbag, still smiling.

'So ... I really think I will have to ban these two from playing Quidditch ever again,' she said, looking from Harry to George and back again.

Harry felt the Snitch fluttering madly in his hand.

'Ban us?' he said, and his voice sounded strangely distant. 'From playing ... ever again?'

第19章 狮子与蛇

"我想他们应该受到比关禁闭更重的惩罚。"乌姆里奇笑得更甜了。

麦格教授猛地睁开眼睛。

"很遗憾,"她说,同时努力报以对等的笑容,这使她看上去像患了牙关紧闭症,"我的意见是算数的,因为他们在我的学院,多洛雷斯。"

"哦,实际上,米勒娃,"乌姆里奇皮笑肉不笑地说,"我想你会发现我的意见是算数的。咦,放在哪儿了?康奈利刚刚发来的……我是说,"她假笑一声,在手提包里翻找着,"部长刚刚发来的……在这儿……"

她抽出一张羊皮纸打开来,做作地清了清嗓子,开始宣读。

"咳,咳……《第二十五号教育令》。"

"又来一个!"麦格教授情绪激烈地叫道。

"不错,"乌姆里奇仍面带微笑,"米勒娃,实际上,是你让我看到了我们需要一个新的条令……记得你推翻过我的意见吗?当时我不同意格兰芬多重组魁地奇球队,你去找邓布利多,他坚持要让球队比赛。我不能容忍这种做法。我马上和魔法部部长联系,他也认为高级调查官必须有权剥夺学生的特权,否则她——也就是我——连普通教师的权力都不如!现在你看到我不让格兰芬多重组球队是多么正确了吧,米勒娃?可怕的脾气……好了,我现在宣读新法令……咳,咳……高级调查官今后对涉及霍格沃茨学生的一切惩罚、制裁和剥夺权利等事宜具有最高权威,并对其他教员所做出的此类惩罚、制裁和剥夺权利具有修改权。 签名:康奈利·福吉,魔法部部长,梅林爵士团一级勋章……"

她卷起羊皮纸放进手提包里,依然面带笑容。

"所以……我想我不得不禁止这两人再打魁地奇球。"她的目光在哈利和乔治之间来回移动。

哈利感到飞贼在他手中疯狂地挣扎。

"禁止我们?"他的声音遥远得奇怪,"再……打球?"

CHAPTER NINETEEN   The Lion and the Serpent

'Yes, Mr Potter, I think a lifelong ban ought to do the trick,' said Umbridge, her smile widening still further as she watched him struggle to comprehend what she had said. 'You *and* Mr Weasley here. And I think, to be safe, this young man's twin ought to be stopped, too – if his teammates had not restrained him, I feel sure he would have attacked young Mr Malfoy as well. I will want their broomsticks confiscated, of course; I shall keep them safely in my office, to make sure there is no infringement of my ban. But I am not unreasonable, Professor McGonagall,' she continued, turning back to Professor McGonagall who was now standing as still as though carved from ice, staring at her. 'The rest of the team can continue playing, I saw no signs of violence from any of *them*. Well ... good afternoon to you.'

And with a look of the utmost satisfaction, Umbridge left the room, leaving a horrified silence in her wake.

'Banned,' said Angelina in a hollow voice, late that evening in the common room. '*Banned*. No Seeker and no Beaters ... what on earth are we going to do?'

It did not feel as though they had won the match at all. Everywhere Harry looked there were disconsolate and angry faces; the team themselves were slumped around the fire, all apart from Ron, who had not been seen since the end of the match.

'It's just so unfair,' said Alicia numbly. 'I mean, what about Crabbe and that Bludger he hit after the whistle had been blown? Has she banned *him*?'

'No,' said Ginny miserably; she and Hermione were sitting on either side of Harry. 'He just got lines, I heard Montague laughing about it at dinner.'

'And banning Fred when he didn't even do anything!' said Alicia furiously, pummelling her knee with her fist.

'It's not my fault I didn't,' said Fred, with a very ugly look on his face, 'I would've pounded the little scumbag to a pulp if you three hadn't been holding me back.'

Harry stared miserably at the dark window. Snow was falling. The Snitch he had caught earlier was now zooming around and around the common room; people were watching its progress as though hypnotised and Crookshanks was leaping from chair to chair, trying to catch it.

'I'm going to bed,' said Angelina, getting slowly to her feet. 'Maybe this will all turn out to have been a bad dream ... maybe I'll wake up tomorrow and find we haven't played yet ...'

第19章 狮子与蛇

"不错,波特先生,我想终身禁赛比较合适,"乌姆里奇说,看到哈利艰难地试图理解她的话,她笑得更开心了,"你和这位韦斯莱先生。我想,为了安全起见,这位小伙子的双胞胎兄弟也应被禁止——如果他的队友没有拦住他的话,我相信他也会袭击小马尔福先生的。我要没收他们的飞天扫帚,把它们安全地保管在我的办公室里,以确保没人违反我的禁令。但我并非不讲情理,麦格教授,"她转身对像冰雕一般瞪着她的麦格教授说,"其他队员可以继续打球,我没看到他们有暴力倾向。好了……祝你们下午好。"

乌姆里奇带着极度满足的神气走了出去,留下一片恐怖的沉寂。

"禁赛,"当天晚上在公共休息室里,安吉利娜声音空洞地说,"禁赛。没有找球手和击球手……我们还能干什么?"

根本感觉不到他们赢了球,哈利到处只看见沮丧和愤怒的面孔。队员们意志消沉地坐在炉边,只有罗恩不在,他自从比赛结束后就没有露面。

"真不公平,"艾丽娅麻木地说,"克拉布在哨响后打出游走球怎么算?她禁止他了吗?"

"没有,"金妮伤心地说,她和赫敏坐在哈利的两侧,"克拉布只被罚写句子,我听到蒙太吃晚饭时笑着说的。"

"弗雷德根本没动手也被禁赛!"艾丽娅捶着膝盖愤恨地说。

"没动手不是我的错,"弗雷德的脸色非常难看,"要是你们三个不拦着我,我准把那个小畜生打成肉泥。"

哈利难受地看着漆黑的窗外,下雪了。他抓到的飞贼在公共休息室里一圈一圈地飞着,人们像被催眠了似的盯着它看。克鲁克山从这把椅子跳到那把椅子,想要抓住它。

"我去睡觉了,"安吉利娜慢慢地站起身,"也许这只是一场噩梦……也许我早上醒来会发现我们还没有比赛……"

CHAPTER NINETEEN   The Lion and the Serpent

She was soon followed by Alicia and Katie. Fred and George sloped off to bed some time later, glowering at everyone they passed, and Ginny went not long after that. Only Harry and Hermione were left beside the fire.

'Have you seen Ron?' Hermione asked in a low voice.

Harry shook his head.

'I think he's avoiding us,' said Hermione. 'Where do you think he –?'

But at that precise moment, there was a creaking sound behind them as the Fat Lady swung forwards and Ron came clambering through the portrait hole. He was very pale indeed and there was snow in his hair. When he saw Harry and Hermione, he stopped dead in his tracks.

'Where have you been?' said Hermione anxiously, springing up.

'Walking,' Ron mumbled. He was still wearing his Quidditch things.

'You look frozen,' said Hermione. 'Come and sit down!'

Ron walked to the fireside and sank into the chair furthest from Harry's, not looking at him. The stolen Snitch zoomed over their heads.

'I'm sorry,' Ron mumbled, looking at his feet.

'What for?' said Harry.

'For thinking I can play Quidditch,' said Ron. 'I'm going to resign first thing tomorrow.'

'If you resign,' said Harry testily, 'there'll only be three players left on the team.' And when Ron looked puzzled, he said, 'I've been given a lifetime ban. So've Fred and George.'

'What?' Ron yelped.

Hermione told him the full story; Harry could not bear to tell it again. When she had finished, Ron looked more anguished than ever.

'This is all my fault –'

'You didn't *make* me punch Malfoy,' said Harry angrily.

'– if I wasn't so terrible at Quidditch –'

'– it's got nothing to do with that.'

'– it was that song that wound me up –'

'– it would've wound anyone up.'

Hermione got up and walked to the window, away from the argument, watching the snow swirling down against the pane.

第19章 狮子与蛇

很快，艾丽娅和凯蒂也走了。过了一会儿，弗雷德和乔治也怏怏而去，对路过的每一个人都怒目而视。金妮不一会也走了，炉边只剩下哈利和赫敏。

"你看到罗恩了吗？"赫敏轻声问。

哈利摇摇头。

"我想他在躲着我们，"赫敏说，"你认为他会在——"

就在这时，他们身后传来嘎吱声，胖夫人向前转开，罗恩从肖像洞口爬了进来。他脸色非常苍白，头上沾着雪花。看到哈利和赫敏，他一下子呆住了。

"你去哪儿了？"赫敏跳起来急切地问。

"散步。"罗恩嘟哝道。他还穿着魁地奇球袍。

"你好像冻僵了，"赫敏说，"快过来坐！"

罗恩走到炉边，瘫在离哈利最远的一把椅子上，没有看他。飞贼在他们头顶上盘旋着。

"对不起。"罗恩看着脚尖喃喃地说。

"为什么？"哈利问。

"我以为自己能打魁地奇。"罗恩说，"我打算明天一早就提出离队。"

"如果你离队，全队就只有三个球员了。"哈利没好气地说。见罗恩困惑不解，他说："我被终身禁赛。还有弗雷德和乔治。"

"什么？"罗恩叫起来。

赫敏把事情的经过告诉了他。哈利受不了自己再讲一遍。赫敏讲完后，罗恩显得更痛苦了。

"都怪我——"

"你又没让我揍马尔福。"哈利恼火地说。

"——如果不是我在场上那么没用——"

"——跟这个没关系——"

"——是那首歌让我紧张——"

"——换了谁都会紧张——"

赫敏站起来走到窗口，离开了争论，看雪花在窗前飘舞。

CHAPTER NINETEEN   The Lion and the Serpent

'Look, drop it, will you!' Harry burst out. 'It's bad enough, without you blaming yourself for everything!'

Ron said nothing but sat gazing miserably at the damp hem of his robes. After a while he said in a dull voice, 'This is the worst I've ever felt in my life.'

'Join the club,' said Harry bitterly.

'Well,' said Hermione, her voice trembling slightly. 'I can think of one thing that might cheer you both up.'

'Oh yeah?' said Harry sceptically.

'Yeah,' said Hermione, turning away from the pitch-black, snow-flecked window, a broad smile spreading across her face. 'Hagrid's back.'

"别这样行不行?"哈利爆发道,"没有你在这儿一味自责就已经够糟了。"

罗恩没有吭声,难过地看着自己湿漉漉的袍摆。过了一会儿,他闷声闷气地说:"这是我这辈子感觉最糟的一次。"

"我也一样。"哈利痛苦地说。

"好了,"赫敏说,声音有点发颤,"我想有一件事可能会让你们俩都高兴起来。"

"是吗?"哈利怀疑地问。

"嗯。"赫敏从漆黑的、飘着雪花的窗前转过身来,莞尔一笑,"海格回来了。"

WIZARDING WORLD